Old King's
Highway

Mt. Moriah

Mt. Provenance
*

Charity Street

Pinckney Street

Jewett's
Pond

Temperance Vale
Cemetery
*

Berwick
Avenue

*

Grace Episcopal
Church

*
Ravensworth
Park

Glen Mawr
Manor *

Hazelwit

Volga Avenue

Union Avenue

Juniper
Park

Winterthurn River

River Road

St. Bride's *

terthurn

N
W   E
S

MYSTERIES
OF
WINTERTHURN

———

OTHER NOVELS BY JOYCE CAROL OATES

———————

A Bloodsmoor Romance
Angel of Light
Bellefleur
Unholy Loves
Cybele
Son of the Morning
Childwold
The Assassins
Do with Me What You Will
Wonderland
them
Expensive People
Garden of Earthly Delights
With Shuddering Fall

Joyce Carol Oates

MYSTERIES OF WINTERTHURN

a novel

E. P. DUTTON, INC.   ·   NEW YORK

Copyright © 1984 by The Ontario Review, Inc.
All rights reserved. Printed in the U.S.A.

No part of this publication may be reproduced or transmitted
in any form or by any means, electronic or mechanical, including
photocopy, recording or any information storage and retrieval
system now known or to be invented, without permission in writing
from the publisher, except by a reviewer who wishes to quote
brief passages in connection with a review written for inclusion
in a magazine, newspaper or broadcast.

Published in the United States by
E. P. Dutton, Inc., 2 Park Avenue, New York, N.Y. 10016

Library of Congress Cataloging in Publication Data
Oates, Joyce Carol
Mysteries of Winterthurn
I. Title.
PS3565.A8M9 1984   813'.54   83-8961
ISBN: 0-525-24208-2

Published simultaneously in Canada by
Fitzhenry & Whiteside Limited, Toronto

COBE

Designed by Nancy Etheredge

10 9 8 7 6 5 4 3 2 1

First Trade Edition

A signed first edition of this book has been privately printed by The Franklin Library for Raymond, most exacting of readers—

———————

*"Depend upon it, Sir, when a man knows
he is to be hanged in a fortnight,
it concentrates his mind wonderfully."*
—SAMUEL JOHNSON

Contents

THE VIRGIN
IN THE ROSE-BOWER

or

The Tragedy of
Glen Mawr Manor

If I—am You—
Shall You—be me?
If You—scorn I—
Where then—We—
Be—?

"IPHIGENIA"

Editor's Note

It is frequently observed by our self-righteous critics that we amateur "collectors" of Murder are antiquarians at heart: unapologetically to the right in matters political, moral, and religious: possessed of a near-insatiable passion for authenticity, down to the most minute, revealing, and lurid detail: impatient with the *new* (whether it be new and untried modes of murder, or new and untried modes of mystery), and enamored of the *old*. Studying the history of crime, as, indeed, history more generally, with the hope of comprehending human nature,—or, failing that lofty ambition, comprehending the present era—cannot interest the purist. For, as the outspoken De Quincey has argued,—Is not Murder an art-form? And does any art-form require justification?

Herewith, I am happy to present that perennial favorite of *aficionados* of American mystery, *The Virgin in the Rose-Bower; or, The Tragedy of Glen Mawr Manor*, which, albeit most informally, introduces young Xavier Kilgarvan to his destiny as a detective *sui generis*. (In Winterthurn City itself the case has long enjoyed a variety of appellations, amongst them, most bluntly, "The Glen Mawr Murders" and "The Glen Mawr 'Angel' Murders," etc. Not one person—including even that exploitive scribbler of murder mysteries, Mr. Mountjoy Price—has had the wish, or the audacity, to refer to this controversial episode of Xavier Kilgarvan's life as "Xavier Kilgarvan's First Case": nor is it this editor's intention to do so.)

How to best describe this old, much-analyzed, yet still tantalizing mystery of more than a century ago! Though it would seem at first blush to declare itself a classic of the *locked-room* variety, and

3

though, doubtless, numberless collectors prize it for that reason, I have always believed that its fame (or notoriety) resides in the fact that, despite heroic effort, *it was never satisfactorily solved*. Or, at any rate, the solution to the mystery was never made public; and the murderer, or murderers, never brought to justice.

And for very good reasons,—as the reader will doubtless agree.

The unexplained murders at Glen Mawr Manor, and in its vicinity, aroused great terror in the inhabitants of Winterthurn, somewhat out of proportion (it seems to us today) to the actual number of violent deaths involved. For a liberal count of corpses, so to speak, yields but four outright murders; and one self-inflicted death. (The deaths, mutilations, victimizations, etc., of a miscellany of animals in the vicinity being of less significance, though, doubtless, still a potent factor in the arousal of fear.) Yet it might be considered that there is such a phenomenon as *soul-murder*, of as great a moral harm as murder of the body: in which case, one, or perhaps two, or even three, additional ''deaths'' might be acknowledged. (For instance, it happened that as a consequence of their horrific experiences, Mrs. Abigail Whimbrel and Mrs. Roxana Murphy were plunged into the abyss of *hopeless insanity*, from which no physician could rescue them. Though it falls somewhat beyond the scope of this history, I should like to record that Mrs. Whimbrel lived to a sickly old age,—well into her ninety-seventh year, it is said—at the Mt. Moriah Hospital for Nervous Invalids, where her grieving family had seen fit to place her; while the fortune hunter Mrs. Murphy,—or Mrs. Kilgarvan, as she might legally be called— suffered an extreme abreaction to a sedative dose of belladonna, administered by Dr. Colney Hatch, and died within twelve days of her husband.)

Superstitious the inhabitants of Winterthurn doubtless were, to have feared, for decades, ''angels,'' or ''angel-figures,'' loosed in the night and frequently in the day: and naïve in their stubborn belief that a preternatural force emanated from the Manor. Yet it were well for the contemporary reader to withhold judgment; and to reflect that our ancestors, though oft appearing less informed than ourselves, were perhaps far more sensitive,—nay, altogether more astute, in comprehending Evil.

Quicklime

Scarcely was it dawn of a remarkably chill morning in May,—indeed, large damp clumps of snow were being blown about like blossoms—when, seemingly out of nowhere, Miss Georgina Kilgarvan, the eldest daughter of the late Judge, appeared, accompanied by her Negro servant Pride, to ring the bell of a tradesman named Phineas Cutter (of Cutter Brothers Mills, on the Temperance Vale Road), and to make a most unusual request. Poor Phineas!—awakened harshly from sleep, afflicted with deafness in his right ear, he must have bethought himself whether this veiled and dark-clad vision was indeed the Judge's spinster daughter, or a specter out of troubled dreams: for how could it be,—nay, how *should* it be—that Miss Georgina of Glen Mawr Manor, heavily clothed in her mourning costume, and as always discreetly veiled, had come on foot to his store to make a purchase of,—*fifty pounds of quicklime?*

Little wonder, then, that Phineas Cutter cupped his hand to his ear, and stammeringly requested of the lady that she repeat her words.

While the diminutive Negro servant stood some yards distant, his crabbed expression giving no sign that he heard, or cared to hear, what his mistress said, Georgina Kilgarvan, speaking in a low, rapid, forceful voice, in which no evident agitation could be discerned, apologized for having disturbed Phineas at an unnatural hour; in truth, she did not know the precise time, as clocks at Glen Mawr vied with one another, in telling the time,—for they had been tampered with, it seems, since her father's death,—but that unhappy fact had no bearing here, and she did not wish to pursue it. The situation was: she found

5

herself in immediate need of a certain gardening substance, a compound of some sort,—lye, lime, quicklime? she could not recall precisely—only that it was a most potent material, employed commonly
by gardeners,—a whitish substance with disinfectant and purgative
powers: lye, or lime, or quicklime,—spread on organic materials, she
believed, to hasten their decomposition; to effect a general cleansing, a
purifying of that which was rotting and foul,—and evil,—and a source
of contagion: *quicklime*, she thought it. As she was a gardener, albeit
on a modest scale, she required this substance for her garden, and
wished to purchase fifty pounds of it, without delay, which her servant
would carry home for her: for it was her firm intention to begin work
on her rose-garden that very morning.

Speaking now in a more peremptory tone, and still without raising her veil, Miss Georgina Kilgarvan explained that she had not cash
on her person, but, ''as her father had done business with Mr. Cutter
for many years, and his father before him, with Mr. Cutter's father, she
was confident that he would trust her to pay in the usual manner; and
would simply bill Glen Mawr,''—this being information of a totally
needless sort, as business with Glen Mawr was always transacted in
that manner.

Phineas Cutter is to be forgiven for his somewhat dazed response to the lady's request, for the situation possessed that exquisite
air of the utterly *rational* conjoined with the *irrational* that is a characteristic of dreams: the vision of a tall, dark-clad, veiled lady, her seal-
skin cape falling majestically to her feet, her manner courteous, yet
edged with a faint air of impatience, or contempt: the which was
wondrously heightened by the very early hour, and the soundless, yet
wildly melodic, disportment of soft, wet, giant clumps of snow that
swirled about and clung melting to her black bonnet and cape. Ah, it
might have been that one of the ''life statues'' from the nearby cemetery had roused itself, to make a teasing visit,—these statues being
uncannily realistic in their proportions and stances, though executed
in chill stone; or might it be a prank of some sort, played upon him to
test his credulousness,—someone who had got himself up in disguise,
as the ''Blue Nun'' of Glen Mawr Manor? (For it had happened more
than once in the past several years that Cutter Mills, like many another establishment in the area, had been visited by pranksters,—or
outright vandals: and though the wily culprits always eluded capture,
it was generally believed, and charged, that they were young men of
''good family,''—spoiled youths whose notion of amusement it might
well be to overturn Phineas's outhouse, or tie his billy goat atop his
roof, or, indeed, trick him into thinking that Erasmus Kilgarvan's eldest daughter was paying him a visit.)

As Miss Georgina was altogether herself, in flesh and blood,

Phineas quickly bestirred himself to comply with her strange request: for, like any tradesman, he feared provoking displeasure in his customers, and particularly in a member of the Kilgarvan family. Miss Georgina had acquired a reputation for eccentricity over the years, and for dealing somewhat punitively with shopkeepers, tradesmen, servants, and the like, who failed to meet with her exacting standards,— to the extent to which it had begun to be said, before her father's death, that one would as readily deal with Erasmus Kilgarvan as with the "Blue Nun." (Behind her back Miss Georgina was thus called, in reference to her perpetual costume, of long, full, oft shapeless dresses and skirts, of no shades other than navy or midnight blue, or black itself; and silk-lined capes of varying degrees of antiquity; and dark, austere bonnets, and hats, in the styles of bygone seasons. She was invariably veiled, not only in public but, it was said, frequently in private as well: though, in truth, so few persons encountered her in recent years, since her resignation from the faculty of the Parthian Academy for Girls and her gradual withdrawal from society, that such observations must have been the fruit of mere rumor. The veils consisted of the sheerest gossamer; or were smartly dotted in black velvet; or were made of a somewhat disfiguring species of netting; or, more frequently of late, they were of so darkly opaque a gauze, the observer was hard put to imagine a human face within, and a pair of secretive watchful eyes—! Little wonder, then, that when Miss Georgina Kilgarvan appeared in public, whether in the relative seclusion of church services at the Grace Episcopal Church on Berwick Avenue or on the street, small children openly gaped at her, and the unmannered amongst the adults covertly stared,—for the remarkable woman did very much resemble a *nun;* or, it might be said, a handsome and self-possessed species of *witch.*)

Phineas made the offer of delivering the sack of quicklime to the Manor somewhat later in the day: but Miss Georgina irritably interrupted him, and stressed again her need for the "gardening substance" straightaway. So Phineas brought Pride with him, into the storeroom, that he might hand over the unwieldy sack; and, perhaps, discreetly inquire of the old Negro what on earth was bedeviling his mistress, to make her behave so queerly—! For he had heard,—or, rather, his wife and daughter had made mention of the fact—that, since the abrupt death of Chief Justice Erasmus Kilgarvan of the Winterthurn County Court, some weeks previous, things were in great upset at Glen Mawr Manor; and one or two servants had already given notice. There were rumors too of Miss Georgina's cruel treatment of her two young half-sisters . . . And was not Simon Esdras Kilgarvan, the Judge's brother, lapsed into a very odd state of mourning, or grief . . .

Old Pride, however, gave evidence of disdaining Mr. Cutter's friendly chatter, no less emphatically than his mistress; and did not deign to cast a rheumy eye in his direction, or allow his very black, and very wrinkled, face to relax into a smile, though poor Phineas did his best to "draw him out." Thus the transaction was completed, in a most businesslike fashion: and Phineas Cutter stood in his doorway, wiping his hands on his overalls, to watch mistress and servant glide away into the swirl of snowflurries, with no backward glance. *Lye, lime, quicklime,—ah yes quicklime!—fifty pounds, please,—for my roses, Mr. Cutter, please,—at once,—with no delay: and charge it to the Kilgarvan account.*

In speaking of the incident afterward, particularly as the months and years passed, Phineas Cutter could not resist embellishing it some-what,—noting that the "Blue Nun's" gloved hands visibly trembled; or that the stark pallor of her skin was discernible through her veil; or that her voice betrayed agitation, and guilt. In later years he was to in-sist, without, it seems, being conscious of the falsehood, that mistress and servant exchanged many a "significant" glance in his presence; and that Miss Georgina found it necessary to lean on Pride's arm, as they walked away. Ah, and had not the woman's *black, piercing, uncanny eyes* fixed themselves most disturbingly on his face—!

Withal, there was something appealing, and even romantic, about the scene: an air of the poignant and the melancholy: and the haunting. For was not Miss Georgina a most enigmatic figure, in her mourning costume, with a mantle of soft melting snowflakes on her head and shoulders, delicate as the finest lace? And was it not an act of thoughtless desperation, *never to be explained*, that a lady of her social station should come on foot, upward of three miles, along a rough country road, before the sun had well risen,—thereby exposing herself to all manner of gossip and speculation?

This, on the morning of May 3, some hours before the discovery of the death of Miss Georgina's infant cousin, up at the Manor.

Yet Phineas Cutter remained standing in his doorway for some min-utes, gazing into the distance, though Miss Georgina and her servant had long since disappeared; and the snow began soundlessly to melt. Was there not something pitiable, and half tragic, about Erasmus Kil-garvan's eldest daughter, Phineas thought; had it not been her fate to be sorely disappointed,—nay, humiliated—many years ago, in an affair of the heart?

Trompe L'Oeil

Impatient with waiting. With longing. So lonely. Hungry. These many years. Impatient to love. To nurse. Our time fast approaches . . .

It was near midnight of May 2, not more than six hours before Phineas Cutter was to be roused so discourteously from his sleep, that Mrs. Abigail Whimbrel (Miss Georgina's cousin by way of her mother's family, the Battenbergs of Contracoeur) started from her sleep, for the second or third time since retiring: and suffered so foreign a sensation through her being,—part nervous excitation, part languor of a heavy sensuous sort—she halfway feared *some unnatural presence had slipped into her bed-chamber.*

"Who is here?—who dares disturb us? I shall ring for a servant—!"

With trembling fingers Mrs. Whimbrel lit the oil lamp by her bedside table: and saw nothing that might be deemed out of the ordinary, save, perhaps, the wildly distended shadows caused by the lamp's flame, and her own most uncommonly pale reflection in a bronze-frosted mirror on the facing wall. Though possessed of an enviably placid, and even quiescent, nature, and very rarely, for her sex, prone to outbursts of emotion or hysteria,—save at those inevitable times when female vicissitudes make war, as it were, upon mental equilibrium—Mrs. Whimbrel bethought herself that she must rise from her bed to examine the room and check once more the slumber of her infant son, who, having been fretful earlier, had been placed by his nurse, at Mrs. Whimbrel's adamant request, in a wicker crib close by her bed.

But all seemed well in the bed-chamber, though Abigail contin-

9

ued to feel some uneasiness at the lushly decorated room into which
Cousin Georgina had put her: and at a queer undefined agitation of the
air, which may have been the consequence of ill-fitting windows, or mismatched floorboards underfoot, belied by the gaily elegant French carpets, and, indeed, by the lavish furnishings on all sides. Yet her mother's heart was consoled by the depth and peaceableness of her baby's
slumber, and by the perfection,—ah, would it never fail to pierce her
heart, as if taking her unawares?—of his tiny being. "Why, then, sweet
Charleton, if *you* are undisturbed, I am quite the fool to stir up a fuss,"
Abigail whispered. For some fond moments she stood gazing into the
crib, taking note of the infant's tiny rosebud of a mouth (which looked
to her as if, damply pursed, it awaited a stealthy kiss); and the near-
imperceptible quivering of his eyelids (did he dream?—did he, perhaps,
dream of *her*,—and of his happiness at her breast?); and the ravishingly
charming way in which his hands, loosely shaped into "fists," rested
on the white eiderdown coverlet. Though knowing herself foolishly
indulgent, she could not resist brushing a fair silky curl from the
baby's forehead; and leaning as gently as possible over the crib, to impart a ghostly kiss upon that same brow. That Mrs. Abigail Whimbrel
doted overmuch upon Charleton Hendrick Whimbrel II (named for his
paternal grandfather, the distinguished General Whimbrel of the
Patriots' War of 1837) was a consequence of the fact that this youngest
of the Whimbrels' several children would be the last child God would
entrust to her care: for so her family physician had told her, and she
knew it must be so. Ah, would it not be afterward adjudged an act of
singular imprudence, to have brought the baby to troubled Glen Mawr
Manor—where, it took no very prescient imagination to perceive, neither mother nor baby was *entirely* wished-for at the present time.

   "We shall not be here long, and Cousin Georgina shall be rid of
us,—poor unhappy creature!" Abigail murmured aloud, with more
forcefulness than she had intended: for, of a sudden, little Charleton
opened wide his liquid-blue eyes, and appeared, for an instant, to stare
up at her. Did he truly wake?—or was he yet safely asleep? Ah, God's
most exquisite little angel, entrusted to a mere mortal's care—! With
relief Abigail determined that he had not actually awakened, which
was, of course, altogether to the good: for, when he had cried and
"carried on" earlier in the day, shortly after their arrival at the Manor,
Cousin Georgina had not been charmed: informing Abigail somewhat
needlessly that Glen Mawr was ordinarily peaceful,—nay, perfectly silent—and that the clamor of a baby's angry wailing was distinctly out
of place. Startled, yet laughingly, Abigail had protested that little
Charleton's crying was scarcely an expression of anger, but only of
colicky discomfort, and upset at unfamiliar surroundings,—quite natural, in fact, in a baby of his tender months. Georgina seemingly

attended to her words with courtesy; yet, a minute later, she reiterated her own observation, in a grave voice, adding that *the men should dislike it in particular,* as any sort of noise interfered with concentration. Seeing Abigail's startled look, perhaps, Georgina at once bethought herself, and amended that Uncle Simon Esdras should not like it,— "being very sensitive of late to undue distractions and interruptions that threaten progress on his *Treatise.*" A faint rubescent flush to the elder woman's cheeks, at her innocent, yet piteous, "slip of the tongue," and a stiffening of her mouth, warned Abigail against attempting commiseration at this awkward moment.

"It is altogether natural that poor Georgina 'feels' her father's presence, as if he were still alive," Abigail observed, with a small *frisson,* "—for, indeed, at Glen Mawr, it does seem the case that the 'great man' has but stepped out of the room, and will shortly be back!"

Little Charleton again stirred, and made a whimpering, mewing sound; and, in some agitation, Abigail stroked his warm brow yet again, and adjusted the coverlet, and his tiny pillow; and essayed to comfort him with a familiar lullaby of the nursery, for, alas, he must not begin to cry so quickly!—

> *Little Baby Bunting*
> *Father's gone ahunting*
> *Gone to get a new fur skin*
> *To wrap the Baby Bunting in!*
>
> *Little Baby Bunting*
> *Father's gone ahunting . . .*

For some precarious seconds it seemed he might wake, and throw himself into a spasm of wailing: for was Abigail not, despite her maternal solicitude and boundless love, a most fearsome *giantess* in his vision?

Fortunately, however, he did lapse into sleep: and the relieved mother returned to her bed, with the intention of reading, as sleep, for her, now seemed cruelly distant: and perhaps not desirable. Thus it was, she took up her Bible, and essayed to read, that her soul might be calmed; and the disagreeable confusion of her thoughts, of but a few minutes previous, quelled. Yet she halfway wondered whether, in truth, those thoughts had been hers at all; or some queer product of her sojourn here, in this intimidating guest room,—the "General's Room," it was known as, or the "Honeymoon Room"—where Cousin Georgina had insisted she must stay, as it was the "only decent room kept in readiness for visitors." She had, she feared, insulted her cousin by her initial response to it, in protesting that it was far too grand, and too formal, and, she knew not why, too *chill* a space, for her to inhabit alone. Might she and Georgina not share a bed,—or, at the very least, a bed-chamber for the night—as they had done upon several occasions in their girlhood? But this wistful query was seemingly *not heard.*

All incongruously, and, it seemed, with not the faintest trace of mockery or sarcasm, Georgina said of a sudden: "Dear Cousin, I cannot wonder that you are disappointed in us,—that you find our way of life at the Manor much reduced from what it was. While Father lived this house too lived: his step, his voice,—nay, his very breath— reverberated throughout. But, ah!—no more of that; for I see by your frown that I am being morbid. And poor Georgina, poor spinster, *is forbidden to be morbid*, by Dr. Hatch himself. Yet it seems naught but 'plain dealing,' to observe that we are, since that catastrophe of late March, an etiolated sort of household, at best: three sisters in stunned mourning, and a bachelor uncle so bemazed, I fear, by his brother's death, he has yet to comprehend its import. No, no, dear Abigail," Georgina said, turning stiffly aside, as if she feared a precipitous embrace, and again speaking with puzzling incongruity,—her thoughts, it seemed, hopping hither and yon: "we are obliged to be frugal now at Glen Mawr, as, I am told, Father's finances were left in a confused state; and it will be many a month, or year, before we are on an 'even keel' once again. We must be humble. Thérèse and Perdita quite understand, for they are not,—praise God, they have never been— *spoiled girls*; and Uncle Simon shall be made to understand. It is not our lot, you see, to dissipate our income in idle pleasures,—to throw the Manor open to visitors, and relatives up and down the pike,— though of course, being hospitable, we should like very much to do so. Ah, would I were a writer of romances, and a heroine of the lending library, and not, as Fate would have it, a mere *poetess!*—though, it seems," Georgina said, with a bemused twist of her lips, "I am scarcely that, any longer."

It is not to be wondered at that Abigail found herself quite nonplussed at this trailing, yet lugubrious speech: in truth silenced, with as much dispatch, as if her elder cousin had rudely bade her be still. ("Why, I had sought only to share her bedroom for the night," poor Abigail, stung, inwardly murmured, "and have been served a stern admonition not to expect *luxury!*")

As it was the custom for most of the members of Abigail's family, excepting of course the very youngest children, to read the Bible twice daily, either in the company of others or alone, it is perhaps comprehensible that her mind sometimes drifted from Holy Writ to attach itself to matters of a profane nature: yet this proclivity seemed the more emphatic, and the more irresistible, as Mrs. Whimbrel lay stiffly propped up with pillows, in her lonely bed,—alas, many miles from

her home in Contracoeur and her belovèd Mr. Whimbrel—and essayed
to read, with a silent shaping of her lips, from the Epistles of John. Ah,
how vexing!—how nettlesome! For, though the spacious bed-chamber
was silent save for the mournful ticking of a pendulum clock on the
mantel and the low persistent murmurousness of the wind against the
several windows, she could not, it seems, attend to the Word of God:
but felt her thoughts urge themselves in another direction, very like a
willful horse straining at the bit.

Her attention was drawn to the facing mirror, which, though
lightly frosted in bronze, displayed with some clarity both herself and
her bed, and the extraordinary *trompe l'oeil* mural by Fairfax Eakins
that had been commissioned by Phillips Goode Kilgarvan some
decades previous and painted directly on the wall and a portion of the
ceiling. A small golden plaque announced the title "The Virgin in the
Rose-Bower," and Abigail Whimbrel was capable of discerning certain
religious elements and motifs in it,—the Virgin, for instance, held
the Christ Child somewhat awkwardly on her knee; yet, withal, she
thought it a decidedly queer painting, and marred by a pagan,—or
might it be Popish?—extravagance of flesh.

Of a sudden, answering to a whim she would have been hard
pressed to explain, Abigail rose from her bed, and went to the door, and
laid her ear against it; and, hearing nothing, *firmly bolted it.* She then
went to each of the tall windows, in turn, and locked them as best she
could, saying to herself the while: "Albeit I am at Glen Mawr, and not
in a strange inn or hotel, I know myself and Charleton unquestionably
safe,—yet shall sleep the more soundly, for knowing too that the room
is *secured from within.*"

She then returned to her bed, and bethought herself that now, at
last, she might darken the room; for nothing could possibly harm her,
save the childish phantasms of sleep. As Cousin Georgina would be
gravely insulted to discover the precautions she had taken, Abigail resolved to rise long before dawn and to undo all the locks and bolts,—
there being little risk of her oversleeping, as Baby should stir, and fret,
and cry for his first repast of the day, not long past five o'clock.

Scarcely had Abigail settled into an ancient mohair chair in Georgina's
drawing room, and carefully arranged her skirts and petticoats, and
taken up her cup of tea,—scarcely had she exchanged greetings, and
subdued smiles, with her young cousins Thérèse and Perdita (who had
come downstairs to tea, it appeared, with timid reluctance, clad in
unflattering dresses of black mousseline, with drooping collars, loose
sashes, and distinctly tattered hems),—when Georgina essayed to
apologize for the fact that Abigail and her baby had been met at the
train station by one of the Manor servants only, and not by Georgina

herself, or Simon Esdras: the excuse coolly offered, *that they were otherwise employed.* To this "apology" that had very much the air of an affront, poor Abigail could but murmur an assent; and busied herself with her tea, and inquiries after the health of the Kilgarvans, while her eye moved about the room to take in what it could,—a portrait in oils of the late Chief Justice in his judicial robes, above the mantel, most imposing in its muscular harmonies of shadow and light; a somewhat untidy stack of books, set beside Georgina's chair; the inert though wheezing form of a large mastiff,—Jupiter his name—lying sprawled on the carpet near Abigail's feet, with as much agèd aplomb, as if he slept in some secluded place. Her own keen èye following Abigail's, Georgina observed, in a low, dry, uninflected voice, that she hoped Abigail would not report back to Contracoeur "on the doubtful state of our household: for it is a fact I cannot disguise, that the servants have been fickle of late, and will get themselves dismissed. Alas as Father has said, it is the times—!"

Abigail Whimbrel essayed some suitable reply, though feeling most perplexed: for how was it possible, Cousin Georgina seemed not to *like* her; or even in a way to *know* her? Nor did the younger sisters contribute any element of smiling freshness, or vivacity: lapsing into silence after making their dutiful,—nay, forced—replies; and gazing with brooding and melancholy eyes at the carpet. When Abigail's sociable voice subsided, naught was heard save the ticking of a mantel clock, which struck the ear as not fully rhythmic; and the sighing, laborious breath of the old mastiff; and, distantly, from upstairs, the renewed crying of little Charleton. (Ah, how he had fretted on the train!—giving both Abigail and his nursemaid a great deal of pleasurable trouble. But now that he had nursed and had been put to bed for his afternoon nap, Abigail resolved that she would not run away upstairs at his bidding.)

The subject was revived, of the abruptness of Erasmus Kilgarvan's death,—the distinguished jurist having died in the courtroom, in full session, some six weeks previous: the which animated Georgina for a while, so that her narrow eyes shone, and a faint blush shadowed her cheeks. Yet this too ran its course; and it was with an ironical voice that Georgina concluded: "Thus you find us, his daughters. *His* heiresses. Left quite behind. As you see. Ah, dear Abigail, you *must* not judge us harshly, and frown upon us so prettily!—for we are not at all *morbid*; but only,—*his.*"

Abigail stammeringly protested that she did not judge at all: but had come to Glen Mawr solely out of friendship, as she could imagine how heavily grief lay upon the household.

"Grief lies upon our household,—I hope I speak for my sisters as well?—no more heavily," Georgina flatly announced, "than might be required."

As no servant appeared to pass about the tea things, Thérèse lay aside her grayish tangle of crocheting, and, with an appealing sort of awkwardness, elected to do so: proffering Abigail a second cup of tea and handing about a plate of crustless sandwiches thickly smeared with butter, and salmon paste,—which, Abigail's keen eye determined, was *not* overly fresh. This half-sister of Georgina's, nearly three decades her junior, was now fourteen years of age, yet childlike in both manner and appearance: her pinched face being neither pretty nor actually plain,—her slender nose with its subtle Kilgarvan crook, and her small sweet mouth, being features of decided promise,—while her dark eyes, it almost seemed, were hooded, and sunk too deeply in their sockets. Abigail had heard that Thérèse was passionately religious, and an outstanding scholar: yet how forlorn her expression, how dim and melancholy her smile—! Nor did it contribute to her charm that her right eyelid quivered, as if she feared a harsh word, or a blow from an invisible hand: a singularly unfortunate trait in a young lady of good family.

As to Perdita, the youngest of the sisters, and by far the most comely,—this child made so little effort to please, with scarcely a smile for her Contracoeur cousin, or more than a mumbled reply, Abigail knew not what to think. She was decidedly pretty, or more than pretty: with a heart-shaped face, and delicately curving brows, and the Kilgarvan nose, and thick-lashed eyes which, even when narrowed, gave a hint of spirited intelligence, or willfulness. Yet her air was aggrieved and sullen; her skin so pale as to suggest anemia, or greensickness; and her lower lip swollen with pouting. (Though perhaps it was actually swollen: Abigail noted a bruise of a flavid purple, singularly unflattering, along her jaw: and scratches on the backs of both her hands. A clumsy child, along with being sullen,—prone to mishaps and falls.) Though Abigail made every effort to provoke a smile in her, and to draw her out in conversation, she stubbornly held her ground, as it were; and sat in her chair with a comical sort of formality, her backbone resolutely straight, and her head held rigid, in imitation,— Abigail supposed it must be unconscious—of her late father, who had, as all the family knew, a mania for correct posture; and much contempt for those who did not observe it.

Abigail was startled, however, to note that, while Georgina was preoccupied in extracting from a pile of condolence cards one of especial significance she wished to show Abigail, the twelve-year-old Perdita secured two or three of the salmon sandwiches from off the tray, in a deft, covert, and, as it were, rapacious motion,—and

devoured them with a greedy avidity more appropriate in a starving animal than in a charming young lady! Detected, she flashed unrepentant eyes at Abigail: yet remained stonily unsmiling: and would not
warm to her cousin.

As Georgina spoke of the gratifying number of condolence cards
and letters she had received since Erasmus's funeral, Abigail took
pained note of the spinster's waxen pallor, which might have been becoming, in the fashion of the times, in a woman some years younger,
or possessed of more agreeable features: but was decidedly unflattering
in Georgina. Though but three years older than Abigail, Georgina gave
every appearance of being a dozen years older: for her high, narrow,
finely wrinkled brow was the more deeply creased when, it seemed,
she was struck by a vexatious thought,—which, to judge from her
manner at tea, was fairly often. At the Judge's funeral, Abigail recalled
with what stiff, numbed, yet unfailingly efficient propriety Georgina
had behaved: having made most of the funeral arrangements herself,
and seeing, however cursorily, to the comfort of the many visitors who
had journeyed to Winterthurn to pay their final respects to Erasmus
Kilgarvan. Brisk, and forthright, and coolly gracious, her eye not
reddened from crying, nor her slender hand given to trembling, the
"Blue Nun" had not failed at her duty, no more than she had failed,—
as everyone whispered—to manage Erasmus's household for most of
her adult life: and to take on the responsibilities of mistress of Glen
Mawr, after the somewhat clouded death of her father's second wife,
when Thérèse and Perdita were very young children. (Of the actual
manner of death of the sickly and, it was said, *unnatural* Hortense
Spies,—who had married the middle-aged Erasmus when scarcely
more than a girl herself—Abigail knew very little: and deemed it best,
as all the family counseled, not to inquire.)

A most enigmatic portrait Miss Georgina Kilgarvan now presented to her cousin's kindly, yet anxious, eye: her cheeks distinctly
hollowed, yet her eyes possessing a mica-like glint, or glitter, that bespoke some suppressed excitation: and did she not retain, for all her air
of a spinster's stiff posture, a girlishness,—a most appealing artlessness—of old? Abigail had gone away to boarding school at the
Canandaigua Episcopal Female Seminary some miles to the west,
where her cousin Georgina was already a student,—nay, one of the
"leaders"—and she could see, in the Georgina of the present, certain
remnants of that schoolgirl, in whom high spirits, willfulness, and a
penchant for sarcasm contended. She would have liked to inquire, discreetly, after Georgina's poetry: as to whether she had in truth abandoned it,—as, it was said, her father wished; but knew not how to
introduce the subject. (Georgina had published a few poems, under
the nom de plume of "Iphigenia," which Abigail had had pointed out

to her, in one or another of the magazines: difficult, obscure, riddle-some, and, it seemed to Abigail's untrained eye, needlessly disagreeable verse!—which baffled the intellect with its clotted syntax, and the ear, with its failure to rhyme. As a schoolgirl at Canandaigua she had quite intimidated her teachers, as well as her fellow students, with her *promise* as a poetess; yet her development afterward, so far as Abigail and others in the family could determine, was most disappointing.)

At Canandaigua, Georgina had been the editor of *Canandaigua Bluets*, the young ladies' annual anthology of *belles lettres*; she had been the leader of expeditions "into the field," to observe birds, trees, wildflowers, and the like; she had walked away, as it were, with many of the honors,—in such divers subjects as Latin, and French, and Elo-cution, and the Classics, and English Literature; she had blossomed, to the amazement of all the Kilgarvans, from a taciturn, withdrawn, sickly miss, given to inordinate brooding, to a forthright and hand-some young lady,—which must have pleased her father, as he had feared, with great justification, an unwholesome sort of influence from Georgina's mother, who had died when the girl was but ten.

She had then gone away to New York City, to the continued amazement of the family, there to matriculate at Barnard College: and insisting upon taking her residence, not with anyone she knew (for several distant cousins, of an older generation, lived there), but in a boarding house for young single ladies in Morningside Heights. Pre-cisely how long Georgina stayed there, Abigail could not recall: but remembered dimly that she had returned home to nurse her ailing fa-ther, once or twice, and then had been pressed into returning home permanently, without taking her degree. Erasmus had suffered an ulcerous condition, it was said; or heart pains; or gout; or,—but Abigail could not recall. (It was a massive stroke that had finally killed him, striking him down dead: yet all remarked how unexpected such a blow was, as, for a gentleman of his years and industry, he had enjoyed un-commonly good health—!) Settling back into her home at Glen Mawr, Georgina had acquired an excellent position as an instructress at the Parthian Academy for Girls, some nine or ten miles away, in Winterthurn City; and had adjusted herself with little complaint, it was said, to having her "wings clipped,"—though not ceasing, evi-dently, to write her curious little verses.

All unexpectedly, she had been courted, in her thirty-second year, by a gentleman of poetical and musical inclinations, by the name of Guillemot,—whether Maurice, or Malcolm, Abigail could not re-call; but, as this somewhat mysterious personage was exposed as a cra-ven *fortune hunter* (or so family legend would have it), the courtship had been most unceremoniously terminated, with no official engage-ment; and so much distress on poor Georgina's part, it was said she never fully recovered: quitting her position at the Academy soon after, and "taking the veil,"—which is to say, turning by degrees into a spinster of eccentric habits and dress. Ah, unhappy Georgina!—Abigail recalled with pain a visit she and Mr. Whimbrel had made to Glen Mawr, some eight or ten years ago, when, shown into this very drawing room by the butler, they had surprised Georgina at her desk, in the act of poetical creation,—and so discountenanced her, she clasped her writing materials to her bosom and ran out of the room like a frightened rabbit; and refused to come downstairs again, no matter how sternly Judge Kilgarvan commanded her. "My daughter is shamed, it seems, to be discovered at her scribbling," Erasmus had said, with every attempt to make light of a most unsettling incident, "yet she persists in the folly: and will not even shrink from publishing the results! Perhaps, dear little Abigail, *you* might whisper some sense into her ear—?"

But Abigail had no more dared approach her elder cousin at that time than she did now, on any terms intimate, or at all direct.

Thus it was, Georgina had passed through her girlhood, and her young womanhood, with, it seemed, a dismaying swiftness: known now through the city as the "Blue Nun"—a figure of pity, curiosity, and not a little trepidation. When they had come to the Manor to inform her of Erasmus Kilgarvan's untimely death, it was reported that she leapt from her chair like a doe pierced through the heart, by the hunter's bullet; that for long minutes she stared frozen into space, her blanched lips shaped to an eerie smile; and that, finally, as the enormity of the shock made its impress upon her, her face drained of all blood, and, gasping and choking, her fingers tearing at her bodice, she sank heavily to the floor. "O dear Father! O God! Where is Thy pity—!" she exclaimed, before descending into blessèd unconsciousness.

Thus, Abigail's melancholy reverie, the while Georgina spoke of those acquaintances, public officials, associates of the Judge's, and certain relatives who had,—or was it that they had *not?*—expressed the proper degree of sympathy upon the tragic occasion. Thérèse and Perdita sat stiffly motionless, as if daring neither to concur nor to object,—though Abigail gathered, from a slight tremor of Thérèse's lip, and a more emphatic sullenness on the part of Perdita, that the sisters had heard these complaints many times in the past; and found them tiresome. With especial ire Georgina took up the subject of the "other Kilgarvans" of Winterthurn City: this being a family of very limited means, dwelling near Wycombe Place, and headed by Erasmus's young half-brother, Lucas, who had been struck from their father's will some years before,—for what particular reason, Abigail did not know. All atumble came Georgina's words now, as if she had been awakened from an oversolemn trance, and might at last vent her spleen. "Just barely, dear Abigail, could they restrain themselves, at Father's gravesite," she said severely, "the *pack* of them: Mr. and Mrs. and great hulking boys, with little pretense of displaying even a hypocrite's sorrow; and many a hint of the savage triumph they felt at viewing poor Father's casket. Mr. Lucas Kilgarvan, the *half-breed*,—nay, do not wince, dear Cousin, for I shall call him that, as Father did: the profligate,—the ruffian,—the ingrate,—the *toymaker*,—whom I shall never call Uncle: nor any of those brutes, cousins of *mine*. No, Cousin Abigail," Georgina said, though Abigail had made no motion to interrupt, "we can never forgive Lucas for the despicable publicity he sought, in contesting Grandfather's will: nay, and pursuing the case to the highest court in the state. How mortified poor Father was!—and Simon Esdras as well, for all his reserve. Never,—never—can we forgive: we *dare* not."

Abigail said, with tentative boldness: "Cousin Georgina, I fear you exaggerate the situation, for I was present at the funeral, and at your father's gravesite, and it did not strike *me* that Lucas and his family behaved—"

"Nay, you are not very perceptive," Georgina said, "or, it may be, you are too *good:* for Goodness, as Father has said, stumbles and gropes in the dark, possessing but a single eye; and depending upon the rest of us for,—for guidance."

So rudely silenced, Abigail bethought herself how best to reply, and sipped nervously at her tea, which she could not taste: the while her infant son's crying sounded faintly from upstairs and agèd Jupiter stirred, and fretted, and sighed in his slumber, with a most human species of resignation. As if following the course of her thoughts, Georgina continued the assault, saying that it was scarcely a secret that the "pack" of Wycombe Street Kilgarvans rejoiced in Erasmus Kilgarvan's death; that it was highly likely they had engaged an attorney, to seek again a reversal of the will; that it was altogether obvious at the funeral that the sons,—the youngest in particular—were restless, and insolent, and clearly *bored:* being, after all, mere animals,—loutish boys.

Abigail gently protested that she could see no basis for alluding to Lucas Kilgarvan and his family as a *pack:* for was not Lucas in truth a Kilgarvan, despite the unfortunate falling-out between himself and his elder brothers; and was not his wife a De Forrest,—the De Forrests being old Winterthurn stock indeed; and were not the sons more properly designated *young gentlemen* than either *louts*, or *boys?* For the eldest, Bradford, must be at least twenty-five years of age; and the youngest, Xavier,—for was not Xavier the one with the curly black hair?—must surely be sixteen years old, and quite grown up. Moreover—

At this, however, Georgina appeared inordinately distressed;

and drew a grayish lace handkerchief out of her sleeve, with which she dabbed at her upper lip and brow; and murmured in an agitated voice that it quite baffled her why Abigail should wish to take *their* side, since she evidently preferred Erasmus Kilgarvan's family, to visit. Nor was it comprehensible to Georgina why Abigail should make it a point to designate Lucas's sons by *name:* there being a particular anathema in the household regarding *Xavier,*—the which word Georgina pronounced as if it were a foreign term, and vile. Abigail could not resist displaying surprise at this revelation: and Georgina continued hurriedly to explain that the boy in question, "Xavier," had behaved most atrociously in the cemetery, paying but a perfunctory attention to the minister's words, and casting his eyes,—indeed, his *bold and smoldering gaze*—where he would: upward to the clouds, downward to the earth, to one side, to another, upon Georgina herself, and, most invidiously, upon Perdita. "Why, the insolent creature stared at me as if desirous of penetrating my innermost thoughts," Georgina said, breathing now somewhat shallowly, "and as to his motives for contemplating my sister, I dare not speculate. Yet I should not have minded the insult to us, and to Father's memory, if my shameless little wench of a sister had not, all coyly, and with but a clumsy attempt at secrecy, *gazed upon him in return.*"

An involuntary twitch in Perdita stimulated Georgina to press onward, and to declare, with an ironic smile for Abigail's benefit, that Perdita naturally denied the charges: "For she is most adroit in feigning both innocence and tears. Yet it would require a far more clever child than she to fool 'Miss Georgina': for *I saw what I saw, and what I cannot see, I can surmise.*"

This perplexing outburst was met by silence: for poor Perdita sat stiffly immobile in her chair, with no more spirit than a wooden doll,—albeit her lower lip trembled, and the tight clasping of her hands indicated significant distress. Abigail glanced from one sister to the other, feeling most awkward indeed, and wondering if the subject had grown too urgent to be deflected by a lightsome remark, or a query on some neutral matter. How very pale Georgina had grown, and how queerly her dark eyes glittered! "Might it be that some innocent question regarding the late Judge's personal papers, and whether Georgina had plans to edit them, would 'save the day'—?" Abigail inwardly murmured. Yet she felt very much the schoolgirl, beneath Georgina Kilgarvan's unflagging gaze, and dared not speak.

Then, all boldly, though in a palpitant voice, Thérèse sought to defend her sister: saying that Georgina was surely mistaken, as *she* had noticed nothing amiss in Perdita's behavior, whether during the funeral service, or in the cemetery. "Albeit we were all distracted by the occasion, Perdita no less than you and me," Thérèse said hurriedly, as if she feared being interrupted, ''—yet I would swear to it, that she did not misbehave, in such a way. We have covered this ground in the past, Georgina, and I must reiterate, though risking your anger, that both Perdita and I were totally taken by surprise when, upon our return home, on that most harrowing of days, you so violently excoriated our cousin Xavier—''

"Ah, you delight in his name!" Georgina said. "Doubtless you luxuriate in the mere sound of it,—the purulent syllables—the *melody!*"

"Why, Georgina, Xavier *is* our cousin, and he *is* a Kilgarvan," Thérèse falteringly said. "How should I *not* know his name?"

Georgina commanded her to be still, and to hold her tongue for the remainder of the hour: else Cousin Abigail should carry back to Contracoeur the remarkable news that the Kilgarvan sisters, though in mourning for their father, enjoyed nothing more than discussing young boys over tea. Perdita, it seems, was a "past mistress" of deception, though plying the world with an angelic face calculated to wring the hearts of fools. Of divers morbid, unclean, secret, and thoroughly perverse practices, indulged in (she had no doubt) by the "pious" Thérèse no less than Perdita, Georgina would not speak; nor did she allow herself even to think; and she recommended a like attitude for Abigail, in regard to her young children.

For some painful seconds it appeared that Perdita might succumb to angry tears, which, Abigail feared, would the more antagonize Georgina; but the child held herself in commendable control; until, of a sudden, another spasmodic twitch overcame her body, and she raised her eyes,—ah, how darkly brilliant, how wondrously insolent, those eyes!—and said in a voice eerily matched to Georgina's, in tone and rhythm: "You lie. It is not true. I have no friend in him. This 'Xavier.' I have no friend. I know no one,—and no one knows me. I love no one,—and no one loves—''

"Quite enough," Georgina said. "You will go upstairs at once: your tea is concluded."

Abigail sought to intercede, but none of the principals paid her heed: and it struck her as significant that Georgina should speak these words with an air of gratified triumph; and that Perdita, though visibly trembling with rage, should rise with such dutiful alacrity, and make an old-fashioned half-curtsy in Abigail's direction, and straightaway leave the room. "Such impudence," Georgina said softly, "fairly begs for the whip: but must content itself by going without dinner."

Briefly, when the tea things were about to be cleared away, and Abigail was quite fatigued, Simon Esdras made his belated appearance,—with such mumbled apologies, it was impossible to know what he said.

Though the white-haired gentleman was unfailingly amiable, with a low bow and a gracious smile for Abigail, that lady suffered the distinct impression that her uncle *did not recognize her:* and it seemed most impolitic for her to introduce herself. All clearly, Simon Esdras's attention was elsewhere, doubtless back in his study: and the tea he vaguely sipped, and the several sandwiches he ate, failed to make any tangible impression on him. Inquiring after the ladies' health,—making idle and witty commentary upon the weather,— stirring three or four sugar cubes in his tea, with inexpert turns of his spoon: thus Simon Esdras, the "private thinker," navigated the shoals of the drawing room, with little expenditure of his spirit. "Ah, yes?— hmmm!—*yes*,—so it has invariably struck me, indeed!" he murmured, with a kindly crinkling of his eyes and a thin, though benign, smile.

Simon Esdras, now in his mid- or late sixties, had been a youthful prodigy who had published, at the age of nineteen, a monograph addressing itself to the epistemological foundations of mankind's perception of existence,—its precise title being *A Treatise on the Probable "Existence" of the World.* (Neither Abigail nor any other member of her family, alas, had had much success in penetrating the elaborate coils and clots of Simon Esdras's prose: though harboring no doubt that their brilliant relative was correct in his reasoning.) So far as Abigail knew, subsequent works from Simon Esdras's pen had failed to make a like impression upon the philosophical world, doubtless as a result of their unusual difficulty, and challenge to "the complacency of American and European thought": but Simon Esdras was not in the slightest deterred, and was said to be in pursuit of his vision with yet more vigor than before. "Had I been of a temper to 'suffer fools gladly' in the academic world," Simon Esdras once observed, in a rare moment of self-commentary, "I should by now be unquestioned in my position, at the very pinnacle of that tiny, and most devilishly slippery, pyramid of professorial rank: but lacking such latitudinarianism, in social no less than philosophical coinage, I must content myself with the triumphs of solitude,—and of Posterity."

In his person, the philosopher struck an altogether amiable, and even unassuming, figure, being rather more "roly-poly" than not: of conspicuously less than medium height: with a small, high, adamantly round belly: a moon-shaped face in which hazel eyes were widely and innocently set, and the Kilgarvan nose decidedly snubbed, to exude a boyish air. Thus it seemed to Abigail a wondrous thing, and entirely to her uncle's credit, that, being a gentleman, and well aware of the disparity between his intelligence and that of his companions, he behaved with an utter lack of pretension; and turned upon the world an expression of guileless and acute *interest*, in conjunction with an air of the *unfocused*, and the *unjudging*. So it seemed that, while his outer eye moved about normally, his inner eye fixed itself upon other matters entirely, of a private nature. He beamed upon Abigail; he engaged Abigail in lightsome parlor chatter; he took no notice of Perdita's absence, nor, indeed, of the tense "atmosphere" into which he had so artlessly stepped; the while the fine mechanism of his brain pursued its arcane interests.

When Thérèse proffered him the plate of sandwiches, he smilingly helped himself, observing generally that it mattered not a whit to him *what* he ate, or even *that* he ate, so long as he should be freed of vexatious metaphysical questions as to the *actual substance* of what he ate; or, indeed, *why* he ate.

Abigail then inquired after Simon Esdras's health: for which polite query he thanked her: but said that, as he was no hypochondriac, he rarely troubled to analyze his interior state, or even to take notice as to whether his heart beat, or no: this too being a topic largely given over to females. "Inner or outer weather," the white-haired philosopher declared smilingly, "it is all the same, to me!"

Again, the ladies laughed, though not with an excess of exuberance; and, as she saw Simon Esdras was about to take his leave, Abigail proffered her condolences once again to him, hoping that he would soon recover from the shock of the Judge's untimely death. These words gave Simon Esdras pause, it seemed, for he frowned fleetingly; and set down his cup at so crooked an angle, tea slopped into his saucer. Yet it was in a charmingly placid voice that he said: "Madame, it is doubtful that any event, in *time*, can be proven *untimely:* for does not the very statement fly in the face of Logic? If one dies, moreover, it follows that one has died neither before nor after 'his' time, but precisely *at* 'his' time: the simple proof of the matter being, *that he has died.* Why, dear lady, do you think it logical, or even possible, that we might die *before*, or *after*, 'our' proper times—?"

Poor Abigail could not determine whether this question was merely rhetorical or serious: thus she fumblingly essayed to answer it, while Simon Esdras smiled in her direction, but gave little sign of attending to her words: and, of a sudden, laying his napkin down, declared that he must be off, for his work beckoned, and he had not "*time* to deal with such knotty subjects, even with persons of demonstrated brilliance like herself."

After he had made his gracious exit, the ladies sat in subdued silence; then Abigail ventured the opinion that Simon Esdras *was* a most original genius, of which the family had good reason to be proud: yet it must give him pain to be pressed into drawing-room conversation of the usual sort.

"No, dear Abigail," Georgina said, "such trivial matters cannot

give Uncle pain; for I have reason to believe, he has rarely experienced
so vulgar a thing in all his sixty-odd years. Pain, as you must know, is
too common altogether: it is but a female prerogative.''

*. . . How inappropriate for Baby & me to be placed in this opulent bed-
chamber,* Abigail took note in her diary, to which she had restlessly
turned when, it seemed, Holy Writ failed her, *a room for a General &
his bride, surely,—a room for a queen—yet one's soul is dwarfed in
such chill splendor: & Baby & me much the better served to be housed
in more humble quarters.*

The General's Room, or, to give it its more notorious appellation, the Honeymoon Room, was executed in conspicuously ornate
French style: which is to say, more precisely, in the "Americanized"
manner of the Louis Seize revival style of the France of Napoleon. Its
original decor must have been eighteenth-century, as it had been prepared for General Pettit Kilgarvan and his beauteous young second
wife, a daughter of Thomas Pinckney's, a full century before; in the
1870s it was redone by Georgina's grandfather, the somewhat eccentric
Phillips Goode, whose stated aim it was to see all three of his sons,—
Erasmus, Simon Esdras, and young Lucas—firmly ensconced at the
very pinnacle, as he phrased it, of their chosen professions: and to see
Glen Mawr Manor established as one of the premier "jewels" of the
Winterthurn Valley: money being no problem, for a gentleman of Revolutionary blood who had increased his fortune tenfold in those unparalleled years following the War Between the States.

Thus it was, Phillips Goode heard word of the fashionable ar-
chitect Richardson, and his controversial "monumental" style, and
hired him, at great expense, to redo several rooms at Glen Mawr, the
most resplendent being the room in which Abigail now found herself:
which boasted not one but two exquisite French fireplaces, decorated
in filigree, mosaics, and mirrored surfaces; and numberless graceful
niches, for the display of costly *objets d'art;* and an entire wall
magnificently covered in morocco, or a most cunning imitation; and
gilt-framed mirrors with etched glass, in designs of gay floating
cherubs, ivy, roses, and the like,—the which reflected, to Abigail's
way of thinking, singularly disagreeable ghost-images of herself. The
room's furnishings, in a bold composite of Louis Seize, Italian Renais-
sance, and something approaching the medieval, had all been provided
by the famed Herter Brothers of New York City, and were most impressive indeed: yet the outstanding feature of the Honeymoon Room
was its several Fairfax Eakins paintings, in ingenious *trompe l'oeil*
style,—the which Phillips Goode had hoped would call wide cultural
attention to Glen Mawr, and to his role as a patron of the arts.

The most ambitious of these paintings was a mural that covered much of a wall, and part of the ceiling, freely copied from a fifteenth-century German painting known as "The Virgin in the Rose-Bower" (artist unknown). While speaking with Abigail earlier that day, Georgina had said in a somewhat uncharacteristic moment of frankness that her late father bitterly regretted the fact that his sire had been so extravagant as to have Eakins paint his masterpiece directly on the wall. "So it is, and always shall be, that Glen Mawr's splendid 'Virgin in the Rose-Bower' blooms unseen," Georgina said, her voice low with passion, "—a great loss to all lovers of our native American art."

Doubtless it was a principle of aesthetic harmony, Abigail thought, that the artist had executed the mural with so resolute an eye for balance and symmetry: for all the figures, despite their floating, and careening, and lurching about, had been placed upon a sort of grid,—this being the central trellis of the rose-bower, which looked, to the superficial glance, rather like a spider's web. Abigail made a show of admiring the Virgin, though, in her surly medieval, or Teutonic, guise, she seemed little desirous of awakening admiration in the viewer; and wondered aloud, to Georgina, whether it *might* result in some such predicament,—being *divine*, that is, while at the same time being *human*. "Indeed," Abigail observed, with a slight shudder, "*I* should find it a distinctly uncomfortable position to have given birth under such circumstances: and to take up the mantle, as it were, of maternal responsibility, at the request of Our Lord Himself. And, also, oh dear!—how it should disturb Mr. Whimbrel as well!—the role of St. Joseph being somewhat ambiguous, as I recall."

It was not the figures of the Virgin and Child, however, but those of the angelic host, executed in flamboyant *trompe l'oeil* style, that gave the mural its disconcerting effect. One or two angels were painted in a conventional flat manner; but all the rest appeared in motion; and alive; and in three dimensions. Several of the more developed angels, executed with their heads, shoulders, and torsos out of proportion to the rest of their bodies, gave the uncanny impression of leaning out of the wall,—so much so that Abigail had to resist the childlike impulse to raise an arm, that she might ward them off. There were upward of a dozen of these remarkable cherubs: some recognizably,—and altogether shamelessly—male; some daintily feminine; some more sensuously and unapologetically female; and one or two of indeterminate gender. Ah, what a cornucopia of wings!—large, and absurdly small; straight, curved, bent, and hooked; feathered in silky black, or silver, or white; or feathered not at all, it seemed, so much as *scaled*. As if the artist had been lazily indifferent to his craft, the quality of the angels' faces differed widely, some being most skillfully rendered, and others but hurriedly. One or two possessed the rubicund heartiness of the Germanic or Dutch nationality; some clearly de-

rived from a more delicate Latinate heritage; some, with pronounced
cheekbones, and sly, slanted, almond-shaped eyes, betrayed Mongol
blood. There were complexions of so stark an alabaster white, the wan
Georgina seemed healthy set beside them; while the more portly
angels exhibited a florid puffiness, of the kind associated with sybaritic
overindulgence—! And how puzzling, too, the contrasting facial expressions: rapt adoration in one; indifference in another; and *hauteur*;
and faint repugnance; and bemusement; and childlike wonder; and,—
but did Abigail's affrighted eye mislead her?—*frank lascivious interest*,
directed toward the chaste Virgin herself.

So entranced was Georgina, she seemed to have forgotten Abigail altogether in her frowning admiration of the figures: and only
roused herself to observe, finally, that she never entered the Honeymoon Room without being reminded of those mysterious words of St.
Theresa's,—"An angel with a flaming golden arrow pierced my heart
repeatedly. The pain was so great that I screamed aloud, but simultaneously felt such infinite sweetness that I wished the pain to last eter-
nally . . . It was the sweetest caressing of the soul by God."

Uttering these words in a reverent tone, Georgina was, of a sudden, overcome by a fit of coughing and breathlessness; and shrank
from Abigail's solicitousness, as if wishing not to be touched. Abigail
was reminded of a scene of many years previous,—why, at her own
wedding-day banquet, in her parents' Contracoeur home:—when
Georgina, in the midst of the fish course, began to cough and choke
with such violence that it was feared she might have swallowed a
bone: and Judge Kilgarvan suggested, in a brusque but not unkindly
voice, that she betake herself upstairs until she was recovered from her
fit, and less flushed, and "fit again for decent eyes." Poor Georgina!—
she who was so proud, and so fastidious in her bearing, and so self-
conscious! With her napkin hiding half her flaming face, she had had to
suffer not only the discomfort of the coughing spell (caused by nothing
more substantial than a mouthful of Burgundy wine) but the humiliation of feeling all eyes in the dining room upon her: and knowing
that her artful pompadour had been shaken loose, and certain swaths
of false hair, designed to disguise the thinness of her own, revealed to
the keen eyes of the ladies.

Now, as then, Georgina had steadfastly resisted aid; and Abigail,
feeling rebuffed, took note of the ghost-reflections of herself and her
cousin in one of the large mirrors: the one tall, pale, alarmingly thin,
with a skin that seemed to radiate white heat; the other much shorter,
and plumper, and healthier in her skin tone and general bearing,—yet,
it seemed, far less *intriguing*. Though they stood near each other, the
two women gave every impression of being absolute strangers; figures
in a coolly executed mural, that hinted of no tender ties of blood and

kinship. "Nay, do not fuss, Abigail," Georgina managed to say, when her breath was shakily restored, *"I am quite all right."*

Impatient with waiting. With longing. So lonely. So hungry. These many years. O cruel belovèd Mother: our time now approaches.

She had nodded off to sleep, it seems, her diary sliding from her lap and her stubbed quill pen quite lost in the languorous folds of the bed. Yet she was able to bestow another kiss on Baby's warm brow; and to give the wicker cradle a final rocking caress; and to extinguish the lamp's flame, that voluptuous shadows might rush forward, from the bed-chamber's niches and mirrors, to embrace her. *O Mother. O belovèd. O cruel. These many years . . .*

Why did the sight so disturb?—angels with the cruel-hooked wings of bats or vultures, all apulse with their secret life, the painted flesh they inhabited, which did not satisfy them. An angel most lewdly stroked the strings of his mandolin while a companion angel, female, with peacock's feathers of an oily slickness, strummed at her harp, squinting and dimpling. Abigail's head had grown heavy in the space of a few seconds. Her calfskin diary had been spirited away: ah, and the pen!—would not ink despoil the bed linens?

A baby or midget angel no larger than a rat, with comical wings that were but wisps of down sprouting from his shoulders, crouched at the Virgin's chaste foot, piccolo in hand, and carmine lips pursed in an attitude of kissing, or sucking: such boldness!—but then he was naught but a babe, and knew no better. Surprised by pain, Abigail whimpered aloud, pushing the small head from her breast. Why, how was it possible, Charleton had slipped into her bed, and burrowed beneath the covers, and opened her nightgown? He had never done such a thing before: and now his lips were greedy, and pulled with an amazing violence at poor Abigail's nipple—! *Impatient. Impatient. O cruel belovèd . . .*

Close about her were fluttering wings, and high-pitched anxious cries, and a tumult of flesh,—ruddy, and creamy-pale, and starkly white; on all sides mouths, sucking lips, bared teeth; eyes that winked and glittered. *O Mother: cruel Mother! We have waited so long!* Abigail drew breath to scream but could not utter a sound, for, of a sudden, the babe's gums grew teeth, of a remarkable sharpness, which fastened in her flesh and could not be shaken away. Flushed cheeks,—dimpled bellies,—mouths, and lips, and tongues: so many: and Infant Jesus's ravenous mouth at her breast, wildly sucking her life from her. *It is our time. It is our time. You cannot resist.* "Monsters," Abigail cried, "—and devils: how dare you touch me thus? *I am not your mother."*

Yet it seemed she could not resist: and the lapping and sucking noises grew louder: for if, in a frenzy, she pushed one heated face aside, did not another, equally greedy, nudge forward to take its place? All desperately she tugged at the forelock of a great shambling boy-angel, a creature but flimsily clad, with protuberant blue eyes, and garish flushed cheeks, and lardy thighs and buttocks so disfigured by dimples, they appeared pocked: but tears of angry despair ran hotly down his cheeks,—how then could she deny him? "But spare Charleton! Spare my Charleton!" Abigail pleaded. Both her breasts, though already streaming blood, were taken up, in ravenous mouths, and sorely abused: no angel being willing to give way until, sated, sighing, he sank beside her, burrowing and clutching close. "I am sinful,—yet blameless," Abigail murmured. "O dear God have mercy—" The very wall beside her head echoed in uncouth laughter, amidst the drunken sound of pipes, and horns, and mandolins, and tambourines. Slippery as an eel, an infant cherub crawled exhilarant to the foot of the bed, beneath the covers, to suck, with unparalleled audacity, at Abigail's toes—! Whereupon a swoon of such incalculable sweetness overtook her, she had no breath with which to protest: and no words: for it seemed the very Devil clutched her fast in his grip, and would not release her.

The Keening

———————

Our time is six weeks previous; our setting, the gravesite of Chief Justice Erasmus Kilgarvan, in the Temperance Vale Cemetery. For it is here that a most puzzling event occurred, even as Reverend De Forrest led a small contingent of mourners in a final prayer for the repose of Mr. Kilgarvan's soul.

Of a sudden, it seemed that a peculiar alteration of the air defined itself: the wintry sun, though hidden all morning behind cruel-ribbed banks of cloud, now glared forth, and harshly illuminated certain granite and marble surfaces in the cemetery; and, with especial malevolence, the high-polished surface of Erasmus Kilgarvan's ebony casket. Why, it seemed for a disconcerting instant that the very stones might speak! Then, to the amazement of all, an uncanny sound lifted: faint, musical, aggrieved, yet subtly angry; of so eerily poignant a quality, it could scarcely be attributed to the cry of a mere bird or animal. Yet it did not seem to be human: nor was it issuing from any of the mourners assembled close about the Kilgarvan tomb.

Numerous persons glanced up in surprise, and some alarm. But none of the deceased's daughters was weeping; Miss Georgina in particular, standing stiff beside her uncle Simon Esdras, her face nearly hidden behind a black muslin veil, gave no outward sign of distress. The sound retreated; then lifted yet again, and defined itself as a high-pitched tremulous wail, or *keening*, of such inexpressible grief, it was all but unbearable to hear.

Ah, what a temptation it was, for the youngest of the mourners, to investigate the source of the sound: but of course no one wished to interrupt Reverend De Forrest's concluding prayer. Even young Xavier Kilgarvan stood his ground, his head bowed in an attitude of prayer, though his sensitive nerves were roused at once; and he knew himself in the presence of *mystery*.

I hope it is not to young Xavier's discredit that he felt some small disappointment that the funeral ceremony at Grace Episcopal Church had proceeded with no remarkable interruptions: for there had been a most alarming rumor, spread promiscuously through town, that divers lowlife persons would rush into the church to disrupt the prayers,—these being enemies of the deceased. But all had proceeded with a tedious sort of solemnity; and the lengthy funeral procession, snaking its slow way through town, had rather more evoked awe and frowning apprehension than any visible expression of malcontent. Then, too, the late Chief Justice had been provided with a substantial police escort,—the which assuredly discouraged acts of mischief.

"Can it be," young Xavier inwardly wondered, "that my hateful uncle will be laid in his grave in *peace?*"

A curious sort of impiety, one might think: but it must be recalled that the boy had been fed, since earliest childhood, all sorts of confused tales of the way in which his father, Lucas, had been disinherited by Phillips Goode Kilgarvan, on that gentleman's very deathbed: to the great advantage of Erasmus and Simon Esdras. And, too, at the time of the Glen Mawr murders, Xavier was but a fresh-cheeked lad of sixteen, who liked to imagine opposition, and actual enmity, where perhaps there was naught but indifference.

Though it was often charged against Xavier Kilgarvan, in later years, that he had been a Free Thinker, or an Anarchist, or a traitor to his class,—indeed, a born troublemaker—from boyhood onward, the facts are otherwise: for our young man, though bristling with every sort of adolescent impulse, and nursing, as it were, a smoldering species of resentment, was very much a child of his time. It would have greatly incensed him to hear reasoned arguments against the Episcopal Church; or against his conception of the Divine Power of the Universe. (Fortunately, the youth had been but slightly exposed to such atheistical notions as Darwinism, Communism, and Anarchism, though he had found Mr. Reade's curious *Martyrdom of Man* in a secondhand bookstore, and intended to peruse it soon.) While kneeling at his daily prayers Xavier oft pondered over certain principles of faith which vexed him, as they were so slippery to grasp; but he had not the sensibility of the doubter. Already, though hardly more than a child in years, he had essayed to bring together the fundamental principles of his religious faith and his "detective's" faith,—for he had long fancied, in secret, a career of crime detection. "The Universe is so constructed,

I believe, that *balance* and *justice* are inherent in it," he thought, knitting his smooth brow, "—God the Father being the highest manifestation of Truth, and Jesus Christ our sole means of apprehending that Truth. Yet," he sighed, running impatient fingers through his curly hair, "—I must confess that these are but words to me; and I am bound to put my faith in,—faith."

As it was Lucas Kilgarvan's stubborn dream that, of his several sons, one or two at least might become gentlemen, despite the family's loss of fortune, he had enrolled Xavier in the prestigious Winterthurn Academy for Boys: albeit the tuition was extremely high, and Mr. Kilgarvan might well have used the money to settle some of his debts. At school, however, Xavier managed to excel in most of his studies; and evinced a quick, inquisitive mind, to the delight of his teachers. He was discovered to have a natural if undisciplined flair for drawing; an energetic sort of talent for music; and, in his spare hours, he liked to construct experimental models for his father's toymaker's workshop (albeit his successes quickly bored him, and his failures roused him to fits of ill temper). Unknown to his parents, he had acquired, since the age of thirteen, an alarming appetite for nickel-and-dime novels of the trashiest,—nay, the most lurid—species: and surreptitiously exchanged with his classmates every manner of adventure tale, of the Wild West, the Seven Seas, and "crime detection," which the majority of the Academy boys read with shameless avidity when they ought rather to be studying their Caesar.

He was proud rather than vain, despite his angelic good looks, the main source of his irritation being the fact that his family had "come down" so visibly in the world: for he knew how the Kilgarvans of Wycombe Street were oft designated, with chilling dispatch, as the "poor" Kilgarvans,—to distinguish them from their wealthy relatives who lived at Glen Mawr. And, ah!—how deep the insult cut into the sensitive youth!

Likenesses of Xavier Kilgarvan as a boy betray such classic masculine beauty, it is not to be wondered at that Miss Georgina should suspect her young cousin and her young half-sister of "romantic" mischief: for, with his Grecian profile, and his dreamy opal-gray eyes, and his olive-pale complexion so readily suffused with warmth, and, framing all, his abundant, lustrous, ebony-black curls,—how should Xavier fail to suggest a type of precocity that is both innocent and childlike, yet gravely unsettling,—and, withal, especially disturbing to those who have had some experience with romance of the more delirious sort, and its attendant tragedies? (For it was well known through Winterthurn that poor Georgina had suffered a broken heart in her youth.)

So it came about that Georgina imagined that her handsome

young cousin Xavier,—whom, in truth, she scarcely knew!—was boldly staring at her, with the intention of "penetrating" her brain; and that he cast improper eyes upon Perdita,—even as the party of some thirty mourners stood assembled on one of the loftiest ridges of the cemetery, before the noble granite mausoleum of the Kilgarvans.

Indeed, in his restlessness, Xavier had allowed his gaze to settle upon the twelve-year-old Perdita: and it began to perplex him, that this mere child, whom he had hardly noticed in the past, now radiated so somber, yet so potent, a girlish beauty, he found himself quite strangely absorbed. "Girls" as such interested him not at all; "romance" was but a word,—and an unappealing word at that. And he quite naturally felt some animosity toward all the Kilgarvans of Glen Mawr,—whom it pleased him to consider his and his father's enemies.

It was while Xavier stood staring in his cousin's direction that the air so radically altered, and the sun seemed to burst forth from a dozen blinding angles, reflected from tombstones on all sides; and the unearthly keening sound materialized, to the distress of the mourners. Alas, what was it?—from whence did it issue? Rising as if from the grasses underfoot, or falling with exquisite lightness from the boughs of the agèd beech trees,—an expression of sorrow lightly tinted, it seemed, with anger,—now joined by another, and that by yet another: a chorus of grief never before heard in Winterthurn.

Then, of a sudden, before it could be distinctly *heard*, the sound dropped away.

Xavier Kilgarvan's senses were roused at once, but he knew not how to behave: and bethought himself that perhaps he had imagined it, and must not cause any disruption while Reverend De Forrest continued with his prayer.

Scarcely five yards away stood Miss Georgina herself, who betrayed not the slightest awareness of having heard anything out of the usual: a commanding presence, even on this morning of grief, in a black silk-and-wool mourning costume only spartanly adorned with ribands, and a very plain black hat, and a fur-lined woolen traveling cape (from out her mother's trousseau of forty-odd years previous, it was whispered, and, alas, somewhat moth-eaten): her head only slightly bowed, as if pride in the midst of her unparalleled sorrow, and in her station, kept her thus erect,—and, indeed, scornful of weakness. *Does all of Winterthurn watch?* the stiff-backed spinster seemed to muse. *Very well, then: I shall deprive them of any spectacle.*

All covertly, though, I suppose, somewhat rudely, Xavier observed his elder cousin: noted the splashes of damp on her traveling cape; noted her mismatched gloves—though each was black, their subtly warring textures proclaimed them unmated; noted the way in which her black muslin veil was sucked arrhythmically against her nose and mouth, and then released, and again sucked back, by the action of her hoarse breathing, leaving a patch of damp . . . Studying the "Blue Nun" thusly, Xavier felt a small pang of pity for her, rather than sympathy, for she *had* been entirely devoted to her father; and, though she had always turned a chill eye upon his entire family, rebuffing even Mrs. Kilgarvan's overtures of friendship, he could quite see that her life was "tragic" in the loose sense of the word. *"Cousins* we are said to be, by blood," Xavier thought, "yet *strangers* we are in fact: though more irrevocably divided than most strangers, in that we can never become *friends."*

Close beside Miss Georgina stood Simon Esdras, in whom Xavier had a more than ordinary interest: for he had closely perused his father's agèd copy of *A Treatise on the Probable "Existence" of the World*, which was said to have been published on the philosopher's nineteenth birthday: and found it a most tantalizing and knotty document, quite incomprehensible as to its meaning! Xavier had inquired of his father what the argument of the *Treatise* was—in brief: Did the world exist, or no; or was there merely the *probability* of its existing? But Lucas Kilgarvan had said he didn't know; and was of the opinion that the *Treatise* was proclaimed an act of youthful genius, and its author touted as another Spinoza, or Aristotle, by philosophers on both sides of the Atlantic, precisely because one could discern no "argument" in the book at all. The first *Treatise* was followed by a second, after a space of more than a decade, and though this monograph— *A Treatise on the "Probable" Existence of the World*—was said to thoroughly refute the claims of the first, Xavier could make very little sense of it; and tossed it irritably aside after a few hours' examination. (Which, indeed, was the general response, for the second *Treatise*, according to Xavier's father, "fell upon deaf ears," and received no reviews or notices, save one indignant dismissal in the English journal *Mind.*) At the age of forty-seven Simon Esdras published a third *Treatise*, by way of a private press located at Nautauga Falls, but this, *A Treatise on the Probable Existence of the "World,"* Lucas Kilgarvan did not own; and Xavier had not yet taken the time to locate it, in the public library, or to borrow it from the headmaster at the Academy: for he had begun to mistrust his ability to reason philosophically. The third *Treatise* was said to have met with slightly more enthusiasm than the second, though not proclaimed a work of genius: which disappointing response so outraged Simon Esdras, he declared he would henceforth boycott the world of philosophy, and never publish again. Yet a slim pamphlet of thirty-odd pages did appear, on his sixty-second birthday, with the formidable title *A Prolegomenon Concerning a Treatise on the "Probable Existence" of the World,*—this privately printed document exciting interest in only one fellow thinker, of whom no one in Winterthurn had ever heard: Charles Sanders Peirce, at this time residing in lonely exile in a small Pennsylvania town three hundred miles away. (It was believed that Peirce's lengthy letter to Simon Esdras proved gratifying, and somewhat restored his faith in the ability of the philosophical world to recognize his gifts: yet, such was Simon Esdras's indifference to social occasions, and his scorn for the "folly of seeking out persons in the flesh," that he and Peirce were never to meet; nor did their correspondence continue.)

Nonetheless, Xavier harbored some interest in his uncle: and might well have tried to befriend him had not the older gentleman behaved ambiguously in the matter of the contested will (announcing himself as indifferent to its outcome, yet profiting, nevertheless, from the judgment against Xavier's father); and had not the Manor been declared "off limits" to him and his brothers, by all adult parties involved in the dispute. "For he is, at the very least," Xavier reasoned, "an unusual relative; and might very well have something to teach me." But if Simon Esdras had any awareness of his four nephews, let alone any special interest in the youngest, he had certainly never given any sign: and when the curious wailing sound began, and, for an accidental moment, Xavier and Simon Esdras locked eyes, there appeared to be no recognition in the older man's silvery-gray gaze,—nor did his affable countenance betray any agitation beyond a fluttering of pale eyelashes. An enigmatic personage, indeed!—for Xavier thought him, in his lifelong willful seclusion in pursuit of Truth, more remarkable even than his renowned brother Erasmus; and decidedly more "colorful" than Xavier's own father.

The queer luminous-gray tone of Simon Esdras's eyes, enhanced by the lenses of his pince-nez, reminded Xavier of cats' or owls' eyes,—reflecting rather than absorbing light. Yet, in his somewhat shiny black suit that fitted him so indifferently, a narrow swath of stubble unshaven on his chin, he had so unstudied and *human* an air, it was impossible not to feel a measure of affection for him: and Xavier fancied he saw a distant smile playing about his thin lips . . .

Clothed in identical black capes of a heavy cotton-woolen fabric that possessed an unflattering sheen, wearing kindred black hats that might well, by the look of them, have been handed down by Georgina, the sisters Thérèse and Perdita maintained their wooden posture, at Simon Esdras's left elbow; and stood with heads meekly bowed, and cheeks agleam with tears, even as the eerie keening sound arose—though Xavier believed he could discern a nervous tic in the elder's eye; and sweet little Perdita, startled into glancing upward, revealed, through the gossamer veil that chastely covered her eyes, a gaze of extraordinary intensity. (And was not the reddened tip of her nose uniquely charming, Xavier thought; and the tremulous air of her pale parted lips; and her tiny foot, tightly encased in a black kidskin shoe, which peeped out, as it were, beneath the hem of her heavy dress?) But in the next instant, as the sourceless noise dropped away, the sisters the more resolutely bowed their heads, and clasped their dark-gloved hands against their bosoms. Did they hear? Xavier wondered. Or did they not? Yet he forbade himself to stare; for he knew that, at the very least, rude behavior on his part, at his uncle's gravesite, would only distress his mother.

Xavier listened closely but heard no further sound, save Miss Georgina's hoarse rapid breathing; and the random and forlorn calls of birds. The irreverent notion struck him that the dead man had awakened of a sudden, to discover himself imprisoned in his satin-lined coffin,—as, indeed, he had imprisoned so many criminals in the course of his career: and those faint wailing cries of sorrow and anger,—might they not be his, sounding distantly from out the coffin? A most disagreeable fancy!

But Xavier deemed himself too much a rationalist to believe in such things. "That the dead are thoroughly dead, to this life at least, no matter how they are transmogrified in Heaven (or in Hell)," Xavier thought, "I take to be self-evident, and shall never question. Such superstitions are for the untutored, and certain members of the female sex." Yet he could not resist the judgment that, if any gentleman in Winterthurn deserved so hideous a fate as to awake imprisoned in his own coffin, it was Chief Justice Erasmus Kilgarvan.

When news of Erasmus Kilgarvan's death spread through Winterthurn, it was greeted with some measure of incredulity, for so vigorous had the elderly jurist been, so very much in the public eye, that one might have thought him indestructible: with his ruddy flushed skin, piercing silver-gray eyes, sturdy, compact, and rather bullish body, and, with-al, his air of ceaseless energy: the very *power* residing in his soul. That he was felled by a stroke while addressing the courtroom seemed in a way apt, for, as the outspoken Miss Imogene Westergaard observed, upon hearing the news of her neighbor's demise, it was the only way in which old Erasmus might be cut down,—by a lightning-bolt, so to speak, issued with no warning.

Though Erasmus Kilgarvan was a familiar and much-admired presence about town, dining out four or five evenings a week, in private homes, or in one or another of his clubs,—amongst them, the Winterthurn Yacht Club and the prestigious Corinthian Club—he was one of the more temperamental of the several well-to-do "bachelor-widowers" in Winterthurn society: and could not always be trusted to suffer fools gladly in his hosts' drawing rooms. Gregarious and even somewhat sybaritic as he was; loving rich foods, alcoholic spirits, good-natured ripostes, and anecdotes of a colorful or even slightly risqué nature; a "jolly fellow"; a "man among men"; a gallant amongst the ladies; an indefatigable charmer when he wished to be so—nevertheless he held the Law in such high regard, he might fly into a rage if certain ideals, judgments, or sentences were questioned; and had acquired, over a period of forty years, a reputation as a jurist of stern and unparalleled *purity*. (Which is to say that, unlike the majority of his associates, and even his "cronies" in town, Erasmus Kilgarvan could not be bribed: nay, not even swayed by sentiments of a personal or pragmatic nature.)

It was a matter of debate amongst the ladies as to whether the Judge's porcine features inclined toward the handsome, or toward the disagreeably smug; or whether the striking effect of his bald, blunt, bulletlike head was felicitous, or otherwise; nor was there widespread consensus as to whether he had "treated" his two wives well, or had behaved admirably in summoning his daughter Georgina back from New York City, where she had been attending college, that she might nurse him back to health,—and remain with him as his companion, forever afterward. (As to the matter of the suitor, Mr. Guillemot: a number of the ladies frankly believed that Erasmus had driven the feckless young man away—but this is idle conjecture, and not to be credited.) Debatable too was the Judge's procedure, in scrupulously following the *letter of the Law*, and complying with his senile father's wish to disinherit his half-brother Lucas *completely*: and the continued wisdom of his severity, in regard to his three daughters. (Georgina, it seems, soon ceased to give him any difficulty, and settled in, as it were, to a life of domestic seclusion, in her early thirties; at the time of Erasmus's death, Thérèse and Perdita were driven each schoolday morning to the Parthian Academy for Girls, by the Negro servant Pride, and picked up again each afternoon, promptly at three o'clock: rarely allowed to visit their classmates' homes, and only once or twice yearly given the privilege of staying late for tea, at the headmistress's residence.) Such systematical severity, some observers thought, inclined to excess, for the girls *were* young and attractive, and might have enjoyed harmless schoolgirl friendships; but others, perhaps more reasonably, believed Erasmus eminently practical in wishing to shield his daughters, at their impressionable age, from certain unpleasant facts of life. Had not the world grown disagreeably motley and fast-paced, in the past several decades?—and had not poor Georgina herself been cruelly wounded, by her headstrong ventures into it?

"It is only out of love that Erasmus acts with so adamant a paternal solicitude," Reverend De Forrest frowningly said, "and I think we would all be grievously in error to offer criticism where we are only ignorant."

Though controversial in these divers ways, Erasmus Kilgarvan was assuredly *not* controversial in his fierce devotion to the Law, and in his unbending efforts to render justice where it was due. As his associates of many years argued, the Judge was, in truth, loath to condemn and punish; but, as he dwelt in a fallen, sinful world, where innocence might well be defined as the *unfulfilled potential for evil,* and guilt itself was but *a matter of degree,* he was obliged to take his responsibilities seriously: and is to be forgiven, I hope, for his steadfast belief that he was ordained by God, as well as by the State, in his judicial role. "Mercy is a luxury," he frequently said, in defending a prison sentence of especial harshness, or, indeed, a death sentence, "while Justice is notoriously frugal. The one is very easy to scatter about, and will draw friends, as honey draws flies; the other wins precious few friends, and numberless enemies. But when God shows us our duty, *we must follow it.*" Nor would he consent to surrender his onerous burden, when advancing years brought with them certain vexing infirmities,—gout, dyspepsia, shortness of breath and temper, and a growing deafness in one, or both, ears.

(As to whispered slanderous charges that Erasmus Kilgarvan naturally inclined toward the prosecution in any case, and was apt to express sardonic views over the strategies,—whether bumbling or expert—of those defense attorneys unfortunate enough to argue before him, these are, I think, quite groundless; and enjoy coinage only in a slacker, more lenient era, when life and property are so cheaply held even by jurists, that negligible sentences are handed down daily, and criminals are soon freed, to commit further crimes against the innocent.)

Heavy fines, incarcerations of many years, death by hanging: these sentences Erasmus Kilgarvan delivered with an air of solemn vigor that contrasted wondrously with his puckish private manner, revealed at the Corinthian Club, where he could unbutton, as it were, and relax, and speak frankly. Rarely did he jest at the expense of the poor wretches he had sent to the gallows; but he was not so intolerably pious a judge as to forbid his drinking companions to do so. Dr. Colney Hatch, in reminiscing over the grand old days of Erasmus Kilgarvan's reign in Winterthurn, expressed the view commonly held, that it was an inexplicable oversight that the Judge was never named to the Supreme Court of the United States: a miscarriage of justice that must have deeply wounded the principal, though, being a gentleman to his fingertips, of course he never breathed a word about it. As Reverend De Forrest said of Judge Kilgarvan in his heartfelt funeral oration, he labored "not for earthly glory, but in the service of his God." And this judgment, I think, remains uncontested.

The most luridly publicized of the numberless cases tried before Erasmus Kilgarvan was, as the reader might recall, that of Miss (or

Mrs., as she titled herself) Hester Vaugh, a good many years before the
time of our present narrative. This painful, and, indeed, still controversial case, studied in law schools until the present day, brought
Erasmus Kilgarvan to the attention of the populace; and subjected
him to numerous charges and insults delivered by a particularly noisome gaggle of "Suffragettes," led by Miss Elizabeth Cady Stanton.
(Indeed, the Hester Vaugh case, and Judge Kilgarvan's refusal to alter
his stand on it, was very likely the initial cause of the rift betwixt him
and his young half-brother, Lucas.) The young woman, Vaugh, seventeen years of age at the time of her arrest for infanticide, had been a
common housemaid in the domestic establishment of a family named
Poindexter, in South Winterthurn; evidently of loose and unformed
morals, she allowed herself to be seduced by her employer, and was
impregnated; and, after being evicted from the household by her
gravely offended mistress, she possessed no more presence of mind
than to *illegally trespass* on property owned by the Empire State–
Chesapeake Railroad,—giving birth to her bastard offspring in an
unheated tenement building, in such crude and filthy conditions that
it was not to be wondered at, that the infant survived a scant hour or
two.

All of Winterthurn was outraged, though the more proper sort of
lady did not wish to acknowledge her awareness of the scandal; several
gentlemen of the cloth made Hester Vaugh the subject of their
sermons, on the tragic fruits of sin and the ever-growing immoralism
of the times. After a much-publicized trial of some ten days, attended
by hundreds of persons and presided over by Associate Justice Erasmus
Kilgarvan (at that time but a youthful figure of thirty-eight), a jury of
twelve Winterthurn citizens found the defendant *guilty of murder in
the first degree:* guilty, indeed, of an "unnatural dereliction of maternal duty, in bringing about, by failing to prevent, the death of a helpless infant."

The Vaugh person was duly sentenced to death by hanging, in
compliance with the statute: but, before the execution could be carried
out, one or another muckraking journalist from downriver seized upon
the lurid tale, and inflated its significance (with such emboldened
headlines as A WINTERTHURN TRAGEDY: FALLEN MAIDEN & DOOMED BABE),
bringing it to the attention of the idle and captious throughout the
Northeast,—including, as it turned out, the rabble-rousing Suffragette
group headed by the Stanton woman. What a misfortune for Winterthurn City, and for the earnest young Judge Kilgarvan—! Where the
twelve gentlemen of the jury had seen a *murderess* of the most loathsome sort, compounding brutality with immorality, the free-thinking
women saw a hapless *victim;* where Associate Justice Erasmus Kilgarvan had seen an unrepentant criminal who must be hanged by the neck

until dead, certain overliberal persons saw a heroine who deserved freedom and the opportunity to "remake her young life,"—if not, indeed, sentimental pity and acclaim in the gutter press.

Was there ever such a perturbation in all the annals of Justice of Winterthurn!—with aroused and oft-uninformed passions on both sides; and families divided in sentiment; and meddlesome editorials and articles not only splashed across the Northeast but featured in England and on the Continent,—where, it is to be assumed, native-born criminals were in short supply.

The State Supreme Court, however, was not to be intimidated by the picketing of its stately halls, by free-thinking women and their hangers-on; or by a particularly meretricious series of articles entitled MALE JUSTICE & FEMALE SUFFERING, which appeared under the by-line of "Nellie Bly" (one Elizabeth Cochrane) for the *New York Tribune*. After due consideration of the original conviction and sentencing, and a close examination of the trial's proceedings under Erasmus Kilgarvan, the Supreme Court unanimously ruled to uphold the conviction; and issued a solemn statement, in which all the Justices concurred, that as death on the gallows commonly followed a conviction of murder in the first degree, Hester Vaugh's sentence was altogether just: and the Supreme Court saw no reason to interfere in the transactions of the lower court in this instance.

So it was, upon a pleasantly sunny day in June, by happenstance on Erasmus Kilgarvan's thirty-ninth birthday, the Vaugh murderess went to the gallows at the state prison in Powhatassie: so emaciated and broken she had to be carried to the platform in a chair (for, to compound her sin of infanticide, the unrepentant woman had attempted, in clumsy wise, to commit suicide by refusing to eat): so lost to all sense of decorum and Christian honor, she screamed at the chaplain who attended her, and vowed that she would return,—"in what guise I know not"—to take her revenge. Despite her weakened condition she was said to have put up a considerable struggle, and did not expire for some minutes, though her neck was snapped at once.

Thus, the notorious Hester Vaugh case, or scandal,—which had the unlooked-to effect of enhancing Erasmus Kilgarvan in the eyes of certain citizens: though that gentleman never ceased to explain that he had but followed the recommendation of the jury, and harbored no especial rancor for the defendant, any more than he harbored a stealthy sympathy. "Justice is duty," the youthful judge often said, "and the precise calibration of justice is a most exacting duty. But no man of the Law shrinks from such a task."

(The reader may be interested to learn that, despite her coarse threats of revenge, Hester Vaugh assuredly did *not* return to Winterthurn in any guise: nor did the Poindexter family, or the twelve jurors, or, indeed, Erasmus Kilgarvan himself, suffer any unusual consequences as a result of the trial and its sordid publicity,—beyond, that is, the ordeal of embarrassment itself, which, many of the principals said, was punishment enough. For the better sort of Winterthurn citizen, then as now, rightly shuns the vulgar glare of *publicity.*)

As for the more recent case of the contested will of Phillips Goode Kilgarvan, which had taken place some three years before Xavier's birth: evidently it happened that, on his deathbed, the eighty-seven-year-old gentleman had taken it into his head to *disinherit* his youngest son, for what specific reason or reasons was never altogether clear (though Lucas had angered and disappointed him numberless times, by failing to establish a career for himself, and by marrying with precipitate haste, and by neglecting to show proper filial regard): this decision being made of a sudden, with, it seems, his very dying breath, in the company of four upstanding witnesses,—Erasmus, Simon Esdras, Dr. Colney Hatch, and the Kilgarvans' attorney, Mr. Henry Peregrine. That the dictated will which was to negate all pre-existing wills possessed an air of the febrile, the disordered, and the rash; that Phillips Goode's signature was decidedly shaky, and granted to be his only by the sworn insistence of the witnesses; that certain abusive remarks pertaining to "tainted blood" and "half-bred blood" were not excised,—these troubling factors should not, I hope, sway our thinking on the matter, for, though the litigious young Lucas Kilgarvan fought the will up to the highest court in the State, and went about town sorely abusing both his brothers, and swore that his father had been coerced, or that the entire will was a fabrication, the final judgment was *against* him and *for* his brothers: the Justices of the Supreme Court ruling unanimously that a father has the privilege of disinheriting an unruly son, up to the very moment of death, provided he is, as the witnesses swore Phillips Goode assuredly *was*, "of sound mind and body."

A most disagreeable case, which caused many a tongue to wag in Winterthurn and elsewhere: but, in truth, an altogether simple one, in which fairly clear principles of law were evoked. (As to the whispered innuendos regarding Lucas Kilgarvan's "tainted blood,"—and the reader will recall that Georgina spoke of Lucas as a "half-breed" as well—this relates to the fact that Phillips Goode's second wife, Miriam D'Ivers of Mt. Moriah, was said to have been very distantly related to a French settler by the name of Camille D'Ivers, who had, in the early 1700s, taken for a mistress, or actually wed, an Oneida Indian squaw, which unfortunate union evidently resulted in issue. So many generations later, after the passage of so many turbulent decades, one might well conclude that the "taint" of mixed blood had been entirely dissolved, in Anglo-Saxon solution: but this supposition Phillips Goode did not make, it seems, once the fiery passions of romantic love had ebbed, and the flaws in the woman he had wed became distinct. Whether the old tale of tainted blood, or, indeed, the "blood" itself, had any actual influence on Lucas Kilgarvan's behavior, one cannot presume to judge: but it was a matter that Xavier, of all the Kilgarvan sons, took most to heart, and rarely allowed himself to speak of, for his adolescent pride was sorely wounded; and he could not abide it, that any of his schoolmates might pity him for so ambiguous a connection . . .)

Of Winterthurn mysteries of a minor and domestic sort, none excited sympathetic comment more frequently amongst persons of society,—not excluding even Erasmus Kilgarvan's most intimate male companions, who had known him all their lives—or aroused more speculation, than *why*, and *how*, a man of such superior intelligence and proven canniness (at forty-three the youngest Chief Justice, at the county level, in the State's judicial history) chanced to marry not one, but two, women of *inferior mettle*,—leaving the luckless man a widower twice over, with three daughters on his hands.

The first wife, Miss Vivian Battenberg, who died when Georgina was but ten years of age, had been so self-absorbed, neurasthenic, and negligent in her household duties as to have failed to appear downstairs at the Manor, fully clothed, for the last several years of her life; the second, Miss Hortense Spies, was a yet more pathetic presence at the Manor, dying under clouded circumstances (the consequence, it was said, of a spiritual malaise of an hereditary sort) when Thérèse was not yet three years of age, and Perdita a sickly babe of ten months.

Indeed, even Erasmus Kilgarvan's detractors could not fail to feel some pity for him, tinged with a measure of impatience, that he should twice err in choosing a mate: and, withal, prove incapable of siring a male heir to propagate his name. (Doubtless it angered him greatly that his half-brother, Lucas, should prove so very manly as to have fathered *four sons:* and these lads, by way of a young woman no more physically robust, it would seem, than either of Erasmus's wives.)

That a young man in his twenties might succumb to the blandishments of a beguiling face and figure (Miss Battenberg of Contracoeur being as pretty a débutante, in her season, as the Valley boasted), or the yet more subtle temptations of a considerable fortune (for the Battenbergs had invested, like the Kilgarvans, in munitions manufacturing and related enterprises, at that most fortuitous of times in our history,—the late 1850s),—that, in short, he might precipitously *fall in love*, to repent at leisure, was not, in itself, puzzling: for, certainly, a number of Winterthurn marriages, embarked upon with touching idealism, soon ran aground upon the hardscrabble realities of daily life; and the riddlesome failure of charming young ladies to mature into worthy wives and mothers. (As an aside, I should mention here that Dr. Colney Hatch, the physician most frequently employed by the leading families of Winterthurn,—the Kilgarvans, the Westergaards, the Von Goelers, the De Forrests, the Peregrines, etc.—had oft expressed the intention of publishing a scientific study on this troublesome subject, closely investigating female incapacities as they are exposed in divers stages: childhood, puberty, early marriage and motherhood, menopause, and senility. He had hoped to establish an actual correlation betwixt the *anatomy* of the sex and its social, moral, and intellectual *destiny:* but, so overworked was this zealous gentleman, so frequently was he called, oft-times in the middle of the night, to the boudoirs of hypochondriacal ladies who feared they were dying, and who *must* have him, that, I am afraid, he dissipated his energies; and, like many another dedicated physician of the older type, he surrendered all hope of fame, in the service of an indefatigable round of patients—!)

The melancholy love match betwixt Erasmus Kilgarvan and Vivian Battenberg, ending in the virtual disappearance, or ''fading away,'' of the once-lively beauty, was, as I say, scarcely remarkable in itself. What puzzled Erasmus's relatives and small circle of intimate acquaintances was the poor man's misfortune, after an interval of seventeen sobering years, to marry *yet another* weak-minded, childish, and chronically neurasthenic woman in Hortense Spies: as prone to idiopathic disorders, household mishaps, and day- and night-time chimeras of the most morbid sort as the first Mrs. Kilgarvan. Phillips Goode threw up his hands in despair, as it were, over his eldest son's perplexing taste in women. ''To sire sons who will survive for more than a few days,'' he said, ''it is necessary to marry more than a pretty face, or a bewitching instep.'' The old gentleman was said to have been more broken in spirit than his son, after the premature birth, and death within a week, of a baby boy baptized Phillips Goode Kilgarvan II,—this piteous infant born after a labor of some twenty-odd hours, of the second wife Hortense. (At this time Thérèse was not twelve months old; and Perdita, of course, had not yet been born.)

Dr. Colney Hatch, whose experience with the Kilgarvan household was authoritative, thought it a tragedy for Erasmus that both wives, in their differing ways, were poorly suited for childbearing, and, indeed, for conjugal relations of the most conservative sort: the one being of a meager, bony frame, and inclining toward anemia and lightheadedness; the other, of a spongy sort of plumpness, and inclining toward hemophobia. In addition to the common admixture of female complaints, originating in the uterus, each young woman suffered from a propensity for respiratory and digestive upsets; unforeseen allergies to those medications Dr. Hatch most frequently prescribed; fits of hysteria brought on by needless speculation upon the nature of salvation, damnation, Heaven, Hell, etc., which their brains were ill-equipped to ponder; insomnia; neuralgia; hypesthesia; bouts of hyperpnea; postpartum depression, the more exacerbated by sore, inflamed, easily bruised breasts, whose maternal milk was tainted by watery blood; and, most enigmatic of all, a veritable cornucopia of minor injuries, brought about, it seems, by sheer clumsiness of comportment—for there was never anyone in all of Winterthurn City like the mistresses of Glen Mawr Manor for toppling downstairs, colliding with doors, shelves, partitions, headboards, and the like!

Alas, that such gentle, pretty, sweet-natured creatures should prove so awkward, and so prone to accident, as to be forever bruising and banging their heads, torsos, pelvic regions, and thighs; cracking their ribs and blacking their eyes, in nocturnal tumbles from bed (caused, it was thought, by paroxysms of night-time terror); scratching, cutting, and even stabbing themselves, with letter-openers, hat-pins, carving knives, and the like; loosening their teeth; dislocating their fingers; spraining their wrists and ankles; even rupturing their spleens, in falls into the cellar that would have been comical had they been less pathetic. The first Mrs. Kilgarvan had accidentally set fire to her lovely brown hair, by leaning too near a candle; the second Mrs. Kilgarvan had so roughly shut her smallest finger in a closet door, the nail had turned black and fallen off. The one lost all appetite, and would have starved herself had not her husband and her physician forcibly intervened; the other acquired wild, exotic, ungovernable tastes, and would have gobbled down glue, starch, raw beans, berries, pen nibs, etc., had not the same gentlemen kept watch. Shortly after Georgina's birth, the first Mrs. Kilgarvan expressed so deranged a horror of nursing (for, she claimed, her infant girl was insatiable in her hunger, and wanted not merely mother's *milk*, but mother's very *blood*), and of cohabiting with her lawfully wed spouse, that she took to hiding in remote corners of the Manor, not excepting the "dungeon" in the oldest section of the cellar, which, in Colonial days, had been used as a sort of informal prison for misbehaving slaves, tenant farmers, and the like—! (Upon one shameful occasion, when a number of the Judge's associates were gathering in the drawing room, for an evening of whiskey, cigars, and forthright political discussion, the distraught Vivian Kilgarvan, at first nowhere to be found, was finally tracked down, so to speak, by the incensed husband himself, in a fetid corner of the cellar, where, naked inside her fur-lined traveling cloak, she sang to herself, and rocked to and fro, holding against her bosom not her own flesh-and-blood babe Georgina but a mere porcelain doll—!)

After the death of the first Mrs. Kilgarvan, the household quieted considerably: there being, apart from the numerous domestic staff, only Erasmus and his brother Simon Esdras (who, deeply absorbed in the writing of his *Treatise*, rarely troubled to come downstairs to dine), and the motherless waif Georgina,—a diminished family, assuredly, yet not, it seems, an entirely unhappy one. Sober, subdued, retiring, but contented: a halcyon period that came to a rude end when a meddlesome Battenberg dowager, visiting the Manor unannounced, declared that it was "unwholesome" for a thirteen-year-old girl to live alone with her father and her eccentric uncle, in a household bereft of feminine influence. Far from being insulted or enraged at this intrusion into his domestic affairs, Erasmus Kilgarvan seems to have conceded the Battenberg lady's point, and to have agreed to send his daughter away to school,—to the Canandaigua Episcopal Female Seminary, in a bucolic region some two hundred miles to the west; and though the widower must have suffered pangs of inordinate loneliness in the great house, he did not seek remarriage for nearly two decades.

As for Miss Hortense Spies, the second Mrs. Kilgarvan,—the marriage seems to have been ill-advised from the start, for Erasmus was some twenty-five years older than his comely young spouse; and his ever-increasing judicial responsibilities, as well as a certain crankiness and irascibility of manner, militated against an idyllic household. (All of Winterthurn speculated, too, as to the nervous hostility betwixt wife and stepdaughter—for were they not, Hortense and Georgina, *very nearly the same age?*) An early pregnancy; the birth of Thérèse; a second pregnancy, resulting in the death of the infant Phillips Goode II; yet another pregnancy, perhaps following too closely upon the others, resulting in the birth of the undersized Perdita,—and soon afterward a lapse into such wayward and unpredictable behavior, her distraught husband could no longer allow her to appear in public.

How, and why, answering to what cruel logic, did this perverse change come about?—that the second Mrs. Kilgarvan should, after a space of nearly two decades, strive to emulate the first, *as if by unnatural sisterly rapport:* Miss Hortense Spies, of one of Winterthurn's oldest families, so sweetly docile, so unfailingly devout a young Christian woman, who in her virgin artlessness had rejected, it was said, any number of gentlemen her own age, as they seemed insufficiently "fired by idealism,"—she of the full soft bosom and hips, the wavy chestnut-red hair, the childlike addiction to comfits, chocolate, and honey: shading, alas, by degrees into a slovenly attired harridan with bruised eyes, her fair skin raked by her own nails, her manner oscillating betwixt a leaden despondency and a shrill shrieking hysteria—? Dr. Hatch, finding evidence of fresh bruises, scratches, and cuts on those parts of his patient's body it was his professional duty to examine, confessed himself perplexed by the situation, for, it seems, the young Mrs. Kilgarvan had taken to *punishing herself*, even to the point of whipping her soft body with a riding crop!—which morbid practice, she had dully explained, "was nothing more than she deserved: being foul, sinful, and of no more worth than a piece of barnyard filth." Dr. Hatch firmly demurred; pointing out to the wretched woman that so mistreating her body, and thereby rendering herself ill-suited for the solemn duties of wifehood and motherhood, was in itself a sin, and must displease God greatly: whereupon the patient began to sob with all the abandon of a spoiled, sickly child, and her husband, who had been pacing nearby (the examination having taken place behind a screen, in the master bedroom at Glen Mawr Manor), fell of a sudden into such despondency, he began to shout and curse at her; and so forgot his friendship of long standing with Dr. Hatch, he ordered him from the room, as if the respected physician were a common servant—!

(Dr. Hatch afterward confided in an acquaintance, at the Corinthian Club,—which palatial retreat on Berwick Place the Judge frequented less regularly, as his marital situation presumably worsened—that he could not comprehend the sinister metamorphosis, save in terms of *an hereditary malaise*, in virulent union with *female pathology of an undefined sort*. Nor did his customary methods of treating such disorders, involving vinegar douches, vigorous daily purges,—by way of Epsom salts, laxatives, and cold-water enemas—and bloodletting,—by way of a rare subspecies of leech affixed to the female genitalia—appear to be having much salutary effect. "So mysterious is the alteration in young Mrs. Kilgarvan," the good doctor said pensively, "that, were one not a rationalist, and fervently on the side of progress, an hypothesis of 'demonic possession' might well be entertained.")

More and more frequently, the willful young woman absented herself from society; refused to heed her weeping baby girls; refused to admit Dr. Hatch into her presence; grew feverish over the reading of meretricious female romances,—among them *Villette*, found beneath a cushion in her boudoir after her death; and hid away, for long hours at a time, in the cavernous unheated attic, or in the chill Honeymoon Room (where, in a happier season, she and her bridegroom had spent their wedding night), or, most perversely, in the farthest reaches of the cellar with its low-beamed ceiling, and its numberless cobwebs, and its damp earthen floor. The alarmed housekeeper, subsequently dismissed by Judge Kilgarvan, told him she had distinctly heard her mistress *conversing with someone in the cellar:* a woman, it seemed, who had answered her in low, languid, drawling, somewhat mocking tones! (Though, of course, there was no one in the cellar—apart ᵣ ᵒm the unhappy Mrs. Kilgarvan herself.)

As a consequence of the irresponsible tattling of servants, all of Winterthurn was to learn the tragic circumstances of Mrs. Kilgarvan's death, but a few days before the third birthday of her elder daughter: discovered, in an airless and foul-smelling corner of the cellar, dying in retching agony of a self-administered potion (diagnosed by the county coroner as *rat-poison paste, made of arsenic*), with a note scrawled in a miniature childish hand pinned to her bosom: *'Tis my own doing & no other—my belovèd Husband Erasmus is blameless—O pray for him & all who remain behind in the Vale of Tears: do not pray for Hortense, as she is* DAMN'D & THE DEVIL'S OWN.

(It was poor Georgina, returned at the end of a day of teaching at the Parthian Academy, who found the wretched woman only minutes before her death,—seeming to know by panicked intuition, as the servants afterward said, as soon as she set foot in the house, that *something frightful had happened.* And how she did cry and carry on, surrendering to helpless spasms of tears!—the stiff and rarely yielding stepdaughter now grieving for her father's young wife with as much selfless abandon as if it were her own mother, or sister, whom she had lost.)

Though it was widely claimed that Judge Kilgarvan had died most unexpectedly, seized by a massive stroke that paralyzed him in midbreath, and sent him crashing to the floor before the affrighted eyes of the entire courtroom, not a few persons had quietly noted, over a twelve-month or more, the elderly gentleman's increasing impatience with servants, and with his daughter Georgina, and a general acerbity of manner that might have betokened ill-health.

The Kilgarvans of Wycombe Street had themselves witnessed one of the Judge's more flamboyant outbursts, approximately three weeks before his death, when, leaving Grace Episcopal Church after the Sunday service, he had, it seems, lost his footing on a patch of icy sidewalk, and flailed out in a sudden rage against Miss Georgina, raining blows upon the abashed woman's head and shoulders with his walking stick, and shouting epithets of such vulgarity as one would have supposed a gentleman of his breeding and character would not know: the while the "Blue Nun," veiled as always, and encumbered by her heavy black skirts, meekly withstood the assault, until such time as Erasmus's arm wearied, and servants hastened to their aid.

Witnesses to this display of temper were deeply troubled, and many did their best to erase it from memory, for, in truth, this flush-faced old man with the clouded bulging eyes, and the head sleek and bald as a bullet, was *not* Chief Justice Erasmus Kilgarvan, in his essence: and they were hard put to interpret his spittle-flecked words,— "You are invincible! You shall conquer, in the end! *You*—and *you*—and *you!*"—uttered in rhythm with his blows, as tears sprang from his eyes, with as much despairing vehemence as if Miss Georgina were not one woman, but many.

(Young Xavier Kilgarvan carried away with him this shocking spectacle of his "uncle"—or, to be precise, his "half-uncle"—behaving with such brutish anger, on the very steps of Grace Church; and is to be forgiven, I think, for the satisfaction with which he pondered it. Yet even Xavier, so prescient in certain things, was quite astonished at the news of the Judge's death—for, it seems, he had gloomily imagined the old man to be *immortal*.)

As to the circumstances of Erasmus Kilgarvan's death, which even his enemies could not fail to think unbefitting a person of his stature and dignity: these were especially ironic, in that, by sheer coincidence, he was handing down a sentence of some severity (upward of fifty years in the State Correctional Facility for Men at Powhatassie), when the convicted felon rose to his feet, and wildly waved his fist, and began to shout incoherent words to the effect that "God has claimed vengeance as His alone,"—whereupon Judge Kilgarvan was so stupefied at this rare act of impudence, in the hallowed marble-and-stucco interior of the domed Winterthurn County Courthouse, in *his* courtroom of so many years, that a weakened blood vessel in his brain snapped: and the poor man went mute in the midst of his speech: and, of a sudden bizarrely mottled (in lurid patches of crimson, pink, and white), in the face, fell to the floor clawing and tearing at his high starched collar, and at the neck of his judge's black gown. *And was never to rise again from where Fate had pitched him.*

So public a death, in so defiled a context; so cruelly timed; so ignominious as to its particulars—these factors rendered Erasmus Kilgarvan's death especially ironic; and could not fail to provoke the more superstitious amongst the populace into claiming that the convicted man *had called forth Divine wrath upon Judge Kilgarvan*. Alas, so hoary, and reasoned, and dispassionate a jurist, who had passed judgment on wrongdoers of every stripe, not excepting criminals of good and sometimes superior intelligence (which, as all practitioners of the Law will attest, adds a special challenge to the task): struck down, as it were, by the maniacal ravings of one Horace

Godwit, of that tribe of poor whites who dwelt in the scrubby foothills south of Mt. Provenance, in the most wretched sort of squalor and moral debasement: how should the humiliation of it not outlive him, and taint his honor? It was the more unfortunate, that Godwit was a creature of the lowest sort, possessing, or feigning to possess, a sub-normal intelligence; that his trial had involved testimony so frequently lewd, the courtroom had had to be cleared of all spectators, including men; that a most poisonous and snarled congeries of tales had emerged, involving forced prostitution in the notorious lumber-men's brothels at Rivière-du-Loup, some ten miles northwest of Winterthurn City . . . Throughout the fifteen days of the trial, Judge Kilgarvan had exhibited an admirable formality that quite masked his abhorrence for the defendant, and for certain of the prosecution's witnesses (one of them being a Dr. Holyrod Wilts, a physician and, it was rumored, abortionist, in the hire of the brothel owners): he had displayed very little of the sickened revulsion he must have felt, as, by degrees, it came to light that Horace Godwit, though self-defined as a farmer, was actively involved in the brothel trade, and had sold several of his daughters (both legitimate and illegitimate) into white slavery: and, beyond this, most unspeakably of all, he had committed certain gross and unnatural crimes with his very own daughters,—*the youngest being but eleven years of age.*

Scarcely is it to be wondered at, then, that Erasmus Kilgarvan, interrupted in midspeech by this wretch's vainglorious outburst,— *"Vengeance is mine, sayeth the Lord! Vengeance is mine!"*—suffered so extreme a shock to his sensibility that his strained nerves broke; and, one side of his mouth twisting upward in a grimace of commingled rage, incredulity, and grief, he fell crashing to the floor, with as much stunning weight, it almost seemed, as the bronze bust of his own likeness, in Roman style, which had, but the previous autumn, been ensconced in the high-vaulted foyer of the Courthouse, alongside likenesses of George Washington, Abraham Lincoln, Julius Caesar, and, not least, Moses and Solomon, in their stern-browed manly glory.

As Reverend De Forrest concluded his remarks, stressing, a second time, the unsurpassed moral integrity of the deceased, and his devotion to the commonweal ("whereby public justice was ever favored above private interest"), the keening sounds lifted yet again, light, rarefied, melodic, sweetly elusive: and this time Xavier felt so inexpressibly yearning a sensation,—ah, how potent! how heart-swelling!—he could barely force himself to remain stationary, in reverent silence.

From whence did the haunting cries derive?—and what was their airy substance? Xavier sensed a kindred restiveness in the younger people present: his brothers Bradford, Roland (or Wolf, as he was often called), Colin—poor Colin, at nineteen as much a feckless *boy* as Xavier himself, and infinitely better-natured!—and, some yards away (but did he dare to look?—he must!) those altogether *strange* and *forbidden* cousins of his: Thérèse with eyes resolutely downcast, her prayerbook clasped to her meager bosom; Perdita betraying some agitation,—for surely she *did* hear the cries—and forgetting herself so completely, she chanced to raise her eyes, and to send darting glances about,—the which were scarcely diminished in their intensity by her veil, but, oddly, wondrously, enhanced!—or so it seemed to the lovestruck Xavier, who stared, and stared, as the sounds of an indefinable sweetness pulsed through his veins, and finely, lightly, tantalizingly, vibrated along his spinal column. And would she glance at him? And would he suffer the shock of *seeing*, and of *knowing*, as their eyes locked—?

So it was, the young cousins seemed to discover each other *for the first time:* and Xavier Kilgarvan, his adolescent blood in a tumult, his heart perceptibly accelerating its beat, experienced one of those lightning-strokes of yearning,—in which desire, passion, and love of the highest degree of purity are commingled—that not only illuminate our lives with ferocious intensity, but pierce them in two, and alter them forever.

The Spectacle
in the
Honeymoon Room

By eleven o'clock in the morning of May 3, news of some "unknown and hideous catastrophe" at Glen Mawr Manor,—whether involving Simon Esdras, or the "Blue Nun," or the young sisters (who had not arrived for classes at the Parthian Academy), or another, unnamed party—had begun to spread through Winterthurn City with such uncanny swiftness that the boys in Mr. Pitt-Davies' mathematics class learned of it: and Xavier, being informed by a scrawled note from young Ringgold Peregrine, crudely tossed onto his desk, that MURDER had been committed at his relatives' grand house, was so astonished, and so gripped with a sudden panic (for, it must be confessed, the phantasmal image of Perdita was rarely distant from his imagination, and, in thinking of the Manor, he thought solely of her and her well-being), that, rather more with trancelike compulsion than brash defiance, he rose at once from his seat, and paid no heed to his startled schoolmaster,—not even to mumble a word of apology or excuse—and ran from the room.

So distressed was young Xavier, he left the Winterthurn Academy for Boys by way of the front entrance on Berwick Place, caring not a whit if he should be espied: and ran along the street, stopping passers-by to inquire of them, if they knew what had happened at the Manor: with so little of his customary concern for his appearance, and for the decorum of his public behavior, that he minded not if one or two persons smiled at the spectacle of a youth dressed in the smart green blazer of the Academy, hurrying along, with his tie blown back over his shoulder, and his mop of curls all disheveled.

Along crowded Berwick Avenue he ran, pausing breathless to inquire at the tobacconist's, if anyone there had heard the news; bursting into the near-deserted offices of the *Gazette*, where the female employees stared; intruding in a private conversation betwixt a couple alighting from a carriage; threading his way through traffic along Union Avenue to make his impatient inquiry to several clerks, two Negro bootblacks, and a number of startled and offended gentlemen, in the high-domed gilded lobby of the Winterthurn Arms. But no one knew how to reply to him: and many persons quite amazed him by not knowing to which "Manor" he referred.

Down narrow Charity Street, where he paused to make a futile inquiry at the Sweet Shoppe; down Pinckney; down Hazelwit; again crossing Union Avenue; inquiring of pedestrians, news vendors, policemen, drivers of hackney cabs, the German proprietor of a butcher's shop on Water Street who thought him crazed,—until, panting, he flung himself through the doors of the brownstone police headquarters at Water and Railroad: where, to his near-sobbing disappointment, he was turned brusquely away, and ordered to take his leave with more restraint than he had entered.

"But surely you can give me some information," Xavier protested, "for I am a relative of the Kilgarvans—I *am* a Kilgarvan— and must know whether a murder has been committed at the Manor: and whether a young girl has been injured."

But the police lieutenant behind the desk reiterated his command that Xavier leave the station; for not even high-and-mighty Academy boys could burst into headquarters, and cause a commotion.

Xavier then ran, in greater distress than before, westward along Railroad,—now approaching Wycombe Street, which, for divers reasons, he wished to avoid—in order that he might confront his brother Colin, who worked at a livery stable close by: the plan quickly formed in his fevered brain that he would borrow cash from his brother, to hire a hackney cab to take him out to the Manor, a considerable distance away. "For it may be," the breathless youth murmured, "that *she* is in particular need of solace; and may even be awaiting my arrival."

Colin, alas, would prove incapable of lending Xavier so generous a sum,—less out of guarded frugality than as a consequence of his own indigence; so it happened that Xavier had to humble himself, and take the clattering Union Avenue trolley to the very end of the line; and, after that, to hike afoot nearly three miles along the Old River Road, until he came to the great arched gate of Glen Mawr Manor—which, as he might have foreseen, was locked fast, and guarded by sheriff's deputies.

Though a more enterprising adventurer or "detective" might have slipped stealthily away, to scale the twelve-foot limestone wall surrounding the Manor at a sequestered place, or, even, to approach it from the river (a challenge Xavier, Colin, and numerous schoolboy acquaintances had, in fact, taken on a half-dozen times in the past),—though Xavier knew from his habitual gorging of pulp novelettes (celebrating such ambiguous heroes as Eugène François Vidocq of the Parisian Sûreté, and the Bow Street Runners, and Inspector Bucket of Scotland Yard, and America's own George B. Jashber) that he might do better to investigate the "scene of the crime" himself, no matter the consequences,—he seems to have been sufficiently discouraged by the deputies' remarks as to give up, for the afternoon, such hopes: and to content himself with learning, from a deputy named Clegg (an acquaintance of his brother Wolf's), the following imperfect account of the "catastrophe" that had befallen the Glen Mawr Kilgarvans, sometime during the preceding night . . .

By eight-thirty o'clock the household was nervously undecided; by nine o'clock, in a tremor of alarm and apprehension, for no one, including Mrs. Whimbrel's devoted Irish nursemaid, knew quite what to do,—whether to continue knocking, ever more forcibly, at the bolted door of the Honeymoon Room; or whether to discreetly withdraw, under the assumption that Mrs. Whimbrel simply wished to slumber the morning through, and would appear downstairs, with little Charleton, when she wished.

(Yet, as the Irish girl half-tearfully repeated, it was *very* unlike her mistress to lie abed so late, for, back home, she rose each morning at seven o'clock, punctually; and the baby had never yet slept past dawn. Thus it seemed to her incontestable,—though she surely did not wish to cause any upset—that something had gone amiss; and why, indeed, *should the door be locked?*)

So the minutes passed, in whispered agitation; and none of the domestic staff knew what strategy to take.

Miss Georgina had arisen even earlier than was customary, it seemed, and had gone out, accompanied by old Pride, no one knew where: whether she had gone on an errand, afoot; or whether she had perambulated along the mist-shrouded bank of the river, in prayerful meditation, as, even in inhospitable weathers, she oft-times did,—no one was to know until, some hours afterward, the proprietor of Cutter Mills, on the Temperance Vale Road, would report his mystifying transaction with her: which only served to aggrandize, rather than diminish, the mystery. (Nor would the elderly Pride condescend to explain, to either the authorities or his fellow servants,—for he was of a sour and taciturn disposition, and generally disliked, even by the Negroes.)

As midmorning waxed, however, and the damp flurried snow began to melt, and the overcast sky gave way, by degrees, to a sunny expanse of blue more suitable to the season, it did become evident that something had happened to Mrs. Whimbrel: and that Miss Georgina must be summoned: for Simon Esdras rarely rose before eleven o'clock, and, even then, could not be relied upon to offer any advice concerning the household,—such matters being too trivial, and too vulgar, for his attention. (Both Thérèse and Perdita stood about confused, in their school uniforms, yet little inclined to leave the Manor: nor did the old Negro ready the carriage to take them into the city: for, it seemed, this was a weekday morning quite out of the ordinary,— though what was amiss no one knew, or dared to contemplate.)

Called forth, Miss Georgina responded with some irritation, as, to her way of thinking, her cousin might sleep until noon, should she so wish: nor did it seem entirely infelicitous that the Whimbrel infant had not yet begun to wail. But she rapped at the door soundly enough; called out Abigail's name; rattled the knob; and even pressed her ear against the oaken panels, yet could hear nothing. (The Irish nursemaid, and one or two of the Manor staff, had similarly applied their ears to the door, earlier,—and heard, or seemed to hear, noises within, of an indefinable nature.) "It seems Mrs. Whimbrel sleeps," Miss Georgina said, with knitted brow, and downcast shadowed eyes, "—and very soundly. Yet, I suppose, she cannot be allowed to sleep forever."

At this, Thérèse hurried forward, and asked if she might be of assistance: but Georgina, scarcely glancing at her, told her to return to her bed-chamber,—for what help might *she* be, unless she could reduce herself to a vapor, and wriggle through the keyhole? Some yards away, at the head of the stairs, little Perdita stood, sucking at a forefinger; but had more discretion than to approach Georgina. "The Honeymoon Room is locked,—decidedly locked—occupied—sequestered—taken over, indeed," Georgina murmured, again rattling the doorknob, and drawing back her lips in a joyless smile that revealed pale gums, "but, I suppose, it cannot be allowed to remain so, forever." And yet again she rapped on the door, with such sudden violence that one of her knuckles began to bleed.

So the morning of May 3 passed, with wretched slowness: and several of the servants took note of the curious fact that Jupiter, far from sniffing and nosing about the upstairs hall, as one might have expected of him, betook himself, shivering, and whimpering like a cowardly pup, to hide beneath the kitchen stairs—!

At last Simon Esdras was summoned, and came to join the others, at first vexed at being called away from his work (for he but dimly recalled that a houseguest had come to stay at the Manor, and had forgotten altogether that it was a niece from Contracoeur, with a babe in arms): then, realizing the gravity of the situation, he too rapped upon the door, and turned the knob, and called out, to inquire if something was amiss—but was greeted, like the others, with silence. By now, Miss Georgina's composure had begun to erode; like Thérèse she paced aimlessly about, and wrung her hands, and returned to knock on the door, with ever-increasing agitation. Simon Esdras commanded Mrs. Whimbrel to unlock the door, as everyone was gravely upset; he expressed his great disappointment in her that she should be so thoughtless as to throw a household of womenfolk into disarray; raising his voice, and betraying a faint tremor of alarm, he warned that her parents and her husband would be notified of her behavior, and that she should *never again be welcome at Glen Mawr.*

Alas, not even these threats could bestir her!—and now clocks throughout the house were chiming ten-thirty; and it became obvious that drastic measures must be taken.

Simon Esdras removed his pince-nez, and absently polished them on his sleeve, the while, in a voice of methodical and uninflected calm, he stated the logical alternatives: whether to smash the door in or remove it from its brass hinges; or to order one of the menservants to scale the outer wall of the house, and break a window. As Miss Georgina seemed not to hear, or to comprehend, he repeated himself: and again repeated himself,—"The one; or the other? The door; or the window?"—while a dozen servants milled uselessly about, and Thérèse sobbingly prayed aloud that no one was harmed.

How long the household might have remained at this snarled impasse, had not the child Perdita so precociously acted, one cannot speculate: but, of a sudden, she appeared running from the back stairs (where she had disappeared unnoticed), an ax from the woodshed in her slender arms, and an expression of affrighted resolution on her face—! It may have been that she proffered the unwieldy instrument to her uncle, or to her eldest sister, who shrank from touching it: or to one of the servants: but, as no one accepted it from her, she made the decision to use it herself; and, demonstrating a remarkable strength for one so tender in years, and so delicate of frame, she simply began to batter at the door,—once, twice, thrice, and yet a fourth time, and a fifth!—as the heavy oaken panels cracked and gave way, with sickening shrieks, beneath the ax's mortal blows!

Thus it was, little Perdita, gasping for breath, her wavy hair all atangle about her heated face, broke in the door of the Honeymoon Room: and exposed the hellish spectacle inside: which was of a species that defies description, even as, being viewed, it stuns and repulses the eye,—and threatens the observer with faintness.

For there, reclining gracelessly on the antique canopied bed, amidst bloodstained sheets, and torn silken spread, one plump white breast bared as if for nursing, lay the vacant-faced Abigail Whimbrel, scarcely recognizable as the robust woman of the previous day: humming tunelessly beneath her breath the old nursery rhyme of "Baby Bunting"; and, with piteous maternal solicitude, pressing against her bosom the limp, lifeless form of her belovèd baby: the which tiny figure could be seen even from a distance of some yards, to have suffered a savage assault,—part of the throat and torso, and much of the back of the tender head, having been, it seemed, *eaten away*.

"Iphigenia"

In later years it was thought that Miss Georgina Kilgarvan began to publish her queer, crotchety, unmelodic poesy only after the disappearance of her suitor, and the death by "misadventure" of her young stepmother: but in truth this was not the case, for even as a schoolgirl at the Canandaigua Female Seminary she had placed, as it were, stealthily, certain riddlesome poems in the very literary magazine it was her responsibility to edit, under divers cóy pseudonyms—one of them being "Iphigenia."

As to what purpose lay behind this subterfuge, and why, indeed, the name "Iphigenia" had been expressly chosen: why a young miss still in her teens should lock herself away in her room, or prowl about the woods like Crazy Eliza of old—a madwoman of Colonial years still celebrated in ballads, oft-times of a bawdy nature, in the hill country—brooding, and shunning company, and scrawling lines in a school notebook that might have been put to better use; and what, in fact, her obscure versifying meant: no one, not even Georgina's childhood acquaintance (for it would be to inflate the significance of their relationship, to call her *friend*) Miss Clarice Von Goeler, could have said.

Certain early verses, published under her own name, did not displease her family, and even gave promise of some native talent: for, consider the solemnity, the precocious wisdom, and the near-perfection of the rime, in these lines penned by Georgina in memory of her deceased mother:

56

All that, poor mortal, to thee blinds, to God is day,
And all our fates, He knoweth:
Thus rest assured, 'tis no confus'd way
The spirit eternal goeth.

(Owing to an unfortunate falling-out between the two families,—the Kilgarvans of Winterthurn City and the Battenbergs of Contracoeur—following close upon the untimely death of Georgina's mother, it happened that Georgina was not able to visit her mother's grave for many years, and then in secret defiance of her father's wishes: for the Battenbergs had been quite bellicose in their insistence that their daughter be buried at home, in the Battenberg family plot in Contracoeur; and Erasmus Kilgarvan had been so despondent, and, it may be, had harbored so potent a silent fury against his departed wife, that he had not protested. Nor had Georgina been allowed, owing to the Judge's extreme sensitivity on the subject, to speak of her mother in his presence, let alone betray effusive tears and sentiment. Yet, when with childish hope she presented him with this little poem, it was said that he knit his brow, and brushed tears from his eyes, and gripped his daughter's arm with sudden passion, murmuring: "Ah, yes, 'tis so; 'tis ever so!—*All our fates, He knoweth—*")

With the passage of time, however, as Georgina grew into a tall, willowy, headstrong young miss, a queer admixture of the outspoken and the taciturn, the gregarious and the reclusive (for while she thrived, as it were, upon the rougher sort of schoolgirl athletic activities, and had an insatiable appetite for chairing meetings, she nonetheless rejoiced in solitude, and could vanish for hours at a time),—as she encountered new and alien influences, in New York City primarily (and precisely what those influences were, with whom she was intimate while attending Barnard, no one in Winterthurn, not even Miss Von Goeler, was to know),—as, in short, she left behind the simplicities of childhood, and took on the knotty complexities of adulthood, her poetical talent was by degrees corrupted, and a new and ever more strident voice asserted itself, to the despair of all. Now there were rude jarring images, and dashed-off lines; a penchant for the sickly, the morbid, the willfully unfeminine; an air not of Christian calm, but of pagan febricity. It was scarcely a secret in Winterthurn that those poems by the poetess "Iphigenia," appearing irregularly in journals of such varying prestige as the local *Gazette*, and *Hudson Valley Leaves*, and *Vanderpoel Review*, and *Atlantic Monthly*, were by Miss Georgina Kilgarvan of Winterthurn: scarcely a secret, too, that her family very much objected to them, and were responsible for the eventual curtailment of the poetess's "career,"—though, as it would turn out, upward of five hundred of these incoherent scribblings were to be found, in packets of creamy-rose stationery, held together by yarn looped through them in the spine, amidst the spinster's personal effects after her death.

That "Iphigenia" was a foreign-sounding name, arcane, enigmatic, suggestive of the exotic and the forbidden, no one could doubt: that it had been chosen for reasons of subterfuge and coyness, seemed altogether plain. A Greek goddess?—a mortal woman?—a personage from Attic tragedy, whose fate might be as repulsive to consider, as it was distant from the self-evident truths of Christian doctrine? Such speculations freely aired themselves, amidst acquaintances of the Kilgarvans, and, indeed, those who scarcely knew them at all,—for Winterthurn City was, in those times, so modestly populated (containing some twenty thousand persons, if South Winterthurn were included) as to allow everyone to know everyone else, and to gossip, whether idly or maliciously, with unstinting zest.

And who should not think it a matter for speculation that Miss Georgina Kilgarvan, the Judge's daughter, should so forget her station in society, and her obligations to her father's rank, as to wish to publish, for the smiling perusal of all, such overexuberant lines as these,—

> Blow,—winds! Toss,—sea!
> 'Tis but my Soul
> In shameless hunger—
> Of Thee!

and,

> In my skull the mourners tramp'd—
> & church bells sounded, to & fro—
> The very air turned—Inky—
> 'Til Your love drew me thru—

and,

> Father of All—
> Sin do—appall—
> Thy Love so near—
> E'en terror, endear—

Meritorious Christian sentiment, yet was the tone of such verse not somehow improper?—were the rhythms not too forced, too sprightly, indeed, too suggestive of female excitation? It was suspected that the *Winterthurn Gazette* published a dozen of Miss Georgina's poems, over a period of years, solely because the elderly proprietress of the "Poetry

Page'' had long been a champion of Georgina's, harking back to Georgina's schoolgirl days; it was known that *Hudson Valley Leaves*, a ladies' venture exclusively, required of its contributors that they help defray printing costs, and agree to buy up a number of copies of each issue in which their work appeared. As to what possessed the poetry editors of the more distinguished journals to publish, even sparingly as they did, "Iphigenia's" awkward effusions,—no one in Winterthurn could have said. Even Miss Clarice Von Goeler professed surprise: for *her* religious odes, though strictly metered and unfailingly rimed, were consistently rejected by both the *Vanderpoel Review* and the *Atlantic Monthly.*

As Xavier Kilgarvan was balked in his earliest effort to gain access to the *scene of the crime,* or, by firsthand detection, to attempt to *penetrate, pierce, unravel, illuminate,* or in any wise *solve,* the mystery of the infant Whimbrel's death, he directed his boyish energies to poking about, as it were, in agèd back issues of the *Gazette,* kindly provided for him by a librarian: and, in his confused hope that he might, all by accident, hit upon some stray *clue* regarding the catastrophe, he stumbled upon a number of "Iphigenia's" poems, dating back to many years before his own birth. The most memorable of the verses he copied out, he knew not altogether why, in a school notebook,—

> *Know, Sweet Babe—*
> *Thy Father's hand—*
> *Rudders—all thou fearest—*
> *'Tis of Him—of* HIM—
> *(& not of* ME—)
> *These Seraphim sing—*
> *Thou hearest—!*

Slaughtered Lambs

It was at the very end of May, on a humid, overcast, hazily warm morning,—now some twenty-six days since the tragedy at Glen Mawr Manor—that Xavier recklessly played truant from school, and inveigled his brother Colin into accompanying him, that they might investigate a report of "mysteriously slaughtered lambs" belonging to a farmer named Upchurch, whose property bordered that of Glen Mawr Manor: a boyish excursion that not only would result in no clear *evidence*, *clues*, or *leads*, so far as Xavier was concerned, but would cause, for reasons ever to remain obscure, an actual rift between the brothers.

In brooding over the incident afterward, Xavier would not know whether to blame himself,—for, indeed, Mr. Kilgarvan, sensing his son's unwholesome interest in the "mystery" at the Manor, had expressly forbidden him to pursue it ("You are not to go anywhere near Glen Mawr," he said, so forgetting himself that he gripped Xavier's shoulder hard, and made the slender boy wince, "not because the place is accursed, not because your relatives would, in any case, turn you away, but because *I*, your *father*, forbid it")—or whether to blame the queer hurtful malaise of that spring morning, which, quite apart from the piteous and sickening spectacle of the mutilated lambs themselves, suggested some causeless rift in the human soul: the heavy, settled, hazy air of a premature summer subject to random incursions of chill, from a capricious northeast wind that blew across the mountains. What most disturbed the youthful "detective" (for so, in truth, the sixteen-year-old schoolboy secretly thought himself) was that events from this date onward seemed to proceed not only with a logic of their own but with a logic *antithetical to his wishes:* which was never the case, so far as he could determine, in the adventures of Sherlock Holmes, C. Auguste Dupin, George B. Jashber, or the canny Pudd'nhead Wilson.

Xavier is to be forgiven a certain canniness of his own, verging, I suppose, upon actual improbity, when, while sulkily acceding to his father's unusually harsh admonition, in his innermost heart he thought, *Xavier Kilgarvan does what he wishes,—what Mystery requires of him, to be solved.*

So it was, he enjoined Colin to absent himself from a morning's work at the livery stable on Railroad Street, and to bicycle some ten miles out into the country, that they might investigate this most recent in a series of unexplained incidents involving livestock, in the general vicinity of Glen Mawr Manor. (Over a period of several weeks there had been isolated reports of slaughtered and part-devoured kids, piglets, calves, and spring lambs; a yearling pony and a fully mature sheep had died from a loss of blood.) As to what predators were responsible for these assaults,—the sheriff's office could offer only the theory that they had been committed by a pack of wild dogs, unusually vicious coyotes, or actual wolves (for, in these years long past, timber wolves still inhabited the mountainous terrain surrounding Mt. Provenance). It goes without saying that the more ignorantly superstitious amongst the country folk murmured of certain fabulous creatures about whom mountain legends had long accrued,—the giant snowy-white "King of the Wolves," batlike flying reptiles with hooked beaks, great bloodsucking vampire bats, et al.; and since whispered rumors had spread of Mrs. Whimbrel's incoherent mutterings, before her collapse, of "angels" and "angel-demons," it naturally followed that such shadowy creatures were sighted as well,—though in no case could witnesses agree upon a description. (Nor did anyone really know what Abigail Whimbrel had raved of, in her dazed and delirious state, on the morning of May 3: for so far as the authorities were concerned, her near-unconscious condition precluded anything approaching testimony, or a reliable account.)

When the Kilgarvan boys arrived at the Upchurch farm, the sheriff and his deputies had already departed, and Upchurch, discovered in the act of burying the dead lambs, did not seem overly pleased to see them approach: for there had been a great many "gawkers and gapers," as he expressed it, milling about his property through the morning, and he was sick of busybodies tramping in his pasture. Xavier swallowed his pride, and asked only if he and Colin might "examine" the corpses: whereupon the shrewd Mr. Upchurch, handing over his shovel to Xavier, told him they were welcome to examine all they wished, if their stomachs could bear it; provided they com-

pleted the job of burial,—making certain that the lambs were buried
at least *four feet deep*, so that scavengers should not unearth them.

Xavier readily assented to this proposition, and Colin, less readily: for the elder boy, being rather more acquainted with manual labor
than his brother, looked upon it with less favor.

Before Mr. Upchurch excused himself, Xavier dared to ask him a
few questions regarding the lambs: and was informed that the three
corpses had been discovered very early that morning, in the lower
pasture; that the bleating of the ewes (which continued still,—an
uncanny, stirring sound not unlike a human keening) first aroused the
farmer's attention; that nothing *quite* like it had happened in the past,
though, in Upchurch's grandfather's time, white-furred wolves some
ten feet in length made forays into barnyards when their natural prey
was scarce in the mountains,—albeit no one had ever trapped or shot
one of these creatures, nor had they been sighted in the past thirty
years. Frank Shearwater, the sheriff of Winterthurn County, was of the
opinion that wild dogs were responsible for the slaughter, and so
Upchurch intended to set out steel-jawed traps to protect his livestock;
but, as he told the boys with some bitterness, he halfway wondered if
he should retain a Berwick Square attorney ("Berwick Square" having
reference to professional gentlemen—lawyers, physicians, stockbro-
kers—of a reputedly élite, or in any case costly, stature) to inquire into
bringing a lawsuit against the Kilgarvans of Glen Mawr Manor, since,
in the opinions of many country people, it was from the Manor these
"predators" came. Seeing the boys' startled expressions, Upchurch
went on to say that the entire clan of Kilgarvans,—harking back to
Colonial times—were a bloodthirsty lot, as apt to turn upon their own
kin as upon outsiders: and it was not so very surprising, to those who
knew of their ways, that an infant should be killed up there, since
numberless queer things had transpired in the Manor, over the
years,—though he was not one to speak idly and irresponsibly. His
neighbor Phineas Cutter, however, told a most suspicious tale indeed,
of the "Blue Nun," who had awakened him before dawn on the very
morning the killing was discovered . . .

The farmer spoke with such cold vehemence, and with so
furrowed a brow, that neither Xavier nor Colin was inclined, as the
reader might well imagine, to reveal his identity; or to choose to interrogate the older man much further. Xavier said, in a faltering voice,
that he did not quite see *how* any predators, as such, might come from
the Manor: for he had heard that the Kilgarvans' mastiff, though toothless with age, and surely innocent, had been summarily shot by one of
the sheriff's deputies, at the sheriff's command, when, at the very
first, it was imagined that the dog had somehow killed the baby—and
the Kilgarvans kept no other beasts at the present time. This reasonable objection Upchurch negligently brushed aside, and reiterated his

notion of bringing a lawsuit against the "high and mighty" Kilgarvans: for whether the predators be *natural* or *unnatural* creatures, whether, like dogs, they *crept along the earth* or, like "demon birds," they *flew*, there was growing suspicion in the neighborhood that the Kilgarvans, and only they, were responsible for the slaughtered livestock. In turning abruptly away, Upchurch wagged a forefinger at Xavier, and instructed him to bury the lambs deep, and carefully, before he left.

As exhilarating a prospect as it had seemed, earlier that morning, to *investigate with their own eyes* the several slaughtered lambs of which they had just heard (news of any kind spreading swiftly through the city, well in anticipation of the *Gazette*), the actual experience was altogether different: for neither boy was truly prepared for the stark, pitiful, *palpable* reality of the small corpses. Xavier, being easily sickened, and inclining toward the squeamish, had to resist with all his strength the impulse to gag; and the sudden childlike desire to weep, or to run away. For the *physicality* of the dead lambs (involving, as it did, the presence of buzzing bottle-green flies, and swarms of red ants) was nearly too much for him, and struck him, he knew not why, as a kind of betrayal . . . When the great Vidocq came upon murdered men and women, or, indeed, had a hand in murdering them himself; when Jonathan Whicher of the original "Scotland Yard" examined a corpse; when such amateur detectives as Dupin and Holmes arrived at the scene of a crime—why, it had never seemed to greatly distress them that an actual physical presence lay before them: nor did it strike the reader, by way of the language employed, that *something had truly occurred* of an *irreversible* and *irremediable* sort. For now, blinking and staring at the dead lambs, Xavier saw not only *victims, corpses,* and *evidence,* but fellow sentient beings who had, not long previously, been alive; and were now dead. And he felt a sickened paralysis, as the unwanted thought entered his brain that, even should he solve the mystery, even should there be a "mystery" to be "solved," the lambs would not live again: for their time on earth was over.

Such niceties of thought did not suggest themselves to Colin, who merely grunted in disgust: observing that the lambs were, indeed, "dead and done for,—wounded in the necks": that there was nothing else to be seen, or learned: that Upchurch had played them for fools, and they well deserved their ill-luck, in being required to dig a grave four feet deep in such resistant, clayey soil. For emphasis, Colin gave Xavier a sharp little blow on the upper arm; and muttered that he had half a mind not even to assist him, since this wild-goose chase was primarily Xavier's doing.

Xavier coolly replied that he would be pleased to dig the grave himself; and that he hoped to gain more from the investigation than Colin's cursory discoveries.

So it was, Xavier swallowed hard, and forced himself to examine

the pitiful creatures more closely, while Colin, contented with turning
them over with his foot, stood with arms akimbo, whistling thinly
under his breath. Xavier blinked tears of helpless sympathy from his
eyes: for, ah! were the baby animals not sweet, and innocent, and
comely, even in their stiffened postures?—was not the odor of their
spilt blood and violated flesh poignant?—did they not seem to gaze at
him, through fine-lashed eyes, with expressions of such soulful intelligence, he could well frighten himself with thinking he stared into a
mirror? *If these be but animal corpses,* the youth uneasily pondered,
how shall I feel, confronted with a human corpse? He would, he resolved, beg of the county coroner, Hans Deck, that he might one day be
allowed admittance into the morgue,—thereby to see an actual corpse,
and to steel himself against cowardly responses.

Gradually, his strength, his calm, and his reason returned; and
he took out of his jacket his artist's sketchbook and a piece of charcoal,
that he might quickly limn the spectacle before him; telling the
disgruntled Colin that he had lately made inquiries into the techniques
of killing employed by certain canines, and believed that these lambs
must have been killed by another sort of creature after all. A dog
plunges to the kill by hamstringing an animal, and ripping out its
stomach; a coyote, by crushing the larynx, thereby inducing strangulation; a wolf . . . "One can readily see that these lambs have been attacked from above," Xavier said, "for note the deep puncture marks
along the spines, and on the necks: and is it likely that these marks
have been made by *canine teeth?* Rather more likely by claws, or
talons. It is said that dogs and coyotes will eat their way through their
prey by way of the hindquarters, and into the stomach, whereas these
victims have been assaulted at the neck, and the rear of the head,—as, it
seems, Abigail Whimbrel's baby was assaulted—and, too, not one rib
has been cracked in all three: and canines rejoice in cracking ribs as
they feed. Ah, what a pity, that the pasture is all grass, and there are no
prints, for then we should assuredly *know*—! Do you not think it suspicious, too, Colin, that so little of the carcasses has been devoured—?"

As Colin's interest in the slaughtered lambs had rapidly
diminished, and was not to be pricked even by his brother's surprising
recitation of facts, still less by "suspicion," his reply was but a murmur of bland assent; and he detached himself from the scene, to drift
off in the direction of a most idyllic pond, or waterhole, a short distance away at the foot of a grassy slope. If Xavier was somewhat disappointed in his brother's response, he gave no sign, but continued with
his rapid sketches, making one after the other with such dexterity
(though, it should be said, not always with scrupulous accuracy), it
almost seemed his fingers moved of their own volition: and allowed
him that curious, and somehow *elating,* sensation he invariably had

while drawing, or composing tunes at the piano,—of the more enhancing his senses by their simple employment. For did it not seem to
him, as he sketched the dead lambs, and the contours of the pasture
about them, and the irregular outline of a hedgerow beyond, even as he
attempted, with deft rough strokes of his charcoal stick, to suggest the
texture, and the hazy glowering oppression, of the sky overhead,—did
it not seem that, by these efforts, he could suddenly *see more?*—that it
might be his privilege, in the next minute or two, to *see beyond?*

As, in the first confused minutes when Mr. Shearwater, the county
sheriff, and several of his deputies arrived at Glen Mawr Manor, late
in the morning of May 3, it seemed to be the consensus,—most vociferously, though disjointedly, expressed by Miss Georgina Kilgarvan—
that a pet dog, grown unaccountably vicious, had attacked the baby
during the night, it seemed only reasonable that the deputies seek out
the cowering, quivering, clearly terrified creature, in his burrow beneath a stairway: and, with very little hesitation or compunction,
execute him at once. Thus, the summary end of the agèd, near-
toothless, arthritic Jupiter, a mastiff of yet-noble proportions, who
had, in his prime, been Judge Kilgarvan's especial favorite: subject to
this cruel dismissal, for being suspected of an act not in his character,
and performed *in a locked room.*

That Jupiter was responsible for the infant Whimbrel's death is
plainly absurd; yet there were to be a number of persons, among them
the stubborn Simon Esdras, who insisted that this was so: though not,
for one reason or another, the ''Blue Nun,'' who afterward changed her
opinion, to concur with the coroner's report,—that the specific cause
of death was unknown, but rats (of the gigantic Norway species) were
most likely to blame. As for the bereft mother's ravings of *angels*, and
angel-demons, and *Baby Jesus*,—these were so clearly the consequence
of a disordered imagination, drawn in part from a remarkably lifelike
mural painted on the wall and ceiling, that they were dismissed as
worthless: albeit Mr. Shearwater and his men treated Mrs. Whimbrel,—as, indeed, they treated the entire Kilgarvan household—with
unfailing if guarded courtesy.

Initially distracted, and speaking with a frightened stammer,
Simon Esdras rallied by degrees: and seemed finally to take solace in
the ''tragical syllogism,'' as he expressed it, that, *as Jupiter had been
responsible for the outrage, and Jupiter had been removed from the
scene with such dispatch, the task of the authorities would seem to be
completed:* and they might now take their leave. For naught remained for the principals save the usual exigencies of grief, yet another visit to the churchyard,—this time, he supposed, far away in
Contracoeur: and he very much doubted he would be able to attend.

So far as Thérèse and Perdita were concerned, their stunned and bewildered air, their youth, and what gave every impression of their genuine ignorance, quite precluded them from giving testimony: nor were the servants helpful, beyond a few much-repeated statements, and some contradictory information, of minimal worth. When, later in the day, Phineas Cutter reported the visit of Miss Georgina to his establishment, and the nature of her purchase, Mr. Shearwater returned to speak with her; but satisfied himself as to her innocence, as it were, regarding any especial information. (Miss Georgina, though visibly shaken, and drained of that palely radiant energy which oft-times suffused her, answered the sheriff's several questions in a small, still, yet never inaudible voice; and made an excellent impression on him,—for had he not heard idle tales of the "Blue Nun" for many years?—in her somber but freshly ironed black muslin housedress, with stand-up collar in Belgian lace, and impeccably starched cuffs. *Why* she had gone out so unusually early in the day,—*why* she had made her purchase of fifty pounds of quicklime not seven hours, it was estimated, after the tragedy,—was explained very simply: she realized that her need for the gardening aid was pressing, as it had been her intention to work *that morning*, indeed, through the morning, in the rose-garden at the rear of the house, which had been shamefully neglected of late; and which her belovèd father had particularly prized . . .)

Meeting young Harmon Bunting, the assistant pastor of Grace Episcopal Church, who was, it seems, on his way to the Manor to offer the solace of their common faith to the Kilgarvans, Sheriff Frank Shearwater shook his hand, and spoke with him for several minutes, happening to mention, in an abashed aside, that he had long been curious as to Miss Georgina's *true self*,—for tongues did wag in Winterthurn City, and his own womenfolk were not guiltless!—but found their interview, though brief and formal, highly gratifying, and rewarding in its own way. This attempt at a species of camaraderie between Mr. Shearwater (who was well regarded in the county, but scarcely well born), and Mr. Bunting (the descendant of the Joshua Bunting who had, some *two hundred thirty years previous*, led an entirely successful attack against a bastion on the Winterthurn River, manned by the settlers of New Sweden), came to very little, as the youthful pastor would never stoop to common gossip about one of his parishioners, let alone a personage of such distinction as Erasmus Kilgarvan's eldest daughter. In a courteous, but unmistakably prim, reply, Mr. Bunting said that an interview with a lady must invariably be highly gratifying, and doubtless rewarding as well: but he could not imagine why, in this hour of fresh grief, poor Miss Kilgarvan had been harassed.

Despite the findings of the authorities, and a lengthy article on the front page of the *Gazette*, calculated to have a calming effect upon the inhabitants of the area (for Mr. Osmyn Goshawk, the editor and publisher of the paper, had always had the highest regard for Erasmus Kilgarvan), it *was* the case that tongues wagged and wagged, with an ever-increasing fervor, in the days and weeks to follow. The coroner's suspicion of *Norway rats*, made public, was scandalous and titillating, indeed: all of Winterthurn City, from the most affluent households descending to the most impoverished, reasoned that it should never be outlived that *rats* of any sort might be acknowledged at Glen Mawr Manor,—the "Showplace of the Valley," as Phillips Goode had boastfully named it. Yet the verdict came too quickly, and perhaps even too plausibly, to satisfy: and was brushed aside by many, with as much elated contempt as the notion that the Judge's agèd mastiff had been guilty. A brutal deed it had been, but had it necessarily been the work of a mere *brute*—? Might not a human agent (whether mortal or demonic) have been involved—?

So disagreeable were most of the rumors and speculations that spread through the town in May, so improbable the reports of "eyewitnesses," that I hesitate to include here more than a brief sampling, drawn from R. S. Gilder's copious study, *The Kilgarvans of Glen Mawr Manor: An History and an Interpretation* (1899); but such an approach is required, if the reader is to grasp the mentality of the times, and the fulsome barrage of fables, fancies, tales, and outright lies that the youthful detective confronted, in his unflagging, if oft-times directionless, search for the Truth.

The Westergaards, whose seventy-acre estate was contiguous with Glen Mawr on the east, claimed to see, at dusk, "undulating figures of an unearthly luminosity" playing in the pine and beech woods belonging to the Kilgarvans: but had no success in identifying them, let alone capturing them (as young Valentine Westergaard wished to do). Miss Imogene Westergaard, the outspoken and somewhat free-thinking heiress daughter of the Colonel, twenty-seven years old but fired with the verve of a self-proclaimed spinster twice her age, insisted that these "undulating figures" approached her, with an air of actual enticement, while she walked her twin Irish terriers along the river path: but that the dogs' frenzied yapping drove them away. (Level-headed as Miss Westergaard was in most respects, observers believed that her testimony could not be taken seriously, in this case, as her clumsy descriptions of *angels, cherubs,* or *vaporous human infants* resembled too closely the ravings of Abigail Whimbrel, and had doubtless been influenced by them. And Miss Westergaard's ire was the more fueled, when, attempting to visit Georgina a fortnight after the tragedy, she was told by a most discourteous black butler that his mistress was not in: and cared not to receive visitors when she was.)

As for Miss Georgina,—of a sudden everyone whispered of her, and knew fresh news of the "Blue Nun," oft of a highly contradictory and implausible nature! For instance, it was said that she had locked herself in her bed-chamber, and refused most foods; that she disciplined herself harshly,—taking purges of a violent nature, administering enemas and douches of the most pitiless sort, injuring herself with hat-pins, candle-flames, riding crops, etc.; that she would communicate only with old Pride, and then through a locked door. Ringgold Peregrine, Henry's son, a corpulent, sweet-natured, idle youth, swore that he had seen Miss Georgina walking in the woods, at the edge of Juniper Park: that she was dressed in her habitual mourning clothes, which must have been uncomfortably warm in the sunshine; that she was heavily veiled, with a dark velvet hood, instead of a hat, completely covering her head; that she carried what Ringgold supposed to be a walking stick at first, but which was, in fact, a riding crop . . . What was surprising was Miss Georgina's behavior: for, as she walked along, hurrying, in a swaying erratic stride, of a kind young Ringgold had never observed in a lady, she paused frequently to swipe at the ground with the riding crop, *as if something invisible were creeping along beside her and nipping at her ankles.* Despite the congenital slothfulness for which Ringgold was known amongst his schoolmates, he was, it seems, well mannered enough when the situation arose: and knew that, as a Peregrine, it might well be deemed his responsibility to "protect" Miss Georgina Kilgarvan if she required protection,—for it was most unusual, indeed, to glimpse a lady of Miss Georgina's stature strolling without an escort in Juniper Park. Ringgold therefore called out to her, to ask if she needed assistance: whereupon Miss Georgina behaved yet more oddly, in glancing over her shoulder at him for the briefest of instants (with what expression—whether surprise, alarm, chagrin, ire—he could not discern through her thick veil), then turning away, and walking hurriedly deeper into the woods, *with no word or sign of recognition.* Poor Ringgold, already somewhat short of breath, stood on the path staring after her, in utter perplexity, and watched as her somber figure disappeared into the woods, with very little sound,—for, indeed, it seemed to him that even the birds had ceased their chattering, and the squirrels their raucous scolding, as the "Blue Nun" passed rapidly beneath.

(When this tale was told to Xavier, however, by the excitable young Ringgold, it was most skeptically received: for, as Xavier pointed out, Ringgold had not so much as glimpsed the lady's face, nor had he the slightest shred of evidence that she was swiping at something invisible,—for, if it were *invisible,* how might it then be seen? Such "eyewitness" accounts could scarcely be taken seriously, Xavier scornfully said, as if, for the moment, he were Monsieur Dupin, or Sherlock Holmes himself, confronted with a particularly obtuse individual,—and, indeed, the reliability of amateur witnesses is notorious throughout the history of crime.)

Equally unreliable, and colored with a surprising cruelty, were the divers tales told of poor Thérèse and Perdita, who had bravely returned to classes at the Parthian Academy, that they might not fall behind their classmates: for now, it seems, it was openly observed, by even those girls who had been amiable enough in the past, that the Kilgarvan sisters were most odd; had been odd from the start; sighed too frequently in the classroom, and wept too frequently in the cloakroom; aroused scorn by working so very diligently at her studies, in the case of Thérèse, and impatience, by an excess of brooding, in the case of Perdita; kept to themselves, or, conversely, failed to keep sufficiently to themselves,—for if Perdita approached a group of girls they coolly turned aside, and Thérèse's deskmate of many months now shrank from her, and requested of the headmistress that she be moved elsewhere. For, it seems, the sisters offended not only by their presence but by an odor that emanated from them, of something most rank, chill, unclean, and sickly. (Like singed feathers, one girl claimed. Like wet fur, claimed another. Like milk just beginning to turn; or agèd soiled clothes; mildew; mold; rot; waste; dark brackish unspeakable blood.)

Felicity Peregrine widened her periwinkle-blue eyes and lowered her voice to a whisper, as she swore she had seen *Thérèse's shadow detach itself from her and drift away*, on one of the school's graveled walks; Mary-Louise Von Goeler evoked frightened giggles by swearing that she had, entirely by accident, touched Perdita's wrist, *to discover that the girl's skin was clammy and cold*, as that of,—why, she would not wish to say. And how fierce was the expression Perdita turned upon her: darkly bright eyes ablaze like a cat's, with ill-suppressed fury!

And all the Parthian girls agreed that the Kilgarvan sisters knew more than they acknowledged regarding the death of the Whimbrel baby,—more, certainly, than the fools in the sheriff's office suspected.

(When these reckless accusations were repeated in Xavier's presence, he had all he could do to keep from bursting out in rage; and felt the insult against sweet Perdita as keenly as if a razor-sharp blade had been drawn against his unprotected skin.)

The headmistress of the school, Clarice Von Goeler (a maiden aunt of the cruel talebearer Mary-Louise), had long made it her mission to befriend Thérèse and Perdita, both because she pitied the girls, being motherless; and because she yet cherished her girlhood friendship with Georgina, who was, in her steadfastly loyal view, "one of the

very few outstanding *individuals* of her acquaintance,—of either sex.''
Though the relationship between Clarice and Georgina had long since
atrophied, for no reason Clarice could discover, she continued to
write little notes to Georgina from time to time, inviting her to accompany her sisters to tea at the headmistress's residence, or to dinner, or on a Sunday excursion along the river to one of the majestic old
inns: most of which invitations, despite their gracious tone, and un-
forced offer of sympathy and affection, went unanswered. (For in this,
and in a host of related issues, the Judge's daughter quite betrayed her
heritage, in her shocking *rudeness*.) Miss Von Goeler was a tall,
flaxen-haired woman of young middle age, healthily colored, forthright, yet, upon occasion, given to periods of introspection: reserved,
one might say, out of stubbornness rather than timidity: with very little patience for gossip, scandal, and the like. So it was, when thoughtless persons asked of her what the ''Blue Nun'' was truly like, or how
matters truly stood at Glen Mawr (as if, indeed, Clarice had set foot in
the house for some ten or twelve years), she was likely to flare up in a
temper, and reply that ''it was no one's concern, and a vulgar sort of
diversion, to make such queries.'' A tale making the rounds, which
was repeated to Xavier's mother by a lady friend, had it that the headmistress had called both Kilgarvan girls to her office to speak in private with them, and to ask if she might be of assistance: with the
startling consequence that Thérèse burst into speechless sobs, and little Perdita grew very white in the face, saying, in a voice of quivering
pride, ''Thank you for your pity, Miss Von Goeler, but we do not *require* it, and we do not *wish* it,''—or words to that effect (for the story,
as one might suspect, underwent numerous alterations and embellish-
ments as it spread through town).

     As he had so long led a life of willful seclusion, and could
scarcely be said to thrust himself upon the attentions even of the
enlightened public, Simon Esdras Kilgarvan escaped general notice,
and was the subject of few tales. So it was, the Kilgarvans of Wycombe
Street were astonished one evening at the dinner table when, in his
usual blithe and unthinking manner, Wolf told them that his circle of
friends,—by which he meant the Rock Barrens racetrack circle, which
included young Valentine Westergaard and Calvin Shaw—had quite
solved the mystery of Glen Mawr: it was Simon Esdras who had
murdered the baby, for he would have had a key to the bed-chamber,
and only Simon Esdras, of all the household, was *unquestionably mad*.
So bluntly, yet so casually uttered, these words did not evoke the response Wolf had anticipated, even from his brothers; Mrs. Kilgarvan
pressed her hand to her bosom, in mute consternation; and Mr. Kilgarvan, after a moment's shocked silence, told his son that he was no gentleman, but a lowlife ruffian, to speak in so coarse a way at the dinner

table,—and of his own uncle. "You will excuse yourself at once, and leave us," Mr. Kilgarvan said. "But, sir," Wolf protested, attempting a smile, "surely you must understand that our theory is not *altogether* serious." "The more scurrilous, then, the lot of you," Mr. Kilgarvan said, with trembling lips, "and you *will* take your leave at once."

It was not long after that evening, however, when reports spread of Simon Esdras,—or a white-haired gentleman who closely resembled him—in any number of unlikely places, including the rougher areas of South Winterthurn, and the unlicensed establishments of Rivière-du-Loup. Whether he drank to dazed excess, or tried his inexpert hand at gambling and cards, or consorted with women of a certain unspecified category,—none of the talebearers was prepared to say. It *was* the case, however, that Simon Esdras now attended church more faithfully, including even Wednesday evening services (to which he escorted Thérèse and Perdita,—Miss Georgina being temporarily invalided); and he caused a stir by showing up, unannounced, at a meeting of the Thursday Afternoon Society, having mistaken the day's program of verse recitation by Miss Iris Kathleen Hume for a symposium of some sort on a Scottish philosopher, of whom no one in the Society had ever heard. On the more somber side, he had taken to dropping in at the Corinthian Club, which he had not visited for forty years, and wandering about both downstairs and upstairs, *as if in search* (so observers believed) *of his dead brother:* with a most mournful, distracted, childlike expression on his pink-flushed face, and a wistful smile for all who came forward to shake his hand. Only a night or two prior to the Kilgarvan boys' adventure at the Upchurch farm, Valentine Westergaard chanced to encounter the philosopher on the granite steps between the Club's stately gryphon figures, and, seeing that Simon Esdras smiled toward him in a somewhat stupefied manner, put himself at his aid, and offered to escort him home. According to young Westergaard, the old gentleman breathed a sweet liquorish breath, yet behaved, in a sense, in no more tipsy a way than usual: plucking at his sleeve, and inquiring of him whether Heraclitus was correct in asserting that one cannot plunge into the same river twice; or whether, to reason more adroitly, Simon Esdras Kilgarvan was correct in asserting that one can either not plunge into the river (sic) once, which is to say, at all, as the "river" is but a figure of speech, or not not plunge (sic) into the "river," as the river is ubiquitous, and carries all mortals along, to we know not where. When Valentine did no more than chuckle uneasily, not grasping that an actual proposition had been put to him, Simon Esdras repeated it, in a high petulant voice that betrayed an uncommon anxiety. "So it is, young man, you must choose," the philosopher said, "—Heraclitus, or Kilgarvan: which is it?" Canny though young Westergaard was, and a very devil at cards and horses, he had no mind for the knottier issues of philosophy, and answered in a vague cheery tone that he "would put his money on *Plato*,"—the only philosopher of whom he had heard, and by whom his grandfather the Colonel swore: which answer was, as it turned out, most brilliant, as it not only impressed Mr. Kilgarvan but silenced him for the remainder of the drive home. Then, at the Manor, he shook Valentine's hand and offered him formal thanks, for having "pricked him in his sophist slumber": for Plato, though mad, doubtless contained a yet more ubiquitous Truth, that "river" and "he-who-plunges" are similarly unreal, or, conversely, "real" to the same degree. "In any case," Simon Esdras said, with a sudden sunny smile, "I shall think hard upon it: and it may be, after all, that Erasmus *yet lives*,—and none of us must die."

Upon returning from a business trip to Vanderpoel and the western reaches of the Valley, Bradford Kilgarvan reported the alarming news that the family's very name, once so distinguished, had become, of late, shrouded in mystery and confused scandal: that Erasmus's entirely natural death was being whispered of as "unnatural" and "unexplained": that not one, but several infants, had died at the Manor: that the "Blue Nun" was most irresponsibly linked with a woman, not even an ancestress, of the late 1790s,—harking back beyond Phillips Goode's time—who had, it seems, poisoned several husbands in Winterthurn. Alas, many an old shameful tale, attached as much to the Kilgarvans' neighbors as to them, was being resuscitated, and passed off as new—!

Protest as Bradford assuredly did, with as much gentlemanly tact, forbearance, and good humor as he could summon forth, that these stories were greatly exaggerated, and that, in any case, the Kilgarvans of Glen Mawr Manor were very different persons from the Kilgarvans of Wycombe Street,—yet he failed, in his own estimation, to greatly alter those notions. Still more worrisome was the puzzling development that those store owners or managers (among them the overseer of the Children's Floor of the great Brant Brothers Cast Iron Palace, in downtown Vanderpoel) who had, in the past, unhesitatingly ordered Mr. Kilgarvan's toys in considerable quantities, because of the very name *Kilgarvan*, now professed less enthusiasm; and agreed to order, it almost seemed with reluctance, certain specialties of the Winterthurn workshop (the wooden Noah's Ark, the fretwork humblybeg, the ever-popular "crying" doll, above all the splendid rocking horse) that were belovèd of the children of the well-to-do, and not available elsewhere, from other toymakers or suppliers. Bradford was deeply insulted when one shopkeeper, while placing his order, expressed the hope that the toys should not prove "dangerous": for he had heard—why, he knew not precisely *what* he had heard!

Informed of such perfidious matters, Lucas Kilgarvan at first flared up in manly anger: then, within an hour, lapsed into that listless melancholia to which he was, it seems, prone. Never did he utter aloud a word of complaint or self-pity, not to his belovèd wife, not even to his most trusted son Bradford: yet it was evident that he suffered: and that, after so many years of unflagging industry and deserved praise for the masterly craftsmanship of his custom-made toys, he still could not rest in the assumption of *financial stability*. So it was, year upon year, the effect, it seemed, of the virulent animosity his elder brother had conceived for him, for clouded reasons . . .

Young Xavier, sensing these things, did not violate his father's pride by speaking of them: but vowed with the more heated fervor that he should one day restore his father's fortune to him, and his reputation; that he should exorcise for all times even the rumor of his father's (and his own) "tainted blood,"—baseless though it was, and trivial. But, ah!—was the very name of *Kilgarvan* now accursed?—might he be forced to leave Winterthurn to realize his destiny?

While gazing at the slaughtered lambs, and covering page after page of his sketchbook with deft, feathery strokes in charcoal, Xavier slipped, by degrees, into a pleasurable light trance: and, his restless brother being otherwise absorbed in wandering about the lower pasture, Xavier felt his spirit expand, and grow ever more airy and insubstantial, the while thoughts of a most exotic species seemed to lift from the trampled grasses underfoot, and fold him in their warm embrace . . .

Of a sudden, Xavier was forcibly reminded of a dream he had had the previous night, bearing upon little Perdita, in which the lovely child had appeared,—in what attire, for what purpose, whether with hair loosed or no, the youth was shamed to recall—in his bed-chamber, by luminous moonlight: a vision of such fleeting sweetness, he had felt it imprinted upon his very being; and awoke with strangulated breath (alas, to naught but his too-familiar room, in which, close beside him, Colin slumbered with deep rasping breaths,—the blameless sleep of any healthsome lad).

Now, not a yard distant from Upchurch's lambs, this dream-image reappeared: and in the next instant vanished: nor could Xavier, though his heart strained, and desire leapt in his wrists, summon it back. Instead, other shapes appeared, of a graceful tantalizing nature: winged, it seemed: floating: gentle: transparent. A tiny hand, the palm heated, the fingers surprisingly strong, insinuated itself into his, to force the stick of charcoal away.

Not clearly audible, yet unmistakably near, a voice murmured his name, and called him *Cousin:* being joined by another, and yet a third: high-pitched, melodic, sweet, yearning, familiar yet unutterably strange. *Xavier! Dear Xavier! Dear Cousin!* He felt a warm breath on his cheek and throat; felt his curls saucily tousled; his tense shoulders stroked; his sides, his torso, and, ah! the more saucily yet, *his very nipples,*—the while hairs stirred on the back of his neck, and his flesh lifted in goosebumps. *Cousin, sweet cousin! O most comely of boys! O, are you ours!* Enthralled, Xavier stood without moving, scarcely daring to breathe, as a pair of damp lips brushed boldly against his, in the first kiss of a *forbidden kind* the innocent youth had ever experienced. Soft-caressing voices sounded close about his head, fine as the humming of honeybees; and, with motions both timid and brazen, the tiny invisible hands stroked, and pinched, and plucked, and essayed to tickle, through his clothes. *Dear Xavier! Dear Cousin! Can it be, you are ours! O sweetest of boys!* The dream was so fraught with slow-pulsed pleasure, the voices so irresistible in their pleading, Xavier feared he might be on the brink of sin: and made an attempt to rouse himself, and to wake, as he oft-times did in the early morning, by jerking his head suddenly upon his pillow to shake off the languorous shackles of sleep.

So it seemed, for a moment, he *was* awake: and naught before him,—the piteous small bodies of the lambs, the farmer's coarse-handled shovel propped against a fence, the very slant and contours of the grassy slope—had been altered a whit. Yet, in the next pulsebeat, he heard again the heated, urgent voices, and felt again the numberless impatient fingers, and wondered if he should die of such suffocating sweetness!—for the incantatory *Cousin, dear Cousin, O Xavier, O beautiful boy!* rose to near-rapture, washing and lapping about him.

From whatever source the necessary strength derived,—whether some hastily recalled passage of the Book of Common Prayer, or an imagined admonitory phrase of one of his detective-heroes, or, indeed, the healthful impulses of his own virgin soul—Xavier managed to rouse himself a second time, and to wrench his hand free of the steely little fingers. His lips of their own volition shaped a silent prayer,—*O release me!*—and in that instant the youth fully awakened: to discover himself crouched on trembling legs above the dead lambs, his body both uncomfortably heated yet chill, and his clothes dampened with perspiration.

The voices, of that haunting mellifluousness, had abruptly fled *as if they had never been:* and Xavier blinked dumbly, to see his precious sketchpad and charcoal stick had fallen at his feet.

"How stange!—how disagreeably strange!" the lad bethought

himself, stooping to retrieve his things. "And yet, why should I suffer any upset, for a mere dream?"

As Colin had, it seems, thoughtlessly wandered off, Xavier made the decision to dig the mass grave by himself: which laborious and unromantic task had at least the salutary effect of waking him yet more fully, and driving from him all dream-phantasms, pleasurable or otherwise—! In other circumstances he might have contented himself with doing his task as quickly, and as offhandedly, as possible,—for, of the Kilgarvan boys, he ranked with Wolf, as frequently unreliable in household matters: but, as Upchurch had so sternly charged him to dig the grave four feet deep, and to cover the lambs well, Xavier toiled to fulfill these requirements, oft pausing to catch his breath, or wipe at his damp brow, or, indeed, turn hurriedly aside that he might overcome a sudden spasm of nausea.

When, at last, he finished his laborious chore, his back ached most cruelly, and blisters had already formed on his hands: but the pitiful creatures were at least hidden from sight, beneath a mound of fresh dirt: and Xavier did not think that Upchurch could criticize him, or complain of him, or rank him with the mere gawkers and busybodies who had tramped about earlier. "So it is, Xavier Kilgarvan must acquire a reputation for being altogether *dedicated*, and, indeed, *professional*," Xavier declared inwardly, propping the shovel up against the fence with care.

His mood was somewhat dampened, however, when, having found his brother napping just beyond the pond, in a cozy sort of bed or burrow he had fashioned in the tall grasses, Colin turned upon him a most uncharacteristic expression: both groggy and startled, and distinctly peevish: his broad, high-colored, handsome face reddening, it seemed, with irritation or obscure embarrassment. While asleep he had evidently been bitten by flies or mosquitoes, as upward of a dozen red, puffy, ugly miniature wounds now appeared on his face and throat; he had scratched at these with such unconscious violence that several were bleeding; and his fingernails were edged with his own blood. Seeing his belovèd brother thus, and being greeted with a surliness he had not expected (for, in the mornings, it was always Colin who woke easily, with a fresh, sunny smile, and an immediate appetite for breakfast, and Xavier who lashed out with childish ire), Xavier felt a pinprick of alarm: might something have happened to Colin in his sleep?—and why, indeed, had he chosen to sleep at so unpropitious a time?—for the boy was husky and broad-shouldered and possessed, it seemed, of twice Xavier's energy, and generally scornful of those who required daytime naps.

It took Colin but a few seconds to overcome his grogginess, and to rise to his feet, assuring Xavier, with a negligent wave of his hand, that he was *quite* all right,—though stupefied with boredom, and resentful as well, of having been ''dragged along'' on one of Xavier's foolhardy adventures.

Xavier halted in his path, for he had, it seems, anticipated some brotherly gratitude, if not actual surprise and admiration, for his labor in burying the lambs unassisted: but, as this was not forthcoming, and Colin continued in his ungracious temper,—averring, with a curl of his lip, that he was heartily sick of ''detection,'' and halfway thought he should report the morning's excursion to their father—Xavier too lapsed into a sullen silence; in which mood the boys bicycled home.

Alas, Colin exacted a subtle sort of revenge, in pedaling with such consistent swiftness, and no ostensible effort, that he soon left his panting brother behind; for the younger boy had not the strength in his leg muscles, or the lung capacity, to keep pace with him. That this was performed, as it were, unintentionally,—that Colin seemed merely not to notice Xavier's absence beside him—made the insult all the more cutting. Too proud to call after his brother, Xavier doggedly pedaled in his wake, watching Colin's broad, bent shoulders, and the muscles that rippled across them, and the unflagging motions of his legs, until, by degrees, as the country road dipped, and rose, and twisted, and dipped yet again, the older boy passed out of sight.

"If I-Am You-"

It was on a sun-drenched afternoon in early May, some thirteen years before, when the air of Parthian Square shimmered greenly in the wake of a brief shower, and all the world, it seems, was giddy with the scent of lilac, that Miss Clarice Von Goeler of the Parthian Academy for Girls (at this time but the headmistress's assistant, and a popular instructress in Music, Elocution, and Deportment) had so curious an adventure while accompanying her friend Georgina Kilgarvan to Dr. Hatch's office on Berwick Square that she brooded over it for months,—for years: and only after Miss Georgina's shocking death, not two weeks before her forty-third birthday, did she speak of it to several of her female relatives: the studied consensus being, they could make no more sense of the incident than of ''Iphigenia's'' clotted poesy of old . . . !

In brief, the event came about in this way: Clarice was in the midst of conducting her third-form girls in a spirited recitation of an ode to spring by John Greenleaf Whittier when, of a sudden, the door was flung open, and two distraught girls burst into the room to say that their teacher, Miss Kilgarvan, had been overcome by an attack of breathlessness,—that she had gone red in the face, and staggered from her desk,—that she had fallen to the classroom floor in a faint,—*and gave every impression of ceasing to breathe.* Whereupon, without a second's hesitation, Clarice hurried down the corridor to her friend's classroom, to discover, with infinite relief, that Georgina had partway revived, and was being assisted to her feet by several girls. Indeed, the dazed woman was feebly protesting that she was quite all right now,—

77

she was quite restored to herself,—and they had no need of milling about, and coming so close: for she could not recall having given anyone permission to leap from her desk . . .

How luridly colored was Georgina's handsome face, blotched with hectic red, yet waxen-pale beneath!—how stupefied with fear, her rapidly blinking eyes!—though she made a show of attempting to stand erect, and refusing further assistance, declaring, in a voice so weakened it scarcely sounded like her own, that she did not wish to be touched, as she was now fully recovered,—*and must complete the day's lesson.*

Clarice, however, could not be so easily dissuaded. It was self-evident, in her opinion, that Georgina was distinctly unwell,—for was she not, even now, short of breath, and swaying on her feet?—no matter her protests, the class must be dismissed, and she must allow Clarice to take her at once, by hackney cab, to Dr. Hatch,—the physician's office being but a few blocks distant, near the city hospital. Georgina essayed to stand her ground, reiterating, with enfeebled breath, that she had quite recovered, that it had been a trifling attack of light-headedness, and that, under no circumstances, was the headmistress,—or, indeed, anyone—to be informed—for she must, she *must,* remain with her class, she *must* complete the day's lesson, else—

"Georgina, you are not yourself,—you *are* ill," Clarice interrupted, in a voice both alarmed and chiding, "and if you possess a whit of the common sense we expect of our students, you will acknowledge that fact."

At this, Georgina drew breath to contend, but was, it seemed, overtaken by a fresh wave of dizziness; and, to the startled concern of all, did a most uncharacteristic thing, *in bursting into girlish tears.*

(That Miss Kilgarvan, the most exacting disciplinarian at the Parthian Academy, the instructress most feared, most admired, and, alas, most frequently imitated behind her back, should succumb to a fainting spell in her classroom, let alone copious tears,—why, was this not wondrous?—was this not delicious?—in truth, was it not remarkable? For so sternly fixèd was Georgina Kilgarvan's character, in the minds of Parthian students, that those who had not witnessed the outburst could not believe it: and were queerly resistant to being convinced. "Why, I might more readily believe, as the Spanish peasants do, that a statue of the Virgin Mary has shed tears," one of the bolder young ladies asserted, "than I might believe, or wish to believe, that Miss Kilgarvan has shed tears.")

As Winterthurn City girls of a near-identical age and social background, Miss Clarice Von Goeler and Miss Georgina Kilgarvan had been drawn together, at the Canandaigua Seminary: though Georgina's homesickness was decidedly less pronounced than Clarice's, and her penchant for solitude, and the studying of inhospitable texts (works of Aeschylus and Sophocles read in the original), and the scribbling of idiosyncratic rhymes had a dampening effect upon their friendship. Clarice had no less a "personality" at the school than Georgina, and was not the sort to pursue an acquaintanceship where but a modicum of encouragement was offered: so it came about, it must be said to Clarice's secret sorrow, that though she was in truth Georgina's "closest" friend at Canandaigua, she was not, in truth, a "close" friend—!

Yet ties between them, of a sort, did exist: for each sensed herself the *unmarriageable*, if not the *unlovable*, type: and so busied herself with activities of a rich diversity, and a generally unflagging air of intellectual vivacity, that no observer, of either sex, might have known whether it was indifference, or timidity, or private fear, that most potently governed her soul. Physically, too, they were alike, in being taller by several inches than the average girl, and less naturally given to gracious motion; the one possessed of fine dark hair and eyes, and the long, aquiline, slightly hooked Kilgarvan nose; the other blond, with frank hazel eyes, and a snubbed nose, and a somewhat stolid jaw. Both loved poetry, and aspired to composing it: but though Georgina, as editor of *Canandaigua Bluets*, consented to publish several of Clarice's poems, she refrained from uttering a word of praise,—which tacit disapproval, or dislike, wounded Clarice's feelings.

Ties there were, however, of whatever intangible kind, for, after graduation, when Georgina went bravely away to study at Barnard, and Clarice remained closer to home, at the Nautauga Falls College for Women, an unexpected correspondence ensued: this being one of those odd relationships that bloom, as it were, through the mails, with surprising vigor, and even a modicum of affection. How flattered,—indeed, how warmed—how *delighted* Clarice was! Whether Georgina truly cared for Clarice's lush impressions of her college, and of her professors, or whether she derived greater pleasure from her own writing,—lengthy, acerbic, "dashed off" letters chock-a-block with vivid descriptions of such features of New York life as elevated trains, A. T. Stewart's gigantic dry goods store, Fifth Avenue and Park Avenue on Sunday mornings, the "demonically inspired" sermons of Henry Ward Beecher, which, it seems, Georgina had ventured to Brooklyn several times to hear,—it would be difficult to say: but when Judge Kilgarvan fell ill, and summoned his daughter home, the epistolary friendship was abruptly terminated; and, to Clarice's bewilderment and hurt, no "real" friendship took its place. They visited each other, and had tea in town, and attended meetings together of the Thespian Society, and the

Junior Ladies' Auxiliary of the Corinthian Club, and the Thursday Afternoon Society; yet Clarice had the distinct feeling that Georgina sometimes looked upon her with actual fear,—that she should suddenly presume upon their girlish "postal" intimacy, and deeply embarrass them both.

After both young women joined the faculty of the Parthian Academy, however, and became, in a manner of speaking, "professionals," their relations were somewhat easier. Clarice might freely complain of the headmistress's crotchets, or of the board of trustees (a gathering of elderly females to whom the tumult of the 1850s had marked "the beginning of the end"); Georgina might complain of the frivolity of their young charges, and their inability to master the rudiments of English grammar, albeit they knew the latest slang. If Clarice complained, from time to time, of her family (for Mrs. Von Goeler had greeted Clarice's thirtieth birthday not as an anticipation of the disgrace of spinsterdom, but as an acknowledgment of it), Georgina demurred from offering complaints of her own,—though Erasmus Kilgarvan had taken a simple-minded sort of young lady for his second wife, not three years before, and rumor had it, through Winterthurn, that stepmother and stepdaughter were *not* the very best of friends. Nor did Clarice and Georgina make reference to those awkward little "poems" that appeared from time to time, in the *Gazette* and elsewhere, under a conspicuous nom de plume.

Yet, through the years, it was Clarice's hidden sentiment, not only that Georgina was in truth her closest and dearest and most *sisterly* friend, but that, in some ill-comprehended way, she possessed the like value in Georgina's heart . . . !

"But I suppose we shall never speak of such things," Clarice sighingly observed, "for they are so very vaporous, where is the vocabulary to engird them? And I should be, no doubt, as tongue-tied as Georgina!"

The fainting spell in the classroom occurred approximately eighteen months before the arrival in Winterthurn of young Malcolm Guillemot, and initiated a period of such capricious ill-health that Georgina thought it best to take temporary leave from her teaching responsibilities: the chronology of which was to be twisted about, in later accounts, so that it would seem, more romantically, that Mr. Guillemot,—or his abrupt withdrawal from the scene—had precipitated Georgina's illness. (In truth, as many persons knew, Georgina Kilgarvan had always suffered intermittent and inexplicable "lapses of health": being robust one day, and weakly pale the next; possessed of a normal appetite upon one occasion, and sickened by food upon the next. Though never before given to actual tears, she was susceptible to dark, raging moods, and sometimes forgot herself in the classroom, raising her voice against her abashed, frightened students, out of proportion to their sins. She scorned certain excesses of the "weaker sex,"—thought the perennial invalids about town were self-pitying babies, undeserving of sympathy,—yet was often invalided herself, for three or four weeks at a time. A tale was told of her, that when Miss Verity Peregrine pressed upon her a packet of iron tablets, that she might build up her strength and make her coloring more attractive, Georgina archly replied, "Attractive to *whom?*"—and refused the offer. There were periods when she seemed to affect a deliberate carelessness in her toilet, and in her apparel, wearing dresses that hung on her like sacks, as if to disguise her inordinate thinness; and to refute the very notion of feminine responsibility.)

As Dr. Colney Hatch was the Kilgarvans' family physician, he must have been familiar with Georgina's vicissitudes of health; yet, when Clarice brought her into his office, patient and doctor behaved with a most puzzling formality,—Dr. Hatch being as distant, and as stubborn, as Georgina. For just as Georgina adamantly claimed that she was *not unwell*, and *did not wish to be touched*, so the frowning physician declared that he would not examine any patient of his, or, indeed, any person at all, who did not wish to be examined. Clarice impatiently interrupted to say that Georgina assuredly *was* unwell; and that any fool, simply by glancing at her, could discern it: but neither patient nor physician would budge, there being a distance of some five or six feet between them. "I cannot understand this," Clarice cried, looking from one to the other, "and wonder if I am in the presence of madmen!"

Dr. Hatch was a middle-aged gentleman of moderate height, inclining toward the stout, with a grave, dour expression, and heavy jowls, given a "sparkle" of sorts by the flash of a gold tooth, and the gold-rimmed bifocals that fitted his face so compactly. His reputation in Winterthurn City was impeccable; he had never married, and was a deacon at Grace Episcopal Church; he mingled with the very best families, and had memberships in the very best clubs; he inspired in his patients respect if not affection; his word was law in medical matters; one can scarcely imagine that he suffered insults lightly. Yet, when Clarice spoke as she did, the good doctor refrained from losing his temper: and, though coloring markedly, contented himself with repeating in a quiet voice that he would not "subject to any examination, any person who did not freely wish to be examined: excepting of course children, who had no jurisdiction over themselves."

Clarice appealed again to Georgina, without success; and yet again to Dr. Hatch, without success. For, though Georgina looked altogether sickly, her complexion mottled and her eyes ringed in

shadow, though her breathing was audibly quickened, and she had
need to support herself, however unobtrusively, by resting against a
table,—Dr. Hatch kept his distance from her, his gaze now affixed to a
point somewhere in space, beyond his visitors' heads, and went on to
speak of the importance of unfailing morning regularity: which was,
he believed, the cornerstone of all forms of regularity, and of good
health. "Congestion in the head is most likely a consequence of congestion in the bowels," Dr. Hatch said, "—both being symptoms of an
overwrought nature, in the female sex in particular, when the strain of
unaccustomed *ratiocination* takes its toll. Thinking, reading, writing, etc.,—these place an inordinate strain on the system, and bring
about any number of disorders. Purges are a necessity; douches with
vinegar or salt solution; enemas, of the cold-water variety; and the
like. A week of enforced rest might be prescribed,—or two weeks, or
three: but, as I say, I do not press my services upon any person who has
not come willingly to my office, and who has not freely requested my
opinion." The physician fell silent, wiping his hands on a handkerchief, his manner no more forceful than previously, but no less firm.
As he seemed about to bow and take his leave,—Clarice and Georgina
being in his waiting room, and not in an interior office—it seemed to
Clarice that she must protest yet again: but what might she say?
Georgina had turned away, to adjust her hat, and to more firmly secure
a strand of hair that had worked itself loose at the nape of her neck; her
expression was both drained and gratified, apprehensive, yet relieved;
how like a frightened child, Clarice observed, who has escaped some
punishment or duty—!

"Thank you, Dr. Hatch," Georgina said, with a wild sort of
good humor, as, her long fingers working blindly, she adjusted a hat-
pin skillfully through the crown of her hat. "I shall take your advice to
heart, as it were: and trust that, if a bill is forthcoming from your office, it will be mailed to *me*, at the Parthian Academy, and not to my
father at home."

With a slight bow, Dr. Hatch murmured that he should not of
course think of billing her: for no examination, and no consultation,
had in truth taken place.

Some days later, as she was leaving for school, Clarice discovered, to
her delight, a small wicker basket hanging from her doorknob, filled
with sprays of lilac,—of lavender, deep purple, and white hues: most
beautiful, indeed most captivating, to both the sense of sight and the
sense of smell. She brought it inside, to discover, beneath the lilacs, a
poem written in Georgina's blunt though meticulous hand, inscribed
"to C.—," and signed "Iphigenia."

''RIDDLE-WISDOM''

If I—am You—
Shall You—be me?
If You—scorn I—
Where then—We—
Be—?

Quickly Clarice reread these enigmatic lines, and again reread them,—
with the unlooked-to result that, of a sudden, she burst into tears: for
she did not,—ah, she could not!—make any sense of them, or of her
unhappy friend: and she knew beforehand that if she were to confront
Georgina, to inquire of her what the ''Riddle-Wisdom'' was, and what
mystery appeared to govern Georgina's life, she would be greeted by a
chill, stony demeanor: and not a word of explanation, or affection.

The Corpse

As young Xavier Kilgarvan privately thought himself a pitiful sort of detective, having failed to investigate the *scene of the crime* at Glen Mawr Manor, and having, moreover, yet to examine an *actual corpse* (or even to gaze upon one not formally attired, and meticulously groomed, by the undertaker's skillful hand), he resolved to make amends: one day soon, he knew not precisely when, to make a bold sortie against the Manor: and one day *very* soon, to view a dead body at the county morgue,—for he had several times appealed to Mr. Deck that, when a likely corpse was in his keeping, Xavier might be summoned.

All too quickly, it seemed, in the first week of June, word came to Xavier that he might drop by the morgue, at his convenience: the message brought to him by a mystified neighborhood boy while Xavier was in the midst of his morning chores. (He had been prevailed upon by his father to aid Mr. Kilgarvan's Negro assistant Tobias in packing several dozen boxes of toys for railway shipment, a task he particularly disliked: for was it not tedious, and menial, and mechanical?—was it not dismayingly brainless? Xavier especially resented packing dolls, for, being breakable, they required a great deal of attention, and he was sure to be blamed if any accidents occurred en route. Also, though he had seen it for years, Mr. Kilgarvan's famed "Bonnie" doll, with its faint kittenish cry that emanated from its midriff, and its hinged eyelids that snapped open so starkly, never failed to startle him: for the glassy eyes, whether brown, or green, or the blue of the clearest sky, always stared, it seemed, directly at *him*.)

So it was, he made his decision to slip quietly away, though but a quarter of the toys had been packed, and Mr. Kilgarvan was certain to be angry with him: for he could not, he reasoned, allow such humble exigencies of his *personal life* to interfere with his *profession*. (As for Tobias, being fond of Xavier, and, in any case, possessed of a charitable disposition, he assured the lad that he did not mind in the slightest being left to pack the crates single-handed: for, by so doing, he could satisfy himself that they were done properly.)

As Xavier ran by way of alleys, lanes, and footpaths the short distance to Courthouse Green, where, at the rear of the stately domed courthouse building, certain county functions were housed,—the sheriff's headquarters, the jail, the morgue—he felt buoyed along by a wondrous sort of elation: and all the sights, sounds, and odors that presented themselves to his confused delectation seemed but the expression of a single grand *substance*, and overarching *purpose*. Indeed, since having taken on the secret mantle of the Detective, Xavier often felt that *anything* and *everything* was significant: and bore, he knew not immediately how, upon the mystery at Glen Mawr Manor, *if only he possessed the wit to interpret it.*

This certainty began to ebb somewhat, as, now breathless, the boy entered the drab and near-windowless stucco building that housed the morgue, and was greeted with little hospitality by an elderly filing clerk, who seemed not to know his name, or why he had come. If he did not wish to identify the body that had just come in, if he was not a relative, then what was his business at the morgue?—a question put to him with such chill indifference, Xavier would not have known how to reply; and was saved by Hans Deck's intervention.

"The lad has come not to identify our 'John Doe' of the moment," Mr. Deck bemusedly said, allowing a companionable arm to fall upon Xavier's shoulder, "but, I believe, to identify Death."

So it was, Xavier was led along a narrow and near-lightless corridor, to a refrigerated chamber at the rear of the building, which gave the uneasy impression of being subterranean: and presented, with no propaedeutic courtesy, with an actual corpse,—the dead body of a youth "freshly killed" in a brawl out the Old Winterthurn Pike, in the region of Rivière-du-Loup. With a gesture somehow lacking in finesse, Mr. Deck whipped off the soiled white sheet that covered the man, to reveal, to Xavier's affrighted eye, a naked masculine body,—a body badly abused—a body so demeaned by divers imperfections (pimples, warts, moles, boils; misshapen and filth-encrusted toes; slack fatty tissue at the waist, belly, and thighs; an Adam's apple painfully prominent; discolorations or bruises virtually everywhere; eyes open in glassy idiocy; bloodied lips agape, to reveal irregular and yellowed teeth)—that Xavier could but blink, and stare, and swallow, and blink the more: for he had expected to see something quite different, *though he knew not precisely what.*

Though Hans Deck's reputation in the city was that of an upstanding but somewhat chill and disagreeable personality, a consequence, doubtless, of the somber trappings of his trade, he spoke most congenially,—indeed, almost warmly—to poor Xavier, who stood staring down at the corpse on its slanted porcelain table, with no more boyish vivacity than that of an actual relative of the victim, and no more conversation than a mute. "'Tis Death you gaze upon," Mr. Deck said, in a near-tender voice, "—the poor fool that was, the 'John Doe' who had lately inhabited that flesh, having fled forevermore."

Xavier made an enfeebled attempt to respond to this, and to ease himself away from the elder gentleman's comradely arm, which lay, still, upon his shoulder; but Mr. Deck gave no sign of hearing, and continued, in a grave, low, caressing voice, to explain that the dead man was most likely about twenty-eight years of age; that, under the cognomen of "Buck" he had been employed upriver, at one of the lumber camps; that, in a drunken state, he had been so badly beaten about the stomach, torso, and head (the back of the skull being broken,—would Xavier care to see?), he had died of internal injuries, of a multifarious nature. As to *who* had killed him, or *why,*—it was doubtful that Shearwater could make any arrests, or would even trouble to attempt them, for no witnesses might ever be found to the slaying: and, indeed, it had probably not been a "slaying" as such, since the brutish young man would doubtless have beaten his opponent or opponents to death, in similar wise, if circumstances had been but slightly altered. "Such legalistic niceties do not concern us," Mr. Deck said,—now giving "Buck" a playful rap on the shin bone with his knuckles,—"who deal primarily with the flesh; and limit our musings to it."

At this, Xavier faintly essayed another response, for it had struck him,—with the force of both the wildly comical and the horrific—that the luckless young man possessed a coarse sort of family resemblance to the male Kilgarvans: there being something about the hard slant of the brow, and the husky set of the chin, and even about the dark guileless eyes that reminded him of his brothers, Bradford and Colin. But this observation was too weakly asserted for Mr. Deck to hear; and the gentleman was in any case expostulating on several pathological conditions (exclusive of the violent hemorrhages that had caused death) of uncommon interest to be found in the corpse. For instance, the divers sores,—*pustules, tubercles, blebs, scales, crusts, fissures,* and *papules;* liberally scattered across the body, with the innocence of mere freckles—were, as Xavier might know, the unmistakable symptoms of venereal disease, in its secondary stage: a scourge and a warning of God that young men must behave with propriety at all times, and resist the wiles of the female sex,—apart, that is, from the blessèd marital bed. "For it is very much as Reverend De Forrest would have it," Mr. Deck said, "that so repulsive a disease is, in a sense, an actual boon of God, for its efficacy in warning us against the snares of the flesh. Why, last month, I had on this selfsame slab an old codger so rotted with his sins, you could see his actual brain through a hole the size of a silver dollar in the roof of his mouth!—a hellish sight, I assure you, yet most powerfully instructive. Though *he* had been too far gone, for years, to profit from it. But I trust," Mr. Deck said, in a more kindly tone, "your father has well acquainted you with such wisdom."

In truth, Lucas Kilgarvan had somewhat abrogated his paternal duty, in postponing a discussion of this nature with his youngest, and most sensitive, son: for even the unperturbable Bradford, and the raffish Wolf, and the stolid Colin, had evinced considerable upset at being exposed to the harrowing daguerreotypes in Dr. Horace Motley's *A Recent History of Disease and Pathology*, and Dr. Findley Litz's famed *Scourges of God*,—these being the two most frequently employed texts in Winterthurn City, in these years, for enlightening young men to the *facts of life.* Yet such was Xavier's caution that he did not wish to question Mr. Deck more closely, as to the nature of this "wisdom."

Of interest as well, the coroner said, seizing a particularly bruised flap of skin in the lower region of the deceased's belly, was this evidence of advanced abdominal hernia: which must have given the young man a great deal of discomfort. And, too, had Xavier's keen eye taken in the malformation of several toes; the oversized and apish nature of the genitals; the concentration of pustules at the navel; the sickly rotted teeth; and the general *unwholesomeness* of the corpse,—apart, that is, from the actual markings of death? "Dr. Hatch, who dropped by late last night, on his way home from the hospital, paused to see what our 'catch' of the day was: and informally diagnosed one of his ailments as a kidney disorder, which would have resulted in a particularly odious death, by way of uremic poisoning," Mr. Deck said, in a voice both sympathetic and chiding, as he lifted the corpse's battered lips to show his gums; and,—as Xavier involuntarily winced—lifted up his eyelids to show his yellowed and bloodshot eyeballs. "Colney works very hard, as you know; yet he told me he is eager to acquire our 'John Doe' for his dissection laboratory at the hospital,—many of the corpses sent him being, it seems, badly deteriorated, as a consequence of extreme old age and indigence," Mr. Deck said. He pinched the corpse's cheek, and chuckled, saying that "Buck" was fortunate to be finding his way to Dr. Hatch's professional hands: for *bodysnatchers* of the most shameless sort were operating throughout the state, digging up the dead in paupers' cemeteries, and elsewhere, and peddling them,—why, God knew where!—this "business" having become quite a scandal in recent years.

Xavier could not even bring himself to murmur an assent to this speech, as, by degrees, the warmth of his skin had yielded to the metallic chill of the morgue; and his earlier ebullience had long since ebbed, to be replaced by a sensation of light-headedness and nausea. Ah, his hopes!—his schoolboy intentions! He had wished to query Hans Deck *closely* on the matter of the Whimbrel infant's death, and whether the coroner's office, or the sheriff's office, had ascertained that rats' teeth would make the sort of wounds and marks to be found on the baby; he had hoped, after a sort of camaraderie had been forged, here in the morgue, that he might prevail upon Mr. Deck to show him divers reports, records, even photographic evidence (if such existed), pertaining to the death. But all this was swept away on a rising tide of nausea that terrified as it sickened: and Xavier recalled with especial horror the breakfast of boiled eggs, sausage, kidneys, and buttermilk pancakes liberally soaked in maple syrup that he had devoured with so innocent an appetite not four hours previous.

"Unlike Alexander the Great," Hans Deck said cheerily, "I require no slave beside me, to whisper in my ear that I am *mortal:* so long as I stay close to my sanctuary here, hidden away behind the Courthouse so very cozily—!"

It then happened that Mr. Deck lifted one of the corpse's limp, hairy, badly bruised arms, to let it fall back heavily upon the table; and, it seemed, poor "Buck" responded with a flicker of startled displeasure about the eyes; with the consequence that Xavier felt his vision spin, and his very soul go cold, and his knees lose all their strength: and saw the floor rear up to strike him with an amazing suddenness—!

In short, the hapless youth *fainted*,—as his elder companion gazed upon him with a bemused and pitying eye.

"'Tis only Death," he murmured, "—Death, and not Life: and how might mere *Death* injure you, my boy?"

At Glen Mawr Manor:
The Dungeon

I

A fortnight after his visit to the Winterthurn county morgue, Xavier made a decision to brave Glen Mawr Manor itself,—no matter who forbade it, or warned against it; or what fears he himself harbored. For he had suffered so potent a dream the previous night, he knew himself *fated*. "And if I am in danger," he thought with somber childlike resolve, "God will protect me, for my purpose, surely, is good."

It may have been a source of further encouragement to him to learn, by overhearing a fragment of a conversation between his mother and a lady friend, that Miss Georgina Kilgarvan was said to be confined to her bed at the Manor: and that so goodly a percentage of the Manor's domestic staff,—both whites and Negroes—had departed, since early May, that most of the rooms were shut off; and Henry Peregrine, the family's attorney for several decades, was strongly advising the Kilgarvans to decamp, and live elsewhere in Winterthurn for the time being. (Not only was the great old house falling into disrepair, but, as certain servants and tradesmen whispered, it seemed to be haunted by the faint, pitiable, yet unfailingly horrific wails of a baby, which emanated from the walls and ceilings at any hour of the day.)

As to any further official developments of the case: there were none. Nor did Mr. Shearwater, or his deputies, or any of the city police, take it kindly when they were questioned of their "progress" in the matter: for while they could not consider the case closed, they scarcely wished to consider it open, for divers reasons. (It was rumored that a lowlife secret society, whether the Knights of the White Camelia, or the Brethren of Jericho, or an unknown third, had taken it upon themselves to make an unofficial investigation of the case, to see whether the foul deed might have been committed by one of the Kilgarvans'

Negro servants: their prime suspect being the elderly Pride, who had long displeased whites in the area with his truculence, and his failure to ingratiate himself with them. No persons of good society would have anything to do with such riffraff "vigilante" groups, which had, it seems, sprung into being spontaneously, in the troubled year 1865, though doubtless drawing upon old Copperhead sentiment, which had been strong in the Valley: Mr. Kilgarvan in particular denounced them as "un-American," "un-Christian," and "un-human," and worried that Mr. Goshawk's *Gazette* did not take a firmer stand against them. So it was, Xavier knew very little about them; and the rumors, in any case, may well have been groundless.]

A firsthand particle of information pertaining to Mr. Simon Esdras Kilgarvan was gleaned, as it were, accidentally, while Xavier was in the cobbler's shop on Charity Street, on an errand for his mother, and happened to overhear a conversation between Mrs. Harrier Von Goeler and old Miss Verity Peregrine. The philosopher had been overindulging in alcoholic spirits of late, with a childlike innocence, and unfortunate results, in numerous places about town,—not only the staid Corinthian Club, where he might be watched over, but in less decorous establishments along Water Street, and even in South Winterthurn, where only the name *Kilgarvan* might be known. It was said that he had startled Reverend De Forrest by speaking of Erasmus as if, in some way, he were yet alive, but behaving "reprehensibly"; and by musing at awkward length upon the need,—now fallen to him—to propagate a male heir, to carry on Glen Mawr's tradition. "For Erasmus, despite his tiresome pride in his manhood, and the disagreeable *heatedness* of his blood, did fail most shamefully along these lines," Simon Esdras averred, with a melancholy shake of his head, yet, it was reported, a queer sort of smile.

Xavier knew himself summoned to the Manor, and fated for,—he dared not guess: when, very late of a Sabbath eve, past two o'clock by the solemn tolling of divers church bells, he woke startled from a dreamless slumber to see, gliding across the floorboards of his room, in a long white nightgown of some filmy material, barefoot, with her wavy hair atumble down her back, *none other than the diminutive figure of his cousin Perdita.* As in life, whether "spied upon" in church by Xavier, or glimpsed somewhat more by accident, leaving the Parthian Academy in the company of her sister, the young girl did not deign to notice him, or to acknowledge his existence by more than a *frisson* of her head and shoulders, so too in this most intimate of contexts she did not glance in his direction: nor did she seem to take cognizance of the fact that Colin slept beside him, faintly snoring, in his customary heavy slumber.

Xavier was so astonished, he rose on one elbow to stare, and quite risked losing her, for all his clumsy boldness: but, it seemed, the lovely girl was possessed of too much pride, and too deeply imbued a sense of propriety, to be thus routed. Making no sound, gliding on her small, white, exquisite feet, Perdita passed through an effulgence of moonlight, the silken ribands at her breast lightly fluttering, and her slender arm upraised: for she was holding a sprig of lilac to her lips, the heady fragrance of which was, in that very instant, released most powerfully into the air. "How is it possible! How,—and why!" Xavier inwardly whispered, the while, all agape, he rudely stared; and felt his besotted heart knocking against his ribs.

Since that harrowing day in the cemetery, now many weeks past, when Xavier had heard that melodic, teasing, never-explained sound sift out of the very air,—and had seen, for the first time, truly, his youngest cousin (who, until that extraordinary moment, had impressed him as being but a sallow-faced peevish child, of no interest to a youth his age)—why, he had behaved most strangely, in wandering out of his way in the city that he might, by chance, catch a glimpse of her: lounging about the base of the bronze memorial to Nathan Hale in Parthian Square, for instance; or strolling with hearty nonchalance along that stretch of Berwick Avenue where the ladies' millinery and glove shops were located,—for someone had mentioned seeing Thérèse and Perdita, in the company of the dowager Mrs. Bunting (young Harwood Bunting's mother), entering one of these little stores. None of these actions need have been deemed "spying"; but Xavier uneasily supposed that that was his intention, for his heart leapt a dozen or more times when, mistakenly, he believed he had caught sight of Perdita: or,—such was the youth's infatuation—when he believed he had caught sight of Thérèse! Once, while moodily walking along the lower end of Water Street, in a rough sort of neighborhood, Xavier had found himself staring at a freight train that rattled past: the locomotive with its fanning white smoke, that, in its chugging and wheezing power, suggested to him some urgency (and, alas, some futility) residing in his own breast; the noisy clattering cars, thirty or more, that appeared to be empty; the caboose with its pair of unlit red lamps, and a hollow-cheeked porter lounging at the rail, gazing blankly toward Xavier. And how abrupt it was, the sudden cessation of noise, when the last of the cars had passed!—like a restoration of sweet calm to his own troubled soul. He had been brooding overmuch, of late, of Perdita; and Mrs. Whimbrel (now confined, it was said, to a hospital, that she might not do harm to herself or her remaining children); and of certain problems within his own household; and of his secret failure as a "detective,"— the which glamorous enterprise was scarcely what he had expected, being, it began to seem, virtually impossible to undertake.

Now Perdita, in pale diaphanous attire, her wavy tresses loosed upon her shoulders, and her delicate heart-shaped face turned just slightly aside, had, it seemed, come to *him:* tiptoeing noiselessly past his moonlit window, a spray of lilac raised to her face, that she might inhale its rich sensuous aroma, with dark nostrils just perceptibly widened, and thick-lashed eyes nearly closed. Her awareness of him,— for it was a certainty, his beating heart informed him, that she *was* aware—made the long wondrous moment all the more enchanting: for she would soon glance at him over her shoulder,—would she not?—ah, would she *not?* Xavier stared, and stared; his parched lips moved to utter her name; but no sound issued forth; nor could he, as he realized of a sudden, move any of his limbs or his head, *being paralyzed.*

"She has died, up at the Manor," Xavier thought, going cold with fright, "and this form is but her spirit, her departing ghost! And I am too late to save her!"

Taking no notice of him, or of the sleeping Colin beside him, the graceful figure advanced to the whitewashed brick fireplace in the inner wall, and, as Xavier stared, in a veritable paroxysm of amazement, her slender fingers groped for, and deftly found, the loose brick that had long been Xavier's secret; and eased it soundlessly out; and took, or seemed to take (for the fireplace was partly in shadow, and Xavier could not be certain what he saw), a ruby ring he had hidden there long ago—!

Silent, and resolutely unhurried,—though, surely, she must know how passionately he watched—Perdita slipped the ring on her finger: and seemed about to glance back over her shoulder at Xavier when, of a sudden, a clattering on the cobblestones outside caused her to vanish: for it was the milkman's horse and wagon, and no longer two o'clock, but four-thirty!—and Xavier woke dazed and agitated with the name Perdita on his lips.

He knew it was naught but a dream, and he would not succumb to the temptation of rising from his bed, to check his hiding place in the wall: for long ago he had found a ruby ring in the street, covered in filth, and had thought he might present it to his mother,—and hid it away,—and afterward wondered guiltily if he had done wrong, in not reporting it—and, alas, it *was* too late,—and the ring *was* beautiful,— and so he had most irresponsibly procrastinated, and dared not reveal his find. Now, it seemed, the dream-spirit of Perdita had come to make her claim: though assuredly Xavier had but imagined her presence—?

Yet, in the morning, when, unobserved, he went to the fireplace to grope behind the brick,—he discovered to his astonishment that the ring was missing after all.

It *was* missing, and in its place had been left a dried and shrunken sprig of lilac,—its tiny blossoms scarcely more than dust, and its sweet fragrance long since vanished.

II

After so uneasy and protracted an anticipation, Xavier found his approach to Glen Mawr,—by way of the handsome half-mile avenue of pink-toned gravel only slightly overgrown with weeds, and edged in sumptuous bridal wreath, with a double row of gracious old plane trees on either side—surprisingly unimpeded: and it was only as he ascended the great stone steps of the mansion, which were semicircular, and of the size and weight of ancient millstones, that he grew somewhat nervous, imagining himself observed. And yet, what harm might come to him? And on so splendid a June morning? It had been the youth's strategy to approach Glen Mawr in no craven, stealthy way,—by the rear, for instance, ascending from the river—as one or another of his detective heroes, of doubtful integrity, might have attempted: he was a Kilgarvan, after all, and thought it wisest to make his approach as openly, and as innocently, as if he *had* been summoned, and could not possibly be denied entrance. (For the occasion he had dressed in a somber cotton-and-woolen suit, with a stiff-starched white shirt, like any young gentleman making a formal visit to so noble a house, having explained to his mother that he was embarked upon an adventure of sorts,—but hinting to her, not altogether honestly, that it had to do with summer employment. "And will you be applying to Osmyn Goshawk, as your father has suggested?" Mrs. Kilgarvan anxiously asked. How Xavier replied to her, with a courteous murmur that succeeded in conveying both a negative and a positive response, and an embarrassed disdain for the very question,—I do not know: but it should not be held against him that, at the onset of his "career," he must needs now and then tell fibs to his mother.)

Yet, forthright though he was, and unhesitatingly as he had rung, and then rapped, for entrance, no one came to the door: and for some painful minutes, *knowing* himself observed, he paced about, hands in his pockets and head bowed, as if brooding whether to depart. His face colored slightly; he grew uncomfortably warm; and thought it an impractical decision, after all, to have dressed so formally, as if for church,—for if the Kilgarvans denied him entrance, why, then, it might well be, Xavier should have to force his way in by surreptitious means. Was not Glen Mawr partly his father's and, through his father, his own?—by all *moral*, if not precisely *legal*, necessity?

Thus he paced about beneath the great-columned portico, and cast his eye upon the tall stone urns, with their Egyptian cast, on either side of the door; and upon the numerous tall, narrow, English-style windows of the façade, which cloudily reflected light, and gave the illusion of a ghostly human presence beyond. (Imposing though Glen Mawr assuredly was, with its steep slate roofs, and massive stone-and-stucco chimneys, and ornamental trim in Italianate style, the fact that nearly half of the windows had been shuttered, both upstairs and down, very much detracted from its aesthetic harmony: and gave, so Xavier thought, an appearance of shabbiness and neglect.)

In the company of other boys, Xavier had frequently trespassed upon the forbidden territory of Glen Mawr, approaching it from the rear, which is to say from the river: for Juniper Park at its easternmost extreme was naught but a great woods, shading into the Glen Mawr forest, and one might unknowingly leave the one and penetrate the other, if warnings against trespassing were infrequent; or had been torn down. But, from the river, one soon came to a high stone wall, cruelly spiked at its top, and littered with glass: which, while whetting schoolboy appetites for adventure, did a great deal to thwart them. Xavier had never seen the terraced "Japanese" garden his grandfather had insisted upon building, at inordinate expense, into the hill beyond the wall; nor had he seen the various subordinate buildings attached to the house,—the washhouse, the bakehouse, the meathouse, the gardeners' sheds, the old slaves' quarters (which, his father bitterly declared, was more sturdy a structure, being built of brick and stucco, than the ramshackle wood-frame house,—formerly an inn—where the Kilgarvans of Wycombe Street were forced to live): but of course he had been told of them: and had long imagined a haughty sort of grandeur where, now, in the morning's hazy warmth, with the sweet scent of bridal wreath and rambling rose undercut by a deeper, harsher, yet not unpleasant odor of lichen, toadstools, and rotting leaves, he was forced to revise his estimation: for the Manor, which had been intended to be so conspicuous a showplace in the Winterthurn Valley, a testament to Phillips Goode's lavish good taste, as well as to his fortune, had indeed fallen into decline,—and why his eldest son had allowed this, with *his* fortune, was legitimately to be wondered at.

("Perhaps, Father, he feels guilt for his crime against you," Xavier once suggested, when the subject had come up, as it frequently did, "and is ashamed to hire workmen to do repairs, or even to hire new servants as the old die off, for that reason." But, though the well-phrased statement had doubtless pleased Mr. Kilgarvan, he could not bring himself to concur, saying, with a wry shake of his head, that so reptilian a criminal as Erasmus Kilgarvan would never identify himself as a criminal, let alone suffer so human an emotion as simple shame: "For all that he does, my boy, is perpetrated, in his eyes, as an expression of rectitude,—and not personal wish." Xavier had thought for a moment; then said, with flashing eyes, and a spirit of angry bitterness not unlike his father's own: "Why, then, he *is* invulnerable!—and can even God discover a way to punish a sinner *who does not sin?*")

As these troubled thoughts sifted through his mind, and caused a pulse to beat behind his eyes with such sullen forcefulness, he frowned in pain, Xavier heard a faint tapping, and his murmured name: and saw, at a casement window nearby, leaning out, the figure of a slender young girl in black,—*lovely Perdita herself.*

With hurried, cautious gestures, as if she feared being detected, Perdita motioned to him to come beneath the window, that she might help him climb inside: and was, for that purpose, lowering a mourning shawl, in black brocade richly fringed, for him to grasp. "The front entrance to our house is always kept bolted," the girl told Xavier beneath her breath, in a low, melodic, rippling voice that seemed, in its murmurous beauty, to vibrate along his very nerves.

So it came about that Xavier recklessly ran to the window, and, with protestations of extreme gratitude, climbed into the house long forbidden to him, as readily as any of his adventurer heroes might have done; and, one might surmise, with considerably more childlike abandon. What felicity, her presence at the window!—and what rare courage, in a girl of her age, to invite an intruder into her very home: nay, to lend him her own small white hand, in so doing!

Scarcely able to catch his breath, Xavier managed to utter only her name,—"Perdita"—in a choked, and somewhat incredulous, voice.

"Yes," she whispered, "but quick, quick—come inside: and take care that the window is bolted behind you."

Perdita looked very much as she had looked at her father's melancholy gravesite, in March, and less as she had looked in Xavier's bed-chamber the previous night: though beauteous enough, with a perfect petal-smooth skin and fine, fierce, dark-lashed eyes, she was inordinately pale, even to appearing sickly; and was possessed of a precocious air of bereavement which, about the eyes in particular, expressed itself in subtle, fleeting modulations of irony. Alas, only twelve years of age, and so irreversibly mature! With a gesture as much of impatience as solicitude, she urged Xavier forward, that she might draw the brocaded shawl safely in, and fasten the casement windows.

For a long awkward minute, then, the cousins stared at each other, with unabashed exultation; but dared not touch. Xavier could not yet altogether believe his good fortune, but stood panting, and blinking, and essaying feebly to smile, as if fearful that some sudden rude motion of his, or unguarded gesture, might cause Perdita to ''vanish'' on the spot: and only by degrees, as the vertiginous hammering of his heart slowed, did he see that this was no faery child, but a very real young girl: *his* Perdita.

''You are very brave to allow me in,'' he said in a rapid, lowered voice, glancing over his shoulder, ''for I know how your sister,—I mean your eldest sister—despises all of my family. And I *know* I cannot be welcome here.''

So softly and shyly did Perdita speak, Xavier had to bend to her, to hear: ''Well,—*you* are very brave to come here,'' she said.

The large, deep-set, liquid-bright eyes were as Xavier hungrily remembered them, or nearly; the chestnut-brown hair was less lustrous, it seemed, but wonderfully thick and wavy, despite the spartan style into which it had been twisted; the small mouth,—now smiling, or straining to smile—was as lovely as any besotted youth might wish. Had Xavier not, in his fevered dreams, often envisioned those lips,— had he not, in truth, pressed his own desperately against them? So strange as they were, were they not also familiar?—as known to him as his own mirrored countenance?

Perdita, though several inches shorter than Xavier, was not so diminutive as he recalled from the day of the funeral; nor would the casual eye have dismissed her as a mere child. A palely blooming *womanliness* lay within the timidity of *girlhood*, evidenced by a graceful and innocent coquetry of her wrist, shoulder, and chin; and the graceful white curve of her throat. (Xavier saw that her slender fingers were *ringless*.) As for her ill-laundered mousseline dress, in a gray so harshly dark it might have been black,—Xavier noted only that its tight stand-up collar and narrow-ribbed bodice were executed in fine bobbin lace, and that its layered skirt was too long, and tattered about the hem. Yet even this attire, with its air of the cast-off and scorned, was, in his eyes, as becoming as a silken gown of the gayest hue—!

Surely this *was*, yet *could not be*, the enchanting specter-girl who had trespassed Xavier's bed-chamber the night before, and stolen away his prized ring, to leave a sprig of desiccated blossoms (which he carried now in his vest pocket, close to his heart) in its place—?

Thus, like any gently bold young lover, Xavier dared to grasp Perdita's hand in his: finding it chill, and fragile-boned as the smallest song sparrow, and slightly resistant, with a natural maidenly restraint. Speaking softly, with as much trembling formality as he could summon forth in the presence of his belovèd (for so dramatic, extreme, and *adult* an expression is not inappropriate in this remarkable context), Xavier stated his mission at Glen Mawr: his simple and straightforward request to examine the room in which the tragedy had lately occurred, that he might see, with his amateur's eye, if any *clues* remained; and his proffering of any assistance lying within his power, to both Perdita and Thérèse, if they required it.

Perdita abruptly withdrew her hand from his, and turned shyly away; seemed about to speak; then, after a blushing hesitation, said that she could not quite comprehend his meaning, in offering her and Thérèse "assistance": but hoped, certainly, that he did not mean to insult. ("For Glen Mawr is our home," she said. "We were born here: we know no other place.") So far as an exploration of the Honeymoon Room, or even much of the house was concerned, she saw no pressing reason for the examination, but no reason to impede it: as Xavier was her cousin, and must mean well. She doubted, however, that he would discover much of value, as the sheriff and his men, and a noisome troupe of police, detectives, and "experts" of divers kinds, from as far away as Vanderpoel, had poked about for days and found nothing. "Save evidence of rats?" Xavier asked.

But Perdita had already turned away, to lead him on his search, a forefinger to her pretty lips, and her manner both stealthy and playful, as if this were, to her, but a child's game: and she and her cousin both children.

They passed through the Judge's library, a long, narrow room paneled in black walnut, with a faded carpet underfoot, and, above the mantel, a somewhat dark portrait, in oils, of their famed ancestor General Pettit Kilgarvan, whose likeness Xavier had frequently studied, with boyish curiosity, shading into anxiety, whether that great man's blood might yet flow, in some wise, in his own veins. Upon the mantel was a cast-iron bull, in belligerent stance; and, lying atop a table, as if it had just been set down, Erasmus's gnarled *Don't-tread-on-me* walking stick. Xavier paused, to take note of the great mahogany desk, which must have measured six feet along its width; and the several leather chairs; and, upon the bookshelves, rising to the shadowy ceiling, leather-bound tomes stamped in gilt, of the multivolum'd works of such giants of the law as Nathan Dane, and James Kent, and Ephraim Kirby, and Joseph Story, and Theophilus Parsons, and the great Lemuel Shaw himself,—these names being dimly known to him from his father's remarks, and Mr. Kilgarvan's embittered pursuit of

Law. Xavier was about to take up one of the books, but Perdita dissuaded him, saying that they must hurry; and must not touch anything. "For Georgina, when she is well again, will discover it at once. Every object in this room, Cousin, has its particular placing, and cannot be disturbed even by the maids,—else Georgina flies into a rage."

Xavier followed his companion into the foyer, which opened for two stories, and pleased the eye rather more than did the Judge's library, as it was less shrouded in shadow. The painted and gilded ceiling was supported by tall, somewhat thick Grecian columns, with much ornamentation at their base; the floor was of a pallid milky-red marble, badly discolored, and beginning generally to crack; opening off the foyer were several stone archways of a medieval character, executed in red sandstone. How potently Xavier's heart flooded with a sensation of *resentment*,—for such palatial pretensions, and such ill-used wealth, denied to him and his family!

"Yet," the heated youth inwardly murmured, "I would scorn to live here, if the Manor *were* open to me: for some insults are past forgiving."

"Cousin, come! Why are you lingering?" Perdita whispered; and, with girlish solicitude, pulled at his wrist.

They ascended a broad, curving, majestic staircase (as splendid, Xavier was forced to admit, as any he had ever seen in Winterthurn,—in the homes of the De Forrests and the Peregrines, for instance); and to the carpeted landing, where, overhead, an enormous crimson-and-gold fanlight was ablaze with sun. Here Xavier's sharp eye lit upon what he perceived to be a *clue* of some sort,—for was it not peculiar, indeed, that the fine-carved mahogany banister should be so crudely scarred, as if by the strokes of an ax, for a space of several yards? He stopped Perdita, and inquired of her, in a whisper, whether Judge Kilgarvan was responsible for these angry markings: but Perdita, scarcely glancing at the banister, told him that it was but an "historical conversation piece," going back for generations,—to when the British General Gadwell and his officers had occupied Glen Mawr, in '77; and the General had shouted for his men to hurry downstairs; and, losing his temper, had ridden his horse to the landing, raging and hacking at the banister with his sword, when they did not quickly enough obey.

Chastened by this explanation, Xavier allowed himself to be led the rest of the way upstairs, in silence; and along a dim-lit corridor, hung with numerous portraits in oils of faces too blurred to be recognized, though he did not doubt they were kin of his; and to the very doorway of the Honeymoon Room,—the oaken door itself being partly smashed, and hanging as if drunken upon its hinges. "Here,—it is very much as it was,—excepting of course for what the intruders have done," Perdita said. Xavier followed slowly in her wake, blinking, and looking from side to side, with the air of a frightened child: for was this the *scene of the crime,* to be entered so readily?—with so little ceremony? "I wonder you are not terrified to go inside," Xavier said awkwardly, "or even that you have not mended the door with some sturdy wood, and nailed it shut." Perdita glanced at him, in genuine surprise; and frowned; and asked, with a wan, droll smile: "But *why* should we be terrified of a mere room? Unlike Cousin Abigail Whimbrel, we live here by rights: and have lived here all our lives."

Xavier entered the room guardedly nonetheless, his eyes rapidly darting from side to side: yet, apart from the opulence of the furnishings and the excessive ornamentation of the walls and ceiling, which he adjudged as comically vulgar, though doubtless costly, he could see nothing immediately remiss, or "suspicious": save perhaps the wider of the two fireplaces, and its spacious chimney, which looked as if it might accommodate an adult figure (might an assailant have climbed down into the room from the roof?); and the several *trompe l'oeil* paintings, which fascinated, yet finally repelled, with their deliberate air of the *artificially lifelike.* As for the place of death,—the carved antique bed with its silken canopy, and its look of inappropriate splendor—Xavier had only to approach it, and to draw his hand along the brocaded cover, to sense that all that had been remarkable about it had fled. Yet here it stood, before him: and here he was, at the *scene of the crime* at last. "So it has happened that my good luck has prevailed," Xavier said, as much to himself as to Perdita,—"for I now stand in the very place in which the Whimbrel infant died, and the unhappy Abigail Whimbrel went mad."

"Yes, it is a pity: she should not have pressed herself, and her hapless babe, upon us," Perdita softly said.

Xavier but half attended to her words, moving about the room, staring, and stooping, and sniffing, and blinking; noting uneasily how his mirrored reflection aped him, from a dozen glassy surfaces, commingled with overelaborate etchings of ivy, roses, grapevines, etc., and designs in bronze and white, painted directly on the mirrors: his image, and that of the pale-browed Perdita who watched him, brought together in a sort of minuet, in utter silence. That an unspeakable incident of an unknown species had transpired in this bed-chamber, not many weeks previous; that it might very well have been an actual, though senseless, murder; that its cause, or its agent, *might* be sought out one day soon, and exposed, and explained, and "solved"; that what lay in the beclouded realm of the *mysterious* could be transposed, by the rigorous logic of detection, into the *comprehensible,*—was this not remarkable? For, after all, Xavier reasoned with mounting excitement, God Himself is a presence underlying, and giving unity to, all ostensibly discrete phenomena: what appears to the untutored eye as Chaos

may be read, by the proper intelligence, and by the proper faith, as Order. He had not yet worked it out, to his own satisfaction, nor did his
detective-heroes pause to brood over such matters,—being, of necessity, caught up in *action*; but he was certain, he knew not altogether
why, that his Christian faith, and the upbringing which his belovèd
parents had provided, would have much to do with his prowess as a detective. "Ah, if only one could remember *forward*," the youth inwardly murmured,—as the multifariousness of the room before him, and,
indeed, the room diffracted into numberless rooms by mirrors, so
threatened to overwhelm him that the pain between his eyebrows, in
the hard-boned region of the glabella, grew for a moment more severe,—"and all that is now baffling, vexing, and mysterious, could be
read as History!" Yet, though he paused to draw breath, the euphoria
of his heartbeat continued.

     With reverent fingers he examined the great canopied bed,—the
heavy goose-feather pillows, encased in fine, spotless white linen; the
various quilts, comforters, coverlets, linens, etc.; the horsehair mattress, which gave evidence of having been recently and very vigorously
cleaned, yet yielded, still, numerous faint stains and discolorations;
and then the silken tapestries draped about the bed; and the minutely
carved posts. True, there was nothing helpful here: and Perdita's bemused attention made him self-conscious: but he was confident that,
in any case, he *was* following a correct procedure. How more directly
might George B. Jashber have approached the situation; or Sherlock
Holmes; or, indeed, the shrewdly bumptious Pudd'nhead Wilson, who
had, as it were, pioneered in the science of *fingerprinting*,—at this
time virtually unknown in the States, and sneered at in both Paris and
London? And there was the imperturbable C. Auguste Dupin, whose
words now echoed, for some reason, in Xavier's brain, as if the great
man were personally directing him: *"Perhaps it is the very simplicity
of the thing that puts you at fault."*

     But Xavier, now standing with his hands on his hips, and sur-
veying the room more generally, could not see how so lavishly glittering a surface, replete with so many differing textures, colors, and
dimensions,—the very paradigm, it nightmarishly seemed, of the great
world itself—might be reduced to any sort of *simplicity*. Or did he
merely lack eyes to see that which stared him in the face—?

     Perdita said, in a lowered voice, that the agents of the baby's
death were evidently rats,—a giant species—a species hitherto unknown at the Manor—that made their way by some undetermined
method into the room, on that tragic night, and had not been glimpsed
again since: the which should have rendered poor Jupiter blameless, in
her Uncle Simon's judgment, yet did not: and did not Xavier think
Uncle most cruel to persist in blaming Jupiter? As Xavier did not know

how best to reply to this artless query, he murmured an assent, taking care not to allow his gaze to fix upon his cousin with an inordinate boldness: for the danger was, it seemed, his impassioned blood might too strongly beat, and cause Perdita to become frightened: to "vanish," as it were, from out his rapt vision—! In a gentle voice he inquired of her whether she did not think it somewhat peculiar that giant rats of an "unknown species" might attack a sleeping baby, and so disappear,—into the walls, or the ceiling, or the very air—as to leave no trace behind: whether some other agent, not, perhaps, an animal at all, might be sought? Perdita bit at her plump lower lip, and appeared to be thinking deeply; then averred that no other agent might be sought, as there *was* no other agent: for, after all, the bed-chamber had been locked and bolted before Mrs. Whimbrel retired. Xavier asked if no one had heard the baby's cries during the night, or any sound from the mother: and again Perdita looked puzzled, and stared half-smiling at the carpet; and said, with a childish want of guile: "Ah, but babies often cry,—do they not?—and wail, and fuss, and soil themselves, and cause a great commotion. It is thought by some to be their attraction, I suppose, that they are so *uncalculating in their effects*; by others, a disadvantage that, when aroused, they always sound as if they are being killed. So, though I cannot recall having heard the sound of a baby's crying, on that night, I do not believe I would have supposed it remarkable,—there being, after all, an actual baby under our roof at that time."

Xavier was so fascinated by his young cousin's low, soft, somewhat husky voice; and her lovely eyes; and the sweet simplicity of her manner,—that he found her words rather more logical than otherwise; and decided he must not ask whether the house yet echoed the baby's cries, and was, in vulgar terms, "haunted," for so foolish a question, hinting of rank superstition, would surely strike the wrong note. Nor did he wish to ask whether Perdita,—or, indeed, anyone at the Manor—knew how avidly it seemed to be wished, in town, that the old house *be* haunted.

Next, he busied himself in examining the fireplaces, and the chimneys,—with no conspicuous results; and the several tall windows, and their faded draperies; and the closets with their showy mirrored doors; and various items of costly furniture,—couches upholstered in silks and satins, chairs of rococo design, bureaus of mahogany deeply carved in plumes, fruits, scrolls, et al., and a massive black walnut armoire in Oriental design, cunningly mirrored, with no less than two dozen drawers, each empty save for tissue paper, and the dried bodies of dead insects. Alas, and he felt the compulsion to examine each drawer thoroughly!—the while the pulse in his forehead dully throbbed, and his starched collar pricked against his throat. Doubtless like Sheriff Shearwater and the rest, he diligently searched for a *secret passageway*, but found nothing save dustballs, and mouse droppings, and cobwebs, and the husklike corpses of yet more insects. His head throbbed the more when, by accident, he saw in a mirror-maze of countless angles and diffractions the lovely face of his cousin in an expression,—ah, how sweet! how subtly ironic! and, it seemed, how *fond!*—of patient amusement at his industry.

He then turned his attention to the heavy gilt-framed mirrors; and the *trompe l'oeil* paintings, which, all along, had been a source of distraction to him: a pulsatile movement, shading into actual writhing, in the corner of his eye: colors that were too strident, human or cherubic figures that were too insistent,—about, it seemed, to rouse themselves from the wall and lean into the room,—amidst a tangle of grasses, vines, grapes, and rose bushes in which roses luridly bloomed, like damp, pouting, crimson-pink mouths. As a very young boy Xavier had been fascinated by such blatant virtuoso demonstrations of the artist's skill in "tricking the eye": he had often stared at a small oil in his Grandmother De Forrest's drawing room, of a pet monkey with a jeweled collar caught in the act, by his mistress, of making off with a massive bunch of purple grapes,—the "trick" of the painting being its illusion of possessing three dimensions, as the guiltily affrighted monkey leapt (or so it eerily seemed!) toward the viewer. For some years, Xavier had imagined such japery to be synonymous with "art," and had essayed to imitate it, with disappointing results; then, with the passage of time, he had lost interest, and now gazed upon such things with ill-concealed scorn, no matter how others continued to admire them. This mural of Fairfax Eakins, for instance, ranging across much of a wall, and a goodly portion of the ceiling, was intended, it would seem, to express a *holy sentiment*, as the Virgin Mary and the Christ Child were nominally at its center: yet, as the most superficial glance suggested, the purpose of the painting was simply to amuse and to titillate, with angels' heads, shoulders, torsos, elbows, limbs, wings of divers sizes and shapes, leaning, or falling, or plunging out of the wall, upon the viewer's head. Indeed, the more Xavier stared, the more distaste, shading into actual revulsion, he felt: for were the angels not ungainly, in their overly "realistic" flesh?—and their dazed, or vacuous, or smug, or leering, or contemptuous, expressions not highly offensive? How queer, their wings!—hooked like a bat's in caricature; or tall and befeathered; or scaled; or possessed of a peacock's brilliance.

As he stared, Xavier was gripped by a childish sense that the angelic host was, in turn, observing him, with expressions of withheld mirth: a comely androgynous figure seemed about to wink at him, holding a flute to its lips; a puffy-faced adolescent angel, of about Xavier's age, seemed to have arched his eyebrow a bit higher, tilting in

Xavier's direction; a more sinister creature, with talons instead of feet, and the drooping black-feathered wings of a bird of prey, was regarding him with scarce-concealed hunger,—and derision. How queerly unsettling, this "religious" subject!—and with what virtuoso flippancy it was executed!—as if, in a sense, the painter had secretly regarded his work as profound, even while he mocked the viewer, and his wealthy patron, with every stroke of his brush.

Xavier observed to his cousin, who stood a discreet distance away, her hands clasped before her, that he had not, within memory, encountered so *bizarre* a painting: for one could not interpret it as reverent, nor could one dismiss it as willfully sacrilegious; one could not mock it, as it *was* a mockery; and one could certainly not ignore it.

Perdita murmured that she could not follow her cousin's abstruse logic, and had so little training in aesthetics, she wished to make no judgment on the matter: save to observe that, as she quietly phrased it, "angels *may* turn demon, with the passage of time,—if starved of the love that is their sustenance."

At this moment, a drop of water, or some more viscous liquid substance, which had been forming by degrees in the narrowed eye of an angel overhead, grew suddenly heavy enough to fall: and Xavier instinctively put out his hand to catch it: a *teardrop*, one might almost fancy, or, judging by its faint crimson stain, a *blooddrop*,—which the bemazed youth, scarcely thinking what he did, brought to his lips to taste.

"It's blood," he murmured,—and his heart lurched.

But in the next instant he had sufficiently recovered himself to observe, in a more composed tone, that the ceiling must be leaking; that rainwater must have accumulated in the attic overhead, to make its way through intermittently, under pressure,—for this was one of the countless vexations the Kilgarvans of Wycombe Street had with *their* house; roofs being evidently very costly to repair. Perdita startled him by taking his hand to examine it: but by now the drop had vanished, and only a faint crimson discoloration remained in the palm— the consequence, no doubt, of rainwater dyed by paint.

"Blood, you say,—blood?" Perdita said, her eyes darkening, and her voice urgent. "Yet how might it be *blood*, dripping merely from the ceiling?"

"No, it was not blood," Xavier said. "I am certain, Cousin, it was not blood,—only a raindrop."

"And yet,—you tasted it: I saw you bring it to your lips."

"Yet it was not blood, for how could it be blood, as you say?" Xavier asked, disguising the uneasiness he felt. "As to why I tasted it,—I do not know: an infantile sort of impulse, perhaps, for which I cannot account."

As no further drops fell from the ceiling,—the pale angel's eye being, evidently, now dry—Xavier moved away, to make a final cursory examination of the room: and to tax himself with Monsieur Dupin's admonition as to the *simplicity* of the situation. "Yet," he thought, "is it not invariably, and smugly, the case that any human situation can be defined as *simple* by those who dwell, as it were, above it; and refined out of temporal existence by one or another authorial stratagem? For if one dwells here below, in the very midst of the puzzle, the navigation of the next hour,—nay, the next *minute*—is a challenge."

Perdita docilely agreed to lead him upstairs, into the attic, that he might examine the space directly above the room; though, as he told himself sternly, he must not expect to find anything so remarkable as a pool of blood. While the young people were making their cautious way along the corridor, to a back stairs, Xavier was startled to hear a voice or voices nearby: but was assured by Perdita that they were in no danger of being detected,—it was doubtless Uncle Simon reading aloud a passage from his *Treatise*, in the solitude of his spartan room, that he might, as he said, test the resiliency of his prose to see whether it possessed that *steely thinness* which all metaphysical pondering required, to save it from muddle. ("It is said in town," Xavier whispered, "that Uncle has been behaving strangely of late: being, first of all, far more often *seen*; and several times in the company of an unknown woman, many years his junior." Blushing prettily, Perdita seemed at first loath to reply; then leaned to Xavier, and murmured in his ear with childish ire: "It is not so. It cannot be. They lie: it is as Georgina says, they always lie. Uncle works on his *Treatise* upward of twelve hours daily; Father's death has very much impressed upon him the nature of,—as he says in *his* words—the 'intractability of the phenomenal world,' and the fact of his own impending mortality. So it is, he works near-constantly,—and rarely leaves home.")

As Xavier might have foreseen, the cavernous low-ceilinged attic of Glen Mawr, airless, stifling hot, disagreeably abuzz with flies, proved no less "intractable" than the Honeymoon Room: being a veritable graveyard of stored and cast-off things, draped with sheets, and awash in such a profusion of odors (of dust, mildew, rot, moth-crystals; the droppings and decayed corpses of mice, birds, bats, etc.; the desiccated shellac coating the taped surfaces of dressmakers' dummies; etc.), the luckless youth felt sickened within the first minute of his entry. But Perdita bravely led him forward, through a maze of steamer trunks, upright cartons, paintings, furniture, ladies' hat-boxes mounting to the ceiling, mirrors in whose grime-coated glasses twin images, scarcely of "boy" and "girl," eerily floated, and all the melancholy useless paraphernalia of a household: bringing him, by instinct it seemed, to the approximate area he desired, directly above the Honeymoon Room. But, ah!—was he not disappointed to see that, indeed, no *pool of blood* lay underfoot, but only a coating of dust,—or, rather, numberless coatings of dust, through which the footprints of various years might be dimly discerned, amidst the tinier pawprints of mice.

Gamely, Xavier made an effort to investigate, he knew not precisely what: and felt the more self-conscious, and a bit of a dandy and a fool, under the close scrutiny of his cousin. With a gingerly motion he drew a dust-heavy sheet from off an ottoman, in itself discolored by dust, to discover naught but a little gathering of dead moths, their wings turned to paper, and their bodies but dried husks. Elsewhere, in opening with fumbling fingers a lady's hat-box tightly bound with twine, he frightened up a mouse, whose panicked scuttling quite startled both himself and Perdita, and made the pulse behind his eyes throb the more sullenly.

So malodorous was the air, and so inhospitable the general terrain, he could not bring himself to stay for very many minutes; and busied himself poking, and prying, and sniffing, about a massive sideboard of Chippendale design, rather more because its numerous drawers were *locked* than because it aroused his suspicions. This ungainly piece of furniture, not unlike one belonging to his De Forrest grandparents, was perhaps eight feet in length, with excessive Oriental ornamentation in mock-bamboo trim, and bird "claws" for feet, and raised sections at either end, housing a series of drawers with bamboo knobs. The high-gloss French finish had long since faded; the lavish cornucopia carvings on either side of the splashboard were all but obscured in dust; so layered with grime was the oval mirror, Xavier would have been hard put to recognize his own image there, afloat in a cloudy sea. Two of the drawers opened easily, and were empty; the others were locked; as was the large central panel,—a fact Xavier's boyish self told him must be *suspicious*, but his more mature self supposed meant very little. Yet he poked and pried about, under his cousin's sweet gaze, as methodically as possible, for, even so prematurely in his "career," he knew that he must not surrender to the tide of *doubt, hopelessness,* and *near-sickened self-contempt*, it seemed to him altogether reasonable to feel at this juncture.

Alas, how opportunely it always happened, at precisely such "calm" moments in the adventures of Xavier's detective-heroes, that a *clue* of some sort thrust itself forward; or even a sudden eructation of danger. But, sadly, this was not to be Xavier's experience in the attic; and it was with an air of somewhat shamed disappointment that he gave up, and followed Perdita back to the stairs. All fleetingly it crossed his mind that, even here, in this unprepossessing region, he *was* being observed: and could not help himself from glancing uneasily about. But of course there was nothing to be seen; and, apart from the idle buzzing of the flies, nothing to be heard.

"And now, perhaps, dear Xavier, you might take your leave," Perdita said, with a worried glance to both sides, as the young people stealthily descended the stairs, "—for while Georgina is confined to her sickbed, and not likely to discover us, I cannot answer to poor Thérèse's wanderings,—or to old Pride, who might turn up anywhere, in 'guarding,' as he imagines it, our household; and I am certain the tyrant carries tales back to his mistress, about all of us."

Xavier felt the wisdom, and the reasonableness, of his companion's words; and surely his own instinct urged him to escape, with great relief, to the freshness of the June sunshine,—indeed, to all the vast, unfettered, healthsome world beyond Glen Mawr Manor! But some measure of detectively stubbornness resided in his breast; and, it may have been, a romantic disinclination to leave little Perdita: for when again might he hope to see her?—when again, to stand so close beside her, to gaze upon her enchanting face, to exchange such intimate confidences? More than once, during the course of the past hour, occupied as he was with *investigation*, the cunning youth had stolen a glance at his cousin; and felt the forbidden knowledge that he might, *if he wished to press hard enough*, dare to brush his lips against her cheek,—nay, against her very lips! Now it came over him again, with the force of delirium, that it was within his power, *if he so wished*, to take Perdita's small hand, and fondle it; to caress her shoulders, and her lovely neck; to bring his warm lips close,—ah, very close—to her ear, her throat, her mouth; to confess to her, in a low, tremulous, yet altogether sincere voice, that he believed he was in love with her: if *love* was not an offense, or an outrage to her tender ear.

But he dared not risk such boldness: and contented himself with drawing very close to her, and stooping to murmur in her ear, whether he might explore, however briefly, the *cellar:* and then, he promised, he would be off,—and never trouble her again on such a fool's errand.

Perdita's cheeks faintly colored, as if taking heat from Xavier's warm breath; and a childish frown appeared between her delicate brows. She reiterated her suggestion that he leave, and quickly,—for a considerable space of time had passed since his arrival. (To his uneasy surprise, Xavier saw by means of a grandfather's clock nearby that *more than two hours had elapsed!*—with the brevity and fluidity of less than one.) Still he persisted: touching as if by accident the girl's arm, and her slender shoulder: and promising that he would remain belowstairs only ten minutes, or less: and then he *would* be gone.

After a prolonged hesitation Perdita sighed, and essayed to smile, with a droll and innocently coquettish upward turn of her eyes, saying that she might as well acquiesce; that she was after all accustomed to such: and only hoped that Georgina would not find out and, when the strength in her arm returned, subject her to a sound whipping. When Xavier evinced surprise at hearing this, Perdita somewhat irritably drew away, saying that neither she nor Thérèse had ever been punished, by Georgina or by their dear father, without having brought it on themselves: and she, Perdita, was by far the worse offender. "But surely you are not actually *whipped?*" Xavier said, staring at her. "For it was altogether rare that my father ever laid a hand to *us,* over the years: and Wolf was particularly deserving as a boy." Perdita shrugged her shoulders, and made a charming little grimace, saying that "Justice was a more precious matter than mere Mercy,"—that, in any case, she had only used a figure of speech: *whipping* to signify *scolding.*

Being led down a narrow stairs to the cellar, Xavier had prescience enough to take, from a shelf, a waxen stub of candle, and to light it, that they might see some six or eight feet before them—but, alas, not very clearly. He was reminded as they descended, Perdita just before him, of an old fairy tale or legend his mother used to read to him, oft-times as he drifted off to sleep, of children entering a dark wood: a boy and a girl, alone and lost, or soon to be lost: clutching at each other in fearful desperation. Yet it seemed to him, even in the face of the murky and ill-smelling cellar, with its earthen floor, that to be *lost* in such a space, in lovely Perdita's company, would prove a delight indeed—!

So they descended; and walked stumblingly about; assailed by divers odors of mustiness, and rot, and drainage, and rich dark earth, and food gone rancid; and Xavier's sensitive nostrils picked up a faint smell of something decaying, or feculent,—which so disgusted him, he halfway wished to turn back. Perdita whispered that she knew very little of the cellar, save that it did not extend beneath the entire house, but only the central area; that it frequently flooded in the spring; and that there *were* rats, surely, throughout,—for which reason, she said, shivering, she wished not to stay there very long.

Still, Xavier wished to poke about, so long as his candle lasted. He followed the sound of trickling water until he came to a stone wall embedded in the earth; he followed the scent of decayed fruit until he came to a storage room; he groped about until his hand brushed against an iron grating, and sizable iron hinges, on a heavy oaken door,—a dungeonlike chamber, it seemed, not very distant from the stairway, but recessed beneath it.

He asked Perdita what this was, but she seemed not to know: a part of the fruit cellar, perhaps: though why a mere storage room should have a door with an iron bolt, and a grated opening, *very* like a dungeon cell, she could not say. Xavier tugged at the door, which,

though difficult to move, and creaking on its hinges, was unlocked;
and went boldly inside, his candle aloft, to reveal, amidst somber
cobwebbed shadows, a windowless space of some ten feet in diameter,
of an irregular circular shape. Divers odors assailed him, of a kind he
did not care to identify: and he felt for a moment he might be ill.
Though, upstairs, he had been uncomfortably perspiring for some
time, he now began to shiver, so that his teeth came near to chattering;
and the sensitive hairs at the nape of his neck stirred. What place was
this? What human presence even now emanated from it? Though altogether empty, and starkly devoid of any "evidence," it seemed to him
a place of unmistakable damnation.

Perdita whimpered that they *must* leave, but Xavier paid her no
mind, stooping to examine the hard-packed earthen floor, in which a
multitude of footprints might be discerned, most with compact little
heels, as of a lady's tiny shoe; and squatting to examine some
scratchings, or actual writing, in one area of the stone wall. "It is nothing," Perdita said in a frightened voice, in which an air of impatience
might have been discerned. "It is very old, and worthless, going back
to ancient times: I beg of you, Cousin, do come out." But Xavier squat-
ted now on his heels, holding the tremulous candle-flame aloft, that he
might, with painstaking difficulty, decipher the letters so crudely
carved in the rock: for, it seemed, there was a message of sorts here,
and a most remarkable one, in the form of *verse*. Ignoring Perdita's entreaties, and even her shy pokings against his shoulder, and the brush
of her knuckles against his hair,—which would, doubtless, at another
time, have greatly aroused him—Xavier haltingly read out these
words:

> Herein, a broken Sinner—
> Ah, engorged in Shame!—
> Godly Husband & Father—
> Blessèd be Thy name!
> If—You will forgive—
> & I rise to Your bosom—again—

"But the verse breaks off," Xavier said aloud, "and the rhyme is not
completed." Nor could he, by groping about, and peering along the
stretch of the damp chill rock, locate any further markings.

So absorbed was the impetuous youth in his search, he was but
dimly aware of Perdita's distress, or ire; and of the strain upon his back
and thighs; and the sickly throbbing of his head. How strange was this
discovery, and what exultation flooded him—! Now he knew that he
had not been mistaken to believe that *anything* and *everything* possessed meaning: and that, with luck and persistence, *he* should deci-

pher it. He inquired of his companion who might have scratched that verse into the rock, and when, and why: if the language did not suggest to her that of her own sister Georgina;—assuming that Perdita was familiar with her sister's odd poetry, as he was. Irritably, in a voice of uncharacteristic harshness, Perdita said that the "doggerel" he had quoted dated back, as she had explained, to "ancient times": that, many generations ago, before anyone who now lived was born, certain "criminal" Indians, slaves, and servants had been sequestered in the cellar of Glen Mawr, for safekeeping, *she* knew not altogether why: but so her father had chanced to mention, and so it must be true.

As he was examining with his fingertips the abrasive, marred surface of the stone, to see if he might discover any further markings, Xavier failed to fully attend to her words, or her reiterated plea that he at last come *out:* for, she declared, she could not breathe in so foul a place, and felt sickened to her very soul. Xavier murmured an assent; but was inwardly cursing himself that he had not the wherewithal to make a rubbing of the verse,—tissue paper and charcoal being all that he would need. "Next time," the perspiring youth bethought himself, "I shall come better prepared."

Not a minute afterward, while he was still vainly groping along the wall, he felt an emanation of sharply cold air: and only chanced to look over his shoulder, at the very moment the oaken door swung shut, and locked!—with a remarkable force, as if it had been blown by a violent wind, or angrily pushed. And, ah!—with what horror he saw that Perdita was no longer close behind him, but had, it seems, "vanished": nor did she answer to his strangulated cry, as he sprang to the door, to discover that it was bolted from without.

In this precipitant motion, the unhappy boy dropped his candle-stub, and *the airless space was engirded in darkness.*

So numbed was Xavier by this remarkable development, he could scarcely grasp the sequence of events, still less what he might do: and such was his pitiful gallantry that, for the first several minutes, he could not comprehend that sweet Perdita had slammed the door upon him; and imagined that she might be in danger, and requiring of his aid. Thus it was, he murmured only her name, repeatedly, beseechingly, as if it were a summons,—or a plea,—or a prayer.

"Perdita—!"

But no sound responded,—save the tranquil trickling of water across rock.

The Lost Suitor

As to Miss Georgina Kilgarvan's aloof, faunlike, yet, it was claimed, unfailingly courteous young man, Mr. Malcolm Guillemot,—believed, in truth, to be two or three years her junior—there had seemed to Winterthurn a substantial gathering of facts regarding him, in the twelve-month space of time during which he "courted" Georgina: yet, as these shards, ellipses, impressions, and mere innuendos (frequently contradictory) failed, it seemed perversely, to add up to a uniform portrait, general mystification and disappointment were felt on all sides. Of the actual likelihood of Miss Georgina Kilgarvan becoming a bride, there was an informal consensus amongst the Kilgarvans' set that this would never transpire: but a contentious division as to whether the match must fail because Chief Justice Erasmus Kilgarvan would never give up his cherished daughter (and to a young man, it was whispered, of exceedingly modest resources,—both his father and grandfather being Presbyterian ministers in a neighboring state); or as a consequence,—so the men jocosely predicted—of Mr. Guillemot's *delayed good sense.*

Indeed, it was a perennial debate as to Miss Georgina's virtues in the comparative light of those of other Winterthurn heiresses of her generation. A goodly contingent of ladies, the older matrons in particular, held that Erasmus's eldest daughter was a decidedly handsome young woman, with fine sharp "snapping" eyes, and a smile that charmed when it would, and an excellent carriage,—albeit there was sometimes a haughtiness in even her warmer manner that unsettled where it wished to please. Yet numerous other persons, amongst them detractors of the Judge, or those who had actually felt the deadly whiplash of his scorn, deemed her *sour,* and *petulant,* and *frankly plain:* as if the defiant *unprettiness* of her verse were matched by her public manner. Miss Kilgarvan was a *lady,* it was granted,—but only by virtue of her station, and not her character.

For was "Iphigenia" not, like her poetry, a vexing sort of puzzle: intransigent, offensive, with an air of concealing far more than she yielded—?

Of the thirty-odd ladies present at that meeting of the Thursday After-noon Society, at which the visiting lecturer Mr. Guillemot recited in a high, impassioned, slightly quavering voice his "renderings into English" of certain lyric poems of Heine, some declared themselves most struck by his large, wide-set, sensitive brown eyes, their gaze affixed, it seemed, in space; and by the marblelike smoothness of his narrow brow; and by the charming way in which, as if windblown, his silky fair hair fell in two distinct "wings" about his delicate face. Others, no less equally impressed, took note of the stylish cut of his frock coat and trousers, in a subtle hue of heather beige; and the propriety of his ascot tie, in russet satin; and the subdued richness of his vest, embroidered in scarlet, beige, and creamy silk. It was afterward debated as to whether the young visitor had recited his translations with a lisp, or no; and whether he had, at the podium, rocked gently to and fro, with the mesmerizing rhythms of the verse. And the ladies were in amiable disagreement concerning the effect of his performance: the most controversial of the pieces being Heine's "Die Götter Griechenlands," which, some averred, was almost *too* powerful in certain of its lines,—

> *And you also I recognize,—you too, Aphrodite:*
> *Golden once, and now, alas, silver!*
> *Though the charm of the bridal gown adorns you,*
> *Secretly I dread your beauty;*
> *And if your chaste body should delight me*
> *Like other heroes, I would die of terror.*
> *As a Death Goddess you reveal yourself:*
> VENUS LIBITINA!

—these final words being uttered by Mr. Guillemot in so impassioned a tone, his very voice seemed to shudder.

Afterward it was asserted, altogether erroneously, that Malcolm Guillemot had been gazing upon Miss Georgina Kilgarvan throughout his performance, and that he had, from the first, directed his recitation toward *her.* Clarice Von Goeler, who had accompanied Georgina to the meeting, knew that this was hardly the case, and was to recall, for

years afterward, with a pang of jealousy, how avidly Georgina had hung
upon Guillemot's every syllable,—how, indeed, the young woman had
leaned forward in her seat, her neck and shoulders near-quivering with
strain. During the question period, when tea and sandwiches were
being served, Georgina had somewhat recovered herself, and asked the
handsome visitor whether it was a valid supposition, or a mere
whimsy of her own, that "all poetry was, in a sense, *translation*, or
artful rendering, of the Unknown depths of passion, into the Known
strictures of language."

Precisely how Mr. Guillemot essayed to answer this riddlesome
question of "Iphigenia's,"—whether in truth the startled gentleman
had answered it—very few witnesses could afterward agree. But that
he had, for the remainder of the hour, fixed his attention pointedly
upon Miss Georgina Kilgarvan, all concurred.

Thereafter, in the weeks and months following, Georgina and Mr.
Guillemot were frequently seen together, alone, or in the company of
Georgina's father,—riding in the Judge's handsome brougham, along
Berwick Avenue, or the River Road, or through Juniper Park; in the
sumptuous tearoom of the Winterthurn Arms, or amidst the quaint
wrought-iron tables and chairs of the Charity Street Sweet Shoppe; at
an open-air watercolor exhibit on Courthouse Green; at an acclaimed
production of *Lohengrin* at the Grand Opera House in Vanderpoel. Less
frequently, doubtless out of reserve, they were seen together as a couple at one or another of the season's social events: the lavish Peregrine-
Shaw nuptials, the Annual Strawberry Fête of the Ladies' Auxiliary of
the Corinthian Club, Colonel Westergaard's fox-hunting weekend (at
which, it should be hastily reported, very few of the guests actually
rode horseback, let alone beheld foxes torn to pieces by impassioned
dogs); Mr. Guillemot slender, pale, affable enough, yet distinctly reserved; and Miss Kilgarvan flushed with girlish pleasure, yet shy, it
seemed, of being observed, by the parents of her students in particular,—as if she feared being criticized, or held up to contempt, or jeered
at behind her back.

Very odd it was, that, during even those halcyon months of Romance,—deemed to be Georgina's first—the clotted and indecorous
verse of "Iphigenia" continued to appear, in such divers publications
as *Hudson Valley Leaves*, and *Godey's Lady's Book:* as the sport of editors, it was whispered by Georgina's detractors; or as a consequence
of actual bribery.

Though Georgina never spoke of Malcolm Guillemot to Clarice Von
Goeler, or to any of her female acquaintances, in any terms less than
resolutely impersonal (as "Mr. Guillemot, the poet and translator"), it

would have required no inordinately acute eye to discern that the Judge's daughter was at last in love; and artlessly so. For was her complexion not touched with a rosy sort of warmth, and less sallow than anyone had ever observed?—was her gaze not bright, and direct, and less overshadowed by irony? Though held to be slightly stiff in Mr. Guillemot's actual presence, or given to nervously fluttering her fan, like a very young girl, Georgina was, it seemed, blessed with new energy, in other contexts: for she taught her classes at the Parthian Academy with inspiration and zeal (as even those girls who hated her were forced to admit), and did her charity work with less ill-concealed impatience; and was one of the Winterthurn organizers in a course for ladies in "first aid," offered by the local hospital. (It had struck Georgina with the air of a revelation that, by the adroit use of one's fingers, *one might actually do something to affect the well-being of another.* Though professing, like all the ladies, an extreme horror of the very sight of blood, and a "weakness about the chest" aroused by any thought of physical distress, Georgina applied herself diligently to the instruction: learning emergency procedures to be followed in case of divers accidents and crises,—woundings, drownings, strokes, heart attacks, chokings, the breaking of arms, legs, etc., and childbirth. How deftly her long fingers worked, applying tourniquets, and gauze bandages, and splints; with what utter absorption she practiced cleansing wounds, and making injections; giving artificial respiration; learning even to induce vomiting; even how to give enemas, in theory at least. Long after the course was over, and the majority of the ladies had forgotten all they had learned, Georgina carried about with her, in her handbag, a compact kit filled with the paraphernalia of the trenches, so to speak: gauze strips, ammonia in vials, compresses of numerous sizes, bandages and bandage scissors, inoculation needles, etc. Sadly, she had no occasion to practice her new-acquired skill, so far as anyone knew,—save when pretty young Mrs. Shaw, pregnant with her first child, sank into a swoon in the midsummer airlessness of Grace Church; and was revived within minutes, by Miss Georgina Kilgarvan's alacrity in breaking open a vial of spirits of ammonia beneath her nostrils. And even in so doing, poor Georgina risked censure, for the public nature of her "performance," as certain persons—including her own father—called it: and for her conspicuous intrusion upon territory that might be said to have been reserved for Dr. Colney Hatch, or another gentleman physician.)

Georgina Kilgarvan's *spinsterish irony,*—held in abeyance, as it were, for the duration of Malcolm Guillemot's courtship—was to return with some grim ferocity after that gentleman vanished from her side: and the zealousness of her teaching at the Parthian Academy was to drain away, like water from out a cracked vase: and, not least to disappear was her handiness at proffering "first aid" in public,—though no one was to know whether she continued to carry her medical kit about with her, over the years, hidden away in her alligator handbag.

A decade later Lucas Kilgarvan was to recall, with some poignancy, two enigmatical experiences of his, pertaining to his niece and her erstwhile "suitor" (this term requiring quotation marks, as no engagement, official or unofficial, was ever mentioned): each of which he was prevailed upon to recount to his youngest son, who begged him to tell all he knew of Georgina's past, in the weeks and months following the initial tragedy at Glen Mawr.

The earliest incident was of fairly little significance, involving, as it did, Lucas's failure to draw Malcolm Guillemot out in commonplace conversation, and to establish some sort of congenial masculine rapport between them, on the late-morning train to Nautauga Falls, one winter's day. After having introduced himself as the younger brother of Erasmus Kilgarvan, and the somewhat youthful uncle of Miss Georgina (there being but seven years' difference in their ages), Lucas inquired warmly of Mr. Guillemot whether he would like to join him in the club car for a cigar; or, somewhat later, for lunch in the dining car. Would he, at the very least, like to share a hackney cab at the Falls—?

But the watchful young gentleman was too shy for such abrupt camaraderie; or too shrewdly valued his privacy to allow Lucas to intrude (he made it a point, it seemed, to keep his place in his book of Longfellow's verse, while Lucas spoke with him); or,—so Lucas reasoned afterward, with a flush of humiliation—he knew very well the strained relations between himself and Erasmus, arising primarily as a consequence of Lucas's opposition, in his late teens, to the "justice" of the notorious Hester Vaugh case. (Ah, the brashness of youth!—for not only had Lucas quarreled with Chief Justice Erasmus Kilgarvan over the finer points of Miss Vaugh's *guilt*, and the law's definition of *infanticide:* he had also gone about town denouncing his brother: and had even penned an intemperate letter to the *Gazette*, which the Goshawks had, all surprisingly, published. Erasmus was never to forgive him, and never to forget,—and, it seemed, Malcolm Guillemot was privy to this knowledge.)

"To be snubbed by 'Malcolm,' " Lucas hotly murmured, "—why, it is like being thrown off course, mounted upon a stallion, by a mere *butterfly*."

As to the second, and more complex, episode: this transpired one Sunday evening in June of the following year, near the end of Mr. Guillemot's friendship with Georgina, as it turned out (though no one knew at the time,—indeed, an "official announcement" was generally expected, amongst the Kilgarvans' social set). The setting was Juniper Park, near the splendid old band pavilion: the time, not long past dusk, when fireflies had made their first tremulous appearance of the night; and many a child had at last fallen asleep in his mother's lap; and the Winterthurn Marching Band,—some thirty-odd gentlemen, livened as much by jovial high spirits as by musical skill—had temporarily laid aside their instruments, to allow for a half-hour's intermission in their concert. Lucas Kilgarvan, a new straw hat rakishly set atop his head, had been sent by his wife to fetch ices for herself and the boys,—Xavier being but five and a half years old at this time—and had, all by accident, been detained by the milling crowd: with the unforeseen, and, indeed, sincerely unwished, result that he chanced to overhear snatches of a decidedly queer conversation, between a husky-voiced young woman and her male companion: the very voices, Lucas gradually realized, *of Georgina and Mr. Guillemot.*

As their words were sporadic rather than even, and seemed at times to drop away altogether into silence, Lucas could not have vouchsafed that he heard what it seemed he heard; nor could he have sworn whose voice, amidst the general merriment of the crowd, was *whose,*—for Georgina's oft-times inclined toward the low, the dry, and the sardonic; and Mr. Guillemot's, toward the thin and high-pitched.

Fired by a melancholic urgency as they were, were these words not, at the very same time, touched,—ah, so cruelly!—by the comical?

". . . soon, then. For it is my . . ."

". . . cannot. You *know* I cannot."

"Indeed, please!"

"Nay, I beg of *you:* please."

". . . a matter of . . ."

"You are cruel."

". . . stubborn."

". . . a matter of expediency."

"You *know* it cannot be."

"Until such time as . . ."

"But you *know* he will not."

"Yet it is my . . ."

". . . beg of you, please!"

"And of *you* . . . !"

After a pause of some awkwardness, during which time Lucas felt his face heat with the guilty ambiguity of his position,—for was he not, in truth, *eavesdropping?*—at last Georgina said, in a tone of resignation: "How much more merciful if one were a brass instrument, all noise and confidence, and no contemptible creature of mere *flesh* . . ."

By the time Lucas could make his escape undetected, to return to his youthful family on the far side of the pavilion, his ices were badly melted; and his mood grown sober, with pity for his unhappy niece.

It must have been in early autumn that it was belatedly discovered that Miss Georgina's "gentleman" had not been glimpsed for some weeks; and, of a sudden, tongues began to wag; and female relatives made discreet inquiries at the Manor, as to Mr. Guillemot's availability for one or another social occasion. Georgina was confined to her room with an illness, declared to be *minor*, and requiring no solicitude: then again, it was said that she planned an ambitious journey abroad, to Paris, Florence, and Rome; and would be leaving presently. Crueler still, and quite without foundation, were rumors that the Judge's daughter had been precipitately *jilted*; and that Erasmus's chagrin was such, he would seek revenge through the courts, directing a "breach of promise" suit on behalf of his wronged daughter—! So ubiquitous, and so slanderous, was this persistent rumor that Henry Peregrine, the Kilgarvans' chief attorney, saw fit to refute it upon several occasions in Winterthurn drawing rooms: yet did poor Georgina no especial favor by angrily declaring that "the abused young lady had suffered heartbreak and humiliation enough, without such nonsense being noised about."

A yet more pitiless rumor, and equally without foundation, was that, like the specter of Crazy Eliza of old, the Kilgarvan heiress wandered about her ancestral home in a shamefully disheveled state, barefoot, unwashed, her hair loosed to her hips, and tangled with leaves and burrs. Singing such mournful and near-tuneless little songs, it was said, as "My Love's A-roaming," and "The Ghostly Swain," and "Shall You Come Home Again, Michael O'Meara?" she braided her hair with willow straw, and affixed, to her meager bosom, such wildflowers,— bluets, anemones, tiny asters—as, it seemed, most enhanced her waxen pallor. In this, she was closely watched at all times by both a nurse and a manservant, sworn by the Judge to absolute secrecy: for, ah! would it not have been scandalous indeed, if such things were generally known—?

The "Little Nun"

———

Poor Thérèse Kilgarvan—!

It could not have failed to escape the sensitive young girl that, of late, careless persons had begun to distinguish between her and Perdita by speaking of the "Plain One," and the "Pretty One"; nor that she was sometimes called the "Little Nun," in contradistinction to the "Blue Nun,"—both terms being inexcusably cruel. It was natural that Thérèse, motherless as a child, should have turned gratefully to God for solace; natural too that, like many another Winterthurn girl of her age and station, she should have been drawn to *goodness*. Thus, how unfair, to be spoken of so slightingly behind her back—!

"Can you guess what they call us when they imagine we cannot hear?" Perdita once asked Thérèse, with a sly creasing of her brows; but the elder wisely turned away, with a prim admonishment that, as such things were not for their ears, why should they condescend to hear? "For, dear sister," Thérèse said, with a trembling lip, "I do not wish to think evil of others, any more than I wish to hear evil of myself."

Thérèse was not yet four years of age when her mother died; and it was her and her sister's lot to be reared, in the main, by her half-sister Georgina, their elder by some twenty-eight years. ("What a pity it is," Mrs. Lucas Kilgarvan frequently observed, "that relations between the two houses are so blighted! For Thérèse and Perdita are good, sweet girls, clearly lonely, if not starved for female companionship,—other than that of Miss Georgina's, I mean. And I, who have sons but no daughters, should have dearly loved to 'mother' them!")

Though a "little nun" in a sense, in her Christian behavior,
Thérèse was hardly immune to ordinary schoolgirl sentiments. So far
as Georgina allowed, she participated in divers harmless activities at
the Parthian Academy; and, though not overly popular with her
classmates, she was, in general, not disliked by them,—until very recent times. Now, though the proud young girl never acknowledged
whisperings and innuendos, and the rude stares of certain of her
classmates, it did not escape her that she and Perdita were singled out
for censure: sometimes pitied, and sometimes contemned, for being
Kilgarvans and dwelling at Glen Mawr.

"Let them mock us, and say what they will!" Perdita said
fiercely. "They will pay for it all, one day—!"

"Nay, nay, dear sister," Thérèse replied at once, "you must not
speak in such desperation!—surely it is a sin!"

Being a maiden of tender years, and yet more tender passions, Thérèse
was quite ashamed to discover herself, *at her father's very funeral*,
staring for long unwavering minutes at her cousin Xavier,—the
youngest son of the detested Wycombe Street Kilgarvans, of whom, all
her young life, she had heard such disagreeable things.

Yet, ah!—was Xavier not handsome?—and fresh-cheeked?—and
innocent in his bearing?—and quite oblivious, it seemed, of the
ignominy borne by his father?

Xavier was not truly a cousin of Thérèse's, but a sort of half- or
quarter-cousin; for his father, Lucas, was but a half-uncle of hers, and
descended from the D'Ivers side of the family. (Which is to say, by way
of Phillips Goode's second wife, Miriam D'Ivers,—who, as family legend had it, was the distant descendant of an unsanctioned liaison between a French settler of wayward inclinations and an Indian woman.)
In his youth, Lucas had been interested in breeding and racing horses;
then he had studied law,—until, it was rumored, Erasmus's great success discouraged him; for a year or so he had attended the Episcopal
Theological Seminary in Hartford, Connecticut; he had married too
young, against his father's wishes; he had borrowed recklessly on the
strength of his future inheritance, to set up a foolish sort of business,—
a *toymaking workshop!*—scarcely a profession for one of his social
stature. "A contemptible failure," Erasmus Kilgarvan oft murmured,
"and a traitor to his heritage beside."

(Yet Thérèse and Perdita soon learned that toys from the
Wycombe Street carpentry shop were greatly prized by children, and
remembered with especial fondness by those on the brink of growing
up: the lovingly crafted dollhouses with their miniature furnishings,
and tiny inhabitants; the custom-made rocking horses, designed for

individual children; the ingenious jigsaw puzzles limning familiar Winterthurn scenes; the Noah's Ark with its procession of charming animals, all in pairs, save the phoenix; the trains, boats, wagons, galleons, turtle-seats, and sleighs for dolls; most famously, the "Bonnie" doll that blinked, and stared, and slept, and woke, to issue a most human mewing cry, very like an infant.)

At Glen Mawr, Lucas Kilgarvan was known as a *common perjurer* as well: for, it seems, he had done that most unforgivable of things,—he had lied in court, under oath. Neither Thérèse nor Perdita knew a great deal about the case, as such matters were kept private amongst the adults; yet it was no secret that their grandfather had, on his very deathbed, repented of his leniency toward the ne'er-do-well amongst his sons, and struck him from his will: with the consequence that Erasmus and Simon Esdras were then the sole heirs; and Lucas, acting out of both greed and desperation, and, no doubt, a craven desire for revenge, contested the revised will up to the State Supreme Court, with no success. Georgina, who rarely condescended to comment upon such activities, as she called them, of the *Lilliputian "Big" World*, once said of their despised young uncle that he quite deserved his fate for going his own way so wantonly. "One knows not whether to pity him as a fool, or abhor him as a monster," Georgina said, "for marrying, and setting up shop, and whelping four,—or is it five?—sons, on the gossamer strength of a *future inheritance*."

Yet, during the funeral obsequies, Thérèse had been struck, quite against her inclination, by Lucas's somber, stricken, kindly visage: and the hint of a tear gleaming in his eye: and the grief that seemed to announce itself in his very posture. And how intently he had stared at the handsome ebony casket, as the pallbearers bore it to the mausoleum: a look of such appalled bewilderment, and childlike loss, it might have been that he mourned his brother after all.

Briefly, Thérèse considered Mrs. Kilgarvan, whose semblance of warmth and maternal solicitude, Georgina had warned, might not be trusted; and the several husky sons,—Bradford, Roland, Colin,—great hulking louts, as Georgina called them; until her eye fell upon the youngest, Xavier,—and quite hooked, and snagged, in sudden girlish sentiment.

"But I must wrench my gaze from him," she thought, "for, surely, my feelings verge on sin; and Father will never forgive me, if he but suspects."

So it happened that the "little nun," hidden behind her dark tulle veil, and dressed in discreet mourning attire, succumbed to Fate: one of those haphazard ecstasies, or fancies, which we of superior age and experience must not too readily dismiss. For was not this child's very namesake St. Theresa herself, transformed by a similar passion,—the *virginal bride*, one might say, of a parallel ecstasy?

Nay, it is wrong for us to too swiftly brush aside adolescent passions; particularly as, in this case, they are to have such significant consequences.

From that day onward, Thérèse uttered many a prayer that God might absolve her of her unwholesome "love" for Xavier Kilgarvan. Yet, perversely, she prized the tender image of her cousin's angelic, yet decidedly masculine, beauty; she dreamt of his dark curly tresses, and his olive-pale skin, and the artless grace of his being. And though he never gazed upon her, she imagined, with a shudder that ran through her slender frame, how powerful it would be, how exquisite a shock, if he ever did.

By degrees, poor Thérèse lapsed into imagining, in her most distraught hours, that Xavier, though scarcely more than a boy, might prove an actual source of aid to Perdita and herself,—that he might be a savior of sorts,—albeit the notion was confused and blasphemous. (Yet certainly it was not Thérèse's fancy that she now saw Xavier so often, in Parthian Square, or along the shady streets near school, strolling with customary schoolboy swagger and never glancing in her direction?)

So it was with both amazement and chagrin that, one mild June morning, she chanced to look out the window of her bed-chamber, to see Xavier himself approaching the house, in plain view: meeting with her sister Perdita as if by prearrangement: and climbing, with boyish insouciance, *into the very house—!*

"What business have they together? How have they managed to communicate with each other? Ah, dear God, if Georgina learns of this—!" So Thérèse muttered aloud, near-overcome with jealousy; and for a long time she could not move from her casement window, as if all her limbs had grown leaden.

"Can it be," she wondered aloud, "that they are sweethearts?— that Georgina's suspicions are true?"

Thérèse stood at attention behind her closed door, and listened intently; but heard nothing. Where was Perdita taking Xavier? And how had it come about that Xavier dared to approach Glen Mawr? Alas, it was a wicked sort of game, Thérèse thought,—and Xavier had best be aware that he was not really welcome in this house.

Many a time Georgina had stormed that Perdita, for all her prettiness, was "of the Devil's party,—stamped with His look about the eyes": and, in truth, Thérèse sometimes halfway fancied there was truth in the charge. For only a wicked, wicked girl would aid a young man in entering a house by stealth, where he was not wanted, and where in fact he was forbidden . . . .

The agitated girl went to her bed, to kneel beside it, and pray to Jesus Christ that all might be well: that no evil be perpetrated beneath her father's roof. So fervently did she pray, so extreme was her distress, that she grew suddenly exhausted; and lapsed into a light fitful sleep; from which she roused herself some time later, confused and shaken.

"Heavenly Father, let it be but a dream, and *he* in no danger—!" she murmured aloud.

But some disquietude of the air, some subtle, yet unmistakable, alteration of the household, warned her that all was not well. Thus she left her room, trembling, to seek out Perdita,—in vain; and to hurry along the many corridors of the house, looking for,—why, she knew not *what:* Xavier himself, or a phantasmagoric figure out of her own dream-fancy?

Her womanly instinct led her at last downstairs, to the gloomy depths of the Manor: where, at once, she heard piteous sounds,— appeals for help muffled through a wall's thickness,—and, ah!—the enfeebled pounding of fists! In that instant she knew what naughty game Perdita had played: for, some years previous, when they were both mere children, Perdita had enticed Thérèse into the cellar, under the pretense of an innocent prank, and had locked her, for one terrifying hour, in the fruit cellar, or "dungeon," as it was sometimes called, beneath the stairs,—a mere child's game, doubtless, yet most frightening to Thérèse.

"Why, did you think I would never let you out?—did you think I would throw away the key, and let you starve to death?" Perdita had asked, her eyes grave with insult. "Why, then,—*you* are very wicked!"

So it was, caring not at all for her appearance, or for the condition of her smock, or collar, or morning-cap, or stockings,—whether her cheeks be rosy, or stricken with pallor—Thérèse hurried down the cellar stairs, and made her groping way to the chamber in which Xavier was confined: and, with but a minute's fumbling effort, managed to force open the rusted sliding bolt,—and free the stricken youth from his prison.

Poor Xavier, to be glimpsed at such a moment!—covered in dust and cobwebs and grime,—badly soaked in perspiration, so that every particle of his clothing was damp, and his person gave off a rank barn-yard odor,—his "gentleman's" fingers torn and bleeding,—his voice hoarse from shouting, and from great wracking sobs that scarce befitted a man: how could he display the proper manly gratitude to the young girl who had rescued him?—how could he even restrain himself, to gaze into her face, and murmur words of civil thanks?

Well, it must be ingloriously recorded here that Xavier simply fled: giving but the most distracted of nods to his benefactress,—indeed, did he not push roughly past her?—and, with never a backward glance, sobbing still and panting, he ran from the house, and along the pink-pebbled drive, to the stony portals at the road, and beyond,—ah, as far as his panicked legs would take him: not a remnant,—nay, not a shred—of his former confidence remaining. Poor boy! Not a coward, perhaps, yet surely not the hero he had wished to be!

Thérèse had whispered after him, "Farewell, dear Cousin, and for your soul's sake, never return again!"—but of course he did not hear.

"The Accursèd Kilgarvans"

It were best to skim lightly over the next several months in this history, both in the interests of editorial brevity and that we might allow poor Xavier to recover, as it were, some diminished sense of his Kilgarvan pride, and some small hope of his "professional" future: there being, in any case, no events of especial significance until the fatalities of the autumn,—save perhaps a curious incident reported to have occurred at Phineas Cutter's home, very early one July morning. (This negligible happenstance—much embellished, I am sure, by repeated narrations, and by the eagerness of common folk to participate in the tragedies of their betters, was: when Jabez Dovekie, the burly red-haired iceman employed by Hazelwit's Ice, arrived to make his delivery at the Cutters', he found Mrs. Cutter and her daughter Ariela in a state of dizzied alarm: for, when they had come into the kitchen that morning, it was to discover a "winged creature thumping and fluttering against the window,"—at first glance a small bird, or bat—but *very* desirous of entry, and *very* malevolent of aspect. The somewhat too impetuous Ariela had gone to the window, to tap at it, and frighten the creature away, but had recoiled in screaming consternation: for the thing was neither bird nor bat, it seemed, but possessed a *tiny wizened human face*,—that of an infant greatly aged, and most hideous to gaze upon! When the iceman arrived, Ariela had but partly recovered, and her mother was close to swooning as well: but so bold was Dovekie, and so little disposed to believe women's nonsense, that, with but a moment's hesitation, he strode outside to investigate: finding no demonic creature, nor any evidence of one, save a gigantic moth of unusual iridescent beauty, beating its powdery wings in a cobwebbed corner below the rain-gutter,—which he seized in his great ham of a fist, and destroyed in an instant. Despite the moth's uncommon size, it offered no resistance to its human assailant, but very nearly dissolved to dust in his hand, which did not wash off, or wear off, for over a week: giving Dovekie a most peculiar aura, one hand bronzed and darkened by the sun, and the other covered in a faint margaric powdery sheen, said to glimmer in the dark. As to whether the winged creature possessed a human face, wizened or no,—Dovekie said laughingly that he had not noticed, having no time for such women's giddiness; but knowing only what must be *done*.)

This apparition of sorts was hurriedly attributed by many to an influence of Glen Mawr Manor, not many miles distant; as were two untimely deaths,—that of old Pride, the Kilgarvans' Negro servant; and Miss Imogene Westergaard, one of Winterthurn's most renowned heiresses—which occurred in mid-September, each in the vicinity of the Kilgarvan estate.

It was, in fact, against the rear wall of the Manor garden, part-hidden in a clump of wild rambler rose, that Pride was found, by one of the few servants remaining in the Kilgarvan employ: the luckless old man having been hanged by his neck, and somewhat mutilated, and even "branded" about the chest and back, with the letter *B*—these countless *B*'s being of about three inches in height, and made to overlap, with the impression of a manic exuberance in the seared flesh:

This unsightly death was attributed by some to a supernatural agency emanating from the Manor,—the abode, as certain observers began to openly say, of "the accursèd Kilgarvans"—and, by others, to obscure rites of voodoo vengeance, peculiar to the more primitive races: but no satisfactory explanation was ever arrived at: and, in the light of matters deemed more pressing, as they involved white citizens of a certain elevated rank, the "mystery" of Pride's demise was soon forgotten; or spoken of only in whispers, by local Negroes. (It seemed, however, that the old man was as stubborn in death as he had been in life, and oft returned to disturb persons in divers settings in Winterthurn: the fresh produce markets on Water Street, the dry goods stores, the feed supply mills, etc., which, in life, he had patronized with a lordly air, in the name of the Manor; and the near-deserted servants' wing at the house, where, it was said, he liked to tramp heavily about, groaning and cursing "all the long wretched line of the Kilgarvans, back to Adam, and beyond." Upon several occasions he was sighted on Berwick Avenue, driving a clattering ghost-carriage, drawn by a matched team of ghost-horses; and once, in the most extraordinary visitation, he was seen by the Von Goelers' cook, grinding a pungent mixture of mocha and java coffee beans, in an iron coffee mill nailed to the kitchen wall—! No explanation could be offered for any of these appearances, the last-named being, of course, the most suspect,—for was not the Von Goeler cook a black herself, and notoriously given to spooks and suchlike fancies? Thus it was, young Xavier Kilgarvan was quite surprised to hear his own father *defend* the likelihood of ghosts: for where rank injustice has been perpetrated, and the Law is of no avail, shall not a man's spirit seek some manner of balance, or restitution?—or the meager solace of revenge, in committing mischief? Given to moods of marked sobriety since the death of his elder brother, Mr. Kilgarvan chided Xavier for his shallow,—nay, adolescent—skepticism: and quoted Dr. Johnson on the subject of the supernatural: "A total disbelief of ghosts is adverse to the opinion of the existence of the soul between death and the Last Day." To this, the dismayed youth replied that a belief in "ghosts" might countenance a belief in virtually anything else: for what might *not* be explained by the supernatural, or the Unknown? He thought it plausible that all human events had human causes, or causes to be rationally examined: in the instance of the lynched Pride, surely a *human agent*, close to home, was—

"But since you not only lack proof of your charge," Mr. Kilgarvan testily interrupted, "but lack the means to acquire that proof, you might be better served by believing in the Unknown, or what you will; or, at the very most, holding your tongue." Which so disconcerted the lad, he offered no further commentary on the subject.)

As for the death of Miss Imogene Westergaard, which so badly shook Winterthurn, and usurped attention from all else,—until the fatality involving Simon Esdras later in the autumn: when it happened that the headstrong young heiress failed to return from her morning walk with her dogs, nearing seven-thirty, her brother Valentine, breakfasting somewhat earlier than usual, rubbed his eyes of a sudden, and murmured in a queer stricken voice that "something had gone amiss,"—he knew not what: and, with no hesitation, rose from the table to run out in search of his sister, who had long provoked disapproval and worry amongst her family by insisting upon making her way *unescorted;* and continuing to exercise her Irish terriers by walking along the river within a scant quarter-mile of Glen Mawr Manor. Indeed, in recent months, when even able-bodied workingmen and tradesmen could be prevailed upon to approach the Manor only with difficulty, it seemed that Miss Westergaard was more adamant than before in *her* refusal to be cowed, as she phrased it, by "superstitious idiocies." So impetuous had the young lady been, and so certain of the beneficent force of her personality, she had several times attempted to visit with the reclusive Georgina, to no avail: and, refusing to be discouraged by the "Blue Nun's" signal lack of interest, never neglected to include her, and her young sisters, on invitations to tea at Ravensworth Park—this being the historic name of the large sand-stone-and-granite house in which Colonel Westergaard and his family lived. As to her motives for so persistently forcing herself where clearly she was not wanted, Miss Westergaard was said to have laughed in delight, and made the claim that it was in *that* the challenge lay: "For where we are *wanted*, why, then, our victories are sorry trifles indeed! It is only where we are *not wanted* that imagination waxes rich." In spurning several eligible suitors, since the night of her débutante ball some eight years previous, Imogene Westergaard had, of necessity, angered and even alarmed certain persons, who had made no secret of the fact that her bluestocking-spinster stance was most nettlesome: the more so in that, unlike, for instance, poor Georgina Kilgarvan, Imogene *was* uncommonly attractive; and in the full flush of womanly health.

It was in a charming grove of beech and dogwood, not many yards from the Kilgarvan property, and about thirty feet from the river, that Imogene's body was discovered, not long past eight o'clock, by her distraught brother Valentine: who, so overcome at first by the sight of the poor, bloody, abused body, could not comprehend that his sister was no longer living; but knelt by her side, and tried to revive her, with many a protestation of chiding grief. His upset was such, he had not noticed the bludgeoned bodies of the twin Irish terriers, lying but a short distance away, where it seemed they had been negligently tossed, into a tangled patch of briars.

Poor Imogene Westergaard was discovered to have died of multiple wounds, inflicted by an unknown weapon, most likely a knife: Hans Deck estimated these wounds,—which were of a crude, gaping, barbaric nature, wildly distributed about the neck, bosom, forearms, and legs—to be "beyond one hundred; indeed, countless." In all likelihood the young lady had been overtaken on the river path, and attacked from behind; and thrown to the ground; and murdered; and, as the piteous flattened and bloody grasses would indicate, dragged on her back to the little grove of trees. Yet her attacker had not seriously hoped to hide her body, as the grove was very near the path; nor had he attempted to disguise it, by covering it with branches, leaves, dirt, etc.

The mystery was the more compounded, and attributed, not least by the more credulous, to the *supernatural influences* of the area, in that no footprints were to be found in the softened earth surrounding the body, save of course Valentine Westergaard's: and no marks, no evidence, no *clues*, were ever to be located,—though Mr. Shearwater and his deputies claimed to have busied themselves for days, in examining the scene of the crime; and questioning certain lowlife persons, residing in South Winterthurn, who were known to have a distinct motive for seeking revenge against the Westergaards. (But a scant six years previous, Colonel Westergaard had aroused much interest, and not a little wrath in some quarters, by, of a sudden, firing unionized workers in his several factories along the river, and importing some one hundred Chinese laborers from the Pacific Coast, who, far from wishing unionization, were willing to work for contracts offering a modest $25 per month: and very diligently and uncomplainingly, it was said. A certain smoldering resentment yet continued in the area, however, so far as the discharged workers and their families were concerned; and it was generally known that threatening remarks, of a drunken nature, had been directed against the Colonel from time to time.)

Despite the efforts of the law enforcement officers, however, and one or two initially promising leads, the person or persons who so brutally killed Miss Imogene Westergaard were not apprehended: which naturally stirred superstitious imaginings all the more. "Yet it cannot possibly serve the community, or Justice," the beleaguered Mr. Shearwater said, with some exasperation, "to arrest anyone at all, and urge him to confess: though it begins to seem that such a move would be greeted with approval on all sides—!"

So disheartened was Xavier Kilgarvan by his humiliating, and altogether terrifying, experience at Glen Mawr,—of which, it should be here recorded, the abashed youth tried hard not to think—that he yielded for some days to his father's stern admonition that he keep his distance from the scene of the "new" crime; and not go poking about, or even making discreet inquiries. It was notoriously easy to offend the old Colonel: and Valentine himself, though a most charming young gentleman, and a bosom friend of Wolf's, was known to possess a mercurial temper.

After a week's stoic resistance, however, Xavier felt that he could keep away no longer: and stealthily proceeded to the scene of the crime: only to find every square inch of the area tramped over, by hundreds of footprints; and many of the lower branches of trees torn off, and small rocks dislodged, making any investigation useless. It had been a brainstorm of his to search the river for the murder weapon, which, thus far, the sheriff's office had not done: but this muddy and exhausting enterprise, taking the better part of a steamy September afternoon, yielded no fruit apart from tangled fishing lines and hooks, agèd rusted strips of wire, shards of glass, waterlogged dolls, parts of baby buggies, and parts of rowboats. Having cut his foot somewhat severely on a sharp piece of metal, the luckless Xavier limped to shore, to sit disconsolate on the bank, and watch the blood emerge, drop by pitiless drop, from his flesh, and fall into the slow-churning water. "At such 'uneventful' times in a detective's experience," he sullenly bethought himself, "it is more or less the rule that *something urgent will happen:* yet I have no fear that, today, anything at all will occur,"—the which humble prophecy turned out to be true.

The Fatal Wedding Night

As the testimony of Mrs. Roxana Murphy,—or, I should say, Mrs. Simon Esdras Kilgarvan—was to prove no less incoherent than that of Mrs. Abigail Whimbrel some five months previous, it was never to be known with any degree of accuracy, or chronological fidelity, all that transpired in the accursèd Honeymoon Room, on the night of Simon Esdras's ill-advised wedding to his "fancy woman": or, indeed, what wild and altogether uncharacteristic species of masculine bravado,— provoked, it may have been, by an excess of alcoholic spirits, including the costliest of French champagnes!—had encouraged the philosopher to bring his bride to Glen Mawr, on that wind-tossed October night; in cruel defiance, as Winterthurn afterward whispered, of Miss Georgina's express wishes. (As it happened, the "Blue Nun" was so discountenanced, and so deeply abhorred the prospect of spending even a single night beneath the same roof with the "newlyweds," that, forcing herself up from her invalid's couch, she fled the Manor altogether, her two half-sisters in tow, and secured the entire top floor of a boarding house for gentlewomen, on an elegant tree-lined street off Berwick Square: this being the place, and, assuredly, nowhere else, the distraught spinster spent the night of October 9, when her uncle met his hideous death.)

After the discovery, in the morning, of this fresh, and, some would say, *needless* tragedy,—poor Simon Esdras having been assailed and mutilated, much like the Whimbrel infant, and Mr. Upchurch's spring lambs; and the unfortunate Roxana, a bride of less than twenty-four hours, propelled into hopeless madness—it came to be reported, through town, that Simon Esdras had quite deliberately chosen to spend his wedding night in the very room imagined to be *haunted:* and that he had done so out of willfulness, and contempt for superstitious fears, in full confidence that, *as the "rabid" Jupiter had long ago been removed,* the room was totally free of danger,—indeed, was it not the most luxurious and desirable of honeymoon settings in all of the Valley? And it would cost him not a single penny—!

In boasting of this plan a fortnight earlier, Simon Esdras had told Osmyn Goshawk, all smilingly, and with a childlike enthusiasm, that the more he considered the unusual circumstances of his betrothal, the more *obliged* did he feel, as a rationalist no less than a Kilgarvan, to refute the sickly nonsense accruing to his ancestral home: for did not common sense, no less than the discipline of Logic, suggest that, as there can be no Evil per se, apart from evil persons, evil creatures, evil actions, etc.,—the nod being given here to Aristotle, and not Plato— there can be *no Evil residing in (mere) (extended) Space;* which is to say, *in a mere room?* One might consider, too, whether Hume's astringent notions of *causality* and *acausality* might not apply; whether Leibniz's *monad-vision* might not be relevant; whether certain elementary propositions in Simon Esdras's own *Treatise on the "Probable" Existence of the World,* penned some thirty-two years before —viz., "A spatial object must be situated in nonspatial, or Infinite, space"; "What possesses the property of *being,* cannot *be* expressed"; "Only propositions may express Logical Form (but) cannot contain it,"— might not prove helpful as well. With a most charming faint blush, and a lowering of his eyes, the philosopher confided to Osmyn that, at the present time, his own fiancée was not yet fully convinced of this argument; but he had every reason to hope that she was "coming round" to his position. Indeed, this robust young widow, formerly the wife of a Railroad Street tavernkeeper, had naught about her of false decorum, or simpering female coyness; and possessed, in his proud opinion, more common sense in her *littlest finger or toe* than all of the Winterthurn ladies combined. "She has said, it would give *her* infinite pleasure to spend our wedding night at Glen Mawr: indeed, to spend all the remaining days of our lives there, as 'lord' and 'lady' of the Manor, so to speak," Simon Esdras said, with a deepening blush, and a slight wavering of his affable smile: for, as Osmyn later reported, it was so remarkable a thing for Simon Esdras Kilgarvan, of all persons, to be *affianced,* he seemed to contemplate it with a faint air of incredulity himself; and uttered his words as if they might be those of another.

As to whether so simple an emotion as *fear* might not dictate one's actions,—Simon Esdras replied to this hesitant query of Osmyn's in a somewhat loftier tone, saying that the amorphous state of mind to which the term "fear" attached could not exist, apart from the term itself: and, as there was no language *ab initio*, it was a logical impossibility; and one to be dismissed from all serious consideration. "As every 'grammar' secretly communicates its own *picture-proposition* of the Cosmos, what is illusory may be for some functional,—as, I believe, my compatriot Charles Sanders Peirce has argued, in somewhat more clumsy terms," Simon Esdras stated, raising his forefinger, as if to discourage his companion from interrupting, "—the paradox then being, is the functional illusory *in fact*, or merely *in theory*?" Poor Osmyn Goshawk felt quite lost by this abstruse reasoning, though, as he afterward said, he had not in the slightest *doubted* the logic of Simon Esdras's argument; and was certainly nodding as the elder gentleman so amicably spoke. Indeed, the original question relating to fear was soon forgotten, as the philosopher proceeded vigorously to investigate, point by point, divers concepts that refuted, or even annihilated, opposing theories. Somehow, too, the matter of *syllogistic necessity* arose ("All X are Y,—E is X,— ∴ E *is* or *is not* Y"), having to do with the deceased Erasmus: about whom Simon Esdras spoke in a most peculiar manner,—part chiding, part gloating, yet, withal, in a tone of puzzled sobriety. "Thus I know it my duty,—and in this dear Roxana concurs," Simon Esdras murmured, "—to succeed where, it seems, my brother so ingloriously failed: *and thereby to invent a revolutionary Logic*, imbued with the fresher air of the New World, and free of all Old World and Attic muddle."

To this, Osmyn Goshawk nervously acquiesced; as, it seems, he could scarcely quarrel.

The ladies were less patient, and far more scandalized, in reference to the "wayward Kilgarvan bachelor," as certain observers called him: for they considered that, at his advanced age, when he might better have been thinking of Last Things, he was very much remiss in falling in love (as Mrs. Harrier Von Goeler put it) with a "pair of gypsy eyes,"—and eyes scarcely innocent of a veritable battery of tricks of crude cosmetry. "Roxana Murphy," whether *Miss* or *Mrs.*, was a woman by no means young, yet given to brash youthful ways; and decked out (as the witty Mrs. Von Goeler again observed) like a steamboat of old,—all frippery, all noise, part gambling casino, part floating brothel. Her tavernkeeper husband had died, it was said, under circumstances never satisfactorily explained; while perhaps not totally atheistical, she inclined toward the indifferent, in matters of religion,—claiming to be upon one occasion, Methodist; upon another, Baptist; upon yet another, "lapsed Catholic"! Most outrageous was the woman's studied *haughtiness* when, by accident, she and her gentleman escort encountered members of the Kilgarvans' social set, of

old; for, it seems, "Mrs. Murphy" coolly declined to ingratiate herself
with the Winterthurn ladies: and stared stonily past their flower-
bedecked hats, while harmless amenities were exchanged. The
hussy!—the trollop! Any fool, save Simon Esdras himself, could see
how shamelessly she plotted to marry him for his money; and to
overleap the lowliness of her station by becoming mistress of Glen
Mawr Manor,—whose portals, in the days of Erasmus Kilgarvan, a
creature of her ilk could not have hoped to enter. Alas, if only Simon
Esdras were not a mere babe in matters of the corporeal life—!

Since the subject bordered upon the indelicate, if not the frankly
indecent, the ladies could speak but obliquely of it: and oft-times
surrendered to stammering blushes, at what was almost, though not
quite, voiced. Yet how could it be that the aging philosopher, for so
many decades scornful of the material, not to say the biological, world,
was now yielding to an impulse most gross, and most enigmatical—?
How could it be that Simon Esdras was capable of noting a female figure, of any sort, let alone responding to it?—he who had, as it was
whispered, so vaguely attended to the melancholy fates of his pretty
sisters-in-law, *with whom he shared a household*, as to have perenni-
ally confused the two women, up to the very morning of Hortense's
funeral. His belated sentiments regarding the tradition of primogeni-
ture they could, perhaps, more readily comprehend; but even these, as
Simon Esdras elaborated upon them, and upon his *Kilgarvan duty*,
soon struck a note of unworldliness, and frank absurdity. "It may have
been that Simon Esdras too thoughtlessly dismissed the world of *existence*, in favor of that of *essence*," one of the bolder of the ladies
speculated. "Yet, at his age,—for I believe he is nearing seventy?—he
may find it somewhat arduous in making his way back."

This witty if slightly suggestive remark provoked both blushes
and restrained mirth: and the yet wittier observation, by a still bolder
lady, that, judging by Mrs. Murphy's air of expediency, as well as her
proven cunning, no very great problem should present itself in
"getting" her with child,—and providing the elderly bridegroom with
an heir.

It was at the very end of June that Simon Esdras began behaving in a
conspicuous manner, affecting a dandy's costume,—consisting of
white duck trousers strapped under kid boots, and immaculate white
linen coat, and snowy vest, and flowing coppery-silk ascot—and appearing about town, alone or with the brazen Mrs. Murphy, at social
occasions to which, it seems, he had not invariably been invited. A
lawn tennis fête at Shadow-Wood House, the ancestral abode of the
Peregrines; a recital given by the piano students of Madame Charpen-
tier, in the old Buonaparte Mansion; the Culpp-Flaxen nuptials, in the

First Presbyterian Church; divers baptisms, weddings, confirmations, and funerals,—including of course that of poor Imogene Westergaard, which the philosopher attended by himself, eyeglasses sparkling with boyish wonder, and mouth fixed in a queer half-smile, both censorious and grieving. To the Colonel, and other stricken Westergaards, Simon Esdras explicitly declined to offer his condolences; but was heard to murmur repeatedly, with many a quirky shake of his head, that "it was all a bungle,—an error, a muddle,— a *vulgar mistake:* and they were best served by transcending it, or dismissing it forthwith."

One brisk Saturday afternoon in late September, as Xavier was slipping unobtrusively from the dusty recesses of the Pinckney Street Book Shop,—where, unknown to his parents, he had placed an extravagant order for several books on Continental criminology, as well as a monograph on Sir Francis Galton's controversial theory of *fingerprinting*— he chanced to encounter his Uncle Simon Esdras, with the redoubtable Mrs. Murphy on his arm: the smiling gentleman attired in snowy white, with a vest of some knit material, in magenta, and a blood-red carnation in his lapel; the lady dressed with a matching boldness, in many layers of shimmering apricot-colored silks, and a slope-brimmed organdy hat, and an excess of Venetian lace. Xavier could not prevent himself from blushing as Simon Esdras not only deigned to recognize him as a nephew, and to hit, after several jocular tries, upon his actual name: but insisted that Xavier join him and his lady for a spot of tea, in Charity Street.

(Which remarkable invitation Xavier certainly could not decline,—nor did he regret it afterward, as this would prove the last time he saw Simon Esdras alive.)

Yet, dazzled as he was by his uncle's circumlocutory manner of speech, and by Mrs. Murphy's blooming and perfumed presence,—for, indeed, Simon Esdras's fiancée did possess snapping "gypsy eyes," which she fixed upon young Xavier with especial interest—he could not concentrate with any degree of success on what was being presented, or argued, or implied, or insinuated; nor did he derive much satisfaction from his tea, or the several mocha tarts and almond puff pastries urged upon him, by the silent, but smiling, Mrs. Murphy. Within a fortnight, Simon Esdras informed him, he and his charming companion would be *man and wife,*—the offices to be performed by a county justice of the peace, with as much brevity as possible; but this action should not mean, as certain gossipers would have it, any disrespect for his late brother,—on the contrary, in fact. "If one posits a belief in the *immortality of the soul,* which is the foundation stone, I believe, of the Christian way of thinking," Simon Esdras said slowly, "one must acknowledge it as self-evident that the soul, being immortal, and bodiless, and no longer taken up with the vagaries of the flesh, cannot concern itself with the pettinesses of this world: thus, our actions *here* are not relevant. If, however," he said, now laying a warm hand on Xavier's wrist, and gazing solemnly at, or toward, him, "one posits a belief in the *mortality of the soul*, one must acknowledge it as equally self-evident that the soul, being mortal, perishes with the body: thus, the actions of the living cannot possibly be relevant,—as any fool might conclude." To this carefully modulated speech, both Xavier and Mrs. Murphy assented: though Xavier had begun to feel the strain of the situation, and suffered a boyish wish to be elsewhere. Why did it strike him with such queer potency that his elderly uncle, though no less self-possessed than he had ever been, and fairly glowing with health, and a touching sort of pride in his female companion, was yet shadowed by,—by Xavier knew not what: an invisible fluttering or rustling, as of wings: an air of the *fateful*, and even the *doomed*, quite at odds with the cheery white wrought-iron tables of the Sweet Shoppe, and the conspicuous finery of the majority of the customers, and, indeed, the tarts and puffs and ices being daintily consumed. "Nay, it is only my irresponsible imagination," Xavier sternly chided himself, "which has never yet served me well, or proved itself reliable."

The awkward session concluded with a surprising alteration of tone on the part of Simon Esdras: who lifted his glasses to rub roughly at his eyes, and to reiterate his position that no disrespect for his late brother could possibly be intended, or inferred, regardless of what his niece,—that "most irrational and unhappy Georgina"—chose to believe: for did they not live in an enlightened era, in the closing decades of the nineteenth century, with fresh advances in science and invention and Logic being made on all sides?—and were the pristine motives of a *gentleman in love* to be questioned, by a morality couched in the prejudices of the Dark Ages? Testily, as if his silent companions had challenged him, Simon Esdras said that he so despised the vagrant muddle of superstition, he would no more condescend to question it than he would, for instance, inquire of the Sweet Shoppe manageress the recipe involved in making one of these pastries. Through the decades of his life he had never succumbed to any sort of failure of reasoning: and he had always evinced a fastidious impatience with such, whether it manifested itself in the coarsest species of peasant religion or in the infinitely more refined, though scarcely less nonsensical, species embodied by the proud Christian Church, in its numerous factions!—this impassioned speech being uttered in a voice of sufficient volume, as to enable all the patrons in the shop to absorb it if they wished.

"And, in addition," the now somewhat flushed philosopher

said, ''whether the world be 'real,' or but 'illusion': whether its existence be 'probable,' or only 'possible,' *or a mere airy bubble residing in a mad person's brain:* I, Simon Esdras Kilgarvan, refute it thus!''—all brashly, and unexpectedly, seizing his fiancée's plump hand, and raising it to his lips, with a ferocious disregard, it seemed to the blushing Xavier, for all who might overhear, or frankly stare.

At Glen Mawr Manor:
The Attic

That *The Mystery of Glen Mawr Manor; or, The Virgin in the Rose-Bower*, was solved by the youthful Xavier Kilgarvan only in a manner of speaking, and that, I am afraid, *unofficially*, is to be explained by the peculiar circumstances surrounding his secret visit to Glen Mawr, some ten days after Simon Esdras's funeral: and by the sudden on-slaught of illness,—diagnosed by Dr. Hatch as a particularly virulent strain of *brain fever*—that laid him low for nearly two months, bring-ing with it not only such inevitable symptoms as a high temperature alternating with convulsive chills, and frequent terror of unseen things, and raving and incoherent speech, and loss of appetite, but *partial amnesia*,—so that, though the bold young detective may be said to have successfully plumbed the depths of the "mystery," he was un-able afterward to recall its crucial details, save in broken, jumbled, and hallucinatory guise. As this circumstance was coupled with the tragic death of Miss Georgina Kilgarvan,—who, though she lingered for eleven weeks as a consequence of an ingestion of *arsenic paste*, never regained consciousness—it came about that the cause of the divers atrocities, and the source of an incalculable terror amongst the citizenry, was both discovered,— and lost forever!

In contemplating this state of affairs some years afterward, and his own descent into illness in particular, Xavier Kilgarvan yet brooded over whether he had been inordinately luckless or, indeed, blessed by his Maker. "For if God had wished me to remember, in unfailing de-tail, why, then, I should certainly remember," Xavier considered, "and, as that is not the case, and what I recall is most *horrific*, and *repellent*, and, indeed, *unspeakable*,—surely it is all to the good?"

It was on the mild, moonlit, yet capriciously gusty, night of October 21, not long after church bells had sounded the hour of eleven, that Xavier satisfied himself that his brother Colin was deep in slumber; and slipped stealthily from their bed-chamber, and down the back stairs; and out into the lightless lane, or alley, directly behind,—where the clever lad had placed his bicycle, in readiness for the adventure at hand; and his schoolboy's satchel, in which he had jammed such gear as he reasoned a detective might find useful: matches, and tallow candles; and ropes of varying lengths and textures; and a handsome double-bladed steel knife borrowed, with no precise acknowledgment, from his brother Wolf; and divers tools from Mr. Kilgarvan's workshop, similarly borrowed. As Xavier had no doubt that he would return home well before dawn,—before, even, the hooves of the iceman's horse sounded against the cobblestone of Wycombe Street—he did not greatly concern himself that any of these items might be missed; or that he himself might be missed. "I shall pedal out to Glen Mawr as quickly as possible, and examine the Honeymoon Room once again, and see what there is to be seen, with no witnesses," he inwardly resolved, "and return at once, with no wasteful lingering; or childish diversions of a foolhardy kind."

(As to what Xavier meant by the slurred reference to "childish diversions,"—this had to do with his shameful imprisonment in the fruit cellar, and the circumstances of his rescue, some months before. Unable to grasp the motive, or the meaning, or even the nature, of Perdita's prank, Xavier sometimes questioned whether, in truth, it had actually been deliberate,—or an accident resulting from a sudden fright, experienced by the delicate girl; or even a sudden gust of wind, snaking its way down the stairs, to strike the heavy door with exceptional force. Withal, the abashed youth, who still prized his cousin in his innermost heart, found it most felicitous, in general, not to dwell upon the puzzling incident; nor even to recall Thérèse's kindness.)

While we envision Xavier zealously bicycling along the near-deserted streets of Winterthurn City,—southward, and eastward, along Wycombe, and Pinckney, and Hazelwit; past Parthian Square with its great plane trees; past Courthouse Green, where the sturdy columns of the Courthouse glimmered pale in the half-light; to the darkened expanse of the picturesque River Road, which will carry him, in less than ninety minutes, to Glen Mawr—it were well to record certain elements of the scene that doubtless made very little impression upon Xavier himself: the ceaseless rippling play of the river's shadowed waves on his right hand; the patches and wisps of cloud blown across the moon,—itself an etiolated presence in the autumn sky; and the unnatural dreamlike silence that engirded all, beyond the mournful sound of the wind high in the trees.

And, too, as Xavier so fearlessly pedals along, it were well for me to record, that the youth would have made this second investigation of the scene of the crime some days earlier, but had been prevented by the unreliable behavior of his brother Colin: who, since the excursion in late May to the Upchurch farm, seemed to have suffered some minute, though distinct, alteration in character, so that Xavier could not foresee when he would retire for the night, or, once abed, when he would sink into his customary sensual abandonment, of deep slumber; nor could the perplexed Xavier predict whether Colin would *remain abed*,—for every fifth or sixth night, it seemed, he gave the impression of waiting, with cunning, until Xavier slept, so that, with uncharacteristic stealth, *he might slip from his bed, and from the room.* (Brooding over the puzzling metamorphosis in his brother, who was, of late, given to frowning and twitching silences, and outbursts of irascibility, and sudden displays of temper,—which manifested themselves in jabs, pokes, and actual blows, directed against Bradford and Wolf, as well as Xavier, and Colin's own friends—Xavier could not decide whether, of late, Colin had taken to running with a set of "young bloods," as Wolf did; or whether he had succumbed to a romance of some unknown sort, with a girl of questionable upbringing. It was Xavier's conclusion, after many hours of *ratiocinative detective work*, that Colin,—and no spectral apparition—had stolen the ruby ring Xavier had secreted in the fireplace; but of course he could not prove his suspicion, and hardly dared raise the issue with Colin, save in oblique and sly asides, which, to his way of thinking, provoked guilty flushes in his brother's face and a decided evasiveness of manner.)

Despite the daring, if not the actual recklessness, of this night's undertaking, Xavier felt very little trepidation as he approached the front gate of the Manor, which was chained and bolted shut: for it was scarcely a secret through town that the great old house was now completely empty of human inhabitants, and that the authorities had counted it a superfluous task to close off the entrances, and board up the doors and windows, and post signs warning against unauthorized visitors,—for who in his right mind, as Norland Clegg had remarked to Xavier, would choose to trespass in that ghoulish place; or even to venture onto the property itself—? "He would have to be a consummate fool, indeed," the sheriff's deputy had said, with a bemused shake of his head.

To this, Xavier had of course murmured a politic assent; but privately shivered, with an indefinable, yearning anticipation,—a sense, it almost seemed, of being on the verge of deliciously, ecstatically, *finally* awakening; of being roused from a slumberous trance, to the purity of uncontaminated oxygen; and to some remarkable vision, which, though thrust upon him from *without*, yet corresponded to something uniquely his own, from *within* . . .

Of late, the activities of home and school that had long absorbed his energies seemed both tedious and futile, the preoccupations of mere boys: he disappointed his teachers by daydreaming in school, he disappointed his father by daydreaming in the workshop, he quite worried his mother by unaccountable silences and sulks and absences, and, ah!—his shrinking from her touch. (Mrs. Kilgarvan supposed it normal that a youth of sixteen years should no longer wish to be caressed and petted by his mother; but she *did* miss the special attachment, for she considered him her baby still.) The family took note that Xavier's moody countenance brightened only when the subject of the "mystery" at Glen Mawr was raised; and then he was likely to say the most disagreeable things,—for instance, that any fool could see that Imogene Westergaard had not been murdered by the same agent that had murdered Mrs. Whimbrel's baby, as "the modes of death were radically different."

Indeed, as Xavier once said at the breakfast table, the "mystery" of the situation was, in a manner of speaking, why all of Winterthurn wanted to link the disparate deaths—!

With but a little difficulty, Xavier managed to gain entry to the forbidden house by way of a pair of French doors, opening onto a side terrace, that had been boarded shut in a most slovenly and desultory manner: and, not yet needing to light a candle, as a consequence of the moon's diffuse glow, made his way, neither hastily nor with an excess of caution, through a shadowed drawing room that smelled of dust, to the high-domed foyer, with its Grecian columns, and wide curved stairway, and air of arrogant ostentation that had so stung the youth's pride and envy some months before: ah! and roused him to a yearning for justice, or for revenge, that had thrummed along his fevered nerves—! Not wishing to pause, and to risk the incursion of a melancholy thought, in sudden recollection of Perdita, Xavier ascended the staircase as swiftly as discretion would allow: and, with a dreamlike alacrity, found himself in the upstairs corridor: scarcely daring to breathe as he approached the doorway of the dread Honeymoon Room, in which his uncle had lately died, and his bride had been so affrighted, it was said the unhappy woman would never regain her sanity . . .

Here, overcome by a sudden spasm of shivering that, to his shame, caused his teeth to rattle, Xavier did pause, but only for a minute: and, fumbling to light a candle, proceeded to enter the room,—which impressed him, beyond the sickening beat of his own heart, as wondrously tranquil. Steeled against attack, the very hairs on the nape of his neck astir, Xavier came forward with his candle aloft, that he might glance swiftly on all sides, and breathe in the air of this forbidden place,—a singular, yet not entirely repulsive, admixture of dust, and damp, and age, and melancholy splendor, faintly tinged with the odor of blood. He paused, listening: but no sound ensued: and, it seemed, even the night's capricious wind had ebbed. His eye gleaned, from the divers contours, shapes, shadows, and glassy surfaces, no evidence of any presence save his own: and that, a pale ghost-figure, hesitant of step, and indeterminate of age, gender, and identity, ensconced in utter silence, within the gilt frames of the numberless mirrors. Only the enormous *trompe l'oeil* mural,—the grim-visaged Virgin with Child, surrounded by a host of floating angels—drew his attention, and this but momentarily. "A mere room,—four walls, and a ceiling, and a carpeted floor," he murmured aloud, "—yet what secrets does it contain?"

Here, sprawled across the blood-soaked bed linens, one hand, it was said, trailing against the floor, and his ravaged head tipped back at a most grotesque angle, Xavier's Uncle Simon Esdras had been found by his manservant, on the morning of October 10, *stone dead:* his bride half-hidden, in a far corner of the room, crouched on her haunches and swaying slightly from side to side, blood liberally splashed upon her beribboned white nightgown, and her expression,—so the terrified servant told the authorities—more frightful in its *vacuity* than his master's had been in its anguished horror. Untouched, evidently, by the agent that had so barbarously killed her bridegroom, Mrs. Murphy,—which is to say, *Mrs. Kilgarvan*—proved so bereft of her senses, she took no notice of the servant as he approached, or, later, of Mr. Shearwater and his deputies: but strenuously resisted their efforts to aid her, and, in the end, had to be borne bodily out of the chamber of death, writhing, and squirming, and twisting mad as an eel, her scream, as it was afterward reported, the more horrific,—for being silent.

That this hideous scene had transpired less than a fortnight previous, in this very space, struck Xavier as remarkable, for now all was peaceful indeed; and, as he busied himself lighting candles at strategic positions in the room,—including the twelve candles, part-melted, of a many-branched candelabrum set upon the bedside table—Xavier wondered at a sudden infusion of his own strength, returning to him in waves; and a sense of mingled excitement, and boyish belligerence. Was it not within his grasp, conceivably, to resolve this mystery before the night was over?—and to bring his findings homeward, in triumph? How amazed all would be who knew him, and had too readily dismissed him as a mere schoolboy—! With a delicious rapidity his fears now transformed themselves into certitude, and muscular excitation: for Xavier could not help but feel, even in this place of slaughter, that God watched over him,—nor even that God's especial love for *him* might be, in certain spaces, suspended.

Thus it was, he prepared himself for his vigil: taking a seat in a chair equidistant from the bed and the door, but pushed back prudently against the wall; and drawing his legs cautiously up, to sit "Indian style"; with his satchel close beside him, opened, in case he had sudden need of Wolf's knife, or any other handy implement for self-defense. (As for the great canopied bed itself, which had witnessed such inexplicable suffering,—though the offensive bed linens had been taken away, and replaced by a spotless white eiderdown coverlet,— Xavier had no more the stomach to too closely investigate the condition of the mattress than he had the temerity to stretch out on the bed. He much envied the casualness with which certain detectives and police investigators examined such blood-soaked evidence, but had begun to doubt whether he would ever acquire it.)

Doubtless it was the influence of the host of candles burning in divers areas of the bed-chamber, their commingled glow being most gentle, and soothing, and harmonious, and suffused with a romantic sort of beauty: for it was not many minutes before, falling into a light drowse, Xavier began to think of his cousin Perdita; and remembered with a pang that irradiated pleasure through his being, even as it stung, the perfection of her heart-shaped face,—the petal-smooth pallor of her skin,—the haunting conjunction in her of the *childish*, and the *woefully mature*. Ah, if only she were with him now, how exhilarated he should be, despite the loneliness of his watch—! He recalled a church service of some Sundays previous, before Simon Esdras's death, when his eye had moved upon his cousin's bent profile, in a pew not far distant: lingering sadly, yet, as it were, hungrily, upon it: taking no note (I am sorry to say) of Thérèse, who sat beside her, in no less girlishly devout a posture. Far overhead, as if in Heaven itself, the organ sounded its thunderous chords, and the congregation reverently sang,—

> *Praise God from Whom all blessings flow!*
> *Praise Him all creatures here below!*

—and Xavier felt the breath of an angel close beside him, feathered wings in such rapid motion, it were as if a hummingbird had drifted near, warm, and perfumed, and delightful to the eye!—yet startling him into waking, so that his head jerked upright, and his eyelids fluttered, and, for a moment, he scarcely knew where he was: languorously embraced in a dream, in his own boyhood bed; or many miles distant, in a forbidden chamber of his "ancestral" home. There was some confusion, too, as to whether Perdita had been his guide to this place, or whether he had made his way alone . . .

He stirred in his cushioned chair; and looked uneasily about; seeing nothing that hinted of life, or motility, save his own dim and vaporous reflection in a mirrored door nearby that caught other like reflections, to toss them, it seemed, back and forth, most vertiginously, from one side of the room to another, and one corner to another, to Infinity. He rubbed his eyes, to goad himself to greater wakefulness; and saw that the French furnishings of the room, and the glittering chandelier, and the bronzed, gilded, and glassed surfaces, and, not least, the remarkable painting by Eakins, were indeed impressive; and wondered that he could have been so unfeeling as to have missed their uncommon value earlier,—in truth, to have judged them as ostentatious and vulgar. "Or is it," the perplexed youth inquired of himself, "a consequence of the recent tragedy, and the spillage of Kilgarvan blood *in this very space*, that accounts for an air of the solemn, and the exalted?"

At some distance there sounded the faint tinkling laughter of children, predominant among them a girl's high-pitched breathless titter: yet was she to be chastised for being merely restless, and silly?—and not at all naughty! Xavier's eyelids drooped; his head began to nod on his shoulders; all evenly, and deeply, his breath came and went. "Yet I am not asleep," he declared boastfully, "for that would be a most tragical error, in this *damned place*."

A tall, willowy, slope-shouldered angel, burdened with the most comical wings,—narrow, and oily-black, the feathers densely curled —drew near the boy in the chair, and murmured something sly, and puckered his lips as if to kiss: but, in the next instant, vanished utterly—!

Whereupon more laughter sounded. And the exhalation of breaths was such, every candle-flame in the room cowered: and one or two actually went out.

The released fragrances of jasmine, rosewater, lilac. A closer, more intimate odor, which Xavier could not identify. Ah, if he might burrow, burrow, burrow!—to the very foot of the bed, beneath the heavy quilt! *But that is forbidden. As certain scents are forbidden.*

So rapidly did the paired hummingbirds draw near, they revealed themselves as bats, with cruel hooked wings, and tiny red-glaring eyes. Xavier reached out smilingly to stroke them,—for he was but a baby, and could not know wickedness—but recoiled at the chill leathery touch of their skin. Very white, very wet, their small needlelike teeth! *O do not hurt me,* Xavier begged. *Where is Momma, that she would allow them so near—?*

Mrs. Kilgarvan closed the book of nursery tales, the one with the Cat and the Fiddle and the Cow and the Moon embossed in red and gilt on the cover. All silently she laid the book aside; and rose to her feet; and blew out the candle, *though Xavier was fully awake and pleaded with her not to leave him alone in the dark.* Stooping to kiss him, she smelled of eau de cologne: Xavier stared helplessly at her through his sleep-locked eyelids. If she loved him, how could she leave him alone in the dark—?

Now the Virgin Mary in her somber blue robes deigned to glance in his direction; and, on her lap, the Christ Child cast a peevish jealous gaze: for was not Xavier as comely, and far more manly?—thus two cherubs whispered, their breaths close upon Xavier's face, and their plump fingers running lightly over his body. He stirred; he shivered; he groaned aloud,—yet in exquisite silence; he watched them with apprehension through his closed eyes; while still the Virgin Mary regarded him with an air of intense concentration, her eyes like burning agates, her skin so whitely hot, no mortal would dare draw near.

Caressing,—tickling,—pinching,—most brazenly *stroking:* thus the pretty cherubs hovering over Xavier; while in the near distance a hornpipe sounded, high and lewd; and a mandolin, strummed with yearning fingers; and something very like a child's tambourine. Xavier would have squirmed free of the cherubs' fingers, but, alas, was he not paralyzed, in his every muscle?—in even his neck, and his head? Nor could he truly open his eyes, to gain freedom, and to recall his soul.

"Unclothe yourself! O beautiful boy! You are not ashamed, surely? For you are one of us,—oh surely!"

"*Is* he ashamed? Then he must be chastised!"

"He must be set right!"

"Sweet Cousin, most handsome of brothers—"

"Sweet Xavier, do not resist: ah, yes: like *this*—"

"But he is ashamed!—he does not love us!"

"He dares not love us!"

"He is cruel!—he is wicked!"

"Unclothe him at once!"

"O beautiful boy, *our own*—"

Blushing, Xavier cowered, and squirmed, and protested in a child's affrighted voice,—but in silence; all passionately he would have pushed away the hot, shameless, pinching, poking fingers,—had he been able: but, alas, was he not trapped in the lurid comfort of sleep, paralyzed through his being?—was he not so amazed, at the sly pinches of his earlobes and nipples, the rough strokes against his thighs, a cherub's fleet kiss, a ghost-bite, a sucking sensation beneath the downy curve of his jaw,—so amazed, and, indeed, so overwhelmed,

that anyone should touch him in such secret wise, he dared not draw
breath?

And, ah! what an intoxication astir in the air!—angels with eyes
that glared with love, and skin white-hot, and wings giddily beating!—
now a breath perfumed, it seemed, with the most fragrant of dried
flowers, from out Mrs. Kilgarvan's potpourri jar; now a breath
bespeaking the shadowed interior of the milkman's empty cans, a
most disagreeable, yet alluring, blend of the metallic and the rancid!
The tender notes of a flute grew ever more high-pitched, and higher
still: and now the random kisses turned to bites: teeth, lips, tongues;
the most greedy of mouths, the most emboldened of caresses; the fluttering of dark-feathered wings, the eructation of harsh laughter; a
commotion in the air, a frantic beating, *beating*—

"You are devils," Xavier murmured aloud, "and you dare not
touch *me.*"

Whereupon, of a sudden, he was catapulted to wakefulness,—
and saw that he was alone in the near-darkened room: that most of the
candles had gone out: and that, beating close about the many-
branched candelabrum, was naught but a cloud of harmless insects,
primarily gnats and moths—!

Yet the perspicacious youth was not so disarmed by relief, nor so
enfeebled by the terror of his dream, that it did not occur to him that
the cherubs might be both *phantasms,* yet *real:* for were not his exposed hands bitten, and lightly bleeding; and was it not the case,
which the felicity of a nearby mirror at once resolved, that his forehead, and cheeks, and jaw, and throat,—nay, and even the upper region
of his torso, where the shirt had been surreptitiously drawn away—
showed distinct evidence of biting?—and of bites *too carnivorous in intent* to be explained away by the happy coincidence of a cloud of
insects, drawn to the candles' flame?

His Kilgarvan blood pulsing hotly through his veins, fueled as
much by a manly sort of outrage, at this offense against his body, as by
the delectation of fear, Xavier withdrew his brother's knife from his
satchel, and opened the longer and more wicked of the blades; and,
atremble with caution, slipped from his chair, to investigate yet again
the area of the canopied bed, and the mural of lunging and pouting
angels overhead,—the which, it now seemed to his eye, quivered with
a most inexplicable species of emotion, subdued, withheld, yet potent
with rage: nay, did not the tallest, and most husky, and most rubicund
of the angelic host frankly stare at Xavier, with silver protuberant eyes?
And did not the pale angel who had, long ago, wept a blood-dimmed
tear, to fall upon Xavier's astonished palm, now gaze upon him with

eyes of exquisite yearning?—the poignant hunger of Desire, but hunger nonetheless!

"You *are* devils," Xavier said aloud, "though you be hidden inside mere paint, and that fading, and cracking, and flaking away into airy nothingness! Yet is it not altogether *preposterous*, and *contrary to reason*—" Thus he drew nearer to the painting, which yielded, for all its conjurer's bag of tricks, but two sober dimensions, the which, surely, hid no mystery; and had not the power to bite human flesh, still less to devour it. At this instant, however, his keen eye may have picked up some small scuttling or scurrying noise overhead, caused by a mouse's passage; or the muffled crackle of silver tissue paper,—of the sort commonly used to line bureau drawers, for purposes of tidiness; or, indeed, the agitated confluence of divers elements, not least the roused tumult of his own heart, which stirred yet a second wakefulness,—*that of memory*. Thus it was the youth murmured aloud, scarcely before he knew the import of his words: "Why, they are in the attic overhead: *that* is their hiding place!"

So it was, Xavier made his swift, and doubtless reckless, way, to the gloom-embowered attic of Glen Mawr, which he had so fruitlessly investigated under Perdita's guidance, many months before; and which, it seems, he had totally forgotten, as his investigation had proved not only sterile, but most humbling. Ah, how courageous!— how unhesitating!—to penetrate that place of shadows, with naught but a candle-stub to light his way, and his brother's knife to protect him! "If only Perdita were here once again," Xavier inwardly murmured, "how blessed should my passage be!"

Lacking that sweet presence, however, Xavier did not at all poorly, in reconstructing his footsteps, as it were, amidst the dizzying assault of scents,—and smells,—and stenches: and in defiance of an atmosphere of panicked desperation, the more enigmatic for its being *silent as the grave*. Making but one or two blundering turns through the maze of furniture, cartons, and boxes, and bumping his head against an unseen beam but a single time, Xavier arrived, panting, at the item he sought,—the massive Chippendale sideboard with the bamboo trim, and the ebony finish near-obscured by dust, and the numerous locked drawers, which, on his earlier venture, he had failed to open. "Here,—dear God, it is *here*,—here and nowhere else—that the devils reside!"

—Thus the jubilant words torn from the boy's throat, to ring most oddly in that place of desolation, with their tone of exuberance and gloating triumph.

Not hesitating so much as a minute, yet, withal, not without a measure of calm, and deliberation, and exactitude, Xavier made dextrous if unfamiliar use of the steel-bladed knife to pry, and chip at, and finally loosen one of the center drawers open: and bravely yanked it out: to see, therein ensconced, a sight that quite *froze his blood*—for, alas, there is no fresh expression in our native tongue that will here serve, with as much linguistic appositeness, or candor. In brief, Xavier's stunned eyes were fixed upon what gave every impression of being not one, but an ill-matched pair, of *infant corpses:* so badly mummified with the passage of time, their skins had darkened, and turned leathery; and their part-opened eyes, fringed by the most minute of lashes, had hardened to a substance akin to milky glass. Two human babes, or, more precisely, their mummy remains: tidily, and, it may have been, lovingly, wrapped in strips of torn wool, that had dried and hardened with the pitiable flesh to leather: the wire twisted about their throats so deeply embedded, and so rusted, Xavier's eye could scarcely perceive it at first, by the candle's flickering light.

Yet still unhesitating, and acting with the same dispatch, Xavier pried open the second drawer, and then the third,—discovering in one a similar pair of infant corpses, and in the other but a single corpse, though of a somewhat older child, very like two or three months of age. These, like the others, had suffered the cruel entwining of wire about their throats; and had been wrapped in similar ''swaddling clothes''; and placed with care in the drawers, amidst silver paper lining. How small, how perfect, the infant faces, surprised in their napping repose!—eyes, and eyebrows, and noses, and mouths, wondrously perfect, in *Kilgarvan miniature;* and perfect too the tender heads, and wisps of fair hair, and all the flexed and frozen fingers—!

Having exposed such horrific treasure, Xavier swayed above it, and felt his senses begin to reel, for could it be, he was actually *seeing* what his gaze absorbed?—and no dream-caprice, or idle schoolboy fancy, sullied his imagination?

''How,— and *whose—''*

—These being the only words, chokingly uttered, of which the affrighted youth was capable, before all breath left him, and all strength ran from his legs; and a corner of the sideboard careened upward most sickeningly, to deal him a sharp crack on the head: and to blot out his senses, in merciful oblivion.

Felo-de-Se

Though Winterthurn talked of little else for months, and speculations of the most inventive sort ran rampant, it was never to be grasped what connection, if any, lay between Miss Georgina Kilgarvan's criminal act of self-destruction (performed sometime in the midmorning of October 22, in the gardener's supply shed at Glen Mawr) and the abrupt cessation of killings, atrocities, and divers "hauntings" in the area: for indeed it was the case, as both official documents and local legend attest, that, with the incapacitation and eventual death of the Judge's spinster daughter, *all preternatural incidents stopped.*

Thus no one doubted,—though no one, excepting not even the most irresponsible of observers, could explain why,—that the "mystery" out at Glen Mawr was at last exorcised.

As the unhappy woman sank into a coma from which she never awakened,—save, from time to time, to writhe, and twitch, and fight with unseen figures, and moan out such enigmatic phrases as "O why . . ." and "It *cannot* be . . ." and "Where have you gone . . . !"— it was impossible for the authorities to question her: still less was it possible for them to issue formal charges against her for the crime of "attempted suicide," or *felo-de-se,*—as serious an offense against the statute, as the crime of murder itself. Dr. Colney Hatch, who was in close attendance upon the dying woman, insisted that she revealed nothing to him, in all the long weeks of her decline: nor did various hospital assistants, report anything out of the ordinary: nor Reverend De Forrest: nor, indeed, poor Georgina's own grief-stricken relatives, including her half-sisters Thérèse and Perdita.

Thus it was, the secret lay interred with the "Blue Nun," in the Kilgarvan mausoleum in the old Temperance Vale Cemetery,—whence it cannot be retrieved.

(As for the luckless Xavier, who felt such horror, incredulity, and sickened repugnance for all that, however broken and fragmented, he was able to recall of his experience in the attic,—it should not be held against the youthful detective that, after his illness of many weeks, he shrank from contemplating the "mystery": for did this fruitless exercise not invariably bring with it a quivering of his delicate nerves, and a heaviness in his heart, and a piercing staccato pain through his head? Most specifically, Xavier dreaded recalling the febrific vision he had had, while lying in a state between consciousness and unconsciousness on the unswept attic floor,—an unlooked-to vision of his cousin Georgina gliding on silent feet, austere as always, and veiled in her mourning attire: making her way to the Chippendale sideboard, and, stooping, gathering the small corpses from it, with many an ejaculation,—of ire, of sorrow, of weeping despair. One by one she lifted the mummified figures, with scarcely a glance at her helpless cousin at her feet,—who visibly suffered a cruel bleeding wound to the head, and might well, for all she knew, have required emergency medical attention. Poor Xavier!—knowing not whether he woke, or slept; or had been catapulted to some dim-lit anteroom of Hell itself.

Indeed, Xavier Kilgarvan was never to know, *with any degree of certainty*, whether this figure of the "Blue Nun" was naught but a hallucination; or Miss Georgina in incomminute flesh and blood. All resolutely, and, as it were, proudly, she ignored him while gathering her pitiable brood to her bosom, that she might secret them away, and bury them for all time: doubtless with the aid of that quicklime she had bought in such indiscreet haste, many months before. *Where* she buried them Xavier was never to know, nor did he seek to know: but when he came partway to his senses in the morning, and pulled himself, with great difficulty, to his feet, his fevered eye took in the fact that *the drawers of the sideboard were now empty,*—empty of everything save tattered and stained silver tissue, and a host of dead insects, dried and insubstantial as flakes of leaf!)

Epilogue:
Mr. Guillemot's Testimony

It was precisely eighteen years following that event-filled autumn,—long after he himself had suffered expulsion, in a manner of speaking, from Winterthurn—that Xavier Kilgarvan, while registering for a bachelor's suite in a small hotel near Gramercy Park, in New York City, chanced to note the shaky signature of *Malcolm Guillemot* several lines above his own: and gasped aloud with certainty that this must be the very same gentleman who had been Miss Georgina's "suitor" of a season long past.

Thus, though Xavier was embarked, at this time, on a most obdurate and teasing case (in consultation with a prominent toxicologist in the employ of the District Solicitor of the County of Manhattan), he took steps to seek out Mr. Guillemot, that he might tactfully,—in truth, very indirectly—question him regarding the tragical Georgina: though it must be said that, through the years, the "mystery" of Glen Mawr was not one Xavier Kilgarvan cared to contemplate with any pleasure.

And his investigation *did* yield fruit, of however an ambiguous sort: causing him to reiterate inwardly those familiar words of Monsieur Dupin's: *Perhaps it is the very simplicity of the thing that puts you at fault.*

Though unusually frail of build, and so pale his skin possessed a bluish translucence, Mr. Malcolm Guillemot not only was willing to speak with Xavier (who presented himself as an "interested party") of his Winterthurn adventure of thirty years before; but roused himself to

149

speak with some passion, in an unfaltering high-pitched voice. Had
Xavier not known the gentleman's approximate age, which could not
be much beyond sixty, he would have supposed him far older: belonging, indeed, to a distant generation. As some of his monologue in the
hotel's dining room, amidst the genial hubbub of voices and the tinkling of tea things, was indecipherable to Xavier's ear, and a great deal,
I am afraid, was rambling and superfluous, it is a severely edited version I shall offer here.—

       ''. . . thus, young man, as was our wont in those days, I re-
peated my hopeful proposal to said lady . . . and was yet again
rejected! . . . this being (so I was kindly advised) naught but a
maiden's stratagem . . . indeed, a necessity of sorts. Being but a foolish sort of youth then . . . in truth, two or three years younger than
the lady . . . I felt the prick of stung vanity, no less than that of wounded sentiment! . . . yet bethought myself, that the lady *was* enamored
of me, if looks, smiles, allusions, and innuendos of divers sorts might
be trusted. (Though I hope I am not being ungallant in so saying, it oft-
times struck me that the lady was more enamored of *me*, than I of
her.) In any case, my pride (if not my masculine fervor for possession)
would not allow me to withdraw from the field . . . for I *was* quite
fond of her . . . her high qualities of intelligence and sensitivity . . . her frequent displays of wit . . . her lapse, so to speak, to girlish
sweetness . . . being most admirable qualities: albeit conversation did
not invariably sparkle between us, and sometimes we fell each into a
blushing silence . . . from which it was the very Devil to wriggle
free! . . . and one did not always regret an interruption from the father
at that juncture.

       "Thus, yet again I girded my loins, to propose a most heroic
third time, while strolling with the lady in the English garden at Glen
Mawr . . . for that was, I believe, the name of the estate; and while we
were strolling, the lady's arm crooked lightly through mine, I nervously repeated my plea, *that she consent to be my belovèd wife.* To
my surprise, then, she behaved most amazingly: by choking with
laughter, and drawing away: and wiping tears from her flushed face,
with the sleeve of her crêpe dress—! Then again, before I could make
any response whatsoever, she gripped my arm most forcibly . . . indeed, in an excitable and playful manner (which, I must confess, I ill
knew how to interpret) . . . and drew me to a side terrace of the
house . . . where her father (who was, as perhaps you know, a high-
ranking judge in the state), and several gentlemen of his age and approximate rank, were seated at cards. So baffled was I, and so stricken
with surprise, I allowed myself to be 'dragged forward,' with a numb
and stiffened gait, and presented, as it were, to the company! . . . as
the lady gave way to her unseemly mirth, and, with her fingers still

closed hard about my arm, cried out in a strident voice: 'Father! O do excuse me! Father dear! *Do* excuse me! For but a minute! 'Tis but a minute!—nay, a half-minute! Gentlemen, *do* excuse us! Father, my friend Mr. Guillemot has given notice *for the third time* that he seeks your eldest daughter's hand in marriage: and that he should like to speak in private with you, at your convenience. Do you hear, Father?— at your convenience! *Do* excuse—!' And so on, and so forth, in this remarkable vein, all the while laughing soundlessly, and gasping for air! Precisely how long this wretched scene continued I cannot say . . . though, poor fool, I stood transfixed with horror, where a shrewder gentleman would have fled . . . my regard for the lady (I scarcely need note) having vanished at once, as if 'twere mere smoke blown by the wind.

"The Judge skillfully hid his shock and disgust at this outburst (for I have no doubt that is what he felt), and uttered but a few well-chosen words, in a voice of restraint, to the effect that his daughter should betake herself at once into the house . . . as she must be suffering from heat stroke . . . and was in danger of collapse. Whereupon . . . ah, how painful! . . . how piercing the memory! . . . the lady released her terrible grip on my arm, and lapsed into silence at once, and turned away, in immediate obeisance to her father's command . . . hurrying in a most graceless fashion . . . her skirts catching about her legs, and her hat askew . . . indeed, all but *running* into the house, before the eyes of the staring gentlemen!

"And so, young man, I left Glen Mawr Manor.

"And I never set eyes upon the lady again.

"And, as the 'feeling' I had cherished for her vanished with such alacrity, upon that summer's day, I felt no inclination to communicate with her ever again . . . or, ever again, to return to Winterthurn."

In the privacy of his suite Xavier Kilgarvan recorded his notes for the case, in his customary code, though his hand trembled, and every fiber of his being quivered with repugnance. At last he threw down his pen, and murmured aloud, "No,—it is too loathsome: and two of his daughters yet live," and, after but a moment's hesitation, committed the offensive notes to the fire,—with which impulsive gesture *The Virgin in the Rose-Bower* must, alas, be finally laid to rest.

DEVIL'S HALF-ACRE

or

The Mystery
of the
"Cruel Suitor"

She cried, "O Love! is this thy doom?
O light of youth's resplendent day!
Must ye then lose your golden bloom,
And thus, like sunshine, die away?"

—"SHE SUNG OF LOVE"

Editor's Note

_____

As it is so frequently, and so unfairly, charged against connoisseurs of Murder and Mystery that we remain a snobbish species, with a marked predilection for crimes of high life,—the unsolved murder of a duke weighing more valuably with us, for instance, than the solved murder of a shopkeeper; and that our preference runs to the classic in all cases, whereby *who* committed the murder must take precedence over all other considerations (viz., *how? why? for what purpose?*), I am happy to present in these pages a new rendering of an old favorite, *Devil's Half-Acre; or, The Mystery of the Cruel Suitor*. This controversial episode in the career of Xavier Kilgarvan took place some twelve years after the Glen Mawr horrors would appear to have run their course: and lodged so deeply, and so bitterly, in the detective's soul, it is no exaggeration to say that the sensitive young man never entirely recovered from its grim lesson,—albeit he did present to the incredulous world an absolutely correct solution to the mystery.

The case, long popular with those persons in our midst who, though dearly loving Crime, are easily angered by Injustice, is no less complicated in its background and details than *The Virgin in the Rose-Bower*; yet, withal, clearer in other respects. The conservative mystery lover will object that the case fails to conform to the purest standards of the genre (the question of *who* committed the several murders being, for the most part, ancillary to whether he will be exposed,—which is to say, whether the ambitious young detective Xavier Kilgarvan will get his man, or suffer professional humiliation); and that the victims, being mere factory-girls of the lowest social caste, fail to excite interest in themselves. Yet its attractions are self-evident; and it did not surprise me that a veritable fusillade of studies of the case, comprising books of scholarly ambition, no less than the usual run of publications, exists surrounding it. (As the volume you hold in your hand cannot boast any pretension of scholarly thoroughness, I have not included a bibliography of materials pertaining to Winterthurn's "Cruel Suitor" and his unforeseen fate: but must warn the credulous reader against the notorious *Ballad of the "Cruel Suitor"* by Mountjoy Price, a shameless novelistic treatment of the case, a best-seller in its time, in which our idealistic Xavier Kilgarvan is transmogrified into a vainglorious dilettante detective named "Zachariah Kilpatrick"; and the wily Valentine Westergaard, into "Yancey West, Esq.")

I shall not, I hope, undercut the suspense of the narrative by noting, for the benefit of those readers unfamiliar with the rudiments of the case, that, to this very day, amongst the more punctilious of crime collectors (and, certainly, amongst descendants of Winterthurn's more prominent families), it is not at all granted that Injustice finally held sway,—or that Xavier Kilgarvan *did* get his man! Again, the reader must form his own conclusion, as this editor has done, regarding the mysterious nature of guilt of a *moral*, *legal*, and *actual* sort.

Devil's Half-Acre

Accounts of Xavier Kilgarvan's involvement with the "Cruel Suitor" of Winterthurn generally begin on a placid Saturday morning in June, not many years before the turn of the century, when, on their way to swim in an abandoned stone quarry nearby, several young boys happened upon the body of Eva Teal, in its queer posture: *kneeling*, it almost seemed, yet pitched stiffly forward, to rest upon her bloodied elbows and chin, against the side of a massive boulder: in that region of rockbound desolation two miles south of Winterthurn City known since Colonial times as the *Devil's Half-Acre*. (So infamous had this area become in recent months that, when news of the girl's death first spread through the city, a common response was naught but a pitying headshake, and the murmured remark: *"Will such girls never learn—!"*)

For the corpse of poor Eva Teal, already stiffened in *rigor*, brought to a tragical count of *five* the number of young girls to be found murdered in, or very near, the Half-Acre—!

And, as of June 8, the law enforcement officers,—both the county sheriff and his men, and the Winterthurn City police— professed themselves baffled by the heinous crimes: and altogether helpless in preventing further crimes to be committed.

As the problematic influence of *place* will figure not only in our narrative, but in the defendant's plea for his innocence at his trial, I think it strategic for me to *digress*, as it were; and to provide for the reader a brief summary of the history (both authentic and "legendary") of the

Devil's Half-Acre. For, while to some knowledgeable persons the very name of the place connotes lawlessness, and mystery, and, indeed, the demonic; in others, I am afraid, it strikes no familiar chord at all.

According to Dr. Manfred Poindexter's five-volume *A Pictorial History of Old Winterthurn* (1884), the Devil's Half-Acre was given its name by the original Dutch settlers along the river, who, struck by the sinister appearance of the rocks and boulders in the area, fancied that they had been "strewn about, as if by a giant's or a demon's hand." In addition, the eye was disconcerted by numerous inexplicable fissures and ravages in the earth, and "unnatural" vegetation, as if, at one time, a violent upheaval of some sort had occurred; and much that was normal and ordered, became fantastic.

Even before the Half-Acre acquired its singular reputation, sometime in the 1750s, the locality was popularly believed unsuitable for human habitation: being considered a favored abode of the Evil One and His consorts, and to be traversed by no God-fearing Christians. Not only was the cheerless landscape decidedly out of scale to the ordinary eye; not only did it give the disconcerting impression of being about to heave itself awake, out of a stony slumber of centuries; not only was there, commingled amongst the boulders, a species of dwarfed or stunted tree, not known to grow elsewhere in the Valley,— but the sickly and decaying stench of the adjacent marshland hung over all, particularly when the wind was still; and the curious sound of the Winterthurn River's "Roaring Rocks," some miles away, imparted an especial air of malevolence. (These Roaring Rocks, long a tourist attraction in the area, are a series of hollows, caves, ravines, and the like, on the southerly bank of the river, through which a subterranean stream ceaselessly flows, producing a ghostly roar, and an infinity of echoes of this roar, as, all invisibly, they dash from rock to rock!)

Thus Nature has, for whatever incalculable purpose, created a most desolate, yet, it should be confessed, romantic half-acre or so: the eerie potency of which I have myself ascertained, in a recent visit to the area, when I essayed, afoot, to trace the probable peregrinations of the "Suitor," and his detective-antagonist. Ah, how chilling and unnerving a visit it was!—the more so to one like myself, accustomed to a sedentary life, and comforting environs! Though in latter days a clandestine spot for lovers, and even, it seems, for the bolder sort of picnicker, it is likely that the Devil's Half-Acre has changed very little in the decades since Eva Teal's piteous body was discovered there; and the pervading stench of the marshland, and the melancholy rumble of the Roaring Rocks, not at all.

For some decades, however, the area was known by another name,—the *Bishop's Half-Acre:* in reference to one "Bishop" Elias Fenwick, who prowled at night amongst the boulders, by the full moon, for what purpose no one knew. This deranged gentleman, it should hastily be explained, was by no means a bishop; but, according to legend, a defrocked preacher of some minor heretic sect,—Anabaptist, it may have been, or Free Evangelical. (Likenesses of Fenwick, made by local artists just prior to his death in 1759, show a startlingly sensitive countenance, yet, withal, decidedly peculiar, as a consequence of the man's hollow staring eyes, and bristling eyebrows, and disordered white hair, which lifted in a sort of mane about his head.) For some years in the 1750s he was allowed, by a tolerant community, to wander about where he would, and to deliver his impassioned sermons to the trees, rocks, and clouds, until such time as he was suspected of "chastising" a half-witted servant-girl: whereupon relatives of his were sternly commanded by the authorities to put him under lock and key.

So it was, the "Bishop" came to be secured in a cellar, with an earthen floor, and no windows or ventilation at all; yet, *at the same time*, it began to be whispered through the settlement that he oft conducted, by the moon's spectral light, a kind of witches' mass, or Sabbath, in the Half-Acre—! These illicit celebrations were, of course, performed in absolute secrecy; and were attended not only by the riff-raff of the community but, upon occasion, by its most pious citizens,—though such attendance, it scarcely needs be said, was vehemently denied by those persons, when they were queried of it.

Now, whether the unfortunate Elias Fenwick sincerely imagined himself a bishop, of an unknown church; whether his actual alliance was with the Devil; whether, in fact, he *was* the Devil in corporeal form,—no one wished to state categorically; and Dr. Poindexter's history hints that these several theories may all have been true;—or commonly believed to be true.

In any case, according to Dr. Poindexter's account, Elias Fenwick came to a singularly disagreeable end. Provoked, it was thought, by the mesmerizing light of the full moon, he somehow managed to escape his lodging place in the cellar; and to forcibly abduct a twelve-year-old neighbor boy (who, in some versions of the story, had aspired to befriend him in his imprisonment), whose battered, mutilated, and grievously outraged body was discovered, early the following morning, amidst the boulders of the Half-Acre.

Not many hours afterward, the "Bishop" was himself discovered, fleeing along the Powhatassie Pike, with no attempt at disguise; and brought back to Winterthurn by a lively contingent of men, to be hanged, within the space of a few days, on Courthouse Green. (This summary execution being impossible to forestall, though compassionate persons argued that, as Fenwick was mentally deficient, he might not be considered *guilty* of his crime, in the normal sense.) The

"Bishop" died upon a gibbet hastily assembled on or near the present site of the liberty pole, facing the Winterthurn Courthouse; he was guarded by a strong body of uniformed militia; and in an atmosphere reported to have been "excitable," as hundreds of persons crowded into the square, from all parts of the Valley, and as far away as Mt. Moriah, Contracoeur, and Yewville. A morbid note was added to the ceremony when the murderer proved so resistant to the rope, he writhed, and kicked, and danced, and leapt, for *upward of ten fearful minutes*, and it was believed by the gaping crowd of spectators that he was, in truth, the Devil; and could not be killed. But two of the sheriff's men grabbed hold of his ankles, and pulled down hard, and harder still, that, at last, his neck might crack, and his soul be released from his mortal body.

After Fenwick was, at last, declared dead, his remains were delivered to a local surgeon, who had applied for the honor that he might examine, and dissect, and analyze, the madman, according to the somewhat crude science of the day. The skull was duly sawed open; the brain removed; the skeleton articulated; the heart, lungs, liver, stomach, et al., examined,—and all with disappointing results. For, albeit Fenwick was covered in filth and vermin, and suffered such minor abnormalities as enlarged tonsils, and numerous boils, and monstrously overgrown toenails (rather more like talons, it seems), he might well have been considered, in other respects, *a normal man*. No visible sign of his madness could be discerned: nor his alliance with the Devil.

However, as the public had clamored for the right to acquire souvenirs of the execution, the "Bishop's" skin was carefully removed from his body, and tanned; and portions of it were doled out for use in the manufacture of pocketbooks, and similar mementos, to be sold throughout the colony. It scarcely needs to be said that his remains, such as they were, could not be admitted to any churchyard; so he was buried in the Devil's Half-Acre, beneath a clumsily chiseled epitaph said to have been of his own creation,—

ME UNHAPPY RACE

HAS RUN A PACE

MY DWELLING PLACE IS HERE

THIS STONE IS GOT

TO KEEP THE SPOT

THAT MEN DIG NOT TOO NEAR

1759

In succeeding generations the Devil's Half-Acre retained its aura of the forbidden, for, as one might imagine, the rock-strewn area, and the

marshy region beyond, and even the nearby highway, were widely believed to be haunted by both the "Bishop" and his luckless victim:
which aura was scarcely lightened by the hurried necessity, in 1864
and '65, of burying upward of four thousand Confederate prisoners in
the vicinity. (These unfortunate men, many of them beardless youths,
had been crowded onto Sandusky Island, into a space that, having been
constructed to hold no more than three thousand men, was taxed in all
its resources to hold eleven thousand—! Indeed, so virulent were dis-
eases on the island,—smallpox, dysentery, cholera, influenza—and
so frequent the incidence of infection and gangrene, it is a wonder that
even more of these military prisoners did not die; and find their final
resting place, as it were, in enemy soil.) Yet, though tales were whispered, through the years, of brawls, duels, assignations, and secret infant burial, in the Half-Acre, it was the gaunt specter of the "Bishop"
that continued to reign.

Not many years before the first of the "Suitor's" girls was found
in the Half-Acre,—which is to say, Effie Godwit, some six months before Eva Teal—it happened that the Suffragist Fanny Flaxen arrived in
Winterthurn City, "stumping" for a wild diversity of things:
woman's right to vote; woman's right to practice birth control;
woman's right to practice celibacy,—thereby escaping the horrors of
venereal disease, claimed to be, by the more bellicose of the Suffra-
gists, *rampant throughout the land.* Miss Flaxen would not heed the
wise counsel of Miss Clarice Von Goeler, at whose residence she
stayed, that she temper her speeches with moderation, and caution: or
that she refrain from voicing her outrage that *houses of ill-repute* were
allowed to exist,—nay, to flourish—in the northerly communities of
Rivière-du-Loup, New Egypt, and Black Rock, amongst others. Nor did
the thirty-eight-year-old woman seem to think it an ominous note, as
Clarice Von Goeler did, that the local police, and the sheriff's office,
declined to offer protection for Miss Flaxen when she spoke at the Armory.

Thus it came about, that the assemblage gathered to hear the
fiery Suffragist's speech, on a most airless and humid September evening, was not altogether the assemblage she might have wished:
consisting primarily of idlers, and hecklers, and jeering youths, with
scarcely more than a dozen ladies of good family, who were in sympathy with the Suffragist cause. From the very first, when Miss Flaxen
began to speak, albeit in a well-modulated and reasonable voice, the
dissidents gained hold: booing, and hissing, and shouting imprecations, and making lewd gestures, and wildly stamping their feet: until
such time as the gas-jets were extinguished, and a group of masked, or
hooded, gentlemen, who had been waiting at the rear, stormed forward, amidst much confusion and trepidation, though some applause,

to "take" the luckless Miss Flaxen!—the which was done by summarily bundling her in a horse blanket, and thrusting a gag in her mouth, and carrying her away,—to the Devil's Half-Acre, and to a most piteous despoiling.

Though it was an open secret in the city that the Brethren of Jericho had been responsible for the abduction, and the "punishment" that followed (which is to say, whipping, sodomizing, and branding with *B*'s across the victim's torso), no witnesses ever came forward to make charges: nor did the chief of police of Winterthurn, or the county sheriff, deem it pragmatical to pursue the matter. "As they were masked or hooded," Mr. Shearwater pointed out, "it would be very difficult indeed to establish identities amongst the Brethren: and not even Miss Flaxen, it seems, is able to offer a reliable description." Since it was generally thought through Winterthurn that the Suffragist had acted most brazenly, in peddling her wares, as it were, where they were so distinctly not wanted, more than one observer, of both sexes, murmured that the lady might be accused of having *provoked the assault:* and having whipped the Brethren into a rage, which could not fail to have disastrous consequences. (No one of good family belonged to this secret fraternal organization, and many shunned the members as mere riffraff; yet the consensus was, the Brethren, though altogether foolish in their capes, hoods, scarlet cummerbunds, spurred boots, gloves, et al., did not ordinarily mean harm: and might, in their patriotic inclination, and their zeal to uphold the Christian morality of the community, comprise a nascent force for good.)

In any case, Fanny Flaxen was found unconscious in the Half-Acre, but a few hours after her abduction: her stripped and badly mutilated body tied across one of the great rocks: and her memory impaired forever afterward, as to precisely what had befallen her in Winterthurn.

"Damsels of the Half-Acre"

It was naught but chance that the body of sixteen-year-old Eva Teal was discovered in the Half-Acre that morning, within twelve hours of her death: for, the reputation of the area had grown so intimidating, very few persons wished to traverse it. (The boys who discovered the corpse afterward confessed, that they had taken a shortcut through the Half-Acre only to demonstrate to one another that they were not afraid to do so—!)

After all, Eva Teal was not the first, nor the second, nor the third, nor even the fourth victim, of her approximate age and social station, to have been found dead in the Half-Acre, within a twelve-month: the luckless girl was in fact the *fifth* to be counted among the "Damsels of the Half-Acre."* And, as the police were proving incapable of finding the murderer, having arrested, and let go, a veritable army of suspects, it is no wonder that, in the popular imagination, the monster might strike again, at any time.

Though it was to be Xavier Kilgarvan's speculation that two additional names might be added to the list of the murderer's victims, albeit their bodies were not found in the Half-Acre, I shall provide for the reader, here, the names of those victims whose bodies *were* found

---

*"Damsels of the Half-Acre" proved the most catchy of the various names affixed to the victims, by one or another of the sensationalist newspapers. Though the appellation evidently originated with the *New York Tribune*,—an especially offensive publication that quite upset the more conservative residents of Winterthurn City—it was taken up with gleeful alacrity by most of the other papers; and cannot legitimately be excised from this narrative.

therein, and who were so much talked of in those days. Prior to the morning of June 8, we have,—

Miss Euphemia ("Effie") Godwit, 19 years of age; a country girl of "doubtful" reputation; born in the Mt. Provenance area, in a family of fifteen children; employed in some uncertain capacity in the notorious Hotel Paradise, in Rivière-du-Loup; found dead, having been repeatedly stabbed, in a remote corner of the Half-Acre, in late December of the preceding year.

Miss Dulcinea ("Dulcie") Inman, 17 years of age; of Fisk Street, South Winterthurn; a milliner's assistant at the time of her death in mid-January.

Miss Tricia Furlow, 16 years of age; of lower Railroad Street, Winterthurn; a scullery maid at Shadow-Wood House (the Peregrine estate) at the time of her death in late March.

Miss Florette Sparks, 18 years of age; of Tyre Street, South Winterthurn; the sole support of her widowed mother and agèd grandparents; an employee of the Foxcroft Shoe & Leather Works Company of South Winterthurn at the time of her death in early April.

Added to which dolorous roll was now,—

Miss Eva Teal, 16 years of age; of Cadwaller Street, South Winterthurn; survived by a mother and married sister, Iris; an employee "of varying merit" of Shaw Brothers Textiles, of South Winterthurn, at the time of her death in early June.

Since each of the girls had endured unspeakable torments before her death, and since each of the bodies had been found in the same general area, all but the most captious of observers agreed that the murders were the work of a single hand; and gave evidence of conforming to some unknown perversity of design. Ah, many were the "amateur-experts" of Detection, some of whom had traveled from as far away as San Francisco, and even London, England, who had strained their ratiocinative powers in the task of *deciphering a code* herein!—to the ill-disguised contempt of the local law enforcement officers, who, while having very few leads of their own to follow, knew at least that a luxuriant puzzling over *names, initials, months of the year, days of the week, dates, hair and eye coloring*, and the like, not to mention anagrams and acrostics formed by the victims' names, would prove a fruitless activity. (Here, I suppose it must be said, in some embarrassment, we have an early manifestation of the deleterious effects of *crime literature,*—whether the esoteric works of Poe or the newly popular works of Conan Doyle—upon the impressionable amateur.)

As for the appellation the "Cruel Suitor," which caught the public's fancy early on, and has held fast ever since,—this poetical and, in truth, altogether astute designation seems to have arisen from testimony at the inquest into Dulcinea Inman's death, when one of the dead girl's weeping acquaintances reported that Miss Inman had confided in her, not a week before her death, that she was "being courted" by a gentleman, in the utmost secrecy: for, it seemed, while this gentleman was enamored of *her,* he had earlier affianced himself to a young lady of his own social set; and was not free, at the present time, to declare his heart. As to the name of this suitor,—this was less clear; nor had Miss Inman indicated with any confidence his exact place of residence, save to boast to her friend that it was "across the river,"—which is to say, in a more affluent sector of the city.

Handsome, gracious, genteel, "wondrously well-mannered," and charitable as Miss Inman's suitor was,—for he was always pressing small gifts upon her—he had, it seems, a fault or two: being surprisingly mercurial in his temperament; and possessive; and jealous; and inclined at times (Miss Inman claimed she had no idea why,—surely she gave him no cause) to be *cruel.* He might grow sullen with no provocation, or, yet more alarmingly, he might burst out with the most cutting remarks; he might pinch her, in play, yet not *altogether* in play; he might twist her slender wrist; or squeeze her shoulder, and shake her; or even slap her: and all, Miss Inman had said, *for no reason she could discover.* "Yet it seemed that his good qualities outweighed the bad," Miss Inman's friend testified. "For what reason, otherwise, would poor Dulcie have put up with such behavior?" (At which point the gentlemen who were conducting the inquest could not forbear exchanging significant glances with one another. *For what reason, in-deed!)*

As none of the suspects in Miss Inman's murder answered to this curious description, the authorities were inclined to dismiss such talk of a "gentleman suitor" as mere girlish phantasy, scarcely worth being recorded. For what shop-girls, and servant-girls, and factory-girls, of South Winterthurn or elsewhere, did not concoct somesuch absurd notion out of the very air?—either in innocent self-delusion or, more wantonly, that they might impress others.

Frank Shearwater, the much-respected sheriff of Winterthurn

County, doubted that the girl's testimony could be allowed any credence at all; and regretted that he could not in some wise suppress it,
to keep it from the newspapers and the rumormongers: for careless
talk of a "gentleman suitor," or a "cruel suitor," could not fail to influence further witnesses, and, as it were, contaminate the police investigation.

Which seems to have come about, indeed,—for of the five girls
eventually slain, all but one (Miss Euphemia Godwit) had confided in a
close acquaintance, or a sister, that *she* had been chosen as the object
of a secret adoration, by a gentleman "whose name could not be revealed."

As the reader who is familiar with Xavier Kilgarvan's career may recall, the young "consulting detective" had been traveling abroad for
some months at this time; and, quite by happenstance, returned to
Winterthurn City only four days after the discovery of the fifth victim's body. As, in his characteristically meticulous way, he will examine the details pertaining to each of the earlier deaths, I shall
refrain from setting them forth in this space; and concentrate upon the
curious circumstances surrounding Eva Teal's death, and the "presentation" of her body in the Half-Acre.

Alone of the five victims, Eva had been placed (unless the exigencies of the death *rigor* had forced her thus) into a supplicant pray-
ing position: her lacerated jaw and elbows steadying her against a rock,
and her bloodied wrists, though untied, nearly meeting behind her
bowed head: her childlike stubbed fingers spread in an attitude of frozen fright. An expression both strained and obsequious yet showed on
her blanched face, which had not, oddly, relaxed after death, so that it
would have demanded a charitable eye, to see in this heart-rending
countenance those "pretty," "charming," and "alluring" features
for which, it seems, the young girl had been known. (Newspaper
likenesses of Miss Teal, or "Eva," as she came to be called, vary widely, as a consequence of the skill of the artist, and the degree of his
wish,—following the order of a calculating editor, doubtless—to em-
phasize the victim's *angelic*, or *seductive*, traits. Yet the most au-
thentic-seeming of the drawings show an ordinary, and even vulgar,
species of comeliness: Eva's eyes disingenuously round, and close-set;
the nose snubbed; the mouth rather full and slack, inclining toward
the sensual.) When the luckless creature was found in the Half-Acre,
her appearance was of course grievously ravaged; and only the crudest
of authorial sensibilities would wish to limn it here. However,—most
piteous of sights!—the girl's fair brown hair was yet charmingly
curled, as if for a Sunday's excursion; and her tattered green poplin
dress, prettily decorated with white velvet ribands by Eva's own hand,

was indeed, as her mother later testified, the victim's "Sunday best." (Other items of feminine apparel,—amongst them a hat, gloves, and undergarments of divers sorts—were nowhere in evidence.)

Death had been most savagely inflicted upon Eva, by way of repeated stabbings about the torso, belly, and thighs: upward of one hundred strokes, as the county coroner, Hans Deck, estimated. Not until some hours later, however, when the body was being prepared for identification in the morgue, did another factor somewhat embarrassingly come to light: which is to say, Eva appeared to have been strangled as well, by a thin gold chain so tightly twisted about her neck, it had sunk deep into the tender flesh; and a small gold cross had been wrenched off the chain, and *placed flat on the victim's tongue,*—as a mockery of the communion wafer, perhaps. (Which grisly element, as we shall see, would give credence to the theory of *ritual murder*, allegedly practiced by Jews against Christians in earlier times.) Eva's jaws were badly bruised, and the teeth bloodied; but, as *rigor mortis* had long since set in, it was not to be wondered that the coroner had failed to note this detail.

Being of a naturally conservative character, Mr. Deck declared only that Eva had met her death in a "suspicious" manner: very likely *not* self-inflicted (as it was a truism of the trade, strangulation must be invariably homicide), nor yet accidental; her misfortune executed by an "unknown assailant, or assailants." As to the precise hour of death,—Mr. Deck vaguely ascertained that it might have been at any time within a span of, say, twelve hours: roughly between the hour of 7:00 of the previous evening and 7:00 of the morning of June 8. Whether the body had been violated in a carnal manner, Mr. Deck chose not to explore, as it had oft been his experience that such information was difficult to obtain, and, in this case, the great number of lacerations would doubtless obscure the evidence. And, too, when girls of doubtful reputation and family were involved, promiscuous sexual activity rendered a verdict the more problematic and disagreeable: witness the earlier examples of "Effie" Godwit (rumored to have been intermittently employed by the Hotel Paradise, one of the most notorious of the Rivière-du-Loup brothels, and *approximately four months pregnant at the time of her death*), and the sweet-faced scullery maid Tricia Furlow (rumored to have seduced a goodly number of the male servants at Shadow-Wood House, and even the young master, Ringgold Peregrine, himself). The sheriff, Mr. Shearwater, observed that Eva's mother and sister both insisted that Eva was a good Catholic girl, who never, or rarely, "kept company" with the opposite sex: whereupon Mr. Deck cannily replied that such an insistence is never *not* made, in repellent cases of this sort.

Of nearly three dozen persons closely questioned by Mr. Shearwater and his deputies, a small number provided information that appeared to be moderately helpful; and several stood out as likely suspects,— these being Eva's brother-in-law, Lyle Beck, a husky, sullen, and unusually bellicose hackney driver, in his early thirties; and a most pathetically frightened young man named Louis, who lived directly below the Teals, in their crowded tenement building on Cadwaller Street; and the distraught office manager of the Shaw textile mill, Isaac Rosenwald, a Jewish gentlemen of forty-one years of age, who had been called in for questioning as a consequence of an anonymous tip received by the authorities. (This piece of information, written in an eccentric hand, part stiff and part flowery, as if the writer had sought to disguise his or her handwriting, was sent to Mr. Shearwater by way of a Negro messenger boy, sometimes in the employ of the Barraclough horse trainers, and prized for his reticence, so far as the identities of his gentleman customers were concerned: nor did he seem to recall, at this juncture, who had sent him on his errand. Apart from this "tip," however, the office manager Rosenwald had already been charged, by certain of Eva's co-workers at the mill, with having "shamelessly favored" her, and, by others, with having "displayed animosity against her"—!)

These leading suspects, and some eight or ten other men, ranging in ages from fifteen to fifty-nine (most of them being residents of the lowlife neighborhood, adjacent to the factories, mills, warehouses, etc., of South Winterthurn, in which the Teals lived), were considered by Mr. Shearwater to have unconvincing alibis regarding their whereabouts on the night of June 7, and through the early morning of the eighth; and, though few of them were ascertained to have actual criminal records, their characters were such that so repulsive and unnatural a crime as that committed against Eva Teal was not beyond their powers. (Ah, how eagerly, and with what civic zeal, informants stepped forward to tell their tales to the authorities!—so long, of course, as they were promised the cloak of anonymity. The Shaws' unpopular office manager was not alone in being denounced by persons wishing to aid in the investigation, for Lyle Beck, and Louis, and any number of men in the neighborhood, *not excluding the parish priest*, were eventually named; and even a half-witted and grotesquely obese boy, the son of a German tavernkeeper, who was brought cringing to the sheriff's office,—a creature so deficient in mental capacity, and so sickly, it quite beggared understanding why anyone would wish to cause him trouble.)

Both Mrs. Teal and her married daughter Iris insisted, with some vehemence, that Eva had been an uncommonly good girl, and had had no enemies; that she had never flirted with any men or boys; that she had always acquitted herself diligently at the mill; and never failed to bring home every penny of her weekly wages,—which is to say, $2.50, for some seventy-two hours of labor. So far was she from being one of the troublemakers amongst the mill-hands, that she shunned their very company, for being "coarse" and "ill-bred": so pious a Catholic was she, as to have never missed a single Sunday's communion,—save perhaps as a consequence of sickness, when it had been necessary for her to eat a small breakfast before going to mass. Her eyes angrily aflame with tears, Mrs. Teal lashed out against "certain Orientals" in the neighborhood who, it seemed to her, stared at her and her daughters most brazenly,—indeed, at all the white women and girls on the street; while the more hesitant Mrs. Beck (herself but a girl of no more than twenty, and hugely pregnant) averred that it "should not surprise her if the Jew at the office,"— which is to say, Isaac Rosenwald—had lured her sister away to murder her for being a good Catholic girl, and shrinking from his advances. "Under the pretext of worrying about a negligible injury of Eva's, Mr. Rosenwald once took her by cab to a doctor across the river," Mrs. Beck said, "and as Eva was not her usual chatterbox self in reporting the adventure to us, I cannot think but that something went amiss: this incident having taken place shortly after Easter. Moreover, is the Jew not *ugly—!*" she said with a fastidious shudder.

The Teals' testimonies, though convincing at the time, were badly undercut by revelations made by other witnesses, who lived in their neighborhood or had worked at the mill with Eva: for, it seemed, Mrs. Teal enjoyed the reputation of being a "shameless liar," who presented herself as a widow when, in truth, her drunkard husband had abandoned her, to live downriver with a girl half his age; and she so frequently quarreled with Eva, over the matter of Eva's slovenliness about the household, and persnickety ways with her own toilet,—and, most damning of all, her "popularity" with the opposite sex ("whether boys yet in short pants, or grizzled old rips three times her age," as one of the older mill-hands sourly phrased it), that several tenants in her building had risen up in arms to ask that the Teals be evicted. As to Iris Beck,—it was known through the parish, as a friend of Mrs. Teal's confided, that Iris and Lyle had married rather more out of dire necessity than romantic inclination; and that Beck not only was a drunkard and a brute, who abused his simpering wife, and "made overtures" to Eva, but was rumored *to have a second family elsewhere*, doubtless under another name. The sheriff was concerned to know whether Beck had ever displayed any actual brutality, or threatened such, to Eva, in the presence of the witness: but it seemed he had *not,*—or, rather, being on his good behavior before other parties, he had confined his bullying to his wife, who was well habituated to it. Iris was the more discredited as an impartial judge of her sister, another neighbor woman claimed, for it was known that she had always been jealous of the younger girl's curly hair and sparkling eyes: and had, upon more than one occasion, loudly quarreled with Eva in the street, and declared she would "gladly see her fry in Hell."

Several girls of Eva's own age, who worked either at the Shaw mill, or at one or another of the South Winterthurn factories, wrung the hearts of their male queriers by weeping as they described their belovèd Eva: who had always a smile, and a witty rejoinder, and ofttimes a present (if only a wild daisy or lily plucked from a field) for a friend; and who was so utterly lacking in guile, it seemed always to break her heart when a cruel or spiteful remark, uttered behind her back, was told to her. True, Eva could not always keep pace with the more experienced workers at the mill, whose impatience she sometimes provoked by her spells of fatigue, dizziness, "sick headache," and the like, particularly as their shift stretched into its later hours; and it was held against her that the foreman sometimes excused her early, or neglected to reprimand her for making mistakes. It was true too that Eva contrived to meet her beaux while telling her mother she was visiting a friend, or attending mass: and that, out of sheer vivacity and playfulness, she sometimes "flirted" in the street, believing herself safe in the company of her friends.

Since perhaps the age of thirteen Eva had let drop hints, of an innocently vain sort, that she had numerous admirers whose names she must keep secret; and, in recent months, she had quite surprised her friends with certain purchases made across the river,—a straw sailor hat with a smart blue band; a pair of charming shoes with mother-of-pearl buttons and zebrawood heels; various cloth flowers, ribands, strips of lace, etc.—which seemed at last to bear out the truth of her imaginings. (Indeed, yes, one of Eva's friends told Mr. Shearwater,—the green poplin dress *was* surely one of these purchases: for it could not have been more than a week old at the time of Eva's death, and had raised quite a storm with Mrs. Teal when it was first brought home.) Eva had coyly hinted of a "gentleman suitor'" and took no pains to hide certain bruises at her wrists, or bumps, scrapes, cuts, etc., on her face,—murmuring only, with both trepidation and delight, and not a little pride, that "members of the masculine sex were so very curious, in their moods of jealousy, and adoration, and again jealousy, one could never hope to predict their behavior—!"

One of the girls speculated that these purchases of Eva's might have come by way of an innocent source,—for there was an elderly woman who kept a tearoom on Fisk Street, and who, though irascible generally, had always admired Eva for her "spunk" and "dash": as for the bruises,—it was no secret that Mrs. Teal, when drunk, beat her daughter; nor did Lyle Beck restrain himself from displaying his bad temper in Eva's presence. (The tearoom proprietress was so shaken by the girl's death, and so in terror of the authorities, she could not even be questioned: but averred only that she knew nothing of Eva Teal,— and could not have recognized her in a cluster of other girls. Eva's mother and brother-in-law, it scarcely needs be said, angrily denied ever having laid a hand on Eva, either in chastisement or in play.)

Though named countless times as a troublemaker in the neighborhood, and a youth "particularly taken with" Eva, the nineteen-year-old Louis, who was variously employed as a stable boy, dock worker, day laborer, etc., cravenly denied having approached Eva at any time; and declared, most outrageously, that he did not know her name; and had not recognized her likeness (this, a charcoal sketch rendered by a local artist) when it was pointed out to him in the *Gazette*. This ill-featured youth, whose cheeks and forehead fairly bristled with pimples, and whose left leg was shorter than his right, as a result of childhood rickets, so vigorously denied all knowledge of the slain girl that he roused the irritation of the authorities, no less than their professional suspicion, and fairly begged, as it were, to be taken into immediate custody. (Indeed, after several hours' interrogation of this young man, which came to as little as that with the half-witted German boy, one of the sheriff's deputies, Norland Clegg, averred that, so far as *he* was concerned, they had "got their man"; and he could wish for nothing more than to be allowed, in private, to extract a full confession from the wretch.)

Yet, as the day's investigation somewhat haphazardly advanced, a host of other names was thrown out to the authorities,—among them (indeed, many times repeated) that of Isaac Rosenwald; and that of Valentine Westergaard, who had been glimpsed, the previous Sunday afternoon, strolling along the south bank of the river with Miss Eva Teal,—or a diminutive and lively young miss who closely resembled her; and—the most malicious suggestion of all—that of Dr. Holyrod Wilts, who had been interrogated at great length, albeit fruitlessly, regarding the death of Effie Godwit, some six months before. (The suggestion that Eva might have had some connection with Dr. Wilts was malicious, indeed, deeply insulting to the girl's memory, in that Wilts was known through all of Winterthurn as the man to see for certain illegal operations; and it was even rumored that he was associated with the Hotel Paradise out at Rivière-du-Loup,—which is to say, the most infamous of the North Country "sporting houses.")

Though Dr. Wilts handily provided an alibi for that shadowy space of time during which Eva had been murdered,—indeed, had he not been absorbed in a twelve-hour poker game at Rock Barrens, with a dozen other gentlemen, including Fergus Barraclough himself?—he submitted with resigned goodwill to police questioning; for he was accustomed to it by now, and accustomed, as well, to walking free afterward. Shunned by such upstanding professional colleagues as Dr. Colney Hatch, his very name spoken with disdain, and usually *sotto voce*, by persons of genteel background, the portly and ill-groomed "physician," who was never without a rank-smelling pipe, had been served subpoenas by many a county grand jury over the years; and by yet more coroner's juries. Still, no formal indictment had ever been handed down against him, and he had never stood trial: his professional colleagues, however harshly they might speak of him amongst themselves, never uttered a word of censure regarding him publicly: nor had one ever stepped forward to testify against him in the matter of divers "suspicious" deaths of females, of clouded reputation, through the years. A most enigmatical person!—who had, it seemed, no office address, in Winterthurn City or elsewhere; nor even any place of fixed abode.

As to Eva Teal,—Dr. Wilts peered at his inquisitors, through gold-rimmed glasses that clutched tight his plump face, and insisted for the fifth or sixth time that he was not only unacquainted with the girl but, may God strike him dead if he lied, *knew nothing of her whatsoever.* He thought it most perverse and unwarranted of the authorities, or of anyone else, to doubt her virtue: for, if she were employed by the Shaws, at that clacking relic of a mill-factory on the river, where, in winter, the girls were in danger of frostbite, and, in summer, of heat stroke (as temperatures in the mill might rise to 118 degrees, on the very worst days), how should the poor thing have had the *time*, if the *energy*, to stray from the path of righteousness? No, he had not known *her*; but if he might offer an unsolicited professional opinion, in confidence,—this murmured with an unctuous smile that revealed a flash of gold fillings—the matter of the penitential position in which the girl was found, the savage brutality of the assault, and, withal, the placement of the cross in the mouth suggested to him an *unmistakable ritual murder*, of a kind once commonly practiced in Middle and Eastern Europe, by Jews.

Having been handily advised by an acquaintance in the sheriff's office,—most likely by Norland Clegg—that his name had, once again, been mentioned in a disagreeable context (for the dashing young Mr. Westergaard had been previously linked, however tangentially, to three or four of the piteous "Damsels of the Half-Acre"), Valentine Westergaard went of his own accord to headquarters, to offer such aid as he might supply in apprehending the "monstrous villain loose amongst us": and creating quite a stir along the lower reaches of Union Avenue, in his handsome two-seater gig, with the crimson damask cushions, and the laminated rosewood trim, and the swaying silver fringe, drawn by a high-stepping dappled mare with braided mane and tail, and driven by Valentine himself. "In any case, it is not *grievously* out of my way," he explained in his mellifluous voice, "as I am wanted at the Racquet Club upriver, for luncheon, precisely at one."

Though genuinely desirous of aiding the police investigation, and, withal, inordinately charmed by the manner of these uniformed persons, so much his inferior in rank, Mr. Westergaard professed some initial breathlessness, and faintness, when confronted with the air of the building: and had to be assured that the "queer, somewhat *rancid*" odor in Mr. Shearwater's office, undetected by the other gentlemen, could not possibly derive from the remains of Eva Teal, as the morgue was some distance away; and, in any case, altogether odorless in itself, as the corpses were kept under refrigeration, and could not possibly decompose.

Mr. Westergaard received this information with a flurry of gratitude; yet begged Mr. Shearwater's pardon, if he yet felt constrained to order one of the men to raise the several windows in the room so far as they would go (which suggestion was immediately complied with): and if he did not linger long in the place. "For there is a perfumy sort of scent, of corruption both bodily and spiritual,—and aesthetic—which wafts about those squalid places, in which Pathos, whether explicitly or by circumlocution, displays itself," Mr. Westergaard hurriedly explained,—raising to his mouth and nose a handkerchief of the most delicate Belgian lace, that he might breathe more comfortably— "against which we gentlemen must steel ourselves: for, as the experience of others has taught, it is *most seductive*."

Though known about town for the fanciful munificence of his dress, said to be provided exclusively for him by a Parisian tailor, and costing a goodly proportion of his income, or allowance (for Valentine, despite his privileged position as Colonel Westergaard's sole heir, was kept "under tight rein" by the elderly man), he seems to have dressed with conspicuous sartorial restraint in venturing down to lower Union Avenue: wearing not a tight-fitting velvet jacket with a cambric ruff, or an embroidered linen shirt, or a flowing foulard tie, or sharply tapered trousers, or kidskin boots of the most delicate eggshell hue, or his satin-lined opera cape, or, indeed, his lavender gloves, which were held up to especial censure by the gentlemen of his social set, while admired by the ladies: but an English-cut tweed jacket, in a subtle aubergine shade; and an ascot of small checks; and spotless white flannel trousers; and, resting smartly on his tight-curled reddish hair, a hat of some idiosyncratic design, in white linen, with a graceful sloped brim and a noble crown, into the band of which a swan's-down feather, dyed crimson, had been inserted. Languidly settling into a chair facing Mr. Shearwater's desk, Valentine chose to remove neither his hat nor his beige gloves; and continued to hold his handkerchief fastidiously to his nose, for the duration of his half-hour visit.

Though it was assuredly not necessary for him to do so, the gallant young gentleman identified himself in full, providing his age (which was thirty-two) and his address (his ancestral home was Ravensworth Park, his private "digs" were at Hazelwit Square, just south of Berwick), in a voice deliberate enough for the stenographer to follow, with no need for repeating. As it was a matter of some embarrassment for Mr. Shearwater to broach the subject of his "whereabouts" on the night of the murder, Valentine graciously anticipated the question, and murmured, with a faint blush of embarrassment on *his* side, that he and several friends,—Roland Kilgarvan amongst them, and, he believed, Calvin Shaw, and Lloyd Poindexter, and one or two others—had just returned from Nautauga Falls, where they had watched some very pretty fillies trot: and Valentine was contemplating a major purchase, if minor points could be worked out, and a small loan arranged,—though, as he hurriedly continued, with a nervous twitch about his shoulders, he did not want it noised about that he was interested in acquiring a certain horse, as parties at the Falls would only take advantage of him. In any case, after their return on Friday evening,—or had it been Friday, after all?—after their return they had a late supper in Hazelwit Square, and played at cards, and drank companionably, well into the early hours of the morning: at which point Valentine excused himself to retire to bed, while two or three of his friends remained at cards. "Or so it seems to me," he said, adjusting his scented handkerchief to his nose, the while his glistening bottle-green eyes traveled from face to face, "for I *was* inordinately exhausted at the time, as my friends will attest: and slept straight through to noon of the following day."

If the authorities wished to verify his "alibi," Valentine said, with an ironical arching of his pale eyebrows, they could of course consult his friends; and they *would* have wished to consult his servants, save for the awkward fact that he had been obliged to dismiss the lot of them a week or two ago,—as it had come to light they were robbing him blind, and taking advantage of his trusting nature and childlike ignorance, in the matter of household finances. Thus it was, his former servants had all scattered,—had, he supposed, fled Winterthurn altogether. On a more informal basis he had recently acquired a footman of sorts,—not an actual footman, in livery, but a young acquaintance, of sorts,—a somewhat rough-hewn person, good-hearted, and not at all badly educated—who unaccountably admired him and liked to hang about his digs, as it were, to chat with him when Valentine was in the mood, and run errands, and the like: but, alas, this amiable youth had *not* been in Hazelwit Square on that fateful night: and no useful testimony was forthcoming from him.

At this point Valentine courteously paused, with a fluttering of his pale-lashed eyes, and a leisurely recrossing of his legs,—and an oblique glance at his bejeweled pocket watch, drawn inconspicuously from his vest. In response to a question put to him, with some hesitation, by Mr. Shearwater, he explained that he had evidently made the acquaintance of Miss Teal,—as, the previous season, he had made the acquaintance of Miss Dulcie Sparks—no, it had been Dulcie *Inman*, had it not, and *Florette* Sparks?—at one or another of those insufferable charity "Musicales" the Winterthurn Assembly sponsored, with the hope of improving the lot of workers by exposing them at a tender age to divers forms of culture. Poor Valentine was so susceptible to the blandishments of elderly ladies, Miss Verity Peregrine in particular, he found it nearly impossible to refuse: and allowed, with a droll twist of his lips, that Miss Peregrine knew well how to play to his vanity, by cajoling him into participating in the program, alongside other amateur *artistes*, though he scarely imagined himself musically gifted—!

As to which Musicale it had been, when the charming little curly-haired shop-girl had sought him out, with the hope, as she phrased it, of receiving counsel from him on a matter of gravest significance to her,—Valentine could not recall: it might have been at Christmas: or then again, at Easter. Upon both occasions he had succumbed to the ladies' requests to sing one or two ditties while accompanying himself on the dulcimer,—which trifling contribution to the evening's entertainment had been, it was said, greatly successful: and so Valentine supposed it must have been, judging by the spirit and duration of the applause. The shop-girls had crowded about him afterward, not unlike butterflies, or pretty moths,—their delicate wings all beating, their eyes aglow—a veritable *greed* for culture evidenced in their faces! Valentine had sung that surpassingly lovely song "There Is a Garden in Her Face," and then, "She Sang of Love," and a modest little tune of his own composition entitled "Shall You Appear, O Evening Star?"—and it pierced him to the heart, and quite moved the Assembly ladies as well, that such a multitude of little shop-girls,—or were they mill-hands?—should fancy that Valentine

sang to *them:* to each of them, individually. "But such, gentlemen,"
Valentine said, with a shrug of his shoulder, "is the mysterious power
of Art."

So it came about, he knew not altogether how, that the girl arranged to meet him, upon one or two occasions,—or it might have
been three—to wangle from him small sums of money, with which to
pay certain debts incurred by her widowed mother: under the pretext
(thus he realized, in sober retrospect) of seeking advice. All wide-eyed,
and girlish, and disingenuous, and beguiling, little Tricia,—that is,
Eva—had inquired of him what course to take, as some elder gentleman had begun to display an unwholesome interest in her; and she
knew not where to turn, as this person (whose name she refused to
give) controlled her livelihood. And if she brought the sorry tale to her
mother, she feared her mother would be angry at *her.*

"There you have it, my friends," Valentine said sighingly, "a
situation not lacking in pathos: yet far less 'special' than the girl
seems to have thought."

Valentine responded politely to two or three questions, put to
him by Mr. Shearwater and his deputies, his somber green gaze moving
from face to face, and lingering a bit on the little stenographer, who sat
to the rear of the sheriff's desk, her eyes downcast, and her fingers so
rapidly moving, one might have fancied them mechanical. His white-
trousered legs were casually crossed, and one small slender foot
wagged arrhythmically, with the sporadic flow of his words,—which
impressed the small gathering of men as most artless, unstudied, and
forthright. It was clear that Valentine Westergaard felt the awkwardness of the situation: the remarkable fortuitousness of his having
known, however slightly and briefly, those girls doomed for the Half-
Acre,—doomed, it might be said, to become the stuff of headlines, and
sensationalist newspaper stories, read avidly throughout the East.
That it was but an accident could scarcely be contested, but, ah, how
queer an accident—! "Indeed, it bespeaks more of the cunning ingenuity of *Art,* than of mere inchoate *Life,*" Valentine broodingly pondered, as, folding his handkerchief meticulously in twain, he signaled
that the interview had run its course. "One is forcibly reminded, however, by the splendid noontide sun, and the fragrant breeze wafting
through the window, of those apt words of our American authoress
Miss Susan Warner,—'What need we of *Art* on a June afternoon?' And
so, gentlemen, if you will excuse me, I must be off."

The enigmatic phrase by Miss Warner was voiced so gently, yet
so compellingly, by Valentine Westergaard, it hung quivering in the air
for some minutes after he had taken his leave; as did the sweet, subtle,
potent fragrance of his expensive eau de cologne.

———

There could not have been a more painful contrast between young Mr. Westergaard, with his exquisite good manners and his eagerness to cooperate with the investigation, and Mr. Isaac Rosenwald,—who, from the first minute he entered the sheriff's office, escorted by a burly deputy, radiated a most disagreeable air: a commingling of alarm, disdain, agitation, and, it might have been, *guilt.*

Seating himself with a show of perplexity, and reluctance, Mr. Rosenwald gripped the arms of his chair, and began at once to speak, in a voice that could not fail to displease, as it was both whining and commandeering. He expressed his shock, and grief, and repulsed horror, at the loathsome crime that had been committed: the fifth crime of its type within less than a year: and a very poor advertisement as to the efficacy of the local police force. A tragedy it assuredly was that Eva Teal had been murdered; an outrage, in his opinion, that it had not been prevented; yet he could not comprehend what connection there might be between *that incident* and *himself.* As office manager for the Shaws, he had a slight,—a very slight—acquaintance with a number of the workers; he knew the foremen somewhat better; yet did not truly know *them* either, as he lived in Winterthurn proper, just off South Wycombe, and never mixed socially with any of the mill employees . . . Indeed, since coming to Winterthurn City from Brooklyn, five years before, he had led a bachelor's existence by his own choice. His landlady would attest to his sobriety, and disdain for frivolous behavior; his employers, he hoped, would attest to his diligence. Moreover, . . .

Thus Isaac Rosenwald rattled on, as it were, in a nervous, irritable, nasal voice, while he remained pitched slightly forward in his chair, and his hands gripped the arms so forcibly, the knuckles whitely glared. He was forty-one years old at this time; yet, withal, younger in manner, and inclining even toward the brash. Mr. Shearwater and his deputies,—and, later, the chief of police of Winterthurn City and *his* deputies—would attest to his *behaving suspiciously* under examination: for did he not shift about in his seat, and did his narrowed dark gaze not leap irresolutely from face to face, fearful, it seemed, of settling anywhere? (An unpleasant impression was produced, moreover, by the cloudy distortion of his eyes, by his glasses: which looked, in the words of one observer, ''like tiny pike lunging.'') Mr. Rosenwald's hair was black, and wavy, and somewhat oily; thinning at the crown of his narrow head, so that the pale scalp glimmered through. His complexion was sallow, and doubtless unhealthy; his nose bony, and thin, though the nostrils were distended, and hairs grew conspicuously within; his lips were of a rich carmine shade, and disproportionately fleshy, the upper lip of an equal thickness with the lower, which is most unusual. All noted with what superciliousness he spoke when, he fancied, *he* directed the subject,—quickly limning for his listeners his educational background, in Brooklyn and elsewhere (which doubtless was impressive to persons who had not troubled to complete high school: for he not only had graduated from college, but had an advanced degree, in business administration, from New York University: and had, for a brief while, attended theological school in Manhattan: and knew, by his own boast, German, French, and a "smattering of Russian")—yet becoming visibly apprehensive when, of a sudden, a line of questioning was introduced that was clearly not to his liking (when, for instance, Mr. Shearwater interrupted to inquire bluntly of him *his whereabouts on the night of June 7*). Indeed, as one of the deputies later confided, anonymously, to a reporter for the *Vanderpoel Sun*, so pronounced a commingling of the *arrogant* and the *frightened* was scarcely uncommon in criminals of the most brutal stripe: yet was a curiosity (or so it would seem!) in a Jewish gentleman with his background, and entrusted to a position of considerable authority by the Shaws.

Mr. Rosenwald's interrogation lasted well into the evening, and became, at times, somewhat heated, as the "suspicious party" sought variously to dismiss the import of the situation, with contempt, and a snort of incredulous laughter; then again, to counter it, with chill sobriety, and a rapid-fire species of logic; yet again, more piteously, to deflect it,—by dwelling upon his reputation (for "reputation" he dared to call it) for upstanding moral behavior, both at his place of work and elsewhere. (When, by their line of questioning, Mr. Shearwater and his deputies hinted that veiled accusations had been made, by other witnesses, as to Mr. Rosenwald's morals,—his lewd advances to the mill-girls, his particular interest in Eva Teal—it was a remarkable thing to note how furious he become; yet, withal, how *frightened*.)

"For it is a matter of common knowledge, is it not," Mr. Shearwater commented,—not, as it was afterward reported in the *Sun*, in an accusatory tone, but in a tone of forthright affability—"that Jews will 'spare' Jewesses their attentions of a certain sort, while pursuing Gentile girls?"

This was hotly and rudely denied: and dismissed as "the most contemptible sort of rubbish,"—which, as one might imagine, scarcely flattered the sheriff of Winterthurn County.

Next, a line of questioning was pursued as to when Isaac Rosenwald had last seen Eva Teal: to which the flushed gentleman applied himself with an inordinate urgency, perched now at the very edge of his chair, and his breathing pronounced in its shallowness. He could not say when he had last *seen* her, if his inquisitors meant, when had his eyes last *alighted upon her:* for, like thirty-odd employees in the shop, all of them females, Miss Teal had doubtless come upstairs to the office, sometime on the afternoon of Friday June 7, to receive her paycheck: which was handed over to her (yes, he had ascertained before coming to the sheriff's headquarters,—Eva *had* received her wages for that week), not by Mr. Rosenwald himself, but by one of his assistants. For this was the usual procedure. For the office manager had more important things to do than to hand out paychecks; and hear complaints and "sob stories"; and deny advances on the next week's salary; and the like. Moreover,—

At this point, Mr. Rosenwald was sharply interrupted, and asked again, a most simple question: *Had he seen Eva Teal in his office on the afternoon of June 7?—however "seen" might be construed.* Whereupon, his thin cheeks flushed in anger, he allowed that he might have "seen" her; but had not talked with her; and had not,—ah, assuredly!—enticed her into his office, and locked the door, and forced his "lewd" attentions upon her.

This display of unseemly irony, or brazenness, was met, for a moment, with shocked silence: whereupon Mr. Shearwater, doubtless intending a coarser irony of his own, inquired of Mr. Rosenwald whether it was his penchant to behave thusly with the majority of the young females "under his thumb," or only with Eva Teal.

Thus outfoxed, as it were, Isaac Rosenwald stared blinking at Mr. Shearwater; and it was some seconds before his parched lips moved,—to indicate that so despicable a joke, in this context, was not worthy of a reply.

"If you choose not to reply, Isaac," Mr. Shearwater amiably observed, "that is your prerogative."

As to the actual evening of June 7,—here, it quickly became clear, Mr. Rosenwald's replies were evasive, and suspicious indeed. For though he had accepted an invitation to dinner with a family named Liebman, of South Winterthurn, and was expected at their home at six o'clock, *he had failed to appear:* and had evidently (for which he was grievously sorry) caused the Liebmans, Mrs. Liebman in particular, some hours of worry, as the woman had taken it into her head that Isaac had been attacked by thieves, or beaten wantonly in the street: such incidents being more and more common in the city in recent years, as the population of South Winterthurn increased, with the rise of the mills. With a flicker of displeasure, as if he resented most forcibly this intrusion into his private life, Mr. Rosenwald told his questioners that he had been reluctant to accept yet another invitation from the Liebmans, not because he disliked them, but because he believed he might be misleading them as to his interest in their eldest daughter; and, since they were the kindest and most generous persons in the world, and worried inordinately,—excessively, he thought—about his welfare, he shrank from taking advantage of them, or disappointing them. Thus, his *reluctance*; as to why he had failed to appear,—the shameful truth was, he had *forgotten*: or had a vague notion that he was expected the following night.

"You had *forgotten* the engagement—?" Mr. Shearwater inquired, with a faint crinkling of his brow. "Yet it has been your boast of yourself, several times today, that you are unfailingly scrupulous in your behavior,—whether professional or otherwise."

"Yes, I forgot the dinner engagement," Mr. Rosenwald said irritably, "which I hope, sheriff, is not a capital offense amongst the citizens of Winterthurn! Albeit, if you speak with the Liebmans, as, I suppose you will, they will tell you another story," he amended, shifting miserably in his chair, "for I was so loath to hurt their feelings, I felt pressed to explain to them that I was taken ill, and went suddenly to bed, to be nursed by my landlady: which of course was not the case, as I spent the evening, until nine-thirty or ten o'clock,—or perhaps a little later—walking restlessly about."

" 'Walking restlessly about,' " Mr. Shearwater said neutrally. "And during this space of time you were accompanied by—?"

"By no one."

"Ah, by *no one!* Yet, doubtless, you were sighted by *someone!*—over a period of three or four hours, in the midst of the city, that would be difficult to avoid."

"I am certain that I was sighted by *someone*, as I walked about," Mr. Rosenwald said in a quickened, nasal voice, "but I scarcely paused to take affidavits from witnesses, sheriff!—and very much resent your line of questioning."

"Yet it might be, Isaac," Mr. Shearwater said, "that you will more resent another line of questioning. Therefore—"

"From about the hour of five-thirty until ten o'clock, or ten-thirty," Mr. Rosenwald interrupted, "I admit to the sin against Christendom of walking about, alone, in the area of Juniper Park,—and along the river—and back to my boarding house by way of Union Avenue: during which time I admit to the sin of being so asocial as to have refrained from entering any of the taverns in the city, it is the pleasure of Winterthurn's citizens to patronize,—in astonishing numbers, on the weekend nights especially. Indeed, the predilection for alcohol amongst certain persons,—the predilection to indulge in it, to drunken excess, in the most noisome sorts of 'neighborhood pubs'—has long baffled me. For even the mill-girls, who have toiled so many hours for their pittance, cannot always resist the temptation to throw it away, as it were, on gin—!''

"And *you* do not treat them?" Mr. Shearwater inquired.

"*I—!* Treat *them—!*" Mr. Rosenwald said, with an expression of genuine repulsion. "I hope, sheriff, I can find better investment to make with *my* pittance."

"In any case, you would say that you 'walked restlessly about,' from approximately five-thirty until ten-thirty, on the night of June 7: that you were accompanied by 'no one,' yet very likely observed by 'someone,'—albeit you cannot provide us with any names," Mr. Shearwater contentedly observed, the while the little stenographer's fingers flew, with, it seemed, a renewed zest. "And though you must know, by way of the newspapers at least, that Eva Teal met her death sometime between the hours of seven in the evening and seven in the morning, you 'resent the line of questioning': and perhaps deem it irrelevant?"

"I am greatly sorry that Eva died; in truth I am stunned by the news," Mr. Rosenwald said, vigorously rubbing his eyes,—his wire-rimmed spectacles, for the moment, thrust askew upon his forehead—"yet I cannot say that the *fact of her death,* no less than the precise *span of time during which she might have died,* has the slightest relevance to me. And that is all I shall say on the subject."

This brave, and even somewhat fiery, speech failed to evoke in Mr. Rosenwald's listeners the precise response he wished: yet, so overwrought had the wiry gentleman become, he seemed not to notice, and rubbed at his eyes the more vigorously, while muttering under his breath words to the effect that "such stupidity,—such incompetence—is not to be believed!"

After a courteous pause, Mr. Shearwater shifted to another subject, and inquired of the "suspect,"—for by now, in the minds of all his interrogators, this severe term was not inappropriate—how he accounted for the fact that several employees at the mill, who begged to remain anonymous, accused him of routinely making lewd and lascivious advances: and of alternately "favoring" certain girls and "bearing grudges against them": traveling about town with them in cabs, and otherwise: *and taking them to the office of an unnamed physician, for an unnamed purpose.* "Moreover," Mr. Shearwater said, in no haste, while Mr. Rosenwald gaped at him with an expression of such incredulousness, one or two of the deputies felt constrained to look away, that they might not burst into ribald laughter, "—moreover, it was reported to our office, by a witness very close to the dead girl, that you *did* have a personal connection with her, however you conspire to deny it: this selfsame witness feeling obliged to say, with a great show of reluctance, and not a little terror at the gravity of her words, that it 'should not surprise her if the Jew at the office had lured Eva away to murder her, for being a good Catholic girl and shrinking from his advances,'—or words close to these." Mr. Shearwater contemplated Mr. Rosenwald, who sat, still, in his attitude of utter shock, the blood slowly draining from his face; and even from his fleshy lips. "Yet I suppose you deem it irrelevant, and unworthy of your time, to comment—?"

After some minutes, when he had recovered sufficiently to speak, Mr. Rosenwald expressed, in a faltering voice, bafflement,— nay, disbelief—that such vile accusations had actually been made: such cruel slurs upon his reputation,—such slander! If uttered at all, they could not have been made by anyone who truly *knew* him: but only by someone who envied him his position, and wished him harm. For his relations with the mill-girls, while never less than formal and businesslike, were, in his opinion, unfailingly congenial: why, he was quite certain they were fond of him,—a small clique at least: who could be relied upon to tell the truth, and set the record straight, if the authorities contacted them.

"As for the notion that I, Isaac Rosenwald, should wish to 'lure' a girl away, for any purpose whatsoever,—that I should know, or care to know, whether she might be Catholic!—*that* is even more preposterous," he said, with a sudden upsurge of feeling, "and I refuse to rise to the bait of commenting upon it; particularly as the slanderer is anonymous."

"So it is a false accusation, as well, that you enjoyed a *personal connection* with Eva Teal?—a mysterious connection, pursued beyond 'business hours,' as it were?" Mr. Shearwater asked.

"Ah,—*that*," Mr. Rosenwald said, in an enfeebled voice, "why, *that*: but was it Eva Teal, indeed, or—another girl, perhaps— I— But was it— *Was* it—"

Thus stammering, and staring with tear-dimmed eyes at the floor, Mr. Rosenwald shifted uneasily in his chair; and seemed incapable of replying, for a full minute or more. Ah, how much the picture of Misery, and Confusion, and Guilt he appeared—! And how intently his listeners regarded him, as if, indeed, he were a rare species of insect,—loathsome, and poisonous, yet, withal, fascinating. One of the deputies here overstepped his position by saying, in a low, challenging voice, that if it was not Eva Teal he recalled, might it have been another of the girls?—the girls of the Half-Acre?

Fortunately, Isaac Rosenwald did not hear this remark, or did not comprehend it, but drew in his breath to explain, with blanched lips, that the incident alluded to had been a simple one,—or, perhaps, a complex one—that it was "off the record," in terms, that is, of his position at the mill: that *his* employers knew nothing about it, as he had not wished to antagonize them by bringing it to their attention. For, as doubtless it had already come out (so Mr. Rosenwald said wearily, with not a little bitterness), relations between him and the Shaws had grown strained of late, for reasons extraneous to this investigation; and, having been "burnt," as it were, in attempting to intercede with them, on the behalf of certain abused workers, he had grown timid indeed; and feared they might have discharged him some months ago, were it not for the likelihood that Mr. Harrier Von Goeler wished to hire him, to oversee his gloveworks. Thus it was, Mr. Rosenwald said sighingly, removing his glasses that he might polish their misted lenses on his sleeve,—thus it came about, all innocently, that he had escorted one of the girls to the office of a young physician of his acquaintance, that she might be treated for a slight scalp wound incurred in the mill: not knowing,—which is to say, not recalling—whether it was Eva Teal or another of the younger girls.

As Isaac Rosenwald was to be interrogated tirelessly on this subject, by both the sheriff and his men and other authorities, at later dates, it were well to present the simple facts of the incident, and to abbreviate the telling. It seems that Eva Teal, never one of the more reliable of the workers, had grown drowsy, or fatigued, near the end of her twelve-hour shift; that her hand had wavered, and her head drooped; that, being hasty in her toilet, she had failed to use enough pins to keep her tresses in place,—with the unfortunate consequence that a strand of hair escaped her cap, and caught in the loom, to be torn out, in the space of an instant, with what fearsome shrieking the reader can well imagine. (For though the girls in the mill,—indeed, in all the mills and "sweatshops" of South Winterthurn—were forever succumbing to accidents, negligible and otherwise, each incident might have been the first, to judge by the horrific screams, sobs, curses, faints, and occasional slaps and blows it provoked: and one might well sympathize with the exasperation of the foreman, who had to contend not only with spilled blood, and broken and severed fingers, and mashed hands, and mangled arms, and gouged eyes, and the like, but with the frequent breakdown of the costly machinery, which invariably retarded production: and which never failed to evoke the wrath of the owners.)

However, Eva Teal was undeservedly fortunate, for her lapse of attention resulted in but a trifling injury,—a bit of hair lost, and a raw spot, no larger than a quarter, on the right side of her head—albeit a fair amount of blood streamed down her smock; and presented a savage and distasteful spectacle. Her foreman was so incensed, he brought her over to the office, that Mr. Rosenwald might discharge her on the spot, and pay her the wages she had earned that week: but, all uncharacteristically (for the "Jewish gentleman" who ran the office was much feared, and generally disliked), Rosenwald took pity on her,—

doubtless for her extreme youth, and simplicity of manner, and the commingled tears and blood with which her costume was stained. "It was my fault, sir, and I am very sorry,—it was my fault, and I am very sorry": thus the weeping girl exclaimed, with the hope of disarming her critic, and winning his sympathy.

So it came about, that Isaac Rosenwald declined to dismiss the terrified girl; and responded with such unusual warmth as to allow one of his office workers to attend to her, in his own washroom; and to use his towel, which became bloody, and unsightly indeed. When, afterward, she presented a more decent appearance, Rosenwald insisted upon escorting her (in truth, by trolley: for he shrank from paying the fare of a hackney cab) across the river to Pinckney Street, that she might receive proper medical treatment; and an infection be avoided. And all this, remarkably, was paid for *out of his own pocket:* and even Eva's weeping gratitude was brushed aside, with some embarrassment and impatience.

(No report of this curious transaction was ever made, officially, for the Shaw family did not hold themselves liable to pay damages, medical expenses, and the like, if an accident occurred in their mill,— these accidents being invariably the result of slipshod work, stupidity, laziness, or outright sabotage, on the part of covert "agitators"; and Eva Teal would certainly have been dropped from the payroll. And, it may have been, Mr. Rosenwald feared more for his own employment.)

As to whether it was true that Eva, either alone or in the company of her blushing girl friends, oft-times found excuses to drop by the manager's office, to wish Mr. Rosenwald a good day, or even to leave a trifling present for him, with one of his assistants, Rosenwald was unwise to deny,—and then to recant,—and again wonder if his memory failed him,—while presenting a picture of extreme unease to his interrogators. For if so many witnesses claimed that it was so,—that Rosenwald had even been heard to call Eva by name, and to smile at her,—why, then, did the gentleman wish to deny it; or to feign a most uncharacteristic weakness of memory?

Near the end of this initial interrogation,—which lasted for more than seven hours, and left the hapless Rosenwald quite fatigued—it was put bluntly to him that all five of the Gentile girls found in the Half-Acre had been viciously mutilated, as if in anger: and that Eva's gold cross had been torn from her chain and placed, doubtless mockingly, in her mouth. Were these savage acts to be construed (as a Winterthurn man of science had suggested) as *ritual murder,* of Jewish origin, performed upon Christians?—for thus Frank Shearwater phrased it, rather more in the spirit of lightsome experimentation than not. Whereupon Rosenwald reacted so extremely,—with such panic, and breathlessness, and a violent tremor of his hand—that he presented a very suspicious figure indeed; nor did his reply, issued in a mere whisper, evoke confidence: "That is preposterous,—preposterous—for everyone knows there is no such thing as 'ritual murder'!"

The Scent of Calla Lilies

So few mourners, apart from their immediate families and a sprinkling of neighbors, had troubled to attend the funerals of Miss Effie Godwit, Miss Dulcie Inman, Miss Tricia Furlow, and Miss Florette Sparks,—the Godwit funeral in particular having been a most niggardly and shamefaced affair, held in a wood-frame Methodist Church, in Mt. Provenance,—that no one, not even Winterthurn's chief of police, might have foreseen the immense crowd, numbering *above two thousand persons*, that attempted to attend the solemn high mass offered for the repose of the soul of Miss Eva Teal, in St. Ursula's Roman Catholic Church, three mornings after her death. Ah, what a barrage of mourners!—of men and women, and even children, so queerly distraught, so white-faced with grief, or apprehension, or anger, or excitement, one might have imagined Eva Teal to have been a prominent member of South Winterthurn's community, and not a sixteen-year-old mill-girl possessed of but a small circle of acquaintances in her lifetime, and no clear reputation whatsoever at her death.

Jostling one another in the street; openly weeping or cursing; thronging into the church's narrow aisles, to push their way into pews; gaping at the white coffin with the brass candles, and the resplendent floral displays, so dramatically placed beyond the altar railing: thus the swarm of "mourners" for Eva Teal, who had, as word of mouth suggested, and the newspapers confirmed, suffered an unspeakable sort of atrocity, at the hands of a Jew: the more outrageous in that the Jew (his name given out to be "Rosenfeld" in the *Vanderpoel Sun*) had not yet been arrested by the police; nor had he even been discharged from his position of sinister power by the Shaw family.

There was even a brief flurry of a rumor,—leaping like wildfire amongst the jammed pews—that the Jew, the murderer, the "Cruel Suitor" himself, was so brazen as *to be hidden there in their midst,* that he might mock Christian grief firsthand: a rumor fortunately laid to rest by the vehement white-haired pastor of St. Ursula's, before any disruption resulted. (For what a catastrophe should ensue if any innocent gentleman, swarthy of complexion, or accursèd with a "Semitic" nose, should have been mistaken for the loathsome "Rosenfeld"—! Even in this sacred place, men were openly murmuring that the Jew should be dragged from his home and hanged, and spared the formality of a trial: for thus the exclamatory banner headlines, and heart-wrenching features, and "confidential" interviews in the *Sun* seemed to suggest.)

No sooner had this invidious rumor been quenched, and a modicum of calm imposed, when the black-garbed mother of the murdered girl, seated at the very front of the church between her married daughter and her flush-faced son-in-law, made a sudden effort to rise, and cried out in breathless anguish, "Eva!—O Eva!" Whereupon numberless persons in the congregation (by no means of the female sex exclusively) echoed her, and succumbed to hysterical sobbing, with here and there the threat of fainting, or actual collapse: so that the priest was once again obliged to climb to his raised podium, and restore order.

Thus, some twenty minutes late, the somber high mass began; with two inordinately small, and clearly frightened, altar boys in attendance; and the priest, in his noble vestments, chanting his Latin in a high, quavering, yet wondrously commandeering voice,—verily a species of exotic mumbo jumbo to some of the spectators, yet withal irresistible.

(Indeed, judging from the gaping and ill-bred manner with which a goodly percentage of the mourners comported themselves, in the church's soot-darkened interior, very few had been acquainted with the murdered girl, or with her family; and not many more were conversant with the arcane Roman Catholic rite. The frequent ringing of an invisible bell startled them; the heavy, pungent, unwholesome scent of incense disquieted; and it was an awkward matter to be always standing when they were meant to kneel, and kneeling when they were meant to sit, and sitting when, of a sudden, like zombies, others rose unhesitating to their feet—! Sonorous and formidable the rich Latin phrases assuredly were, but utterly incomprehensible: and incomprehensible too the rapid crossing motions made by those rapt in prayer,—one or two fingers touched lightly to the forehead, to the breast bone, to the left shoulder, and to the right, with unfailing mechanical precision by children no less than adults!)

There was no mistaking, however, the import of the white, white coffin, surrounded by banks of flowers, beyond the altar railing,—nor the impassioned message of the priest, when finally he left off his Latin to speak English, and a wondrously frank English at that,—

"May God have mercy on the soul of Eva Teal: and may He strike His swift sword of justice against the man,—nay, the *fiend*—who has done this terrible, terrible crime!"

At the rear of the airless church, sitting on the center aisle, with his hat perched on his knee, and his white-gloved hands gripping his cane, Valentine Westergaard observed to a companion that the Popish ceremony was most impressive indeed,—for all that, it *was* comical; and overdone as a carnival ball; and made the bone of the skull vibrate with tedium; and the blood subside; and the nostril's fine hairs bristle, in reaction to the stink. Yet, withal, the hoary-headed old priest was captivating, in his imitation of Jehovah speaking from out a cloud: and the altar boys in their spotless white surplices were irresistible, as Raphael's angels. "*Quite* the religion in which to die, if not to live!" Valentine murmured enviously. "And how quaint to have prayers said for one's soul,—when one has none, I am sure: or, at any rate, that poor child had none."

His young lady companion signaled him, with a pretty frown, to please be still: for though Miss Mary-Louise Von Goeler had consented to come with him to the Teal service, for the secular purposes of "amusement" and "edification," she found herself now deeply moved,—indeed, pierced to the heart; and it was naughty of Valentine to say such things when all the world knew he meant not a word.

So the handsome red-haired gentleman settled himself, with as much grace as possible, in the cramped pew; and stared hard at the costumed priest, and the charming altar boys, and the swinging chalice, and the gilt cross upon which an awkward effigy of Jesus Christ hung; and of course at the gleaming white coffin; and the profuse banks of flowers on all sides,—sent in honor of Eva Teal by a wide diversity of Winterthurn citizens who had never heard of the girl in life, nor would ever have troubled to bestow a second glance upon her. (A simple white linen card upon which *Ravensworth Park* had been scrawled, in Valentine's hand, was affixed to the most exquisite floral arrangement of all: a mass of white gladioli, and white calla lilies, and white mums, and white carnations, and white multifoliate roses of faultless beauty, in the very center of which a single crimson rosebud had been placed, to great effect.)

All surreptitiously, Valentine drew a scented handkerchief from out his vest, that he might dab lightly at his eyes,—in which tears of indeterminate origin *did* well—and shield the lower part of his face, in a casual hope he might be spared the grosser of the odors assailing him from certain of his fellow human beings (who failed to bathe frequently, or adequately); and from the shadowed interior of the church itself, which had witnessed, over the decades, a great deal of purposeless mourning. Withal, Valentine allowed that he found the heady scent of calla lilies most fragrant; most intoxicating; which was invariably the case. Enchanting, too, the wink and glitter of the ornate candles' flames, as they were reflected in the "virginal" white coffin, with a look,—ah, how fearsome! how delicious!—as if the frail soul within were reviving.

So caught up in the spirit of the ceremony was Valentine Westergaard that, by its conclusion, tears did freely flow across his smooth cheeks, and he had quite mastered, to his lady companion's mingled surprise and disapproval, the art of "crossing" himself: two fingers touched gracefully to the forehead,—and to the breast bone,—and to the left shoulder,—and to the right. *Enchanting—!*

"Our Accursèd Profession"

In his twenty-seventh year Xavier Kilgarvan had, all unwittingly, made a modest "name" for himself, as a result of his inspired work on a certain notorious murder case in Manhattan (this, the Senator Halsey–Countess Wielkopolski Scandal, which quite dominated the news of that season but is now forgotten, by all but connoisseurs with an especial interest in dactyloscopy, in the history of crime detection); in his twenty-eighth year he made the curious decision to retreat, as it were, from his own success, and from an embarrassing species of renown,—promulgated with tireless energy by the *New York Journal*; and to hazardously seek a wider type of knowledge, in the area of crime detection, as elsewhere, by embarking upon a most ambitious journey abroad. Alone, with no experience, and very limited funds, the heroic young man chose to visit not only the British Isles and Europe, climes by tradition hospitable to American travelers, but such distant and formidable regions as Western Russia, and Turkey, and North Africa; nor had his intention been to slight the noble vastness of the East (into which, it was lately reported, his friend of schoolboy days Ringgold Peregrine had most mysteriously vanished): for, indeed, did not all the world lay before him,—beckoning to him that he should make no pretense of *comprehending* it, or *analyzing* it, or, indeed, *mastering* it, but only *submitting himself to its wonders!*

Withal, the strenuous journey was abruptly terminated, when, of a sudden, while frowning over a letter of his mother's, forwarded to him in a British hotel in Tangier, Xavier believed he could discern in its words a queer and unsettling malaise *to which Mrs. Kilgarvan assiduously did not allude.* True, she had from time to time discreetly confided in her youngest son that his father, though spending more hours in his workshop than ever, remained thwarted in terms of profits, and oft-times infuriated: for not only was the fastidious crafts-man required to observe how the crudest, flimsiest, and cheapest man-ufactured toys outdistanced his in sales,—nay, soared quite beyond them, as an actual horse, prancing and kicking up its heels, might gal-lop merrily away, to leave a mere rocking horse behind!—but he was constrained to endure, often with a stoicism shading into bitterness, the reasoned arguments of his eldest son that, by taking a bank loan of sufficient magnitude (which Bradford, in his felicitous new position as a vice-president at the First National Bank of Winterthurn City, would aid him in securing), he, Lucas Kilgarvan, might join the race,— *and successfully compete in the marketplace.* And, too, Mrs. Kilgar-van alluded upon occasion to a certain disquiet, regarding the wildly fluctuating nature of Wolf's fortunes at the racetrack and suspected, but not known, irregularities in his private life (for Wolf, now a hand-some young man-about-town of thirty-two, lived in surprisingly luxu-rious "digs" facing the fashionable northern edge of Juniper Park); and was more frank in her maternal worry that Colin, long estranged from the family in certain regards, should grow more estranged still,—and vanish from their lives altogether. (Ah, the vexing riddle of Colin!—the subtly *guilt-provoking* riddle of Colin! Xavier never pondered upon the subject without wondering uneasily how he, Xavier, had in all inno-cence contributed to this queer alteration in his brother's behavior,— nay, in his very soul: yet, torment himself as he would, and did, he had forgotten why the thought should strike him at all; and why he should feel so debilitating an emotion as *guilt*.)

"For am I,—can I be—my brother's keeper?" Xavier bethought himself, thousands of miles from home, "—the more so in that *that* brother, once my closest companion, has scarcely troubled to speak with me at length in a dozen years: and goes his way with the unnerving authority of a sleepwalker, never in want, and never quest-ing."

Well comprehending, with a woman's especial sensitivity, yet with a mother's keen solicitude, how Xavier in his lonely pride yearned to hear news,—ah, any news, be it even treacherous!—of his lovely cousin Perdita, Mrs. Kilgarvan took care to intercalate, in each missive, how this or that suitor was rumored by Winterthurn society to have "advanced," or "fallen behind," in the prolonged competition for her hand: with the adjuratory postscript that Xavier was not to worry himself, with cousinly apprehension, that the haughty girl should err in her choice,—or, indeed, that she would finally make any choice at all. Now Osmyn Goshawk appeared to advantage; now Angus Peregrine; now a beetle-browed Annapolis graduate, of whom no one in Winterthurn had ever heard; now the wealthy Calvin Shaw; now Valentine Westergaard,—but the names were too many, and had the effect of canceling one another. ("For I think it altogether likely," Mrs. Kilgarvan observed, "that neither of old Erasmus's daughters shall ever marry: since a species of distaste, or actual fear, seems to have passed to them, regarding the conditions of Holy Matrimony. And now that they are given a comfortable home with the dowager Mrs. Spies, and have even come into a little money of their own, who in Winterthurn is to gainsay them—? Most unhappy of girls!")

"As to *that*,—the issue of whether Perdita shall marry, or no," Xavier exclaimed aloud, with an irritable swipe of his hand through his hair, "Mother will be proved mistaken one day: for I quite believe it within my power, *if I try but hard enough*, to make her my wife; and to mend her troubled soul forevermore."

Never failing to include local news of a beneficent sort, and brimming with warm tidings from friends and neighbors, Mrs. Kilgarvan's letters yet communicated, between the lines, as it were, of her perfectly executed script, that indefinable air of *malaise*, of which I have spoken: nor did it fail to escape her son that, in recent months, she had all mysteriously ceased urging him to return home soon. (For like many another lady of her time and social class, it worried her inordinately that her son's "grand tour," while assuredly not lacking in cultural richness, might awaken him to other, less agreeable pleasures and appetites; and shake the foundation of his Christian faith.) Many months before, in December, Mrs. Kilgarvan had made glancing reference to a certain crime that had occurred in Winterthurn,—or, more specifically, in that "lawless and godforsaken" region beyond the city, the Devil's Half-Acre;—a crime perpetrated upon a young woman of sordid parentage (the illegitimate daughter, it was said, of the infamous Horace Godwit,—himself newly paroled, after having served but twelve years of his fifty-year sentence), and proven loose morals (being employed as a "chambermaid" at the Hotel Paradise, in Rivière-du-Loup). This "case," Mrs. Kilgarvan made haste to inform her son, was *not* one which would prick Xavier's interest, as it was very different, she believed, from the matter involving the Senator and the Polish Countess, to which Xavier had applied himself with such diligence, and unexpected success, the year before: as naught but riffraff were here implicated; and, more importantly, the sheriff had expressed himself as confident, only the other day, that they would soon arrest the murderer. "How odd it is, and decidedly unwholesome, that I, of all persons, should so much as take notice of 'crime'!" Mrs. Kilgarvan ruefully exclaimed. "For such is the effect,—dear Xavier, I cannot think it but *invidious*—that you and your 'career' are having upon me."

In his reply, Xavier apologized for the sinister influence attributed to him; yet quietly observed that all persons, no matter their goodness and the innate purity of their hearts, must realize that "crime" is scarcely a random and isolated phenomenon in life, but one which *parallels* them,—and is, alas, often contiguous with them. "True, the results are commonly hidden away in the 'Devil's Half-Acres' of the world," Xavier observed, "but the origins,—ah, the origins are often far closer to home!" Thus, though he quite understood how she, and Mr. Kilgarvan, and the great majority of the relatives, disapproved of his choice of a life's occupation, he would not apologize for that occupation, no more than he would reconsider it. For which he hoped she would forgive him!

These matters being aired, Xavier then went on to press for additional news of the Godwit case: had the murderer been taken into custody, had the trial date been set, was it generally believed that the police had assembled strong evidence, etc. To these queries, however, Mrs. Kilgarvan, oddly, failed to reply,—which seemed but an oversight at first: and then, as it happened, two or three letters sent to Xavier were unlawfully confiscated in Turkey, which may have contained the information: until, at last, with the passage of weeks, Xavier quite naturally forgot the subject, in his heady absorption with *his* news.

(And, ah!—how splendid his trip was proving, how rich, how rewarding! Despite the flattering attention paid to him in New York City, where, indeed, his species of detective work was unique, Xavier knew himself but an amateur; a rank beginner; an apprentice or acolyte of sorts, who had a great deal to learn from his betters. Accordingly, he sought out professional colleagues on the Continent, and in England, with gratifying results. The renowned,—and famously eccentric—Alphonse Bertillon not only had made Xavier graciously welcome at the Paris Sûreté, but had given him an audience for many hours, explaining, with a great display of emotion, the methodology of the new science of anthropometry,—or *bertillonage,* as it was alternately called;—and exacting from him a promise, which he gave in a somewhat faltering voice, that he, Xavier Kilgarvan, would be the first to pioneer in the new science in America.* At Scotland Yard, Xavier found himself scarcely less welcome, for there, by an excellent stroke of luck, the young detective's work in Manhattan was already known;

Bertillonage, already beginning to be superseded by the newer science of fingerprinting, at the time of Xavier's meeting with the famed Bertillon, is a method of criminal identification, now quite forgotten, in which suspected criminals were laboriously measured: sizes and shapes of noses, ears, heads; length and breadth of the trunk, fingers, forearms, legs, feet, etc. I hope the reader will forgive Xavier for having failed to lead a crusade in his native country for this cumbersome means of detective work, despite his rash promise.

and his impassioned interest in dactyloscopy,—which is to say, finger-print detection—could not fail to gratify such persons as Sir Francis Galton, who, at Scotland Yard, had "pioneered" in this field. And numerous other new ideas and techniques, in the science of forensics, were discussed during the ten days of Xavier's visit, proving almost too fecund for the young man to absorb. Whether death be caused by fire, or whether a person *already dead* has been cleverly burned; whether hanging be *suicide,* or *homicide;* how a near-decomposed corpse might be identified; newly discovered experiments in testing for the presence, in the bloodstream of a victim, of morphine, or insulin, or divers sorts of "foolproof" poisons; whether there be an actual *physiology of crime,*—argued most convincingly by certain men of science, in England and elsewhere; whether there may lurk within each individual,—as the great Herbert Spencer so forcibly argued—an *older, incoherent, bestial,* and altogether *amoral* "ancestor," scarcely known or intuited by the waking mind, but parasitic upon it, and highly dangerous: indeed, capable of monstrous eructations of violence. These matters, and more beside, were discussed with Xavier Kilgarvan freely and unstintingly; for he must have impressed his English hosts as an altogether winning, and wondrously *serious,* young gentleman.

Even Xavier's firm-stated resolve that he would, through life, keep to a sort of amateur status, and be but a "consulting detective" who had the option of accepting or declining clients—depending, as the youth fervently declared, upon their *moral rectitude,*—did not annoy the professionals: for they quite sympathized with his desire to remain free from all compulsory entanglements. So long as Xavier enjoyed the benefit of a modest annuity, willed to him by his De Forrest grandfather, and so long as, from time to time, he might receive payment for his services,—which was wonderfully the case in his "saving" of Senator Halsey's life—what need was there for him to put himself in harness, so to speak, and become a grim *professional—?* "You are quite right, Mr. Kilgarvan," the chief inspector of Scotland Yard said, with a sigh, "to understand, so early in your career, that ours is, all sensationalist glamour aside, an *accursèd profession.*")

Nonetheless, Xavier's spirits could not have been more buoyant, after these fertile conversations; and he wrote at length, and most eloquently, to his mother, of his secret hope for the future of mankind,—that "crime, if not the criminal heart itself, might someday be eradicated by the *intelligent, pragmatic, and systematic unification of the numerous forces for Good.*"

Ah, how wondrous it would be, if this eradication might come about within his own lifetime!—yet, to be realistic, Xavier supposed he must not expect *that.* "It will be enough for me to know, Mother," he said, "that I have contributed, however modestly, to the *partial eradication* of crime during my career. Beyond that,—why, 'tis God's will, and not man's!"

So it was with dazed dismay that Xavier returned at last to Winter-thurn, to learn of all that had transpired in his absence, to which his mother had not alluded: the initial surprise being sprung upon him when, shortly after disembarking from his steamship, in New York harbor, he chanced to buy several newspapers,—amongst them the excitable *Journal*, which gave a three-column headline, and an illus-tration, to the subject of an alleged "ritual murder, of secret Jewish or-igin," perpetrated not a week before in Winterthurn City: nay, not a single murder as it developed, but very likely *five*, and all by the same man!

Though chastising himself for so doing (as Xavier knew at first hand the cynicism of the popular papers of the day, that cared scarcely a whit for truth, but only for selling copies),—though biting his lip hard, and forbidding himself to be influenced—he did read the some-what incoherent story; and studied the beak-nosed, thick-lipped, heavy-jawed simian likeness of the prime suspect, a "Mr. Isak Rosenfield"; and quite frustrated himself, and caused his stomach to lurch in revulsion, as he tried to extract, from the lurid columns of type, some semblance of *fact*, and *chronological sequence*. (As this early story in the *Journal* is replete with errors, oft of a vicious sort, there is little need for the reader to sully himself, in perusing it over Xavier's shoulder: but it may be of interest to record that naught but a hurried mention was made, at the story's conclusion, that other suspects were said by police to be considered: the focus being on a first-person "anonymous" account, by a fifteen-year-old mill-girl, of her having been "unspeakably and obscenely abused in 'Rosenfield's' very office; and of having seen there a certain filth- and blood-encrusted towel, which, the Jew boasted, was *stained with Christian blood*.")

By the morning of June 13 it was announced by the Shaw family that Isaac Rosenwald had been "permanently relieved" of his responsi-bilities as general office manager for the South Winterthurn mill; by the morning of June 14, the sheriff of Winterthurn County, Frank Shearwater, announced that Rosenwald had been arrested "on suspi-cion of first-degree murder." He was taken immediately to a cell in the county jail, a most unprepossessing building of gray concrete and stucco, to the rear of the Courthouse and not far distant from the county morgue,—trundled away in some haste, and with as much se-crecy as possible, as, even at this early date, the law enforcement officials feared for his safety.

Now all of the Valley newspapers, excepting the staidly conservative *Winterthurn Gazette*, ran three-column or banner headlines proclaiming the arrest: and speculating excitedly on the crime, or crimes. In the *Nautauga Falls Bulletin* it was charged against the suspect that he adhered to "an alien religious dispensation"; in the *Powhatassie Union-Journal*, that he had no religion whatsoever, but prided himself on a "notorious Jewish agnosticism." While the *Vanderpoel Sun* blazoned forth in righteous denunciation of the Hebrew gentleman's "predilection for young and helpless Christian virgins," the *Nautauga Falls Dispatch* revealed fresh evidence of a "cornucopia of sickly, unnatural, and perverse appetites" in the suspect. As Rosenwald's connection with Miss Eva Teal was well established, and a number of affidavits had already been sworn by witnesses placing them together on the "fatal day," focus began to shift to relating in what ways the suspect had been involved with his earlier victims,—Miss Effie Godwit, Miss Dulcie Inman, Miss Tricia Furlow, and Miss Florette Sparks;—and if, and when, and how frequently, he had been sighted in their company. It was held against him in all the newspapers that he had "willfully deceived" a family named Liebman, whose hospitality, over the years, he had accepted; it was hinted that a "romantic betrayal" of some undefined species had taken place between Rosenwald and the eldest Miss Liebman. Even the *Winterthurn Gazette* pronounced it an "unlikely" explanation that, on the evening of June 7, the suspect could account for his actions only by insisting that he had "walked restlessly about" for many hours: returning to his boarding house at nine-thirty, or ten o'clock, or ten-thirty: when in truth (so the *Gazette* had learned, in a confidential interview with Rosenwald's landlady) he had not returned until *nearly eleven o'clock—!* "He was ever a quiet, secretive man," Mrs. Buzard said, "giving no hint of his innermost thoughts, or of his religious practices: though oft-times revealing a most finicky appetite, in the matter of his meals, and whether they be cooked too well, or not enough; whether his mail be perused by the other boarders, or by myself,—an entirely unwarranted presumption. Many a time he returned to his room past dark; and from below one could hear him walking about,—pacing, or *prowling*, it seemed—with a light, stealthy step."

The *Contracoeur Tribune* interviewed Eva Teal's sister, who charged that the suspect had forced his victim, against her will, to accompany him to the office of "an infamous local physician," for "certain unknown services": this, very near the time when the body of Florette Sparks (a resident of Tyre Street, which intersects with Cadwaller) was found in the Devil's Half-Acre. "And ever afterward, until the day of her death," Mrs. Beck said, "my sister displayed evidence of an unnatural fear, though she would not say *why*, or *who* was responsible; and oft-times I observed her saying her beads, or fingering her little gold crucifix, which she wore about her neck, in the hope it might protect her from harm."

The *Vanderpoel Sun* created something of a sensation by running a three-part feature on the history of "ritual murder, as practiced by Jews," from medieval times to the present, with such experts as the Reverend Benjamin Tusk of the First Presbyterian Church of Winterthurn, and Professor of History at Hamilton College John Francis Flood, and Professor Emeritus of Religious Studies at Harvard University Cornelius Jones, amongst others, contributing. (Withal, a controversy arose as to whether blood from the victim must be let *while the body is hanging upside down*, a sufficient distance from the ground: or whether, in modern times, the ritual was performed more handily, with a vessel simply placed beneath the slashed throat to catch the spilling blood. Also, it was unclear amongst the gentleman experts whether a *crucifix*, or a *cross*,—or, indeed, any Christian token whatsoever—was required in the ceremony.)

The editor of the *Sun* held it a curious thing that of the several thousand persons of Jewish heritage in the Valley, not one wished to make an official comment on the custom: *save to deny that it existed at all, or had ever existed!*

It was reported that a grand jury was being hastily assembled to consider the evidence amassed thus far, and to determine whether an indictment of murder in the first degree might be handed down against Isaac Rosenwald,—as public sentiment, stirred by the newspapers, and by a midnight rally in Courthouse Green under the spirited auspices of the Brethren of Jericho, ran strongly in that direction.

These matters Xavier Kilgarvan found most distressing: and shameful: and shameful too, the quality of the police investigation thus far,— whether that of the sheriff's office or, more recently, that under the direction of the local chief of police, Mr. Munck, a portly and irascible gentleman with an uncommonly flushed face. Hans Deck's coroner's report on Eva Teal,—which was made available to Xavier only after several applications—gave evidence of having been filled out in haste; and the coroner's jury, comprised, it seemed, of Mr. Deck's courthouse cronies, had not a single question to ask of the witnesses, the law enforcement officers, and the coroner himself. Thus it was, no expert pathologist had been called in to examine the body: not even to determine whether sexual abuse of any sort had been involved, and semen present: or to ascertain whether the victim had met her death in the Devil's Half-Acre, or had been carried there afterward. The vagueness of the span of time during which the girl might have been killed struck Xavier as unsatisfactory indeed, for, surely, it must be possible to fix a more specific hour,—though several persons with whom Xavier spoke, including Mr. Shearwater, expressed surprise that he should think so. "You must remember, Mr. Kilgarvan," the sheriff said, with a neutral sort of smile, "that you are not in Manhattan at the present time, still less in Paris and London: Winterthurn works according to its own methodology, which has not, I think, very often failed us over the generations."

Blushing hotly, Xavier bit his tongue, for he certainly did not wish to offend: and was deeply grateful that, to his own pleased surprise, the sheriff agreed to release to him a copy of the confidential transcript of the witnesses' interrogations, in exchange for a pledge that he would show the material to no one, and say not a word about it,—"most particularly *not*," Mr. Shearwater cautioned, "to any of this drove of 'crime reporters' who have set upon us."

Xavier carried the weighty manuscript off, with immense excitement, and, within a few hours, had given it an initial cursory reading,—scarcely knowing what to think, or whether, so early in the case, he *should* allow himself a thought or two. (For he had learned from painstaking labor in previous cases,—not excepting his single "famous" case, of which, alas, I have not space to speak here—that it often proved a disastrous temptation to seize upon a solution too quickly: for when passion, and effort, and God's grace of soldierly strength, rushed into a *solution* whereby a *premise* must be imagined, why, it was the very Devil to undo it—! "Nay," he said scoldingly, "Xavier must not surmise that *X*, or *Y*, or, it may be, *Z*,—or, most certainly, *V*—is our 'Cruel Suitor,' for that cannot, so early, be a helpful approach.")

And, moreover, he did have numberless questions to ask of the law enforcement officers, that could not be answered by the transcript: nor by his initial investigation of the Devil's Half-Acre, which, it fairly sickened him to discover, had been so trampled by the curious and the morbidly inclined, since the previous Saturday, that no evidence was to be found. Ah, what fools the police were, not to protect the area!— and what diplomacy and tact he must therefore exert to say not a word of their failure to secure fingerprints from an allegedly bloodstained rock, against which the victim had been propped: and to follow a procedure of virtual idiocy in assiduously washing the blood from off the rock, so far as they could,—that the sight of it not offend the eye!

All courteously, however, Xavier inquired of the sheriff, and of those deputies who had been witnesses, whether, in their opinion, the boulder in question had been *stained* with blood,—or *splattered:* which question provoked both mirth and disquiet, and eventual disagreement,—for three persons swore that it had been stained, while two swore that it had been splattered, and a recalcitrant third, that it had been *dabbed with blood*, as if by a brush. ("Which helps me very little," Xavier reasoned, "for doubtless I put the notion in their minds, and but reap the harvest of my own suggestion.") Yet he concluded that it was highly probable, that the victim *had* been assaulted elsewhere, and brought to the Half-Acre dead, or dying. "Which would mean, then, that a considerable quantity of blood was spilled somewhere else," Xavier thought, with a small pang of certitude, "—and not so very distant from the Half-Acre, perhaps!"

Yet the question of precisely *where*,—and how he might locate it, in all of Winterthurn—quite dazzled him.

His patience was put to a more severe test when Mr. Shearwater somewhat awkwardly informed him, in reply to yet another question, that the dead girl's clothes had been *purposely destroyed*; and not a scrap of lace, or a button, remained—! "For such was Mrs. Teal's request," the sheriff said, "and, under the circumstances, we did not wish to upset her."

"Do you think it would upset her if the body were exhumed?" Xavier asked.

"Exhumed—! When it has only just been buried—!" Mr. Shearwater exclaimed, with a sharp look at Xavier, and a marked expression of distaste. "Why, young man, *I* should be upset under these absurd circumstances."

"But it may prove necessary," Xavier stubbornly said, "that the body *be* exhumed."

"Necessary? How might it be 'necessary'?" the elder man inquired, with equal stubbornness. "It might be requested by the District Solicitor,—it might be requested by my office, or Munck's,—but that it is 'necessary,' I cannot see. Nor can I altogether see, Mr. Kilgarvan, how this matter concerns *you*."

This quick rejoinder stung the youthful detective as much for its abrasive truth as for the insult behind it: so that he felt his face suffuse with heat, as if he were but a boy still, to be handily put in his place. Nevertheless, he thought, "Why, then, I shall *make* you see!—only give me time!"

Here, Xavier rose stiffly to his feet, to shake hands in parting: and believed he could discern, in the frowning Shearwater's manner, a begrudging sort of interest, or affection,—for how many like-minded persons might there be, after all, in Winterthurn?—in all of the Valley? Xavier had once read, and taken to heart, the principle that, since Detection is so inordinately lonely a pursuit, it therefore follows that all detectives are kin. And was there not a brotherly,—or, at the very least, an avuncular—grip in the elder man's handshake?

Thus it was, at the door, Frank Shearwater relented for a moment, and confided in Xavier that he *was* somewhat startled at the way in which the public had wished to leap to conclusions regarding the murder: for it seemed to him, as it seemed to one or two others, that Eva's brother-in-law, the hot-tempered Beck, was a more likely suspect than Rosenwald; and there remained the nineteen-year-old Louis as well,—for this loutish and ill-featured youth could no more account for his whereabouts on the night of June 7 than Isaac Rosenwald: and his continued denial of having known Eva was outrageous, indeed: and a stable boy employed at the livery at which Louis sometimes worked, had reported to the police that, at about the time of the Furlow murder, in March, Louis had slyly hinted, or boasted, that *he* knew something about the Devil's Half-Acre which he would never reveal. "And, as you will see, if you study the transcripts, there are one or two other 'suspects' as well," Mr. Shearwater vaguely said, "—in a manner of speaking."

At this, Xavier expressed surprise that Isaac Rosenwald had been arrested at all. But, it seemed, the matter had been forcibly taken out of the sheriff's hands; for Munck,—and, more importantly, the District Solicitor, Hollingshead—were lately convinced that Rosenwald *was* the murderer of the five girls, and that he would readily confess: for he was being subjected to a severe regimen of interrogation at the present time, under Munck's direction; and showed signs (it was rumored) of wishing at last to cooperate.

"But if he is *not* the murderer, what will that avail them,—or us?" Xavier exclaimed.

Mr. Shearwater responded not at all to this query, as if he had failed to hear it; but, in a somewhat weary voice, with an irritable rubbing of his chin, he reiterated his surprise,—nay, his alarm—at the way in which the "cause" of Rosenwald had been snatched up by so many divers groups: the public; and a good many of his professional colleagues,—not to mention the Mayor, and *his* colleagues; and Winterthurn's Congressman Dorsey, who had already "made a study of the case," he claimed, and would stand behind the police 100 percent; and of course the newspapers, in Albany, and New York City, and Boston, as well as in the locality: as if they should *know*, because the police had *suggested*, that Rosenwald was the "Cruel Suitor"—!

"Yet, Mr. Shearwater, the reason for that cannot be much of a mystery," Xavier drily said, "as Rosenwald happens to be a *Jew*; and, all hypocritical pretenses aside, Christendom has not been overly favorable to Jews through the centuries."

This too the older man failed to hear, or to acknowledge; as he continued to rub absently at his chin, in an attitude of puzzled and vexed contemplation; saying yet again that he was,—well, yes, *surprised* and, it may be, somewhat worried as well: for, though he had known Winterthurn had, in general, greatly feared the murderer, and prayed that he might be discovered,—though, as a law enforcement officer, he had known with what terror certain persons, young girls in particular, had lived these past months—it would not have struck him as a possibility that the law-abiding, and peace-loving, and, withal, resolutely *Christian* community should rouse itself to so immediate a fervor regarding this Rosenwald: who was, after all, but a suspect in the case: and not yet even arraigned by the grand jury, let alone found guilty. Mr. Shearwater confessed that he found it an embarrassing experience simply to walk along the street, as so many persons crowded about him, to shake his hand, and to thank him profusely; uttering such imprecations against the murderer,—the monster—the *Jew*—that he scarcely knew how to respond: and Hiram Munck was meeting with the very same phenomenon, which, beyond the initial surprise, now seemed to gratify. The Jericho Brethren were most vociferous in their thanks, and congratulations, and praise for the police; and, at their rally the other night, which one or two of the deputies felt required to attend, several speeches called for a march to the jailhouse, that Rosenwald be hanged at once, and the county spared the expense of his trial! Of course naught came of this, nor would, as the man *was* under arrest, and would be dealt with in a legal fashion, and *would* be proven guilty,—if he were guilty.

After a moment's silence, Mr. Shearwater observed, in a somewhat altered tone of voice, that it did partake of the miraculous, how things fitted together in the investigation,—how, indeed, a sort of unexpected narrative emerged,—if one began with the premise that Isaac Rosenwald, *and no one else,* had committed each of the five murders. "For a great deal that is now unexplained, and frankly bewildering," he said slowly, "is, by this method, resolved."

Xavier then observed, with an amused grimace, that it was a cumbersome method, surely, and scarcely scientific, or even rational, to *begin* with any such premise, under any circumstances, and work defiantly forward, disregarding the vast multifariousness of contingencies, evidence, alternative murderers, et al., when such factors failed to support the scheme. "For thousands,—nay, millions—of persons *might* have committed these crimes," Xavier said, laughing, "and it will hardly do as police work to choose one, and assemble a case against him. Why, it has yet to be established, to my skeptical mind, that there is but a single 'Cruel Suitor,'—though the odds, as common sense would dictate, are surely in that direction. And, under certain circumstances, as we all know, even outright confessions do not resolve mystery, but make our task at uncovering the truth the more overwhelming, in that history becomes sealed."

Whether Mr. Shearwater was closely attending to these forceful words of Xavier's, which one cannot fault for their wisdom, and for their evidence of an intuitive grasp of the *principle of detection,* or whether some troubling reverie inwardly distracted, he seemed to rouse himself, to say, at the door, his heavy hand descending upon the younger man's shoulder, and his leathery creased skin of a sudden creasing the more, with an expression of fleeting pain: "Ah, indeed!—*yes!*—truly! You are right, my boy, quite right!—ours is an accursèd profession."

The Faithful Maiden

Toward dusk of a preternaturally sultry and airless June day, not a fortnight later, I am sorry to say, the slender figure of the young detective might have been observed climbing, with some guarded haste, the overgrown hill above Volpp Avenue, beyond the weatherworn ruins of the old Quaker church, and into the desolate churchyard itself: his steps so cautious, and his manner bespeaking such vigilance, yet withal such *hope*, it would have required no unusually astute eye to surmise that the young man was a lover,—or, more plausibly, a potential lover—bent upon an assignation; and scarcely, at the moment, a detective absorbed in the pursuit of Truth.

For this was indeed the case: and though I hesitate to present such extraneous information, which cannot fail to perplex and annoy the connoisseur of mystery, and does, in truth, disappoint this chronicler himself, I believe it is necessary in that a more complete portrait of Xavier Kilgarvan emerges, by degrees: his romantic obsession with Miss Perdita Kilgarvan having some parallel (though I am at a loss as to its nature, or how to assess it) with his obsession for the exposure of Mystery itself. For, ah! is he not heroically single-minded, and methodic, and zealous, and devoted, to her who has not, over the span of twelve long years, granted him more than a few words, and a measured smile or two,—a smile that never failed to pierce his heart, though it was rather more guarded than otherwise, and faded as quickly as it appeared? And is there not a hint, in the eagerness of his very posture on this overwarm June afternoon, and in the frowning apprehension of his stare (fixed upon the high stone wall surrounding Mrs. Willela Spies's garden—more specifically, the door in the wall), indeed, in the boyish intensity of his manner, that invites disappointment?

Thus it was, minutes cruelly passed; dusk grew ever deeper, yet brought with it no diminution of the heat, or relief from the unnatural airlessness. As the church bells of Winterthurn City variously sounded, in dolorous sequence, the hour of seven-thirty, and then of eight, Xavier Kilgarvan watched with yet more mindfulness the little door in the wall, which, by degrees, was dissolving into shadow: and drew in his breath sharply when, for a moment, it appeared,—but, alas, only *appeared*—to be opening. In a voice in which manly impatience vied with a childlike air of reproach, he murmured aloud: "Why is she late?—but will she come at all?—but she has promised!—and no one forced a promise from her. Yet *is* she late, for perhaps I misunderstood the time?—and it may be she is unavoidably detained: they say poor old Mrs. Spies has become quite tyrannical in her dotage, and affrighted of death, and must be indulged." And so on, and so forth, in this vein, while he so forgot himself as to pace about in the weedy graveyard, scarcely conscious of the agèd stone tablets and markers close about him, and even underfoot,—fallen, broken, and moss-bedimmed as they were, their Quaker modesty and piety the more effaced by the pitiless passage of time. A casual stroller on the street, or a passenger in one of the carriages that infrequently passed, might well have started at the dim figure on the hill, insubstantial as an apparition: and possessed, it very nearly seemed, of the dogged purposefulness of such.

"She *shall* come," Xavier consoled himself, half in ire, "for I cannot have mistaken the sincerity of her tone, or the appeal of her lovely eyes: and did she not hint that she had an especial message for me, pertaining to the Teal case? Teal, alas, and the others—!"

(Though in the same instant he severely bethought himself, as to how his sweet cousin could possibly have any information, or any advice, to tender to *him* on so disagreeable a matter.)

No need for him to pace about so restlessly, and to allow his pulses to flutter, for, indeed, it was self-evident that Perdita *would* come by stealth to meet with him in the Quaker churchyard, if she had so promised: and, all amazingly, she *had* promised: and even shyly returned the light squeeze of his fingers, and gazed, for a remarkable moment, directly into his eyes,—no matter that, all about them in the Peregrines' gilded drawing room, others continued amiably to chat, and to put frivolous questions to one another, above their tea cups. Ah, how beautiful she had been, attired all in white muslin, with tiny lavender rosebuds stitched to her bodice, and to the hem of her voluminous skirt!—her chestnut-brown hair framing her delicate face, and her eyes darkly aglow, and her nose so charming, with its distinctive Kilgarvan crook!—Xavier's cousin, yet so pronounced a stranger to him, and, withal, so "strange" in her aura, it might have been that he had never gazed upon her heretofore, or heard her exquisite name pronounced. Nearly of his height, and with the subdued radiance of the midsummer moon, Perdita was far more comely of form, and assuredly more graceful, than she had been as a mere girl of twelve: now an accomplished young woman of four-and-twenty, of excellent family, whose hand in marriage was eagerly sought,—so rumors spread daily through town, overlapping and contradicting one another—by a gratifying diversity of gentlemen, both old and young, and unfailingly "eligible": as Xavier could not, in truth, consider himself eligible, with his meager annuity and doubtful prospects. Yet it seemed to him not at all farfetched that he alone might win,—or might already have won—her heart: and that his success in solving the murders, if it came at all, might,—ah, he knew not *how*, nor *why!*—bring with it some sort of financial largesse.

(As to his personal attractions: though Xavier Kilgarvan was by no means a creature of preening vanity, like certain Winterthurn gentlemen of the younger set, he was not afflicted with that tedious disability, *false modesty;* and had known, from the cradle onward, that he possessed a rare species of masculine beauty, or charm, that could not fail to please,—or, at any rate, to intrigue—the opposite sex. At twenty-eight years of age he might be said to be at the very zenith of his attractiveness; and could surmise, from the response of young women both abroad and at home, that he cut a striking figure indeed, being of slightly above moderate height, and lean, and lithe, and muscular,—though not to excess, which is always displeasing to the civilized eye: possessed of smooth olive-tinged skin, inclining, when he was in roused high spirits, toward the warmly rosy: and given to a most engaging and artless smile that quite banished all evidence of brooding from his features. The fine-sculpted look of his cheekbones, nose, and lips was even more pronounced, and more compellingly "classic," than it had been when he was a lad of but sixteen years; the opal-gray dreaminess of his stare, no less arresting; yet, it must be said, since the age of twenty-five or so, his propensity to frown, and squint, and grimace, with the vexatious rigor of thought,—for, alas, the youthful detective was always *figuring matters out*, whether they were of any significance or no—had begun to take its toll: and fine, white, near-invisible lines, discerned as yet only by his attentive mother, oft-times appeared on his brow. An habitude toward *absentmindedness* in social situations had earned him, in certain quarters, the reputation of inclining toward the eccentric,—albeit the fetchingly eccentric: for even when Xavier Kilgarvan's mind was clearly elsewhere, puzzling over clues, and plotting out situations, and trying on, as it were, viable "suspects," he was never rude, or impolite, since his Kilgarvan good manners were inbred in him; and behavior that in some persons is arduously acquired seems to have been, in Xavier, instinctive. It is true, his air of childlike simplicity had long since faded, just as his lustrous dark hair was less curly than it had been in his boyhood,—indeed, less thick and springy withal, as, when he lay abed with brain fever, a considerable quantity had fallen out, and had failed to grow back to its former healthsomeness. A faint, near-imperceptible, yet eerily luminous scar, of the size of a pebble, could be discerned at his left temple, near the hairline,—the legacy, as it were, of his horrific experience in the attic of Glen Mawr Manor, a dozen years previous; and an object of some annoyance to Xavier himself, who fancied it must be more prominent than it was, and particularly distracting to young beauties like his cousin Perdita. "Yet the wretched mark is my 'baptism,' for better or worse," Xavier gravely consoled himself, "the sign of my dubious wisdom,—indeed, for better *and* worse." In his years as a student at Harvard College,—where he had studied, with varying degrees of zealousness, such subjects as History, and Mathematics, and Physics, and Chemistry, and Psychology [Professor James's theories of the "unconscious" being particularly intriguing to him], and English Literature, and Philosophy from the Greeks to Spinoza and Kant, and the Classics, and Archaeology, and, ah! what did young Xavier Kilgarvan *not* take up!—he had come to see that all the academic disciplines were paradigms of the detective's search for Truth: that life itself might be imagined as a pursuit,—a hunt—an impassioned quest—requiring both diligence and bravery, and not a little resignation, as to the nature of one's "baptism." For Xavier Kilgarvan, even as a youth in his twenties, was too reasonable a person, and too obedient to God's will, to regret any necessary loss of innocence,—so long as it was balanced by wisdom. Indeed, since that fearsome morning when, all unprepared, he had gazed upon the very face of Death in the county morgue, he believed he had come a gratifying distance, and had learned a great deal: albeit he supposed himself but a novice in the vast field of crime detection, as in life itself, set beside his seasoned and stoical elders. "Yet, perhaps, with Perdita beside me," Xavier excitedly murmured, "I shall possess the courage to do virtually anything: and to fulfill the destiny God has chosen for me.")

Thus is it ever, the appeal,—nay, the forthright *prayer*—of youthful Love!

Though from time to time, as it were casually, Xavier sent a card, or a brief letter, to both his girl cousins,—most particularly from his recent trip abroad, when he sent a half-dozen cards bearing succinct and resolutely "impersonal" messages—it had happened that, within the space of twelve lengthy years, Xavier and Perdita had met but a few times, and always in the presence of others, when communication of any significance was impossible; and the hapless Xavier found it most difficult to interpret his cousin's glances, and shy chill smiles. "She is fond of me, that is evident,'' he thought, ''and it is impossible that she should not sense my feeling for *her.* Then again, alas! perhaps I am mistaken, and it is as people say,—the Misses Kilgarvan will never marry, or even allow themselves to become engaged, as they fear and abhor men: and I cannot help it that I, who would only adore and honor her, am a *man—!''*

The ''Misses Kilgarvan,''—late of the accursèd Glen Mawr Manor—were rather more whispered of in Winterthurn City than, in truth, they were actually known: for, following immediately upon the death of their sister Georgina, the girls were taken up by pitying relatives in Contracoeur, and then in Nautauga Falls; they lived for a full year with Miss Clarice Von Goeler, who, as the proud executrix of ''Iphigenia's'' poetical remains, was assembling a volume of the late poetess's work; they attended various schools for girls of good family,—amongst them the Rockport Seminary for Young Ladies, in Rockport, Massachusetts; and the Dundee School in Cornwall, Connecticut; and Miss Chernsworth's Finishing School in Albany, New York. Judge Kilgarvan having died virtually intestate, his financial affairs in an alarming tangle, the girls could count on no reliable income from that source: nor did anyone wish to purchase the Manor: and when Simon Esdras's idiosyncratic will was deciphered, it seemed that the philosopher had chosen to leave his badly attenuated fortune, and ''forthcoming proceeds from on-going editions of the *Treatises,''* not to his pauperized nieces but, most remarkably, to his younger half-brother, Lucas Kilgarvan,—who had been, it was now generally acknowledged through town, grievously cheated of his rightful inheritance, many years before. (Lucas Kilgarvan is to be forgiven, surely, for his somewhat cynical response to Simon Esdras's belated thoughtfulness, as the ''fortune,'' after taxes, attorneys' fees, court costs, et al., came to naught but $119.09; and the several *Treatises* had fared so poorly with the reading public, it was discovered that the author yet owed his printers money,—well beyond the sum of $119.09, as Lucas's luck would have it. ''Now I am twice damned,'' Xavier's father exclaimed, with a laugh of angry resignation, ''for I find myself no less penniless than I was, as a 'wrongfully disinherited' son, while burdened now with the reputation of being an heir to a considerable fortune—! May the Devil take all philosophizing,—and all philosophers to boot!'')

As to Miss Von Goeler's selfless project, *The Collected Poems of ''Iphigenia,''* in three slender volumes,—this publication was financed wholly by Clarice herself, and no costs were spared, in seeking out the most skilled printer available (in New York City, as it turned out), and insisting upon the finest quality of paper, type, artwork, etc., with covers in a richly dark crimson calfskin, and letters in Gothic gilt of a most arresting design. As the tragical poetess

had scribbled well beyond five hundred poems, in addition to those she
had published, and these were in creamy-rose stationery packets, with
the Glen Mawr seal at the top and gay-colored yarn looped through the
spines, Clarice had instructed the printer to preserve this homely for-
mat, so far as he was capable: and to scatter throughout the pages of
the three volumes certain pencil sketches, and pen-and-ink drawings,
that had been discovered amidst Georgina's papers. Her exacting toil,
over a period of many months, in editing "Iphigenia's" poems, was, as
Clarice repeatedly told the curious, purely a labor of love: for she had
little doubt not only that Georgina Kilgarvan possessed a rare species
of poetical genius, but that, one day, the public should discover it,—
and buy the *Collected Poems* in great quantities. Toward that end, she
had arranged it so that all the profits would go to Thérèse and Perdita,
and not a penny to herself: a provision that had inspired initial mirth
in observers, who could not fancy such barbarous verse selling at all,
but that was met with deep gratitude on the part of the sisters, who
could count on very little income from any source,—until such time as
they might be wed, when, it was promised, old Mrs. Spies would provide a dowry of modest proportions. (Though Thérèse had excelled in
school in such demanding subjects as Greek and Latin, and had a particular flair for translation, it was considered by Willela Spies to be in
bad taste for the twenty-six-year-old woman to seek gainful employment in Winterthurn, as if, in Mrs. Spies's words, she were but a common shop-girl: and it was all poor Thérèse could do to arrange to give
tutorial lessons, for a token fee, to the sons and daughters of the well-
to-do. As for Perdita herself,—she had been overheard to murmur, in
one or another Winterthurn drawing room, that, had she a "stake"
with which to begin, she might as readily make her fortune by betting
on the horses, like the gentlemen, as by seeking out someone to marry.
"For if gambling be a sin against God," the impetuous young woman
said, "is it not a far more grievous sin to gamble one's very *self*, than
merely with money?")

     At the Peregrines' tea the previous day, Xavier had managed to
disguise the inordinate excitement he felt at meeting Perdita once
again: yet, so flooded was his very being with sensation, which moved
like splashes of warm sunshine through him, he could scarcely speak
to her, save to murmur perfunctory words and phrases; and to offer
compliments of a familiar sort. Ah, what a vision the girl presented, in
her full, rustling, sweeping white muslin frock, so very prettily decorated with lavender rosebuds, and ribands of lavender velvet!—her
gleaming hair artfully arranged in bands, and braids, and spit-curls,
and poufs, the better to set off her heart-shaped face—and her manner
an exquisite mixture of the grave, and merry, and sly, and innocent,
and the coquettish: very unlike her sister, who comported herself with

somber dignity, and smiled but sparingly. It was said of Perdita,—indeed, Xavier had first heard the tale from his brother Wolf, who had it on good faith from Miss Amanda Shaw—that while an innocent girl of sixteen, at the staid Rockport Seminary, she had so inflamed the passions of a Mathematics instructor thrice her age, that the unhappy gentleman had had to be finally discharged from his position at the school, thereafter to lapse into the lethal vice of alcoholism: this tragedy having evolved, evidently, *with not the slightest shred of awareness, let alone intention, on Perdita's part.* (For, despite certain saucy mannerisms,—rolling her eyes, sniffing loudly, smirking—Miss Perdita Kilgarvan was acknowledged, by even those classmates who hated her, to be a good Christian girl: as chaste and pure of spirit as of flesh; and quite guiltless of caring a whit to attract the opposite sex.)

More recently, since returning from Europe, Xavier had been intrigued by clouded rumors of a secret engagement Perdita had unwisely entered into, with the ne'er-do-well eldest son of the Versfields of Philadelphia and Nag's Head, New York,—which is to say, the fabled Versfields of the old whaling and shipping fortune:—an alliance that resulted in catastrophe, and actual death, so far as the impetuous young gentleman was concerned. (The Versfields had so strenuously objected to their son's choice of a wife, he had taken his father the Commodore's sloop out alone, under the influence of alcoholic spirits: with the consequence that a sudden gale arose in the Sound, and the sloop was overturned, and wrecked, and young Versfield drowned . . . Or so one version of the scandalous tale went. Xavier had been both amused and vexed to hear a variant, in which a triangle of sorts had arisen amongst Perdita, her unacknowledged fiancé, and his younger brother: whereupon both brothers, besotted with liquor, had taken out the sloop, to fight a duel upon its heaving deck: and again the sloop was overturned in a gale, with, this time, the deaths of both brothers . . .) Thus it was, Xavier could not forbear politely inquiring of Perdita, in a lowered voice, whether she had recovered from the shock of a "certain untoward incident, of which he had heard,"—with the result that the chestnut-haired beauty had stared at him in some puzzlement, her gaze frank and direct, and her manner altogether guileless, as she assured him she knew not precisely what he meant: and hoped he did not make reference to the several tragedies of a dozen years ago,—which is to say, the deaths of her father, and her uncle, and her half-sister—which, with God as her witness, she fervently hoped she would *not recover from,* as such would be evidence of a shallow soul, indeed.

Shortly thereafter the social event became distinctly unpleasant for Xavier, as Mrs. Willela Spies, grown stout, and arthritic, and hard of hearing, evinced far more curiosity than Xavier found comfortable pertaining to his "career," of which the lady had heard jumbled and comical reports. Speaking in a veritable voice of brass, Mrs. Spies interrogated the blushing young detective as to whether it was true that he had worked closely with Scotland Yard, in pursuit of the notorious fiend Jack the Ripper: and whether it was true, as her London relatives had said, that the fiend had finally been discovered to be "of Hebrew stock." Xavier was not so discountenanced by this nonsense as to fail to speak in a forcible voice in reply: to explain,—alas, to the entire drawing room, which had paused to listen—that he had certainly *not* been involved in the search for Jack the Ripper, since the investigation had occurred years before; and that the six murders attributed to "Jack the Ripper" had most likely been committed by a Russian military surgeon who had lived, for a while, in London's East End, under a diversity of aliases: and who was, it seemed, suspected of an unsolved Parisian murder as well, involving a woman of the streets barbarously slaughtered. The madman had escaped London, and was presumed to have returned to his native land; and was assuredly *not*, Xavier said, of "Hebrew stock."

Undeterred, Willela Spies pursued her subject, though it was scarcely appropriate in Shadow-Wood House, in mixed company: now bluntly alluding to Winterthurn City's own "Jack the Ripper,"—and what a vast relief it was, for the womenfolk in particular, that the monster had been at last apprehended. In this, the room generally concurred; and even Xavier's mother, who surely thought the topic distasteful, and would never have commented directly upon it, joined in the consensus. Whereupon Xavier, for a moment forgetting himself, rose to his feet and declared that, in his opinion, the "monster" had not yet been apprehended: but was still at large. "For the investigation has scarcely begun," he said, "and the case against Isaac Rosenwald is so shoddy as to be comical." Doubtless he spoke rashly, carried away by the exigencies of the moment, in stating that no reliable grand jury would hand down an indictment against the luckless suspect, at least on the basis of the evidence at hand: and, if they did, no honest prosecuting attorney could prove his case: and no jury would find the man guilty. "For it is naught but ignorant passion and prejudice that have railroaded Rosenwald to jail, at the present time," Xavier said firmly, "and these are not, I hope, sufficient to find a man guilty of murder in the first degree, under our law."

Ah, what a storm was thus released, in the Peregrines' elegant drawing room!—for not only did the disagreeable Willela Spies object to Xavier's forthright statement, but numerous others, including the Reverend Harmon Bunting and his mother, Mrs. Letitia Bunting, and all of the Von Goelers who were present, and Mrs. Shaw, and elderly Colonel Westergaard, and the canny Henry Peregrine, who antagonized Xavier by asking, "If the Jew Rosenwald is not the murderer, then who is?—for someone, after all, is guilty!"

Though much aroused by this ignorant remark, Xavier managed to calm himself, and to hold his tongue; for he knew he was obliged to exercise greater prudence than to discuss the case in so casual a setting,—as if it were but drawing-room conversation, and not a matter of the greatest significance. Had he not already spent hours,—nay, arduous days—of his time, puzzling over the probable chronology of events leading to the murder of Eva Teal; had he not brought several raging headaches upon himself, in attempting to make sense of the divers coroner's reports, transcripts, et al., pertaining to the Teal murder, and the murders of the other young women,—these documents, it scarcely needs be said, giving evidence of shockingly inept police work; had he not suffered a veritable cornucopia of frustrations in seeking out such personages as Mrs. Teal, and Mrs. Iris Beck, and Lyle Beck, and the ratlike Louis (who continued brazenly to deny that he had ever set eyes upon Eva Teal), and Rosenwald's landlady, Mrs. Buzard (who had of late seemingly invented an "Isaac Rosenwald," to serve up to journalists,—and a most suspicious character he was, indeed); had he not, sometimes in disguise, ventured into the malodorous neighborhoods of South Winterthurn to speak, as it were idly, with whomever he might encounter—? All artlessly Xavier had put questions to a dozen or more of Eva Teal's co-workers at the mill; and her foreman; and random parishioners of St. Ursula's,—who had, alas, proffered wildly conflicting versions of the murdered girl, and the suspect Rosenwald. He had sought, but had failed to find, the redoubtable Dr. Wilts; he intended very soon to seek out Valentine Westergaard, who was, at the present time, said to be visiting relatives in Newport, and sailing, and playing polo,—quite as if nothing had transpired in Winterthurn to give him pause, and to subdue his naturally effervescent spirits.

Was Valentine Westergaard the "Cruel Suitor"? Might the answer to the puzzle be as simple, and as terrible, as that—?

Thus Xavier brooded, while about him the other guests continued to talk, and most outrageously: veering from the subject of Rosenwald to that of an essay in the current issue of *McClure's Magazine*, by one Burton J. Hendrick,—"The Great Jewish Invasion of America"—which Eberhard Von Goeler had read in its entirety, and pronounced highly informative; from this to the subject of "ritual murder": and the employment of Christian blood, in matzo bread, during Passover,—though no one present knew what either matzo bread or Passover was. As one of the murdered girls had been employed in the kitchen of Shadow-Wood House, and her brazen advances had, it seemed, so dismayed young Ringgold that he had felt obliged to leave,—alas, to leave the very country, and to travel God knew where!—it was natural that Henry Peregrine speak for some impassioned minutes on the subject, though, by his own admission, he had never set eyes upon the girl; nor had Ringgold ever spoken of the matter directly to him; or (evidently) to anyone. After a pause, during which the ladies assiduously fanned themselves, the white-haired Colonel Westergaard spoke ramblingly, albeit reproachfully, of a similar problem that had transpired at Ravensworth Park some years previous,—this, the wanton advances of a chambermaid of tender age, no more than fifteen, toward poor Valentine, who had, in the privacy of the Colonel's library, dissolved into actual tears at the shame and confusion such behavior provoked in him. "Ah, it came to an unfortunate conclusion, as I recall," the Colonel said, sighing, "—yet, on balance, I would rather suffer the blight of some small scandal than lose my only grandson to the Far East, as, it seems, poor Henry has lost his son."

From this, the subject drifted to that of the loose morals and unnaturally precocious experience of certain young women of the lower classes; and the pity of it, that the "Cruel Suitor's" victims were so lost to all decency, and, withal, so careless of their own lives, as to venture into the Devil's Half-Acre with the apelike Rosenwald, or with anyone at all. Some genial attempt was made to draw Xavier Kilgarvan back into the conversation (for the disapproval of his furrowed brow could not be mistaken, nor the nervous drumming of his fingers on the arm of a chair), as Henry Peregrine inquired of him whether it was the most advanced European theory, or no, that a propensity toward crime was *inherited*; and whether certain unmistakable *criminal characteristics*,—long limbs, protruding ears, thin upper lips, low brows, simian features, et al.—might be discerned, to alert police, and the public, as to who criminals in their midst might be. Though he surmised it but a transparent ploy to placate him, Xavier did speak for several minutes, in a reasoned, and altogether lucid, manner, as he thought the issue a crucial one: and most misleading, as the theories of Cesare Lombroso (who had tirelessly measured the skulls of many criminals, and noted their "animal" characteristics, in the 1870s) were now largely discredited. Albeit he had meant to say but a few words, Xavier found himself developing his position: that while ignorant, inept, frequently brutal, and easily solvable crimes *might* be likely to be committed by "animal-like" personages, it was often the case,—ah, in his limited experience, it *was* the case!— that crimes of greater cunning and subtlety were likely to be committed by persons who gave every impression of being wholly human, and civilized, and even, upon occasion, refined. "As to the 'Cruel Suitor,'—one cannot help but recoil in disgust at the nature of his horrific crimes: for, in the five murders we know of (I should not be surprised, in truth, if there have been more), there is not only the irremediable fact of Death itself, but the fact of the murderer's marked anger, as if he disapproved of his victims,—in somewhat the way certain persons in this room disapprove—and wished to punish them. A monster, it is said; a madman; a fiend. Yet I suspect," Xavier said, with hot-flushed cheeks, "when he is finally captured, the 'Cruel Suitor' will prove no more monstrous, or mad, or fiendish, than any one of us here assembled."

Which astringent observation, it scarcely needs be recorded, struck a most disagreeable note in the Peregrines' drawing room.

As the church bells through Winterthurn City began, yet again, their cruel tolling,—sounding now the hour of eight-thirty—Xavier sternly admonished himself for playing the fool, and for having waited so long: as Perdita had clearly chosen not to meet with him, or was unavoidably prevented from so doing, by one or another exigency of Mrs. Spies's household. Thus he was about to turn away when, of a sudden, his pulses leapt at the vision,—ah, how long, how steadfastly, awaited!—of the garden door opening at last: and a slender, lithe, enshadowed female form gliding through.

Her magical name escaped from his lips, unbidden; and, scarcely knowing what he did, Xavier hurried down through the churchyard, like a man lapsed into an enchantment: stumbling against the tilted and broken grave markers, and not minding that mischievous briars gripped and tore at his trouser legs. "Perdita—" he murmured, his hand pressed flat against his breast, as if to placate his tumultuous heart. "As you had promised, so you *are* come—!"

He would wrap her in his embrace; he would clutch her tight; he *would* press his heated lips against hers,—for thus his manly pride, no less than his desire, bade him. For he quite believed,—nay, was he not convinced, to the very roots of his being?—that his sweet cousin harbored feelings for him of a like urgency, and strength, as his for her.

Thus Xavier made his way, with blind and precipitate haste, to the stone wall that bordered upon the Spies property, while the ghostly female figure made its more restrained way to him,—and it was not until but a few yards separated them in the sultry midsummer gloom that Xavier's staring eyes forced him to acknowledge all that his pounding heart refused: that this young woman was not Perdita, after his long wait; but in fact Thérèse, the older sister, she of the dour pallid skin and great mournful eyes—!

A most humiliating surprise, indeed; and so injured did poor Xavier feel,—and crestfallen, and numbed, and shamed, and very slightly touched by anger, that, for a minute or two, he could scarcely attend to the young woman's profuse apologies, and her abashèd, even cringing, expression, as she sought to explain that Perdita was "indisposed," and had taken to her bed early; and that she, Thérèse, had been sent,—ah, she knew how inadequately!—in her place, to make this heartfelt apology; and to deliver a missive.

Dazed as he was by this painful reversal, and wounded, like a child, to the heart, Xavier yet recovered enough poise, or semblance of good manners, to thank Thérèse for her solicitude; and even to make some mechanical overture toward conversing with her,— for, after all, Thérèse *was* his cousin, no less than Perdita; and he *did*, he supposed, feel a dim stirring of affection for her, or, at the very least, interest: for he knew she was generally believed to be of uncommon intelligence, and wondrously well read, and, withal, the very pillar of kindliness, generosity, and Christian piety. And she had once,—had she not?— given him aid, in some near-forgotten minor matter, up at Glen Mawr Manor many years ago.

So it was, standing most awkwardly in the derelict melancholy of the old Quaker graveyard, amidst brambles, and shattered granite, and vexatious mosquitoes, Xavier gallantly refrained from asking for Perdita's missive at once, that he might (as his yet-palpitating heart urged) turn away to greedily peruse it: inquiring in a voice that betrayed but a token of the sharp disappointment he felt, as to Thérèse's health,—and that of Perdita: and making glancing mention of the tea laid out at Shadow-Wood House the previous day, which his mother had greatly enjoyed, save for the introduction of a certain distressing subject, and the animadversion roused against Xavier; which, he allowed, surprised her far more than it could ever surprise *him*. "Yet I suppose I should apologize, to you and your sister, if not to the others,—ah, hang the *others*, they are such bigots!" Xavier said, half-laughing. "For I did not mean to willfully upset the ladies, with a dilemma here in Winterthurn, of which they can be expected to know very little."

This forthright speech surely struck poor trembling Thérèse to the heart: for, as the reader will recall, she had, a dozen years previous, fancied herself in love, *and most irrevocably so*, with her dashing cousin: and being the most haplessly faithful of maidens, she had nursed, and tended, and shrunk from, and exulted in, and despaired over, that potent fancy, or emotion, through the intervening years!— for not even the most craven and unabashèd pleas to Our Heavenly Father had secured her release. Yet Xavier's actual presence,—not fancy, not dream-phantasm, not vaporous memory—so discountenanced her, she could not fully attend to his words; and most gracelessly handed him Perdita's letter; and then said, as if snatching haphazardly, and somewhat desperately, at a subject to detain him: "Ah, a dilemma?—it is a dilemma? A *dilemma*, Xavier, you say—?"

Whereupon Xavier, giving the stiff envelope a furtive caress, as he slipped it into his vest pocket, made the somewhat disjointed reply that whereas most crimes are but crimes, though upsetting enough, and crying out for reparation, the "Cruel Suitor" presented a dilemma as well: for where public sentiment so furiously urged punishment upon a suspect (and that luckless person, as the authorities neglected to point out, but one of several), it would be a tricky business to save him from the noose,—unless of course the actual murderer was apprehended, within a few months; and made to confess. "Which, considering his low cunning," Xavier commented, "strikes me as unlikely, indeed."

So intently did Thérèse stare at Xavier's face, so greedily, as it were, did her starved eyes seek to absorb him, she failed to grasp the import of his words; albeit she nodded a ready assent, and, despite the sluggish warmth of the June evening, hugged her linen jacket close about her, as if she were overcome by cold. "Ah, it is a tragedy, then,— I mean in potential,—a *dilemma* and a *tragedy* both," she said, with a slight stammer, "and we are obliged to pray to God for guidance, if the gentleman,—I mean the Jewish gentleman—for as you have called him a 'gentleman,' Xavier, I am sure he *is:* if he, whose name I seem to have forgotten—if he is innocent, as—as—you seem to imply."

"Then again," Xavier distractedly said, "he *may* be guilty: for I have often been astonished, in both my limited experience with crime and my somewhat more ambitious reading in the history thereof, at where guilt *may* reside: and cannot claim omniscience."

At this, poor Thérèse fell miserably silent: for though she desperately wanted to retain Xavier's wavering interest, so sensitive was she to every shade and nuance in his manner, and every flicker of expression in his face, she understood full well that he wished for nothing more than to escape her: that he might, with a shameless greed of his own, read the doubtless slapdash letter Perdita had penned. (For Perdita was not in the least "indisposed," nor had she retired early to her bed-chamber, though this was given out to Willela Spies as the reason for her absence from tea, and from the evening meal: nay, on the contrary, the flighty miss had been unable to decline an invitation, made in careless haste, from Valentine Westergaard and a few of his circle,—amongst them Mary-Louise Von Goeler, and Calvin Shaw, and Felicity Peregrine, and, it may have been, Xavier's own brother Wolf—that she join them for a midsummer eve's excursion on the river, on Valentine's lavender-sailed sloop, beyond Sandusky Island: very likely to partake of a lavish supper at one or another of the riverside inns. Ah, what bitterness gnawed at Thérèse's heart!—what righteous ire, what childish spite! For while a sense of simple justice urged her to disabuse Xavier of his trust in the deceitful Perdita, a more profound,—and, indeed, most numbing—sense of Christian charity forbade her to utter a word. "For I dare not trust my own instincts in this matter," the unhappy girl admonished herself, "as my love for Xavier must blind me to all that is low, and petty, and degraded, in my own female nature.")

So it was, Thérèse bit her lip; then proffered the subject of Perdita's health, as a kind of bait, which had the desired effect of ensnaring her companion,—though she could only reiterate, with blushing emphasis, that her sister was "feeling not altogether herself, as a consequence, doubtless, of the unusual humidity," but would surely regain her customary vivacity upon the morrow. This assurance did seem to gratify Xavier; who had no more pride than to make further inquiries regarding Perdita: whether she did not find it a strain on her delicate nerves, for instance, to take up residence again in Winterthurn, after the divers tragedies of her girlhood: and whether it was a matter of worrisome distraction, that so many suitors,—as the gossipmongers would have it—were competing for her hand.

"Ah, there are not so *very* many," Thérèse stiffly rejoined.

Yet, as this topic drew Xavier's extreme interest, poor Thérèse was obliged to develop it: hoping that her interrogator,—so uncommonly observant, it seemed, in other regards!—should fail to take note of the commingled pain and adoration in her face, and the significance of her faltering voice. She spoke of Mr. Osmyn Goshawk, who had long been attentive to both the sisters, after their father's death, and who had,—ah, most considerate of gentlemen!—applied for both their hands, at different times: his first choice being Perdita (so the blushing Thérèse was obliged to say), and his second, herself. She spoke of the Reverend Harmon Bunting, who, with his widowed mother, had been assiduously attentive to them both, years ago; and who, as a bachelor minister, was much in need of a wife: whether Perdita (again, the gentleman's first choice) or Thérèse. An upstanding man of God, sure to rise in the ranks of the Episcopal Church, painstaking, exacting, utterly scrupulous in every matter, large or small; his prim, pinched, rather waxen face verging, it sometimes seemed, upon the sternly attractive; and the rare power of his sermons from the pulpit—!

Thérèse then hesitantly supplied the names of a half-dozen other rivals for her sister's hand, amongst them Henry Peregrine's nephew Angus, who was making such a name for himself in Boston, where he practiced law; and Calvin Shaw,—albeit he was a fickle sort of gentleman, addicted to gambling and horses, and doubtless destined to bachelordom. As to the young Annapolis graduate of whom Xavier had heard, and the Versfield heir, and Valentine Westergaard himself,—Thérèse grew close-mouthed, and said that such rumors were baseless; indeed, most disagreeable. She paused,—seemed about to speak further,—shyly raised her eyes to Xavier's face,—murmured that, as a Latin tutor for Jody Shaw, and Roddy Spies, and one or another boys in their teens who were acquainted with the circle to which Valentine belonged, she was in a position to say that,—ah, she knew not precisely *what*: and had best hold her tongue.

By degrees the mist-shrouded sky had begun to lighten; and a gauzy moon, of singular luminosity and proportions, made its belated appearance; and the creatures of the night, invisible in the tall grasses of the churchyard, and in the wild wooded area farther up the hill, began their dolorous song. Perdita's missive pressed against his breast, and its subtle lavender fragrance rising to his nostrils, what wonder that the young detective wished heartily to be gone, that he might all avidly peruse it?—despite the fact that, in the moon's pale glow, with a white radiance suffusing her skin, and her great haunted eyes affixed to his own, Miss Thérèse Kilgarvan struck a most compelling picture, indeed. Alas, that her beauty was so somber, so chaste!—and so easily mistaken for plainness!—the greater injustice being her identity as *Perdita Kilgarvan's* older sister.

Xavier took care to escort the trembling Thérèse to the rear of Mrs. Spies's garden, where the narrow wooden door yet stood suggestively open; and scarcely noted that, in her sudden shyness, the arm she slipped through his was wooden indeed, and every movement of hers stiff and ungainly. It seemed too that, of a sudden, she had gone mute, where a scant moment before she had been very nearly chattering,—a most puzzling, *most* mysterious young woman, who shrank from him even as she required his assistance in descending the hill, and in extricating thorns and brambles from her heavy skirt. At the garden door Xavier bethought himself to inquire of her what she had intended to say regarding her tutorial charges,—or had it something to do with *Valentine Westergaard?*

For a pained space of time the agitated young woman stood quite tongue-tied, as if desirous both of scurrying away and of acquiescing to her companion's question; her gloved fingers plucking nervously at one another, and her shadowed eyes fairly shrinking from Xavier's penetrant stare. Then, as Xavier was about to bid her goodnight, and turn away, she murmured, in a voice so tremulous Xavier could barely hear: "Only that,—dear Cousin!—you must be ever vigilant against Valentine Westergaard, as he has conceived an intense dislike of you —or so Roddy Spies has said,—and,—and—you see, I cannot comprehend *why*,—only that it seems to be so,—in which case,—O dear Xavier!—do not go riding or boating with him, or dining, or,—I know not—whatever sorts of diversions gentlemen might do,—for it seems— Nay, you must excuse me, Cousin: Mrs. Spies will be asking after me—"

Whereupon the pallid young woman betook herself, in some haste, into the garden,—leaving Xavier Kilgarvan to stare after her speechless.

"...Your Adoring Cousin"

As to Perdita's secret missive, I shall waste no time in coy subterfuge, or authorial procrastination, but record it, herewith,—

Dear Cousin Xavier:

"Give Woman wings & she is either angel or beast,"—thus Father oft said—& Dear Xavier can he have been mistaken with his wisdom!—Nay it is *doubtless so*,—for I have broke my promise to you—& seemed to know beforehand that I should do so— Alas *must* do so,—being not abed these many hours but upon my *knees*, affrighted & shamed!—I mean of my own Passion, sweet Cousin,—as well of *yours*—& *You*.

In a weighty old tome smelling of dust & time, my Guardian Angel Thérèse (for thus I playfully chide her,—ah, she is so good!—& hath a beauty in her soul that makes mine quite sullied, as Iago would know),—my Angel Thérèse discovered & read scoffingly to me, of the cruel things claimed of our Sex thro' the ages. Such as,—

> Woman has not a soul (this, the Chinaman's fancy)
> Woman is barred from Paradise (the Mohammedan)
> Woman is but *half human* (Aristotle & Hippocrates)
> Woman is so foul,—nay a very bunghole of pestilence & rot!—'tis better the human species lapses to extinction, than that Man succumb to her wanton-

218

ness (thus say Ambrose & Tertullian & many
another elder of the Church)
Woman is all that man is not: *Woman is not all that
Man is.*

Thus, dear Xavier, you must agree, 'tis impossible that you & I
shall ever know each other, across this dread Abyss. When I recall how boldly you squeezed my hand (& I but an ignorant girl
of 12!) & *pressed your heated lips against my cheeks,* in Glen
Mawr's enshadowed cellar, why, my Virgin heart quakes, & my
conscience shrinks away, in appalled shame! So fierce & hot-
blooded & intemperate are you, & so *Kilgarvan,* I dare not trust
you even in the Quaker churchyard, where 'tis said tiresome
dour-faced ghosts troop about amidst the mosquitoes & the
bats! Nay, sweet Xavier, *I dare not trust myself in your embrace,*
who has vowed to be Virgin on her wedding day.

(& if God will grant me thus, VIRGIN THEREAFTER.)

Nay, I jest. My fevered pulses jest. 'Tis the moon's sly tide. I
mean the secret Female tide. I mean,—but I dare not whisper
what I mean, for fear of making you blush. Thus, these jests.
Feeble ploys only. For, were you here with me now, secreted
away in my bed-chamber,—

(Alas, old Willela summons me, that I must simper, & sigh, &
oversee her endless prattle, & settle her cushions behind her,
who might be better served,—thus the Devil counsels!—by having them mashed hard & firm against her face! But Nay.)

Well,—she calls; & the pauper Perdita must obey; & shall break
off with (dare I whisper it?) a *kiss,*—'til such time as we will
meet again. Sweet Xavier, you dwell already in my heart,—as I
pray I dwell in yours—& shall murmur Farewell; with this
warning,—

DO NOT VENTURE ALONE INTO THE DEVIL'S HALF-ACRE
UNTIL SUCH TIME AS YOUR ADORING COUSIN

Perdita

WILL ACCOMPANY YOU HAND IN HAND,—& ARMS ENTWINED,
—LIPS SEEKING LIPS,—ETC.

This remarkable *billet-doux,* of a licentiousness and daring
scarcely imaginable in any young woman, let alone one of good breeding, our amazed hero read with trembling alacrity, by one of the flick-

ering gas-lamps of Volpp Avenue. And as the multifarious thoughts, desires, and low impulses that flooded his being, for hours thereafter, are not fit to be recorded in print, I shall forbear doing so,—and leave the overwrought young detective to his folly.

The Doomed Man

It was on the overcast and singularly hot afternoon of July 1 that, after hearing vehement testimony by a motley assortment of witnesses, and such crucial persons as Sheriff Frank Shearwater, and Chief of Police Hiram Munck, and District Solicitor James William Hollingshead, a county grand jury unanimously moved to hand down an indictment of *murder in the first degree* against Isaac Rosenwald: being, as it was afterward explained to newspaper reporters, "distinctly prejudiced" by said suspect's feeble defense of himself, and his "sullen," and "craven," and "uncooperative" demeanor throughout: and having been, in any case, under great pressure to arrive at this verdict, as a result of vociferous urgings by men who gathered daily outside the Courthouse,—whether actual members of the noisome Jericho Brethren (though unrobed, and unmasked), or hot-tempered citizens, or mere idlers, of the sort that oft congregated in Courthouse Green in the more hospitable months of the year, for want of worthy employment. And, when news of the long-awaited indictment quickly spread through the square, how jubilant a chorus of voices arose!—and wound its way from block to block, through much of the city, and across the river to South Winterthurn, where a like clamor of triumph sounded, most particularly in the Cadwaller Street area; where, it seems, numerous ill-informed persons believed that an actual trial, and an actual verdict, had transpired, and *that the Jew would be soon hanged.*

(All this, it scarcely needs be said, was duly reported in the newspapers; and even the *Winterthurn Gazette* saw fit to emblazon the verdict in two-inch headlines, and to include a crude pencil sketch of the accused man by a local artist, which emphasized a low brow, a rapier-like nose, and lewdly thick lips.)

Following the grand jury's announcement, a flurry of interest in the case again arose, and it became most problematic to determine whether the campaign of the *Sun,* and the *Nautauga Falls Bulletin,* against Mr. Rosenwald's attorney (a gentleman, it was noted, of "New York City training and Hebrew alliance") was the crucial factor in the unfortunate violence done against him, in his hotel room on Union Avenue; or whether, roused by public sentiment that any lawyer, of any persuasion, should have the audacity to defend a murderer of such proportions, a small mob of men acted on their own volition, in beating him so badly, he had to be hospitalized straightaway,—and was obliged to make the prudent, though belated, decision, to withdraw from the Rosenwald case.

At this time too it began to be reported, in the Valley papers, that a group of Utica students,—including, it seems, several young men from the Baptist seminary—formed a secret fraternal organization, friendly in spirit to the Brethren of Jericho (whose membership in recent months, through the entire state, had increased most remarkably), but narrower in their interests: an organization not named in any of the papers, though its title,—the Kill Kyke Klan—was by no means a secret.

So disgusted was Xavier Kilgarvan with the newspapers, he had long since ceased provoking a headache, and gastric upset, by too thoroughly perusing them, with the occasional exception of the *Gazette:* thus it was, he knew of these matters only indirectly, and by way of what was mentioned to him at home,—though Mrs. Kilgarvan never spoke of the "repulsive" case, and Mr. Kilgarvan, being much caught up in the designing and fashioning of his toys, seemed but dimly aware of developments outside the workshop. When Bradford came to dine, bringing with him his fiancée,—the pretty Miriam Burke, Mayor Burke's daughter—he spoke with careful neutrality on the matter, as, while *he* believed the case against Rosenwald was insubstantial indeed, the Mayor was "all fired up about it"; and he did not wish to offend his prospective father-in-law, who was inclined to be hot-tempered. Wolf rarely dined with the family, but sometimes dropped by, at about tea time, on his way elsewhere,—upon which occasion he could not resist chiding, and teasing, and very nearly abusing, his youngest brother Xavier, by inquiring why he looked so morose and dissatisfied of late, for, after all, was not the "Cruel Suitor" safely under lock and key, and prevented from further slaughter; or was it the case,—ah, how wickedly innocent this query!—that Xavier had *fallen in love—!*

"I hope the lady is not Miss Thérèse Kilgarvan, our 'bluestocking' cousin,'' Wolf said, with a stroking of his curled mustache, and a provoking comradely wink, ''for I should be most fearful of a sister-in-law possessed of such intemperate piety, and skill at ancient languages; not to mention her questionable history as an heiress of Glen Mawr.''

To this tormenting observation, Xavier did not condescend to reply; though a dark flush of his face surely signaled the malevolent Wolf that his words had found their target.

As to Colin, who had, for some years now, been the despair of his parents,—at thirty-one years of age, he gave rather more the impression of being a hulking youth of indeterminate sensibility than the cherished son of genteel parents; and from his way of life,—whether at the Barraclough estate, where he sometimes found employment, or in the waterfront area, or in South Winterthurn—he had picked up numberless coarse mannerisms, and coarser habits of slang, which could not fail to distress his mother in particular. Xavier, who had long pitied him, and wondered at him, and felt an obscure guilt over him, now deemed it a mercy that Colin so rarely troubled to visit Wycombe Street, and yet more rarely succumbed to Mrs. Kilgarvan's invitation to dine with the family on Sunday. That Colin's alteration was a *mystery* of sorts, Xavier supposed, given the happy promise of his youth, and his early enthusiasm for helping Mr. Kilgarvan in his business; that it was at best but a commonplace mystery, and one which would yield no especial reward if pursued, Xavier did not doubt. And, ah!—what a crude, queer, half-comical and half-threatening appearance Colin lately presented, being most days but carelessly shaven, with strands of grease-stiffened hair falling into his eyes, and a wide slack grin, and the blunt bluff insouciance of a Hereford bull that pushes and nudges where he will, with no fear of being stopped. Not the least of Colin's queerness had to do with his outlandish carnival air, for, while attired primarily in soiled workingman's clothes, with overalls, and hobnailed boots, and a much-notched leather belt, and shapeless ''railroad'' caps, he sometimes added touches of an improbable dandyish sort,—an embroidered vest that fitted his muscular chest like a girl's bolero jacket, being far too small for him; a silk ascot tie in peacock tones, which he knotted in slovenly fashion about his neck; and a perfumed lace handkerchief that peeped, as it were, from out an overall pocket! (It was Xavier's optimistic opinion that his brother retrieved these cast-off items from the trash, perhaps in the back alleys off Parthian Square, or Berwick; or that he had been given them by a kindly gentleman for whom he ran errands. Bradford, however, confided worriedly in Xavier that he feared Colin was a thief: that he stole these things, and doubtless others: and that he would one day bring great shame and humiliation on the family. ''As if I have not had to struggle, since boyhood,'' Bradford sullenly said, ''to overcome the

prejudice against us, as sons of the slandered 'half-breed': nay, as innocent bearers of the very name *Kilgarvan!*")

Xavier chose to share with no one his growing fear of Colin, and
what Colin's future might yield: since the husky young man evinced
no embarrassment at accosting Xavier on the street, if he chanced to
see him, to ask mockingly of him that Xavier "lend" him money; or
buy a tip regarding the horses, or even the *murder mystery,*—as Colin
called it. (For Colin hinted strongly that he knew of persons, who
knew of persons, who might be of aid to the young detective in sniffing
out clues, or whatever; yet the several times Xavier fell for this bait,
and was rewarded with a mumbled name and address, invariably of
South Winterthurn, his mission came to naught.) It was Colin, however, who told Xavier of the Kill Kyke Klan of Utica, New York; and
Colin who averred, in a rare moment of brooding solicitude, that *he*
should not want to be the luckless Rosenwald, subjected every day, it
was said, to interrogation by the police; yet holding firm; and antago-
nizing his enemies the more by his refusal to "crack." When Xavier
queried Colin of all that he knew, or had heard, regarding Rosenwald,
and his "enemies," and the new-formed Klan, and the Brethren of Jericho, he rarely received a satisfactory answer: for the nettlesome
Colin then changed his tone, and his manner, and laughingly commented that *he* could not be dragooned into joining such tedious organizations, and be required not only to swear pledges (to preserve
the Christian family, and liberty, and white supremacy, and the Constitution, et al.) and to wear hoods and vestments, but to *pay actual
dues* for the privilege of doing so—! "Damned fools, they are," Colin
said, with his wide jeering grin, "and nobody shall talk *Colin Kilgarvan* into joining them, unless dues are paid to *him.*"

"But has anyone approached you, to join?" Xavier asked, with
some concern. "Who has approached you?"

Whereupon Colin rudely thumped Xavier on his shoulder,
rather more by way of dismissing the question, and bidding him farewell, than wishing to impart actual pain,—though actual pain *was*
imparted.

It was a few days after the grand jury's decision, when the atmosphere
about Courthouse Green had slightly calmed, that Xavier received, to
his surprise, permission to speak with the accused man,—which had
been refused numberless times since his arrival in Winterthurn, on the
grounds that he was not a relative of Rosenwald, nor "professionally"
involved in the case.

Having steeled himself against the discomfiture of meeting a
man greatly demoralized by his plight, and, withal, brutishly ugly,
Xavier was inwardly shocked to discover that Isaac Rosenwald was gra-

cious, and eagerly cooperative, and so far from resembling an ape or monkey, that Xavier could not possibly have recognized him from the "likenesses" the newspapers had published! Indeed, apart from his cruel-puckered eyes, which blinked incessantly (for, it seemed, his glasses had been broken, and there was no possibility of their being replaced), and the drawn and haggard appearance of his face, and one or another nervous tic, Rosenwald struck Xavier as quite personable, and even fairly attractive: very much, in fact, the kind of gentleman with whom he might wish to cultivate a friendship, if circumstances allowed.

As Xavier had been granted but a half-hour visit, and this beneath the beetle-browed scrutiny of the jailkeeper, he wasted no time in introducing himself; and stating the aim of his interview; and explaining that his interest in the case was purely that of an amateur,—he was no employee of Pinkerton's,* and no police informer, and, he hoped, no meddlesome crank who would make things worse by his attentions. Nor was he, he hastened to make clear, a reporter for any newspaper, or one who hoped to exploit his meeting with Rosenwald by selling his story to the highest bidder.

Thus the air was cleared, after some initial awkwardness; and the accused began earnestly to recount all he knew,—which was in truth very nearly nothing Xavier did not already know, from his own perusal of the transcripts, and his questioning of the divers witnesses. Again, Rosenwald's account of his slight acquaintance with Eva Teal; his account of the accident in the mill, and the bloodied towel, and the ill-advised trip to the doctor; and his wandering about,—ah, how unfortunately!—on the night of June 7, instead of going, as he assuredly ought to have done, to the home of his friends. From time to time Rosenwald's voice cracked, or ascended to a reproachful whine; but for the most part it was as well modulated as Xavier's own, and his manner wondrously reasonable,—indeed, Xavier began uneasily to think, as their conversation continued, was it not *too* reasonable?—for the prisoner gave evidence of knowing very little of the newspaper campaign being waged against him: a consequence, Xavier supposed, of the jailer's censorship. Nor did the unhappy man know the extent to which the invidious term *ritual murder* was being bandied about, by

---

*Though it was never officially announced, word had spread in certain Winterthurn circles that the Shaw family had commissioned Allan Pinkerton's National Detective Agency to determine if Isaac Rosenwald was in truth the murderer of Eva Teal,—and if the murder had taken place on property owned by them. Whether Xavier Kilgarvan had only heard this rumor, or whether he had sighted a professional detective known to him, in the city, I cannot say: for nothing came of the Shaws' commission; and no private detective save Xavier Kilgarvan himself is on record as having investigated the case.

persons who scarcely knew what they were saying, but knew, assuredly, what they *felt—!*

(By the by, Xavier had traveled all the way to Cambridge, to
spend several days at the Harvard library, doing research into the subject of "ritual murder" as allegedly practiced by Jews, against Christians: and came away quite sickened with his findings, which spoke
very badly for Christendom, and did not augur well for Isaac Rosenwald. Though he had thoroughly satisfied himself that "ritual murder" in this context was but a fictional notion, he could not pretend to
believe that his argument, or, indeed, that of any informed and con-
scientious person, would prove persuasive against local sentiment.
Why, the atmosphere in Winterthurn City had grown so subtly con-
taminated of late, even the ladies in Mrs. Kilgarvan's circle now
alluded in whispers to this arcane ritual, as if they knew whereof they
spoke—!)

As he spoke with Isaac Rosenwald, and saw how the pitiable
man warmed to him, and clearly wished to grasp his arm, or his hand,
had not the jailkeeper retained his frowning vigilance, Xavier came to
feel that it was just as well,—ah, it *was* just as well!—that Rosenwald's
few visitors, and his attorney, had shrunk from informing him of the
gravity of the situation. For, after all, what could the poor man do in
his solitary jail cell? (It was said the other prisoners shunned him, and
that, after a number of threats, he had had to be locked away in the oldest and most remote corner of the jail, for his own protection.) As it
was, though near-blind without his glasses, Rosenwald spent hours
each day penning letters,—to persons in authority, like the Governor
of the State, and, indeed, the President of the United States; and to
newspapers; and to divers Jewish organizations. (As to whether these
impassioned missives were mailed,—Xavier had discreetly inquired
of several persons; and, having received only evasive replies, did not
doubt that the letters were being withheld; or even assembled by the
prosecution, to build its case against Rosenwald.) He was occupied fur-
thermore, he told Xavier, in writing a "frontal attack on the glaringly
inept police work" he had encountered; and in preparing an article on
"rank anti-Semitism in America, in the 1890s," to be submitted to the
prestigious *McClure's,* or *The Atlantic Monthly.*

Alas, Xavier thought, to accuse bigots of bigotry!—so frontal an
attack, he feared, could not fail to inflame them the more. (It might be
mentioned that, by this time, even Frank Shearwater had "come
round" to supporting the grand jury's decision: indicating to Xavier, in
a manner both vexed and mysterious, that there was "more to the case
than he knew," which would be revealed at the trial.)

Nonetheless, Isaac Rosenwald assured Xavier that he had confidence, withal, that things would turn out favorably for him. For, after

all, he *was* innocent, which meant that another was *guilty*, and might at any time be apprehended; and he had faith in the court system; and in justice; and in the common sense of most men. To this, Xavier murmuringly assented, though it moved his heart that, sickly as he appeared, and thin to the point of emaciation, Rosenwald should state his position in such optimistic terms. Why, as he was *not guilty*, how could the prosecution *prove that he was?*—a logical impossibility, Rosenwald declared, with a snort of derision. "And should my captors force me to confess," he said in a lowered voice, as Xavier rose to take leave, "I will take advantage of the public's attention at my trial, to deny the confession, and to proclaim to the world how I have been mistreated. And should I be sentenced to death," Rosenwald continued, in a louder and more vigorous voice, his reddened eyes now rapidly blinking, and his hands trembling, with the desire to reach out, and to clutch Xavier's own, "why, even then, as I am marched to the scaffold, I shall continue to protest my innocence: and use Winterthurn's very scaffold as a platform for announcing my plight *to all of America.*"

Thus it was, the detective came away from his long-sought interview more deeply troubled, and shaken, than he had anticipated: and broke his habit of a long, brisk, rambling walk at dusk, to go instead to the gentlemen's bar of the Winterthurn Arms, and down a glass of bitters,—or two: a most uncharacteristic gesture, I am bound to say. His harried brain reviewed the case yet again, and again he stumbled upon the issue of the *span of time* during which Eva Teal must have been killed: and the most exasperating point, that Mrs. Teal refused to consent to have her daughter's body exhumed ("For has the poor girl not suffered enough at the hands of 'gentlemen'?"), and that Hans Deck, Frank Shearwater, Munck, Hollingshead, et al., could see no reason for it. Alas, the obduracy of such persons!—and their willful, and, it almost seemed, spiteful, ignorance, in resisting Xavier Kilgarvan's proffered aid!

  "Still," he consoled himself, his spirits rising by degrees, as the tankard of bitters was depleted, "still, I *shall* triumph, eventually: for, as the great Hans Gross has told us, 'Every crime engenders clues'; and when I at last come upon an actual clue, I will snatch it up to my bosom, as if it were the rarest jewel."

"Too Fast Have
Those Young Days Faded"

As Valentine Westergaard had been acquainted, however obliquely, with each of the "Damsels of the Half-Acre," it did not surprise those who knew of the young gentleman's generosity (and, as his friends laughingly charged, his penchant for rank sentimentality) that, after their tragic deaths, he quietly arranged for lilies of divers species to be placed at their graves; and masses to be said for the repose of their souls,—four of the five girls having been, quite by happenstance, Roman Catholic. Obeying, doubtless, an inbred sense of *noblesse oblige* (for the Westergaards were one of the very oldest families in Winterthurn,—indeed, in the New World itself: their fortune having been made in the eighteenth century, in the brisk shipping trade between the West Indies and West Africa, where rum was exchanged for slaves, at enormous profit)—and obeying too a dictum of the heart which his drawing-room manner could never suggest, Valentine personally saw to it that small sums of money were sent, now and then, to the victims' families; or, at any rate, to those still residing in Winterthurn. (For, in addition to the seven members of the Furlow family, who had quite disappeared from their slum dwelling on Railroad Street, it seemed that the ne'er-do-well father of Dulcie Inman had similarly vanished: to no one's regret, assuredly, as Inman, a slaughterhouse worker, was both a drunkard and a bully, and had taken to staggering up to the front gate of the Westergaards' Ravensworth Park, at any hour of the day or night, demanding to see the "young master.")

Undeserving though they doubtless were, both the Godwit and the Sparks families had received unspecified gifts from Valentine;

whose daughters had spoken of him, to them, as the gentleman who sang with the voice of an angel,—played a most exquisite instrument called the dulcimer, and sang, ah! how beautifully!—such songs of love, and parting, and nightingales, and springtime, and Death, as they had never heard before: a gentleman inordinately handsome, and wondrously attired, with curled hair, and the slightest suggestion of a lisp; who could be most grave, like a preacher,—then again gay and witty and charming; and never *quite* predictable. It was said that Valentine had been particularly attentive to both Mrs. Teal and her married daughter Iris, in the weeks following Eva's death, and had even sent one of the menservants from Ravensworth Park down to Cadwaller Street, to be of assistance in the early days of grief and confusion; and to provide the distraught women with food and drink,—alas, Mrs. Teal soon proved inordinately fond of Jamaican rum!—when, for some days, it appeared that the shock of the brutal murder, and the noisome attention it drew, had brought them to the very edge of collapse. And this protracted generosity was in defiance, as it were, of Valentine's own sense that Mother Teal should like nothing better than to "sink her talons into him, and her sharp greedy beak": and his fastidious aversion to a female of her low breeding, and propensity for emotional displays. "Yet she *is* sweet Eva's mother,—or shall I say *was?*" Valentine murmured wonderingly, "and sometimes it is possible,—I do not say it is *easily managed*—to see the daughter in the mother: the dear 'naughty angel' in the old harridan with her gross flaccid face."

(For in such mock-cynical asides,—as all of Valentine's friends and social acquaintants, and, not least, his admiring relatives knew—the young gentleman played at rousing himself from his predilection for sentiment, and melancholy, and all the softer emotions. "There was never a more gracious and kind-hearted young man in all of Winterthurn than your Valentine," Miss Verity Peregrine assured Valentine's mother, at the time of the embarrassment caused by the chambermaid Molly O'Reilly, when Valentine was but a youth of twenty-six. "Yet one wishes he were not *quite* so witty!—albeit we know he means not a word he says, and is but a small child at heart.")

Though Valentine and his impetuous older sister Imogene had never been close,—indeed, in Imogene's succinct phrase, each had "grated upon the other, like a knifeblade against a grindstone"—it was noted by all how violently her death shook him; how deep, and protracted, and, as it were, poetical, was his mourning; and how adamant the brother was that the sister had *wrongfully died*,—for, had the headstrong young woman not insisted upon walking her terriers near accursèd Glen Mawr Manor (for so the inhabitants of Ravensworth Park were wont to speak of their neighbors' estate, amongst themselves), she should be living still, and brightening the house with her high, gay, nervous laughter, and her strident voice, and, withal, her magnificent presence. Alas, had she not been warned to avoid the vicinity of Glen Mawr a dozen times?—had she not seen, or fancied she had seen, "preternatural" shapes, in that area near the river? "How ironical that, though it was Imogene's willfulness for which we all adored her," Valentine moodily observed, "it was that very willfulness that brought about her death." For upward of a year afterward Valentine sighed, and slunk about, and secreted himself away in his bed-chamber, that he might apply himself to Holy Writ; he took on certain airs and mannerisms of Hamlet, and, indeed, directed his tailor to fashion *Hamlet-like* mourning costumes for him,—these, of the finest black velvet, that, in certain lights, yielded a wondrous grape-maroon sheen; and silky black shirts, with flowing collars and ruffled cuffs, and oft an embroidered design, in dark crimson, across the breast; and a most arresting winter coat, of exquisite black cashmere, in "Cossack" style, trimmed with sable,—in which outfit Valentine had his portrait painted by the Philadelphia artist Thomas Eakins. (Though he pronounced the painting a "slanderous failure" afterward, as Eakins had given his likeness,—for what perverse reason, Valentine could not guess—an insipid weak chin, and a pointed nose, and eyes of so unnaturally bright and hard a green, they brought to mind the iridescent hues of certain huge carrion flies!—and were assuredly *not* Valentine's own.)

It may have been at this time that Valentine composed several of his sweetest and most melancholy songs, which, some years later, so pierced the hearts of his female listeners, of all ages, at the Winterthurn Armory Musicale. Though his tenor voice was perhaps somewhat thin, and inclined to waver, and his long beringed fingers on the dulcimer frequently stroked an infelicitous note, there was no faulting the potency of his art, and the heart-rending loveliness of his words,—

> *One kind kiss before we part,*
> *Drop, drop a tear,—and bid adieu!*
> *Tho' we sever, my fond heart*
> *Till we meet shall part for you!*
> *One kind kiss before we part*
> *Drop, drop a tear,—and bid adieu!*

And again, a yet more haunting lyric, composed, the young man claimed, at Imogene's very bier,—

> *She cried, "O Love! is this thy doom?*
> *O light of youth's resplendent day!*

Must ye then lose your golden bloom,
And thus, like sunshine, die away!"

As to the little chambermaid Molly O'Reilly, employed some years previous by the Westergaards,—she who was to acquire, throughout Winterthurn, an unenviable species of "fame": this precocious girl, not fifteen years old at the time of her death (as the Colonel recalled), but a mere *fourteen*, had so affixed her amorous musings upon the young master of Ravensworth Park, and had so lewdly abandoned herself to daydreams featuring him, that, all incredibly, *she fancied herself with child by him.* (That the reader of genteel background is both shocked and puzzled by this assertion, I can well imagine: for it is against our inclination to believe, or to wish to believe, that a girl of so tender an age, whether of the working classes or no, should convince herself of such a matter,—nay, that she should be sullied enough, by the crude facts of the physical life, to be *capable* of such conviction. Yet it is perhaps not out of place here, in this discussion, to mark that such morbid and febrific imaginings on the part of girls scarcely past childhood,—indeed, such purulent phantasms of *naked and unmasked wish*—had frequently been noted by Dr. Colney Hatch, who had been assembling, for upward of twenty years, a treasure trove of evidence pertaining to the divers weaknesses of Woman, and the general inferiority of the sex: thus, one can conclude that the O'Reilly delusion, if not its sordid aftermath, did not surprise him greatly, when it was brought to his attention. I think it a pity, if not an actual tragedy, however, that Winterthurn's most eminent physician so wore himself out with his *practice*, in ministering unto the area's numberless female invalids, that he had no time to present his *theory* in book form; and suppose it must have been a painful surprise to him when, later in life, he discovered that findings *precisely analogous to his own* had been published by two gentlemen writing in the German language: the famed Dr. Hans Gross, whose *Criminal Psychology: A Manual for Judges, Practitioners, and Students* Xavier frequently consulted, and the yet more renowned Sigmund Freud, whose musings on the moral inferiority of Woman, and the fantastical nature of her psyche, have been studied throughout the world.)

Thus it was, the fourteen-year-old chambermaid Molly not only conceived of this unlikely development, but was possessed of no more shame than to broadcast her plight back-stairs at Ravensworth,—in the kitchen, in the wash-shed, in the smokehouse, anywhere amongst

---

*Albeit my research has unearthed a rival composer for "She Sang of Love,"—one Thomas Moore, who died in 1852, and whose *Irish Melodies* had once been popular through America.

the servants where her tears and ceaseless complaints might be tolerated. An orphan, having been born of a very young girl likewise employed at Ravensworth, who had died of childbed fever, with no father's name to bestow upon her babe, this Molly was, it was said, a pretty enough child: with flaxen curls, and wide-set blue eyes, and a dusting of freckles across her round face; cheerful and lively, most days; very possibly *too* cheerful, before the onset of her delusion; and, as it turned out, far too lively,—and impetuous.

Through three, or four, or five lengthy weeks in the springtime of Valentine Westergaard's twenty-seventh year, when the young man was troubled sufficiently, by an indecision as to which of the arts to pursue (for it was Valentine's ironical fate to be talented both in *music* and in *poetry*), this bold young miss "kicked up a fuss" amongst the domestic staff; then, of a sudden, toward the end of May, when the pathos of her situation had been daily worsening, she contrived a remarkable fib,—in truth, several fibs: and confided in one or two of the kitchen help that, at last, the young master was "coming 'round"; he *did* confess to loving her; and regretted having abused her; and wished now to elope with her, to California; and make her his lawful wedded wife. The solicitous young master had secured, however, from a midwife who dwelled in Mt. Provenance, a rare species of mushroom,—a prodigy of Nature which, in the magical soil of the mountain, grew to a height well beyond five feet; and was possessed of unusually potent purgative qualities. This mushroom, when taken as medicine, would, Molly was told, cure her of the "problematic growth" in her belly; and make her pure again; and fit to be a gentleman's bride. "For Mr. Westergaard regrets that he cannot marry anyone *not* a virgin," Molly all artlessly said, "and I would not force such an ignominy on him."

It came about, nonetheless, despite the girl's boast, that, some twelve hours later, her stiffening body was found in a thicket two miles from Ravensworth Park; and the diagnosis made,—by a physician who lived close by—that the desperate creature had taken *poison*: very likely, adjudging from the vomit on her person, a certain species of toadstool, whose lethal properties were well known. As to Valentine Westergaard, and the phantasmal notion that he even knew her name, much less wished to make her his wife,—this was of course sheer fiction: and categorically denied.

Much tiresome fuss ensued, however; and speculation; for Molly O'Reilly's tale of the young master, and his love for her, and plans for their future, was both repeated and embellished, not only by servants in Winterthurn but by certain of their employers. When at last the Colonel was informed, and called his grandson and sole heir to him for an explanation, poor Valentine stood for some minutes struck mute, though trembling in every limb: and then burst into tears: and confessed that, for nearly a year, the wretched girl had been pursuing him most shamelessly,—leaving love notes of a crude, and crudely expressed, sentiment on his pillow; popping out at him from behind doors; stealing up behind him as, sequestered in a quiet corner of the garden, he had been strumming his dulcimer, or steeping himself in Holy Writ. So bold was Molly,—or Milly, or Emmie; ah, the very syllables of these vulgar names irritated!—she tiptoed into his study upon more than one occasion, to toss a nosegay into his lap; and disturbed his sleep several times, through the winter and into the spring, by stealing into his bed-chamber, clad in naught but the most diaphanous of night-time garments. And this, an "innocent" girl of but fourteen years!—whose amorous appetites, no less than the bawdiness of her speech, quite repulsed the twenty-six-year-old Valentine.

Yet, it seemed, when Valentine chastely turned her out, and locked his door against her, she went straightaway to one of the stable boys,—or, it may have been, to one of the groundsmen (for naturally none of the staff would admit it)—with the calculated intention of *getting herself with child*, that she might spite Valentine, and awaken jealousy in him—! (For so the desperate girl told him afterward, scarcely comprehending that he could feel no emotion for her save unbridled disgust: and a hearty wish that she vanish from his sight at once. "Then I shall boast that the child is *yours*," she warned,—the which low threat poor Valentine could hardly credit, as he believed the girl but coarse and ignorant, and not at all wicked.)

Thus, weeks passed; and Valentine sought to avoid her, and even the thought of her. But on that fatal Sunday eve she begged that he accompany her into the forest, for she had something highly important to confide in him, and, all foolishly, he consented: for he *did* feel some pity for her, and a measure of Christian charity. Once they were in a secluded place, a mile or two from the house, she drew from her bosom an herb of some kind, or a vegetable of some pale grayish hue,—for Valentine did not get a clear view of it—and informed him that it was *poison*, and that she would devour it, if he refused to return her love. Though Valentine halfway doubted the veracity of her angry words, he essayed to wrest the "poison" from her, but with no success: for she ran wild as an animal into a thicket, into which Valentine was loath to venture: and devoured the grayish substance before his eyes: and, within minutes, swayed, and fell, and lapsed into hideous convulsions. So terrified and sickened was Valentine,—indeed, affrighted near out of his wits—he ran the full distance back to the house, despite the delicacy of his lungs, and the great shock to his constitution; and, glimpsed by no one, ascended the back stairs, to his room; and fell unconscious across his bed, not to be roused for many hours. And then, ah, what confused shame was his!—for he knew himself bested by a mere chambermaid; and feared that he might never outlive the ignominy of their acquaintance.

Thus, sobbing, Valentine Westergaard confessed all; and, on his knees, begged forgiveness from his grandfather for having made so many foolish blunders, albeit in innocence; and for having, he feared, drawn some penumbrous blight upon the Westergaard name. Doubtless the Colonel scolded him soundly, for old Westergaard, long before his dotage, was not a man to mince words: doubtless Valentine's grief was the more inflamed, and his regret at having ever tolerated, however obliquely, the "unclean attentions" of such a creature: yet the mischief had been done, and naught but the passage of Time, and the solicitude of his family and circle, might help heal the wound.

Both Hans Deck and Dr. Colney Hatch averred that Molly O'Reilly *had* died by way of toadstool poisoning, as she had threatened; and that the death,—so especially piteous in a child of her years—must be counted as *self-inflicted*, under these trying circumstances. No overly fastidious examination being deemed necessary, and an autopsy quite repugnant, it was never determined whether the precocious girl had indeed been with child, or had merely concocted this fancy by way of coercing Valentine: nor was the probable "father" ever named, as, of course, no member of the frightened domestic staff at Ravensworth chose to come forward, even to inform upon another.

Thereafter, when Valentine Westergaard sang in public a certain lyric of a truly poignant loveliness, all the young female servants at Ravensworth, and elsewhere, fancied it was in homage to the tragic Molly O'Reilly: and, indeed, judging by the sentiment, and certain accidents of phraseology, one might so infer,—

> *Has Sorrow thy young days shaded,*
> *As clouds o'er the morning fleet?*
> *Too fast have those young days faded*
> *That, even in Sorrow, were sweet—!*
>
> *Does Time with his cold wing wither*
> *Each feeling that once was dear?—*
> *Then, child of misfortune, come hither,*
> *And I'll weep with thee,—tear for tear.*

But, as the young gentleman had frequently sung these lines before Molly's death, and, indeed, even before Imogene's, we can credit it naught but a chambermaid's delusion,—one, I am afraid, of many.

At Ravensworth Park

These oft-told tales of Valentine Westergaard, Xavier brooded upon time and again, as the summer deepened, and grew ever more sluggish, and his own investigation into the case faltered: for he was convinced that Valentine Westergaard had poisoned Molly O'Reilly,—and murdered his sister Imogene, in a most loathsome fashion—and that Valentine, and no one else, was the "Cruel Suitor." Indeed, was the conclusion not self-evident? How was it possible that all of Winterthurn failed to see? Yet, if Xavier brought the subject up, in however casual a manner,—as in a remark, put to Shearwater, or Munck, or Hollingshead, or, indeed, anyone at all: *Odd, is it not, that Valentine Westergaard is the only person associated with each of the murdered girls?*—his words rang out in an uncanny sort of stillness, or vacuum, not only as if they were not heard, but very nearly as if they had *never been uttered.*

"Why, as a mere boy of sixteen I had known that Valentine murdered his sister, and sensed that everyone around me knew," Xavier inwardly murmured, "albeit such 'knowledge,' in itself, is altogether useless."

Only Wolf, encountered by happenstance on one of Xavier's nocturnal perambulations in the city, deigned to hear Xavier's remark, and to comprehend its precise significance. With a slight stiffening of his handsome features, and after but a moment's hesitation, he said easily: "Ah, but you must remember, Calvin, and Lloyd, and Francis, and perhaps one or two others, were with Valentine for much of that evening, just having returned, I believe, from the track at

Nautauga Falls: surely such companionship constitutes an 'alibi'—?
Why, it is even likely that Colin dropped in, somewhat later, for, you
know, he is quite entranced by Valentine, albeit he has always scorned
him for his dress and manners,— and it is said that Valentine finds him
wondrously droll and amusing.''

Before Xavier could draw breath to protest that he found it impossible to speak with Colin, on any subject at all, Wolf hurriedly
continued: "In any case, Xavier, Valentine should be most distressed
to hear such things by way of you, for, you know, he is an inordinately
sensitive person; and, withal, he is particularly fond of *you.*''

Xavier stared at his brother, to determine if he spoke seriously,
or no; then said, with a studied effort at coolness: "Why, I had thought
he disliked me,—surely it cannot be a secret how I dislike *him!*''

Smiling, and frowning, and stroking one side of his mustache,
Wolf said: "*I* shall not be the one to convey such news to Valentine,
you may be sure.''

"Why not?" Xavier brashly inquired, as his brother hailed a lone
hackney cab that had appeared on the darkened avenue. "Are you fearful of your friend's well-being?''

With a negligent wave Wolf bade him adieu, and laughingly
said: "No,—rather more of my brother's.''

As customs, manners, and niceties of behavior have so sadly altered in
Winterthurn through the long decades separating our present-day
time from that of our narrative, it were well for me to recall the protocol of dining at Ravensworth Park,—indeed, at the majority of the
great homes of that bygone era.

Invitations to Ravensworth being set precisely for the hour of
seven-thirty, no guests dared, or, indeed, wished, to arrive at the front
gate more than two or three minutes before this time; and should any
guests be so rude as to arrive after, it was tacitly understood that they
would never be asked again.

Dinner proceeded with ceremonial calm, and the utmost dignity, never ending before a full two hours; and rarely lasting beyond
that point, as a number of the guests, at Ravensworth and elsewhere,
were invariably agèd, and had need of retiring early. So far as the Westergaards were concerned,—as the Colonel was of an exacting disposition, and insisted upon "running a tight ship," protocol at his table
demanded that, in addition to carrying on, more or less, an amiable
conversation with one's partner, one maintain a strict vigilance regarding the Colonel. That is, when the white-haired gentleman chose
to shift the focus of his attention, abruptly or otherwise, from the lady
on his *left,* to the lady on his *right,* it were well for all the other gentlemen to follow suit, though they be surprised in midstream, so to

speak: otherwise the Colonel's veined eyelids would conspicuously tremble, as if he had been grievously offended; and his staring green eyes, which possessed very nearly the glassy power of his grandson's, would grow more luminous yet. Punctually at ten o'clock, before even the first strokes of the house's numerous clocks began to sound, Colonel Westergaard would signal to a favored manservant, that he be assisted to his feet; whereupon the entire table rose, in one near-coordinated motion, whether all had finished their dessert and coffee, or no. Following this, with no deviance from the pattern within memory (save for the evening when Miss Georgina Kilgarvan had suffered from an embarrassing species of gastric upset, and had had to be hurried away upstairs by the Westergaards' housekeeper), the ladies were escorted to the adjoining drawing room, there to enjoy one of the more lightsome of the liqueurs; and the gentlemen made their way to the Colonel's library, there to indulge in brandy and cigars, and conversation of a more manly sort. Here, there *was* some relaxation, albeit, under the Colonel's narrowed eye, not an excessive amount: and, after precisely thirty minutes, a manservant opened the doors between the two rooms, which signaled the onset of the final part of the evening, when the gentlemen graciously rejoined the ladies for another thirty minutes of sociable repartee.

At this point, the Colonel nodded sharply in the direction of his grandson Valentine, that the young man help him to his feet: and all of the guests, not excluding, upon most occasions, the garrulous Olivia Westergaard, whom liqueur, it was said, made tipsy, went silent at once, as the evening's festivities were formally closed.

The evening Xavier Kilgarvan escorted his mother to the Westergaards', shortly after the first of August, conversation was rather more lively than usual, following this course: during the cocktail period, the upcoming racing season was discussed, at Saratoga, Belmont, and Nautauga Falls,—this topic being led by the Colonel, and enthusiastically developed by Henry Peregrine, Harrier Von Goeler, and Valentine Westergaard, who hoped for "*undeserved* good fortune, as his *deserved* ill-fortune, of the previous season, had quite beggared him." During the soup course, the soup itself (a delicate French turtle's-blood consommé) was praised, and analyzed, and placed in comparison to a like soup, served some days previous, at the Goshawks',—with no conscious insult being intended, though none of the Goshawks was present. The salmon course was accompanied by so prodigious a French wine, that subject quite absorbed the entire table; albeit, near the conclusion, Xavier was interrogated by Valentine Westergaard, as to the degree to which his "sensual palate" had been altered by a recent peregrination to France. (Somewhat discountenanced by this inquiry, Xavier expressed a doubt that his palate had been significantly altered at all, as he could not contrive an interest in such trivial matters: so far as he was able, he ate and drank sparingly: which reply seemed to please Valentine, who made haste to concur with his judgment.)

The following course, consisting of canvasback duck, ushered in a prolonged discussion of débutante balls and cotillions: and focus naturally shifted upon pretty Mary-Louise Von Goeler, who had come out in Winterthurn society but a few years before, and had a few comments to make,—this young woman of four-and-twenty being altogether charming, with close-set gray eyes, and a quick thin smile, and a habit of cocking her head to one side. (As to whether she and the handsome young heir of Ravensworth Park would ever marry,—indeed, whether they would ever become affianced—no one seemed to know, or to wish to speculate.)

During the meat course, the quality of the veal was admiringly discussed, and one or two upcoming social events; and Mrs. Bunting's plans to replace her Belgian linen wallpaper (in her upstairs boudoir) with a lighter floral design. During the game course, the venison was thoughtfully analyzed, as to whether it struck some palates as inordinately salty, or no: and the degree of success of the accompanying Burgundy wine: and the upcoming hunting season, which several of the gentlemen, including the Colonel, anticipated with great relish. (Though not Valentine Westergaard, who risked his grandfather's censure by visibly shuddering, and running a nervous hand through his tight-curled red hair, murmuring the while that though he could abide, he supposed, the disguised *taste* of blood, in meat or soup, he would surely faint quite away at the *sight* of it, in any vulgar quantity. "In which I suspect I am alone amidst the present company, of my sex," he all bravely continued, "unless Xavier too eschews the pleasures of the hunt: for I believe I have heard of my industrious young friend that he has no time for such 'trivial' preoccupations." To which remark Xavier replied, in a curt and startled tone, that he had little time, these days, for *preoccupations* of any sort.)

Next, over salad, Colonel Westergaard initiated a general, though not overly animated, discussion of a yachting competition of some decades past; over cheese and fruit, the subject ranged wide, to include boats owned by several of the gentlemen, and races either forthcoming or already past, and accidents that had, or had not, occurred, by the grace of God. As if inadvertently, mention was made of the Versfield "tragedy," but swallowed up almost at once, as a lapse of taste, before Xavier could turn his attention to it,—indeed, had he heard correctly? Over dessert, the remarkable texture of the meringue was discussed, and the exquisite sweetness of the wine, and a forthcoming marriage, and the prospects of the next day's weather. After which, when the Colonel abruptly rose from his chair, the dinner proper ended.

If the reader is curious as to why, in defiance, as it were, of Thérèse's warning, Xavier Kilgarvan accepted an invitation to dine in the company of Valentine Westergaard,—I suppose it was the case that the frustrated young detective yearned for *something* to transpire, whether dangerous to him, or no: for is not *something* preferable to *nothing*, in such situations—? The impasse at which he found himself, after so many weeks of inquiry, and brooding, and ratiocination, was such that he knew himself close to despondency: and he took it as an ill omen that, on three nights in succession, following his inconclusive interview with Isaac Rosenwald, he had hoped to placate his strained nerves, and raise his spirits to some modest degree, by the more vigorously immersing himself not in work, or in reading,—or, indeed, in composing a strategic species of letter for Perdita—but in solitary drinking, in one or another of the humble taverns on lower Union Avenue. (Albeit young Kilgarvan indulged himself thusly to but a prudent degree,—two or three tankards of bitters, downed over a period of some hours, being the limit of his indulgence.) Also, it happened that Mrs. Kilgarvan was wont to languish for a more varied social life, and very much appreciated being asked to dine at Ravensworth: Mr. Kilgarvan, though duly included in such invitations, being loath to venture into society in recent years, as his toy-designing and -fashioning work consumed all his energy. (To Xavier he said, in a bemused tone, that he could no more sit properly at a dinner table without twitching, and scratching himself, than could his assistant Tobias for all those hours: and he had rather carve puppets and dolls with his own hands than be trapped in a dining room with them, and forced to take them seriously.)

It was true that evenings at Ravensworth, and elsewhere, were somewhat lacking in spontaneity, so far as young persons might be concerned: but the wily Xavier Kilgarvan employed his two-hour stint at the dining-room table, amidst numberless crystal wine glasses, and champagne glasses, and goblets, and antique china, and gleaming silver cutlery of a staggering variety, and God knows what all else,—such legerdemain being required to dine at Ravensworth, it were best to accomplish it, in any case, sheerly by rote—examining, as covertly as he could, the *probable murderer* in their midst; and, at other, freer moments, allowing his thoughts to drift upon his belovèd Perdita, with whom he had not had the pleasure of exchanging a single word in weeks. (So infatuated with Perdita was the young detective, he would not disobey her expressed wish that *she* would summon *him* when the

moment was propitious: for he had come away from one or two
abashed visits to Mrs. Spies's house, at the tea hour, with the admonition fairly ringing in his ears,—though couched, it scarcely needs
be said, in the gentlest of tones—from Thérèse, that Perdita was
"indisposed at the present time," but would communicate with him
soon, if he *would* but respect her wishes. Thus, he contented himself
with writing three or four love missives, in language so restrained, the
young lady should not guess at, or be repulsed by, his passion: and
sending such gifts to her,—a pair of ringed turtle doves; a volume of
Tennyson's poesy; a heart-shaped box, splendidly wrapped, of Swiss
chocolates, from a downtown sweet shop—as he supposed appropriate
for a suitor to send to his belovèd, in such awkward circumstances. Of
the degree of unwholesome fantasizing, and brooding, and excitable
rehearsal of the future, in which poor Xavier indulged, regarding the
visit to the Devil's Half-Acre on which Perdita would accompany
him,—it is very frankly repugnant to this editor to speak; and may best
be passed by, in prudent silence.)

Valentine Westergaard being an altogether more profitable object for scrutiny, by anyone fancying himself an actual *artist of detection*, and not a mere *lovesick swain*, Xavier directed his energies
toward a covert examination of this ambiguous personage, the while
idle remarks and perfunctory queries and simulated little exclama-
tions of interest washed around him, and over him; and the inexorable
progress of the dinner continued. Yet what could be said, in all fairness, regarding Valentine's behavior?—was it *suspiciously natural, excessively charming, zealously proper?* How gracious the heir of
Ravensworth Park was, in his assiduous attention to the lady on his
left (the long-widowed dowager Bunting, devoted mother of the young
reverend), and now to the lady on his right (Xavier's mother herself,—looking very attractive, it seemed to her admiring son, in a
summer gown of some lightsome, gossamer, many-layered material, in
divers shades of yellow; and with the three-stranded De Forrest pearl
necklace looped about her graceful throat; and her eyes girlishly aglow
in the candle-flame: for Valentine's attentions *did* flatter her),—yet it
had always been the case, in Xavier's memory, that the heir of
Ravensworth was unfailingly charming in these circumstances, if not
invariably in others. For, surely, Valentine had acquired a precocious
skill at social legerdemain himself, by his thirteenth year: and might
have performed an entire evening by rote. And, moreover, though it
disturbed Xavier to confess this, he himself was not beyond being
"charmed" by the sinister creature!—and felt a curious thrill of pleasure, or intrigue, when, as if by happenstance, Valentine's pale-lashed
green eyes moved upon him, and some seemingly harmless (or subtly
flattering) remark was aimed in his direction.

Thus, the gentleman's impeccable *behavior.* And though he was in all likelihood a murderer of the most loathsome stripe, who would, surely, strike again, and yet again, if he were not stopped,—it was an eerie yet incontestable proposition that, of all the gentlemen ranged about the table, not excluding the insufferable old boor Westergaard and the pious young prig Bunting (with his new-acquired "pontifical" air), why, Valentine was certainly the most congenial: and the most humorous: and, withal, the most *intelligent,*—that is, following Xavier himself. ("For I *shall* outwit him by and by," Xavier inwardly vowed. "Only, dear God, give me time; and a fulcrum from which to move the Universe.")

So far as Valentine's *appearance* went,—again, in all fairness to the subject, it was highly problematic that any conclusions could be drawn. Young Westergaard's smooth, pale, somewhat low brow glistened with perspiration; and, at surreptitious moments, he employed his linen napkin to dab at his damp upper lip. Yet all of the gentlemen guests, in their high starched collars, and dark woolen suits, and formal white ties, were freely suffering on this airless August eve: the portly Henry Peregrine, as upstanding a man as one might encounter in all of Winterthurn, giving evidence, by the testimony of *his* glistening skin and a frequent expression of panicked discomfiture about the eyes, of being more visibly "guilty" than Valentine Westergaard—! And though Valentine might now and then squirm in his seat, or too urgently drain his wine glass, or so forget himself as to allow his delicate features to shift, for an instant, into a pained grimace: though, indeed, his long slender fingers unconsciously rapped and drummed on the tablecloth, and his sea-green eyes swerved in their sockets, as if seeking out the solace of a clock's face,—Xavier could hardly conclude that he exhibited any excessive uneasiness in these circumstances. (Albeit it gave Xavier some small pleasure to note that Valentine's hairline was receding; and that the creamy ointment, or zinc mixture, which he had fastidiously dabbed on certain tiny pustules about his mouth, had become by degrees more noticeable. "He is under treatment for some foul disease," Xavier thought, "unless I imagine it, in my zeal to condemn the monster to death!")

In all, Valentine comported himself with his usual facility, in making lightsome conversation with one admiring lady, and then with another; raising his eyes to smile courteously in the Colonel's direction; inquiring gallantly of Miss Mary-Louise Von Goeler her plans for the morrow, or her considered opinion of a lawn fête held at Goshawk Manor the previous Sunday; and visibly gratifying Mrs. Kilgarvan by his seemingly unfeigned interest in the impending Burke-Kilgarvan nuptials. ("What a fine couple they shall make, your *Bradford,* and Mayor Burke's *Marian,*—ah, is it *Miriam!*—do forgive me, for transposing a letter or two," Valentine softly exclaimed. "I shall have to tax my powers of imagination to compose a suitable little song for the occasion, if, indeed, I *am* up to the task,—a bachelor like myself who has been left quite behind, it seems, in the species' fervent campaign of *perpetual motion*."} All the while, however, Xavier fancied that Valentine's secret absorption was in *him:* and in performing the unstudied mannerisms of an *innocent man,*—or, it may have been, a mockery thereof.

"Perhaps the villain knows that, since June, I have made discreet inquiries after him, through Winterthurn; and, when he condescends to spend his days in the city, I have bored myself to distraction in trailing after him; and 'keeping vigil,' as it were, on his townhouse in Hazelwit Square," Xavier broodingly thought. "Perhaps too the villain knows how frustrating,—nay, maddening—the enterprise has been: for, of a sudden, it seems the 'Cruel Suitor' has radically modified his ways, to present the tiresome face of innocence to the world." Xavier sighed so audibly that his dinner partner glanced at him, in naïve wonderment, perhaps, that *she* was the provocation; and he took advantage of a spirited discussion further down the table, of the relative merits of the Sweetwater, and the Rose Tree, hunts, to surreptitiously dab at his lower lip, with his napkin. "But he must soon discover," Xavier consoled himself, "that *Xavier Kilgarvan* is not so easily duped."

Ah, while lemon *sorbet* is gravely served by several white-gloved menservants, how felicitous it would be, that the Detective might slip from his corporeal being, to make his phantom way to Hazelwit Square, some six or seven miles distant: there to enter (whether lawfully, or no) Valentine Westergaard's red-bricked Georgian townhouse, his commodious "bachelor digs," and *to examine every square inch of the interior,* from the cellar (where, very likely, part-destroyed evidence is buried, though not so cleverly Xavier could not retrieve it), to the low-ceilinged attic (abuzz, in all probability, with the murderous wasps and hornets of the blackguard's sickened *conscience*). Splashes of maiden's blood,—or streaks, or mere freckled dots, all but invisible to the eye: on a door frame, or against the silken wallpaper of the bedroom, or near-camouflaged on the wainscoting of the library: yet Xavier Kilgarvan should discover them, and examine them with the aid of his magnifying glass: and come away with the necessary evidence to force the police to make an arrest. (For it must be confessed, neither they nor the District Solicitor's office have shown the slightest inclination to search Valentine's townhouse: and the mere mention of the possibility, on Xavier's part, elicited stares of shocked disapproval. "And what might be gained by so desperate an action?"

Mr. Hollingshead has asked, with brusque impatience. "Only the virulent enmity of old Westergaard, and the censure of all the Valley—!")

Though restrained in his attentions to Xavier during the lengthy
meal, save for several pointed questions, and a half-dozen languorous
glances, Valentine lost no time, once the gentlemen retired to Colonel
Westergaard's study for the respite of brandy and cigars (both of
which Xavier was obliged to refuse), in expressing his fascination with
him. Indeed, as they were ceremoniously en route from one room to
the other, Valentine smilingly murmured in Xavier's ear: "Now,
doubtless, you can see why your brother Wolf and I, and some others,
grow restive at Winterthurn's dining-room tables, upon occasion,—
and long to 'kick up our heels,' as it were, like naughty schoolboys!"

In the Colonel's study, amidst the general air of masculine relaxation, Valentine seated himself close to Xavier, to ply him with
flattering questions, and to make him, for some uncomfortable minutes, the center of attention: a position Xavier did not relish, as it
violated not only his intrinsic modesty but his shrewd wish, as an am-
ateur-professional in his art, to maintain invisibility. He asked Xavier
his impressions of Paris, and the Parisian police, and the Parisian
underworld ("It is said the crimes there are more imaginative than our
own,—but I cannot believe it"); he might wish, he said, with a slight
frisson of delight, for an entire evening,—nay, an entire night—to hear
Xavier's discussion of crimes and criminals in North Africa, and the
Mideast ("For one *does* hear such tales back home!—scarcely to be
credited, I fear"). He inquired of Xavier's acquaintance, rumored to be
intimate, with the famed gentlemen of Scotland Yard, of whom, alas,
Valentine had only read; and would probably never have cause to meet.
Were there not remarkable new developments in crime detection,
scarce comprehended by the layman; was there not a sense,—for so
Valentine had heard, from some redoubtable source—that Evolu-
tionary Progress itself was leading to a narrowing of the margin for
crime, and that all crime, if not the criminal heart itself, would one
day soon be refined out of existence?—by the end of the next century,
perhaps: for, alas, there were not very many years remaining in *this*
century—!

Here, Xavier started,—for were these not his own words—*his*
own words mockingly repeated to him in Valentine's insinuating
drawl? Yet he essayed to disguise his amazement, and his growing repugnance at Valentine's physical closeness,—for, indeed, Xavier could
scarcely draw breath without inhaling the pungent fragrance of the
other's eau de cologne—by remarking, in a neutral voice, that Valentine seemed to be uncannily cognizant of Xavier's travels, interests,
and beliefs,—rather more, it seemed, than Xavier of *his*. "Why, that is
easily explained," Valentine said, opening his pale-lashed eyes wide,

and sniffing with evident pleasure at his brandy, "for, as you know, Wolf,—or is he called 'Roland' at home?—keeps me informed of things in which he knows *I* have an abiding interest; and, during the long months of your absence,—fifteen in all, I believe; a *cruel* absence— when we chanced to meet at one or another tea, or reception, or charitable bazaar, your mother delighted in speaking of you, to me: and, upon one or two striking occasions, even read portions of your let- ters,—which impressed me with their rare sensitivity and intelligence, and, not least (for I have pretensions along such lines myself), their capturing of a distinct *literary tone*. Yet, withal, I am bound to say, dear Xavier, it seems to me a tragical sort of blunder for a young man of your capacities, and breeding, and unique charm, to expend his ener- gies in brute matters,—nay, in unspeakable things—better left to such custodians of our civilization as the police, and dear droll Mr. Deck. Ah, I hope I have not displeased you,—for your expression shows some surprise, and ire!—when I mean, my young friend, to do hardly more than repeat, in somewhat more forceful terms, the sentiments your own mother oft shared with me."

For some shocked seconds Xavier could think of no reply: for, while his pride smarted that Valentine Westergaard, of all persons, should be privy to certain of his secret ideals, he suffered a distinct pang of *guilt:* as it was a certitude, his choice of a career had long greatly worried Mrs. Kilgarvan.

These thoughts the yet somewhat dazed Xavier did not precisely *think*, so much as *feel*, while, in a pretense of camaraderie, that meant to prick the interest of several of the other gentlemen, Valentine ranged wider in his conversation, to speak of how very promising it was, and how hopeful for those of Christian belief, that the art of crime detection *was* so rapidly improving: for he had read somewhere, it may have been in a medical journal, that arsenic, through the centuries prized as the "poison of poisons," and, somewhat too callously, "in- heritance powder," was now very easily detected by informed patholo- gists,—albeit, as the lethal substance was all amazingly tasteless, and odorless, and innocently white as sugar, it could never be detected by the victim himself!—an infelicitous state of affairs. Yet was it not the case (though Valentine confessed himself but shabbily informed of such matters) that certain plant alkaloids,—amongst them *belladon- na*, and *cocaine*, and *morphine*—were detected only with great difficulty?

Xavier bit his tongue, for his immediate impulse was to inquire of Valentine why he wished to know about these rare poisons; and why he spoke with such unusual intensity. But he contented himself with stating that the science of toxicology was a new and precise one, like dactyloscopy (fingerprinting), or forensic medicine in general,—and that, in his opinion, the art of crime detection would be revolutionized by the turn of the century. "Only think,—murderers will no longer be able to elude Justice," Xavier said, fixing his gaze unblinkingly upon Valentine's, "and the incidence of crimes will shrink correspondingly."

"Ah, it is marvelous to think so—!" Valentine sighed.

At this point, Harrier Von Goeler intruded into the conversation, to inquire of Xavier what the truth of the situation had actually been, in the matter of the Halsey-Wielkopolski Scandal: and Xavier was obliged to say a few words, albeit he believed he had fairly sickened of the subject, and had earned a respite from it. As he spoke, he could not determine how to interpret Valentine's rapt interest, as to whether it was genuine, or mocking, or, oddly, both simultaneously: for while Xavier hurriedly limned his understanding of the case, and sketched out his own role (which he wished to underplay) in the detection of the crime, and the ferreting out of the actual criminal,—the Senator being, as the world has doubtless forgotten, *altogether innocent* of the strangling death of his mistress—Valentine rested his elbow on the arm of the sofa, and leaned his chin on the back of his hand, and stared, and stared, at Xavier, with unblinking eyes. From time to time he murmured, "Ah! is that so!" or "Not really!" or "You *do* say?"— though never with any discernible air of derision.

As it is the strategy of the present volume to concern itself solely with *mysteries of Winterthurn,* and to but glancingly allude to other cases, or adventures, of Xavier Kilgarvan's; and, indeed, as several other dedicated connoisseurs of crime have dealt in book form with the Senator Halsey-Countess Wielkopolski Scandal,—or Tragedy, as it was alternately called—I shall not devote any significant space to it here. Suffice it to know that, by locating in the Countess's suite in the Plaza Hotel, amidst a dismaying tumble of ripped clothes, bed linen, flowers, overturned and smashed furniture, pots and tubes of rouge, powder, mascara, lip paint, et al., one single oily fingerprint,—indeed, but part of a thumbprint; by having this print photographed, and many times enlarged, that it might be compared, in the courtroom, with a similar magnification of the Senator's prints; and by producing, to the amazement of all, the identity of the *actual murderer,*—Xavier Kilgarvan, in the employ of the defense, was able to save the Senator from the gallows. Not only this, but the sensational trial marked the first time in our history that an American judge,—and, following his directive, an American jury—was willing to accept this arcane species of scientific evidence, and to bring in a verdict accordingly. (For, at this time, the very concept that each individual possessed unique fingerprints, unchanging through his life, was not only unknown but, if

argued, jeeringly rejected, even by intelligent persons: all the spirals, ellipses, circles, whorls, and slanting lines at our fingers' tips being, to
the naked eye, *invisible!*) Thus, Xavier's triumph; and the great leap
forward in criminal detection, whose fruits we enjoy even to the
present day. Yet the young detective's painstaking labor brought him
but a flawed sort of gratification, for the publicity attending the case,
centering upon the murdered Countess, and her grotesquely corpulent
lover, and, by and by, the dashing figure of the youthful "Detective of
Genius," as presented by Mr. Hearst's *Journal* in particular, was so
fraught with exaggerations, errors, and outright falsehoods, and, withal, so alarming in its general tone of strident vulgarity, as to more
greatly demoralize Xavier, as he put it, than the fact of *human
wickedness*, and *crime*, itself. For while wickedness might be said to
spring from some unfathomed schism in the soul, did not the lurid
trickery of the newspapers spring from a most shallow, and easily detected, motive, indeed?—one which cast a blight, as it were, upon
even the triumph of Justice, and the detective's pride in his work. In
granting interviews, Xavier had stressed the fact that he was but building upon the scientific discoveries of others,—namely, William Her-
schel, Henry Faulds, Sir Francis Galton, and one or two other
Englishmen—and that earlier cases upon which he had embarked,
whether as a consequence of his own curiosity or at the request of acquaintances of his on the police force, must be counted as failures; he
had smilingly said that he was *not* the romantic species of detective
about whom amiable entertainers like Conan Doyle spun their tales,—
albeit, as a boy, he had reveled in such fantastical adventures. He had
even made an appeal of sorts to the *Journal* reporter, that the confused
nature of crime detection be explained to readers: for it was something
of a scandal that so very few crimes *were* solved, or even recognized as
crimes; that so many murderers not only went "scot free," but were
never even suspected; that numberless deaths counted as *natural* were,
in harsh truth, *unnatural*. "We have exposed but the very tip,—the
very glimmering of the tip—of the iceberg of Crime," Xavier had
forthrightly declared, "and have, I am afraid, a great distance to go before humanity abandons its old ways, out of necessity."

Yet, though Xavier had spoken as lucidly as possible, though he
had taken infinite pains to present himself as but a dedicated amateur,
with no wish to exploit the misfortunes of others as a way of advancing
himself,—though, repeatedly, he stressed numberless failures of his—
it came about that, in the *Journal*'s tabloid-size pages, day following
day, and week following week, a vainglorious person called "Xavier
Kilgarvan," yet a total stranger to him, sprang forth to mock all he had
said, as a caricature mocks its subject, though undeniably akin to it:
and he soon grew quite sickened with the whole enterprise. Perhaps

the most bitter consequence of the publicity, and one which would surely bear fruit in future years, was the roused animosity of the police,—for which Xavier could not in truth blame them. So it was, he surprised admirers and detractors alike by fleeing to Europe shortly after the Senator's acquittal. "In the years to come," Xavier reasoned, "I must take care not to fall into the hands of those who wish only to exploit me for their own ends; and I must be cautious that the very craft of crime detection does not, by way of me, become cheapened. But how difficult it is to know how to comport myself!—for I am fated to perform in public, and the public will invariably mirror back to me a personage *not myself.*"

These troubled feelings coursed through Xavier while he spoke, with a pretense of sociability, with the gentlemen in Colonel Westergaard's smoke-filled study; and Valentine Westergaard, indolently seated beside him, continued to watch, and to listen, with his air of bemusement. The unsought attention brought a heated flush to Xavier's face: he dearly wished he were elsewhere: and would have been hard put to reply courteously to a blunt question of Henry Peregrine's (as to which side,—*prosecution* or *defense*—he would sell his services to, in the upcoming Rosenwald trial), when, of a sudden, a manservant solemnly rolled open the doors that divided the Colonel's study from the adjoining drawing room, and the gentlemen rose with uniform alacrity, and murmured expressions of delight to once again mingle with the ladies.

"Fascinating, dear Xavier!—fascinating," Valentine said, lightly laying his hand on Xavier's knee, as they rose from the sofa, "and what a pity your discourse cannot continue through the remainder of the evening; or, indeed, the entire night."

Quicksand

The following episode, which occurred a few days after the dinner party at Ravensworth Park, is so anomalous an event in Xavier Kilgarvan's life, and, withal, so repellent,—particularly to those of us whose celebration of Crime Detection is best confined to the study, and the cushioned easy chair!—I had long debated whether to include it here at all: for it seriously detracts from our estimate of Xavier Kilgarvan's high moral worth, if not his credentials as an "amateur expert" in Crime; and advances the narrative but slightly. Yet, as one or two revelations herein are, I suppose, crucial to the reader's comprehension of the whole, I am left with very little choice in the matter: and must beg the reader's pardon for two things,—first, the bizarre philosophical musings to which Xavier succumbs, in his distress (the which I make no pretense of understanding, no more than the citizens of Winterthurn professed to understand Simon Esdras Kilgarvan's divers ravings: for are not such speculations mere twaddle set beside the *hard facts* of science?); and, second, the loathsome physical experience our hero is obliged to undergo, which fairly sickens me to record.

The *setting* is the Devil's Half-Acre, to which, unwisely unaccompanied, Xavier Kilgarvan hiked, by way of the river; the *time*, a sunny August morning, following a night of harsh and cleansing rains,—which, drumming against his roof and his windowpane, had afforded Xavier his most soothing slumber in many weeks; and encouraged the young idealist to muse that, perhaps, the *solution* to the vexing mystery was close at hand.

Thus it was, he betook himself to the Half-Acre yet again; and made another examination of that desolate and eerily *forsaken* place of rocks, boulders, and stunted vegetation,—half fearing, it should be confessed, that his darting eye might fall upon the corpse of yet another murdered girl. (And would not a fresh murder, at this time, constitute a gesture of the most vicious mocking cruelty, aimed against *Xavier himself*, by the monstrous heir of Ravensworth Park?—for Xavier had no doubt that Valentine sensed his suspicion; and quite exulted in it.)

So absorbed in his investigation was Xavier, the minutes speedily passed: and though his pulses leapt with the certainty that some clue, some shard of overlooked "evidence," some wondrous Fact, was about to declare itself to his penetrant gaze, *nothing emerged.* "How unyielding!—how pitiless!" Xavier murmured, shading his eyes from the midmorning sun. "The Half-Acre is more repugnant, because more inhuman, than I remember: these 'strewn-down' boulders as ugly as anything in Nature might be: and, ah!—the heat,—the glare,—the marshy stench,—that curious rumbling noise in the distance, which appears to fade when one listens closely, then resumes the more ominously a moment afterward!—a place forsaken by God, indeed."

These words, and more beside, the disappointed young man so forgot himself as to voice aloud: a mannerism he noted frequently in persons of uncertain mental equipoise, or advanced age: and scarcely wished to cultivate in himself. Yet the Half-Acre *was* a most uncannily desolate place, near-impossible to describe, for it struck the heart very much as Xavier expressed it, and roused all manner of anxieties: for though one might look very hard at a certain spot, satisfying himself that the configuration therein of stony shapes, and dwarfed vegetation, and woodland debris, and the sun's pale glare, hid no secrets,—indeed, at midday, no shadows—as soon as one turned away, or glanced elsewhere, a panicked sort of doubt arose. Xavier was not the first visitor to the Half-Acre to be drawn, with palpitating heart, to the mottled and misshapen boulder upon which (as legend would have it) "Bishop" Elias Fenwick had directed to be carved, or had himself carved, this childish epitaph of his own creation,—

ME UNHAPPY RACE
HAS RUN A PACE
MY DWELLING PLACE IS HERE

THIS STONE IS GOT
TO KEEP THE SPOT
THAT MEN DIG NOT TOO NEAR
1759

—now so badly weathered, the letters could be made out only with difficulty: nor was he the first to wrench himself away, after a few minutes' contemplation, with as much shuddering alarm as if he had been,
all uncomprehending, gazing into a nest full of poisonous snakes—!

Yet, apart from the "Bishop" and his specific history, apart, it
seemed, from any *human* connection at all, the boulder-strewn
wasteland provoked an indefinable anxiety, or panic: and brought to
Xavier's mind certain tales he had read, in college, of the Greek god
Pan, whose invisible presence aroused terror, or panic, in human
beings. In this hellish place very much the same phenomenon might
be observed: for might not someone,—or something—be crouching
close by, slyly edging out of one's vision when one turned to investigate; were there not whispers, or murmurs, *almost* heard; and did not
the ancient tumult of the earth, frozen to stone these many millennia,
yet exude an impetiginous presence,—a restless, yearning, damn'd
spirit, neither inhuman, nor fully human? The paludal feculence of the
nearby swamp, into which, doubtless with minimal ceremony, the
corpses of so many Confederate soldiers had been dumped, boasted,
with every breeze, of ripeness, and decay, and malarial rot; and the
ceaseless thunder of the famed Roaring Rocks some miles distant, at
the river,—of which I had occasion to speak in my opening chapter—
could not fail to upset any but the most phlegmatic of persons.

(Alas, poor Xavier: for, despite the temporary balm of his restor-
ative sleep of the previous night, our young man was, at the age of
eight-and-twenty, far from phlegmatic, indeed.)

Nonetheless, Xavier strode about the rocky half-acre with as
much frowning diligence as if he were making an initial investigation:
brandishing a magnifying glass that promised at every turn to yield up
treasure, yet succeeded only in emphasizing,—nay, *magnifying*—the
very barrenness of the search. Not only did the wretched area fail to
provide Xavier with fresh evidence, it seemed, by way of a certain implacable sterility,—a lunar species of *silence*, and *emptiness*, and *nullity*—to negate, as it were, all that one did know of it: so that Xavier was
by degrees overcome by doubt that any human beings had ever entered
this place; and that any human history, of however malefic a sort, had
here transpired. Alone!—and most lonely! A sliver of yearning entered
Xavier's heart, that he had *not* waited for Perdita to accompany him,—
a yearning of such visceral potency, one knows not whether to deem it
mere lust, or noble desire. "Ah! if *she* were but here,—at my side—her
hand in mine," Xavier exclaimed aloud, to the taunting rocks on all
sides, "how fearless I should then be!—and capable, with God's grace,
of *seeing*, and *knowing*, infinitely more than I do."

But since that day some weeks previous, Perdita had refrained
from writing to him: save a careless scrap of a note, penned to thank

him for the "unlook'd-to but altogether Prized" gift of the pair of turtle doves; and another message, of scarcely more substance, in reply to
one or another of his own letters,—reiterating the plea that he hold
himself distant from her, for the time being at least, as his presence
awakened in her "chaotic & not-to-be-named yearnings, of a kind at
variance with a Virgin's soul": the which hastily scrawled *billet-doux*
exerted so profound and so morbid an influence over the young detective's state of mind, I am almost abashed to acknowledge.

In this malevolent atmosphere, however, Perdita's image could
not long be harbored. In its place, Xavier summoned forth that of Valentine Westergaard: saw again the pallid, simpering, effeminate face;
the too-red hair, its curls unnaturally tight; the rosy insinuating smile,
that revealed slightly yellowed teeth; the greeny glow of the eyes. That
Valentine's slender anguilliform figure, gliding here and there amidst
the oversized boulders, was very much *of* the Half-Acre, seemed to
Xavier incontestable: nay, it would not have surprised him greatly to
whirl about, and to see Valentine but a few yards away, staring fixedly
at him, and smiling. *Dear Xavier!—my dear young friend! How droll of
you to hike out to this most favored of places, at the very hour at
which I had fancied I should visit: and how serendipitous that my loneliness shall now be absolved!*

A sudden knocking of his heart so alerted Xavier, he *did* glance
around,—but saw nothing, and no one: save the whitely blinding glare
of the sun that, as noontide approached, grew, with every minute, the
more ferocious. It angered Xavier that he was fool enough to turn
about so; and to be frightened. For even if Valentine did appear,—even
if, of a sudden, all silently, he did materialize—was not Xavier Kilgarvan "man" enough to confront him? "Why, he is but a fop; a half-man;
a weakling upon which finery is draped," Xavier muttered aloud, that
he might hear himself think over the distant roaring of the rocks, "and
even if he carry his weapon with him, slyly hidden inside his coat, why
should *I* be afraid? The coward attacks only helpless maidens: he
would never dare set hands upon a man,"—and so on, and so forth, in
half-conscious mutterings of this nature.

Nonetheless, Xavier felt a prick of cold terror yet a second time:
and could not resist glancing over his other shoulder: to see, quivering
in the sun's radiant light, an image of sorts, not truly formed, yet visible enough, of the murderer,—the "Cruel Suitor" lounging against the
arm of the sofa, his weak-boned chin resting languidly on the back of
his hand, his placid eyes fixed upon Xavier. *Ah! Yes! Is't so! Really!
Why, my sweet boy, you are a paragon of Idealism!—a "Detective of
Genius," indeed!* Xavier blinked, and stared, and pressed a hand
against his pounding heart, though he knew full well Valentine was
not there, and that he was quite alone. Yet, by narrowing his eyes, he

saw, or fancied he could see, how teasingly Valentine slid his knife,—
for surely it *was* a knife?—from out the inner pocket of his formal dinner jacket. Why, had he carried :: with him into the very dining room
of Ravensworth Park,—was the monster never without it? All suggestively, all seductively, Valentine stroked the handle; and the long
gleaming glittering blade. Unless Xavier's eyes cruelly tricked him,
the handle was in the shape of a cross,—the better to be gripped with
the fingers; and shone golden; most golden; though studded with tiny
precious gems, predominantly rubies. The blade was doubtless made
of steel,—well above twelve inches in length, and about two-and-a-half
inches at its widest point,—catching the noontide's sunlight with especial vigor, and flashing it to Xavier's dazed eye. *This! Why, 'tis but a
mere toy: a child's sword, and not a warrior's: so pretty an instrument,
and so delicate, it quite wears out one's arm, in battle. Should you like
to grip it in your hand, sweet Xavier, to test its modest weight! Only
come here,—come here. Come here—*

The felicitous passage of a yellow butterfly distracted Xavier,
and seemed to waken him: thus he stood, blinking, and sweating, and
panting, and staring into space: and, for a confused instant, blind to
the heaped and jumbled landscape beyond.

After a minute or two, when his senses grew calm again, Xavier
wiped at his clammy forehead with a handkerchief, and exclaimed
aloud, "How damn'd a fool am I becoming, and how craven a coward!"—in a voice that fairly trembled with anger.

For, of a sudden, he was *most* angry with himself,—and cared
not a whit that his familiar headache had started, just behind his eyes;
and that within a few minutes tears would spill onto his cheeks. "Dear
God, I am a fool, and a coward, and an ass, and,—ah, I know not all,"
Xavier said, grinding his teeth. "For there is naught in this hellish
place but *I:* unless, as Milton's Devil so aptly says, *I myself am Hell:*
and is't not somewhat vainglorious, to think so?"

Thus he stormed at himself; and resumed his fruitless examination; employing his magnifying glass with growing impatience, and
no success; stumbling on the inhospitable terrain; near-turning his
ankle; brushing with sudden vexation, mounting to fury, at a second
butterfly,—or was it the identical pretty creature?—that blundered
against his perspiring face. (It were well for the golden-winged butterfly, with its tigerish stripes, and subtle rubiginous patterns, that it
flitted effortlessly away from Xavier's grasp,—or the exasperated man
might have behaved most ignobly, to crush it between his fingers.)
But, by degrees, he did so manage to placate his thrumming nerves
that something resembling a *detective's investigation* followed,—
albeit in such comically sterile ground, there was nothing to investigate.

Still, Xavier knew precisely where each of the murdered girls had been found. Had he not immersed himself thoroughly in the facts?—had he not memorized all?

Not a few yards distant was the much-abused body of Eva Teal, in its rigid kneeling position: the bruised jaw and elbows against that misshapen rock, the wrists close to touching behind her head, so that, at first glance, one might imagine they were tied. A charming poplin dress, in green, prettily decorated with cream-colored ribands, and lace that, albeit machine-made, was altogether charming as well. A gift from her suitor, doubtless. Or, perhaps, Valentine had simply given the child cash with which to buy it. But where were her hat, and her gloves; and her cotton stockings; and her petticoats; and sundry items of underwear, which the sheriff's report had failed to list—? Alas, the dress was so badly torn, and ripped, and bloodied, it had been thought most prudent to burn it: and so it had vanished: and Xavier had heard but the other day that the tiny gold cross found in Eva's mouth was now "missing"—! No fingerprints had been discovered on it because no fingerprints had been sought. It had not crossed the mind of Shearwater, or that of any of his deputies, or Hans Deck, that *fingerprints* would surely be on the cross,—and that they might be detected.

"Ah, such asses!—such feeble excuses for 'policemen'!" Xavier exclaimed, of a sudden: with a renewed rush of his anger, and a thrust of pain behind his eyes. "If only *I* had been in charge—"

Roused by his intemperate outburst, the murdered girl lifted her head, with some difficulty, to gaze at him: her sweet face so sorely abused, and her plump lower lip so bloodied,—indeed, was the flesh not torn partly away?—that, though he had pondered her likeness many a time, in rapt and pitying absorption, Xavier might not have recognized her now. Poor girl!—poor child! If only he might have saved her!

Xavier staggered backward, rubbing roughly at his eyes. It was the noontide heat, the vertiginous glare: he was not himself: he *was* himself, but most agitated. For, alas, the pathos of the situation struck him, as it had so many years previous: even should the murderer be apprehended, and the "solution" proudly proclaimed,—even should the detective revel in *his* triumph—the murdered and abused cannot rise again, to share in such felicity: for their time on our pitiless earth is past: and Heaven's balm most problematic.

"Nay, I cannot allow myself to think along those lines," Xavier cautioned himself, in a panting voice, "not now,—not again—not ever again. For it is a sort of blasphemy, is't not?—to despair in my own powers, and to risk God's displeasure—"

He resolved to give way no more to childish fancies and degrading fears: but to return to the task at hand: noting (with considerable relief) that the phantasmagoric figure of Eva Teal had been disrupted by a small contingent of wasps, and that he was quite alone in the Half-Acre; and safe from all danger.

So familiar had Xavier become with the divers histories of the "Damsels of the Half-Acre," and so long had he ground his teeth, as it were, over their sisterly fates, it was not so difficult for him to envision the corpses in their allotted places amidst the boulders, as the disinterested observer might suppose. To be a detective, it has oft been remarked, is to dine,—and commune,—and sleep—with the dead, if not with Death itself: and to so adroitly braid one's life with one's subject, not a hair's breadth comes between. Thus, Xavier Kilgarvan knew in what deplorable wise Miss Euphemia Godwit had been found, in a corner of the stony graveyard, frozen so stiff amidst the rocks, it had taken an heroic species of effort to free her,—and a singular amount of fortitude, on the part of the sheriff's men. He knew the approximate place,—some eighty feet to the east—Miss Dulcinea Inman had been hastily, and doubtless with contempt, interred, in the vine-enshrouded swamp; and the final resting places, within fifty feet of his own position, of Miss Tricia Furlow,—the kitchen maid who had so "shamelessly" pursued Ringgold Peregrine, the affrighted young man had had to flee the country!—and Miss Florette Sparks, of whom it was said she possessed a "resolutely cheery manner," and a mass of dull-blond curls so profuse, they seemed to fly about her head. Each of the young women had had the fortune,—soon to become misfortune—of having been acquainted with, and doubtless courted by, a certain gentleman, whispered to be handsome, and high-born, and wondrously gracious, and, withal, inclined to be *cruel:* and so it seemed they were made his brides, if not precisely his wives: and suffered the retribution of a most brutal death. "Yet it is not an exaggeration to say," Xavier heard himself whisper hoarsely, "that, in all of Winterthurn, I am the sole person to suspect,—nay, to *know*—that Valentine is guilty: or even to dare make the claim aloud. Moreover,—"

So it was, despite the warning throb of pain in his head, and the tears that now liberally streaked his cheeks, Xavier succumbed to a fit of very bad temper indeed: berating the police for their incompetence, and himself for failing to speak up more forcibly: cursing Mrs. Teal and Hans Deck alike, for their resistance to consenting to the exhumation of Eva's body,—unless, perhaps (for the thought only now occurred to him), they were awaiting *monetary rewards* for their consent; which is to say, *bribes:* the which Xavier *would* offer them out of his own pocket, if necessary, with due contempt. "Nay, I have been too courteous these many months,—I have been too law-abiding,—too 'good,' " Xavier raged, "—while the murderer himself feels not a whit of apprehension, let alone fear; and the luckless Rosenwald is prepared for slaughter; and, I have no doubt, Perdita herself stands aside amazed, that her 'impassioned' suitor so lacks boldness!''

The golden-winged butterfly incautiously brushed too near, and drew Xavier's ire, so that, all unthinkingly, he closed his fist about it, and destroyed it in an instant: flicking its crushed body from his fingers against a rock, and essaying to wipe the powdery remains, yet unthinkingly, against his coat sleeve. At this moment he chanced to sight, perhaps a hundreds yards distant, where the rocky soil of the Half-Acre subsided by degrees to marshland, badly choked in cattails, reeds, scrub willow, and the like, a single glove,—a *lavender glove*— lying in brazen innocence, for any eye to discover!

His—!

Hesitating not a moment, Xavier ran to retrieve the solitary clue,—yet found it devilishly difficult to approach, as it had been blown, or had floated, several yards out, into a puddle of questionable composition: being partly stagnant water, encrusted with a frothy greenish scum, and partly a thick, black, malodorous mud. Alas, to set foot in such foulness!—to be forced to ruin not only his shoes, but very likely his trousers as well! But, holding his breath against the noisome stench, Xavier all bravely splashed out into the puddle, and in triumph seized the "clue,"—indeed, was it not in genuine triumph?— as any fool could see that the glove, despite its unusual hue, was a gentleman's, and not a lady's: and, in all of Winterthurn, could belong only to Valentine Westergaard. "Thus, I will see you damned by *man*," Xavier said, panting, "who are, till now, damned only by *God.*"

It happened, however, that Xavier's progress into the little bog had been more gracefully executed than his egress could be: for, to the detective's consternation, he saw too late that he had unwittingly run out into a species of *quicksand:* and that, with every step, but particularly with a panicked step, he sank several inches more!—and was so dazed at the suddenness, and queerness, of the danger, he could not think how to proceed. To hasten forward seemed altogether unadvisable: to retreat, purposeless: yet to stay in one position, a fatal decision, as, even unmoving, he felt himself being tugged downward, by hideous, implacable, sucking degrees. Casting his eyes wildly overhead, where a meager patch of August sky peeped through a confused lacework of leaves, branches, and sinewy vines, Xavier murmured aloud: "But to die *here,* and *now,*—and in so degrading a manner!''

Yet he could not reasonably believe he would *die,* for saving himself was an utterly simple matter: he had only to maneuver his body (grown frighteningly heavy and clumsy) some *eight or ten yards forward,*—which is to say, out of the clayey sucking mud in which he found himself, to firmer ground: that very ground from which, but a scant moment before, the detective had, all obliviously, stepped—!

Then, he had been altogether safe, though he had not guessed at the conditions, and the qualifications, for his "safety." *Now*, as the bog sucked at him,—for, indeed, it *did* suck, and tug; all how deliberately, how resolutely sucking, tugging, pulling, swallowing!—*now* he was in mortal danger: and cursed himself for his irremediable error. That the simple reversal of Time could not be directed, in such emergencies, struck Xavier as a singular failing of the human will: as wretched a predicament, perhaps, as the habitation of a body.

Now, with astonishing swiftness, he had sunk to his knees; now, all unbelievably, to midthigh; a warm purulent gassy odor was released from the mud that awakened a spasm of nausea in him; he cried out in desperation, and in rage, at his plight; he succumbed to a terror, that he could not fail to sink,—might it be *completely?*—for now the mud had drawn him down yet farther, and,—but *could* it be?—yet farther: and no help was in sight: and no means within reach, that he could help himself,—for, though the marsh was overgrown with scrub trees and vines, none was close by; nor had he a rock, or any firm thing, that his fingers might grasp.

Even now, Xavier reasoned with himself that the substance into which he had so brashly stepped, to retrieve his invaluable clue (held high above his head, in a trembling hand, for safekeeping), could not possibly be *quicksand*, as quicksand per se was not to be found in Winterthurn, to his knowledge: it must be but a particularly odious, and, he supposed, dangerous, species of marsh mud,—so rank, and foul-smelling, and fecal in its composition, it quite beggared defining. Not *quicksand*, which was known to be lethal to mankind, or to any living thing that blundered into it; but mere *mud*,—mere *muck*, mere slimy watery *filth*—which was another matter entirely. Surely so banal a predicament might be overcome by a spirited application of,—but, alas, Xavier knew not precisely what: not wit, not ingenuity, not virtue, not cunning, not patience, not exactitude, not physical prowess, not excellent intentions,—not, indeed, anything he might dazedly call forth as possessed by *Xavier Kilgarvan*.

"But I shall not *die*, for such a trifle," Xavier whispered, "for the possibility is unthinkable: and my murderer should evermore be free."

Nonetheless, he deemed it advisable to put aside his manly pride, and call for help in earnest: nay, shout for help: and scream: and plead that someone in this godforsaken place should come to his aid. Yet this agitation,—coupled, unfortunately, with a sudden and involuntary struggle: a *wrestling*, as it were, with no one and nothing against which to pit his strength,—had the infelicitous effect of causing him to sink yet farther, and yet more rapidly: the loathsome mud sucking now at his midriff, so that it was necessary for him to keep his stiffening arms raised above his head,—an action that, though sounding facile enough, had begun to produce some discomfiture.

"Nay, 'Xavier Kilgarvan' cannot *die*," the now-terrified man pleaded, "for it would violate all that I,—all that we—know of God's love for us: and our expectations of,—of completion, and perfection—"

Doubtless such logic, and its translation into a rigorous grammatical form, afforded the doomed man a scant semblance of *control* of his unfortunate situation: but, I am sorry to say, it had no effect whatsoever in slowing the cruel rate of progress with which the "mud" pulled him down. So it was, he gave over logic yet again: and again succumbed to shouting, and screaming, and begging, and pleading: the which came sadly to naught, as the marsh, and the dank surrounding forest, and the portion of the Devil's Half-Acre it was yet Xavier's privilege to see, were all empty: and even empty of motion: and so unutterably *dead*, no echoes of his pleas sounded. Alas, that Xavier's surrender of his pride, and his abrupt indifference as to his worldly reputation, should seem to have no effect upon the surrounding landscape or, indeed, upon the vast World beyond: was it not some ignoble species of *error*, an uncalibrated *shifting of planes*, an actual rent (as it were) in the *fabric of Reality itself?*

Why, the mere prized fact that Xavier's mother loved him so dearly,—was this not, in itself, sufficient to "save" him?

And,—how queer and disordered, the thoughts buzzing in his skull!—the mere fact that, as he had concluded from a close perusal of Simon Esdras Kilgarvan's early *Treatise*, the probability of the existence of the "World" itself was in doubt; or had been so, at the time of the *Treatise*'s publication.

And, most potent of all, that Xavier Kilgarvan *was* a hero, and knew himself so: willing to risk death (as, it seemed, he was now doing,—his trembling hand yet held high, to keep the lavender glove safe), with no expectation of monetary reward; and, it began to appear self-evident, very little hope of appreciation.

Or was the hideous experience but a *dream?*—from which, bathed in chill perspiration, he would wake, to open his affrighted eyes wide, upon the balm of morning sunshine?

Or,—he knew not *how*, or *why*, or *by what agent*—was it a *test* of his courage? his intelligence? his muscular strength?

Or was the incident a humiliating sort of *moral lesson*, designed to imprint the need for constant vigilance upon his soul?—no matter the detective's confidence in his powers, and his certitude in doing right.

("Well, as I have learned my lesson now," Xavier feebly observed, "the folly *might* lift.")

Yet he continued to sink, all helplessly; and unvoiced prayers shaped his lips; and yet the forest, and the Devil's Half-Acre, and the glimmering patch of blue sky, mirrored naught of his plight. For some tantalizing seconds, the sucking action of the bog appeared to have stopped: and Xavier scarcely dared breathe, let alone move his body, for fear he would provoke it into resuming. His handsome face was so besmeared with mud, and so screwed up in amazed terror, it is altogether likely that he could not have recognized himself; or would have wished to. And as, at last, he was forced to draw a deep, desperate, gasping breath,—why, the very thing happened that he had feared: and he sank another inch or two, the mud being now at midchest.

But it could not be, his buzzing thoughts insisted, that he might sink yet further,—and then *yet further:* for would that not mean his very extinction? And as the proposition was untenable, how might it be demonstrated?

"Nay, it *is* unthinkable," Xavier whispered, with numbed lips. And yet the action of the bog most miserably continued, now accelerating, now slackening in its pace, and again accelerating; and releasing, as before, a most nauseating gas,—these tiny heated bubbles rising to the surface, and bursting, stirred by Xavier's feet. "Unthinkable," Xavier murmured, trying with all his will to hold himself rigid, and not to flail out in panic, "unthinkable: for I *am* 'Xavier Kilgarvan,' and I *am*, after a long hiatus, at last in possession of a tangible clue—! Thus it seems to me in error, and,—I know not: *incongruous, unseemly, unnatural*—that I should die now, in the midst of the story. Why, it seems to me self-evident that I *cannot die*,—that God would not permit it—for all of the world should vanish with me!"

So it was, the doomed detective consoled himself.

As the torturous minutes passed, he found it no longer practicable to hold both arms stiffly aloft; and resigned himself to surrendering, as it were, his left arm to the bog: which, even at this juncture, he shrank from calling *quicksand*. Now it was with inordinate difficulty he drew air into his lungs; and this, owing to its sickly gaseous quality, provoked so violent a sensation in him, he was forced to expel it at once. Some yards distant, a flotilla of golden-winged butterflies all lightly passed, with no more cognizance of the entrapped man than the petrified hulks of swamp trees had cognizance of him: and Xavier sharply regretted that, shortly before his death, he had been intemperate enough to cause the death of one of *these*,—a creature possessed of so delicate, and so wondrously intricate, a beauty, in the minute span of its fluted wings, as to justify all earthly disharmony,—and Mankind's enfeebled wickedness. "Ah, forgive me!" was Xavier's whispered plea.

Now, however, it was too late for such musings, for even the most resolutely optimistic of persons could not help but suspect that Xavier must soon sink below the bog's scum-encrusted surface,—and suffocate, and die an unspeakable death: and, indeed, suffer that most irremediable of insults, *complete oblivion*, and *erasure:* with no trace of him remaining for the world to mourn—! Sensing this, in despairing fatigue Xavier lowered his right arm, which had grown numb: and closely examined the "clue" to which, it seemed, he had given his life: now perceiving it, with a sickened rush of certitude, and rage, to be far too clean,—indeed, was the glove not freshly laundered?—to have lain in the bog since June. "Why, it has been 'planted' to lure me hither,— to my folly,—to my death!" Xavier softly exclaimed: and so revulsed was he by his own blindness, he threw the glove from him with what meager strength his arm retained,—so that it landed a few yards away, caught in an upright jaunty position amidst the reeds, with mocking lavender solicitude bidding him *adieu.*

By degrees, sinking, being sucked so relentlessly downward, to the febrific bowels of the earth, Xavier came to see that this was no merely local and finite a space into which he plunged, but the *primordial, everlasting, boundaryless* Universe. Here, no World existed, for "existence" was but a phantom: this inchoate sprawling lapping sucking substance predated all extension in space, and all time,—and, it scarcely needs be said, quite annihilated the very principle of Individuality. It had been given to him, to be *Xavier Kilgarvan* for naught but the duration of his heartbeat,—for the duration of his lungs' potency: and when these failed, as they soon must, he would pass over, unresisting, into the primordial Universe, where Time had yet to be born.

This, then, is the greatest of Mysteries,—to which there is no solution: thus Xavier's ebbing consciousness bade him understand, as the surrounding marsh, and the forest, and the Devil's Half-Acre, grew dim; and the overhead sun had so greatly descended from noon, it might have been,—ah, how unnaturally!—dusk.

In Courthouse Green

And, all by happenstance, it was *on this very day*,—in truth, the late evening hours of the day—that Isaac Rosenwald met his fate, at the rough hands of the Soldiers of the Second Invisible Empire of the Brethren of Jericho. (The First Invisible Empire having dissolved, it was said, in 1869 or '70, for clouded reasons.)

Doubtless, any reader familiar with the general contours of Winterthurn history, or, indeed, the history of the State, or the era, knows the tragical sequence of events: yet I cannot deceive myself that there do not exist numberless others, born of generations inhospitable to History, who are altogether ignorant of the shameful episode,—declared, all arrogantly, to have been performed by the Brethren so that *Justice would be served, and the murderous Jew not slip away, by one or another knothole in the Law,—the which his New York City attorney would doubtless find.* (For thus the criminal action was explained afterward; and certain newspapers through the State, being so zealous of widening their circulation, and so little disposed to the protocol of common decency, saw nothing amiss in publishing confidential interviews with members of the Brethren, in which the "high Christian-American ideals" of the secret fraternal order were set forth!—and but a modicum of criticism, of their methods, offered.)

As my task herein is to present Mystery, and rarely to dwell upon ancillary factors (however rich in pathos and sentiment they may be), I shall very briefly record the events of August 9, which have been treated elsewhere at far greater length. Suffice it to know that, all unwisely, and under what duress no one was afterward to satisfactorily determine, Isaac Rosenwald at last confessed in full: not only to the abduction and murder of Eva Teal, but, most unexpectedly, to the abductions and murders of Euphemia Godwit, and Dulcinea Inman, and Tricia Furlow, and Florette Sparks, as well,—a considerable triumph for Mr. Munck and his police officers, indeed. The eleven-page confession was signed by Rosenwald shortly after noon of August 9, in the presence of numerous witnesses: signed, it was rumored, with some difficulty, as the guilty man's hand badly shook, and his vision had greatly deteriorated: and he seemed sometimes so queerly dazed, as to have very little cognizance of his surroundings. After this, he was straightaway returned to his private cell, where he had languished these many months; and, within scant minutes, it seemed, word began to spread through the city that Rosenwald had confessed: that the police had had the right man all along: that the "Cruel Suitor" had acknowledged the murders of all five Christian girls, and one or two more beside: that he had done harm to youths as well, while living in another part of the State: that he was unrepentant in his crime: that he was gloating in his crime: that he expressed contempt of his Christian captors, and of Christian justice: that he had named with lubricious delight the divers horrors, insults, and obscenities he had perpetrated upon the innocent girls: that he was an agent of a secret international Jewish organization: that this organization had pledged to free him, by legal means or no, before Passover: that "Jewish money" was pouring into a defense fund, headed by an infamous New York attorney: that he had spat in Hiram Munck's face: that he had boasted of two or three other local murders, believed by fools to be accidents: that he had feigned sickness, in order to be transferred to a hospital, to await his trial: that the hospital was in truth the property of a Jewish organization: that, yes, the police had had the right man, these many months, and naught had been done to him,—indeed, had he not had a holiday from all labor and responsibility, sleeping as late as he pleased, and idling about in the serenity of his jail cell, and gorging himself on food at the taxpayers' expense? And now a lengthy trial must be trotted out, at yet greater expense, doubtless mounting to *thousands of dollars:* with the rigamarole of a judge, and a jury, and Hollingshead, and a defense attorney, and witnesses, and testimonies, and the like: the primary consequence being, an incalculable stretch of time would ensue *before the Jew was hanged.*

Not since Lee's surrender in April of 1865, it was afterward claimed, had word spread so swiftly through Winterthurn,—nor with more jubilation, and roused excitement. But, ah!—to think that *they had had the right man all along, and had not done a thing about it!*

Vigilante executions, or, as they are sometimes vulgarly called, *lynchings,* were not so rare through the Northern states, in these by-gone days, as certain citizens might wish to think; and it is doubtless to Winterthurn's especial shame that, over the passage of years, despite some effort on the part of the county's law enforcement officers, a number of these incidents occurred,—often, it must be acknowledged, beyond the city proper, in the hilly and but sparsely populated terrain surrounding Mt. Provenance, where eructations of lawlessness are not uncommon to this very day; and many a dispute between neighbors has been settled, with distinctly informal means. Indeed, it may yet be a joke of sorts, in Winterthurn City, that there are areas of the countryside the sheriff and his men are loath to visit,—no matter how desperately they are wanted.

(Dr. Poindexter's massive *Pictorial History of Old Winterthurn* might be faulted on this issue, I am obliged to say, as naught but three of the most infamous "executions" are named in his text, and these but glancingly: under pressure, doubtless, of the fact that they have been so long celebrated in ballad form, they could not conscionably be ignored. Nor are other historical records, documents, archives, et al., reliable, for self-evident reasons.)

Earlier in this narrative, I had occasion to speak of the disagreeable case of the defrocked clergyman Elias Fenwick, who, fancying himself an actual bishop (doubtless of some more distinguished sect than his own), seems to have concocted out of deranged fancies a mysterious *sacrificial rite,*—with the unhappy result for a twelve-year-old neighbor boy, that he became the "Bishop's" first known victim: and suffered a most appalling death. In those primitive times, before the Colonies had declared their proud independence of England, Justice was far more swiftly and summarily dealt out than it is now: for, within the space of naught but a few days, *with no lawful trial on record,* the madman was hanged, and a rudimentary autopsy performed, and certain parts of his body preserved for historical and sentimental purposes. (Since having assembled my introductory chapter, I have acquired, by way of a collector who makes his home in Rome, New York, a peculiar item of the size and shape of a bookmark, which, resembling agèd parchment, or leather, is in fact neither: but boasts to be, if the etched legend be trusted, *An authorized strip of the tanned skin of "Bishop" Elias Fenwick of Winterthurn, taken from his left buttock 13 October 1759. May God Have Mercy On His Soul.* A most curious memento of bygone years, is't not?—and one which I shall certainly not use as a mere bookmark, but keep in my *collector's drawer,* for safety's sake!)

Some decades later, in the area of Water Street near its intersection with the Old King's Highway (or, as it is more commonly known these days, the Mt. Moriah Pike), there occurred a singularly repulsive crime, perpetrated by a former slave named Rufus Sayles (or Sales), who was said to have been taken up by an elderly Quaker couple out of pity for his condition; and given work in their dry goods store; and "treated with such Christian compassion, one might have thought the brute their son,"—as one account of the crime would have it. Rufus Sayles being mentally deficient, or by nature exceedingly wicked, he seems to have felt little gratitude for the Quaker couple's largesse; and, so far from realizing himself in their debt, or, indeed, in the debt of the white race generally, he took to "strutting about town," and "giving himself airs," and even, upon occasion, staring most brazenly at white persons of the female sex, instead of humbly averting his eyes, as others of his race, or the redskin tribe, were accustomed to do. As the elderly Quakers were not half so ingenuous in their business methods as they were in their charitable acts, it was long rumored through town that they were secretly far more well-to-do than they wished to appear: that, in all likelihood, they were *wealthy:* their gold coins cleverly hidden about the house, or in one or another of their outbuildings. Thus it happened, not, alas, to everyone's surprise, that, one wintry eve, the Negro crept from his pallet at the rear of the store, and most barbarously slashed the throats of his employers, before they could even rise from their beds: and gathered all the coins, silverware, candle-sticks, etc., he could locate: and fled along the Old King's Highway toward Mt. Moriah, on a horse of but modest strength and speed, stolen from the Quakers' stable. So foolish was Rufus Sayles, or so panicked at the unholy deed he had committed, he failed to secure his booty well enough to his saddle, and blundered so egregiously that an actual *trail of evidence* was dropped on the highway, leading directly to the cornfield in which he was discovered asleep, in a drunken and stuporous slumber!—with the consequence that, when a small posse of men found him, they did not even trouble to rouse him from his slumber, but hacked the fiend to death, *and to pieces*, with their knives. It was said that Rufus Sayles's various organs, including the actual heart, were scattered through the cornfield; and that his dark blood liberally flowed, to enrich the parched soil; and that, on certain windless nights in autumn, his grieving spirit yet roams the acre, claiming that he was most unfairly treated by his white accomplices,—whose names were never known, if, indeed, such "accomplices" had ever existed.

Not many years afterward, in the 1830s, there occurred through the Valley a veritable plague of beatings, floggings, brandings, disappearances, and outright murders, perpetrated by the Anti-Masons: this semisecret organization, later to declare itself an actual *political party*, having come into existence after the ostensible "execution" of a brick-and-stone mason of Batavia, New York, who had meant to betray secret Masonic rituals by publishing them in a book. As the man had been a Royal Arch Mason, and as he *had* disappeared, it seemed to many persons self-evident that the Masons had disposed of him, most likely by throwing his body into the Niagara River; and leaving no trace behind. So it was, the Anti-Masons sprang into existence, to seek revenge for the murdered man; and more generally to seek suppression, and persecution, of the Masons, who were rumored to be blasphemers, immoralists, satanists, and the like. So many were the lynchings and attempted lynchings of the decade, and so confused the local accounts, it would be impossible to set them forth with any degree of historical accuracy: though it is of interest here, I think, to note that the Anti-Masons practiced a form of nocturnal rallies, raids, and terrorizings, not unlike that of the Brethren of Jericho; and that a clear line of descent most likely exists between these noisome bullies and the vigilantes who broke into Isaac Rosenwald's cell and bore him away for execution, in Courthouse Green, not long past midnight of August 9. Indeed, to Winterthurn's shame be it recorded, there were tales of law enforcement officers themselves pledging loyalty to the Anti-Masons; or, at the very least, neglecting to restrain them. And the like held true, I am afraid, when Isaac Rosenwald was abducted.

As to more recent ancestry in the Winterthurn Valley, doubtless the First Invisible Empire of the Brethren of Jericho,—which, being staunchly *nigger-hating*, sprang to life following the end of the Civil War—was made up of traitorous "Copperheads," these being the vociferous Southern sympathizers who had opposed President Lincoln at every turn, and argued that the War was being illegally waged, for the *freeing of the blacks*, and the *enslavement of the whites*. Through the Valley, as through New York State generally, the Copperheads wielded considerable power, at least for disruption and mischief: and it is but infrequently recalled that, in 1863, Clement Peregrine Armbruster, who was both a Congressman of the United States and Mayor of Winterthurn City, had stirred up an amazing controversy as to whether Winterthurn should straightaway expel all its blacks and secede from the Union!—as, in Armbruster's words, "naught but Chaos and Night will follow when the tyrant Lincoln brings white Christian men to their knees." So there can be little mystery about it, that both Republicans and Negroes were often terrorized, in those days: and that the latter suffered most grievously, in being chosen at random to be beaten, flogged, branded with white-hot irons, tarred and feathered, hanged, and burned, that all Negroes might be served a lesson.

As the Second Invisible Empire of the Brethren of Jericho was a secret fraternal organization, naught but miscellaneous details are known of it, and these are highly suspect: for it was rumored that the

Brethren would punish most severely any man who betrayed their secrets, and wreak vengeance even upon his family. It was generally known, however, that only white male citizens above the age of twenty-one might belong: that they must be sponsored by members who would swear to their loyalty, and courage, and "integrity": that they took blood oaths to defend the Brethren against all opposition, no matter if it be legally constituted, or no: that they submitted to arduous initiation rites, involving considerable physical pain, in order to have the privilege of *inflicting such pain upon others.* Their high Christian ideals were freely reported in the newspapers: they were dedicated to the preservation of the white Anglo-Saxon Protestant family, and to Justice, and to White Supremacy, and to the Pursuit of Happiness, and to Morality, and to the Constitution, and to Liberty, and to Free Speech, amongst other pledges. Though their meetings were invariably held in secret, albeit out in the open (owing to their large numbers), so frequently did they rally or demonstrate in public, and even march in military procession, their curious garb came to be known by all: these ankle-length gowns, and swirling capes, and scalloped hoods, of tough cotton fabric, yellow brocaded in black; these crimson cummerbunds and gloves; these spurred leather boots, of high-polished black; these ritual swords, or daggers,—being held up to ridicule by most citizens, yet covertly admired, it must be confessed, by some. (Thus Valentine Westergaard, who visibly shuddered at any mention of the uncouth tribe, and who amused his circle of acquaintances by declaring how distressed he should be if a contingent burst into his townhouse, with the aim of "laying hands upon him, and making him be *good*," yet admitted envy of the Brethren's costume: for *he* dared not appear in public in a crimson velvet cape of his own, trimmed in sable; nor could he quite bring off spurred leather boots; nor dare to thrust a gilt-handled sword through his cummerbund! "Withal," Valentine said sighingly, "I admire the brutes for their inspired synthesis of the *military*, the *ecclesiastical*, and the *carnival*: and for their tact, in shielding us from their brute faces.")

The execution of Isaac Rosenwald at approximately 12:40 A.M. was preceded by a mass rally of the Jericho Brethren in a field some two miles south of town: some of the Brethren disguised in their billowing costumes, and a surprising number in their everyday clothes, with no especial attempt at concealment. All were hotly aroused by the news of Rosenwald's confession, which had, as the long day progressed, become embellished with divers fantastical details, of a kind not even the newspapers had anticipated; and long before Horace Godwit, the grieving father of the murdered Effie, made his drunken appeal to the crowd that vengeance be exacted with no further hesitation, the jubi-

lant chant of *Hang the Jew! Hang the Jew!* was taken up on all sides. As
to the nature of further speeches made to the gathering, and to which
Winterthurn citizens, masked or no, climbed atop a hay wagon, to
add their raised voices to the rest; whence came the dozens of kero-
sene-soaked torches, lit, with the coming of night, to striking effect; or
where the law enforcement officers of the county and the city were
while all the foregoing transpired,—none of this seems to be known
with any certainty, as accounts of the night's famed mischief vary
greatly, and no official reports exist.

Thus it was, some three or four hundred men marched into
town, and then along lower Union Avenue, to Courthouse Green:
their quivering torches held high: and a wondrous euphoria in their
tramping, and stomping, and arm swinging, and chanting. Little is it
to be marveled at that no one dared challenge them: that Hiram
Munck was nowhere to be found,—not in his darkened house on the
edge of Juniper Park, and not, certainly, at police headquarters; and
that Frank Shearwater, confined to his bed since the afternoon, with
pains in his chest and an alarming shortness of breath, could scarcely
summon forth the necessary strength, to rise and take command.

*And where was young Xavier Kilgarvan, who had taken such an
inordinate interest in the case?—why was he, of all persons, not
present?* Thus it was afterward asked by several parties, who were innocent, and sickened, spectators to the hanging: but no answer was
forthcoming.

The doomed Rosenwald, forcibly marched from his jail cell, was said
to have evinced little surprise when the hooded members of the Jericho
death squad burst in upon him: nor did he resist his fate: though, as a
consequence of his weakened condition, and his bad eyes, he could not
always bear himself along steadily enough to satisfy his five escorts.

Apart from aiding him with nudges, and occasional rough
thrusts from behind, however, these men demonstrated a remarkable
restraint, amounting almost to timidity, in their handling of him; and
(as it would be known some months later) actually began to doubt, as
the minutes passed, that Rosenwald *was* their man after all. For he impressed them, despite his haggard and emaciated condition, as a *gentleman*, of a teacherly or a ministerial sort: and not a murderer: still
less the fabled "Cruel Suitor," of which so much had been said—!
However, such misgivings were belated, indeed; for, as one masked
man observed to another, in a muttered aside, their impatient
comrades on the Green should be grievously disappointed, and confused, and angered, if they were now told that the Jew Rosenwald was
not guilty, after so much effort on their part; and had it ever been
known to have occurred that a man taken from his prison cell for exe-

cution was abashèdly returned, *by the selfsame death squad that had taken him hither!* ("Nay,—it is impossible—we should be laughed out of Winterthurn and whipped and branded by our brothers," one of the men told the others; and so, I am afraid, it would have been.)

Thus it came about, with no one interfering, Isaac Rosenwald was led blinking to Courthouse Green, where, by nightmare magic, a great unruly crowd had gathered; and a makeshift gallows had been fashioned, out of crude unfinished planks and boards. Ah, how hellish the sight must have looked to him, his glasses lost, his eyes reddened and dazed: his head ringing with a chant he had long been hearing in his sleep: *Hang the Jew! Hang the Jew! Hang the Jew!* And how hellish too the flames from high-held torches, that cast lurid reflections upward, to illuminate not human faces, but ghost-countenances with naught but blunt shadowed holes for eyes,—the demonic and the childlike here combined, in a way most perverse.

Once the condemned man stood on the narrow gallows platform, however, the noises of the crowd began to abate; and it may have been, as, by torchlight, the Brethren could examine his face, an air of subtle disappointment communicated itself through the park,—for the pale, narrow, thin-cheeked face had very little about it of the Semitic, let alone the brute, or the simian; and it would have required an inflamed species of imagination to suppose that this slope-shouldered man, of less than moderate height, and delicate frame, was the long-sought murderer of the five "Damsels of the Half-Acre"—!

Yet, once begun, such follies cannot, it seems, be halted: nor did a portly berobed gentleman of the cloth, a member in good standing of the Brethren, balk at his task, as he read, in a trembling voice, certain vehement passages from the Old Testament, pertaining to God's wrath, and God's justice, and the fate in store for those who resist His love. Following this, the hooded minister inquired of Rosenwald, if he repented of his hideous crimes, before God, and man: and, even as the dread noose was being lowered, somewhat clumsily, over his head, he took care to hold himself erect, his knees not buckling, and to say in a voice that was heard clearly across the Green: "I, Isaac Rosenwald, repent of nothing, for I have nothing to repent: and only ask of *my* God that He forgive *yours*—"

Whereupon, with a sudden brusque movement, the incensed hangman cut him off in midsentence: and he fell: and suffered some five or six minutes' agony at the end of the rope: and died.

Postscript

The reader will share the outrage of any person of sensibility, to learn that, following this ignominious episode, *not a single arrest was made by the police:* and this despite the fact that, at the actual time of the hanging, some five hundred persons must have been crowded into the square; or watching from rooftops and trees nearby. (There exist daguerreotypes, and pen-and-ink sketches, of the lifeless body, which was not cut down from the gallows until well past dawn: and, ah! how diminutive and childlike the frame, and how placid the countenance, of that ill-treated man! Yet no representations exist of the Jericho Brethren who had killed him: nary a hint of their ghostly, yet stolid, presence at the gallows, and crowded about on all sides: so that, to the superficial glance, it might seem that Isaac Rosenwald had contrived to die by his own hand, at the end of a rope; or had been thus struck down by his Maker, with no human agency involved.)

Yet, as the beleaguered Chief of Police Hiram Munck had occasion to say when questioned, over a period of months, by divers outraged parties,—amongst them the State Solicitor-General, and the American Jewish Committee, and one or another Winterthurn citizen of uncommon integrity—it is well-nigh impossible to make identifications of *masked men*; nor was it any more possible, in these confused circumstances, to persuade men to inform upon one another,—for anyone might accuse anyone else; and mere whispers and innuendos would assuredly not stand up in court. Then too, how might individual arrests be made?—for the police should end up, as Mr. Munck frowningly said, "arresting nine-tenths of Winterthurn City, which *cannot* be done."

The Traitor

Through the long months during which Isaac Rosenwald had been held in custody, there had always been, amongst informed and thoughtful citizens, a modicum of uncertainty (whether voiced aloud, or no) as to his actual guilt,—still more, as to the likelihood of his having murdered all five girls. Yet, following the hanging, there descended upon Winterthurn City, virtually overnight, a remarkable species of *doze*, or *amnesia:* as if, with the erasure of the prime suspect, the dread mystery of the "Cruel Suitor" had itself been erased!—and there no longer remained the need, still less the wish for a need, to pursue it.

"And now, let us pray that he restrains himself!"—thus more than one person was overheard to murmur, with naught a moment's pause to consider the singular import of his words: or how very curious it was, they were so readily understood.

In so complaisant, or, it may have been, so numbed, an atmosphere, one can well imagine the wildly commingled emotions,— amazement, and incredulousness, and simple shock, and derision— provoked by the disclosure, in mid-September, that yet another "suspect" had been arrested by police, as the "Cruel Suitor": and this, so extraordinary a personage, and blessed, as it were, with a name that exuded a local sanctity,—no one but *Valentine Westergaard himself.*

Yet it would have been an egregious error to suppose that Mr. Munck had dictated a warrant for Valentine Westergaard's arrest, without the single-handed effort of Xavier Kilgarvan to assemble an airtight case against the villain: without, indeed, the ceaseless pressure put upon him by the impetuous young Kilgarvan,—who claimed he would expose, and humiliate, and deprive of their authority, such high-

269

ranking officers as Munck, if they did not bow to his will: and acknowledge Westergaard's guilt. Yet more remarkably, he had somehow persuaded the District Solicitor, Mr. Hollingshead, that the State might proceed with confidence in bringing Westergaard to trial, no matter the prowess of his legal defense,—a *coup* much discussed by gentlemen of the bar, in commensal fraternization at the Corinthian Club, or the Winterthurn Athletic Club, very near the vicinity of Courthouse Green: for was not the canny Hollingshead, with an election year imminent, obliged to be most cautious?—and how dared he brave the wrath of Old Winterthurn (which is to say, the reigning families of the Valley, a number of whom,—the Westergaards not excepted—were millionaires many times over), whose donations to his campaign fund, over the years, had been most welcome? "In short, it must be the case that Valentine *is* guilty," these gentlemen concluded, at last, "else Xavier Kilgarvan would have been banished long before this, and sent away in disgrace."

Yet, as an elder felt obliged to point out, with a fond faint smile, and a puckish arching of his eyebrows, "there is *actual* guilt, and there is *proven* guilt: and how commonly is it the case, that the two are espoused?" Whereupon the abashèd gentlemen deferred to him as having, most succinctly, summed up all that might be said.

What has happened to young Kilgarvan, to rouse him so strangely?—to cause him to bear arms, as it were, against Valentine Westergaard?

Thus the question was asked in Winterthurn drawing rooms, and in one or another of the private clubs, or wherever, by happenstance, persons acquainted with both young gentlemen met: the ladies whispering of the amazing development no less than the men, with many a fluttering of a brocaded or silken fan, and a *frisson* of anticipation: for, quite apart from the possibility of Valentine Westergaard, of all people, being an *actual murderer* (a prospect, I might as well point out here, no one could take seriously, as the very concept of *murderer* was to them indistinct), there arose the likelihood of a court trial of unparalleled drama and intrigue, to liven the upcoming season,— one in which, moreover, two young, attractive, and wondrously eligible bachelors would be "locking horns."

Yet the general sentiment was one of shocked disbelief, that the Colonel's grandson, despite his peculiar,—and even, upon occasion, notorious—ways, should be suspected of any crime whatsoever; let alone a capital offense; let alone *this* capital offense. For while much had been whispered of Valentine and his circle, in recent years, and the Molly O'Reilly embarrassment had not been forgotten, it was quite another matter to imagine the elegant young gentleman, with his curled hair, and velvet jackets, and fur-trimmed coats, and lavender gloves, as the *suitor*,—let alone the *murderer*—of mere shop-girls, of South Winterthurn stock! But somehow it had happened that Xavier Kilgarvan, acting out of his own volition, and financing an investigation of sorts out of his own pocket, had arranged to pay the fees of an expert pathologist, on the staff of the Massachusetts General Hospital, that the bodies of *all five of the murdered girls* might be exhumed, and re-examined: with findings rumored to be somewhat different from those of Mr. Deck. (It was even rumored, doubtless irresponsibly, that Xavier had stooped to outright bribery in getting permission for certain of these exhumations,—as the next of kin of the murdered girls, when they could be located, were most reluctant to disturb the slumberous peace of the dead; and were justifiably apprehensive of what an expert autopsy might yield.) Beyond this, Xavier was said to have assembled a thousand-page portfolio, the fruit of many arduous nights and days, when, oft-times in disguise, he had mingled with the inhabitants of South Winterthurn, seeking firsthand accounts from persons who had glimpsed Valentine Westergaard in the company of Eva Teal, or any of the slain girls; or had been privy to disclosures made by the girls, regarding their friendships with Westergaard. (Ancillary to this was the disquieting rumor that the young detective, in piecing together his case against Westergaard, had several times spoken with frightened persons, both male and female, who claimed that, many months previous, they had offered their testimony freely to the police, and had wished to swear affidavits naming *Westergaard*, and not *Rosenwald*, as the object of their suspicion,—being, for their pains, summarily dismissed from police headquarters; and sent away with the admonition that bearing false witness, and interfering with the progress of a police investigation, were criminal offenses. Also, it had come to light that several sworn affidavits, including that of Rosenwald's garrulous landlady, Mrs. Buzard, had subsequently been retracted; and that this information had been suppressed by Hiram Munck.)

Most shocking of all,—and most damning for Westergaard— while he, Wolf Kilgarvan, and one or two others had been attending the races in Saratoga, the cunning Xavier had taken the opportunity of misrepresenting himself to Valentine's servants, and, under pretext of taking measurements for new draperies, had searched the handsome Hazelwit townhouse "from top to bottom," as he boasted: making the discovery therein that, in two of the rooms, the carpets had been very recently cleaned; and the hardwood floors fastidiously sanded; and dappled across the wainscoting, a modest number of bloodstains were to be found,—or, in any case, stains that gave the appearance of being blood. So enterprising had young Kilgarvan been, and so shameless in his intrusion upon a gentleman's privacy, he had forced the lock to Valentine's boudoir, which no servant was permitted to enter: and found therein, hidden away in a massive chest of drawers, the murder weapon itself!—this being an antique dagger, gilt-handled, and studded with ornamental gems, which had come down through the family from the time of the Earl of Westergaard, who had formed so fortuitous an alliance with Richard III and had long remained fiercely loyal to his monarch. The dagger, or small sword, had been, it was said, carelessly wrapped in a silken dressing gown of Valentine's, and secreted away at the rear of a drawer, as a child might have hidden it: in guilty haste, and with no forethought: evidencing so little calculation, the blade of the dagger yet betrayed some very suspicious dark stains, as did the turquoise dressing gown.

(Herewith, I shall include, for the reader's information, two groundless,—nay, utterly fantastical—rumors that evolved from the above, and made the rounds, *sotto voce*, of the very best drawing rooms in the Valley: the first, that the ghostly imprint of Eva Teal's face had been retained on the dressing gown, and would be shown as evidence at the trial; the second, that, upon exhumation, it was discovered that the ghostly image of Valentine Westergaard's face was yet retained on the irises of the murdered girls' eyes!—the which grisly evidence, when demonstrated to the jurors, could not fail to convict poor Valentine. Hearing these things, the accused man was said to have flushed with annoyance, that his ''second-best dressing gown had been despoiled in such a wise'': and that none of the sluts had had the common decency to shut her eyes, at a crucial moment.)

Of the numerous newspapers that had dealt so severely with Isaac Rosenwald, naught but the *Vanderpoel Sun*, and the *Nautauga Falls Bulletin*, and, from time to time, the *New York Tribune*, chose to make an issue of the newest development in the case: and, even in these, until the start of the trial in January, very little space, indeed, was granted it. The *Winterthurn Gazette*, owned by the Goshawks, and overseen by Osmyn, could scarcely ignore such extraordinary local news: yet, as the Goshawks had been compatriots of the Westergaards for at least six generations, and had several times intermarried (albeit not invariably happily), Osmyn could scarcely wish to highlight Valentine's arrest, nor dwell upon its evident necessity. Indeed, it was whispered of Osmyn that he grew increasingly frightened of the news that tumbled, near-daily, into his lap: for, after the lynching of Rosenwald, he had at once closed down the newspaper for a full week,—with the explanation that the presses required cleaning, re-oiling, and the like; and, when the *Gazette* resumed publication, the editorial page had exercised admirable discretion in including but a single carefully phrased piece on the constitutional rights of all American citizens to trial by jury, and due process of law: regardless of their ''probable, or self-evident guilt.'' No mention was made of the curious behavior of the law enforcement officers on the fatal night, save a brief and respectful notice, well hidden on an inside page, to the effect that Sheriff Frank Shearwater, having suffered a heart attack of moderate severity on the morning of August 10, had, from his very hospital bed, resigned his position,—the which he had held, as the article would have it, "with honor and distinction, and oft-demonstrated courage, capability, and integrity,'' for nearly two decades.

With the outbreak of the new scandal, it was not to be remarked upon that all of the Westergaards went into seclusion: nor even that Xavier Kilgarvan's family was so reticent in wishing to discuss his role in the matter. Mr. Kilgarvan toiled away in his workshop for longer hours than before, with only his faithful Tobias in attendance: for, as wholesale orders for his toys had gradually declined, a felicitous reversal in custom-made orders seemed to be in effect, from the more wealthy amongst his clientele,—to whom $800 rocking horses, meticulously crafted, and fitted out with genuine horsehair, mother-of-pearl teeth, a "real" children's saddle, and the like, were naught but charming trifles; and $1,000 dolls, named variously Rosabelle, and Annemarie, and Little Eve, and Salome, were beginning to make their appeal. Never one to readily creep forth into society, as he phrased it, Xavier's father now resolutely declined all invitations; and the reigning worry of the household was that, at the very last minute, he should suffer one of his "neuralgias," and fail to attend Bradford's wedding.

Mrs. Kilgarvan, it was rumored, was aggrieved at her youngest son's behavior, and, perchance, somewhat angered as well, for she could not believe of Valentine what Xavier said,—nay, insisted:—and relations between them had grown strained. Bradford comported himself with his usual dignity when forced to discuss the case, as often happened, with one or another of his business associates, or friends: saying that he knew nothing: that he scarcely felt he *knew* Xavier, grown so fiery of late: and had no opinion on the subject. As for Wolf and Colin,—Wolf could offer but a nervous, or flippant, remark, when questioned; and Colin so brusquely rebuked all inquiries, with a menacing frown, and a perceptible tightening of his fists, it cannot be wondered at, *he* was rarely approached.

Xavier *did* appear mysteriously altered: as if he had somehow aged several years, in a brief span of time: his features discernibly less boyish now, and assuredly less gentle: the facial skin tighter than formerly, across the brow in particular: and a disquieting silver-gray glint, as of mica chips, to his gaze,—which, for so many years, had warmly impressed the ladies as limpid and dreamy, and wondrously appealing. To the casual eye he was perchance no less attractive than he had been; yet his social manner, even when resolutely courteous, and constrained, exuded an air of secret repugnance; and his smile was but measured and ironic. If some incalculable childlike exuberance had faded from his countenance, an air of gravity had well replaced it: and if he now seemed continuously on the very edge of impatience, or even brusqueness, his intrinsic good manners held him in check. It was known that, shortly after the death of Isaac Rosenwald, Xavier had appeared in certain places about town, both public and private, greatly distraught, and "not himself": saying such rash, despairing, and ill-considered things, not only about the Brethren of Jericho, but about the police, and, withal, *the entire community*, that his mother had at last pleaded with him to desist: for outspoken censure of the Brethren might well be considered, at this date, a species of dangerous self-indulgence, indeed; and, surely,—as more than one troubled person pointed out to Xavier—Winterthurn City was no more criminal, no more sinful, no more *human*, than anywhere else, in this fallen world.

All scornfully the young man absorbed this doubtful wisdom; and said in a voice of chill composure: "The world being *fallen*, as you say, I had always supposed our task was to *raise* it."

To some persons of his own age, or younger, Xavier could not fail to strike a prepossessing figure; for it is hardly to be wondered at that a female heart might helplessly accelerate in his presence. (Even so composed a young woman as Perdita, whom masculine attention, in recent years, seems to have badly spoiled,—or, it may have been, wearied—found in her cousin's newly emboldened step, and peremptory manner, a quality very much to her liking: though the troubled young woman did not truly know whether she *liked* what her heart so vigorously bade her to *like!*—there being an incontestably greater comfort in gentlemen of another species altogether, in whom the manly sensibility, as it might decorously be termed, had somewhat atrophied. Thus it was, Perdita quietly observed to Thérèse that their cousin Xavier had changed, she knew not entirely *how*, and could not guess *why:* and Thérèse, in a similarly quiet tone, averred that he *had* changed, at least in manner: and quite oddly. "I do not like the change," Perdita said. "I do not feel comfortable with it." Whereupon Thérèse glanced at her, with an expression of scarcely disguised censure, and said: "But why do you imagine, sister, that it is an obligation of *yours* to like, or not to like, Cousin Xavier's manner: or, indeed, to feel comfortable with it?—for I am not aware that he has ever meant a great deal to you." Biting her lip, Perdita turned away; and with a childish agitation of her brow, murmured, so that her sister could scarcely hear: "He has not. He has never. Not a one of them!—ever.

And so, and so,—why, he has *not*; and he will *not*; and pray do not trouble me again on this subject, Thérèse—!")

To others, however, of the older generations, Xavier's aggressive behavior was disquieting indeed: and provoked many a reminiscence of the time when *his* father, the young half-brother of Erasmus and Simon Esdras, had dared go to court against them: as if any judge, or higher court of appeals in the State, would have found *against* the redoubtable Erasmus Kilgarvan—! (Though it was now generally believed that poor Lucas had been cruelly deprived of his inheritance,—not *illegally*, but merely *cruelly:* and it had been most heartless of his older brothers to have done so.)

Publicly chided for bringing "fresh grief" to the Westergaards, and "fresh scandal" to Winterthurn, Xavier had suffered the infirm Mrs. Spies to rap sharply at his wrist with her folded fan, while a number of persons covertly observed: and did no more than murmur, in a neutral voice, that, surely, *he* brought neither grief nor scandal hither, but only wished to uncover what was already in their midst. Whereupon the elderly lady gripped both arms of her wheelchair tight, and cast a flushed and indignant gaze upon him, and exclaimed, for all to hear who wished: "Ah, then!—you are even more of a disgrace to us than we had dared suppose: not only a low *detective*, but a *traitor to your class.*"

From whence came Xavier Kilgarvan's unusually rancorous energy?—his intemperate zeal for Justice? It was supposed by those who knew him best that the death of Rosenwald had been the "final blow"; and, indeed, he was to say frequently, in the weeks and months to come, that he wished as passionately to clear Rosenwald's name as to bring Westergaard to his knees.

True, certainly: and admirable, indeed: but true only in part,—that Xavier sought revenge against Valentine Westergaard for having been, amongst other things, responsible for an innocent man's death. For we are privy too to the fact that Xavier held Westergaard responsible for *his own death*, as well,—in a manner of speaking.

"Let Your Light So Shine..."

As a consequence of various shrewd stratagems employed by Valentine Westergaard's defense counsel, Mr. Angus Peregrine of Boston (whom, it was said, the Colonel had essayed to contact, while the grim police carriage, bearing Valentine to police headquarters, was yet clattering down Union Avenue!), the case of *The Commonwealth vs. Valentine Westergaard* was to be postponed to late November; and then again,—as the defendant suffered so protracted a malaise, a tertiary species of brain fever was feared—to shortly after the New Year: a tactical maneuver not zealously opposed by the District Solicitor, James William Hollingshead, as, it seems, the trial was approached with great uncertainty, and apprehension, on both sides.

Thus it were practicable for me, in this space, to speak briefly of a miscellany of pertinent matters, before summarizing the trial, and presenting the reader with its unlook'd-to outcome: for several things, I believe, require clarification,—Xavier's evident *escape from near-certain death*; Xavier's new-energized investigation, and its gratifying results; and Xavier's success, at last, in persuading the Law to take Valentine Westergaard in hand, and deal with him most forcibly. (It should be remarked upon, however, that, even before the aggressive young Angus Peregrine arrived in Winterthurn City, posthaste from Boston, Valentine had been most discreet in his replies to police questioning: murmuring naught but, "Ah!—I don't any longer *know*, you know," or "Why, is't so?—but I cannot, you know, *recall:* and must not prematurely agree," or "No,—yes,—but then again, *no:* for memory boggles, so many months later: and, you know, my dears, you must *not* press me to concur, and take advantage of my compliant nature!'' and the like, while dabbing at his forehead with a perfumed handkerchief, gripped in a trembling hand; and essaying to fix his interlocutors with a stare of unwavering and baffled innocence,—*quite* the manner, as the police officers afterward agreed, of one who has murdered savagely, and with not a whit of remorse. Yet, even then, taken by surprise as he was, and, as it were, *trapped*, the wily Valentine managed to contrive some deliciously inspired replies, pertaining to damning testimony by ''witnesses,'' the bloodstains in his house, the lethal weapon, etc.,—the which will be provided by the defense, at his trial, as there is not sufficient space here.)

It was true that Xavier had hired an expert pathologist from the staff of the Massachusetts General Hospital to perform the tasks that no one in Winterthurn was willing, or able, to do: with a number of significant discoveries (that each of the murdered girls, and not only Eva Teal, had been strangled as well as stabbed to death; that Effie Godwit appeared to have suffered previous beatings, contusions, knife wounds, and the like; that Tricia Furlow had died bearing a three-month fetus in her womb; that a semen detection test, so belatedly performed, yet appeared to be positive in the instances of Florette Sparks, and Eva Teal,—indeed, as the perplexed Dr. Dunn reported, it might be the case that *two distinct semens* were yet present in the body of Miss Teal: though he would not wish to swear to it; that, judging from information supplied by Mrs. Teal, and the condition of the victim's duodenum, she had died at approximately 3:00 A.M.,—which is to say, long after Isaac Rosenwald had been reported in his bed). It was true too that Xavier had felt obliged to suspend certain niceties of conduct, for temporary pragmatic purposes, in not only proffering ''cash incentives'' to one or two strategic persons (including of course the canny mother of the deceased Eva), but, by a subtle employment of language, suggesting to them, they might very well be in danger of their lives,—if the ''Cruel Suitor'' was not apprehended.

(''But, dear God, he is dead!—he has been hanged!—surely everyone knows, he cannot harm us any longer!'' Thus Mrs. Teal exclaimed, while fixing Xavier an emboldened, though somewhat apprehensive, look: whereupon Xavier drily replied that, as she must sense, an innocent man had been hanged in his place: and it was *her* obligation, as a Christian woman, to help him name the man who was guilty. Being not altogether sober at the moment, and, doubtless, sickened with a long-lingering guilt of her own, Mrs. Teal could not speak for some wracked moments; then murmured, with a sudden grasping of Xavier's arm: ''Alas, do you mean,—the *other*? For, perhaps,—well, I know not,—it has been so long,—and *he*,—I mean, the other,—why, *he* has been most generous,—in *his* grief, as he says, as well as ours,—or so he has said,—the fine gentleman,—and very different,—ah, you would think so too!—very different from,—why, from what one *expects*—Surely, Mr. Kilgarvan," the confused woman said, yet gripping Xavier's arm, and peering into his face with both anxiety, and a forlorn trace of coquetry, "surely he would not wish to harm me, who has promised generosity to me, for the remainder of my life?" Wherepon Xavier quickly said: "Of whom do you speak, Mrs. Teal,—Valentine Westergaard?" and the reply came as quickly: "Dear God, Mr. Kilgarvan, I hope there is none 'other'—!")

For many an arduous day, and a goodly proportion of the night, Xavier, disguised, had made his way afoot through South Winterthurn, daring to venture into the most opprobrious of "haunts," there to learn what he might of the fine gentleman,—so handsomely dressed, so scented with cologne, so unfailingly good-natured—whose practice it had been, until recent months, to frequent them: and to indulge in what diversions might be available: with not a whit (so it was many times reiterated) of *stinginess*, in his expression of gentlemanly gratitude. Elsewhere, he contrived to speak with girls and women,—ranging between the ages of twelve and seventy-three—who toiled, for a modest wage, some twelve or fourteen hours daily (Sundays naturally excepted), in the textile mill owned by the Shaws, or in the glove factory owned by the Peregrines, or in the canning factory owned by the Von Goelers, or in the paper pulp mill owned by his very kinsmen, the De Forrests: by degrees assembling a disjointed, but wondrously illuminating, narrative of Mr. Valentine Westergaard's role as a sort of fairy-tale prince, amongst a certain segment of the younger female population south of the river. The *heartfelt, impassioned, beauteous* songs Valentine sang at the charity Musicales, accompanying himself on his dulcimer; the attentions he paid to this girl, and to that; the compliments, the excursions on the river, the small pretty gifts, the lengthy idle strolls in the park, the exhilarating rides in his two-seater, out into the countryside,—now Effie Godwit being favored, now little Dulcie Inman, now Tricia Furlow, now Florette Sparks, and now, not least, but, as it seemed, *last,*—Eva Teal herself: who quite roused jealousies amongst her girl friends for having managed to charm Mr. Westergaard for an unusual number of weeks: and for having received from him rather more than her share of nosegays, trinkets, items of apparel, and the like. As much perplexed as outraged, Xavier asked of the girls why they were not more cautious of their "suitor," particularly after the first of the murders; why they were not more frightened, of his very graciousness, and honeyed charm, and "that horrific stare of his,—which possesses all the warmth, animation, and humanity, of *green glass*." But the majority of the girls replied, all artlessly, that Mr. Westergaard was *such* a gentleman, once one was actually in his presence, and the dazed recipient of his attention,—and never seemed to *mean* harm, in losing his temper, or pinching, or slapping,—and was so unfailingly apologetic afterward, and *so* generous in retribution,—why, it was difficult to believe anything unpleasant about him. And, of course, such queer things were whispered, and were *always* whispered, of the attentions one or another of the girls was receiving from this, that, or the other gentleman from across the river,—whether with the name of Westergaard, or Goshawk, or Shaw, or Kilgarvan, or, indeed, *with no name at all*—it was a puzzle as to which information was true, and which not.

"Yes, I see,—I suppose I see," Xavier concurred.

Nonetheless, a number of these young persons had, all bravely, volunteered to tell their abashèd tales to the police; but had been, as we have seen, sent unceremoniously away; and had not dared to protest,—not even when Isaac Rosenwald was arrested, and given out to be the killer, and everyone *knew*, ah, absolutely *knew*, that he was innocent.

"But I had thought it was *known* that the 'Jew' was guilty," Xavier drily observed. "Else why all the hubbub raised against him,—and the numberless testimonies?"

To this, the majority of the girls could supply no coherent explanation. For it was invariably other girls, or women,—"spiteful sorts"—who had borne witness against him, and had even signed their names to affidavits, in the passion of the moment and, perhaps, to win praise from Mr. Munck and his assistants: albeit certain of these affidavits had been later retracted, at the command of a priestly confessor.

"So it was known that Rosenwald was innocent, rather than that he was guilty," Xavier said, taking care to keep his voice from betraying any disgust, or despair. "Yet nothing was done. I mean,—to prevent what happened."

"What would you have had us do?" Thus Xavier was more than once interrogated, with an expression of great perplexity.

In making his systematic inquiries of the mill-girls, Xavier took care to disguise himself as a much older gentleman, yet not too pointedly a gentleman: not, assuredly, of Westergaard's social rank. With meticulously gray-powdered hair, and trim goatee, and wire-rimmed glasses, and a studied and avuncular manner of speech, Xavier gave himself out to be "of the healing profession"; and had never a moment's worry that *he* might be questioned,—for the naïveté of the great majority of the girls was such, they no more suspected Xavier of subterfuge than they had Valentine before him! (Indeed, it crossed the young detective's mind upon several alarming occasions, and sorely plagued him through many an insomniac night, that any of these young females might oblige him,—ah, how prodigiously!—as, it began to seem, Perdita would *never*. From that young woman so very little: from these others, so much: though of course Xavier should feel quite sickened afterward. While traveling about Europe he had succumbed to one or two, or perhaps three, temptations, with an air of the experimental and the provisionary, it scarcely needs be said, but his pledge *had* been to Perdita all the while, or, at the very least, to her image . . . Nay, it did no good to think along such lines: it were best to forbid it. "And yet, how easy it must be,—how easy for us,—in crossing the river,—I mean for Valentine and his ilk, who ceaselessly take advantage," Xavier bethought himself. "And no remorse afterward, I am sure: for where there is no *memory*, how can *remorse* spring to life—?")

In prowling the night-time streets of South Winterthurn, Xavier delighted in several disguises,—that of a waterfront laborer of his own approximate age, though stouter in girth, and far rougher of visage (taking for his model in speech, mannerisms, bearing, etc., his brother Colin); that of a racetrack hanger-on, temporarily down on his luck (taking for his model a cleverly debased version of his brother Wolf); or that of a disgruntled acquaintance of Valentine Westergaard's, of a distinctly lower social class, who had been cheated and abused by him, yet was too cowardly to explicitly seek revenge. To the repentant, and, alas, no less garrulous Mrs. Buzard, whose conscience had, too late, pressed her to declare that "the Jew Rosenwald" had been in truth an *ideal boarder,* Xavier had presented himself as an affable, portly gentleman, a visitor from Powhatassie, a traveling salesman, perhaps . . . Indeed, so mesmerized did Xavier frequently become, in his mustaches, and whiskers, and eyeglasses, and new-acquired modes of walking, and improvised accents, he lamented that he must return to "Xavier Kilgarvan," to whom so formidable a task presented itself as *ridding the world of Evil,*—or, at the very least, of one singularly evil man.

"How mysterious it is!—how much a riddle!—that my 'task' matters not a whit to anyone else," Xavier thought, in droll amusement, "yet is the very air I breathe, *without which I could not breathe,* to me!"

As to the controversial "plundering" of Valentine's house on Hazelwit Square (this term later to be used, with searing contempt, by Angus Peregrine),—Xavier performed the brazen *coup* very much along the lines that gossip would have it, in disguise as an upholsterer's and decorator's apprentice, a cheery young man in a cloth cap, with a valise of measuring tapes, house-plans, and the like, whose speech at the rear door of the house was so utterly convincing, the housekeeper (who had heard not a word from the master on the subject of redecorating) not only allowed Xavier into the house, but gave him free rein, to wander where he would, for upward of two hours—! Assuredly it was a pity, Xavier afterward granted, that this kindly old woman,—indeed, *all* Valentine's fresh-acquired servants—were to be so brutally sacked by the master, upon his return: but, alas! such infelicities cannot be prevented.

Thus it was, the decorator's apprentice, to be excused, perhaps, for his springy step, and insouciant whistling, and scarcely disguised air of *gloating elation*, utilized to the full every minute granted him,—ah, it must have been by God!—in Valentine's resplendent townhouse. What a triumph for Xavier,—what a feast! Nonetheless, he managed to calm his beating heart; and to proceed with as much restraint as possible, in examining the premises *inch by inch;* or very nearly. Methodical, assiduous, wondrously patient: for he *would* not be hurried, here at last in the "Cruel Suitor's" abode: nay not even if he heard the murderer's footfall on the stair—!

Nor was Xavier susceptible, after the first dazed minute or two, to the cornucopia of charms ranged about, in room after room, and on virtually every square inch of wall space: for Valentine's taste inclined, as one might suspect, to the baroque, and the lavish, and the rich-textured, and the playfully dazzling. Velvet draperies of an inordinate lushness; rich-brocaded chairs and divans, in medieval Spanish design; silken wallpaper in bursts of raw color; odd, arresting, doubtless "amusing" *objets d'art*, on every table and mantel; wall hangings by Gustave Moreau depicting languorous *chimères*, and death angels, and wispily clad youths astride unicorns, and sunken cities, and funeral pyres . . . "A riotous garden of fancies *without*," Xavier primly observed, "to disguise the hideous sterility *within*." In the drawing room, which was splendidly decorated in rich greens, purples, and deep reds, and presided over, as it were, by an antique Italian tapestry whose silken threads yet shone with a jewellike radiance, Xavier at once discovered that the Indian carpet had been freshly cleaned,—ah, and somewhat too abrasively, it seemed, as, in certain areas, the emerald-green arabesques were faded, and the fringe had grown distinctly shabby. Grunting with effort, Xavier turned over a goodly portion of the carpet: to discern, with a sharp intake of breath, a sizable bloodstain,—for surely it *was* a bloodstain—on the underside, directly beneath the bleached area. A thorough investigation of the carpet yielded several other stains, smaller in size, but no less blatant to the trained eye; and, though the hardwood floor had been very recently sanded and polished, a sequence of faint stains was yet visible in the grain of the wood.

"So it was, Eva Teal died in this very spot: or greatly suffered here," Xavier murmured beneath his breath, "Eva, or any of the others, I should say,—or, dear God!—any other innocent victim, of whom we know not. For the man is a monster, and capable of anything." For a brief space of time, not numbering, I suppose, above ten minutes, while Xavier continued his meticulous investigation, he felt a tangible sense of apprehension,—of near-explicit dread,—a fleet vision of a girl struck down, her arms flailing helplessly, her bodice stained with blood, her stockinged legs part exposed, and stained too: and Valentine, sinuous Valentine, *his* face all wildly distorted, Xavier might not have recognized it: Valentine rearing upward, with his dagger clutched tight in both hands. "Nay, it is but a phantasm,—a consequence of my excessive excitement," Xavier told himself. The deed, cruel as it had been, *had* been done; and completed; and belonged now to history; and it was not given to Xavier to prevent it, or erase it.

Now breathing quickly, and blinking against the fresh-provoked pain of one of his familiar headaches, Xavier continued the examination: finding, to his delight, a series of probable bloodstains scattered across the ebony wainscoting. And, in an adjoining room, yet more bloodstains, on the wall, and on the underside of the carpet . . . It was probable, then, that Eva, or one of the other victims, had bled most profusely in *this* room: and Valentine, being of a shallow and impatient sensibility, had not troubled to examine the carpet's underside, after it had been returned from the cleaners. And though this floor too had been freshly and assiduously sanded, several faint stains yet remained, which Xavier's magnifying glass revealed: and he did not doubt, with a rising,—nay, fairly galloping—sense of elation, that, when the police ripped up the floorboards of both rooms (as he would insist they must do, once a search warrant was properly prepared), they would discover a considerable quantity of *congealed blood* beneath. Why, it might amount to cups,—to pints,—to actual quarts!—evidence of which Valentine had not the least suspicion, in his emboldened ignorance. "And then we shall have him,—I shall have him," Xavier murmured aloud. "And he shall stare out in dazed terror over the crowd of spectators, as poor Isaac Rosenwald did before him!—with the difference being, *he* will know that *God Himself has directed his execution.*"

Thus, along such intemperate lines, Xavier spoke to himself, with but a peripheral knowledge of what he said. How queer it was, that, as always at such times, *delight,* and *dread,* fought for ascendancy in his heart: as linked, indeed, as the inhalation and exhalation of breath: or the systolic rhythm of the actual heart. As, by inches, he progressed through Valentine's downstairs rooms, and, on his pained knees, made his way up the narrow curved staircase, it came to him that his delight must be his dread: for where else,—how the brooding young man taxed himself!—might delight arise? And of what earthly value *was* mere delight, if not springing from dread?

He recalled his hellish "baptism" of sorts, in the quicksand, or mud, many days previous; and, many years before, within the lugubrious walls of Glen Mawr Manor. But of such things, at the moment, he knew it unwise to think.

The door to the master bedroom was locked; but, as Xavier, though the son of a gentleman, had long ago trained himself in the dexterous manipulation of a skeleton key, this presented no obstacle whatsoever: and he halfway wished that Valentine, off at the races in Saratoga Springs, might be granted a moment's vision, of *this* triumph. The bedroom suite (or boudoir, as its fanciful trappings, and mirrored walls, and odor of heavy incense, suggested) was a spacious area, yet so crowded with furnishings, it had an oppressive air; nor did the peculiar hue of the French wallpaper,—a glazed plum-black—liven the atmosphere; nor an inordinately detailed engraving above the fireplace mantel, by an artist named Toorop, of whom Xavier had never heard, of a vast city of the dead, in which, in childlike yet sinister fashion, naked maidens and youths languidly disported themselves, amidst graceful little mounds of bones. In near-ribald contrast to the somber wallpaper, Valentine's enormous bed was covered in crimson velvet, with numberless brocaded pillows scattered untidily about: the canopy was of creamy satin: and not, Xavier's keen eye discerned, remarkably clean. Indeed, did not the boudoir give off a scent of staleness, an air of the unwashed and the despoiled—? And how Valentine's expensive cologne *stank*, in these close quarters—!

Yet Xavier forced himself to proceed with his customary thoroughness, though his head rang with pain; and the riddle gripped him, as to why on earth he was here, in a murderer's malodorous boudoir, when, in truth, he would rather be virtually anywhere else, for the solace of his soul!

His search, however, was initially disappointing, as no blood appeared to have been spilled in this room; or, at any rate, no stains remained. Valentine's commodious clothes closet, that ran the full length of the room, and was jammed with a fop's resplendent attire, yielded, to Xavier's discerning eye, and to the potent magic of his magnifying glass, no clues whatsoever; nor did a squat bedside table, whose veneered drawers contained, of all surprising things, tinsel-wrapped bonbons and chocolates from the Charity Street Sweet Shoppe. (Xavier's lips curled with a disgust he did not clearly comprehend when, upon examining several of the candies, he discovered that they had been bitten into, showing the impress of Valentine's small teeth, and then fastidiously rewrapped—!)

Atop a second bedside table Xavier discovered a large, unwieldy book of Japanese etchings, covered in fine Belgian linen, whose contents quite shocked him. Indeed, he had never seen anything quite like them: shamelessly frank, yet unfailingly graceful, images of Eros: a diversity of arcane posturings, involving both human beings and beasts; fornications in pairs, triples, quartets, and en masse; ceremonial beheadings and disembowelings,—which particularly offended Xavier, as very little blood was depicted, and that which was, possessed a fraudulent sort of daintiness. "A repulsive *amusette*," Xavier inwardly murmured, with a shudder, "yet altogether appropriate as a bedside companion for Valentine."

He wondered what loathsome practices the room's enormous mirrors had witnessed, their glassy focus being, all remorselessly, upon the luxuriant canopied bed; and to what purpose the heir of Ravensworth Park had traveled about the world, squandering his family's money, in the acquisition of winking, leering, tawdry, distasteful, yet, doubtless, highly expensive works of art. On display, as if in a private museum, were jewel-encrusted (and somewhat dusty) statues of nymphs, satyrs, centaurs, and the like, ill-executed, and engaged in cheerless erotic acts; on the fireplace mantel a most revolting depiction, in flawless white marble, of the subject of Laocoön,—the serpents richly imbued with small precious gems, the human beings contorted in postures of unspeakable agony. Yet more perversely still, Valentine had hung close by his bed a coarse gravestone rubbing in Gothic letters, taken from the tomb of a Westergaard ancestor:

LET YOUR LIGHT SO SHINE BEFORE MEN
THAT THEY MAY SEE YOUR GOOD WORKS
& GLORIFY YOUR FATHER WHO ART IN HEAVEN

Behind a Japanese screen was a writing desk, in laminated carved rosewood, whose drawers, being carefully searched, revealed naught but divers scraps of papers, and scented stationery, and part-crumpled sheets of poesy, scribbled in a lazy hand. Several poems were dedicated to "the naughty Angel E."; one, which caused Xavier to start, was dedicated to "my sweet Doppelgänger X.,"—containing these lines:

O Ecstasy of Death & Priapus,
Our Lord of Saintly Pain—

—which aroused an especial sensation of disgust in the detective.

"It cannot be that this sickly creature thinks of me as a double, still less as a brother," Xavier said, hurriedly returning the sheets of paper to the desk, and closing the drawer with his gloved hand. "Nay, it cannot be anything but idle literary posturing, the product of a diseased sensibility!"

At last, however, his search yielded fruit: and extraordinary fruit indeed.

It was in an immense Regency chest of drawers, in a shadowed corner of the room, that Xavier discovered all he might have wished, in his most greedy dreams: one drawer yielding an untidy heap of women's apparel (chemises, garters, ripped stockings, soiled ribands, and, most damning of all, a cotton petticoat stiffened with bloodstains); another, the long-sought murder weapon itself,—for surely this heavy dagger *was* the murder weapon?—carelessly wrapped in a turquoise dressing gown, and faintly stained, yet, with the blood of an innocent victim. So excited was Xavier with this discovery, he stood for some seconds staring, and staring, his numbed lips shaping the words *So it is: I have you, so it is: I have you*, while Valentine's mantel clock daintily chimed the hour. Indeed, the detective's nervous exultation was such, he did not recall that this weapon in its *physical actuality* had been prefigured by his own *dream-anticipation* of it, in the Devil's Half-Acre: the which curiosity I feel I should mention in this space, as so much vulgar attention is given to "Zachariah Kilpatrick's" rare intuitive and extrasensory powers, in the fictionalization of the case, while in real life, *Xavier was scarcely aware of these powers*, and would have blushed to hear them attributed to him.

So it was, at this moment of triumph, Xavier gazed upon the Westergaard heirloom with both *delight* and *dread* pounding in his ears, and coursing furiously along his veins. Ah, at last!—at last he had "got his man"!—and now he must leave everything exactly as he had found it, and hurry to the chief of police, and to the District Solicitor, and bid them make haste to Hazelwit Square, that the priceless evidence might not vanish—!

Postscript

It occurs to me that I have neglected to explain the way in which Xavier Kilgarvan saved himself, or was saved, from a most pitiable death in the quicksand, in early August: the unadorned reason for this being, *I do not know.*

Yet my discomfiture is not uniquely mine: for, so far as I have been able to determine, no other authority on the life and career of Xavier Kilgarvan knows either!—the wily detective having been most careful, through the years, to keep the details of that awkward experience to himself. Of course, it may certainly have been the case (as Mountjoy Price, and one or two others, suggest) that a mysterious and unnamed personage, who had been spying on Xavier Kilgarvan for some minutes, at last came,—ah, near-belatedly!—to his rescue; and, by brute strength, and a certain felicity of movement, hauled him free of the loathsome muck. Then again,—and here, I am afraid, no significant *mystery* is involved—my firsthand examination of the probable patch of quicksand, into which Xavier so unwittingly stepped, suggests that the substance, though, to this day, foul enough, and doubtless treacherous, was not, indeed, *quicksand* in the strictest sense of the word: but only an uncommonly soft, viscous, abhorrent species of *muck:* and the area itself but a kind of pond, of decidedly finite, and not infinite, dimensions. Which is to say, my experimental measurings with a sturdy tree limb, that could be trusted not to snap, revealed that the pond's bottom was probably no more than five and a half feet below, at least at the time (admittedly, many years after Xavier's accident) of my measurement. Thus, is it not reasonable to suppose that, after so many minutes of near-unendurable panic, and terror, and humiliation, and, indeed, physical torture, Xavier Kilgarvan simply *touched bottom!*

And how he afterward maneuvered himself free of his confinement, in which, as the reader might recall, he had sunk to his very chin; how, with what desperate, inspired, tortuous manipulations of his arms, he at last succeeded in grasping something stolid enough to hold his weight; and how many minutes,—nay, hours—were required, of strain, and toil, and panting, and weeping, and sobbing, and mumbled prayer, to haul himself free: none of this information is available, not even to the detective's most faithful devotees.

Albeit we must content ourselves with the fact that Xavier *did* survive the "baptism of the muck,"—at least in a manner of speaking. As to whether he shook off the chill wisdom derived from that sudden and irreversible *shifting of planes*, and violation of the *fabric of Reality* itself: that is another matter entirely: and the reader must form his own judgment.

A Romantic Interlude

It was shortly before Valentine Westergaard's trial for first-degree murder was scheduled to begin, in late November,—and, indeed, but a few weeks following the much-celebrated nuptials of Bradford Kilgarvan and Miss Miriam Burke—that Xavier, of a sudden, declared to Perdita that he could not live without her at his side, and wished to make her, with as much dispatch as possible, his *lawful wedded wife:* with what ambiguous results, the reader will learn.

Through the autumn the young lovers (if it is not a sentimental exaggeration to call them thus) had been meeting, sometimes in the presence of others, but, more often, in secret: as Mrs. Spies had let it be known, with no excess of diplomacy, that she would not permit a charge of hers to "keep company" with Xavier Kilgarvan,—nay, she would never again allow that low, deceitful, conniving creature, that self-declared Anarchist, into her drawing room. "For he means to bring us all to shame: it is a long-delayed eructation of his *half-breed heritage,*—make no mistake about it! ah, make no mistake!" Thus the corpulent invalid sighed, and fumed, and fussed, and vigorously fanned herself, as if, by the nervous strokes of her wrist, she might drive all thought of *Xavier Kilgarvan* away from her household.

All wisely, the shrewd Perdita held her tongue, and feigned acquiescence, though, in truth, she *had,*—alas, so very oddly, and powerfully!—succumbed to some indefinable spell, or aura, in her cousin: seeing even in his habitual scowl, or the ironical twist of his lips, or, withal, the eerily luminous scar, of the approximate size of a nickel, that sometimes declared itself at his left temple, a species of,—

288

ah, *how* to describe it! *how* to calibrate its potency in her maiden's heart!—a species, it might be said, of uncommon manliness; and urgent charm. His numerous missives and cards to her, she bitterly regretted not having prized, over the years: nor had she, until very recent months, sufficiently valued his gifts. (Albeit Perdita had devoured, in the privacy of her dressing room, and with untrammeled relish, the several boxes of chocolates, bonbons, walnut fudge, and the like, Xavier had had delivered to her from the Charity Street Sweet Shoppe; and, with gloating pleasure, she had, all surreptitiously, dabbed "his" cologne on her delicate wrists, or behind her ears. After the death, by inanition, of the smaller of the pair of turtle doves, Perdita had severely charged Mrs. Spies's maid, that the piteous incident should not be repeated. Indeed, finding the opalescent-feathered creature dead at the bottom of its cage, one chill autumn morning, and its mate quite agitated and forlorn, circling, with a drunken sort of grief, its lifeless body, Perdita had experienced one of the heart-rending pangs of her young womanhood: and stood for some numbed minutes staring into the cage, in voiceless grief, that this,—this outrage,— *Death itself*—should have so violently confounded the morning's sanctity; and roused certain memories, long quiescent, she had wished to erase forever.)

"At least, with God as my witness, the second of the doves shall not die!" Perdita vowed, as stinging tears sprang from her eyes, and streaked her blanched cheeks, "else *I myself* will deservedly die as well."

Elderly Mrs. Spies's heated animadversions against Xavier, which Perdita forbore, with many a hidden wince, and a clasping of her hidden hands, the less artful Thérèse could scarcely countenance: as, it seems, that loyal young woman yet nurtured, in her innermost heart, her love for Xavier,—albeit possessed of uncommonly keen insight, and the habitude of interpreting her sister's moods, passions, obsessions, and the like, over many a year, Thérèse knew well how the forbidden romance blossomed: by what stealthy art *billets-doux* were sent, and received; in what exhilarated trepidation "chance" meetings were contrived, at the public library, or at the Armory's watercolor exhibit, or even,—so emboldened were the lovers!—at Reverend Bunting's Wednesday evening services, to which, pleading her divers infirmities, Mrs. Spies declined to go. Being of a resolutely pious, upright, and trustworthy character, Thérèse would have willingly thrust her bared hand into a candle's licking flame rather than stoop to the ignominy of *spying:* yet, though making not the whit of an effort along such lines, and, indeed, turning her eyes swiftly away if, perchance, she came upon a crumpled sheet of stationery bearing her sister's hand, nonetheless it somehow came about (whether by an osmotic process of sisterly communion, or by a careless or random word dropped by Perdita) that Thérèse knew *when*, and *where*, the illicit lovers planned to meet; and, afterward, the approximate degree of emotive exchange at such meetings. Doubtless such knowledge deeply pained Thérèse, who saw how scant were *her* chances with the dashing young detective: assuredly such knowledge distressed her that, all inadvertently, she was privy to certain secrets of Perdita's life. More than this, the knowledge of a romance that thrived in the interstices, as it were, of her sister's *outward behavior*, greatly puzzled her: as, from childhood forward, Perdita had ever been capricious, and wanton, and fickle, and susceptible to a wild diversity of notions,—save constancy. And, in her evident feeling for Xavier, abloom these many weeks, there did seem to be an element of constancy: and even an air, wondrous in Perdita, of somber meditation and self-scrutiny. Ofttimes, when the sisters were alone, Perdita sighed, and rubbed with such ferocity at her face, Thérèse flinched at the distension of her pretty features; and observed that she "scarcely knew of late *who* she was,—or what the world required of her,—or how, granted her own weaknesses, and penchant for error, she should prove capable of living a morally coherent life: or even (God grant her mercy!) capable of living out her life *to its natural completion.*"

When Perdita lapsed into so queer a mood,—partaking of both self-pity and a chilling species of indifference—Thérèse trembled to answer her, in dread of provoking a blasphemous dialogue (for it was *self-slaughter* to which Perdita obliquely alluded,—the very sin that had overcome both their mother and their elder sister, Georgina); or, what would have discomfited Thérèse yet more, and caused her to blush crimson to the roots of her hair, a discussion of the *forbidden infatuation*. For just as it was known, yet not explicitly known, by Thérèse, the tumultuous nature of Perdita's heart, so it was known, yet not altogether *explicitly*, that Thérèse knew: and a precarious sort of diplomacy obtained, in regard to which the dowager Mrs. Spies prattled on in ignorance. Yet Thérèse shrank from any precipitant revelation, or, what would have been yet more distasteful, any heartfelt confession on Perdita's part: for she abhorred so unlicensed a passion as Perdita harbored, with no less vehemence than she abhorred it in herself.

So it was, as the autumn darkened, Thérèse nursed in her heart certain troubling sentiments; the which were hardly macerated by the near-ceaseless buzz of news, gossip, slander, and outright falsehood that circulated about Xavier Kilgarvan, hardly less than the infamous Valentine Westergaard. Indeed, Thérèse hesitated to confide in her diary, *even in code*, in case, in one of her reckless storming moods, Perdita essayed to read it: and to expose all that crouched hidden in

Thérèse's heart. "Ah, how she should mock and laugh, if she knew!" Thérèse inwardly shuddered. (In addition, I suppose it should here be noted, in the interests of fairly supplying the reader with *clues*, that Thérèse had come to be, all inadvertently, the recipient of certain confidential information, pertaining to Valentine's *guilt*, or *innocence:* which came to her unsought,—indeed, unwished—by way of young Roddy Spies, whose tutor she was at the present time. Knowing not, of course, whether this "information" be strictly accurate or riddled with error, Thérèse nevertheless recorded it, in codified form, in her diary,—and would have been greatly distressed if Perdita, or anyone, blundered upon it.)

Thus, an awkward situation had evolved in the Spies household; and Thérèse so forgot herself on several occasions, as to blurt out a stammering and intemperate reply, when Mrs. Spies spoke of Xavier Kilgarvan as mean, and mercenary, and of riffraff stock, and little better than a Communist, Anarchist, or Free Thinker, in his persecution of poor Valentine. ("Albeit," Mrs. Spies allowed, "Valentine is no angel; nor presents himself as such. Which hardly means that he is the *devil* these slanderers make him out to be—!") It must have been a peculiar breach of drawing-room decorum, the sudden display of a contradictory nature in Miss Thérèse Kilgarvan, of all persons: this most proper of young ladies, whose nunlike demeanor, and unbending standards of deportment, had long cast a chill sort of propriety over all her acquaintance—! Yet, with low quavering voice, and a decided angry flash of her deep-set eyes, Thérèse dared to assert, before teatime visitors, that her cousin Xavier was the very antithesis of all Mrs. Spies named him: not mean, but noble; not mercenary, but as chastely indifferent to worldly success as,—why, as Christ Himself had been.

"If Valentine Westergaard is innocent of the charges made against him," Thérèse all boldly said, "he will have naught to worry about when his day in court arrives."

So uncharacteristic was this outburst, it was received in puzzled silence; nor did Mrs. Spies, after a moment's truculent stare, choose to pursue the subject. And afterward, when the sisters were safely alone, Perdita thanked Thérèse for her courage, in opposing the obese old harridan (these being Perdita's cruel-chosen words, I should hasten to say, and not my own): the more so, in that Mrs. Spies, being of so shallow and vindictive a character, might excise Thérèse,—indeed, Thérèse *and* Perdita—from her will for such trifles. "So it is, *I* sit in cowardly silence," Perdita nervously murmured, "while our dear cousin is traduced."

Being yet distressed by the contretemps downstairs, and little wishing to provoke any intimate conversation on her sister's part, Thérèse made no rejoinder; but betook herself quietly away. Not many minutes later, however, Perdita shyly approached her with these startling words: "Love between cousins *is* forbidden, I believe, Thérèse?— love of a married sort, I mean?—love that necessitates touching, and fondling, and kissing, and,—ah, I know not!—save that it is offensive to good taste, and sternly condemned by many a saint?—Thérèse?—is it not so?—*is it not so?*" The which unwelcome outburst Thérèse declined to answer, pleading a sick headache, and badly frayed nerves.

Though, through the crowded autumn months, the lovers succeeded in meeting but infrequently, and, when at last they were alone together, found themselves stricken by a peculiar species of shyness, it must not be supposed that each failed to comprehend the gravity of the situation: or that Perdita was quite so surprised as she seemed, when at last the agitated Xavier stammered out his proposal.

For, it seemed, he could not live,—nay, he did not wish to live— without her at his side, as his lawful wedded wife: having loved her for upward of a decade, though very often at a miserable distance: and with very little hope to sustain him. While the agitated young woman turned partly away, in a sudden paroxysm of confusion, Xavier continued in a quieter and more forcible voice, to explain how, in truth, he had fallen in love with her on the very day,—God forgive him!—of her father's funeral; but could not deceive himself that his feeling might have been reciprocated, or even understood. For he had been but a callow youth of sixteen at the time, egregiously self-centered (or so he recalled): while Perdita had been an angelic child of twelve.

For some strained moments Perdita could not bring herself to reply, then said, with an air of breathless gaiety, that Xavier must be mistaken,—*for she never had been a child.*

"As for understanding the nature of your feeling, Xavier, if not precisely its depth," Perdita lightly continued, "assuredly I did: and for this Georgina soundly punished me."

"Was she exceedingly cruel?" Xavier asked.

"Ah, exceedingly!—but not, you know, unjustly," Perdita said.

Xavier found himself rather more saddened by this playful assertion than pricked to curiosity; and thought it most prudent to pursue his former subject. Thus, for some minutes, as they walked, in a fine light drizzle, amidst the blighted and desiccated remains of summer flowers (their meeting place being Juniper Park's lavish sunken garden, which, in more hospitable weather, is exhilarating to the eye, but, alas, on so drear and forlorn a November afternoon, cannot fail to rouse sentiments of *decay, mortality,* and *finitude*),—Xavier spoke in a subdued yet impassioned voice, setting forth his high regard for Perdita, and his worry lest that regard be misinterpreted; and his ready acquiescence to any scruples she might raise regarding a union between them (for, though not in truth very closely related as to blood, they *were* related, by way of the objectionable Phillips Goode; and Xavier could anticipate naught but a wildly fluctuating income, dependent upon the vicissitudes of his career; and there was the matter of Xavier's career itself,—which, he had no doubt, struck many persons in Winterthurn as problematic; if not in fact insupportable). "I wonder, indeed, that I dare to approach a person so innocent, and so thoroughly good, as yourself," Xavier said, "for I must confess, my mind has dwelled with dark matters, oft to the exclusion of light, for many years now; and I have so familiarized myself with the atrocities of the Devil's Half-Acre, it sometimes frightens me, to wonder that *I* did not commit them myself—! For I am more conversant with certain details regarding them, I am sure, than Valentine Westergaard himself."

"Ah, Valentine—! He *is* most cruel; and indiscreet," Perdita sighingly said.

"And a despicable monster."

"Yes,—certainly,—a monster," Perdita emended. Then, drawing slightly away from her companion, she said, with a pretty frown: "But, Xavier, must we dwell upon such matters, at this time?—for we have not many minutes together; and the subject is most distressing."

"I am very sorry," Xavier hurriedly said. "I forgot myself: and should not have uttered such thoughts aloud, still less in your company. It is a measure of my obsession with our 'Cruel Suitor,' and his loathsome crimes, that my mind does dwell upon them without regard to,—to—well, sometimes to external circumstances: and I must forcibly remind myself that such matters are not for women's ears; and assuredly not for *yours*. It cannot be wondered at that you shrink from me in disgust, at such times—!"

As if caught unawares, Perdita laughed, and frowned, and drew the hood of her cashmere Capuchin cape more closely about her face; and murmured: "Not disgust, dear Xavier!—not entirely *disgust*. Nay, I am rather afraid that,—I hesitate to say,—it is hardly appropriate— well, I find that I *know not:* and must beg you, Cousin, to change the subject."

Chagrined, it may have been, by Perdita's artful designation of him as *cousin*, the which seemed to frankly preclude *lover*, or *suitor*, poor Xavier walked by her side for some brooding minutes, in silence; and naught was heard but their footsteps on the damp graveled walk, and the cawing of crows overhead, and the faint melancholy rustle of leaves, stirred by a wind from the northeast. Ah, how much more akin was this *day* to *dusk!*—and the withered rose bushes ranged along the path, forlorn testimony to Time's inexorable passing—! The bleak stilled fountains, that in summer so delighted the eye: their green-

stippled basins, into which debris had been blown; the graceful, yet, it
seemed, needlessly arch, postures of Grecian figures, in stone; the
mute starkness of a tall boxwood hedge that essayed to enclose them;
above all, the very tone, the very taste, of the air: these struck Xavier
as wondrously romantic, and compelling; yet, at the same time, were
they not tinged with an air of scarcely definable *dread—?*

"I must make her comprehend the depth of my devotion,—its
seriousness, its gravity," Xavier thought, in some agitation, "yet, how
to find the words? Dear God, I must not fail—!"

Thus it was, the lovers continued but to walk; and to walk with
some small distance between them, as if they feared brushing against
each other. Surely it was true, as Perdita had said, they had so meager
a space of time allotted to them (Perdita was supposed to be taking tea
with a convalescent lady, or invalid, in town,—Xavier had forgotten
the name); yet how queer, how painful, how helpless it seemed, that
these minutes should be misspent—! At last Xavier forced himself to
break the awkward silence, and to ask Perdita, if his words,—if his *proposal*—had offended her: and whether she had any answer to give him:
albeit, he quite understood, the abruptness of his speech must have
discountenanced her. And Perdita drew the hood of her handsome dark
cape the more closely about her face, as if, in maiden timidity, she
wished to hide herself from him; and for a long moment seemed incapable of reply.

She then said, in a low, somewhat hoarse voice, that she had not
been offended by his words,—nay, not offended,—nor entirely surprised: for he had written of such matters, had he not? And she in
turn,—ah, how boldly! how shamelessly!—had written to him in similar wise: and, for the most part, in sincerity. However—

Here, she again paused; and Xavier saw with a pang that her eyelashes were beaded with tears; and that her plump lower lip trembled.
How vulnerable, and how surpassingly beautiful, Miss Perdita Kilgarvan was at that propitious moment!—her profile sweetly graceful, yet,
withal, Grecian, save for the charming Kilgarvan "crook" in her
nose,—and her remarkable eyes, though deep-set, and so shadowed as
to appear bruised, yet ablaze with feeling. Was this not the selfsame
girl who had, as a child of twelve, gazed upon Xavier most overtly, at
her father's very gravesite; had she not,—unless memory was
beclouded by mere whim—penetrated the walls of Xavier's night-time
slumber, and walked, barefoot, and innocently *déshabille*, across the
floor of his boyhood room—? Ah, Perdita!—*his* Perdita!

Of a sudden,—coterminous, it seemed, with the eruption of
some small fracas amongst the crows in the boxwood hedge nearby—
the impulse came to Xavier, communicating itself through the nerves
and sinews of his being, that, to make Perdita assuredly *his*, he must

lay hands upon her, forcibly: that so forthright an action was but what Perdita herself craved: and the purpose for which, indeed, they had conspired to meet, in the November desolation of Juniper Park.

("A beastly notion," Xavier chided himself, with pounding heart, and an uneasy shifting of his gaze, "worthy more of the 'Cruel Suitor' than of *me*.")

Fortunately, the young lady at his side sensed not a whit of this impulse, nor the abashèd distress that followed; and began, at last, in the selfsame lowered, hesitant, guileless voice, to speak; and to speak in so uncalculated,—indeed, so breathless and rambling—a manner, as to quite surprise her suitor. So far as he could recollect, Xavier had never heard any young lady of his acquaintance speak in so frank a wise: yet that which might have gravely offended, if not repulsed, another young gentleman, bewitched Xavier no less than the actual substance of her speech—! For Xavier imagined (with what justification, I cannot say) that, at last, Perdita in her truest self deigned to address him, and had cast aside all factitious drawing-room repartee. All blushing, she averred that she *did*, she believed, reciprocate his sentiment,—that is, to speak frankly, she *did* love him,—however,—however— (And here she broke off for the space of one or two agitated breaths, the while Xavier stared blinking at her,—with what incredulity, and slow-dawning triumph, the reader can well imagine.) However, Perdita continued, scarcely daring to glance at her companion, it must be revealed that she, as an object of his love, was not altogether,—how to phrase it, how most simply to explain?—not altogether *worthy:* nay, not worthy *in the slightest:* as her own wretched mother had not been worthy, at the time of her marriage, or afterward, of her father.

"Why, Perdita, what on earth are you saying?" Xavier burst out, with not an instant's hesitation, "your mother not worthy of your father?—of *Erasmus Kilgarvan*? I should rather have thought," he said, with an annoyed laugh, "the converse was true: for it would have required quite a search, up and down the Valley, to locate a woman even his *equal*."

But Perdita, dabbing at her cheeks with her gloved hands, and blinking helplessly, seemed not to have caught the drift of Xavier's meaning; and murmured emphatically: "Ah, yes,—yes,—you are quite right: his equal was not to be found,—*is not to be found*—and I fear I am but the blighted offspring of that union, Thérèse and I both; and that any good-hearted and decent young man, like yourself, dear Cousin, should be warned against me,—albeit my heart must shatter, to pronounce such deathly terms."

Xavier stopped in his tracks, to stare blankly at Perdita. His pale brow lifted itself in perplexed creases; and his gray gaze took on a

harsh, steely quality. " 'Warned against you'!" he exclaimed. "My darling Perdita,—for you *are*, you know, my darling,—I have never heard
such nonsense, unless it be the fantastical explanations Valentine
Westergaard has advanced, as his defense: yet you speak, it seems, sincerely: and mean not to jest, or to mock, or to toy cruelly with me."

Perdita succumbed to a minute's noiseless weeping; then,
brushing the tears from her blanched face, said, with an air of faint reproach, that she assuredly did not jest or mock at this painful juncture:
nor, certainly, did she *toy with him*. "Indeed, Xavier, *you* are behaving
in a fantastical manner, to suggest such things," she murmured,
shrinking slightly back, as if, in maidenly trepidation, she feared what
she saw ablaze in his face. "You are strange. You are obtuse. *You* jest
and mock: why, are your lips not laid back from your teeth, in a sort of
snarl—?"

All hastily, Xavier made an effort to compose his heated features; and, daring now to grasp his companion's arm, albeit gently, at
the elbow, he assured her that he meant not to criticize, still less to
cause grief, only that, in declaring his untrammeled love for her, he
could scarcely bear her to oppugn it; and so groundlessly. "To suggest
that *you* are unworthy of *me*, of all persons,—to suggest that you and
your remarkable sister share, in some improbable wise, in your mother's unworthiness, vis-à-vis your monstrous father," Xavier said, in a
quavering voice, "why, it is, you know, intolerable to hear: it makes
me quite upset: very like a wire, or a weather cock, that has been
struck, of a sudden, by an electrical charge from the sky,—and
possesses not the wherewithal to *discharge* it."

A fresh gust of chilled air, heavy with moisture, caused Perdita
to shudder, despite the warmth of her long cashmere cape; and Xavier
had to check himself that he might not, with precipitant rudeness, fold
her roughly in his arms. For did not her delicate frame call out for solace, and protection?—did not her startled lips call out to be kissed? Instead, Xavier essayed to explain, once again, with a display of manly
patience, that he *loved* her; nay, *adored* her; *worshipped* her; *wished to
marry her*; and therefore could brook no opposition in his estimate of
her worth,—for to suggest, as she did, even in girlish hyperbole, that,
in some mysterious wise, she shared in her mother's piteous degrada-
tion (though not in her mother's "degraded character,"—that Xavier
would not accept), was grossly insulting: not only to Perdita, *but to
himself*.

Hearing this, Perdita fixed her suitor with a markedly queer
look; and said, in a sharp tone, that she found it an unlook'd-to development in their friendship that, in declaring the motive for her own
lack of pride, she should, all unwittingly, insult *his*.

"Why, you are overbearing in this," she said, essaying to wrest her arm from his grasp. "You *are* rude; and intemperate; and irascible; and have no more my own best interests in mind, than you have your own."

"Because I declare that I love you, and wish to marry you, I am accused of being rude?" Xavier cried out in exasperation. "Why, it *is* no less a fantastical species of 'defense' than Valentine and his attorney have concocted: and were you not so fragile, and so precious to me, I should like to shake such nonsense out of your head—! Is this the teasing manner, Perdita, with which you tempt all your suitors?—the bemazed stumbling little army of us, from balding old Goshawk to,—I know not whom: the insipid Bunting, or the drunkard Shaw? Ah, and even *now*, you cannot forbear looking at me in a most nettlesome and provocative manner,—as if you meant to entice yet more reckless words from me—"

Perdita did at last wrench her arm free of Xavier's grip, and, in a childish gesture, delivered, against his chest, a blow with her small gloved fist: the which was assuredly harmless, yet quite surprised her companion. She cried: "I see that, in loving you, and in confessing my love, I have but proved myself a true daughter of my mother: a low, sinful, damn'd creature, of no more value in God's eyes than one of those cawing crows overhead,—or a piece of mere trash!"

" 'Mere trash!' " Xavier exclaimed. "How dare you speak so?— *you!* Of all persons blessed by God,—in beauty, in grace, and in unparalleled charm—"

"Because you know me not! Because you gaze upon my outward form!" Perdita said hotly.

"As you gaze upon *mine!*" Xavier rejoined. "And hear but the outward substance of my poor groping words,—and twist them, and torture them, until they are unintelligible—"

"And I am most offended, Cousin," Perdita said haughtily, with a just perceptible inflection of disgust at the word *cousin*, "that you should speak ill of my father,—for, rest assured, I heard what you said of him!—indeed, how should Perdita not have heard! 'Monstrous,' is he!—when *you* are the monster, to malign him thus,—and to bully me, to entice me to sin: nay, to have *seduced me*, as a child of twelve, at Father's very gravesite: for do not deceive yourself, Xavier, I grasped, even then, the significance of your unchecked, lawless, lascivious gaze, and sensed how unsparingly brutal would be your touch,—as, precisely, *it now proves to be!*—albeit you disguise yourself as a lover, and a suitor, who wishes me only well."

At this extraordinary outburst, Xavier drew breath to interrupt; and would have forcibly seized his belovèd by the shoulders, to still her, had she not adroitly eluded him. "And I am offended, Cousin," she continued, yet more angrily, "by your frequent evocation of Valentine Westergaard, as if that sickly creature represented some standard of deportment, to which *I* have reference; and by your familiar allusion to my 'suitors,'—as if you, or anyone else, knows a whit of my innermost feelings. I care not for Osmyn Goshawk as a *man*, yet respect him, as an upstanding citizen; and cannot think that it matters greatly that he is near-bald,—any more than it matters, to the world, that Xavier Kilgarvan boasts an overabundance of hair. As for Reverend Bunting,—while no woman could feel any 'womanly' affection for him, it is quite possible to regard him highly and even with awe: for *he* enjoys an intimacy with God's will, quite enviable to those of us who feel a greater compatibility with Satan! As for Calvin Shaw, one of our more dissolute Winterthurn bachelors,—he is no more dissolute, I submit, than Wolf Kilgarvan, and interests me to the same approximate degree.''

Xavier stared at her, his own eyes abrim with tears; and a heartbeat of uncommon ferocity pounding, it seemed, in every part of his body. How faint with desire, how agitated, the young man found himself, at the sound of Perdita's raised, incautious, provoking voice: how dazed, at the sight of her beautiful face, wildly agleam with passion—! He stared; and stared the more; and murmured that she was cruel,—most cruel—that it was self-evident *she did not love him:* that she meant only to toy with him, and torment him, as she had so many years ago, at Glen Mawr Manor,—albeit there was the excuse of her tender age *then*, while now, no excuse whatsoever! ''If, Perdita, you would leave off hypocrisy, and outright subterfuge,'' Xavier said, in a trembling voice, the while his fingers writhed with the desire to take hold of her, ''you might confess that you decline to marry me because I am poor, and likely to remain so; and you require money, and some degree of social rank. You might confess that you find my profession 'low' and 'mean,' following your benefactress's charge: you might confess that you care not a whit whether I live or die, or must endure a lifetime of melancholy and heartbreak as a consequence of your cruelty.''

''And there is *hypocrisy*, indeed!—and the most artful species of *subterfuge!*'' Perdita said, laughing. ''That I must marry a man, merely to save him from a lifetime of self-pity—!''

With no mind to their surroundings, but only to each other, the distraught lovers had long since wandered from the graveled walk, into a wild, grassy, wooded area: where, with the gradual cessation of the rain, a light mist had arisen, in sinuous and irregular fingers: and the dimly glimpsed trunks of divers trees, including white birch, created a glowering, phantasmal, yet not altogether disagreeable aura. So potent was the fine pale mist, it quite obscured the sky and, indeed, much of their surroundings; so that the unhappy pair had only each other to contemplate, save for the ghostly tree-figures in the background. Xavier's heart now beat so rapidly, and so strangely, he half wondered if, by malefic design, Perdita, or someone unknown, had lured them out of Juniper Park altogether, and into the wild forest bounding the Devil's Half-Acre!—there being, without a doubt, a marked alteration of the very quality and texture of the air, and of Xavier's own soul. Glancing about, startled at his unrecognized surroundings, Xavier bethought himself, with a thrill of horror: "Here, in such a setting, amidst such mist, and secrecy, and anonymity,— what should not befall us? *What has not already occurred, not once, but numberless times—?*"

Yet Perdita continued to rail at him, most incautiously; and to tease; and gibe; and, indeed, as he had seen, *torment:* for it was clear now that she did not love him, and would never be his wife. Xavier gazed upon her through tear-dimmed eyes, and felt a wave of vertigo, as if he had drawn near to a mirror, and his own breath had begun to cast a pall of steam over it, obscuring its image. "It is I, in enchanted guise; she is my own soul; yet how she despises me!" Thus the wretched young man inwardly charged, while, still, his steely fingers did indeed "ache" to seize hold of her; and his heartbeat expanded, to pulse everywhere in his roused flesh. That he might lay hands upon her and grip her hard,—and harder still—so that her terrible words might be silenced: so that he might, in abandon of all that was gentlemanly and chaste, crush her in his arms, and press his mouth, all craving and helpless, and ravenous, against hers—! Ah, what bliss! And if she should submit to him, in maidenly confusion, or voluptuous acquiescence; or if she should prove resistant, and fight him with fists, and nails, and teeth,—why, *that* should scarcely matter, with Xavier in so extreme a state!

At this moment, a misstep of Perdita's in the wet grass, or, it may have been, a sudden shrinking on her side from the expression glimpsed in Xavier's face, caused her to turn her ankle: and to whimper aloud in surprised pain. Whereupon, acting with gentlemanly alacrity, Xavier sprang forward to catch her, and steady her in his arms and—

The "Cruel Suitor" Tried

Amongst veteran collectors of Murder, both here and in the United Kingdom, the much-publicized five-week trial of Mr. Valentine Westergaard for the "aggravated and premeditated" murder of Miss Eva Teal (the sole crime for which the defendant was ever to be indicted) is no less prized, to this day, than the grisly murders themselves: the divers unexpected turns of the trial culminating in Valentine's testimony, and the jurors' unforeseen verdict, rendering it a rare and exotic episode, indeed, in the history of criminal law—! Yet the outcome, precisely because it so baffled most expectations, was deemed highly satisfactory by the great majority of the spectators,—if not by certain of the principals, who, it is no exaggeration to state, never entirely recovered from the ordeal.

Indeed, for many years before I had taken on the challenging task of editing, collating, and presenting material relevant to this crucial,—and, I am afraid, not altogether palatable—season in Xavier Kilgarvan's life, I had been well aware of the controversial old case of Winterthurn's "Cruel Suitor": yet had supposed it to be one of those *open-and-shut cases* about which the overpunctilious delight in arguing, to the exasperation of others. Now, however, as my immersion in these old documents has granted me the status of an "amateur-expert" myself,—one whose familiarity with the proceedings allows me the omniscient eye poor Xavier craved—I quite see the grounds for controversy; and why, in certain circles, the "guilt" or "innocence" of Mr. Westergaard continues to stir animated debate. For here, we have to deal not only with the perennial elasticity of such terms, as

300

they are employed by our legal brethren, but their ethical, moral, and even *metaphysical* dimensions as well—! Setting aside the verdict of the twelve gentlemen jurors, and paying heed strictly to Valentine Westergaard's bold testimony in his own defense, who amongst us would have wished to cast the first stone?—and how, indeed, should we have cast our ballots?

Guilty,—or *Not Guilty,*—or,—?

By the time the trial opened, some six months after Eva Teal's body was found in the Devil's Half-Acre, Winterthurn was laid under the spell of pitiless cold; and the numerous events of the past summer (not excluding the fate of Isaac Rosenwald, whose name was now rarely mentioned) seemed remote indeed; and partaking of the febrific uncertainties of that season. As the newspapers in the Valley and through the state had long since seized upon other colorful subjects, it was jarring to the more conservative citizens of Winterthurn that, yet again, and with equal zeal as before, a journalistic "hue and cry" was inaugurated in their midst: virtually every desirable hotel room in the city booked (an entire floor of the Winterthurn Arms taken, for the duration of the trial, by an unnamed "Veiled Lady" and her entourage,—including, it was rumored, five toy terriers and a cockatoo), and tearooms and restaurants crowded, and hackney drivers grown arrogant with their own importance: and, overnight, no question on anyone's lips save,—*Is Valentine Westergaard indeed the "Cruel Suitor"?*

The majority of the newspapers, especially those in the Valley, sided with the defense, and proclaimed the prosecution's case flimsy, and trumped up, and, withal, outrageous: yet even those that clearly delighted in the spectacle of a Gentleman Jack the Ripper (as the several Hearst papers deemed him) showed rather more an inclination to consider Valentine innocent until proved guilty than they had Rosenwald: the oft-stated task of the prosecution being, to prove the defendant's guilt *beyond any shadow of a reasonable doubt;* while the task of the defense was but to stir, in the jurors' hearts, that *selfsame shadow of a reasonable doubt.* Thus it is, under our law, the burden of the prosecution is always more onerous than that of the defense: which, of course, is altogether as it should be, that the innocent are protected from harm.

As for the formidable young Angus Peregrine, a nephew of Henry's, and a graduate of Harvard Law School,—the informed reader is probably most familiar with this gentleman for his later association with the infamous "Boss" Everwald of the Senate (he who was eventually censured by his fellows, after many years of wrongdoing), and for his historic defense of the "Rummage Hill Strangler," amongst other much-publicized activities. At the time of the Westergaard trial, however, young Peregrine was generally known for his success in defending a motley assortment of persons, ranging from the wealthy to the penniless. (For instance, Angus Peregrine volunteered to defend the notorious "Medford Widow," who had, by a conservative estimate, poisoned some eight husbands during the course of her matrimonial career: albeit, at the time of her arrest, the lady was all but impoverished.) Such cases the ambitious young criminal lawyer took on for the excellent publicity they afforded him, and for the sport as well, as he was apt to merrily phrase it, of doing battle with seasoned warriors in the courtroom.

"To enter battle in such circumstances,—when matters of actual *life* and *death* are at stake,—is to feel, to the very marrow of one's bones, that one is at last *alive*," Mr. Peregrine oft-times stated. And, indeed, with his sleekly black, oiled hair, and his slanted brow, and his zestful complexion; with his squat, barrel-chested, yet surprisingly agile body; with his "piercing" eyes and his elastic face that seemed, like any actor's, to spring to life with the stimulus of an audience, expressing now *grave concern*, and now *beatific calm*, and now *heckling mirth*, and now *Christian compassion*, and now *scathing contempt*, before the enthralled eyes of a jury: why, it was a joy for courthouse buffs, no matter their loyalties, to see such a professional outmaneuver this witness, and that; to make of hostile witnesses inadvertent allies of his own; to anticipate the prosecution's strategy by astonishing concessions, and yet more astonishing denials; to "stonewall" at decisive moments; to lead the most timorous of defense witnesses through a mare's nest of questions, to a destination ingeniously plotted, by Peregrine's own hand; and, in short, to make fools out of his adversaries, that *he* should reign supreme.

Needless to say, Angus Peregrine did not always succeed quite so dramatically; and what triumphs he had already achieved, were won after an incalculable siege of sheer labor. So far as the Westergaard case was concerned: that he would be flummoxed, so to speak, by one of his and Valentine's most trusted witnesses,—Colin Kilgarvan, in fact—is not to be held against him, as nearly everyone who has studied the case is agreed, that no attorney could have foreseen so bizarre a happenstance. "Ah, do not mention Winterthurn City!" Angus Peregrine often remarked, with a snorting laugh, over the decades, "—the most lethal climate of my acquaintance: turning some hapless gentlemen into beasts, and others, who would defend them, into fools."

It is a measure of Angus Peregrine's magnanimity, and Xavier Kilgarvan's civility, that they should dine together at the Corinthian Club, when at last the impaneling of the jury was completed,—a tedious procedure, as it proved, lasting an unconscionable five weeks: and that, with very little expenditure of time on social chatter, or inconsequential panegyrics regarding the excellence of the Club's cuisine, the two young men should fall into an intense discussion, not of Valentine, nor even the case at hand, but of the philosophical nature of their opposing positions. Xavier declared, in a curt voice, that, though he could not fail to respect Angus for his success *within* his field,—criminal law being, as he well knew, an uncommonly savage and competitive species of activity—he could not at all respect him *outside* it: and supposed it must be stated, in as frank language as possible, that they were enemies; and the defeat of one would be the triumph of the other. "Indeed," said Xavier ominously, "the defeat of the prosecution, in this case, will be the defeat of Justice itself."

At this belligerent remark, Angus Peregrine evinced genuine surprise, and disappointment; perhaps as a consequence of being four or five years Xavier's senior, and therefore more experienced, and worldly; and being of the tribe of stolid, rubicund, gregarious gentlemen much prized by doormen, *maitres d'*, hotel maids, and the like. Which is to say, he felt a measure of comradely affection for all men who were his equals, and was quite baffled that, upon occasion, they should express dislike or disapproval of him. Thus, while the frowning Xavier picked at the roast beef laid so lavishly on his plate, and limited himself to but a few sips of the costly French champagne Angus had ordered, the more exuberant of the two gentlemen expounded, at length, on the nature of his profession, as *he* viewed it. "Let us say, Xavier, that you have proved,—that is, you believe you have proved—that my client is guilty of the crime with which he has been charged. No, let us go a step further, for the sake of argument, and grant that you, with all your detectively skills, *have* proved his guilt; and that he is, indeed, *guilty*. Why, then, how can you not know,—*you*, who are a Kilgarvan, and a nephew of old Erasmus—that the challenge, for me, rises almost exclusively from that predicament?—which is to say, not the prosecution's 'proof' of guilt, but 'guilt' itself. Were the defendant innocent, and a verdict of *not guilty* naught but his just desert, how should I, Angus Peregrine, be allowed any margin for genuine triumph? In such meager soil, what meager plants might grow? Nay, mere 'justice' no more excites me as a worthy goal than a game of poker in which all players possess equal skills, and identical cards; or an exchange between the two of us, in which, let us say, you give me fifty dollars in paper money for fifty dollars in gold coins." Waxing ever more articulate as the minutes passed, and his companion stared at him in stony silence, the genial Mr. Peregrine waved for another bottle of champagne, and even laid a brotherly hand upon Xavier's motionless arm, while continuing: "The great joy of *my* profession, Xavier, is the converse, it seems, of *yours*. For you make it your task,—and a transparently futile one, I am bound to say—to rid the world of the *in-*

justice of crime: by which is meant, the criminal sorties upon the innocent waged by their 'criminal' brethren. You are a Platonist, perchance, who wishes the Criminal to be dealt with, that Criminality be attacked at its literal base; and Justice restored. I, however, seem to have sprung full grown, as it were, out of my mother's womb, so far as a sense of such things goes: for I cannot any more believe in the abstraction of Justice than I can believe in a child's Eden, from which we were all expelled. Thus it is, Xavier,—ah, do not scowl at me, and fix me with a murderous eye, simply for telling the truth!—thus it is, my friend, I take up with zest the challenge of the Law, and, indeed, rise from my bed each morning at five-thirty, aflame with plans, my skull buzzing with thought, *precisely for these reasons.* Just as 'innocence' per se is not a legal term, so innocence is not a very fruitful state; and my instinct is, save in very rare cases, to shun it like the Devil. Though," the good-natured gentleman said, with a chuckle, as he instructed the wine steward to refill Xavier's glass, "so far as Valentine is concerned, it may even be that he is *innocent.* Or, at any rate, *not guilty.*"

None of this, we may assume, was entirely surprising to Xavier, though all of it was disagreeable,—nay, repugnant; the more so, in that it was communicated to him in so blatantly sunny a manner, it seemed hardly cynical at all—! Taking care to keep his voice subdued, so that no one dining nearby should hear, Xavier said: "But then, is not *your* life criminal too? Is it not predicated upon lies, hypocrisy, and subterfuge of every sort? For, by your own acknowledgment, you prefer guilty clients; you are most comfortable with crime; and derive your energies from it. How would you defend your life, erected upon such a foundation?"

Whereupon Angus Peregrine said, after a moment's unclouded reflection: "My *life,* Xavier, and my *professional career,* must not be confused. For the one has not invariably to do with the other; I hope I have the wit to keep them distinctly separate—! And you—?"

Xavier winced at this friendly query, as if it gave him pain; and replied, in a singularly slow, halting, benumbed voice: "My life and my professional career are,—are—one and the same." So saying, he drained the champagne from his glass without tasting it; as if the knowledge of his unique doom had struck him only at that moment. *"One and the same."*

"Well, I shall drink a toast to such courage," Angus Peregrine said merrily, "and give thanks to Allah, that the width of this table separates us!"

As the irascible and somewhat deaf Chief Justice Francis C. Armbruster presided over the trial, there was, unavoidably, a fair amount of

"empty" time, during which the Judge soundly chastised the prosecuting attorney, or the defense, for some minor error in procedure: for
the eighty-nine-year-old jurist was most roused to life, as it were,
when afforded the opportunity to cross swords with the "Young Turks"
(as he called them, half fondly, and half in contempt) who came before
his bench. To this distinguished old gentleman, James William Hollingshead, at the age of sixty-one, was but an upstart young man with
political ambitions, who spoke in an unseemly orotund manner, less
as if he were prosecuting a case before a judge and a jury than addressing
a huge assemblage. (Indeed, never had the main courtroom of the Winterthurn County Courthouse been so jammed with spectators,—still
less, with such a contingent of lavishly attired ladies! Their slow-
wafting perfumes and colognes, and the sight of their resplendent furs,
and elegant befeathered hats, must have been quite dazzling to the
courthouse regulars: and could not have failed to throw Mr. Hollingshead slightly off course.) Thus it was, the prosecution was so frequently interrupted in its opening remarks, a full three and a half hours was
required for a fairly simple and direct assertion to be made,—viz., the
State would prove that the defendant, Valentine Westergaard, was the
murderer of Eva Teal; that he had deliberately befriended her in order to
take advantage of her youth, naïveté, and misplaced trust in him; that,
sometime between the hours of 3:00 A.M. and 4:30 A.M., of the morning
of June 8, of the previous year, he had, in a manner both *premeditated*
and *bestial*, taken her life, in his townhouse at Hazelwit Square; and
had subsequently transported her body to the Devil's Half-Acre, where
it was discovered some hours later, in a most cruel and mocking
posture. (These charges, it scarcely needs be said, were wondrously expanded by the District Solicitor, who, as the minutes passed, began to
throw off his initial trepidation, that, before a packed gallery, he was
prosecuting the grandson of Colonel Westergaard—! Thus it was, Hollingshead fell into his customary rhythm of speech; albeit Judge Armbruster's queries, and visible expressions of impatience and doubt,
were sometimes distracting.)

It is scarcely to be wondered at that, to the Judge, the high-
spirited Angus Peregrine was a yet more nettlesome figure: for, despite
his sleek balding skull and porcine features, and the girth of his torso,
he seemed but a beardless youth, of less than thirty-five years. How
rich, how artfully modulated, his booming voice!—which quite outdid
Hollingshead's, and Judge Armbruster's own: and therefore required,
from time to time, "toning down" from the bench. (Indeed, through
the course of the trial, Armbruster plagued Angus Peregrine more
persistently than he did Hollingshead; though, as it began to seem, less
out of a spirit of disapproval than out of a spirit of contentious play. As
for the guilt or innocence of the defendant, and the actual substance of

the case,—these were but peripheral matters; and, indeed, as Armbruster was said to have commented in private, he had, in the course of six decades on the bench, "encountered far worse.")

Thus it was, the infamous trial of Valentine Westergaard on charges of murder in the first degree,—which, in those zealous days, carried with it *a mandatory sentence of death by hanging*—was an altogether different phenomenon to experience, either as a participant or as a spectator, than most accounts suggest: which is, of course, true of all court cases, regardless of how *gripping, suspenseful, melodramatic,* and the like, they are given out to be. This fact is a commonplace to those familiar with the vicissitudes of the American criminal justice system; yet must needs be stressed, for the benefit of others. Otherwise, the reader will be perplexed to learn that the majority of the spectators (excepting always, or nearly always, Miss Mary-Louise Von Goeler,—inaccurately described by the more sensational of the newspapers covering the trial, as Mr. Westergaard's *secret fiancée*; and the mysterious "Veiled Lady," rumored to be a European noblewoman; and one or two other members of the female sex, smitten with adoration for the defendant) could not invariably retain their concentration, through the protracted hours of testimony, cross-examination, lectures by Judge Armbruster on abstruse points of law, and the like; but lapsed into daydreams; or essayed to doze, with their eyes open. And one is inclined even to comprehend, if not entirely excuse, the intermittent restlessness, fatigue, and outright ennui, exhibited by the accused man himself,—who had often to "pinch himself in surreptitious wise," as he said, to be primed to a semblance of attention, *even while hostile witnesses were giving testimony against him, of a most damning nature.*

Poor Valentine! Totally unaccustomed to being confined in such a fashion, and, since earliest boyhood, indulged in, in his most wanton caprices, he found himself, of a sudden, both *agreeably* at the very center of everyone's attention yet, *disagreeably,* virtually "imprisoned" there—! He fell into a pique, early on, that Angus Peregrine refused to grant him the privilege of taking the witness stand, whereby he might succinctly, and with withering contempt, deny the insulting charges laid against him; and, by simply *informing* the jurors that he was an innocent man, and sorely abused, bring the tiresome proceedings to an end. But, following the counsel of his grandfather, and one or two knowledgeable gentlemen, Valentine sullenly acquiesced to his attorney's "strategy" and was obliged to sit, hour upon hour, in one or another of his superbly tailored, but somewhat warm, and close-fitting, costumes; leaning his delicate chin upon his knuckles (about which a handkerchief,—supplied fresh to him every half-hour, by his valet—was wrapped, that he might be spared the more noxious odors of the room); frequently sighing; and crossing and uncrossing his legs; his green gaze affixed to the countenance,—if it did not too greatly offend him—of whichever personage happened to be in the witness chair at a given time. ("Alas," Valentine murmured into the bailiff's unprepossessing ear, "it begins to seem that little Trixie, or Molly, or Emmie, or all three, or, indeed, *all*, have quite bested me, in exacting their revenge from beyond the grave *in this odious wise!*")

Fatigued near to the limit of his endurance, by Dr. Dunn's exacting three-hour report on the autopsy he had performed (the which caused, now and then, *frissons* of an indefinable nature to ripple through the courtroom); rendered glassy-eyed, by the slow, halting, lachrymose testimony of that shameless liar Mrs. Teal (who succeeded in wringing a tear from even the most devoted of Valentine's admirers, and quite sidestepped Angus Peregrine's thunderous accusations, by admitting her failures as a mother,—and her "wretched cowardice in accepting 'bribes' from Mr. Westergaard"); bored to distraction by the plodding testimony of Hiram Munck, and several of his officers, as to the "evidence" seized in the Hazelwit townhouse (which items were, with vulgar show, introduced into the trial,—and exhibited by Hollingshead, in scarcely concealed triumph, to the frowning gentlemen of the jury): Valentine succeeded in rousing a specious sort of admiration, amongst the more cavalier of the spectators, when, upon one singularly tedious occasion, *he fell into a light doze!*—and was severely chastised by the old fool Armbruster.

(Even at so vulnerable a moment, when another person might well react with surprise, confusion, or blushing embarrassment, Valentine behaved with impeccable composure: and, with a graceful wave of his hand, as if both thanking the Judge for his solicitude and, at the selfsame instant, dismissing him as one might a servant, Valentine murmured negligently: "Thank you, Your Honor: *I* am at fault, and *you* are most kind." Whereupon the flush-faced Armbruster threatened to clear the courtroom, if such titters, giggles, and, not least, muffled handclaps, were repeated.)

Thus, a seemingly endless procession of witnesses,—of resolutely, and, most unkindly, *hostile* witnesses, under the District Solicitor's tutelage—comprised of total strangers to Winterthurn society, like the alarming Dr. Dunn (whose "scientific" findings regarding bloodstains, semen, the condition of Eva Teal's esophagus, stomach, duodenum, womb, and the like, Valentine found most aesthetically repulsive); and discomfitingly familiar persons, like certain "girl friends" of the deceased Miss Teal (who held stubbornly if agitatedly fast, in the barrage of Angus Peregrine's examination, that, yes, indeed *yes*, they had seen Mr. Westergaard,—"the very gentleman seated at the table there"—with poor Eva, on thus-and-such occasion, and, again, on thus-and-such a day, and,—how wicked of them!—*on the very afternoon of June 7*): the while Valentine was constrained to sit, and sit, and bite his tongue, and endure with manly stoicism a sensation of vertigo and faint nausea provoked by the morbidity of the courthouse atmosphere.

("This is unbearable! This is sheer torture! I cannot see why *I*, who am the principal of this harlequinade, am not allowed to cross-examine these 'witnesses' myself," Valentine poutingly complained in Angus Peregrine's ear, "—for I should dearly love interrogating one or another of these lying little girls, who simpered and preened enough for my attentions last year, and were savagely jealous of Eva's 'success'—!")

It went neither unremarked nor unappreciated by the large contingent of Valentine's supporters, nor by the more astute of the newspaper columnists, that the defendant, though on trial for his life, chose wonderfully *not* to conform to the trite custom of appearing in a *uniform of virtue*, to gull the jurymen, and to sway the sentiments of the vulgar crowd. (In accordance with this custom, hardened criminals costume themselves like clerics, or professional gentlemen of modest fortune; and infamous harlots, like convent-school girls, in somber grays, blues, and blacks, oft with white lace collar and cuffs.) But Valentine Westergaard, who had never done a vulgar thing in public in his life,—"nor a tasteful thing in private," as he liked laughingly to emend—was defiantly not of that sort: for it was his intention to appear in a new outfit each day, in ascending order of sartorial splendor. Thus, on the opening day of the trial, when the garrulous District Solicitor and the yet more garrulous defense attorney presented their opening remarks, and the senile old fool of a Chief Justice sought to interfere, Valentine drew all eyes with the very simplicity, and perfection of cut, of his outfit: this being a silk-and-wool suit executed by his London tailor, in dove-gray and black pinstripes, the trousers gently tapered, and the coat fitting snug at the waist, with a delightful surprise of subtly pronounced, or lifted, shoulders,—the quintessence, as the press noted, of the "Anglo" and the "Latin," in exquisite equilibrium. On the day following, Valentine took care to dress with appropriate sobriety, as Xavier Kilgarvan's pathologist-hireling *would* present his tediously grim laboratory report, and quite sicken anyone who chose to listen closely: selecting for his costume a three-piece French silk-and-gabardine suit of so delicate a shade of powder gray, some of the ladies afterward disagreed amongst themselves whether it was not, in truth, an *eggshell blue:* the hand-embroidered vest, with its miniature pearl buttons, being a decided blue, of that lovely hue known as Mediterranean. As the third day dawned remarkably cold and drear, and testimony by yet more "hostile" witnesses loomed large, Valentine thought it necessary to brighten matters up, as it were, with an ascot tie of saffron-tinted Egyptian cotton, of a sort never glimpsed before in Winterthurn (or in Manhattan either, as a columnist for the *Tribune* duly noted), and, in his buttonhole, a carnation of identical hue; albeit his woolen suit, in a midnight blue that shaded discreetly to black, and his dazzling white starched shirt, possessed the propriety of any young banker's outfit; and drew forth many an admiring comment, even from associates of Hollingshead's. (The tradition of the "Cruel Suitor's flower" dated from this occasion: by which is meant, ladies both identified and anonymous, including the mysterious "Veiled Lady," who had taken an entire floor at the Winterthurn Arms, vied with one another in supplying Valentine with floral pieces for his buttonhole: so that the defendant had his choice, each morning, of carnations, rosebuds, lilies-of-the-valley, dwarf orchids, and the like. And, ah! did this not rouse envy in the other gentlemen associated with the trial—!)

Thus, Valentine's shrewdly calibrated design: to make his début in court, in a manner of speaking, in comparatively conventional (though assuredly costly) attire: to evolve through wools and gabardines to silks, and satins, and velvets, and brocades, and furs; from high starched collars and cuffs, and "boiled" shirt fronts, to loose, flowing, open-necked shirts of East Indian or Moroccan styling; from the chaste dignity of solids, pinstripes, and the more subdued Scottish plaids, to the sybaritic delirium of paisley, and hand-painted Japanese fabrics, and needlepoint design, and Venetian openwork lace, and cotton chintz asquirm with floral figures—! From somber hues he would flare forth in rich lavenders and purples; in golds, lime greens, crimsons, silvers, and multitextured blacks. In readiness was a cape lined in gold brocade, along the lines of a Roman toga; and an aubergine (dyed) overcoat of otter fur; and, not least, his "mourning" overcoat, in Cossack style, with its splendid sable collar. With stealthy cunning he had timed his dramatic transformation from wool or gabardine to the surprise of velvet (this, a suit of so richly dark a green, it struck the untrained eye as black), to coincide precisely with the morning when *his* side of the sorry tale might begin to be told: which is to say, when at last, in the third week, Angus Peregrine launched his "aggressive defense," as the strategy was called; and a magnificent procession of witnesses sprang forth, to take the stand, and swear on the Holy Bible, and declare all sorts of vehement, wholesome, and, withal, much-awaited, facts about Valentine Westergaard, so absurdly accused of *murder.*

And what sport it was, though assuredly an anxious thing for certain of the ladies, to see which flower Valentine would choose for his prized buttonhole—!

Yet, as Valentine freely complained to his counsel, he lay awake nights with the worry that he might miscalculate: nay, how could he *not* miscalculate?—not being able to determine very precisely how long the wretched trial would run; and dreading to appear in the same costume twice; or to ascend too rapidly to his most flamboyant apparel. Despite the Colonel's disapproval,—ah, how tightly the old boy gripped the drawstrings of his purse, still!—Valentine deemed it far wiser to be in possession of too much finery than too little. "For instance," Valentine mused, with a faint crinkling of his forehead, "suppose I *am* sentenced to hang, and have naught to wear: naught, that is, but a costume I have already worn, and which all the world has seen. Dear God, to go out in such a wise!—to cross the threshold into chill Eternity, so very humiliated! Nay, it is an intolerable thought; it is obscene; *it shall not happen.*"

Then, after a brief pause, noting, perhaps, Mr. Peregrine's look of extreme discomfiture, Valentine lightly patted his hand, and gaily said: "But of course I shall not hang, shall I? You may be sure of it!"

It was generally acknowledged, even by Valentine's supporters, and by those newspapers favorable to the defense, that the prosecution,—which is to say, Xavier Kilgarvan—had assembled a most formidable case against Valentine Westergaard: indeed, did it not begin to look like an *open-and-shut* affair—? How very hard, the "hard evidence"!—including the desecrated female undergarments found in Valentine's Regency chest of drawers; and the alleged murder weapon; and the bloodstains on the walls, carpets, and floors; and, not least, the solemn report by police witnesses that a quantity of congealed blood *amounting to several quarts* had been discovered beneath the floorboards of one of the rooms in the Hazelwit house. And, too, the meticulous report of the Boston pathologist, though displeasing to the jurors because of its unremitting *factual nature*, struck a singularly lugubrious note.

The ladies sighed; and fretted; and fidgeted; and looked worriedly about; and longed for a recess; and the solace of hot chocolate and scones, at one or another of the neighborhood tearooms, that they might gauge the depth of the sentiment *for*, or *against*, Valentine. As old Miss Verity Peregrine observed, it was a problematic thing to cast out of one's mind the spectacle of the Westergaard dagger, so luridly despoiled with blood; and those unseemly items of female apparel taken from the chest of drawers. And what on earth could the fastidious Valentine have meant, in squiring silly little mill-girls about town, and presenting them with gifts, and proposals of marriage? "I cannot think that, if he did do such things, Valentine was altogether *himself*," Miss Peregrine falteringly said.

This attitude was taken up, generally; for everyone knew Valentine, and knew his childlike good nature; and how, when he said wicked things, he never meant them,—nay, not a tenth of them.

Then again, as Mrs. Harrier Von Goeler stiffly pronounced, if Valentine had been acquainted with one or two of the slain girls, in an innocent fashion, it was, after all, *his* business, and no one else's.

It quite pricked their womanly, and even maternal, sympathies that so gracious a gentleman was so discourteously treated; so falsely and absurdly accused, of every sort of atrocity (not least, placing a Catholic trinket in the mouth of a dying girl!); forced to sit for hours on end beneath the rheumy gaze of old Armbruster (of whom it was said, he had sent near as many men to the gallows as Erasmus Kilgarvan, in *his* time); and, most distressing of all, as the days passed and the trial's coverage widened alarmingly, made the subject of tasteless cartoons, jests, limericks, and ballads, across the entire continent. (Even England's *Punch* took up the novelty of an "American gentleman,"—was not the very term paradoxical?—who aspired to the savagery of a Jack the Ripper.) It was thought, after the strain of the first seven or eight days, when the "surprisingly bellicose" Hollingshead was presenting his case, that Valentine began to look unusually pale; that one of his eyelids drooped; that his posture was not so much gracefully negligent as it was lax, and weary, and indifferent. Yet, even so, *was* he not handsome!—his eyes so penetrating a green, his skin so flawless, his lips so finely sculpted, his expression so poetical!—thus the ladies murmured behind their fur muffs, while settling themselves into their reserved seats; and staring avidly at their Valentine.

(It might be here remarked, by the by, that some of the prejudice against Xavier Kilgarvan was displaced by an intense dislike of Mr. Hollingshead: and by a mistaken notion that, as the detective did not take the witness stand, he had not so actively participated in assembling the case against Valentine, as all had supposed. In truth, Xavier knew it most pragmatical not to give testimony, as Angus Peregrine would mercilessly attack him, for having gained illegal entry into his client's home; and make him out to be little more than a pilferer. He feared too that, if roused to anger by Peregrine's sophisms, he might lose control of himself entirely, and begin accusing Valentine to his face of the heinous things he had done,—the which, even now, as day after day followed in the courtroom, and so much rhetoric was declaimed, seemed queerly unreal. Alas, in a court of law, when all is followed to rule, does not virtually everything,—whether past, or the very present—acquire the quality of *unreality*?)

(Yet again, it might be peripherally observed that Valentine's female devotees took a dim view of the exotic "Veiled Lady" so abruptly ensconced in their midst: and that Mary-Louise Von Goeler in

particular, long praised for her "loyalty" and "courage" regarding Valentine, was especially piqued. For it must have wounded the proud
young woman's feelings greatly to see how, in the courtroom, Valentine discreetly, and, as it were, accidentally, allowed his unperturbed
gaze to drift about the rows of spectators, until he saw the lady's
comely form: and paused for a beat of one or two intense seconds, before turning away. Most vexing were the rumors, making their way
through town,—from the Rose Tree Hunt Club, to the Racquet Club,
to the Yacht Club, to the Corinthian Club, to the Cricket Club, to the
ladies' dining room of the Winterthurn League, to the Von Goelers'
own drawing room—that the "Veiled Lady" was the heiress daughter
of a Greek shipping millionaire and his Philadelphia-born wife, well
above thirty years of age, and, if not pointedly *infamous* in her pursuit
of men, at least unshackled by certain of the hesitations and scruples
Miss Von Goeler's innocence required. The rumor may well have been
groundless; as Angus Peregrine assured Mary-Louise's father, *he* knew
naught of it: but many an idle tongue had it that *billets-doux* were
being exchanged between the female interloper and Valentine; that the
lady declared herself passionately in love with Valentine, and was
"thoroughly convinced of his blamelessness"; and that Valentine, for
his part, had penned a sequence of sonnets in the lady's honor—!
Cruelest of all was the observation, made by more than one of Mary-
Louise's close friends, that, *even while she gave testimony, as a character witness, in Valentine's behalf,* the fickle young man was
essaying to catch sight of his mysterious admirer, who sat, as always,
in the gallery of the courtroom, clad in a sumptuous lynx fur coat,
with matching hat, and a dark dotted Swiss veil discreetly hiding her
face.)

Once the ebullient Angus Peregrine launched his attack, however, the atmosphere of the courtroom began to alter most tangibly,—
nay, miraculously: all those tiresome and grim things Hollingshead
had "proved" being, of a sudden, open to doubt, if not to contempt,—
or even scornful mirth. Most ingeniously, Mr. Peregrine had hired *his*
"man of science," hailing from the Albany Medical Facility: a physician of advanced years, but undimmed opinions: who, though unfamiliar with the actual anatomical remains of the unfortunate Miss
Teal, nonetheless took his colleague Dunn soundly to task for making
certain "undemonstrable" and, indeed, "farfetched" statements,
under oath, with the meretricious intention of *swaying a jury.* So
scornfully did this bald, rotund, bespectacled medical man attack the
very notion of the pathologist as a person to be taken seriously ("Why,
Your Honor, and gentlemen of the jury, 'pathology' is a close neighbor
of 'palmistry,' in *my* humble opinion"),—so bitterly did he attack Dr.
Dunn in particular (this gentleman, fortunately for his pride, having

returned to Boston some days previous]—and so glibly did he answer Hollingshead's stumbling questions, during the cross-examination, that he provoked waves of outright laughter and muffled applause from the spectators: and old Judge Armbruster was sorely tried, whether to succumb to mirth himself, or rap his gavel and scold the assemblage as if they were misbehaving schoolchildren.

Alas, how torturous a session, lasting well into three hours!— during which Xavier Kilgarvan, seated unobtrusively by himself in a rear row, suffered such pangs of consternation, and fury, and sickened revulsion, he had all he could do to remain where he was, and not flee from the scene of devastation. For it was as certain premonitory terrors had suggested, during many a sleepless night: the merrily cynical Angus Peregrine (whom he had not been able, in truth, to *dislike*) would now systematically destroy all that he and the police had built up, over a period of numberless weeks: and James William Hollingshead was not the man,—indeed, who in Winterthurn City was?—to thwart him.

Thus, at the conclusion of the Albany physician's testimony, naught seemed to be granted as *hard science*, save the mere fact that a female body identified by divers witnesses as "Eva Teal" had been found, in thus-and-such a place, and at thus-and-such a time: whether the deceased had indeed died "of suspicious causes," or by her own hand ("for, indeed, Your Honor, and gentlemen of the jury, *I have seen more remarkable things,—nay, more cunning, and more artful—in my time*"), being, it seemed, but a matter for conjecture and debate.

In the days that followed, while Valentine Westergaard's wardrobe reflected, oft with daring prescience, the happy turn of events, one after another of the State's "proofs" was challenged, and as frequently dissolved in derisory titters, as in sober logic. It would, I think, prove an exercise in needless cruelty to note, with any degree of minuteness, how the testimony of the divers defense witnesses (numbering, most remarkably, above *one hundred*—!) came to take its toll upon the hapless Hollingshead and his assistants; and, not least, upon Xavier Kilgarvan himself, forced to sit for hours on end while Peregrine led friendly witnesses through blatantly perjured accounts,—indeed, through wondrously *articulate narratives* that betrayed, from time to time, the vocabulary and rhetoric of the wily attorney; and forced to sit, to his despair, through *his own mother's testimony!*—for Mrs. Anne Kilgarvan, soft-spoken, hesitant, and, withal, embarrassed at finding herself, for a half-hour's time, the cynosure of attention, had voluntarily stepped forward to speak as a character witness for Valentine: having known him, as she gently yet adamantly explained, since boyhood, and having formed an attachment to him *that approached that of a mother for her son.*

"How is it possible!—how can such a horror be happening!"
Xavier bethought himself, squirming with the sudden throbbing pain
of a headache; and wondering that those seated close about him did not
shrink from him, in surprise at the waves of heat, and mortification,
and savage fury, that doubtless radiated from his being. "And I know
not which horror it truly is,—that my belovèd mother is perjuring herself, for a madman; or that she is not perjuring herself in the slightest!"
Quite apart from swearing to Valentine Westergaard's "unstained
moral nature, and high nobility of spirit," Mrs. Kilgarvan stimulated
some intrigue amongst the assemblage by recounting that, if she remembered correctly,—she had once glimpsed, on Charity Street, a
young lady closely resembling Miss Eva Teal, with her arm all brazenly
passed through that of a dark-clad gentleman with pronounced Semitic
features: which is to say, the very Isaac Rosenwald, who, she had been
given to think, had confessed long ago to the selfsame murder for
which Valentine was being tried—!

"Dear God," Xavier inwardly cried, while pressing both hands
hard against his burning cheeks. "It is *not possible* that this horror is
occurring, but that I am but locked in nightmare,—or in a loathsome
pit of muck."

Yet, it *was* occurring in precisely this wise; and though, from time to
time, Hollingshead, or, more likely, one of his younger and more astute assistants, scored some definitive points in questioning one of
Peregrine's witnesses, it was unmistakable that a total *shift in sentiment* had transpired; and that even the cantankerous Armbruster, who
reveled in quibbling with the defense over wee points of legal procedure, could not but admire the brilliance of the campaign. And, ah!—
was it not a wondrous thing, to see the roses gradually returning to
Valentine's pale cheek, and the old glistening exuberance, to his eye—?

Thus it unfolded, by malevolent prestidigitation, that, according
to the sworn testimony of scores of character witnesses (including the
greatly revered Archbishop Ellery Cruller, who had confirmed little
Valentine in the Episcopal faith), the defendent was a Christian gentleman of the highest moral integrity; albeit his *charitable gestures*,
and his *uncalculated generosity* toward those of a lower social station
than his own, had plainly led him into awkward waters. (And it was
doubtless true too, as several of the gentlemen smilingly averred, that
Valentine, like any red-blooded member of the masculine sex, had
"sown his share of wild oats in his time.")

As to the moral integrity of Miss Eva Teal,—some fifteen
witnesses, of both sexes, swore to it, with many a grim shaking of the
head, that very few of the mill-girls at the Shaw works had had a worse
reputation: whether for laziness and outright mischief in the mill, or

for a slovenliness of her person, or laxity in religious matters, or,—most damning of all—*promiscuous commingling with the opposite sex.* Though it could probably not be denied, that Valentine Westergaard was one of Eva's "suitors" (for want of an apter word), this gentleman was but one of a veritable contingent, of divers ages, social rank, and intentions, *not excluding the Shaws' office manager, Rosenwald;* and could scarcely be faulted for pressing gifts upon her, when it was commonly known, the wanton Eva openly solicited them. Albeit her mother wept copious tears in court, and swore upon the Holy Book that Eva had been cruelly used by Mr. Westergaard, it had long been whispered up and down Cadwaller Street, how the mother urged the daughter to "make herself ever more attractive to him," in the hope that more gifts, and outright cash, might come tumbling into *her* lap. Indeed, as Lyle Beck sorrowfully testified, he had heard by way of his wife (from whom he was at the present time separated), that Mrs. Teal and Eva conspired to blackmail Mr. Westergaard sometime in the future,—if all went according to their plans.

" 'If all went according to their plans'?" Angus Peregrine quizzically reiterated, with a dramatic pause, during which time he glanced significantly at the jurors. "Pray tell us, Mr. Beck, precisely what you mean by that suggestive phrase."

Whereupon another dramatic pause followed; and the bull-necked young man frowned, and shook his head, and essayed to look pained, saying, he wished not to sully the ears of the ladies in the courtroom, with such gross information; nor did he care to further compromise his late sister-in-law's name: for had she not paid in full for her immoralism?—and, in any case, never again would unknowing persons of his sex fall captive to her wiles.

At this, both Mrs. Teal and her daughter Iris began shouting,—nay, shrieking, very like fishwives!—and had to be forcibly escorted from the courtroom by the bailiffs: leaving in their wake a most disagreeable impression, as both uttered shocking things about Mr. Beck and his ancestry, and, moreover, accused the red-faced man of having "sold his testimony to the highest bidder."

"Thus blood reveals itself," Angus Peregrine ominously intoned.

With the passage of hours, the character of the deceased was visited with such opprobrium, it almost became a question why Valentine Westergaard (or, for that matter, any man at all) would have wished to keep company with her. At last Judge Armbruster, in whom, perhaps, a scintilla of gallantry remained, called Angus Peregrine back into the privacy of his chambers; and must have convinced him, that "Eva" had been adequately disposed of; and it might be wise for him to move on, to the next phase of his campaign.

While poor Xavier fairly writhed in his seat, and thought that, at last, he *would* have to flee to the biting salubriousness of the winter air, Mr. Peregrine took up the ticklish issue of the evidence confiscated by police, from out of Valentine's townhouse: and, lo!—it was not *ticklish* in the slightest, but most easily explained.

For, it seemed,—according to the testimony of Mr. Westergaard's housekeeper, his valet, his butler, and two maids—the telltale bloodstains discovered in the downstairs rooms were "without a doubt" the result of a nosebleed suffered by a female domestic, some months previous: the which slatternly creature, since discharged from her post, had neglected to clean up after herself. As for the unspeakable female undergarments, and the despoiled dagger, found in the chest of drawers upstairs,—these were also "without a doubt" items deliberately secreted there by that selfsame domestic, to revenge herself upon her master when she learned of her dismissal. How spiteful she had been!—and how determined to cause trouble for Mr. Westergaard!—albeit he had been inordinately generous with her, and had discharged her with two weeks' full wages.

Upon cross-examination, the servants held fast to their fantastical stories: refusing to allow that the quantity of blood discovered in the house might not be excessive, for a nosebleed. (Albeit, as the housekeeper belatedly acknowledged, there may have been *two* nosebleeds, and not *one*.) Nor did any of them allow that it was a peculiar thing, their having been so abruptly *rehired* by their master, at generous salaries, after they had been unceremoniously *sacked* but a few months previous: for it was known, after all, that Mr. Westergaard possessed a rare, bountiful, childlike manner, and was as unpredictable in his charity as most masters are predictable. So far as the identity of the female domestic went, Mr. Hollingshead was gravely informed that the slattern had departed Winterthurn of a sudden, leaving behind no forwarding address; and, it was later revealed, to no one's surprise, she had given one and all *an entirely fictitious name*—!

So it was, to the despair of the prosecution and its supporters, the *open-and-shut* nature of the case was totally destroyed: and the invaluable evidence assembled by Xavier Kilgarvan, and seized by the police, was in the process of being,—ah, how blithely!—explained away. Such evidence as did exist, and could not be exactly refuted, yet could not be held to *necessarily* prove anything against Valentine Westergaard, no more, say, than it might be held to *necessarily* prove anything against any one of the servants, or any visitor of Valentine's. All the servants swore that the master of the house had been totally in ignorance of the contents of his chest of drawers, as he never had occasion to use it; nor could he have hidden the antique dagger there,—

for, as all recalled, he had complained of its being stolen from his drawing room some months previous.

And who had stolen it from him? Why, the dishonest and conniving servant-girl, whose name no one knew and who had vanished utterly from Winterthurn, leaving not a trace of herself behind.

Being told such things by one after another of the servants in Valentine Westergaard's employ, Mr. Hollingshead lost his temper, and earned a reproof from Judge Armbruster when, flush-faced, he turned with a clumsy ironical flourish to the jurors, and challenged them thusly: "Gentlemen, if you believe the defense, why, then, you are capable of believing anything,—that *black* is *white*, that *up* is *down*, that *God* and *Satan* are one!"

Following this sequence, Mr. Peregrine called to the witness stand Hiram Munck and several of his senior officers; and sternly commanded them to explain to the court, *with no subterfuge*, how it was they had extracted an "airtight confession" from the late Isaac Rosenwald, some months ago; yet had the temerity to arrest Valentine Westergaard for the crimes to which Rosenwald had confessed. In turn, each of the police officers was subjected to so methodical, and merciless, and skilled, an examination, it was wondered how the men could ever show their faces in Winterthurn City again—! (Mr. Munck, as it developed, was to retire from public life within a few months, pleading exigencies of age and broken health.) Either the much-touted confession of poor Rosenwald was *false*, and very likely coerced from him; or it was *valid*,—in which case no grounds could possibly exist for bringing identical charges against Valentine Westergaard.

"Here we have a most baroque species of police work, indeed," Angus Peregrine all drily observed, with a wink at the smiling jurors. "Why, I should not be surprised to open the *Gazette* tomorrow evening, and learn that these indefatigable gentlemen have reversed themselves yet again, and arrested a third 'suspect'!"

Forced to endure hours of this examination,—which might more properly have been called a dissection—Xavier was consumed with a desire to rise from his cramped seat, and wave his fists, and begin shouting: for what might be more hopeless than the impasse to which police bungling, and Hollingshead's ineptitude, had brought them? He clenched his fists, but remained rooted in his place; blinked tears of fury from his eyes; and stoically held his tongue.

Yet there remained the hope that a single astute member of the jury would be unswayed by the defense's trickery; and that, by way of *his* persuasion, the other jurors would gradually see the truth; or, at the very least, the jury would be hung and a new trial called. But when Xavier covertly studied the jurors' faces,—when, in fatigue and mounting despair, he essayed to divert himself from courtroom testimony, by "reading" their thoughts—he could not be deceived that one of them was untouched by Angus Peregrine's assault; or, indeed, that a single one of them gave sign of possessing especial intelligence and sensibility.

Nay, how very *commonplace*, and *ordinary*, and *shallow*, these twelve gentlemen appeared; and how dishearteningly *gullible!*—having been moved to visible outrage by Mr. Hollingshead's presentation, some days before; but now, moved yet more visibly to the obverse position,—and so out of sympathy with the prosecution, they shrugged and whispered amongst themselves when Hollingshead spoke, or dared even to close their eyes, in full view of the court. For even with the damning evidence of the murder weapon in hand,—the stained petticoat, the female apparel, etc.—the State seemed now powerless to stay the tide of Angus Peregrine's mesmerizing narrative: and *his* voice reigned supreme.

Doubtless his tale had its attractions, and might be adjudged as convincing, if the actual truth were not known: for it possessed legendary qualities, and had about it an air of the comfortingly familiar. An open-hearted, guileless, perhaps too-charitable young Christian gentleman, of noble blood, as it were, was lured into a lowlife sector of the city, there to be exploited, with chill premeditation, by an amoral girl, and her mercenary mother; this same guileless gentleman, in speaking too openly of his involvement, being, some months later, as cruelly exploited by the law enforcement authorities,—and by "certain local personalities" who wished him harm, for private reasons. (At this pronouncement, Mr. Peregrine turned his stern, grave, "piercing" stare in Xavier Kilgarvan's direction, whereby the entire courtroom, not excepting Valentine Westergaard himself, followed his lead!—the which frontal assault left the young detective as miserable in his seat, and as flushed with surprise and embarrassment, as any schoolboy chastised in full view of his fellows.)

In Angus Peregrine's utterly simple *exemplum*, the defendant was not only fully innocent of all charges brought against him: he was himself the *violated martyr* of the State: having suffered, over a period of months, far more psychological anguish than any of the victims of the "Cruel Suitor" had suffered. Why, it required no elaborate medical training to gaze upon the defendant, and to see how his health and spiritual well-being had been ravaged, by the ignominy of this slur against his integrity; and by the tortuous proceedings of the trial itself. And all this, Angus Peregrine thunderingly declared,—and all this was to no purpose, *as everyone knew that the murderer of Eva Teal had been discovered, and had been punished for his crime, many months before: this being no one other than Isaac Rosenwald.*

The pronouncement of this dread name,—rarely, or, indeed, *never* heard in Winterthurn City any longer—roused the assemblage to a *frisson* of startled satisfaction: and seemed, indeed, the proper conclusion to Mr. Peregrine's potent tale.

Thus it was, the roles of *murderer* and *victim* were, by shrewd degrees, reversed: and if any of the ladies in the courtroom gave way to tears now, their sentiment was solely for Valentine Westergaard: the murdered Eva Teal being quite forgotten.

And what of poor Valentine?—though splendidly costumed for the day, in a fawn-colored suede jacket trimmed in black leather, and a lavender embroidered vest, and heather-green trousers of an unusual cut, he did appear somewhat peakèd, and even sickly: his eyes dispossessed of their normal luster, and one of the eyelids drooping; a *soupçon* of gray discernible in the curls at his temples; and his old graceful languor now more resembling the lethargy of an invalid or a convalescent, from whom all vital energy has drained. Staring at the defendant as he had done, day upon day, and week upon week,—and shrinking from Valentine's occasional furtive glance, as Valentine sought out *him*—Xavier soothed his nerves with the promise that, should Justice fail, *he* would punish Valentine himself: *he*, Xavier Kilgarvan, would seek revenge for the murdered girls, and for Isaac Rosenwald, and, not least, for the insult of the "planted" lavender glove,—the which outrage Xavier, in his pride, would never forget.

"Yes, I know not *how*, or *when*," Xavier thought, "but if it falls to me to exact vengeance, why then I will have no choice: unless conscience unmans me." Then, his brow furrowed, his gaze grown stony with brooding, he thought: "But of course I must do nothing that would endanger my love for Perdita, or hers,—ah, *hers!*—for me."

The "Footman's" Testimony

So far as an *alibi* was concerned, it had been Valentine's somewhat hazy assertion from the very first, that he had spent the evening of June 7, and the better part of the night, in the company of several of his friends: these being Calvin Shaw, and Lloyd Poindexter, and Roland (or Wolf) Kilgarvan: which gentlemen were duly called to give testimony in his behalf, albeit the climate of opinion in the courtroom was such, one might have supposed such testimony to be redundant.

Led through a series of rehearsed questions and answers, each of the young men confirmed Valentine's story, though it *was* a hazy issue, as to precisely how late they had stayed at the Hazelwit townhouse playing cards and drinking: and only when one of the assistants in Hollingshead's office questioned them closely, and relentlessly, did it emerge that Mr. Shaw had "probably" left shortly before *three o'clock:* and Mr. Poindexter, testifying second, had "probably" left shortly before *two o'clock*; and Mr. Kilgarvan, testifying, most conveniently, last, stressed the fact that he had "most certainly" left the townhouse shortly before *one o'clock.*

All were emphatic, however, that no young woman answering the description of Eva Teal,—in fact, no young woman answering any description at all—had been present at the informal gathering: nor had they ever heard Miss Teal's name on Valentine Westergaard's lips,— that they could recall.

Young Mr. Shaw not only exhibited certain of the less fortunate symptoms of alcoholic overimbibing in his person (which had grown, in the past year or so, unhealthily bloated), but, in his manner, behaved as if he had hastily downed a substantial number of drinks, to strengthen him for the ordeal of appearing in court. Speaking in a slow, slurred, halting voice, he insisted that his friend Westergaard was innocent of the charges brought against him; that no one in Westergaard's circle had ever heard of Eva Teal; that no young female answering to her description had been at Westergaard's residence, that he knew of; and he was fairly certain that Westergaard had immediately retired for the night, following the departure of his friends.

This testimony was more or less echoed, with minor alterations and emendations, by Mr. Poindexter and Mr. Kilgarvan: who, confronted with the hypothesis,—which Dr. Dunn had earlier set forth as *fact*—that Eva Teal had been murdered sometime between the hours of three o'clock and four-thirty, of the morning of June 8, did naught but repeat their statements, like frightened children; that no young woman had been a part of their gathering that night; that they had never so much as heard the name of Miss Teal; that it was preposterous to suggest that Westergaard had committed any act of violence whatsoever that night; and so on, and so forth.

Some days previous, Xavier had waylaid his brother Wolf on the street (as, it seemed, he was never successful in finding him at home), and put it to him bluntly that Wolf was risking charges of perjury if he lied, or "stretched" the truth, in giving an alibi to Valentine, for friendship's sake: and that, over all, it was a sickening thing for Wolf to have become so intimately involved with a creature like Valentine Westergaard.

With marked uneasiness, Wolf answered that his *baby brother* knew so little of his affairs, it were well for him to hold his tongue, and to keep his distance: and to refrain from insulting Wolf, by the mere naming of *perjury*.

Xavier coolly replied that he spoke only in Wolf's best interests,—and in the interests of Justice. For if Valentine were the "Cruel Suitor," as it surely seemed he was, *how* could Wolf protect him?—how could he defend him? Why, it was preposterous,—it was intolerable!

But already Wolf was striding away, with a negligent wave of his hand; already, it seemed, he had passed out of earshot.

And, in court, seated in the witness chair in a pose of strained affability, Wolf had given his testimony so woodenly, and with so marked an air of detachment, Xavier, staring hard at him, thought that he too must be part drunk, or under the influence of drugs: and, surely, not telling the truth. "For perhaps he does not know the truth," Xavier thought. "Perhaps he has never dared ask Valentine . . ."

Thus Valentine Westergaard's *alibi*: which was assuredly fraudulent: but which did not appear to be greeted by the courtroom, or by the jurors, as such.

Yet Angus Peregrine must have surmised that he needed additional ballast, so to speak; and made the move,—disastrous, as it turned out—to summon a surprise witness to the stand, Mr. Colin Kilgarvan, who had actually been in Valentine's presence, or under his roof, during the hours in question; and who would attest, *once and for all*, that Eva Teal, or anyone resembling her, had not been in Valentine's company.

So, yet another witness for the defense came forward: yet another: and swore to tell the truth, etc., with one hand on the Holy Bible and the other defiantly upraised: and took his seat, with some awkwardness and self-consciousness: and began his stilted perambulation through Angus Peregrine's artful dialogue: and then, of a sudden, fell queerly silent.

Mr. Peregrine repeated his question, in a prodding voice, as one might speak to a slow-witted child: but Colin sat mute: mute and staring into space,—or toward that space at the defense counsel's table inhabited by Valentine Westergaard.

Yet again Mr. Peregrine repeated his question, having to do with the sequence of events of that fateful night and morning: but the bull-necked witness could do no more than mouth silent words, while, in plain view of the discomfited courtroom, he clenched his fists on his knees.

All stared at him; even those persons,—not excluding, I am afraid, one or two jurors, and Judge Armbruster himself (for this session immediately followed the adjournment for lunch)—who might ordinarily have been dozing off; and ladies who had been for days contenting themselves with knitting, needlepoint, and the like, under the surmise that the trial was as good as completed, now glanced alertly up.

For, it seemed, Colin Kilgarvan, albeit he most painfully desired to speak, *could not*.

Alas, how brutish a picture Xavier's brother presented, on that chill afternoon, so very near the tragical termination of his life!—hulking, and slack-jawed, and ill-kempt, and possessed of so coarse and ruddy a complexion, one supposed him a day laborer: and could never have guessed he was the son of a gentleman. Encountering him by chance in the back streets and alleys of Winterthurn City, Xavier could never look upon him without inwardly cringing; for not only was his once-handsome brother now uncouth and shambling, his costume a potpourri of odds and ends taken from the trash (or, worse yet, pilfered), but, if Colin's red-lidded gaze fell upon *him*, there was the likelihood that Xavier would be approached, and, not to put too fine a point upon it, extorted, for a few dollars' cash. Nor is it a shameful detail to add that Xavier, being of a decidedly slender physique, and pacific in his manner, feared a drubbing from Colin—who must have weighed, at this time, some two hundred and twenty pounds.

And, it seemed, he harbored no especial love for his younger brother.

His connection with Valentine Westergaard was a cloudy one, owing nothing at all, evidently, to Wolf; indeed, Wolf was said to be keenly embarrassed by this connection, and would not remain in the same room with Colin, at the Hazelwit townhouse. By way of discreet inquiries at one or another of the lowlife haunts it was Colin's predilection to frequent, Xavier had learned, to his discomfiture, that Colin ran errands "after dark" for Valentine: which is to say, he did things of a dubious nature, which the servants could not be enlisted to do, or were incapable of doing. On Valentine's part, it was said that the idle young gentleman thought his "Footman" wondrously amusing, for his combination of the slavish and the quick-tempered: the quality that most endeared him to his master being a *peevish unpredictability*. None of Valentine's men friends could tolerate the "Footman," and none of his women friends had done more than glance upon him, from a distance; all, doubtless, felt distinct uneasiness in his presence; for, despite his slack smile, and slow-blinking eyes, and awkward bodily movements, he *did* radiate an air of the unpremeditated,—nay, the ungoverned and impulsive.

"Why, Colin Kilgarvan is as apt to spit on my French carpet, and clench his great fists, and stride menacingly in my direction," Valentine had once said sighingly, "as he is to thank me, in stammering fulsome wise, for some trifling tip of a dollar or two! I should dearly love to dress the boy in livery, and hire him on at Ravensworth, above the heads of the Colonel's tiresome old 'English' servants,—but must content myself, I suppose, to wait for the old man's death."

Now, the erstwhile "Footman" continued to stare at his master, not many yards distant, the lower part of his stolid face distorted by a wide, thin, mirthless grin; paying no heed to Angus Peregrine's repeated entreaties that he answer the question put to him; indeed, waving his fist haphazardly in the attorney's direction, as if Peregrine were but a pestiferous insect. What malefic gaze passed from master to "servant,"—what message of alarmed and infuriated urgency the trembling Valentine essayed to communicate, while daring not to say a word,—I have no way of knowing, for it has not been recorded; nor are journalistic accounts of the incident reliable. Judging from the witness's writhing contortions in his chair, and the strangulated mouthings of his inaudible words, what he dearly *wished* to utter, he could not; and what he *dreaded* to utter at last burst from him, in a voice slow, benumbed, hollow, halting, dazed,—a voice not recognizably his own, though articulated horribly through him.

Herewith,—I include all that has been recorded of the "Foot-man's" infamous testimony.

"... for sport says Master, for sheer divine sport Master says ... and Colin must obey ... and *she* dare not disobey ... as it is nearing dawn and ah! thè tedium to escort her home! ... the others are prigs Master says and shall not be invited again ... Master says, *Cowards* and not men ... indeed says Master has she not *unmanned* them! ... to their shame be it said ... her tears and her tiresome screams when the cushion is taken away ... 'Poor Eva' says Master for his tears spill onto hers ... it has grown very late ... she is bleed-ing overmuch ... and she is unclean says he ... ah, he is very angry! ... but Colin must not peek: 'Nature is the very pox to be overcome,' says Master, *'but she must be overcome.'* Therefore much scrubbing will be required. It is far worse than the other times. For says Master she is particularly unclean. She is filthy says he and must be punished. Are they not puling cowards to have fled says Master now true divine sport has begun! ... unmanned by mere screams and such ... the scent of blood terrifies the weak ... Tighter says Master and tighter until her foul tongue protrudes, only you and I are equal to the task, as with the other repulsive creatures ... *so determined to provoke manly rage* in their thrashings and sobbings and bloody discharges! For sport says Master now it is time says Master, for sheer divine sport Master says ... and Colin must obey ... it is sweet says Master and *you* are sweet ... for they must be trundled away to the Half-Acre, as it is their place, being unclean ... being most loathsome and unclean ... and afterward all must be aired ... and scrubbed ... and consecrated. They are filthy says Master please take them away, O please, and *you* shall be rewarded ... sweet Colin ... for the odor is fearsome says he ... take them away to the Half-Acre and murmur not a word to me afterward says Master ... for I fear I shall be ill ... But first sweet Colin says Master come and kneel before me, that I might bestow a kiss upon your chaste brow ... .''

At this point, while the courtroom was locked in a veritable paroxysm of attention, and naught but the slow, enfeebled, bemazed, half-human voice of the "Footman" sounded, it suddenly happened that Valentine Westergaard essayed to rise from his chair, with an af-fectation of disdain, or smiling incredulity; and summoned forth suf-ficient strength, to shake off Angus Peregrine's quick grasping of his arm, and, a second later, the much firmer grip of one of the bailiffs; and, turning to the crowded courtroom, with a cavalier sort of smile, and his green eyes glistening, seemed about to speak: but, in an in-stant, as if struck by an invisible blow to the back of his head, lost all strength,—*and fell crashing to the floor.*

The "Cruel Suitor" Unmask'd

As a consequence of Valentine Westergaard's collapse, it was necessary to adjourn the trial for three days: after which, contrary to his attorney's desperate wishes, and, indeed, to the amazement of all the courthouse buffs, the defendant insisted upon taking the witness stand *to testify in his own behalf*,—albeit such a stratagem, at such a point, with prejudice and revulsion now running so strongly against him, seemed hardly less than suicidal.

For, in the interim, Colin Kilgarvan had freely surrendered to the authorities: had freely, if woodenly, confessed to his role as a "willing accessory" to Valentine Westergaard's crime,—nay, to five crimes: not only the abduction, torture, and murder of Eva Teal, but those of the other four "Damsels of the Half-Acre"—! In a slow, dull, benumbed fashion, the thirty-one-year-old man recounted each of the slayings,—or "sports"—with not the slightest hint of remorse, or, pity, or withal, reflective consciousness of his crime: enumerating such details as fairly sickened his interlocutors: and betraying impatience only when requested to repeat what he had said, as if so deliberate an act, requiring a more complex degree of mental organization, irked him. Upon several occasions he simply blinked, and stared into space, and, his lips widening in a transfixed, mirthless grin, averred that his interrogators must ask "Master" about such niceties, as he, Colin, knew naught of *motives*, but only of *facts*. His confession required some four hours to complete, partly because he spoke in so halting and mechanical a manner; and when at last the transcript was prepared, and given to him for signing, he sat motionless before it for a space of twenty minutes, a quill pen in his hand, and his lips silently moving. At last, he signed his name to the document, with a clumsy flourish; and a heaving sigh, such as a brute ox might make; emitting a forlorn murmur,—the first instance, it was alleged, of any betrayal of *human emotion:* ". . . Master says we live amidst surfaces, and the Art of Life is to skate well upon them . . . but Colin has not skated well. . . Colin has sorely disappointed . . . Colin must needs betake himself to the Half-Acre now . . . for his time is past . . .it is finished: never again will Master bid him kneel before him, that the blessing might be said . . .''

Thus Colin Kilgarvan was duly booked as an accessory to Valentine Westergaard's acts of wanton murder, and locked up in the Winterthurn County Jail, under the strictest surveillance; no bail being set; and no visitors allowed, save Angus Peregrine,—who was rebuffed by the prisoner, and sent away with a bleeding nose and mouth. Dr. Colney Hatch was summoned to examine him, with the desire, in particular, of subjecting him to a thorough phrenological measurement: but deemed it unwise to enter the cell with him, even if the prisoner were secured by restraints. Yet it was Dr. Hatch's considered opinion, which was released to all the newspapers, that Mr. Colin Kilgarvan, though *eccentric,* was not *mad:* and that he must bear responsibility for his crimes.

As to the Kilgarvan family's response to this unlook'd-to development in the trial,—it were more merciful of this narrator not to discuss it, for fear of lapsing into the *maudlin,* in delving too deeply into the tragedy; or seeming *callous,* in failing to do justice to all persons involved. Suffice it for me to note here that the catastrophe was such, *Mrs. Kilgarvan never again exchanged words with her youngest, and formerly most belovèd, son. And Xavier,*—well, Xavier shall be dealt with, in time, in a fashion befitting his destiny.

The whispered judgment of numerous staring spectators that Valentine Westergaard, returned to the courtroom after three days' absence, looked *but the ghost of his former self,* was, in truth, only a slight exaggeration: for, possessed now of a prominent, bony, marble-white brow, and deep-shadowed eyes, and drawn and sunken cheeks, he looked a full decade older than his age; and had to be helped to the witness stand by his faithful valet, with as much care as if his legs might buckle beneath him at any moment. So visibly did his upraised hand shake, while he swore the oath on the Holy Bible, it seemed a painful thing to observe,—even by those who had crowded into the courtroom to see him, as it was said, "hang himself."

Not a person amongst the hundreds of spectators failed to observe, moreover, how totally Valentine's *spirit* had seemed to depart from him; how modestly, and even meekly, the defendant was now clothed, in an altogether ordinary gabardine suit,—plain, dull, drab, black, penitential—such as a young minister might wear, ascending to the pulpit of a middle-class church. His shirt was.white, but not dazzlingly so; his collar and cuffs were properly starched, but did not call attention to themselves. And the handkerchief he raised repeatedly to his face, to dab at his wet lips, and, upon occasion, at his rapidly blinking eyes, was naught but simple cotton, bordered in very homely lace.

So enfeebled was Valentine's voice when he first began to speak, Judge Armbruster at once interrupted, with an air of undisguised impatience, and disgust, commanding him to speak with more volume; or forfeit his "day in court."

Thus, Valentine summoned all his strength, and, gazing out into the assemblage with an expression of infinite sorrow, declared that *all Colin Kilgarvan had said of him, was true.*

All Colin Kilgarvan had said, that is, pertaining to *external events.*

So far as *inner events* were concerned, however,—why, there was a great deal that must be added; and explained. For the things that had been performed by Valentine Westergaard's unwilling hands had been, in fact, forced upon him,—by the spirit of a malevolent personage, an enemy to both God and man, *long dead,* but known (as it would be disclosed) to inhabitants of Winterthurn.

So it was, Valentine told his long, convoluted tale, the while every individual in the courtroom strained to hear; and even those persons who had conceived a violent revulsion toward him and wished fervently to see him executed, scarcely dared to breathe, for fear of missing a single precious syllable. How mesmerized, in particular, were the ladies!—their pretty fans more slowly, and yet more slowly, in motion; and their eyes fixed unswervingly upon the heir of Ravensworth Park. For now, at last,—after so many weeks of obfuscation, and the tedium of testimony, by insignificant persons—they were gazing (so intimately, it seemed!) into Valentine's very bared soul: and, ah! what a surprise, to glimpse what lay within. For it could scarcely be doubted that *the defendant now spoke the truth.*

As Valentine Westergaard's complete testimony,—lasting some six hours and forty-five minutes—is available elsewhere, in the official published transcript of the case, and in Professor Myron Haskins's definitive study, I shall abbreviate it greatly here; albeit there are passages of especial poignancy, and a happily inspired sort of lyricism (in the asides to Nature, Woman, the Muse Melpomene, etc.), that might interest the general reader. Nor shall I attempt to communicate, through the oft-times inadequate medium of mere language, the candid, guileless, and somewhat hypnotic effect, of Valentine's words.

All ineluctably, the tragedy was set into motion some eighteen months previous, when, quite by happenstance, in a nocturnal perambulation along the river, the solitary walker, so deep-immersed in a prayerful communion with his Maker, took a mistaken turn; and, thinking himself in the vicinity of the Old River Road and the railroad track, continued hiking unwisely,—and soon found himself lost. (As to young Mr. Westergaard's nocturnal walks, of which no one had known, it seemed, save his late and belovèd sister Imogene,—while hardly more than a boy, of a sudden made parentless by a caprice of Fate, or, it may have been, a canny species of Divine Wisdom, Valentine had taken to spending many hours of the day in prayer: either on his knees, in the private sanctuary of his bed-chamber, or while walking in the wilder and rougher sections of the forest, of Ravensworth Park. Following the untimely death of his sister Imogene, with whom, as all knew, he had been inordinately close, and to whom he had been selflessly devoted, Valentine had, for a space of some months, lapsed into near-despair; he had fancied that the world was indeed, as the Bard had hinted, "weary, stale, flat, and unprofitable"; and that it could yield no pleasure for him. Ah, how pierced to the heart he had been, by poor Imogene's death!—how stubborn in mourning,—how slow to be reconciled! Thus, from that time onward, his prayerful communion with God was the more greatly, and despairingly, intensified, as its outward manifestation was kept *jealously hidden from the world*. "For what lies between the individual soul, and Almighty God," as Valentine quietly stated, "cannot be displayed in Society,— which is to say, 'worn upon the sleeve, for daws to peck at.' ")

Thus it was, one midsummer night, by an evident miscalibration of the moon's trajectory in the sky, Valentine lost his way; and found himself in that inhospitable area some miles south of the river, known as the Devil's Half-Acre.

Ah, if only he had not wandered out of his way, and become hopelessly lost!—if only the moon's solemn refulgence had not betrayed him!—five young women who had died most cruelly before their times, would be living still; and Valentine Westergaard, who had, many years before, pledged to his Maker a lifetime of the *secret performance of Christian charitable acts* (whereby moneys were to be given, anonymously, to institutions, organizations, needy and deserving individuals, et al., with as much dispatch as if by God's own command), should not now be on trial *for his very life*.

But, as the vagaries of Fate would have it, he *was* set adrift in that place of misshapen boulders and stunted trees, with no familiar landmark to give him succor, and, after an incalculable period of stumbling, and staggering, and groping, he heard, with pounding heart, and reeling senses, a voice most horrific, *yet imbued with an eerie authority*, that seemed to come from the very air about him: *I claim you! You are mine! Who goes there,—trodding o'er my grave,—desecrating my slumber:* HE IS MINE!

For, all unknowing, poor Valentine had trod upon the final place of rest, of the bones of Elias Fenwick, who had died better than a century before: nay, who had been publicly executed, in just retribution for his loathsome deeds—! Too late,—ah, *too* late!—the affrighted young man saw how he had blundered; saw the ill-featured rock, into whose pocked and leprous surface crude letters had been carved, in warning:

> THIS STONE IS GOT
> TO KEEP THE SPOT
> THAT MEN DIG NOT TOO NEAR.

Herewith, there ensued some minutes of futile struggle on the part of the mortal Valentine, against his superhuman foe: with Valentine pleading, and begging, and weeping for mercy, that he be released from the erstwhile "Bishop's" grip, and allowed to go his way; and the "Bishop" all gloatingly reiterating his claim that, as Valentine had desecrated his slumberous peace, by trodding so rudely upon his grave, he must forfeit his soul,—and would be required to bring *five brides* to the Half-Acre, for the delectation of Elias Fenwick.

Brides—? queried the sobbing Valentine, who had sunk to one knee, beneath the invisible assault of the fiendish spirit. *I do not understand: brides? young women? living and breathing young women*—?

Whereupon the portentous voice intoned: *Nay,—not living and breathing.*

So potently had the spirit of Elias Fenwick insinuated itself into Valentine Westergaard's being, not even the most adamant pleas to Our Almighty Father proved efficacious; for, as Valentine had unwittingly violated the "Bishop's" sleep of many decades, it seemed that a species of actual curse had descended upon him, in concordance (alas, *how*, and *why*, we are not given to know!) with God's instructions. Thus it was, though the young man valiantly struggled against the fiend, and against his own wretched fate, there was little to be done save acquiesce; for, in truth, not the most minute sinew, joint, or artery, of his tremulous body, was any longer under his dominion,—but only under that of the "Bishop."

These fearsome words Valentine calmly, albeit in a melancholy tone, asserted, the while hundreds of persons leaned forward in their seats, to grant him their absolute attention: not excepting, of course, the twelve gentlemen jurors, who frankly gaped at this most extraordinary of narratives: and Chief Justice Armbruster, who, it might be surmised, had by this stage in his career heard virtually everything.

After a pause of some minutes, during which strained respite Valentine was proffered a glass of water by his white-gloved valet, and a vial of ammoniac spirits, to be shaken beneath his nose, the testimony was resumed: by slow, painful, arduous steps, progressing to the first of the "sacrifices" of the "Bishop's" brides,—which is to say, the death of Miss Euphemia (or "Effie") Godwit, with whom Valentine had become acquainted, in a somewhat incidental and casual way, at one of the charity Musicales held in the Armory. (On his part, Valentine had had not the slightest wish to become acquainted with the importunate young miss,—indeed, he had earnestly sought to discourage her, by alluding to a secret engagement, between himself and a young Winterthurn lady. But, alas, the forward young miss had refused to be discouraged!—with what lamentable results, the world well knew.)

Thus, the first of the Bishop's *five brides* met her destiny,—and poor Valentine, it seemed, was most helplessly plunged into *his*.

For, following this initial horror, which had been performed, evidently, with no *knowledge, volition,* or *inclination,* on Valentine's part, it was but an inevitable step to the sacrifices of those other young women known, in the popular press, as the "Damsels of the Half-Acre": viz., Miss Dulcinea Inman, Miss Tricia Furlow, Miss Florette Sparks, and, not least, Miss Eva Teal.

Each of the "sacrifices" occurred while a kind of mental eclipse overcame Valentine's consciousness; and when, hours later, he woke groggily from his trance, not only had the heinous act been committed, but the body was itself gone,—having been transported to the Half-Acre by an emissary of the "Bishop's"; and very little remained to press upon Valentine the fact that an outrage of some sort had occurred, *beneath his very roof,*—save haphazard splashes of blood, torn, stained, and stridently perfumed female apparel, an extreme lethargy through his being, and the like. Colin Kilgarvan, who had of late forcibly befriended him, was evidently of the fiend's party, and in constant communion with the fiend: knowing how most pragmatically to lure the prospective victims to Hazelwit Square, and how to deal with them, once they were secured: and, afterward, knowing with a most practiced thoroughness how to "expedite" the bodies to the Half-Acre. So inhuman and fearsome a creature as this Kilgarvan, Valentine had never before encountered in his somewhat sheltered life; yet he could no more escape his calamitous influence than he could escape the influence of Elias Fenwick, diffused through his very being.

So it happened, that the five prescribed brides were, one by one, brought to their damn'd husband; and Valentine himself,—ah, how ironically!—was both the *instrument* of this unspeakable horror and its primary *victim*.

At the conclusion of his lengthy confession, Valentine had grown so weakened, he could scarcely hold his head erect; and his delicate hands visibly shook. Yet, all bravely, he summoned forth the shuddering strength for a final effort, and, with tears now unabashèdly streaking his face, softly cried: "May God Almighty have mercy on my soul!—may this Christian court have mercy on my soul! *For the 'Bishop' assuredly did not.*"

The "Cruel Suitor" Judged

It is frequently charged against narratives of Mystery and Detection that "natural" seamless actions are willfully interrupted, in the pursuit of an histrionic effect: that the fluid chronological sequence of events, in that ill-comprehended element we call Time, is most cunningly,—and, upon certain occasions, most shamelessly—distorted, to extract, from the proceedings, the very last droplet of *apprehension, suspense,* and outright *dread.* Thus, the alleged authenticity of History is laid upon a sort of grid, or narrative artifice, with the most egregious of intentions: *that of stirring the reader's emotions.*

Yet it is difficult to see how narratives like mine might be otherwise presented, for, if granted a "natural" and "seamless" form, they would necessitate hundreds of pages: for, only consider, one might fruitfully investigate any number of ancillary themes stirred by the case at hand,—the response of the small Jewish community of Winterthurn, for instance, to the lynching of Rosenwald; or, for another, the response of the Catholic-immigrant community to the verdict finally handed down against Valentine Westergaard. These worthy subjects, in conformity with the rigorous structure of Mystery, must remain unexplored; our concern is solely with the monomaniacal zeal of the young detective.

So far as the prolonged strain of the jury's deliberation is concerned,—this, I shall abbreviate, for it involved eleven long hours in all, and a strict fidelity to the laws of chronological time would be ill-advised. I shall therefore refrain from sympathizing with the torments of waiting suffered by various parties (amongst these, Miss Von Goeler,

whose impassioned loyalty to Valentine had unaccountably increased
with the passage of weeks; and old Colonel Westergaard, whose health
had so deteriorated during the weeks of the trial, Dr. Hatch had at last
commanded him to take to his bed; and Eva Teal's mother, haggard,
and sober, and penitent, who attended mass daily, and said numberless
prayers for the repose of her daughter's soul, and in the hope that her
murderer might "hang high"; and such principals of the case as James
William Hollingshead, and Angus Peregrine, who waited out the
verdict in a Union Avenue tavern, their past animosities drowned in
convivial tankards of bock beer; and the redoubtable "Veiled Lady,"—
now whispered to be an actual *lady*, of birth and breeding, if not precisely of behavior, heiress to Pullman fortunes—who had all brazenly
commandeered the Garden Room of the Winterthurn Arms, and issued
instructions that a "victory celebration" be prepared, for Mr. Westergaard and all his relatives, friends, and supporters, when at last the verdict was announced; and, not least, our hapless Xavier Kilgarvan, who
had been so stricken and demoralized by his brother Colin's admission, he had, through the several hours of Valentine's preposterous
defense, found it highly difficult to concentrate,—assuaging his heart
with the promise that, should the jurors be gulled by this "defense,"
and vote acquittal, *he would himself see to Valentine's punishment.*)

All these hours, and half-hours, and quarter-hours, and minutes, and slow-dragging seconds, of mental anguish, it is a mercy to
overleap: and, in the interests of brevity and economy, to open a door,
as it were, upon the final strained minute or so, when the decision was
announced: The principals reassembled in the courtroom: Judge Armbruster, roused from a nap in his chambers, now settling himself, with
an irritable sigh, behind his bench; the jurors filing solemnly back into
the jury box, and casting their fatigued eyes upon the Judge, and the
prosecutor, and defense attorney, and the sickly red-haired Westergaard; the grave-brow'd foreman of the jury handing over to the bailiff
a folded slip of stiff white paper, to be conveyed to the Judge, and the
Judge, with due ceremony, unfolding it,—and holding it slantwise to
the light,—and frowning,—and squinting,—and at last raising his
spectacles, that he might better read the message,—and pronouncing
to the courtroom, in a voice that betrayed but faintly a tone of
perplexed incredulity, these irrevocable words,—

"*Not Guilty.*"

The Turtle Dove's Fate

———

14 February
MIDNIGHT

My Dear Xavier,—
Belovèd Xavier,—
Sweet Cousin,—
Dearest,—

(You see I know not how to address you,—how to conform to
the Heart's, & the World's, demands!—& have scribbled over
these past five or six days numberless missives, & in despair
torn each in twain. At this very moment,—as Winterthurn's
church bells begin their chimes,—at this moment, yet again my
strength so fails me, I find I am scarcely capable of lifting my
hand, to force my wretched Pen along the page,—knowing the
sorrow my words must cause—as indeed *I am myself pierced to
the heart.* FOR AGAIN I HAVE BROKE MY PROMISE TO YOU, & all savagely & irremediably despoiled my own Happiness. Yet I swear,
'twas not done wantonly.)

Withal, I have performed the horror in such wise, *it is not to be
revoked by God, no more than by Man.* For Perdita has pledged
her word, on the Holy Bible, & 'tis said, such, freely given, cannot be retracted.

Will you forgive me?—ah, I do not dare beg you!—I do not dare
presume!

Simply & bluntly,—& most grimly,—
I, Perdita Kilgarvan, have, in fullest consciousness,—for the
health & safekeeping of my immortal soul (Cousin, does such a
phantasmagoric entity exist?—would Uncle Simon Esdras claim
yea, or *nay*?) & in craven terror of perpetual Damnation in the
fiercest flames of Hell—entered into a formal engagement, to be
yoked in Holy Matrimony to our much-honored Reverend
HARMON ATTICUS BUNTING III: said long-deliberated action, being,
as I said, not wanton; & having been taken, Xavier (Please, will
you believe me?), some two or three days *before* the Tragedy of
your brother Colin erupted, to stun us all; & before the outrage
of the Verdict. (As to this "outrage,"—I wonder, since the imminent Master of Ravensworth Park has been proclaimed from
the very dome of the Courthouse *innocent of all wrongdoing
against my sex*,—& since so many of my sex, for reasons I cannot conceive, persist in believing him innocent, & in adoring
him,—how dare *I*, who could not have qualified to sit upon the
Jury—how dare *I*, Perdita, raise my Skeptic's voice?)

I pen this hurried and shamed missive, dear Xavier, that you
might learn of my impending marriage from my own lips, as it
were; & not noised amazedly about town. The Reverend
Harmon Bunting (whom I am learning by degrees to call
Harmon,—but it is a most taxing enterprise, as I have so long
venerated him, as Reverend Bunting: & wonder at the teasing
propinquity of *Harmon* to *Harmony*,—a mellifluous yet forcible
sound)—this kindly & charitable gentleman of the cloth, & yr.
erstwhile Perdita, have already entered into a union of sorts,
kept secret from the world; but soon to be celebrated at the altar.
Dear One, know that my decision has been made after many a
sleepless night, of anguish, & tumult, & fervent Communion
with God (alas, how *one-sided* this intercourse seems, in my
awkward experience!—a sign, I cannot doubt, of my unworthiness). I so fear Damnation,—*deserved* Damnation, I know, like
my wretched Mother before me—that I must cleave to Christian
Virtue in its most visible & unambiguous form; & align myself
with Good; & shun forever the *hot excesses* of our love,—if
"love" such wildness be—the lawless kisses & forbidden
caresses & ah! I dare not utter *all else*: for I have vowed to Jesus
Christ *never again to muse upon such impurity*. Indeed, once I
am "baptized" MRS. HARMON BUNTING, & no trace of my original
self remains,—shall not a wondrous cleansing & amnesia not be
performed, upon my sin-stained Soul?

As to Mr. Bunting's knowledge of certain *secret excesses* &

promises,—I essayed to speak without subterfuge to him, in the
privacy of his rectory office, yet halfway wondered (as, for
upward of an hour, I wept, & sobbed, & bewailed my fate,—*my
predilection for sin*), whether the chaste gentleman quite
comprehended all that I uttered, in the extremity of my despair:
save to meet my gaze with his own (so healthsome & clear,—
eyes of sea-blue shading to gray—lucid as washed stone): &
speak to me, at unhurried length, of certain admonitions &
teachings of Jesus Christ, & of St. Paul: &, not least, to lead me
in heartfelt prayer: Mr. Bunting *on his knees* in my presence, &
I *on mine*, for near a rapturous hour. Mr. Bunting,—that is,
Harmon—has vowed to be my "spiritual bridegroom," as, he
somewhat grimly murmured, I have had my surfeit, doubtless,
of the *other sort*. So kindly, & charitable, a gentleman!—he has
offered to speak with you, if you so wish: & to proffer you spiritual advice: albeit (thus he frowningly & I know not how justly
emended) he doubted your capacity for Christian wisdom at the
present time,—as, it seems, you have been negligent in
attending church services; & your occupation (*preoccupation*, I
truly think it must be called) leads you to an unwholesome
contemplation of Evil, & an indifference to God.

Indeed, Mr. Bunting has behaved so graciously in all this, & is so
markedly *uncondescending* in his manner toward me, I see at
last why he was called to God, at so early an age (scarcely twelve
years, it seems); & why he has been so long approved of, &
granted somewhat "precocious" favoring, by the exacting
elders of the church.

Thus, the die is cast.

As to *Love*,—why, Perdita must hold her tongue forevermore; &
observe a discreet silence.

(INDEED I shall hold my tongue. For I am NOT FREE TO SPEAK. I am
AFFIANCED. & SOON TO BE WED. & hereby to solemnize my vow,
while church bells faintly & dolorously chime I know not what
hour, with shaking hands I shall remove the beauteous turtle
dove you gave me,—ah, Xavier, so long ago!—I shall remove this
soft-feathered creature, from out its pretty wicker cage: & essay,
with what little strength yet remains to me, *to wring its neck:*
that mercy be at last granted it, for its melancholy, & torpor of
heart. *Requiescat in pace*, O innocent thing!)

This final missive to pass between us, blurred & maculate with
my tears, I shall send by way of my dear sister Thérèse,—who

will not, I know, dishonor its seal; nor attempt to prize from you, in however circumlocutory a way, its unhappy contents. If you like, sweet Xavier, *do hate me:* for I know, I am fully deserving: & doubtless shall cherish, in my innermost being, a memory, or actual living vision, of your impassioned regard for me,—whether it be the folly of *Love;* or the carnivore energies of *Hatred.*

Your despairing Cousin,
& "friend" no
more,—

Perdita

Cousin Thérèse

So benumbed was Xavier Kilgarvan by the catastrophic, and most humiliating, outcome of the trial, and so heavy-hearted, as a consequence of his family's tragedy, it cannot truly be said that he greeted
Perdita's valedictory letter with quite the flood of emotion it would
have evoked, in more equitable and healthsome times: and, quickly
perusing its contents with furrowed brow, and red-lidded and puffy
eyes, in a somewhat discourteous manner (as the trembling bearer of
the missive, poor Thérèse, was forced to stand by in attendance), he
swallowed grimly, and murmured, "Well,—'she should have died
hereafter,' " and discountenanced his visitor by letting the sheets of
scented stationery fall, as if neglectfully, to the carpeted floor—!

(As to this surprising response,—it would have required, I think,
no uncommonly perspicacious lover, to have construed, over the past
several weeks, that Perdita was by degrees, and most deliberately,
withdrawing her affection from Xavier: or had already, in the secrecy
of her woman's heart, withdrawn it: for, proffering but vague and insubstantial excuses, she had failed to honor three or four of their
engagements; and, at the last of their meetings, had behaved in a distinctly inaccessible manner. "Ah, you do not love me any longer, Perdita: *you too are abandoning me*," Xavier cried, scarcely knowing, at
the time, what his uncalculated words meant; or the import of Perdita's white-lipped protestations. "*I,*—abandon *you!* Why, it is as much
a possibility," she said vehemently, "as the earth detaching itself from
the sun, and veering off, of its own wild volition, into the depthless
and lightless abyss of *Nothing!*")

Though she could have had no way of knowing the actual contents of the mysterious letter she had been prevailed upon to deliver, Thérèse had nonetheless understood that the *liaison* between Perdita and Xavier,—for such, she feared, it must be called—was being terminated, and most abruptly, by her sister; and her maiden's heart ached with inarticulate sympathy and pity, for the undeserved sufferings that had, of late, fallen upon Xavier's comely head. How swiftly it had all happened!—and, given the ways of the law, how irrevocably! For while Valentine Westergaard would surely have appealed the verdict, had it gone against him, the prosecution was helpless to appeal: and would have to accept a defeat both absolute, in moral terms, and near-universal, so far as publicity was concerned. For all of the Valley, and much of the State, was abuzz with news of the sudden reversal of Fortune's wheel,—the "Cruel Suitor's" amazing freedom, and the arrest and indictment of his "Footman" accomplice; the evident victory of Angus Peregrine, and the devastation of his opponents. (In truth, as those persons acquainted with the Law well knew,—poor Angus not excepted—this "victory" was so much ancillary to *his* meticulously plotted defense campaign, it could have afforded very little pleasure; and the defense attorney's role in the proceedings was deemed as comical, or pitiable, depending upon one's magnanimity. Mrs. Spies had brought back from her Monday Afternoon Society the scandalous news,—how authentic, Thérèse could not know—that Colonel Westergaard and his grandson were so much in contempt of Angus Peregrine, for his near-fatal error in introducing Colin Kilgarvan into the trial, it was now doubtful that Peregrine's fee would be paid!—and the taunt was, the *hack lawyer* might hire himself another of his kind, to sue for his money, if he thought the public humiliation was not too steep a price to pay.)

As for Xavier,—it was no groundless rumor, but an actual fact, that, immediately following his brother's arrest, his aggrieved mother had suffered a nervous collapse; and lay abed in delirium, calling for her "betrayed son, Colin," and cursing her "traitorous son, Xavier." (Well may the reader express surprise, and doubt, at the extreme terminology I am obliged to employ; yet it is no exaggeration, that Mrs. Kilgarvan, that most gentle and Christian of mothers, in raving, and thrashing about in her bed, and tearing at her bed linen, had fallen to *cursing* her youngest son!—with such vehemence, and such a queer admixture of profanity and *baby talk*, Dr. Hatch soon came to wonder whether she were possessed by a demon. "Albeit it is altogether antithetical to Science," he frowningly said, "to 'believe' in such influences.")

So strained were the circumstances at the Kilgarvan house, Xavier had thought it wisest to decamp,—nay, if truth be told, he had been *evicted* from his home—and had, in haste, acquired a four-room flat in a modest brownstone off Parthian Square, for the months of February and March. It was the wretched young man's intention that he should make discreet appeals to his mother, over an extended period of time; and his hope,—pray God, it will not be fruitless!—that, by degrees, he might be forgiven.

In the sober chill light of midday he knew himself blameless: for, after all, he had but devoted himself unstintingly to the highest ideals of Justice; and had endangered his own life thereby. At other times, however, when his vision was subtly distorted by the abrupt oncoming of night, or, it may have been, by the fracturing of reason, which an indulgence in alcoholic spirits (however measured, and restrained) inspires, he judged himself,—ah, *knew* himself—guilty, in the very terms his mother charged. For, in aspiring so passionately to bring Valentine Westergaard to the scaffold, he had succeeded in bringing his brother to that extremity instead!—the irony of the Law being, Colin Kilgarvan must be charged with having aided and abetted a murder, or murders, in the first degree (whether such acts were performed by a mortal man, or no)—such a crime being punishable by hanging— though Valentine Westergaard had been acquitted of *his* particular charges. And now poor Xavier was wracked by nightmare images, and terrifying waking dreams, of his brother *hanged:* and in that very place in Courthouse Green where Isaac Rosenwald had died, so many months before.

He took no solace from the fact that, in such cities as New York, Boston, and Philadelphia, the verdict in Westergaard's favor had been greeted with incredulity, and outright scorn: the *New York Times* condemning it as "so extreme and farcical a miscarriage of Justice, it undermines not only our faith in the jury system, but our faith in human nature itself." For, closer to home, through the Valley, and in Winterthurn City, sentiments were quite the reverse; and the *Winterthurn Gazette* spoke for the great majority, in hailing the verdict as a "stirring vindication of the American tradition of trial by jury,—nay, a tribute to the American virtues of *common sense*, and *fair play*, and *Christian compassion.*"

As for opinions in society, or in the street,—Xavier shut himself away from them, in wise caution: a pulse beating erratically behind his eyes, and his fingers "aching" to do violence, when he was in the presence of an enemy. "I shall bide my time in silence,—in secret,—in cunning," he consoled himself, "and someday,—why, *someday*—I know not how, I *will* wreak Justice upon his head!"

"He should not dwell alone, and in such melancholy surroundings,"

Thérèse thought, when admitted to Xavier's little parlor, or sitting room, on the third floor of the brownstone. "It cannot fail to be injurious to his spirit; and, ah! what is that odor of staleness, and disarray, and sorrow—?" Somewhat awkwardly, Xavier aided Thérèse in slipping off her heavy woolen cape; and, with an air of frowning gallantry, took from her her muskrat muff, and long white cashmere scarf, to set upon a table; the while the keen-eyed young woman glanced nervously about, to take in the undistinguished proportions, and yet more undistinguished furnishings, of his temporary home.

How dreary it was, and how inappropriate, for *him!*—for, despite the wintry sunshine that slanted through the windows, and gave a sparing sort of glow to the faded chintz draperies, and despite the charming needlepoint carpet that covered much of the scuffed hardwood floor, the parlor bespoke a melancholy indifference, and impersonality: a mere rented place: without a soul, or even a personality: not a setting (so Thérèse half-angrily thought) for a gentleman of Xavier's high worth and character. And how very queer it was, that the parlor walls had been covered, it seemed not long ago, in a silvery striped paper, that wriggled and writhed in the corner of the eye, like narrow fish, or eels; and how incongruous, that the furniture,—a settee with badly faded Aubusson upholstery, a bowlegged French armchair, a tub chair covered in floral chintz—had pretensions, as it were, of grandeur; albeit grandeur sadly past. It was one of those rooms, Thérèse saw, into which a negligent landlady had settled her outworn and outgrown pieces, in the hope that her bachelor tenants might not greatly care, or even notice.

And, ah!—that Xavier Kilgarvan, of all persons, now made his home *here.*

She saw too, with a small cringe of disapproval, and dismay, how littered much of the parlor was, with newspapers,—or sections of newspapers: as if Xavier had laid them carelessly down, and forgotten them; or even thrown them irritably about. And were those not unwashed glasses, here and there upon a table, and on the fireplace mantel; and was that not a *bottle* (whether of wine, or sherry, or some more potent drink, Thérèse cared not to see), set casually on the bare floor beside the divan—?

As for Xavier himself,—Thérèse could not fail to note the strain in his courtesy; the perfunctory, albeit hurried, air of his gallantry; and a near-imperceptible agitation (betrayed, she sadly saw, by a small helpless flutter of the eyelids, as if he feared weeping): for, of course, it was certainly the case that he had been expecting the *younger sister,* and found himself, a second time, cruelly surprised, by the appearance of the *elder.* (Yet so powerful, and so resilient, was Thérèse's love for

Xavier, she counted his mere presence,—and *her* presence close beside him—ample reward for what some persons might, in contempt, call the *humility* of her role, if not its *humiliation.*)

Keenly disappointed as he must have been, yet Xavier did not, in truth, seem altogether surprised: and managed to greet the blushing Thérèse with a modicum of smiling equanimity; and even to shake her gloved hand, with an altogether artless expression of warmth. For he *did* like her: nay, she felt certain that he *liked her very much:* and if only *liking* might yield to *loving*, why then, how the world should be transformed—! "It is only that his senses are bewitched by Perdita," Thérèse thought, half in wondering, and half in disdain, "for I feel confident that *he himself* cannot 'love' so shallow a young woman."

While he frowningly perused,—indeed, seemed almost to *skim*—the letter she had been entrusted to bring him, Thérèse could not forbear studying him, in anxious detail: noting that his handsome countenance had been drained of its usual color, and had acquired, doubtless by degrees over the frigid winter months, that sepulchral pallor much prized by certain members of the female sex,—the which, they fancied, lent them an *angelic radiance* that enhanced their natural beauty. Much the same thing might have been said about Xavier (at least to Thérèse's way of thinking), save that his cheeks had noticeably thinned; and somber shadows encircled his eyes. And his distraction earlier that morning must have been such, he had cut himself while shaving,—not once, but twice, on his tender chin: the evidence of which quite pulled at Thérèse's heart.

After Xavier had read through Perdita's letter, and allowed its pages to fall to the floor, it was clearly time, Thérèse saw, for *her* to take her leave: for Xavier must want to be alone with his sorrow, or, it may have been, his rage: or a wild commingling of both. Yet, with unfailing graciousness, he lifted his red-flecked gaze to hers, and inquired of her whether she might like coffee or tea; or,—was it not midday, or even later?—a glass of sherry.

"You are very kind, Xavier, but I must leave,—I fear I have been the agent of some distress, as it is," Thérèse quickly said.

"Well, *if* you have been," Xavier said, with a pale attempt at mirth, "it is a further discourtesy to hurry off, and leave me to drink alone."

So it was, Thérèse felt prevailed upon to remain; and even accepted a small glass of sherry from Xavier, at which she sipped with extreme caution, finding the liquid stinging to the tongue, and doubtless more potent than she knew. In an attempt to make conversation, she murmured some words of sympathy regarding Mrs. Kilgarvan's illhealth: which remark drew from Xavier a droll smile, and the observation that *she* might visit his mother, if she so wished; but *he*, it seemed, was forbidden.

This disagreeable news Thérèse had already heard, by way of Mrs. Spies and her Monday Afternoon Society; but she pretended surprise, and concern; and said, with a faltering sort of warmth, "Ah, I am sure that will not be for long: as your mother is too reasonable and forgiving a person."

"Perhaps it is *reason* that guides her, in this wise," Xavier said flatly, "to withhold *forgiveness.*"

This rejoinder was not so rude as it appears, on the printed page; but was uttered rather in a spirit of forthright declaration, after which Xavier took a sip or two of his drink, and yet another, and lapsed into brooding silence. Thérèse watched him almost fearfully, and wondered if he might,—ah, he *might*—humble himself, and ask, of a sudden, about Perdita; or, worse yet, confess his futile love for her; and unburden his heart to Cousin Thérèse. ("If this collapse in the formality of our relations should occur," Thérèse instructed herself, the while her maiden's heart beat calmly, "I shall forget my own pride, in commiseration with another's grief; and perhaps our joint tears will mingle.")

But Xavier did naught except drain his glass, which seemed to fortify his strength, and to bring a little color to his cheeks: stooping then to retrieve the scattered pages of Perdita's letter, and, making a show of not so much as glancing at them, shutting them away in a desk drawer.

All timidly Thérèse inquired, whether he had any message for Perdita: and Xavier said, with a cavalier shrug of his shoulder, that there was no message: nor would there ever again be, from *him* to *her.*

Xavier then proffered his visitor more sherry, which was nervously declined: for Thérèse could not think she was really wanted: and, to spare Xavier the strain of her company, must take her leave. Yet when she rose hesitantly to her feet, he did, it seemed, display a sincere regret: again half chiding, that it was not courteous of her,— nay, not very *cousinly*—to abandon him to an afternoon of wintry solitude, and the cheerless prospect of drinking alone.

"Then perhaps you should not drink at all," Thérèse quietly said.

Xavier appeared to acquiesce, though without visible enthusiasm; and, going to get Thérèse's cloak for her, asked ironically what sort of occupation or diversion she might recommend, for whiling away the interminable day,—not to mention the night.

Thérèse blushed under the somber scrutiny of his gaze, and stammered that she knew not, precisely,—she knew not what would please him,—though, she supposed, any kind of fruitful occupation would suffice.

" 'Fruitful occupation'!" Xavier exclaimed. "Why, I have had my fill of *that*; and of 'doing good' as well. It is all a Sisyphean labor, Thérèse. A trial possesses the awesome lucidity of a flash of lightning, I have seen,—by which I mean, it illuminates all the principals, unsparingly, and unforgettably: toiling away in our roles, industrious, and fully absorbed, and each quite convinced we are right: very like miniature gods, worshipping our own godheads. *Prosecution*,—and *defense*,—and *judge*,—and *jurors*,—and *defendant*,—and, not least, the avid pack of *spectators*, hanging upon every syllable: all miniature deities. But I am speaking too wildly," Xavier said, "and am causing you distress."

"Not distress so much as bewilderment," Thérèse hurriedly corrected him, "and surprise. For I read in your words a measure of disappointment, shading into outright despondency; and, ah! dear Cousin, I wish I possessed the means of dissuading you from it!"

"You are very kind," Xavier murmured, helping her with the woolen cloak; and watching as, blushing the more, she wrapped her cashmere scarf several times about her slender throat. "But I fear I am as my mother thinks me,—and perhaps it is Perdita's judgment as well,—a kind of aberration, or contaminant,—'fruitfully occupied,' doubtless—and yet, harvesting what singular fruit!"

Thérèse stared at him in mute appeal; and, for a long impassioned moment, could not bring herself to speak, for fear she would say something irrevocable. Then, at last, in a rush of emotion, she heard herself saying something she had not intended, nor even rehearsed,— the which quite astonished Xavier.

In a quavering voice she confessed that, for many weeks, she had been tormented about her responsibility in withholding certain information from him,—certain confidential information entrusted to her by one of her young pupils (whose name she must not reveal),— which, for all she knew, and taxed herself for knowing, might have made an enormous difference in his approach; and in the outcome of the case. "Even now that the trial is concluded, and the villain freed, I cannot say much," Thérèse whispered, "for I have given my word, with God as my witness; I have vowed *not* to violate confidence; and, ah! what a burden it has been!—and to so little purpose. For I *knew*, Xavier,—I mean, I *half knew*, or had been led to *think* that I knew— that your unhappy brother Colin was in some way involved in Valentine's activities; and that the more you pursued the one, the more you pursued the other; and in exposing one, you would doubtless expose the other."

Blushing crimson beneath her cousin's astonished stare, yet not pausing to reconsider her words,—indeed, scarcely to draw breath, for fear she would stammer and fall silent—Thérèse continued to tell him that (may God forgive her!) his brother *Wolf was not altogether innocent either:* "I mean of certain peripheral matters,—Wolf, and Calvin Shaw, and one or two others,—companions of Valentine's—whose 'crime,' or 'sin,' was in failing to denounce certain outrages, or to forestall them. Do you understand? Do I speak clearly? Your error all along,—if *I, Thérèse,* dare speak of such, in *you*—your error was always in thinking that Valentine acted alone, and unabetted; or, what is more peculiar yet, that he could have done the things he did, without hinting or boasting to his friends, or,—and here I am only speculating, Xavier, for I cannot actually *know*—without exciting their fearful admiration: albeit of course they are not murderers themselves, nor indeed monsters, but only cowardly young 'gentlemen,' perhaps." At this, Thérèse hesitated; and murmured, in some agitation, that she had best say no more,—for, she feared, she had already revealed too much.

As the reader might imagine, Xavier was astonished by his frail cousin's outburst: and begged her to repeat all she had said. One of her pupils had told her—? Had told her,—precisely, what? But Thérèse drew away, saying she must honor the boy's request not to tell a third party these hideous secrets. "The boy is terrified that Valentine,—or, indeed, Colin—will take revenge on him," Thérèse said, "albeit there seems to me little reason for that now. But, I dare say no more: and had wanted only to convey to you, however inadequately, the fact that, dear Xavier, I have long been wretched, in harboring such unspeakable knowledge,—and knowing, moreover, certain things *you* could not have known,—and that no one would tell you."

Xavier followed the agitated young woman to his ill-lit vestibule, and to his door: too stunned, it seemed, to respond at once. As they parted, however, he managed to say, in a stumbling sort of voice, that, no matter the circumstances,—whether Colin had been involved, or no; whether *Wolf,* or *any,* or *all,* of his brothers had been involved—he would have pursued Valentine Westergaard exactly as he had: which is to say, he would have pursued Justice, no matter the personal cost.

"Ah, I knew that was so!—I knew!" Thérèse all breathlessly exclaimed, as she hurried down the stairs.

While crossing windy Parthian Square, Thérèse felt her eyelashes begin to frost over, and her burning cheeks to sting: and had not, until that moment, known how tears spilled from her eyes.

Epilogue

———

All coincidentally, and not in the least, I hasten to say, by crude melo-dramatic design, this narrative closes,—draws away, as it were—with yet a second vision of half-conscious weeping: and eyelashes, and tender burning cheeks, frosting over in the February wind: as Xavier Kilgarvan himself, the following night, stands bruising his bared knuckles on the stolid oaken door of his family's Wycombe Street home,—his desperate energies, I am loath to say, to no purpose. *For the door is closed and bolted against him: and will not be opened.*

Earlier this very day, a Sunday, the distraught young detective was turned away from his family's doorstep, by Mr. Kilgarvan himself (greatly aged and soured since we have last been in his company,—and vehement in his command that Xavier betake himself off: and depart Winterthurn altogether); and, just now, as the hour of eleven is being sounded through the city, by Mr. Kilgarvan's faithful assistant Tobias,—who, with pained reluctance, and not a little shame at his appointed task, explained somberly to Xavier that neither his father nor his mother wished to gaze upon his face, at the present time; or, perhaps, at any time in the imminent future;—albeit Xavier would be hurriedly summoned, if Mrs. Kilgarvan's health suddenly worsened, or her state of mind, regarding *him*, improved.

Words that admit of very little ambiguity, it seems to me: yet Xavier, infused with a spurious sort of strength, and optimism, by drink (of a potency many times superior to that of mere sherry, it might be said), continues knocking at the door: his knuckles now be-

346

ginning to bleed, and to sting most ferociously in the −15 degree F.
temperature: his voice lifted stubbornly and childishly in a plea for
admittance so injurious to his pride ("Please let me in,—dear Father, and Mother,—you must let me in,—for an hour, at least,—
ah, please!—for I am your son Xavier, whom you have always loved,
—*you cannot wish to banish me*"), I hesitate to record it here, for Posterity's judgment.

Thus, while this youngest, once favored, and now, indeed, truly
"banished," of the Kilgarvan sons, persists in his folly,—scarcely noting that the gas-jets beside the door have been rudely turned off, and he
stands in bleak darkness—I shall conclude *Devil's Half-Acre; or, The
Mystery of the "Cruel Suitor,"* by withdrawing, by degrees, from the
piteous scene: retreating by feet, and by yards, and now by a half-block
of darkened brick façades, about which snowflurries undulate: as
Xavier's lean and urgent form is gradually enshrouded, by the fine mist
of snow; and, withal, by the singular gloom of Winterthurn's chill,
when massed snowclouds choke the nocturnal sky, and no chaste-
glowing moon, or diamond-bright stars, shed their light upon the
earth.

Alas, poor Xavier,—farewell!

With infinite relief, I must confess, I end my chronicle at this point;
indeed, at this very moment; for the near future brings with it no
surcease of pain and humiliation, for the Kilgarvan family. As the
obstreperous Colin is so little subdued or chastened by his
new-acquired circumstances, he provokes fights of a brutish nature
(employing *fists, feet, gouging fingers,* and, not least, *teeth*), in his
place of imprisonment, he will shortly be thrown into solitary confinement, and, there, by a means never satisfactorily explained, he
will so despair as to take his own life, by hanging: to be found by his
jailer one chill March morning, *stone dead*, and *unrepentant*.

As to the more canny Roland, or Wolf, with whom we have become but slenderly acquainted,—he has already, in truth, disappeared
from Winterthurn, with the pretense of visiting a business associate in
New York City; but will be reported never to have arrived there,—or,
at any rate, never to have arrived at the address he had indicated.
Whether he fell prey to that lowlife company of gamblers, cardsharks,
racetrack idlers, and their ilk, with whom, it seems, he and the other
"young bloods" of Winterthurn sometimes mingled; or whether, as
some persons afterward insisted, he had, under an alias, joined the
United States Navy, to set sail for Manila Bay with the famed Asiatic
Squadron,—and to sink all the Spanish warships in sight; or whether,
all mysteriously, he *had* simply disappeared from the earth's surface,—

I am in no position to say; nor did Xavier Kilgarvan ever choose to investigate his brother's fate.

As to the beauteous, but, alas, faithless, Perdita,—she and Mr. Harmon Bunting were indeed wed, some three months following her letter, in a small, stately, and pious ceremony at the Grace Episcopal Church: with the Archbishop of the diocese presiding, and a very select number of relatives and friends in attendance,—not including, it scarcely needs be said, Xavier Kilgarvan.

Such familiar Winterthurn personages as Hollingshead, and Munck, and Shearwater fell by the wayside, as it were, within a space of a few months; retiring from public life, and, in Mr. Shearwater's case, forced to his bed, with a heart disorder so serious, he was not expected to outlive the winter. Elderly Chief Justice Armbruster lost strength rapidly, following the trial, and died on the first day of April: stating on his deathbed that he was departing this life "with no great regret," as, he feared, he had "meted out his share of Justice,—and Injustice—in his time."

In the wake of the Rosenwald case, in particular, one gentleman alone emerged not only unscathed but, indeed, near-glorified,—this, Winterthurn's ebullient Congressman James Hanrahan Dorsey, who, in subsequent years, with a goodly proportion of the rural and "poor white" populace supporting him, and the vociferous backing of the Jericho Brethren, was to rise to the enviable office of United States Senator (to which he was elected for four terms): and to not a little national prominence, as a consequence of powerful friendships in the Senate.

Angus Peregrine, as the reader doubtless knows, was launched, all ironically, upon his "dazzling" career as a criminal lawyer of the highest rank,—and one who commanded the highest fees: for, prudently, he did not choose to sue Colonel Westergaard for the money owed him: and, as it happened, the publicity accruing to his success in freeing his client, whether *good*, or *bad*, or distinctly *mixed*, was, in the end, like all such publicity, *good*.

As for Valentine Westergaard,—some months later, near the end of September, Xavier, then living in his bachelor townhouse in Washington Square Park, was the recipient of an altogether guileless, and, withal, warm and comradely message from him, posted in Ravenna, Italy—! For, it seems, Valentine and his "Veiled Lady" admirer (subsequently revealed as Miss Valeria Vanderbilt, an heiress of enviable wealth and reputation) had eloped shortly after the conclusion of the trial; and were yet in the midst of their year-long honeymoon cruise. Valentine's brief message, scrawled in a lazy, looping, languorous hand, in ink the shade of the duskiest of Muscovy grapes, commended to Xavier's ''discerning'' eye the classical beauties of the Northern Italian landscape; and, to other of his senses, the ''exotic & sometimes agreeable *divertissements* of the Marital Bed''; and closed with these enigmatic words, which could not fail to pierce the trembling Xavier to the heart,—

''The 'Bishop' having assuredly decamped from *my* being, pray, sweet Xavier, he does not next settle in *yours.*''

THE BLOODSTAINED BRIDAL GOWN

or

Xavier Kilgarvan's Last Case

Every crime engenders clues.
—HANS GROSS, 1892

Editor's Note

Amongst the more churlish criticisms leveled against the art of Murder and Mystery,—in their classic literary forms, I should hasten to say—is the objection, whether philosophical or aesthetic, to the inevitable *tidiness of the conclusion*, toward which the form instinctively moves: whereby all that has been bewildering, and problematic, and, indeed, "mysterious" is, oft-times not altogether plausibly, resolved: which is to say, *explained*. It is objected that "life is not like that": that mere Mystery, binding together a group of persons for a certain space of time, cannot adequately define them, or proffer a noble vision of life: that it is an affront to our sense of the complex (and doubtless tragic) human condition that the most devilish of mariner's knots are handily untied, to assure what is, after all, a *happy ending*,—the anathema of the modern sensibility.

As if it were not, to all right-thinking persons, a triumphant matter that Evil be exposed in human form, and murderers,—or murderesses—be brought to justice; and the fundamental coherence of the Universe confirmed!

Thus it is, through my long career as an amateur collector of Murder and Mystery, and as the editor of numerous volumes similar to the one the reader holds in his hand, I have never felt the slightest inclination to apologize for my tastes; nor to shrink from declaring that the mystery or detective novel boldly upholds the principle, *in defiance of contemporary sentiment*, that infinite Mystery, beyond that of the finite, may yield to human ratiocination: that truth will "out": that happiness is possible once Evil is banished: and that God, though,

353

it seems, withdrawn at the present time from both Nature and History, is yet a living presence in the world,—an unblinking eye that sees all, absorbs all, comprehends all, each and every baffling *clue;* and binds all multifariousness together, in a divine unity. Without God, I have no doubt that mysteries would continue to exist, and even to proliferate: but Mystery assuredly would not.

To essay, all bravely, to see the whole, and to "remember forward," and never to blink at wickedness,—as Xavier Kilgarvan oft tortured himself to do: thus, in emulation of God, the detective aspires to invent that which already exists, in order to see what is *there* before his (and our) eyes. He is the very emblem of our souls, a sort of mortal savior, not only espying but isolating, and conquering, Evil; in his triumph is our triumph. Even should he fail, is not such failure noble?—for to be human is, indeed, *to fail to be divine;* and no shame must be attached.

In the span of approximately twelve years during which Xavier Kilgarvan achieved a modicum of fame, or notoriety, in his hazardous profession, it became a nettlesome issue with him that his *successes* were so vulgarly emphasized in the tabloid press, and his *failures* rarely reported, as being, perhaps, not sufficiently newsworthy; or too commonplace. (For, up until very recent times, most crimes went not only unsolved but undetected: a "suspicious" death might as well be deemed "natural," for what might have been done about it, in any case? I am shocked that the usually perspicacious De Quincey should offer the rough estimate that, of 230,000 deaths reported in London in a twenty-year period during the seventeenth century, naught but 86 were murders!—the more plausible figure being, to my way of thinking, 86,000.) Such an emphasis, Xavier Kilgarvan felt, blinded the public to the painstaking labor, the daily and hourly "grind," of the detective's work: and woefully misled as to the glamorous ease with which mysteries were solved. (It were well for Xavier that he had long been retired, and settled into the blissful harmony of domestic life, when the first of Mountjoy Price's exploitative detective novels, featuring the dandyish "Zachariah Kilpatrick," began to appear in the 1920s: to eventually earn far more financial largesse for their author, it has been estimated, than Xavier Kilgarvan himself had ever earned—! For these slick, shallow, and infuriatingly breezy works of fiction, some nineteen in all, presented a glib young gentleman who rarely struggled with a cerebral problem for more than an hour, who never displayed fear or apprehension, and never shrank from physical combat: and seemed, at the conclusion of an adventure, precisely the same person he had been at the outset.)

Indeed, so taxing did Xavier Kilgarvan's "accursèd" profession prove, he withdrew from it, all abruptly, in his fortieth year: which is to say, within a scant six months of his return to Winterthurn, to solve the sensational case known variously as "The Rectory Murders," "The Winterthurn Ax Murders," "The Mystery of the Minister and the Society Lady," etc.,—though, for our particular purposes, it bears the title of *The Bloodstained Bridal Gown;* or, *Xavier Kilgarvan's Last Case.* (A close parallel to this title being Mountjoy Price's *The Case of the Bloody Bridal Gown,* a best-seller of 1938: but, beyond this, there is little resemblance between Price's meretricious mystery and the definitive study of the case I have here assembled.) The loss to the profession of Detection was an extreme one, for no American detective, with the possible exception of Allan Pinkerton, achieved as great a renown as Xavier Kilgarvan; and no one at all was so brilliant a detective,—Pinkerton being but a mere hack, set beside Xavier Kilgarvan, and so lost to all standards of gentlemanly decorum, he did not shrink from hiring himself out to the highest bidder, no matter the degree of justice or injustice involved. Yet I suppose it a sad necessity that Xavier Kilgarvan *did* retire at so early an age, whether for purposes of health, or to save his immortal soul, or whatever.

The irony of the situation, as I understand it, after some eight or nine months of painstaking scrutiny into old documents, letters, police reports, and the like, is that Xavier Kilgarvan had no legitimate case to "crack," as the reader will see: but was fully accurate in his exposure of the murderer, and to be faulted only minimally, in his investigative procedure. For, within an admirably brief period of time, the appalling mystery is handily resolved: the murderer, unlike Valentine Westergaard, does not escape God's wrath: and peace and tranquillity are restored to a distressed community. In addition, *a happy ending is provided,*—one both plausible and deserved.*

Herewith, after upward of seven decades, the sole definitive account of the most-publicized mystery of Winterthurn, of a season long past.

---

*Albeit I should mention here, I suppose, that certain carping students of the case, and one or two vociferous monomaniacs, insist to this day that Xavier Kilgarvan did not truly "get his man." Such caviling, however, we need not take seriously, as, amongst *aficionados* of Crime, you will invariably find eccentric personalities who argue, for instance, that Miss Madeleine Smith was blameless of the charges laid against her; or Miss Lizzie Borden; or that Jack the Ripper did not exist, or was a renowned surgeon, etc. The more perverse a notion, the more inclined are certain temperaments to believe it!

"...You Alone Are Our Salvation"

Every extant account of the infamous murders in the Grace Episcopal rectory begins on the afternoon of September 11, with the discovery of the bodies, or with the sighting, not many minutes beforehand, of the "red-haired specter" bearing his bloodied ax: but fresh evidence, to which, it seems, I alone have access, would place the actual beginning of the mystery some twenty-four hours earlier, in a very different setting altogether.

For it was in upper Pinckney Street, near the intersection with Chambers, in the midst of the hurlyburly of a late weekday afternoon,—when hackney cabs, carriages, motor cars, and, not least, clattering trolleys were in full force—that a veiled woman in a cab signaled to a Negro shoeshine boy, that he should come to the curb, and run a simple errand for her. Succinct and direct was the charge, with no wasted words on the woman's side, and immediate compliance on the boy's: for he was accustomed to such requests from the white gentry, and did not think it a curious matter, that a lady whose features were hidden behind a pearl-gray gauze veil, and whose voice was lowered to a hoarse, rapid murmur, should entrust him with an "urgent" message, to be sent at once by way of Western Union,—albeit the telegraph office was but a stone's throw away, and the lady might easily have alighted from her cab, to send it herself.

However, this was evidently not her wish: for the boy was given a thrice-folded sheet of stationery, and several dollars in paper money; and, while the lady remained seated in the cab, to watch after him, he ran without hesitation to the Western Union office, and did as he had

356

been instructed. (Doubtless it was the case that, to the Negro lad, all white ladies were, in a sense, featureless; or hidden from such lowly eyes as his by near-opaque veils. Consequently, he had not the vaguest impression, whether the mysterious lady was young, or middle-aged, or old; whether her manner had been controlled, or agitated; what sort of clothes she had worn,—albeit he had a dim recollection of a dark wide-brimmed hat, adorned with smooth black curving feathers, shielding much of her face, and all of her hair.)

The message had been fastidiously printed in black ink, in tall, perfectly formed (or disguised) block letters, on a sheet of plain white stationery that bore no letterhead, and yielded no fragrant scent, however subtle; as it was unsigned, and, moreover, addressed to *Mr. Xavier Kilgarvan, of 38 Washington Square, New York City*, the telegraph operator was naturally roused to curiosity,—and disappointed that the stammering shoeshine boy could offer no explanation, other than that "a gracious lady had bade him bring the message" to Western Union, and have it sent with no delay.

In its entirety, as it was sent out from Winterthurn City at 5:15 P.M., on September 10, the telegram read:

XAVIER KILGARVAN RETURN TO WINTERTHURN IMMEDIATELY
YOU ALONE ARE OUR SALVATION

A Parenthetical Aside

_____

As to the fate of the telegram, bearing its "urgent" message: though it was delivered with admirable alacrity to the correct address,—which is to say, to the handsome brick-and-stucco townhouse at 38 Washington Square, which Xavier Kilgarvan had purchased some years previous— it happened, unfortunately, that the detective was not at home to receive it: whereupon, there being, evidently, no servant on the premises, it was merely slipped beneath the door: and its terse imperative was to go unread for approximately twenty hours,—within, that is, ninety minutes of the first of the murders in the rectory, some two hundred and thirty miles away.

Had Xavier Kilgarvan not been absent from home; had he received the telegram by the evening of September 10, as the sender had wished,—it is scarcely a farfetched speculation to suppose that the lives of several persons would have been spared, and _The Bloodstained Bridal Gown_ would be unknown to us; and Xavier Kilgarvan's prospering career would not have been so abruptly terminated.

"The Golden Vanity"

Judging from several reports, and from the testimony of her cook and housemaid Bessie Hyde, it must have been at approximately 3:45 P.M. on the warm, airless, and mist-shrouded afternoon of September 11, when, seated at her *escritoire* in the ground-floor sitting room of Jewett Cottage, poor Mrs. Bunting,—that is, Mrs. Letitia Bunting, Reverend Bunting's seventy-two-year-old mother—glanced up perplexed from a letter she was writing to her sister in Nautauga Falls, to see, or to imagine she saw, by way of a wall mirror, Reverend Bunting himself noiselessly entering the room behind her. How queer that Harmon would walk into the cottage unannounced,—how queer, his expression of startled, anguished, and, as it were, *petulant* entreaty! Mrs. Bunting stared: and let drop her pen, taking no notice that it spilled ink on her letter: and stared yet the more: for, without turning, she seemed to comprehend that the image of her belovèd son was not altogether *right:* a clouded, wavering, shimmering, somehow insubstantial reflection, as if seen through water, or obscured by the mists that had settled in Winterthurn since the preceding night. "Why, Harmon, what is it,—why do you look so aggrieved?" the widowed mother said in a low, frightened voice: her eyes catching at his, despite the distortion of the polished lenses he wore, and a certain tremulousness of his facial muscles: and her sense, she knew not why, that the dark-garbed gentleman in the mirror both was, *yet was not*, her dear son. He had halted just inside the doorway and stood tall, stout, swaying, reproachful,—one hand extended, and the palm held upward, in a gesture both supplicant and commanding. "Mother, come! *Mother!*" he

359

whispered, though his thin lips seemed scarcely to move, and the silvery-gray muttonchop whiskers framing his stern face looked, of a sudden, stiff and lifeless as steel wool; and the chill utterance seemed as much to have sounded *within* the lady's head as *without.*

"Why, Harmon,—dear—what is it?" Mrs. Bunting exclaimed.

Pressing a plump beringed hand against her bosom, Mrs. Bunting turned to see, all amazedly, that no one stood behind her: neither her son nor anyone else had entered the somewhat dim little room, with its patterned rosy wallpaper, and its white damask draperies, and its pleasing richness,—indeed, was it not a veritable cornucopia of possessions, assembled over a long and energetic life?—of chairs, and sofas, and small tables, and lamps with painted globes, and china figurines, and framed daguerreotypes, and the like: naught but what might have been,—and even in this, Mrs. Bunting could not trust her blinking eyes—a wisp or tendril of fog that had insinuated its way into the cottage, though all the windows and doors were surely secured.

"Harmon, dear son—what is it? *What—?*"

Mrs. Bunting's affrighted voice sounded most peculiar, in the empty parlor: and when she looked back to the mirror,—this, a good-sized oval framed in carved cherrywood, that had belonged to the Bunting family for generations—she saw that the image had abruptly vanished, and naught but the familiar furnishings were reflected. (Yet, now, had they not acquired an uncanny etiolated aura, to appear, to her dazed eye, not altogether *right—?*)

"I have seen a ghost," Mrs. Bunting murmured aloud; then, but a scant second later, she chided herself, for the thought was preposterous: her darling Harmon was alive, and, indeed, in the prime of life, despite his growing stoutness, and an inclination to exhaust himself with work, and complaints now and then of digestive upsets. Moreover, Mrs. Bunting, for all that she was well into her seventy-third year, and had never, through much of her energetic life, been overly robust or hardy,—being, in truth, a mere *four feet nine inches tall*—prided herself on being an upstanding Christian lady, of Protestant demeanor: loved throughout her son's parish for her unfailing high spirits, and resolute optimism, and oft-expressed faith in the "simple good news of the Gospels": never inclined to succumb to idle fancies of morbidity, or pagan superstition; and little disposed to coddle those persons (excepting not even her troubled daughter-in-law Perdita) whose tempers led them in that direction. Indeed, Reverend Bunting's parishioners marveled at Letitia Bunting's selfless zeal, in heading the Ladies' Altar Society, and helping to organize the Sunday School, and the Young People's Bible Hour, and participating in numerous Winterthurn City charitable organizations, while (as it was whispered) her daughter-in-law shrugged off her responsibilities, with the plea of ill-health, or too little time. Mrs. Bunting's religion, if not precisely a "muscular" species of Christianity, of the kind popularly espoused by prominent clergymen of the day,—and by former President Teddy Roosevelt himself—was at the very least a right-thinking and uplifting sort, merry, sunny, and forthright. Thus it was, the minister's mother found welcoming smiles everywhere: for it was oft claimed that her pert, pink, smooth-skinned face, and her china-blue "twinkling" eyes, and, above all, her hearty *hello*, could virtually transform a sickroom, and bring sunshine where shadow commonly dwelt. For what does it profit us as Christians, Mrs. Bunting frankly believed, to ponder overmuch on the old issues of Hell, and damnation, and God's wrath, and man's fallen nature, seeing that, as the Gospels spelled out so clearly, *Jesus Christ has died for our sins—!*

So it was, this good woman bethought herself, that she could not possibly have seen a ghost, still less the ghost of her son: and would not cause any foolish upset in either of the households,—albeit her heartbeat was yet erratic, and a sickened sense of apprehension arose in her. Here in the cottage, Bessie was busily absorbed in the kitchen preparing for a high tea, to which some eight or ten prominent ladies of the parish were invited, and which both Harmon and Perdita would attend,—the latter, that is, if her capricious health allowed. So Mrs. Bunting did not want to disturb her. Nor would she succumb to the temptation to hurry over to the rectory (some three hundred yards away, along Jewett's Lane), just to pop her head in, as she sometimes did at this time of day: for it was certainly the case that Harmon was taken up with pastoral matters, and, of late, when Mrs. Bunting dropped by uninvited, it struck her that her daughter-in-law's hospitality was distinctly strained. ("Ah, my dear,—I hope I am not intruding!" Mrs. Bunting would call out cheerily, as ready to betake herself out of the parlor, as not: for the diminutive lady prided herself on resolutely *not being* one of those meddlesome mothers-in-law of whom it is common parlance to joke,—albeit her distinguished son, after more than a decade of marriage, made no secret of his dependence upon her, in matters both personal and professional. "Not at all, Mother Bunting,—not at all: pray be seated," Perdita would say, fumbling with a loosened plait of hair, or attempting, with childlike awkwardness and impatience, to adjust one of her stockings. How odd it was, Mrs. Bunting could not help but think, no matter the time of day she visited, Perdita seemed invariably to be taken by surprise: her toilette not adequately completed, her housedress not altogether fresh, and her manner,—ah, her manner!—distracted, or morose, or "nervy." Why, upon one occasion not long before, it was evident that Perdita, though very prettily attired in a pale green brushed-velvet dress, and her chestnut-brown hair for once done up sensibly, had neglected to put on either stockings or shoes: and was barefoot downstairs, in the rectory parlor, *at ten o'clock of a midsummer morning*, when any parishioner, dropping by, might have seen her. Naturally Mrs. Bunting refrained from making any censorious comment, save, afterward, in privacy to her son; nor had she ever spoken directly to Perdita of the unwholesome habit the younger woman had fallen into, over the years, of brewing countless pots of strong black China tea, which, with no sweetening added, nor even a dollop of cream, she drank from morning until night—! And yet Harmon professed to wonder at her nervousness and "high-strung" behavior, and to insist that she see Dr. Hatch on a regular basis.)

Such thoughts fairly streamed through Mrs. Bunting's mind as, seated at her *escritoire*, she made an effort to concentrate on her letter to her sister, and to resist glancing up, every minute or so, to the mirror on the wall: which, though reflecting now an incontestably empty space, yet exuded an air of the uncanny and the disagreeable. "It is absurd,—it is impossible,—and gives great offense to our Maker," Mrs. Bunting chided herself, "to incline to such superstitious notions." Her late husband, Mr. Robert Darr Bunting, Rector of the Church of St. John the Evangelist, of Nautauga Falls, had strongly disapproved of such pagan nonsense; as did her dear son Harmon,—albeit, residing in Winterthurn as he did, he was oft-times confronted (as he frowningly confessed) with matters not easily explained away by scientific or logical proof, or Christian common sense. For instance, in the very vicinity of Grace Church, in a wooded area bounded by Berwick Avenue to the south and Jewett's Pond (or Lake, as it was frequently called, since it measured nearly two miles in circumference) to the north, there had been, over the decades, and, alas, even within the past few months, certain inexplicable occurrences: the consequence, some thought, of "damned spirits" laid to an inappropriate rest, in the sanctified soil of Grace Church Cemetery; or, it may have been, as the elderly sexton Henry Harder believed, the result of a drowning,— whether accidental, or homicidal, or self-inflicted, none knew—that had taken place in Jewett's Pond in the late 1790s. Oft-times, on a clear and windless night, in the depths of the winter, cries for help seemed to emanate from the pond,—shrieks, and screams, and impassioned pleas,—in a voice hardly human, and not to be identified as either male or female; at other times, footsteps sounded heavily in the lane, as if someone were running, though no one was to be seen. Poor Mrs. Bunting was loath to confess that, living in Jewett Cottage as she did (Reverend Bunting having bought the tidy little stone-and-stucco house for her at the turn of the century), she was prone to hear these unearthly sounds, or to imagine she did; and made an effort to believe her son's firm-stated theory, that the cries from the pond were made by shifting or cracking ice, in the frigid depths of winter; and the footsteps were naught but some simply explained phenomena, of wind, loose shingles, creaking tree limbs, and the like.

Yet it seemed that, from time to time, *and not exclusively by night,* spectral figures were seen in the area, arising from the pond and the tall marsh grasses on its banks, and drifting, vaporlike, through the woods; ascending to one or another of the houses overlooking the hollow,—the Pitt-Davies', the Niehardts', the rectory, Jewett Cottage itself. Phantom faces were reported to appear at bedroom windows, to gaze into lighted rooms; unexplained footsteps were heard on stairs; soft whispers, murmurs, and cajolings emerged from the very air. And, ah!—some young girls and women claimed even to be touched, or caressed, by invisible hands: an experience that aroused incalculable terror, and was scarcely to be explained away by level-headed persons like Reverend Bunting. Indeed, Perdita herself had several times complained of a "chill and malefic presence" in the rectory, especially when Harmon was away in the evening, on church business: she heard footsteps overhead, and a soft tuneless whistling that "mocked even as it threatened": one August night, in no way wracked by wind or rain, or given an oppressive refulgence by the full moon (whose "glowering face" oft-times distressed her), Perdita woke terrified from a nightmare to see, pressed against the windowpane, a human countenance,—far too vivid and substantial, she claimed, to be mere wisps of vapor from the pond. (With that characteristic admixture of resignation and alarm that so nettled her mother-in-law,—albeit Letitia Bunting held her tongue on such matters—Perdita allowed her comforters to know that the spectral face, while horrific, was yet "familiar" to her mind's eye: *and did not altogether surprise her—!* "I am wicked,—I have sinned,—even if I have not sinned, why, I *am* wicked," the young Mrs. Bunting said listlessly, "so he shall come for me: and naught but a thin pane of glass separates us.")

Such remarks could not fail to annoy Harmon, who was inclined to believe, like many another resident of the affluent northerly section of the city, that persons who had no business in the neighborhood were responsible for these intrusions: unemployed men pretending to be seeking work: thieves, and parentless children, and riffraff of every sort, spilling out, as it were, of the crowded slums south of the river, where, in the 1890s and the first decade of the new century, thousands upon thousands of men and women had settled,— immigrants from Eastern and Southern Europe; impoverished Negroes from the South; country people forced from their farms by the erratic value of the dollar, to work in the factories and mills of South Winterthurn. "And to agitate therein for higher wages, and fewer hours of work,—and to cast their traitorous votes for Eugene Debs!" Harmon

Bunting drily observed. (Indeed, Harmon had suffered, in the past several years, from what he saw as a "tragic diminution" in the reliability of the American workingman and -woman: gentleman as he was, he found himself ill-suited to contend with the vagaries of drunken gravediggers, indifferent handymen, dishonest servant-girls, and even, for an infuriating spell in 1908–9, a young assistant pastor with a Harvard degree who slyly questioned his superior's theology, and spoke casually of him behind his back. Thus it seemed more imperative to Reverend Bunting every day to "hold the line" and to "stick fast": which virtues he frequently preached from the sanctity of the Grace Episcopal pulpit.)

　　Letitia Bunting would have been a most insensible mother not to take alarm at the number of enemies,—some outspoken, and some covert—her son had accumulated during his tenure as rector of Winterthurn City's most prestigious church; and the poor woman could not console herself as to which might be less fearsome,—the threat of disaster from the "inhuman" world, or that from the "human." For instance, it was whispered that Harmon had made an implacable enemy of Ellery Poindexter, the chairman of the Bishop's Standing Committee, and one of the most wealthy men in the parish: the dispute having to do with technical matters regarding the appropriation of funds for the Episcopal branch of the Colonization Society. (Or so Mrs. Bunting gathered, for she did not wish to ask her son outright; nor did she inquire of him whether the falling out between the men had anything to do with Amanda Poindexter's "crisis of faith,"—an episode, protracted and feverish, much discussed in Winterthurn drawing rooms, for the past six or eight months. For, it seemed, the deeply troubled Mrs. Poindexter, *née* Shaw, was neglecting her familial and social duties of late, including the chairmanship of the Rose Hunt Cotillion, for which powerful office she had, the year before, vigorously campaigned. She had time for naught but the Ladies' Altar Society of Grace Church, which, it was said, she essayed to dominate: and for earnest discussions with Harmon Bunting on church matters, or fine particulars of Episcopal faith. Amanda fretted that she varied greatly in her capacity for belief: on some days she felt strong enough to believe in virtually everything, including such Romish dogma as infant damnation; on other days, her doubts were such, she could not grasp the nature of the Trinity,—which is to say, how Father, Son, and Holy Spirit, being three autonomous, divine, and masculine entities, were yet *one*. Thus, she was frequently a visitor in Reverend Bunting's study in the rectory, while her driver waited outside, smoking a cigarette by the opened door of the Poindexters' Lancia Lambda; or, a summons would arrive from St. Bride's, the Poindexter estate on the Old River Road, that Mr. Bunting was invited to tea, or to dinner, or to an evening of "sequestered conversation," that Amanda's turbulent mind might be put to rest, on some theological nicety. Mrs. Bunting thought Amanda Poindexter one of the more forceful, albeit charming, society ladies of the parish: she had swallowed her hurt, in Christian humility, when, at a large reception some years before, Mrs. Poindexter had gazed down quizzically upon the diminutive elder lady, as if, for a scant moment, she had no idea who she was!—though Letitia Bunting's presence, in her black silk-and-woolen cape and her tiny black kidskin boots, was known through the city.)

In addition, it was rumored that Harmon had in some obscure wise offended Wilbur Elspeth; and Dustan Westergaard; and Bradford Kilgarvan, the Mayor's most trusted aide. More recently,—and, to a mother's worried mind, more significantly—Harmon had had an altercation with a bully and a ruffian, one Jabez Dovekie, who was not even a member of his parish, and assuredly not a gentleman. This near-giant of a fellow, red-haired, and brutish in his person, and doubtless slightly inebriated, had had the temerity to arrive unannounced at the rectory the previous week, *on three consecutive days,* demanding to speak to the pastor: and becoming quite abusive to the housekeeper when it was explained that Reverend Bunting was otherwise engaged. He would make no formal appointment, for, as he said, he did *what* he wished *when* he wished; and would not be bound by the schedules of others. Harmon professed not to be worried about Dovekie, albeit both Perdita and Mrs. Bunting evinced fear, and Mrs. Harwich, the housekeeper, was left shaken by the bully's words; and John Hathorne, the assistant rector, believed the man unstable and unpredictable. Harmon, however, considered him but a bluff, and a fool, accustomed to ordering women about, and men of weak character, but scarcely a man to browbeat *him.* As to why Dovekie was so incensed over Reverend Bunting,—he had, it seems, gone bankrupt some five or six years previous, in his ice-hauling business; he had unwisely borrowed money from divers sources, at very high interest rates; and he (so Harmon now believed) embezzled several thousand dollars from his widowed sister's estate. This sordid matter now seemed to be coming to light, all by accident, as, the invalided woman having experienced a conversion not long before, she was now eagerly desirous of making her peace with God, and with the Episcopal Church: and implored Reverend Bunting to take over her accounts completely, in the service of Jesus Christ. This enterprise Jabez Dovekie furiously contested, as it was but "meddling" in Dovekie family affairs; and involved the "high and mighty" pastor in matters that were none of his business.

Yet another distressing matter, which had been brought to Harmon's notice only within the past fortnight, had to do with certain "scandalous" and "obscene" letters, received intermittently since the previous spring, by several ladies in the parish: these being Amanda Poindexter, Dorothea Carnsworth, both the pretty young Penistone twins, and poor Perdita herself,—of those whose names were known. As such ugly disclosures were not discussed in the elderly Mrs. Bunting's presence, she knew nothing of the actual content of the missives, save that, as Harmon had said in great disgust, they were the product of "a diseased, twisted, and blasphemous mind," which could belong to no one of their acquaintance; but must be the work of a cowardly stranger,—very likely even an enemy of the Church. They had been, of course, penned by an anonymous hand, and sent by way of the regular post: received by the innocent ladies in great consternation, fright, and secret shame: until, after a recent outburst of Mrs. Poindexter's, which had evidently been gravely hysterical, the matter had been brought to light, and the other ladies had, in great distress, spoken out. Mrs. Carnsworth had destroyed the three letters received by her, immediately upon opening them; the Penistone girls had hidden theirs away, half imagining, at the start, that they were but pranks of some kind,—or a new species of Valentine, of French origin; Perdita had burnt three of the five sent to her, but had thought it wisest to save the last two, for, in her opinion, the author of the sickly missives might well be dangerous, and his actions should probably be brought to the attention of the police,—albeit she herself was too overcome with shame to acknowledge her plight. At the present time,—that is, by the afternoon of September 11—the matter had not been officially reported, though Orrin Wick, Winterthurn's new chief of police, had eard disquieting rumors of "threatening" letters having been received by several prominent society women, amongst them Ellery Poindexter's wife.

Such a barrage of worrisome thoughts, streaming through Mrs. Bunting's brain, made it at last impossible for her to concentrate upon the letter to her sister,—the which she had been writing for some minutes while scarcely knowing what she said, and in a hand far less refined than usual. Though the cherrywood mirror reflected nothing out of the ordinary, and the sitting room was, of course, empty save for herself, Mrs. Bunting became increasingly distracted, and was not to be soothed by the familiar heavy tread of Bessie Hyde in an adjoining room, or the cheery twittering of a pet parakeet in the kitchen. At last, inwardly trembling, she laid down her pen, thinking: "I must go to Harmon."

So it was, shortly before four o'clock of that fogbound and inordinately warm September day, Mrs. Letitia Bunting, the widowed mother of Reverend Harmon Bunting, called out to her servant Mrs. Hyde that she was going to pop her head into the rectory, and would be gone but a minute. Attired, then, in her black rain cape, and black bonnet, and carrying her umbrella, she left Jewett Cottage, and, walking as quickly as her legs would carry her, followed the familiar meandering path through the cemetery, past the back of the church, and to the rear door of the minister's residence. So apprehensive was she, while chiding herself for her foolishness, she took no note of the wondrous fresh scent of the wet grass, or the peaceable stillness of the day, or, not least, the languid melancholy of the mist that curled through the gravestones, and lifted into the limbs of the tall trees. How brave and determined, that petite figure!—and how loath am I, to follow her into that scene of carnage!

While the trembling Mrs. Bunting enters the rectory, by way of the rear door,—her knock having gone unanswered, and the door, as always, unlatched,—I should like to pause briefly to supply the reader with a curio of sorts.

This precious item, shortly to be "lost" in Orrin Wick's investigation, is none other than the conclusion of the very letter Letitia Bunting was writing to her sister, on that tragic day so long ago!—just last week brought to my excited attention by a collector in Basking Ridge, New Jersey; and now a part of my crime collection, or Crime Treasury, as I call it.

How Mrs. Bunting's letter was lost by Winterthurn police, and how this page came to be found again, is doubtless mysterious: but the reader must understand that, up until the present time, numberless pieces of evidence, confiscated by police, were routinely lost, or misplaced, or destroyed; or, it might be conjectured, stolen away for sentimental or mercenary reasons. (Which seems to have been the case with the little gold cross found in Eva Teal's mouth: for it has recently come to my attention that this priceless item, or a reasonable facsimile thereof, has been placed on the market by a dealer in White Plains, New York,—albeit for a shockingly high price.)

Herewith, Mrs. Bunting's disjointed thoughts, expressed in a near-illegible hand, and, to my mind, most riddlesome indeed: for why, at this particular time, did her thinking swerve in this purposeless direction; and why,—if "why" be not too fanciful a question—did Orrin Wick lose the page? *Or was it Orrin Wick who lost it—?*

> . . . his choice of a wife & not to be questioned nay not *deliberated* by one who loves him dearly, for 'tis better to marry than to burn as we are told: & doubtless Harmon took such counsel to heart. Yet dear sister how it wounds me that from the first she has rebuffed me & my proferred love! It is known that her own mother was wicked & mad, & died in wretched sin (having swallowed poison when she was but a small child),

whereupon it follows that she contemns me who would be Mother to her.

Dear sister, daily & nightly I pray to God, that the bountifulness of my heart not be so scorned, with that small chill smile & razor-line betwixt the brows, & ah! the darksome blaze of her black eyes which, it seems, *Harmon has never beheld.*

Strait is the gate & narrow is the way which leadeth unto life & few there be that find it. Sister dear, I am most aggrieved.

Such happenings here that cannot be grasped! A "presence" hovers over the household,—unspeakable letters are received by ladies of Christian virtue; Harmon is beset by enemies, who wish him confusion & defeat; Winterthurn City grows daily less recognizable beyond the south bank & ugly to behold & wicked; & she who should be my loving & devoted daughter is stiff in my embrace & hums under her breath when I speak & is subject to moods & spells & humors,—some as a consequence of the Moon's waxing & waning, some springing from her own soul.

Ah, you may well ask, *do they quarrel?*—but I know not: for Harmon spares me such grief.

Yet I cannot hide my eyes to the friction betwixt them & the strain of the household: dear sister how can I fail to *hear* that which is *almost voiced?* She weeps & her lower lip swells in rebellion that Harmon should & must & *will* oversee her income, less from Kilgarvan investments (for Erasmus it seems speculated unwisely) than from royalties from that queer book of poesy,—*The Collected Poems of "Iphigenia,"*—which is to say, poor Georgina Kilgarvan's work, much ridiculed here at home but valued (it is said) elsewhere. I know not the sums involved nor even if they be substantial (for that is unlikely) but Perdita flares up, & weeps, & lies abed, & drifts about the rectory pale & disheveled & "moonstruck," & glory be to God Harmon is strong & taciturn at such times & never weakens as a doting husband might.

Why, but three Sundays ago he spoke from the pulpit most powerfully, on the verse from Matthew:

> *For in the resurrection they neither marry, nor are*
> *given in marriage, but are as the angels in heaven*

& *she* did not attend,—lying lifeless abed with her servant-girl in attendance like a nurse & weeping that her mistress would not eat & oft-times *failed to breathe,* so far as she could observe!

Dear sister, my hand shakes,—I scarcely know what I mean to say, & what will become of us. *Her* moods of despondency & lethargy,—her spells of chattering gaiety; her wild heartbreak & yearning,—spring from I know not what ungodly source, lest it be the old defilement of the blood, inherited from wicked ancestors. For long hours she sits & stares out the window at nothing,—save the close-packed gravestones in the oldest corner of the cemetery. These spells she essays to hide from Harmon & me, but Mrs. Harwich (whose word cannot be doubted) confides daily in me. They date back long before the disagreement over the royalties from her sister's book,—they date back to before her unwholesome attachment to the foundling infant who died last year, of which I have written you. Dare I say it, sister, the spells date back to her return from her honeymoon, now ten,—nay, eleven—years ago!

This daughter whom I dare not embrace,—whom I dare not call Daughter,—she is said to be beautiful, yet can it be beauty of a healthsome sort? Those wild black eyes & dark tresses now streaked with silver!—& her habit of humming under her breath while others speak,—or singing some tune that has snagged in her brain,—whether a trashy popular song like "Meet Me in St. Louis, Louis," or the old ballad "Barbara Allen," or another called "The Golden Vanity," about a drowning it seems, & most sorrowful to hear, in her chill voice in particular,—

> *There once was a ship*
> *And she sailed upon the sea,—*
> *And the name of our ship was*
> *The* Golden Vanity—

With which enigmatic words, Letitia Bunting's hastily written letter breaks off; and was never to be concluded.

The bells of Grace Episcopal Church were sounding the hour of four, in a muted, somber, yet noble tone, when, having received no answer to her agitated knocking, and her yet more agitated calls, Mrs. Bunting bravely opened the door to her son's study at the southwestern corner of the rectory, to gaze upon a spectacle nearly too horrendous for me to transcribe: this, Reverend Harmon Bunting, her belovèd son, lying asprawl on his horsehair divan, with a woman beside him,—a woman not his lawful wedded wife, but Mrs. Amanda Poindexter *in a disheveled state.*

Ah, what an unlook'd-to vision!—the frowsy-haired lady resting her blond head cozily against Harmon's shoulder, and Harmon with his arm slipped about her waist, his outspread fingers lightly resting on her ample thigh!

Surprised thus, and afflicted, moreover, with weakened eyes, poor Mrs. Bunting stood frozen in the doorway, unable to turn aside in tactful embarrassment, or to murmur any sort of greeting or apology: her throat most painfully constricted, the while her heartbeat grew ever more erratic: and her brain, of a sudden benumbed, reluctant to absorb the full horror of the scene,—for is it not invariably so, when the known world shatters irrevocably around us, and, in a scant instant, the dread wisdom is communicated, that *naught will ever be the same again—!*

Yet Mrs. Bunting could not for long deceive herself: for the guilty couple lay on the divan far too stiffly and too awkwardly to be in a natural posture; nor was it natural that neither started, or made any response, when she incautiously opened the door. And, ah! were their facial expressions not decidedly peculiar,—their skulls misshapen, or smashed, it may have been, like crockery,—a good deal of blood, bright fresh glistening blood: *yet-flowing blood,*—befouling their hair and faces, and soaked into their clothes, and gathering in rapid drips in a single hideous pool on the hardwood floor? Why, it seemed to be the case that the gentleman's balding head had been severely crushed, and his iron-gray muttonchop whiskers commingled with bone and tissue; one glassy eyeball bulged from its socket, while the other eye, showing but white, was partly closed; the high starched collar of his white shirt appeared to have been driven, by demonic force, into his badly lacerated neck; two fingers dangled near-severed from his limp right hand; and his skin, that had so recently been ruddy and healthsome, had gone ashen gray in death. As for the lady,—though lifeless as well, and bleeding copiously from cruel wounds in her head, neck, and upper left arm,—she appeared to have been treated with considerably more delicacy than her companion: for her round fleshy face with its half-moons of rouge, and its small close-set staring eyes, yet possessed an air of simpering prettiness; and her expression was one of startled chagrin, rather than animal terror. Lavishly attired in a flounced dress of pale apricot chiffon, with puff sleeves and three-inch tight-buttoned cuffs, an heirloom cameo brooch at her throat and a strand of heavy pearls about her neck, Amanda Poindexter seemed to take up most of the divan, propped awkwardly as she was against Harmon's shoulder, both her bloodied arms outspread, and the hem of her dress raised, all surprisingly, to expose blood-soaked petticoats. So massive and self-contained did the lady seem, even in death, she might have been about to rise petulantly from the divan, to smooth down her skirts, and secure one of the shiny blond switches that had been jarred loose from her coiffure, and put a haughty question to the intruder: "Yes? What do you mean by disturbing us?"

So it was, Mrs. Bunting stood paralyzed a few yards away, a frail figure the size of a child, and essayed to speak,—"Oh, Harmon,—oh, my boy,—my baby,—my belovèd,—what have they done to you?"— while her blinking gaze took in, but could not absorb, a mocking array of *hearts* (paper cut-out hearts, crimson velvet hearts, cinnamon hearts, chocolate hearts) liberally scattered about the bodies. How could it be that she saw what she saw!—that so frightful a vision had been granted her by God: she, Letitia Bunting, who had ever adored Him, and had never questioned His will!

She would have rushed forward to her son,—she would have screamed, to summon help,—but, of a sudden, a hoarse breathing or panting just behind her, which she had been half hearing all the while, defined itself unmistakably, and, with no time for caution, nor even dread, she turned, and uttered a small high wail of surprise,—to catch the sharp edge of the bloodied ax, as it fell upon her upraised forehead.

"The Red-Haired Specter"

Shortly thereafter, according to the testimonies of several witnesses, the figure of a man of unusual height and size, and of coarse,—nay, brutish—physique, was to be observed running along Jewett's Lane, from the direction of the cemetery: lumbering, and heavy-footed, and stooped over in an apish posture, and carrying something in his arms: a red-haired stranger of giant proportions, being, it seemed, seven, or eight, or ten feet tall, and possessed of a "fearsome countenance": a wraith or a specter loosed from Hell, or a mortal man in evident distress—?

Alas, that the afternoon's undulating mists had not only deepened by this time, to meld with a premature dusk, but that a light drizzle had begun to fall, the more to obscure visibility!—for of the several witnesses, only one had had the opportunity to gaze upon the creature at close range, and he was but a child of ten years of age; and grievously frightened by the encounter.

In Jewett Cottage, but an eighth of a mile from Grace Church, Mrs. Bunting's loyal servant Bessie Hyde found herself making frequent trips from the kitchen to the front parlor, that she might gaze, with some apprehension, out the window: the while berating herself for not having offered to accompany her plucky mistress to the rectory. But it was often the case that Letitia Bunting would go about unescorted, briskly tying on her bonnet, and fastening her cape about her, and professing both surprise and chiding reproach that she might be considered advanced in years, and in any wise infirm. So Mrs. Hyde peered into the lane; and waited, and waited, with some trepidation;

consoling herself with the fact that, surely, Reverend Bunting would escort his mother back to the cottage, well in time to allow her to dress for tea . . . Thus it was, the affrighted woman saw the "red-haired specter,"—as, in the earliest phase of the investigation, Jabez Dovekie was so floridly called—running past the cottage from the direction of the church, some twenty or twenty-five minutes (by her confused estimation) after Mrs. Bunting had stepped out. She had known at once that he was a criminal,—most likely a murderer: that he had just committed a monstrous act, and would soon commit another: for, ah!—how hideous, how fearsome, how unnaturally twisted, the creature's face,—and how gigantic he was, whether human, or demonic! Stooped over in brutish fashion, yet running, it seemed, in a most erratic way,—now toward the center of the graveled lane, now in the overgrown grasses at the side,—swaying, and wavering, and plunging blindly forward, as if, in the exigency of the moment, he lacked animal cunning and scarcely knew what he did. "He is fleeing a murder," Mrs. Hyde murmured aloud, cringing behind the curtains, her poor heart nearly stopped, in terror that he would turn into the cottage gate, and break down the door. Albeit the fog had grown particularly dense in the low-lying area of Jewett's Pond, Mrs. Hyde was to insist that she could see clearly enough to discern that the creature's thick, somewhat overlong hair was *red*; that his eyes were *tawny and ablaze*, like smoldering coals; that he wore *workingman's clothes*, and *no hat*; and that he was cradling in his arms an object about the size of a *small child*, gripped to his chest in an awkward fashion, that much impeded his ability to run. Upon seeing this frightful person, scarcely more than forty feet from where she stood, Mrs. Hyde was so gripped with terror, she came near to fainting dead away,—and could give no thought, for some agitated minutes, as to the well-being of her poor mistress.

So powerfully had this horrific vision been impressed upon Mrs. Hyde, she would be capable of identifying the fiend with no difficulty, as she afterward told Orrin Wick: and, indeed, would wholeheartedly give evidence against him, to send him to the gallows, and to Hell,—if he be a mortal man.

In similar wise, and with as much vehemence, Amos Niehardt and his invalided wife, Flora, who lived just up the lane from Jewett Cottage, declared that they could readily identify the "murderer": for, it seemed, the disheveled creature had tramped through Mrs. Niehardt's rose-garden in his panicked flight, and had passed within ten feet of their house. Eighty-two-year-old Amos Niehardt's description of the red-haired figure paralleled Mrs. Hyde's generally, save that he believed the man to be "at least twelve feet in height," and wearing bloodstained working clothes, and possessed of a gargoyle-like face, with red-glittering eyes. Moreover, he was carrying in his arms *the* *limp and flimsily clad body of a comely young woman,—*the rector's wife, Perdita, it seemed! (Nor could Mr. Niehardt be budged from this notion, even when it was explained to him that, at the time, Mrs. Harmon Bunting lay unconscious in her boudoir on the second floor of the rectory, her wrists and ankles bound, and a gag tied about her mouth. "Nonetheless I am certain that 'twas she, and no one else, clenched in the brute's arms," the elderly gentleman stubbornly asserted, "and Mrs. Niehardt will support me, for, though her eyes are poor, and she was lying abed at the time, she remembers how I exclaimed at once that it must be a kidnapping or an abduction, with the rector's wife as the victim.")

As to whether the red-haired man was a "specter" or not,—the Niehardts debated the issue betwixt themselves, but were undecided, for while there were enormous footprints in the garden, arguing for a material source, it had always been the case that the phantasmal cries from the pond, as well as the sound of running feet in the lane, *seemed* real enough when they were heard, but were, of course, of unearthly origin; and both the Niehardts had experienced these alarming phenomena countless times, during the fifty-odd years of their residence in Jewett's Lane. (When Amos Niehardt learned more fully of the ax murders, including that of the much-loved widow Letitia Bunting, he was the more incensed, and voiced the opinion that he hoped "the malefactor *was* but a mortal man of flesh and blood, that he might be dispatched straightaway to Hell.")

Miss Elvira Pitt-Davies, happening to glance out her sewing-room window into the lane at about this time, was startled to see someone passing by in evident haste, with something,—she knew not what, but believed it an inanimate object—gripped in his arms. Alone of the witnesses, however, the fifty-six-year-old maiden lady felt obliged to confess that, owing to the fog and the drizzling rain, it was impossible to see clearly: and she dreaded to involve any innocent person in the case by proffering inaccurate testimony. Indeed, when brought to the station-house to identify Jabez Dovekie, some days later, Miss Pitt-Davies said frankly that she could not: nor could she swear that she had actually seen the running man with something in his arms. Had he been dressed in work clothes; had he been bareheaded; had his hair been red,—Miss Pitt-Davies apologized for her timidity, but, alas, she could not say. "It is a very serious thing to accuse a man of murder, after all," she told police.

(The spacious old Colonial house owned by the Pitt-Davies family, on the picturesque northern shore of Jewett Pond, is perhaps three-quarters of a mile from Grace Church, as the crow flies; and situated well uphill, that its inhabitants might enjoy a view of the pond and its wooded surroundings. I mention the fact in this space as, quite by happenstance, Xavier Kilgarvan will reside there for the duration of the case, as a guest of his former teacher and admirer Murre Pitt-Davies, the headmaster of the Winterthurn Academy for Boys. A splendid white clapboard house it is even today, though so much else in Jewett's Lane, and, indeed, in Winterthurn City itself, has been altered: and one can well imagine Xavier's romantic yearning as, standing at the window of his bedroom on the second floor of the Pitt-Davies house, he could gaze across the pond to the glinting steeple of Grace Church, and envision his belovèd Perdita in her invalid bed, in the adjoining residence—!)

Precisely why the ten-year-old Leroy Craven was playing with his Irish setter dog in the cattails and rushes along the shore of Jewett's Pond, in such intemperate weather, was never satisfactorily explained, albeit neighbors spoke of the boy's habitual queer behavior, and his parents' indifference in disciplining him. Having no playmates, the child prowled about where he would, exploring the muddiest stretches of the pond, and hiding in the rushes, for unknown purposes: talking to himself, and brandishing "javelins" and "swords" fashioned of tree limbs; at times afflicted with an excruciating shyness, so that he ran from residents of the neighborhood, and, at other times, possessed of a kind of demonism, in that he pelted them with stones and clumps of mud from his hiding places. It was said of Leroy Craven, by his parents as well as his teachers, that he was incapable of discerning truth from fancy; yet, it seems, he acquitted himself in a mature fashion, in describing the "red-haired giant" he had seen running blindly along the lane, splashing through puddles, and whimpering aloud to himself, *a bloodied ax cradled in his arms.*

When this nightmare figure first appeared, out of the mist that cloaked the lane, Leroy's dog growled deep in his throat, and laid his ears back: but was, in the next minute, so terrified by the apparition,—or, it may have been, by the smell of fresh blood—that he turned tail, as the expression goes, and ran cowering away, through a muddy stretch of marsh grass. The fleeing dog drew the man's attention at once, but drew it, fortunately, away from Leroy Craven, who was squatting nearby in the grasses, frozen with terror, as he knew he would be murdered,—"chopped to pieces by the ax," as he said—if the man's wild-rolling eyes chanced to light upon him.

For the space of some thirty seconds, a most protracted and dreadful period of time, the panting man stood close by, *within five feet of the child*, as if undecided how to proceed. So near was he, so horrifically near, as Leroy Craven afterward said,—and was to say, indeed, for the remainder of his life, this being its peak—that he could see the beads of perspiration on the brute's forehead, and hear his sobbing breath, and very nearly feel, or so it seemed, the tumult of his heart: he had time,—ah, how would he have *not!*—to memorize every detail of that fearsome countenance, which he would never forget so long as he lived: the wide furrowed forehead, the fleshy nose and jowls, the blunt chin, the dazed expression of the eyes. Whether man, or demon, or a monstrous amalgam of both, the paralyzed child knew not, but felt, as it were, *in the very instant of his terror,* a queer surge of pity for the creature, as he radiated more an air of desperation, than of wickedness.

Yet the front of his jacket was smeared with blood, and there was no mistaking the authority of the long-handled ax he gripped in both hands, its broad evil head covered with dark stains and what appeared to be hairs, and even the handle discolored for much of its length. "It has been used for murder," the boy thought, "and will be used again, if I betray my hiding place."

Fortune smiled upon the lad, however, for, of a sudden, the red-haired man made the decision to throw the ax into the pond, so far as his powerful muscles would carry it: and, his breath still ragged and panting, he turned to run away,—to disappear into the mist,—and to "disappear," in a manner of speaking, for a space of several days.

In the Rectory

By the time Xavier Kilgarvan arrived in Winterthurn City on the 7:05 train from Manhattan,—to the commingled amazement and apprehension, it scarcely needs be said, of Chief of Police Orrin Wick and his officers—the lurid news had spread through town that the bodies of three persons had been discovered in the Grace Episcopal Church on Berwick Avenue, barbarously hacked to death with an ax: that the unidentified murderer was loose in the city: that the beautiful young wife of Reverend Harmon Bunting had been ''grievously and mysteriously violated'' by that selfsame murderer: and that a scandalous ''love nest'' had been exposed,—whether in the hallowed interior of the wealthy Grace Church itself, or in the minister's residence.

In addition, it was believed that the minister's elderly mother, a veritable saint to those who knew her, was amongst the victims: and one of Winterthurn City's most prominent society ladies was involved: and one of the city's most prominent clergymen,—taken in adultery, it seemed, and punished forthwith by a vengeful husband!

Alas, numberless were the variants of these early reports, streaming most promiscuously through the city, in those hours before the *Winterthurn Gazette* could mobilize its staff to publish a special edition: there being the insistence, in some quarters, that the crime must have been perpetrated by a gang of gypsies; or by a gang of blacks; or by a contingent of striking workers in South Winterthurn,—for there was, at this time, a wildcat strike of cannery workers at a factory owned by the Poindexters, now in its third day. Elsewhere it was stated as a fact that the Episcopal clergyman had been ''hacked to death'' by a maddened zealot of a heretic sect of Antichrists; and that both murdered women,—Mrs. Letitia Bunting and Mrs. Amanda Poindexter—had been "obscenely abused" before meeting their deaths. A flurry of fresh rumors reported the death as well of the minister's wife, Mrs. Perdita Bunting, *née* Kilgarvan: with the curious embellishment that all four victims had died at the hand of Ellery Poindexter, one of the deacons of the church—! Then again, it was offered as factual that a contingent of disgruntled servants, including gravediggers recently discharged by the minister, had "mutinied" against their master, and gone berserk, killing more persons than they had intended: and that Harmon Bunting had been subjected to "ritual punishment" by the Brethren of Jericho,—there having been, at this time, several widely publicized incidents of chastisement of clergymen by the Brethren, with the charge that the men were insufficiently Christian, or American; or that they had "misbehaved morally"; or had spoken out against the patriotic group, in public or in private. Yet again, it was hysterically circulated amongst the wealthier citizens of the city that the murders had been committed by a small band of Anarchists from New York City, of Austrian or Russian origin: and that the murders were but the first of a proposed series, in the systematic erasure of all social classes from the United States. In other neighborhoods of Winterthurn, however, it was presented as self-evident, and with some wicked gloating, that the vainglorious Reverend Bunting had been murdered along with his mistress by an infuriated husband, or an agent of the husband: and that the police had already made their arrest: or (this being a peculiar variant) would not be making any arrest, as the wealthy Poindexter clan had taken swift and pragmatic moves to buy them off.

It was nothing short of remarkable, how quickly word spread that, at the very least, *something* had happened up on Berwick Avenue to draw such a bevy of policemen, and so clamorous a throng of spectators, who, despite the rain, not only had gathered on the sloping lawn of the church, but had spilled over, as it were, into the cemetery,—a noisome pack of men and women eager to learn the most gruesome details of the murders, while professing scandalized repugnance; and not above snatching up whatever "souvenirs" were at hand; whether chunks of crumbling stone from the grave markers, or leaves from the handsome hickories and oaks that surrounded the church—! One comely tree, growing unfortunately near the street, and possessed of several low-sweeping limbs, was cruelly vandalized by the crowd, and in danger of being stripped bare of its leaves,—a sobering reflection, as Osmyn Goshawk was to comment in his front-page editorial, on the degeneration of civility and common courtesy in the Modern Era. "The brute devastation *within* the rectory was echoed, if not mocked, by the brute devastation *without"*—so Mr. Goshawk charged.

With the passage of minutes, from late afternoon to early evening, the murmurous throng grew; and both Berwick Avenue and Jewett's Lane soon became clogged with persons of all ages, not excepting children, of a social class not ordinarily glimpsed in this section of the city. From time to time, flurries of excitement arose with the arrival of certain recognized persons (amongst them Mr. Goshawk of the *Gazette*, and Dr. Colney Hatch, now white-haired and venerable, and walking with a cane); and with the false report that, at last, the bodies were to be borne out of the rectory to the waiting mortuary van. (How the onlookers surged forward at this prospect, fairly trampling one another, and scarcely to be held back by restraining police,—and how vociferously disappointed they were when no bodies appeared!) It was wrongly asserted that Ellery Poindexter had arrived *incognito;* it was preposterously asserted that the ax murderer had been apprehended by police, and would be shortly brought back to the scene of the crime. Indeed, what was *not* susceptible to belief, on that notorious autumn day of mists, and drizzling rain, and a red-haired "specter" wielding an ax, and a "love nest" sickeningly befouled with human blood and brains—! All irresponsibly, it was even asserted that Xavier Kilgarvan, who had not set foot in Winterthurn since Valentine Westergaard had walked off scot free, nearly a dozen years before, would now return: a farfetched rumor soon to shade into the truth.

Much confusion and initial bungling, it scarcely need be said, attended the earliest stage of the police investigation into the murders: partly as a consequence (so rumor would have it) of Police Chief Orrin Wick's stunned disbelief that what seemed to have happened, had actually happened,—and in his jurisdiction. No one, not even members of the victims' families, appeared more dazed than the usually vigorous and forthright Mr. Wick, who was observed to have done little but stare at the butchered corpses for some fifteen or twenty minutes, and to give little guidance or instruction to his officers. It was a ghastly enough thing, that three persons should have been murdered in so brutal a way; yet all the more difficult to grasp that an upstanding gentleman of the cloth should have been surprised, as it were, with a lady not his wife,—a lady, moreover, born a Shaw, and married into the Poindexters. And how came it, Mr. Wick asked aloud, that the elderly Mrs. Bunting should have been closeted with them; and why had *she* been killed? (With especial brutality, it seemed: for while Reverend Bunting had suffered some *twenty-three* strokes of the ax, by the coroner's estimate, and Mrs. Poindexter some *nineteen,* the frail Letitia Bunting must have borne the brunt of the maniac's untrammeled frenzy, in suffering more than *two dozen* blows of the weapon, both from its blunt side and its sharp side, any one of which would probably have been lethal: which unspeakable brutality had so extreme an effect upon the elderly woman's eighty-pound body as to make any exact description of it in this chronicle impossible. Suffice it to say that, upon first glimpsing the mutilated corpse, several of the police officers, including Mr. Wick himself, came very close to fainting dead away: and the youngest had to rush from the room, to succumb to a fit of vomiting. For the horror of the scene was such, Reverend Bunting's walnut-paneled study may as well have been an abattoir,—there being blood virtually everywhere, save the ceiling some ten feet above; and unmistakable brain tissue, and fragments of bone, sprayed against the furniture, windows, and wall. Indeed, though the law enforcement officers had seen many an ugly sight in their careers, there was no doubting the fact that nothing resembling this carnage *had ever before occurred in Winterthurn.*)

The bodies had been discovered by Mrs. Poindexter's chauffeur, McPhearson Jones, when he returned for his mistress at four-thirty, and waited, in the drive, for a good half-hour: this being approximately the time that young Leroy Craven, badly shaken from his ordeal in the marsh, was all breathlessly trying to explain what *he* had seen to his doubting parents. Police were summoned: a young patrolman ventured into the rectory, and, seeing the gravity of the situation, retreated at once, to report the news to the central precinct: and, within a short space of time, a sizable contingent of police officers had arrived, all somber and apprehensive. Indeed, so overcome was Orrin Wick when he first examined the butchery (as he called it), he forgot numerous elementary principles of his trade: allowed persons as dazed as he to wander about, and track up the residence with bloody footprints: failed to check the building to see if the murderer was still there, or what doors and windows were locked, or unlocked, or had been forced: failed to order an immediate check of the neighborhood: failed even to check the cellar,—where, as it turned out, poor Mrs. Harwich lay unconscious, having been pushed down the cellar stairs by the murderer, and locked up in the dark. So disoriented was Mr. Wick, and so irresolute his officers, being taken up, in particular, with the mocking array of *hearts* strewn about the study, it was only with the sudden arrival of Miss Thérèse Kilgarvan that thought was given to the minister's missing wife, at last discovered bound, and gagged, and herself insensible, in an upstairs room; and it was only by way of the keen-eyed McPhearson Jones that a badly soiled black broadcloth cap, later identified as belonging to Jabez Dovekie, was discovered on a cemetery path,—and saved from the clutches of the rabid souvenir-seekers.

(It was unfortunate that Mrs. Poindexter's chauffeur could provide police with no information, regarding suspicious persons approaching the rectory that afternoon: for, as chance would have it, on this most fateful of days Mrs. Poindexter had bade him run errands for her downtown, while she visited an hour with Reverend Bunting,—as she was wont to do, of late, one or two afternoons a week.)

It was afterward charged against police that there had been an unconscionable delay in informing members of the victims' families: for Miss Thérèse Kilgarvan had merely "heard news,"—and inordinately confused and cruel news, indeed—regarding a veritable bloodbath at the church; and the Poindexter children learned of their mother's rumored death while at their riding lessons, at the Sandusky Hunt Club. As for Ellery Poindexter,—it soon developed, all surprisingly, that *no one knew where he was:* for he had been missing, it seems, since midmorning. (According to servants, Mr. Poindexter had left St. Bride's at approximately ten o'clock in the morning, having breakfasted late, as he often did, and alone: it had been understood that he would drop by his Hazelwitt office,—for Mr. Poindexter had been, for a few years, a practicing lawyer, while the Law amused him, and he still "kept his oar in" the trade—and then dine with an associate at one, at the Corinthian Club. So far as the club manager knew, however, no such engagement had been planned; and Ellery Poindexter must have dined elsewhere. At Hazelwit Square, it was believed he had spent the day at St. Bride's, suffering from one of his asthma attacks; at St. Bride's, it was believed he had planned to be away the entire afternoon, and very likely into the evening.)

Albeit the coarser element amongst the townsfolk already whispered of Reverend Bunting's "love nest," and a cuckolded husband's revenge, not one of Orrin Wick's officers, and certainly not Orrin Wick himself, did, for an instant, imagine that the distinguished Ellery Poindexter might be the murderer: for he was known to be a gentleman of the highest breeding; his family had lived in Winterthurn since before the Revolution; if possessed of a heavy, saturnine, somewhat ironical countenance, and shadowed, or even clouded, eyes,—if given, as rumor would have it, to a whimsical sort of speculation in railroad and grain stock, and a more explicit sort of gambling at one or another of his clubs,—why, it was nonetheless the case that Mr. Poindexter was a *gentleman:* and whoever had killed the Buntings, and Amanda Poindexter, and had so cruelly abused poor Perdita, was naught but a *beast.*

Within an hour or two of the discovery of the bodies, then, it was very nearly a foregone conclusion that Jabez Dovekie, who had been harassing the Bunting household for a fortnight, and had, so Mrs. Harwich insisted, even threatened Reverend Bunting with bodily harm, must be the ax murderer: for it would have been a simple matter for the brute to take up the gardener's ax from out a nearby toolshed: and no extraordinary effort for him to wield it as lethally as he had, being a giant of a fellow, at least six feet five inches tall, and weighing nearly two hundred forty pounds; and possessed of a mercurial temper, greatly exacerbated by drinking. (The church sexton, Henry Harder, informed police that, when drunk, Dovekie was known to abuse his wife and children; and had acquired a considerable reputation as a scabrous personality, in his West Railroad Street neighborhood.)

Under Dr. Hatch's efficient ministrations, Mrs. Harwich, discreetly removed to Jewett Cottage, began to revive; and at once berated Jabez Dovekie as a monster and a beast, and now a murderer, of the most despicable sort. Though she had not actually glimpsed him in the rectory that day, she had no doubt but that the assailant was he, and no one else: stealing up noiselessly behind her, as she was about to descend the cellar stairs,—striking her between the shoulder blades with what must have been the blunt edge of the ax head,—causing her to pitch head first down the stairs, into the darkness, with no concern as to whether she had injured herself seriously, or no,—and then locking the door behind her, and leaving her moaning with pain. Ah, what a mercy it was, Mrs. Harwich said, that she *had* fainted, and was spared hearing the shrieks and screams of the victims overhead,—which, in truth, she did hear, as if in a dream, and at a distance. "It is he, Dovekie,—it is he, only he, the murderer," the distraught woman said, with surprising vehemence, "for he has long wished harm to Reverend Bunting, and has gazed with salacious eyes upon his wife—!"

Shortly thereafter, Leroy Craven's father brought him shy and abashèd to the police, to tell his disjointed story: with the near-miraculous result that the murder weapon, which might not otherwise have been found, was dredged up from the pond within thirty minutes; and readily identified as having been taken from the Buntings' gardener's shed. It was a remarkable thing, Orrin Wick thought, how precisely matters were falling into place: for, despite some negligible contradictions amongst the witnesses, it looked to be an open-and-shut case, as the expression goes,—an unspeakably savage act of murder, yet most likely unpremeditated.

Thus, a warrant was duly sworn for the arrest of Jabez Dovekie; and a manhunt loosely organized, consisting of police officers, and sheriff's men, and volunteers from the community (amongst them a goodly contingent of members of the Brethren of Jericho,—though they did not officially identify themselves as such). The ramshackle Dovekie house on the west end of town was searched, not, I am afraid, with an excess of courtesy, though it soon became evident that the wanted man was nowhere in the vicinity; and his frightened wife and children knew naught of his whereabouts. Mrs. Dovekie was a short, obese, poorly groomed woman of middle years, her flesh marred by fading bruises, and her expression altogether stunned: she pleaded with the men, as they tossed things about, and slammed doors, and overturned pieces of furniture, that she had no idea where Jabez was;— he had been drinking for two or three days, and hadn't been home to eat or sleep: he had a bad temper, she said, now in tears, and cringing, but he meant no harm,—he was a good man except when he drank, but he meant no harm.

Shown the black broadcloth cap, Mrs. Dovekie stared at it for some painful moments, as if she knew,—ah, she *knew!*—what it portended: but at last she admitted that it belonged to her husband: and then inquired, all ingenuously, where it had been found.

Doubtless the reader has been wondering this while, *What has become of Perdita?*—a question very much to the point; yet one not readily to be answered. For the experience suffered by the minister's wife was so very curious,—nay, perverse and inexplicable—it has never been understood, or satisfactorily analyzed, to this day.

Though his heart had long hardened against Perdita Kilgarvan, his faithless cousin, and his yet more faithless belovèd,—*though he did not love her any longer*, and felt no more concern for her than he would for any woman in her horrendous circumstances,—yet Xavier Kilgarvan was discountenanced, as the reader may well imagine, when, arriving in Winterthurn City as he had been bade to do by the mysterious telegram, he was greeted with a wild diversity of "news": that the distinguished Episcopal minister Harmon Bunting and his family had been hacked to death, by a madman, that very afternoon; that Reverend Bunting and a "lady love" had been surprised by the lady's husband, and hacked to death,—and the Reverend's innocent wife "despoiled"; that a gang of Anarchists had forced entry into Grace Church, and butchered the minister, his wife, and his elderly mother; that three innocent persons had been slaughtered by a madman with an ax,—or four, or five; that Mrs. Bunting, the minister's young wife, had been murdered in her bed and *in her bridal gown*, by her husband and his mistress,—this woman being none other than Mrs. Ellery Poindexter, of all upstanding citizens!

It had long been the canny detective's habit to display not a whit of the emotion he felt,—whether alarm, or dismay, or incredulity, or frank childlike curiosity—so, hearing such extraordinary reports, told him by Pullman porters, cab drivers, and the like, within ten minutes of his arrival in Winterthurn City, Xavier Kilgarvan responded by asking a few subdued questions and keeping to himself the tumult of his thoughts and his droll observation that, knowing the fantastical permutations "news" of this sort invariably takes, it was hardly likely that Mrs. Perdita Bunting had been wearing her bridal gown that day. "*That*, assuredly," the detective thought, "is sheer phantasmagoria."

Nonetheless, this eccentric detail happens to be true: for when, at last, Thérèse, and Chief of Police Orrin Wick, and one or two of his officers, entered Perdita's enshadowed bedroom,—after the unconscionable delay, of which I have spoken—it was to find the cruel-used young woman bound by her wrists and ankles (the twine wrapped around her ankles so very tight, it left red marks in her tender flesh,—while, mercifully, the twine about her wrists had been less forcibly secured, and had, in truth, been worked loose),—and gagged, with a strip of torn linen—and thrown, as it were, across her tumbled bed, attired in the selfsame bridal gown, of oyster-white raw silk, in which, many years before, she had been wed: the gown being now so soaked in blood, the skirt in particular, and the bodice of pearls and satin ribands so hideously splashed, that it was not to be wondered, Thérèse and the others thought that Perdita too had been murdered!—and not, instead, the victim of an assault so vicious and so shameful, it might have been more merciful for her (thus tongues would wag) had, indeed, she died by the same hand that had struck down her belovèd Harmon.

Quickly Thérèse removed the linen gag from her poor sister's mouth, and undid the ties that bound her wrists and ankles; yet, even so, Perdita was but half-conscious that help had come to her, and that she was no longer in danger,—that, indeed, it was her own sister Thérèse, bareheaded and in the simply cut light woolen suit in which she taught, now kneeling beside her. Ah, how piteous it was to see!— the stricken woman weeping, and raving, and begging not to be killed; struggling with her very rescuer; pitching herself in a paroxysm of terror from side to side on the rumpled bed, her loosed tresses wild about her, and ah! the bloodstained silken gown so very close to slipping off one bare shoulder, Thérèse was obliged to tug it hurriedly back in place, for modesty's sake. "Sister! Sister! It is I, Thérèse!" she cried. "Pray do not be so distressed,—you will not be harmed further!"

Yet Perdita blindly struggled, as if it were a nightmare that gripped her, and not Thérèse: begging not to be killed,—pleading for mercy,—then again, pleading for *death*, that her shame might die with her.

"For Harmon will not,—ah, Harmon *cannot*—love me again as his undefiled wife."—Thus the delirious woman murmured, while the men stared, and backed away from the bed; and Thérèse essayed to restrain her by seizing her wrists, and repeating that she would not be further harmed,—her assailant was gone,—she was now in safe hands,—the police were here,—all would be well, with God's blessing.

These intelligent calming words Perdita seemed to hear, and, for a space of some panting seconds, she ceased her frantic struggle: her great dark eyes widening yet further, to reveal a rim of white: and her gleaming chestnut-brown hair,—so strikingly threaded, these past several years, with silvery-gray—spread about her on the disordered bed linen. Then, an infelicitous movement, it may have been, on the part of Mr. Wick, roused her again to terror, that her assailant had returned: and, all accidentally, poor Thérèse received a sharp blow to the face. "Perdita, sister, please calm yourself: you will not be harmed! The police are here, Dr. Hatch has been summoned, *no one will hurt you*"— thus Thérèse fairly begged, while the hysterical woman sobbed, and panted, and wrenched her head violently from side to side.

Yet, even at so extreme a juncture, in her stained and torn finery, and having suffered, it seemed, the most shameful ignominy known to Woman, Perdita could not fail to strike the disinterested masculine eye as beautiful,—indeed, as ravishing: the which sight had so immediate an effect upon the gentlemen, the kindly Orrin Wick in particular, that it is no exaggeration to say they succumbed to an emotion equivalent to *love*,—in its most vaporous, romantic, and insubstantial guise. For, in her writhing distress, in her seemingly excruciating terror, was Perdita Bunting, *née* Kilgarvan, not a most wondrous creature, withal?—possessed, like Lilith, of a beauty both unearthly and greedy; blessed with a luxuriant head of hair, and great stark staring eyes, and a mouth that boasted both voluptuousness and icy chastity; her comely female form, squirming eel-like before their gaping eyes, given the greater power of enchantment, as it were, by the brutal contrast it afforded with the chopped and yet-bleeding bodies of the victims, but a floor away—?

(Herewith, I should add, in haste, that Orrin Wick was, at this time in his lengthy and honorable career, still a youngish man, of about forty-five years of age: devoted to his wife of twenty years, and his three children,—including an eighteen-year-old son, Orrin, Jr., of whom he was inordinately proud: an upstanding Christian gentleman, belonging to the First Methodist Church of Winterthurn City: and, in his arduous profession, the more prized for his diligence, probity, and congenial character, in that he lacked more "glamorous" qualities of the sort wantonly assigned to policemen by the sensationalist press. In stating that Mr. Wick had succumbed to so ill-defined an emotion as love, I am, of course, not suggesting that he knew he had done so,—or that the disheveled minister's wife, now widowed, could have had the slightest awareness of what transpired.)

Thus, Thérèse gripped her sister hard, and even embraced her, to assuage her fears; and the stricken woman, in a somewhat lowered voice, though still sobbing, spoke of a demon,—a monster, a brute

with blazing eyes and white-glaring teeth,—who had stolen up behind
her and taken her by surprise, as she stood in her chemise, about to
wash her hair, unassisted, as, by happenstance, her Nell had been
called away that morning, to come quickly to her ailing mother's
home in Mt. Sweetwater. Gloating and laughing in an untrammeled
bestial manner, this cowardly assailant,—whose face, alas, Perdita
could not glimpse—gripped her in an instant, with no mind for her
pleadings for mercy: and, jeering at her shame and terror, boasted that
he had "exacted his revenge" downstairs, and would now "balance the
accounts" by way of her: to subject her to an ignominy of which (so
the panting woman whispered with tight-shut eyes) it is not possible
to speak in decent discourse.

"Suffice it to say, *he had his way with me*,—'his way' being
most loathsome and contemptible," Perdita said. "And such was my
distress, and the confusion of the moment, I could not fully see his
face, but had only an impression of glaring eyes, and grinning overlarge
white teeth, and hair inclined toward red, I believe,—red grizzled with
gray—a personage who seemed familiar to me, yet, ah!—most unfamiliar, most alien, most monstrous!" She paused, lying now motionless, as if all struggle,—indeed, all strength—had drained from her
slender limbs; and opened her sorrowful eyes; and, speaking to
Thérèse alone, as if, for the moment, not wishing to acknowledge the
presence of the abashèd gentlemen, she said: "He then forced on my
limp body, I know not why, my very own bridal gown,—this raiment
of happier and more innocent days,—ah, Thérèse, *I know not why*,
save that he was a madman, and chortled of revenge!—forced the gown
on me, taking no mind for how it ripped and tore,—for how the delicate pearl buttons snapped off, in his brute fingers, and,—and—from
somewhere, I know not where,—did he return downstairs, leaving me
insensible here?—I know not where,—dear God, my thoughts are
shattered,—from somewhere he dipped his hands in blood,—the blood,
he bragged, of my belovèd Harmon,—and this blood, Thérèse, the
monster wiped on my dress, to despoil its purity forever, and to
'baptize' me, as his demon logic would have it, *as his bride*."

The abused woman's voice had dropped to a scant whisper, and
now, as every fiber of her delicate body quivered, it ceased altogether:
and Thérèse, hugging her close, and paying no heed to her blood-
soaked garment, now began herself to sob, with childlike abandon.

Some minutes passed thusly, with no word spoken, and no
sound in the room save that of the sisters' weeping: whereupon another of Mr. Wick's officers entered the room, and, waking, as it were,
to the men's presence, Perdita began again to rave, and to pitch herself
about, begging Thérèse not to allow them near the bed,—nay, not to
allow them in the room. "Profane,—hideous,—mocking,—unspeak-

able!—*his* touch!—*their* touch!—it must not happen again,—Perdita shall die,—no man must come near,—O Thérèse, do not let them touch me,—do not let them fondle and despoil me,—never, never, *never*—"

At last Dr. Hatch arrived; and was ushered upstairs; and with hesitation approached his patient, as if fearing the extremity of her distress. Her wild eye alighting upon him, Perdita drew back her lips from her moist white teeth, and made, involuntarily, a hissing sound: whereupon the tearful Thérèse again embraced her tight, and explained to her, that it was only Dr. Hatch,—her physician—Dr. Hatch whom she knew well, and whom she had no reason to fear. But Perdita whispered, "No, no,—none of them shall touch me again,—I am raw and bleeding from their cruelty, Thérèse!—pray do not let them touch me ever again!"

Following an intense exchange of whispers amongst Thérèse, Dr. Hatch, and the greatly agitated Orrin Wick (who had, all unaccountably, flushed a bright crimson in being privy to so frank and unabashèd a scene), it was determined that the stricken woman must not be roused to further hysteria. So it was, Dr. Hatch handed a vial of ammonia to Thérèse, who held it beneath her sister's flared nostrils: with the result that she blinked, and swallowed hard, and, the while tears streaked her pallid cheeks, regained some semblance of calm. At this, she would not allow the agèd physician to draw near her bed, for, as she said, she could not abide being touched: and would as readily surrender her life as suffer the indignity of an examination. And, shrinking in womanly modesty, as she became ever more conscious of her surroundings, she begged Thérèse, to beg the police officers to leave the room.

With a gallantry that did him credit, Orrin Wick obeyed this command straightaway, for he could see what the situation was,—knew what it was *his* task to accomplish, that Justice might be dealt out to the brute who had so abused Mrs. Bunting. "It may be that we are arrived too late, to aid certain persons," Mr. Wick said in a forceful voice, "but we are not too late to aid *you*, Mrs. Bunting. Pray do not lose patience with us!"

Once the door was closed, Thérèse again appealed to her sister, that she allow Dr. Hatch to make, at least, a cursory examination: for, under the law, a medical report was required: and Dr. Hatch was obliged to act. But Perdita would not hear of it; despite her condition, she was as wondrously stubborn as ever. "Nay, sister, nay,—it cannot—it *will not* be," she said in a hoarse voice, "for, as I have said, I am raw and bleeding from one brute, and cannot tolerate the touch of another."

It is a measure of Dr. Hatch's distress upon that terrible day, that he did not take offense at these intemperate words: for, it seems, he had allowed himself a glimpse into Reverend Bunting's study,—a glimpse, and no more—and had been quite shaken by the sight. (Advanced now in years, Dr. Hatch had come to think it was the wisest procedure not to interfere overmuch, where interference was unwanted.)

So it was, he turned gallantly aside from his weeping patient, and fixed his gaze to a neutral corner of the room; while, in haste, Thérèse fashioned a curtain of sorts about the bed, that Perdita, with her aid, might remove her bloodstained garment; and slip on a dressing gown of beige silk. Dr. Hatch then cleared his throat, and asked one or two questions, precisely as to how Perdita had been abused; and what injuries she had suffered. "Has there been much bleeding, my dear? And has it stopped? And is there great pain?" he inquired, a writing pad on his knee, and a pencil in his trembling fingers. Perdita cupped her hands to Thérèse's ear, to whisper a reply: whereupon the blushing Thérèse leaned to Dr. Hatch, to whisper this information to him. "Ah, indeed!—ah, dear me, *indeed!*" the snowy-haired gentleman exclaimed, his own cheeks grown ruddy, and his rheumy eyes aglow with indignation. In a shaking hand he transcribed these particulars, so far as he was capable; declared that the examination was concluded; and that the most soothing remedy for Mrs. Bunting's distress, at the present time, was a liberal dosage of laudanum,—"the very medicine, my child, for *sleep* and *forgetting.*"

For which kindness Perdita profusely thanked him, with tear-streaked cheeks; and murmured lowly, "God bless you, Dr. Hatch."

Yet this day of unparalleled surprises was not even now concluded: for, just as the remains of the victims were about to be removed to the mortuary van, and the manhunt for Jabez Dovekie was already under way, there arrived at the rectory, in a hackney cab, a fashionably dressed gentleman in amber-tinted glasses, who said it was imperative that he speak with Chief of Police Orrin Wick at once.

This goateed stranger, of but slender build, and moderate height, gave the impression of being considerably taller,—nay, of being most aristocratic and assured—by dint of his posture; and his bearing; and his tastefully elegant clothes: a navy blue suit in tropical wool, of the finest texture, with a double-breasted coat; a white shirt of narrow pleats with a smart wing collar, and a silken "ancient madder" necktie; and a handsome hat of Panama styling, in autumnal hue. His gloves were of a very pale powder gray; and, as he courteously removed his hat, one saw the flash of lapis lazuli cuff links.

His card he handed straightaway to the amazed Orrin Wick,—

```
XAVIER R. KILGARVAN
CONSULTING DETECTIVE
NEW YORK CITY

"I make my circumstance"
—EMERSON
```

—while, unabashèdly, he proceeded to remove the disguise in which he had traveled: taking off the metal-rimmed amber glasses, and the altogether convincing goatee, and matching wig (of dull-red wavy hair, subtly tinged with gray); and wiping from his cheeks and throat a ruddy species of face powder, which had given him, upon entry into the bright-lit foyer, an air of almost insolent health and well-being.

Ah, it *was* Mr. Xavier Kilgarvan!—albeit somewhat agèd, about the eyes in particular; and possessed of a masklike imperturbability, or an inordinately refined graciousness, which had not always been his. To put the provincial chief of police more at his ease, Xavier Kilgarvan said, in a voice low enough so that it might not be overheard by persons milling about, that he had come to Winterthurn City for reasons he could not disclose, as he did not entirely understand them himself: but it was his presumption he had been summoned hither, by an unknown person, to contend with the mystery at hand. He knew, by now, of the bare facts of the murders of Reverend Harmon Bunting and his mother, Mrs. Letitia Bunting, and of his parishioner Mrs. Amanda Poindexter,—he knew, in a most confused way, that Reverend Bunting's wife had been somehow "abused": and wanted only to proffer aid to the police in seeking out the criminal or criminals. "Please understand, Mr. Wick," Xavier Kilgarvan said, in a discreet voice, while fixing the elder gentleman with the semblance of a smile, "I have come only to assist you and your detectives, if you so wish, for no fee whatsoever; and I give my word as a gentleman, I shall not agitate to 'take over' the investigation, save at your request."

It was an awkward minute or so before Orrin Wick, flush-faced, and staring, yet, at this apparition,—whom, now, he halfway fancied he *did* recognize, the goatee being stripped away—sufficiently collected his thoughts to shake the hand of the renowned Mr. Kilgarvan; and to welcome him to Winterthurn City, after so many years; and, with somewhat less enthusiasm, to the "mystery at hand." For, as Mr. Kilgarvan would learn shortly, there would be little formal investigation required, the identity of the murderer being already known; and only his present whereabouts a question. So it was,—this, remarked with a veritable air of apology!—no mystery accrued to the situation at all: while dreadful enough, and, indeed, unparalleled in its savagery, the case was an open-and-shut one, in which the expertise of a detective of Xavier Kilgarvan's caliber was assuredly *not needed.*

Hearing these words, yet, by some subtle intimation of his smile, indicating that he did not exactly credit them, Xavier Kilgarvan fixed Winterthurn's chief of police with a level, gray, stony gaze, of a just perceptibly ironic nature, and murmured: "*That* remains to be seen,—*that* is yet to be determined. For, Mr. Wick, as you must know,—as our mutual boyhoods in Winterthurn have instructed us—there is invariably Mystery: and not least, where acts of murder are concerned."

Lapis Lazuli

It is, I think, a proven fact of the human psyche, that while Mystery, satisfactorily *solved*, yields immense pleasure (to the degree, perhaps, to which it has appeared intractable), that Mystery which cannot be solved, which defiantly resists all analysis, yields immense displeasure,—nay, an actual sensation of physical sickness, and dread,—*a vertigo of the soul*. For, as the one confirms our hazardous faith in Man's pride, in both controlling destiny and comprehending its innermost secret, the other, all monstrously, denies our instinct for logic, and order, and justice, and sanity, and, indeed, civilization itself,—without which, we should soon find brute existence intolerable.

Thus it was, despite the air of impenetrable equanimity with which Xavier Kilgarvan returned to the city of his birth, and the much-admired coolness with which,—ah, how unhesitatingly!—he proceeded to examine, in detail, the bloody scene of the crime, he could not fail to shake off the oppressive sense of uneasiness, mounting to dread, which commonly stirred in him at the mere thought,—the mere recollection—of Winterthurn: Winterthurn being that region (in the detective's imagination at least) that could not be comprehended, or "solved"—!

The place of my birth, Xavier Kilgarvan oft brooded, *and of my damnation.*

Virtually anywhere else, it seemed, his enviable powers of ratiocination, detection, and intuition rarely failed him; but when his thoughts shifted to Winterthurn, and to his impotence and failure *there*, Xavier Kilgarvan felt, for all that he had acquired Fame and Fortune in the world, helpless as a young child. So far as Winterthurn was concerned, the common laws of Nature were suspended: that which might yield to a systematic attack elsewhere, was obdurate here: the detective might as fruitfully exercise his mental prowess *by beating his head against a stone wall* as by trying to "understand"—! For Xavier Kilgarvan had been too cruelly wounded, by the losses of his brother, and his mother, and his secret belovèd Perdita, to muse philosophically upon Winterthurn's vagaries, in the style, for instance, of Angus Peregrine: who, when the men happened upon each other in Manhattan, liked nothing better than to dwell upon his professional humiliation there,—his "public triumph and his private defeat," as the ebullient criminal lawyer phrased it.

Ah, the bitter mysteries of Winterthurn!—to be brooded upon by night, as one prods an aching tooth, or caresses, all surreptitiously and guiltily, a sore festered past healing! Oft-times, rendered insomniac by memories, Xavier Kilgarvan would lie sleepless in his bachelor's bed, on the third floor of his handsome Washington Square townhouse, turning over and over in his mind, helpless, and enraged, and baffled, and, it truly seemed, *damn'd*, those puzzles he could never hope to solve. What had happened to the good-hearted Colin to transform him, by degrees, into a monster,—a monster in the unquestioning service of a monster; what had happened to the surpassingly generous, and kindly, and loving Mrs. Kilgarvan, she who had, through all Xavier's young life, so unstintingly adored *him*; and, not least, what had happened to lead Perdita in the direction she had, seemingly of her own volition, chosen: defying not only Xavier's love for her but her avowed love for him? *It cannot be grasped, any of it,* the tortured man bethought himself, staring into the dark. *Therefore I should content myself, for the remainder of my life, with only those mysteries within my ken.*

Yet how they plagued him!—how they haunted him! Those unsolved,—indeed, insoluble—mysteries: and, beyond them, a greater mystery, as to how God could allow such transgressions in His world! For it was certainly the case,—as the sympathetic reader, I think, will agree—that even when Xavier had succeeded in ascertaining the truth, some incalculable malevolence prevented Justice from being served: the innocent Isaac Rosenwald treated most grievously, the guilty Valentine Westergaard set free: and Winterthurn City proceeding, withal, *as if naught were amiss.* (At the time of this narrative, in fact, "Isaac Rosenwald" drew blank stares when mentioned, as Xavier discovered within a few days of returning: even so thoughtful a personage as Murre Pitt-Davies had simply forgotten his existence. As for Valentine Westergaard,—he had had the grace not to return to Winterthurn after the accidental death of his heiress wife Valeria, a few years following their marriage, but had "settled in," as one of his relatives said, in the exotic city of Tangier, to devote himself to music, poetry, and love of God.)

Yet it could not be denied that, with the passage of years, the only mysteries that truly engaged Xavier's imagination were those quite clearly insoluble: in truth, of a resolutely personal, and even childlike, nature,—*Why had he been banished from all human happiness?*

Sipping sherry as he oft-times did, or, as soon as dusk snugly fell, rewarding himself (for thus he phrased it) with a generous glass of Scotch, Xavier did not, of course, so much assuage his high-strung nerves as *deaden* them. Upon numerous occasions he fell to musing over certain lectures delivered by Professor William James, which he had been privileged to hear, as a Harvard undergraduate, and he recalled the subject of the *mystery of personality*, and of *religious experience*, which had greatly intrigued him; and of which the distinguished psychologist spoke with immense edification and wit. There was, for instance, that enviable specimen of humanity, the healthy-minded individual; there was the morbid-minded; and the divided; and the second-born, or converted; and, not least, the mystic. There were those so utterly swallowed up in God, they might be said to inhabit sheer joy, not in themselves but in God; there were those mysteriously afflicted by a pathological joylessness called *anhedonia*,—a species of melancholy stubbornly resistant to all remedy. As an energetic and somewhat brash youth of nineteen, Xavier Kilgarvan had considered the latter persons ludicrous, and un-Christian, and, indeed, *sick*: he had joined in the general laughter in the lecture hall when Professor James, in his powerfully modulated voice, had quoted the elderly Goethe on the nature of his long existence: "It is but the perpetual rolling of a rock that must be raised up again forever." Now, in his fortieth year, nearly as famous in his profession as Mr. Pinkerton (and, owing to his integrity, a great deal more respected), Xavier Kilgarvan felt a stab of kinship with the agèd poet; and halfway wondered if *anhedonia* might not be the most intelligent response to God's fallen world. "*Here*, after all, is Hell," the detective idly mused. "Nor are we likely to be out of it, save through death."

The danger of alcoholic intoxication was that it exacerbated the morbidity of this state of mind; its solace, that, with the passage of years, all subtly, it rendered it more palatable. For, save when his brain was afire with ideas, and his workday stretched to as many as eighteen hours uninterrupted, Xavier Kilgarvan was subject to queer fuguelike periods of fatigue and emptiness,—nay, virtual nullity: when he might have compared himself to one of Mr. Kilgarvan's costly clockwork dolls; or, as he had fallen into the habit of imagining, a mirror of sorts suspended over an abyss, reflecting naught but mists, and vapors, and bodiless shadows in motion,—and, when motion stills, reflecting naught.

It had gradually impressed itself upon him, that, in the course of his vigorous career, he had seen everything the world had to offer, in its general outline, if not its particulars: there being, as specialists know, a remarkable pattern of correspondences in Crime. For is it not, at bottom, merely Death that seeks entry into Life, by whatever means?—merely cruelty and disorder, thrust into calm? While caught up in the febrific excitement of a case, the detective was possessed of a boyish enthusiasm, and had not the leisure to ponder along such lines; but, the case being at last solved, his handsome fee received, and the aftermath of no consequence to him, he found, more and more, that he lapsed into a curious state of lethargy, in which,—ah, how unnaturally!—*he did not greatly care what ensued.*

At the time of the Grace Church murders, Xavier Kilgarvan had been involved, by a conservative estimate, in more than two hundred cases, of which some thirty-five are generally deemed major: yet he had never fallen prey to morbid imaginings in the midst of a case, or lost his remarkable energy: for which virtues he had earned an exemplary reputation as being absolutely reliable. Even so, the assertion had begun to haunt him, he knew not from what source, that there is, after all, no innocence in Mankind; *but only degrees and refinements of guilt.*

"Consequently, why should one care *who* kills *whom*; still less *how*, or *when*, or *why*—!" the troubled man bethought himself.

At his most pessimistic, Xavier Kilgarvan, oft in disguise, wandered about the streets of Manhattan by night, to see, on all sides, a multitude of guilty persons: murderers whose smiling countenances belied their sins; murderers yet to commit their sins; or, most terrifying of all, murderers who had managed to erase from their memories *all knowledge of what they had done.* Whether sincere-seeming, or gay, or childlike, or exuberant, or contemplative, or pious; whether dressed in clothes as fashionable and costly as his own, or very modestly,—these persons strolled freely about, "innocent" to all external judgment, yet, withal, oft-times locking their eyes to Xavier Kilgarvan's, in tacit acknowledgment of their sin. *No innocence, do you see?—but only degrees and refinements of guilt:* so the melancholy declaration sounded in Xavier's mind, as he wandered alone betwixt dusk and dawn, scarcely knowing,—or, afterward, remembering— where he went.

(Alas, it must have been a consequence of the numerous wicked assaults upon his body which, over the years, Xavier Kilgarvan had suffered*: for, of late, particularly after an evening of alcoholic indulgence, the detective found himself unable to recall precisely where he had been. Sometimes he woke, as it were, on an unknown street; at other times, while being driven home in a hackney cab; yet, most commonly, in his very own bed, in his Washington Square townhouse, fully clothed, and with not the slightest knowledge of how he arrived there. At such times, wrenching himself awake, Xavier Kilgarvan struggled with bodiless assailants, unknown to him, but intent upon savagely taking his life: and woke with infinite gratitude, tears starting from his eyes, to discover himself safe at home,—albeit his clothes were frequently torn and stained; and he might be bleeding from one or two negligible wounds about the face. These lapses of memory, which brought with them raging headaches for most of the following day, Xavier did not like to think of as *amnesia*, as he knew that to be a pathological condition; and supposed his own problem more minor. Yet how curious it was!—to wake in one of his favored disguises,—as an elderly Roman Catholic priest, or a spoiled young Manhattan playboy, or a middle-aged Italian vendor—with not the slightest recollection of *why* he had got himself up so expertly, and *where* he had been, and *what consequences*, if any, had resulted!)

Ancillary to the sense that he had seen everything the world might offer, at least by way of evil, was the sense that preoccupations of a normal, and even manly, sort were henceforth forbidden him: for those several liaisons with women he had embarked upon, after Perdita's betrayal, were rather more experimental than otherwise, and deeply dissatisfying. Admirers Xavier Kilgarvan had many, of the female gender, and most forthright and dogged were some of them,—nay,

---

*By the time of our present narrative, Xavier Kilgarvan had been struck on the head from behind so often, no one has offered a very convincing estimate; and, with nearly as much frequency, he was stabbed,—by way of instruments as divers as ice picks, nail scissors, fish forks, et al., in addition to knives. Upon one singularly disagreeable occasion, he was trussed up in a tarpaulin, and thrown into the freezing East River; upon another, he was bound with yards of wire, and left in a baker's oven, to die a most wretched death,—saved at the last possible minute, as it turned out, by his own ingenuity. On the West Coast, he was once set upon by a pair of ferocious mastiffs (with ugly scars on his ankles and legs to show for it): in Baton Rouge, Louisiana, he was near-devoured by a three-hundred-pound sow: in a luxurious resort in Barbados, he was nearly pecked to death by an African parrot, of the giant species. In addition, he had come very close to dying beneath the hooves of wild horses; and fifty feet below the surface of the earth, in a mining shaft in West Virginia. Most frequently, as one might suppose, he was *shot at*, though rarely *shot*: for, despite these incidents, Xavier Kilgarvan led a remarkably charmed life, in never having been seriously wounded; or laid up in the hospital for more than a week. The only disfigurement on his face, after these many years, was the pebble-size scar at his left temple, which was queerly achromatic of hue, and grew more livid and pronounced, and, as it were, disfiguring, when his color was up.

quite shameless: but if he succumbed to their blandishments, it was more from a wish to arouse, in himself, certain creaturely appetites and sensations than for reasons of the heart. "So cold!—so icy cold!" one especially wounded lady passed judgment on him, even while pledging herself to love him forever, and to be his bride, if he would have her. Another, in his embrace, grew rigid with cold; yet another, convinced that, after a night of love with Xavier, her blood beat chill and sluggish in her veins, and parts of her body, including her lips, had grown numb—! It was rumored that Xavier Kilgarvan had once been married, in his youth, in distant Winterthurn; and that his young wife had died in childbirth; and that he would never again wed. Then again, it was rumored that he had inherited a fatal genetic weakness, akin to hemophilia; and dared not wed, and sire offspring. Part rumor, and part fact, were the tales told of him, that he had grown wealthy as a consequence of his clients' gratitude: for when the "consulting detective" was not paid in outright cash, he was given lavish gifts of jewels, and *objets d'art*, and racehorses, and yachts, and enviable properties throughout the Northeast.

Out of sheer whimsy, it seems, Xavier Kilgarvan patronized the most exacting (and the most expensive) tailors in Manhattan, so that his wardrobe boasted all variety of costumes, from the elegantly formal to the sporty and daring: he owned any number of tuxedos, and evening garb, and suits of a conservative English cut; and Irish tweeds, and flannels, and houndstooth checks; his shoes were of black lizard, and custom-made. He had a pair of red suspenders trimmed rakishly in gold and leather; and a herringbone Donegal tweed coat, with a full beaver collar, that gave him a zestful air. It had become a hobby of sorts with him to collect cuff links, amongst the most prized of which were a pair made of antique enamel and eighteen-karat gold, formerly belonging to an Italian prince; and another of crystal, sterling silver, and diamonds, with matching shirt studs; and the lapis lazuli pair,—a gift from a female client of advanced years, of the Rockefeller family. While not valuing any of these things very highly, Xavier nonetheless vowed to cultivate, in his numbed soul, a dispassionate "pleasure" in those things considered, by the general run of mankind, to bring pleasure,—with, I am afraid, naught but occasional success.

Oft-times, in the twelve-month preceding the narrative at hand, Xavier Kilgarvan roused himself from troubled dreams, to feel that his blood *did* run cold, and that his very touch was icy; that he was not merely chilled and numbed in himself, but the cause of such in others. If his soul was but a mirror overlooking an abyss,—if his soul was but a nullity, mirroring naught but frantic motion,—how was he, Xavier Kilgarvan, to account for it; and what might he do to transform himself?

"Perhaps I did die in the quicksand that day," he thought, "and the news of my death has yet to reach me."

He had not failed, for instance, to detect the police chief's slight shudder, when the two of them shook hands in the rectory vestibule: for Xavier Kilgarvan's touch, though gloved, imparted chill. Nor, with his acute sense of hearing, did he fail to detect the whisperings outside Reverend Bunting's study during his two-hour examination of the scene of the crime. How calm, how methodical, this "consulting detective"!—how lacking in all human response!—thus the witnesses remarked to one another; and would carry their tales through Winterthurn.

Xavier Kilgarvan prided himself, however, on having at last returned to the dread land of his birth; and for purely professional reasons. He could not be humiliated by throwing himself at his mother's feet,—for his mother was dead; his boyhood was dead; his tenure as a son was dead. Now he was fully an adult, without parents or history. If he must concern himself with Perdita, the minister's wife, why, then, their relationship would be exclusively professional: for he did not love her, and had not, for eleven years, in his waking hours at least, allowed his thoughts to dwell upon her.

With his magnifying glass and tweezers, his gloves not removed, nor his exquisitely fitted tropical wool coat, Xavier Kilgarvan examined, inch by inch, the room in which the savage murders had taken place; and spent some long entranced minutes simply gazing, with his inner eye as well as his outer, at the pitiable remains of Reverend Harmon Bunting, and Mrs. Amanda Poindexter, and poor Mrs. Letitia Bunting: consoling himself with the admonition that, even in Winterthurn, he must be content to analyze only those mysteries within his ken.

The Talk of the Town (I)

Not since the days of the "Cruel Suitor's" reign, now many years past, had the inhabitants of Winterthurn City been so frenzied in their absorption with Crime,—or, as the *Gazette* had emblazoned in three-inch headlines, OUTRAGE: there being, in the days following the discovery of the bodies, scarcely any other topic allowed for discussion than that of the "Grace Church ax murders," as they shortly came to be called. And, quite apart from the hideous murders themselves, and the fact that the murderer was still free, were the scandal of Reverend Harmon Bunting's evident liaison with Ellery Poindexter's wife; and the grave and part-mysterious abuse suffered by the Reverend's wife; and, not least, the remarkable appearance on the scene, *as if by prearrangement*, of the celebrated Manhattan detective Mr. Xavier Kilgarvan.

While as many as one thousand persons gathered on Berwick Avenue, day following day, with no other motive than to stare in silence at the dignified gray façade of the Grace Episcopal Church, those persons belonging to the Buntings' and the Poindexters' social set discussed tirelessly,—over luncheons, teas, dinners, and late-night suppers, in their stately homes, or in their clubs,—virtually every aspect of the case of which they had knowledge: the identity of the murderer being of very little interest, as "Jabez Dovekie" was a name that counted for naught. *But might it be true that Harmon Bunting and Amanda Poindexter had been adulterous lovers?—and had Ellery Poindexter known?*

(As a consequence of wild and alarming rumors, connecting the ax murders with Anarchist activities, or with the striking workers in South Winterthurn, a number of the larger houses became fortified, within a matter of hours: the Von Goeler, the Peregrine, the Shaw, and the Westergaard estates, amongst others, being armed by able-bodied menservants bearing rifles and shotguns, in the event of attack. For, as the elderly Henry Peregrine said, in an impassioned voice, if Anarchists were indeed responsible for the murders, in their announced campaign to level all class distinctions in America, *no one of decent upbringing was safe:* and it was foolhardy to suppose otherwise. So violently negative was public sentiment against the striking workers at the Poindexter factory, even children gathered in the street, to throw stones at pickets, and the police gave themselves license, as it were, to wade into the demonstrators with billy clubs: the result being, within two days of the murders, that the strike was broken, and planned strikes, in other South Winterthurn factories, were most prudently canceled.)

Even so, most speculation on the case centered about the question,—Had Reverend Bunting and his prominent parishioner been involved in a love affair; and had Ellery Poindexter known; or anyone at all—? A goodly number of the ladies, subsequently to be questioned by Xavier Kilgarvan, believed that a love affair betwixt the two was simply out of the question: for no one who had heard a single one of Harmon Bunting's dry, earnest, and unfailingly righteous sermons could envision him as an adulterous lover; and no one who knew of Amanda Poindexter's devotion to her family, and, of late, her preoccupation with Christian theology, could doubt her moral probity. (Albeit it was hesitantly acknowledged that there had been some strain in the Poindexters' union, for upward of a decade: Ellery Poindexter being a "difficult" gentleman, as much dreaded in society as admired, for the acerbity of his wit. Indeed, though Ellery Poindexter had not returned to St. Bride's until past nine o'clock in the evening of September 11, having been mysteriously absent for approximately twelve hours, he had not deigned to explain himself to anyone; nor to proffer anything so crude as an "alibi." A tall, saturnine, slope-shouldered gentleman in his mid-fifties, urbane in manner, though oft-times cruel in expression, Mr. Poindexter was generally known to have been gifted, as a youth, with a myriad of talents: yet proved too indolent, or too indifferent, to cultivate any. When questioned by a noisy contingent of journalists, who had somehow managed to corner him, as it were, en route to Mrs. Poindexter's funeral on the morning of September 13, Ellery Poindexter had replied in subdued, laconic, and, it very nearly seemed, listless tones, that he very much regretted the opprobrium to be suffered by the Poindexter family for years to come: and, it scarcely needs be said, he very much regretted the loss of his

belovèd wife, Amanda,—and the loss of his minister, and the saintly
Letitia Bunting: but, apart from that, he did not wish to comment on
the situation, as police would shortly apprehend the brute who had
wielded the ax, and Justice would be served. As to where he had been
through much of the day, while news of the murders had spread into
every neighborhood of the city,—the gentleman did not condescend to
explain; nor did he rise to a reporter's impertinent question as to why
he had not even gone to the mortuary to view his wife's remains, but
had, very shortly after being greeted with the horrific news, retired to
his bed-chamber, pleading fatigue and an impending asthma attack.
Coarse-mannered as the reporters were,—some of them being attached
to Mr. Hearst's papers in Vanderpoel, Albany, and New York City—
they did not dare to ask the widower his opinion on the scandalous
rumors everywhere in effect: albeit Mr. Poindexter would most likely
have turned aside the offensive question, with a mere flicker of dis-
dainful *hauteur.*)

In naught but whispers and surreptitious asides was the plight
of Mrs. Perdita Bunting discussed, and never, of course, in mixed company: for it was generally known that the lowlife brute Jabez Dovekie
had "had his way with her," following the murders; and that, for what
bizarre purpose no one might guess, the red-haired brute had
fumblingly dressed her in her very bridal gown, that he might despoil
it with blood, and with his own animal excesses. So foul,—so lurid,—
so unnatural a crime was scarcely to be comprehended by persons of
good breeding: for, set beside it, even the ax murders seemed in a way
natural,—which is to say, to the extent to which the taking of a human
life is acknowledged to be a *human proclivity.*

Being a gentleman, and, moreover, Mrs. Bunting's personal physician, Dr. Colney Hatch shunned all questions regarding his patient:
saying curtly that the unhappy woman was under heavy sedation, in
her bed; and was not to be disturbed in any way,—by police officers, by
well-meaning friends, or by "that young detective Kilgarvan from
Manhattan," whose presence in Winterthurn could not fail to bring
disruption. (For it was the case that Dr. Hatch had attended Xavier's
mother after her collapse; and doubtless had been poisoned against
him by her ravings.) Fearing that Dovekie would return to the residence, or that a like-minded maniac would attempt to break in, the
chief of police had assigned two junior officers to watch over the
house, at all hours of the day and night; and, upstairs in Mrs. Bunting's
bed-chamber, either Miss Thérèse Kilgarvan or Mrs. Bunting's maid
Nell was in attendance 'round the clock, to prevent the stricken
woman doing harm to herself, should she be so moved. (Speaking with
somber authority, Dr. Hatch stated that, abused thusly, a decent
woman is susceptible to great self-loathing; and, in line with the foul-

ness of the crime perpetrated against her, may wish to take her own life. So it was, the physician recommended prolonged bed rest; and no excitement of any sort; and thought it an excellent step that the silken wedding gown, torn and stained past redemption, had been burnt by Nell and one of the policemen, in the coal-burning furnace in the cellar. "For it would be an unfortunate development, indeed," Dr. Hatch said, "if Mrs. Bunting should ever again set eyes upon the garment.")

In such scandalous situations it is common practice for members of a social set to "close ranks" against outsiders: and so it was, that those selfsame ladies who had oft expressed their disapproval of Reverend Bunting's wife now shed tears on her behalf, and sent to her invalid's bed any number of floral arrangements, light romances, boxes of bonbons, and the like. That the former Miss Perdita Kilgarvan had been unpopular in Grace Church parish, amongst the ladies at least, was scarcely a secret, as, all irresponsibly, she had left it to her indefatigable mother-in-law to oversee many of the rectory's social evenings; and oft turned a sullen face to friendly overtures, even from officers of the Altar Society; and behaved from time to time in a manner unbefitting an Episcopal minister's wife. (It was widely known, for instance, that the excitable young woman, herself childless, had become morbidly attached to a foundling infant, doubtless of the lowest parental stripe, left at the rectory door one Christmas Eve; and had been inconsolable for weeks, after its death. Then again, the following spring, she had, unbeknownst to her husband, joined a ladies' cycling club, with the brazen intention of bicycling in Juniper Park, in a veritable army of bright-colored stockings, tam-o'-shanters, and bloomers!—this caprice being cut short, as one might imagine, when Reverend Bunting was informed by a parishioner. As to domestic disagreements, particularly Mr. Bunting's management of the "Iphigenia" royalties,—little was known save that hinted at by the long-suffering Letitia to one or another of her most trusted friends, and, by way of them, circulated through town. In general, it was held against Perdita Bunting that she was not worthy of her husband, nor of her own social status in Winterthurn; and that, though she was a fully mature woman of five-and-thirty years, her manner, and her girlish appearance, gave her the air of one far younger.)

Nonetheless, Winterthurn society grieved for her, and murmured not a word when, of the Kilgarvans, only the hardy Thérèse, and Bradford, and the two or three elderly aunts, attended the funeral for Harmon and his mother: both the coffins being closed, out of necessity: though it was known that Harmon had been costumed, by the undertaker, in a stole, cassock, and white surplice,—the proper ecclesiastical vestments of his station. "To think that one standing so close to God, as Reverend Bunting, should be struck down in such wise!"—thus the awed murmur of Miss Verity Peregrine, as soft clumps of earth were dropped on the gleaming ebony caskets.

As for Xavier Kilgarvan's wholly unanticipated involvement in the case,—virtually everyone who speculated on the subject, whether acquainted with Xavier from years before, or no, preferred strong opinions: the consensus being one that would have greatly surprised Xavier, had he known,—for it credited the detective with uncanny powers of precognition, second sight, and the like. How else to explain the sudden reappearance of Lucas's son in Winterthurn, after an absence of more than a decade?—and on the very afternoon of the murders! Not many months before, the *Gazette* had published a laudatory profile on Mr. Kilgarvan, taken verbatim from the *New York Post*, which had stressed Xavier Kilgarvan's "clairvoyant" powers, while slighting his scientific procedure, and, alas, gravely slighting the Manhattan police, with whom he had worked in a totally cooperative manner. Moreover, with the passage of time, and a kind of collective amnesia, in which disagreeable events were forgotten, it came to seem, to many proud citizens, that Winterthurn's own Xavier Kilgarvan was on a par with the famed Sherlock Holmes,—albeit the Englishman was naught but a fictitious creation of A. Conan Doyle, and Xavier was a living and breathing personage, not yet forty years old. Just as Isaac Rosenwald's name was now forgotten, or recalled, hazily, as being that of an unrepentant criminal who had been executed,—just as Valentine Westergaard's name was associated with the Vanderbilts, and with an enviable world of cosmopolitan-international society,—so too had the aura surrounding "Xavier Kilgarvan" undergone a significant change. If the toymaker Lucas had sired a son highly respected in the larger world, surely that cast an agreeable light upon Winterthurn—? Thus it was thought only fitting, and not at all to Orrin Wick's discredit, that, on the morning following the murders, he had invited Xavier Kilgarvan to guide the police investigation,—albeit, as Mr. Wick half apologetically reiterated, there was really little *mystery* about the case at all.

(Almost immediately, however, it was whispered that a minor contretemps had flared up betwixt the police chief and his exacting new colleague: for Kilgarvan objected to the fact that Perdita Bunting's wedding gown had been burnt to ashes,—and with the assistance of a police officer! Nor had the punctilious detective failed to register disapproval of slipshod police procedure, in the confiscating of divers articles of evidence from the rectory, and Jewett Cottage; and in the astonishing way in which Reverend Bunting's study, *and the stairs leading to the second floor of the house*, had been tracked up with bloody footprints. And Kilgarvan had charged, yet more seriously, that Mr. Wick's officers had violated their professional obligations, by having purloined certain clues of a sensational nature; amongst them, a half-dozen of the mocking hearts—whether paper, candy, or otherwise —that had been strewn across the dead couple. Public-spirited anxiety was expressed to the effect that, when Xavier Kilgarvan returned to Manhattan, he might cast aspersions upon Winterthurn police; and it was remarked, behind Orrin Wick's back, that he was in danger of being shown up as a bumbling fool, who could not even catch a red-haired giant of a murderer whom any child could identify—!)

Quite apart from these issues, however, speculation raged over Xavier Kilgarvan, in whose veins there flowed,—did there not?—some sort of "tainted" blood, going back for many generations. It had manifested itself in two of his brothers, Colin and Roland: the one remembered as a monster of sorts, a prowler by night, and, it may have been by way of God's mercy, a *suicide*; the other,—a ne'er-do-well who had fled Winterthurn under the shadow of disgrace, owing numberless gambling debts. Though born a De Forrest of Old Winterthurn, Mrs. Kilgarvan, Xavier's mother, had proved headstrong and wanton even as a girl, in marrying Lucas Kilgarvan *for love:* and bearing him his sons, in near-poverty: and dying what was called, in whispers, a suspicious death,—there being, at her very funeral, rumors of an overdose of the opium derivative *lac-elephantis*. And it was known, too, that the deranged woman, in her last days, had pronounced a curse upon her youngest son: that he wander the earth for the remainder of his life, unless some woman, *as wicked as he*, offered him love.

As for Lucas Kilgarvan,—he had gradually become a total recluse, living in but two or three rooms of his large ramshackle house on Wycombe Street, while, on all sides, a thriving mercantile neighborhood had taken hold, and the streets were filled with rushing vehicles; and the very sky despoiled by an elevated train that passed a half-block from his workshop. Winterthurn society had long forgotten this eccentric gentleman, and ambitious young Bradford Kilgarvan, an aide of the Mayor's, and a vice-president at the First National Bank of Winterthurn City, rarely spoke of him, save in half-embarrassed allusions to his father's trade or craft: for the Kilgarvan Toy Manufacturing Company yet did well,—in fact, thrived—though only two persons labored at the custom-made toys. (These were, of course, Mr. Kilgarvan himself, and his trusted assistant Tobias, now grown gray and stooped with age. A tale was told that Lucas Kilgarvan, who yet called his Negro assistant "boy," could not grasp that the grizzled old man was no longer young, and incapable of lifting heavy cartons: and Tobias remained too solicitous of his white master's feelings to set him right. Yet, this puzzling myopia aside, Mr. Kilgarvan continued to excel in his craft, and was said to drive a shrewd bargain with his wealthy patrons, who were willing to pay amazing prices for custom-made rocking horses, crooning and winking dolls, and other automata. Thus it had been a rumor in the Wycombe Street area for years, that the elderly toymaker had hidden a considerable bundle of cash in his house—!)

It had not failed to strike observers that a secret animosity existed betwixt Xavier Kilgarvan and his elder brother Bradford: for the latter, informed of his celebrated brother's presence in Winterthurn, had expressed genuine surprise, and not a little alarm: and had stammered out some blushing explanation (in Mrs. Harrier Von Goeler's judgment, unconvincing indeed) as to why Xavier was a houseguest of the Pitt-Davies, and not of his. (For, it seemed, alone of his Winterthurn acquaintances, Murre Pitt-Davies had kept up a correspondence with Xavier,—acknowledging himself as one of the detective's most fervent admirers; and expressing pride that he had once been his instructor at the Winterthurn Academy for Boys.) Bradford Kilgarvan, grown sleek and stout and guarded in manner with the passage of years, was very much allied with the conservative faction in Winterthurn City politics, under the guidance of his father-in-law; and could simulate little enthusiasm for his younger brother's career, or for his life more generally. Dining at the Corinthian Club with associates on the night of September 16, when, at last, the murderer Dovekie had been caught, and brought to the county jail in manacles and leg-irons, Bradford had been overheard to say that he supposed his brother would be leaving town shortly: for what remained to attract him—? "A professional detective's *modus operandi* is akin to that of a carrion bird, after all," Bradford said with an air of frowning consideration, "drawn to corpses, that he might feast and glut himself; then, the corpse picked to the bones, off he flies, to seek his next repast!—shameless, and, withal, doomed."

The mother of many a Winterthurn débutante took note that Xavier Kilgarvan, despite the cloudiness of his reputation, would be the catch of the season: for was it not whispered that he had never been in love,—nay, not even enticed into an engagement; and was it not known, that, with a true gentleman's disdain for money, he had nonetheless accumulated a considerable fortune? Mr. Murre Pitt-Davies was tirelessly queried by the ladies as to whether, in the detective's past, there might not have been a tragic love: which might account for his air of brooding, and his near-sullen reserve, and a certain bemused and melancholy expression about the mouth. (So far as Murre knew, however, there had been no tragic love; indeed, no love at all; and, alas, very little friendship. Nor had Xavier remained in contact with either of his attractive young lady cousins, Perdita and Thérèse,—according to the testimony of Thérèse. "I am afraid that Xavier is the most solitary person of my acquaintance," Murre said. "And it can hardly be a coincidence that he is the most renowned.")

Though no longer precisely young, Xavier Kilgarvan possessed the air of a youthful and vigorous man, at least in public: his hair, streaked with gray, scarcely less thick, and springy as ever; and his glacial silver-gray gaze, as forceful; and, ah!—his manly profile as clean and chiseled as that of a Grecian statue. Though very few gentlemen in Winterthurn dressed more stylishly, Xavier gave the appearance of hardly caring whether his costly suits, or his impeccably white shirts, or his numerous pairs of gloves, became soiled in the course of his work; nor did he exhibit the slightest sign of vanity, of a kind one might anticipate in a gentleman thus attired.

Little sensing how their queries nettled her spinster heart, the more aggressive of the society ladies invited Miss Thérèse Kilgarvan to tea with the ill-disguised intent of learning all they could about her dashing cousin. Was it true that Mr. Kilgarvan mingled with the most wealthy and influential New Yorkers; had he come near to being killed numberless times; and did she know why, of a sudden, he had returned to Winterthurn after his long embittered absence?

Now a respected instructress at the Parthian Academy, and something of a bluestocking, the elder Miss Kilgarvan had, at the age of thirty-seven, come at last into a kind of bloom: being far more composed than she had been as a younger woman: and even, in the eyes of most observers, far more attractive. Enjoying an income of her own, part as the consequence of her teaching position and part as the consequence of her share of the "Iphigenia" royalties (which bi-yearly sum was a mystery to her colleagues,—albeit I am in a position to state that they estimated it far too low), Thérèse dressed smartly, though never conspicuously; she had even, to the surprise of most persons who knew her, experimented with that new invention, the "permanent wave,"—with but passable results, her hair being unusually fine. Though she possessed none of the elusive beauty of her younger sister, she was not accursed with Perdita's moodiness, or her short temper: *she* did not frown and screw up her face, and cause a knife-blade of a line to declare itself betwixt her brows, as Perdita did: and when Thérèse smiled, one could be certain she smiled with genuine pleasure, and not in mockery. Some of her students stood in awe of her, feeling no warmth or playfulness in her manner, though admiring her unstintingly as a teacher; others,—indeed, the majority—thought her the most remarkable woman of their acquaintance. For seven or eight years now, Thérèse had been quietly, but assiduously, courted by Murre Pitt-Davies, the headmaster of the Winterthurn Academy; and the two were frequently seen together at one or another of the city's cultural events. Thérèse seemed happy enough in this kindly gentleman's presence, yet it was believed she would never consent to marry him, being,—like her fated half-sister, Georgina, before her—a *born spinster.*

Thus it was, Thérèse colored slightly, and bit her lip, that she might not reply rudely when queried about her cousin. All simply, and with maidenly dignity, she replied that she knew little of his life, whether "professional" or "private." "Indeed," she said quietly, "my cousin is as much a stranger to me now, as he has ever been."

Xavier Kilgarvan's Investigation: At St. Bride's

———

Of more than thirty persons closely questioned by Xavier Kilgarvan in the days immediately following the murders,—which is to say, before the wretch Dovekie was apprehended—it was Ellery Poindexter who proved the least intimidated by the Manhattan detective: indeed, it was Mr. Poindexter who exhibited the most brazen species of *indifference* regarding the situation. For, though he was deeply aggrieved by the loss of his wife, and by the loss of his dear friends Reverend Bunting and Mrs. Bunting, he simply could not see in what wise their deaths related to *him*,—thus the phlegmatic gentleman reiterated, with very little pretense of courtesy.

So assured was Ellery Poindexter's social position in Winterthurn, and so little disposed was he to grant Xavier Kilgarvan a modicum of respect, he allowed the detective but a half-hour of his valuable time,—as he phrased it; and, even so, with calculated rudeness, kept Xavier waiting ten long minutes in a drab alcove of St. Bride's, furnished with mismatched odds and ends. "He is frightened of me, perhaps," Xavier bethought himself, as, growing impatient, he paced about the room, glancing from time to time at his pocket watch,—a charming trinket of gold, pearl, and black enamel given him, in lieu of cash, by a client from Virginia. "For he knows that I alone seriously 'suspect' him,—though, in truth, he cannot truly *know* it."

When, at last, the master of St. Bride's appeared, his rudeness verged on actual insult: for he pointedly avoided shaking Xavier's hand: threw himself into a nearby chair, with no ceremony: and allowed Xavier to know, by way of his unkempt "mourning" attire (a black velveteen smoking jacket with lapels of deep crimson, and badly stained cuffs), and his heavy-lidded indolence, that he certainly had had no significant business beforehand, to keep him from their appointment.

With impeccable courtesy, however, Xavier proceeded to put questions to Ellery Poindexter, in a tactful, yet forthright, manner, as if no grave insult had been proffered by one gentleman, or received by another: for it had long been the detective's covenant with himself, so to speak, that all matters of pride, vanity, and egotism be set aside in the pursuit of his professional duty. Such questions as he asked,—if Mr. Poindexter knew of any motives for the murders, for any *one* of the murders; if he had any theory about who had sent the anonymous letters to his late wife, amongst other ladies; if he had ever heard rumors of a liaison betwixt his wife and Reverend Bunting, or had suspected one; and where he had been, for most of the day of September 11—seemed to Xavier reasonable enough, if not inevitable under the circumstances: yet they roused in Ellery Poindexter a flush of indignation, and a pronounced tic about the mouth, that belied his air of languid indifference. He interrupted the detective in midsentence, to declare that his queries were naught but a waste of time, as the murderer was known, and would surely be made to confess by the police when he was captured.

Not without a semblance of sympathy, Xavier here paused; and affixed his heavy-breathing host with a civil gaze, in which no hint of irritation showed; then ventured to say, in a subdued and unemphatic voice, that there were a half-dozen aspects to the case, minor mysteries, as it were, not to be explained so simply: albeit, from the testimony of eyewitnesses, and considering the prejudice raised against him, it did look as if Dovekie were guilty. However,—and here Xavier smoothly continued, before Ellery Poindexter could draw breath—it was a naïve assumption, indeed, though seemingly commonplace in Winterthurn, that guilt might reside solely in a mere *agent of murder*, and not in his *employer*.

At this, Ellery Poindexter blinked in genuine incomprehension: or so the keen-eyed detective believed.

"For, after all, one might find any number of 'agents,'—any number of persons willing to take up an ax and use it," Xavier quietly said, "for a significant fee."

For a brief moment Ellery Poindexter stared at him, in belligerent silence: then he said, the very notion was "preposterous."

So far as Xavier could gauge, however, it did seem to him that, despite his legal background, and his considerable acuity, the husband of the murdered Amanda had not grasped this principle: so Xavier chose not to press it at the present time, but to repeat one by one the questions he had asked, in a subdued, unemphatic, and, as it were, artless voice that would not offend any reasonable gentleman.

Yet, it seemed, Ellery Poindexter *was* offended: recovering from his surprise and discomfiture, in a matter of minutes: and replying to his interlocutor in a voice of barely disguised contempt. Did he know of any motives for the murders,—for any *one* of the murders? —Why, yes, assuredly, *yes*, of the several thousand members of Harmon Bunting's congregation, upward of a full thousand might cheerfully have wished him dead, for his dry, pedantic, self-righteous, repetitive, and unfailingly *droning* sermons, if not for the priggishness of his face. Had he any theory as to who had sent the anonymous letters to Mrs. Poindexter, and the other ladies? —He was embarrassed to have no theory whatsoever, save a whimsical thought which had passed through his mind, when Amanda, in hysterical tears, had first received *hers:* the thought being, each of the ladies had sent the letters to themselves, as an act of supreme self-adulation. "For I assure you, Mr. Kilgarvan, Amanda was never so much in her element, and never so gloriously 'feminine,' " Ellery Poindexter said, "as when she gave way to fits of hysteria."

As to whether he had heard rumors of a "liaison" betwixt his wife and Harmon Bunting, Mr. Poindexter stated that he had not; nor had he harbored any suspicion, for the mere notion was preposterous, if not obscene,—allowing that one was familiar with the principals, and their tireless air of self-regard and worry over their *prospects for Heaven.* (For, it seems, Mr. Poindexter's wife had become morbidly,— and, some might say, foolishly—wrapped up in theological matters, of minuscule dimensions, as to whether she enjoyed free will, or no; or whether she had been, from the time of Adam, predetermined to Heaven, or to Hell; and whether certain sins were more grievous than others. "The commonplace run of things," Ellery Poindexter said with a sullen smile, "that captivates certain idle ladies, whose appeal to certain vainglorious gentlemen of the cloth is most flattering.") Finally, in reply to the question, *Where had he been through the day of September 11,*—Mr. Poindexter told Xavier, with an air of sighing disdain, that his personal life was his own affair exclusively: he did what he wished, when he wished, with not the slightest sense of being accountable to others, and certainly not to a person outside the Poindexter family,—"still less," as he drily said, "to a 'consulting detective' of dubious reputation": and, as he had neither committed the murders himself nor commissioned an agent to do so, he saw no reason to provide Mr. Kilgarvan with an alibi,—and must remind him, that Orrin Wick, thus far, had been a model of tact and propriety in querying him on this subject. Therefore, unless he was to be formally charged with the murders, he saw no reason for this diverting interview to be continued: but must beg Xavier to excuse him.

Xavier, however, remained seated: and quietly made the observation that Mr. Poindexter did not show inordinate grief for his wife.

Whereupon Mr. Poindexter meditatively stroked his mustache, and said, in a similarly unemphatic tone, that, as he was a *Poindexter*, his grief was scarcely a matter of public show: a principle that a *Kilgarvan* might not comprehend, unless it were spelled out carefully to him.

If Xavier Kilgarvan felt a veritable pricking of his heart at this unconscionable statement, and a flurry in his veins signaling the exhilaration of battle, his handsome countenance maintained its composure: and he but slightly narrowed his eyes, in regarding his opponent, as if, of a sudden, he were gazing into an overly bright light. He then proffered his apology to Mr. Poindexter, for a false, and, indeed, naïve, assumption, as the Kilgarvans themselves had rarely worn their hearts upon their sleeves through the generations; and he could well understand the value of subterfuge. "Still, Mr. Poindexter," he said, as he gracefully rose to take his leave, "it were well for you to realize that, despite the evidence against him, this *Dovekie* strikes me as a hapless pawn,—a mere blunderer of sorts, in a narrative too complex to have been his creation. The mockery with which the presumed 'lovers' were arranged on the divan; the near-incalculable rage and brutality that had felled them; the scattering of hearts; the anonymous letters,—the very *feel* of the crime, in short,—and one or two other clues, which I shall not weary you by mentioning, lead me to suspect that Dovekie is not the man: as perhaps we will discover when I question him."

Breathing hoarsely of a sudden, and plucking at his mustache with nicotine-stained fingers, Ellery Poindexter heaved himself to his feet: and stood, for a long awkward moment, staring at Xavier with undisguised loathing. He said: "Why is it of any concern to you, who has killed whom, or why; or whether the 'narrative,' as you call it, is complex, or devilishly simple? The former iceman, Dovekie, or Doveski, or whatever be his improbable name, is assuredly the murderer: for he was all but caught red-handed, as the expression would have it, and observed by a number of persons, and it is all perfectly clear!—though hanging the wretch will not bring my poor Amanda back, or the Buntings; or restore to Perdita Bunting what it pleases the gallant to call her lost 'honor.' In any case," Mr. Poindexter continued, in a lowered voice, as, perhaps, he had caught sight of a spasm of sheer rage in Xavier Kilgarvan's face, "*you are not one of us, Mr. Kil-*

garvan: you are out of your element in Winterthurn, and will only provoke the Fates.''

Albeit his heartbeat had, at the mere mention of Perdita's name, accelerated wildly, and a piercing pain started betwixt his eyes, Xavier managed to bear himself calmly; and to murmur that the Fates had evidently been provoked to excess but recently, and he could not see how *he* might cause harm. "It is only the truth I seek, after all," he said.

"Well,—you will regret it," Mr. Poindexter said.

"No, it may be that *you* will regret it," Xavier said. "Else why do you stare at me in such hateful alarm; and why, my dear sir, is your forehead beaded with perspiration; and a most distracting tic enlivened about your mouth—? Yet more urgently, Mr. Poindexter, your breath has become so labored, and your color so poor, I halfway fear you are about to have an asthmatic attack.''

Confronted with such unabashèd, albeit chill and formal, hostility, the master of St. Bride's bethought himself for a moment or two; and essayed to control his breathing; and, finally, with a haphazard smile, strolled to the door, to show his visitor out. Ah, the tension that had arisen, so very swiftly, betwixt these two gentlemen!—of so pronounced a quality, I fancy I can feel the quivering of nerves, and the hot spasmodic rush of ventrical blood, even as I transcribe it. True it was, that Ellery Poindexter's sallow skin had become beaded with perspiration; and the left corner of his mouth twitched; and his breathing had grown so labored, it was painful to hear. Yet, at the door, he contrived to shake hands with Xavier; and said, with a semblance of a haughty smile: "If this iceman creature is not the murderer, Mr. Kilgarvan, then who is,—and how might it be proved?''

Half-bowing in farewell, Xavier said, with admirable equanimity: "That is my task,—that is why I am here, and why I was born.''

Postscript

Though Xavier had not troubled to explain the progress of his investigation thus far, to Mr. Wick or, indeed, to anyone,—secrecy being a dimension of his professional strategy—I see no reason not to quickly limn it here, for the benefit of the impatient reader. Within a very brief time he had seen that, judging from the quantity and the trajectory of blood, brain tissue, and fragments of bone, splattered across Harmon Bunting's immense roll-top desk and a section of the walnut wainscoting, the clergyman-victim had been struck down while seated at his desk, in his swivel chair; and his lady companion, Mrs. Poindexter, had been attacked while seated on the divan, facing the desk. How swiftly the murderer had rushed into the room to deal his victims their death blows, and how coldly and savagely he had wielded his lethal weapon, before either of the astounded persons could flee—! (As to poor Mrs. Letitia Bunting,—it was self-evident that she had been murdered simply because she had blundered into the scene of the crime, while the murderer, dripping ax still in hand, hid behind the door.)

Straightaway, then, the murderer had virtually *waded through blood*, in order to drag Reverend Bunting's body to the divan, some four or five yards from his desk; and, doubtless with some difficulty (the inordinate weightiness of the dead oft being remarked upon, in the annals of Murder), to place it in the awkward position in which it was found, with Mrs. Poindexter's bloodied head on its shoulder; and a cruel scattering of *hearts* left across the bodies. "So theatrical a display," the detective inwardly reasoned, "is the work of either a lunatic who seeks revenge of a public sort to assuage his wounded vanity,—a

412

cuckolded husband, in short—or, yet more subtly, an ingenious killer, whether lunatic or no, who hopes to confuse speculation, that his own motive remain a secret.'' Thus it struck Xavier Kilgarvan as highly improbable that Jabez Dovekie was the murderer: and his theory was subsequently confirmed by a thorough examination of the study. For whoever had murdered Harmon Bunting, and dragged his lifeless body to the divan, had been required to move about the room considerably; and Dovekie's enormous bootprints,—matched with those on the marshy bank of Jewett's Pond, and with other footgear of his, confiscated by the police—were to be found only within a radius of a few feet, just inside the door.

These findings gratified Xavier Kilgarvan, as they destroyed Mr. Wick's complacent theory of an open-and-shut case, in which *his* expert services were not needed: albeit he was sorely vexed that he could isolate no footprints or fingerprints anywhere in the downstairs area of the rectory, that might in probability belong to the murderer. His progress thus far Xavier had disdained to share with Mr. Wick and any of his officers, for he had a very poor opinion of their professional acumen; and worried that they could not keep confidence. ''Once I am able to interrogate this luckless Dovekie, then I will know,'' he told himself.

It may have been an error of strategy, as we shall see, for Xavier to have withheld his findings from the police, with whom he seems to have agreed to cooperate: but, ah!—not even a genius of a detective, oft gifted with remarkable powers of intuition, can ''remember forward.''

The Betrothal

So identified with Xavier Kilgarvan, Consulting Detective, was the emboldened motto "I make my circumstance,"—first printed on Xavier's calling cards in his thirtieth year—that it was a rare person indeed who remembered that Ralph Waldo Emerson, and not Xavier Kilgarvan, was the originator of the healthy-minded sentiment; and, of all Xavier's acquaintances and associates, only Murre Pitt-Davies recalled that the full sentiment was "You think me the child of my circumstance; I make my circumstance."

Boldly American, this declaration; and altogether necessary to believe, perhaps, for so self-reliant and solitary an American as Xavier Kilgarvan,—whose heroic task, as we have seen, has been for a quarter of a century to ferret out wickedness where he might find it, in the pursuit of Truth. Yet the reader will forgive me, I hope, for demurring as to the absolute truthfulness of the proposition, for the general run of mankind no less than for the great Emerson himself. (Who, as the reader will recall, suffered such crippling losses in his young adulthood, a full mental recovery was impossible!)

In any case, *circumstance* alone figured in an altogether unanticipated development in the progress of Xavier's investigation,—and in that shadowy domain wherein his private fancies and aspirations dwelt. For, on the fourth full day of his sojourn in Winterthurn, while yet more closely examining the minister's residence, Xavier hit upon not one, but several remarkable discoveries.

Insomniac through much of the night, Xavier Kilgarvan woke restless and agitated well before dawn of September 15; spent an hour perusing his notes, diagrams, character assessments, time charts, et al., pertaining to the case; and an additional hour re-examining those half-dozen anonymous letters that had been put into his custody by the chief of police. (He had by this time singularly crude documents addressed to Mrs. Perdita Bunting, and to the Misses Penistone; and, all surprisingly, the two letters extant, from those received by Amanda Poindexter,—for Ellery Poindexter had had them delivered to Xavier by messenger, but a few hours following their interview. "Ah, can it be Poindexter *is* frightened, and hopes to placate and disarm me?" Xavier bethought himself with a frown. "But he will see, I am not so easily manipulated.")

It scarcely needs be said, that the detective had spent many hours studying these distasteful missives, which alternately scolded, and cajoled, and besought, and accused, the hapless ladies to which they were addressed, in a bold and oversize block-lettered hand. He had examined the hand set beside those of persons whom, given the wilderness of probability, it was not altogether unreasonable to suspect (amongst them Ellery Poindexter, of course; and his chauffeur McPhearson Jones; and Jabez Dovekie; and the elderly sexton Henry Harder; and the assistant pastor John Hathorne; and, not least, Harmon Bunting himself,—for it had early crossed Xavier's mind that the sanctimonious Bunting could very well have been the culprit); but so far as he was able to determine, no characteristic leapt out, as absolutely identifiable, linking the letters with any one of these persons. (Though, subtle similarities might be seen *in each of the hands,*—and in a sample of Orrin Wick's handwriting, perused for mere curiosity.)

Each of the letters had been printed on a single sheet of white parchment paper, bearing a watermark of the most common variety, and kept in stock in copious quantities by several Winterthurn stationers. Each began with the salutation *My Dearest,*—and proceeded, in a rambling, stilted, and somewhat Biblical tone, to chastise the lady for her *sinful ways*, and the *lewdness locked in her heart*; to beg of her, some small favor (a silk stocking, soiled undergarments, etc.), that she might leave in a public place, for her "admirer" to receive; to beseech her not to be *cold, unfeeling,* and *selfish*; to accuse her of frailties common to her sex (amongst them inconstancy, willfulness, vanity, an unclean predilection for men of "brutish physiological type," and the telling of falsehoods "for their very own sake"). One of the ladies was queried, whether she "imagined herself unobserved" in her wantonness; another, whether she guessed how Almighty God scrutinized her while she daydreamed during church services, like a veritable "Whore of Babylon," mocking the very pew in which she sat. It was declared to Perdita Bunting, *née* Kilgarvan, that she was soulless as any member of her family; and to the young Penistone twins, that their hot and lecherous fancies could be read in their "fawnlike eyes." Amanda Poindexter appeared to have aroused the slanderer's especial ire, for the shameless way in which she "draped her Bosoms & Hips in costly finery," and pinched her cheeks to redden them, that she might simulate the "long-lost innocence of girlhood." And so on, and so forth: a sickly sort of evidence, indeed, which aroused in the gentlemanly Xavier naught but disgust.

("How queer it is, that those members of my sex who most despise women, are the very persons who succumb to such obsessions!" Xavier thought.)

So a somewhat disagreeable hour passed; after which Xavier quietly left the Pitt-Davies house, to stroll along Jewett's Lane, and to watch the eastern sky delicately lighten with dawn, above the placid and mirrorlike surface of Jewett's Pond. His eye was naturally drawn to the proud steeple of Grace Church not a quarter-mile distant, and the slate roof of the rectory; and, so oft had he heard the testimonies of the Jewett's Lane witnesses, regarding the "red-haired giant" or "specter," he fancied he could envision the lumbering Jabez Dovekie, ax in hand, making his panicked way down the cemetery hill, and along the lane. Poor fool! Dovekie had doubtless made the most egregious of mistakes, in snatching up the bloody murder weapon to run with it: in a paroxysm of terror, or sheer befuddled drunkenness, believing that he would be blamed for the murders,—as, doubtless he would have been, had he summoned help. "In any case," Xavier *thought*, "as soon as I am able to question the man, I can determine immediately if my theory is correct."

Following this, he hiked the full circumference of Jewett's Pond; climbed through the cemetery to the residence; and inquired courteously of Mrs. Harwich, whether he might look through the quarters again,—excepting of course the suite of rooms on the second floor, in which the invalided Perdita was ensconced.

Like many another member of her sex, Mrs. Harwich felt the detective's subtle appeal, which was all the more powerful, it seemed, for being of a melancholy cast. Not only did this good woman welcome him inside; she insisted upon preparing a hot breakfast for him, far more elaborate than he desired, and obliged him in his inquiries by chattering away, in a nervous voice, on nearly any subject the detective introduced. What sort of person had Reverend Bunting been? — Oh, unfailingly kind, and practical, and moral, and Christian in his every phrase; tireless in his duties as pastor; run near-ragged, as his mother oft-times complained, by the demands of certain selfish parishioners; inclined, it was true, to impatience and exasperation, when his will was crossed; but wondrously well-mannered; and an upstanding gentleman, of old Winterthurn stock. And was he a devoted family man, as well? —Oh, assuredly: *most* devoted to his mother, the saintly Letitia: and never less than civil to his wife, who,—and here Mrs. Harwich's voice dropped—did not appear to behave, much of the time, as a rector's wife ought.

Casually pressed by Xavier Kilgarvan, the housekeeper artlessly prattled of Perdita Bunting's mercurial ways, as soon as she was established in the residence as mistress: charming, and vivacious, and sunny, and gay, with a tuneless little song on her lips, and a warm greeting for everyone who came to the door; and then, with no warning, moody, and dull, and tearful, and white-skinned, so despondent, as she phrased it, "with the old, wicked, ne'er-changing ways of the world," she took to her bed for days at a time. While Reverend Bunting could not be said to be a doting husband, still less an amorous swain,—being, for one thing, inclined in recent years to stoutness and shortness of breath—it was the case that he *was* a respectful husband; and had every right to be coldly disapproving of his wife, when she behaved in such headstrong ways. "Ah, Mr. Kilgarvan, to hear the sudden unprovoked laughter, when she has been mute as the sepulcher, for days!—childlike, and shrill, and savage as shattering glass, ringing out in the gloom!" So it was, Mrs. Harwich did not worry excessively over her mistress's current invalided state, for she believed it would one day pass, and the pale-brow'd lady rise from her bed, when sufficient strength returned. "Albeit now Mrs. Bunting is a *widow*," Mrs. Harwich murmured, with her hand pressed against her bosom, "and must needs see the world forever altered: draped, as it were, in funeral black."

Encouraged by her listener's sobriety and frowning patience, and wishing, it seemed, not to be left too much alone with her duties, Mrs. Harwich spoke ramblingly of her hellish sojourn in the cellar of the house, and the injuries she had suffered; of Jabez Dovekie's persistence, and the brutishness of his manner; of Letitia Bunting's saintliness; of Bessie Hyde's unearned good fortune, in having had so generous a mistress to serve; of Mrs. Amanda Poindexter, who would give orders to her as if she were a mere maid; of the rudeness of Mrs. Poindexter's chauffeur, Jones, who drank; of certain parishioners who were always stirring up a fuss; of the odd behavior of Nell,—which is to say, Mrs. Bunting's personal maid—who had received a message, she claimed, from her ailing mother in Mt. Sweetwater that obliged her to be absent for the full day of September 11,—that very day of unspeakable horror. ("In what way is, or was, the girl's behavior 'odd'?" Xavier Kilgarvan inquired, "—for I have questioned Nell, and she tells me the message turned out to be fraudulent, and *most* baffling: though no less baffling than other aspects of the mystery." "It is odd," Mrs. Harwich said, with some reproof, "in that Nell's mother is always ailing; has been confined to her sickbed, I believe, for years; and so frequently do messages of one kind or another come to Nell, chiding her for not having visited, the girl has grown most callous. Yet, it seems, she was off like a flash that morning, all in tears, and quite agitated,—so piteous in her distress that Mrs. Bunting, *our* Mrs. Bunting, gave her the price of the train ticket outright: and prevailed upon her to accept it as a gift.")

From this, Mrs. Harwich lapsed to her earlier topic of Reverend Bunting's wife, confiding in Xavier that the life of the rectory had been so disrupted from time to time, she had near quit her post of many years; and had been restrained only by Letitia Bunting's wise counsel. It was not generally known, for instance, that, not long after her marriage, Perdita Bunting had succumbed to an unnatural state of nausea, vomiting, vertigo, and overall malaise, diagnosed by Dr. Hatch as a *false pregnancy*, in which, though the young woman appeared to be wasting away to a mere skeleton, she fancied that her belly was bloated, and so obscene a sight in the eyes of the world, she was obliged to swathe herself in loose clothes, or hide away in her darkened bedroom—!

Then again, the young Mrs. Bunting suffered nightmares and night-visions of a frightful nature, in which a spectral figure pressed himself against her bedroom window, and pleaded for admittance: this demon said to be (by Nell, who claimed she had seen it) so cunningly shaped as a man, and a man of some attractions, that it was no wonder the minister's wife fell into hysterics, in not knowing where to turn. ("Some years ago, it was, when Nell first arrived at the rectory," Mrs. Harwich said, "she was awakened by Mrs. Bunting's moans and whimperings, and ventured, all timidly, into her mistress's bedroom,—for the master and the mistress by this time slept apart—to see the young lady, not fully awake, sitting up in bed distraught, her hair tumbled wildly across her bosom and her nightdress, in Nell's words, all in disorder: turning to Nell her great dilated eyes, that reflected the flame of Nell's candle as would the eyes of a cat, and saying quietly, 'He is here,—he has come,—he is bold and impatient,—it is not my will,—it is not my wish,—I cannot be held to account,—I am wed now, and *not his*— O sweet Nell, stay with me tonight, that *he* cannot climb through my window!' And, Mr. Kilgarvan," the housekeeper continued, in a rapt lowered voice, "it was poor Nell's fancy that she did see him, or it,—though for but a fleeting instant, upon that occasion. A most diabolical agent, in that his countenance seemed *angelic!*—and his features regular and cleanly chiseled, like those of a statue of olden times.")

Seeing that her listener frowned, and sipped at his coffee with, it may have been, a hint of impatience,—for such tales *were* farfetched indeed, in the calming light of day—Mrs. Harwich shifted her tone, to say that it invariably happened, following one of these queer episodes, that the mistress either took to her bed or was up and about very early, with an excess of energy, and stern commandments for all.

As for the foundling infant left at the rectory door, one Christmas Eve but a few years back,—Mrs. Bunting was all in a fever to keep it and raise it as her own; and went so far as to "baptize" it with a name so queer, it seemed at first her own invention,—a foreign name by the sound of it, Mrs. Harwich said, which she had never trusted herself to pronounce. " 'If,'—'Iffi,'—'*Iffagene,*' a very queer name," Mrs. Harwich said, blushing, "of a sort never heard in Winterthurn." "Perhaps you mean 'Iphigenia'?" Xavier asked, staring at the woman. "Well,—yes—whatever," Mrs. Harwich said, "but it did not matter, as the Reverend forbade her to keep the sickly thing; and Dr. Hatch's housekeeper confided in me afterward, it was marked with the dread disease of its sinful parents, and would never have lived to maturity."

Pricked by this quaint usage, Xavier Kilgarvan inquired of the woman why she had said the babe *would never* have lived; and was informed, in a near-whisper, that Reverend Bunting and Dr. Hatch had concurred in their judgment that to provide costly medical treatment for the piteous thing, and, as it were, "nurse" it along, would be contrary to God's will. Thus, despite Perdita Bunting's tearful protestations, and threats the unhappy woman made *against her own life,* the foundling was allowed most mercifully to expire: for 'twas clear that God's initial damnation on its head could scarcely be contravened, without risking His especial wrath; and naught but the most desperate of women would wish to adopt a baby under such scandalous circumstances.

"Indeed,—indeed, you may be correct," Xavier said, signaling, by the sudden flatness of his voice, that the subject had begun to bore him, "for is not any act of adoption hereabouts, one of *desperation!*"

Shortly afterward, Xavier applied himself to a re-examination of the rectory, with the thought in mind that he would scrutinize those things which, some days before, he had considered relatively insignificant. For it is often the case that the *interstices* of an investigation yield fruit, when other spheres prove barren.

So it was, he happened across a packet of clippings, yellowed magazine articles, etc., *pertaining to himself,* at the bottom of a steamer trunk carelessly filled with cast-off ladies' clothing,—doubtless Perdita's: and blinked, and stared, and swallowed hard, while leafing through these documents, a number of which he had never set eyes upon before!—for such was the young detective's impatience with the public face of his career, he could not be troubled to keep accounts. A pulse beat strongly in his throat; he felt a chill rising from the dank earthen floor, to his very heart; and a voice of stifled rage instructed him, *The wretched woman has loved you all along, and you she, and yet she has been another man's wife, and now must be his widow.* After a minute, however, Xavier sufficiently recovered himself to cram the puerile clippings back into their envelope, and hide it beneath the untidy layers of clothing: the which momentarily diverted his attention, and assuaged the painful beating in his throat, in that he noted their odd charm,—the bicycling costume in particular, being of a rich blue-brown velveteen, bloomers and embroidered bolero alike. These too, however, he let fall back into the musty interior of the old trunk; and conscientiously shut the lid upon them. "So she has thought of me, from time to time, doubtless solely when her eye hit upon such public notices," Xavier sullenly bethought himself. "Well,—so be it: I cannot say that I have thought overmuch of *her.*"

Xavier then perused the first-floor rooms of the residence, excepting the kitchen and the servants' quarters, finding little of note in the dim-lit music room, or in the parlor, or in the dining room with its mullioned bay window and glass-fronted sideboard: high-ceilinged, joyless, yet unfailingly *proper* rooms, which boasted very little of the personal, or the unique. (A Chinese vase in which four or five peacock feathers stood; a somewhat hazy watercolor of a river scene, perhaps by a local artist,—perhaps by Perdita herself; numerous cut-glass figurines, of dancers, elves, affable "wild" creatures: these, and no more.) "Such is the wintry ambiance of the Buntings' marriage," Xavier thought, with a stab of gratification, "—the bed in which *she,* of her own free will, chose to lie."

In opening the door to Reverend Bunting's study, however, he gave a start, as, for a scant blurred instant he saw, or seemed to see, the shadowed figure of Ellery Poindexter before him: Mr. Poindexter harassed, and breathing hoarsely, as he stooped to grasp someone or something in his arms, to drag it to the divan nearby. And, ah!—the broken and bleeding figure of a woman lay already on the divan, her finery despoiled, her hair loosed from its elegant coiffure, one plump arm stretching lifeless to the carpet—!

An eye's blink, and the hazy scene vanished, as if it had never been: patches of watery sunshine, cast by the mullioned squares of the room's single window, dispersed the hellish apparitions: albeit the detective could smell, with sickened certitude, that very same commingling of the odors of blood, and animal terror, and perfume, and tobacco, and the oily hair pomade that Ellery Poindexter wore, *with near as much clarity as he had smelled it on the evening of September 11.*

This morning, however, the book-lined study with its somewhat faded wallpaper, and its dark wainscoting, and its large and grace-less roll-top desk, possessed no horrors, and, indeed, appeared to be so scrubbed and polished, and resolutely tidied up, one might have mis-taken it for a very ordinary room altogether: a place of laborious and dreary sermonizing, where troubled parishioners came for spiritual solace. Only the absence of several items,—amongst them the leather divan and the blood-soaked carpet—suggested that something unto-ward had occurred.

Fired with a nervous sort of energy, Xavier Kilgarvan proceeded to search the room, tapping assiduously for false panels in the ceiling-high bookcase; investigating the floorboards, and the fireplace, and the antique molding; and, with that indefatigable instinct for thorough-ness which was rarely acknowledged in him (possessing, it seems, none of the "glamour" of other detectively traits), he betook himself to examine, volume by volume, all the books in the room—!

How much time this dull, exacting, and fatiguing task required, I cannot say, save to note that, some hours later, Mrs. Harwich timidly rapped on the door, to inquire if Mr. Kilgarvan should like luncheon: the which invitation was politely declined. Agèd volumes in Latin and German: folios of one thousand pages each: dissertations on every aspect of Christian theology, through the centuries: anti-Papist doc-trines: complete volumes of *The Christian Journal, The New England Preacher, The Journal of the Harvard Divinity School,* and more: col-lections of sermons by various gentlemen of the cloth, of whom Xavier had never heard: and, in a proud calfskin binding, with gilt-edged pages, *The Collected Sermons of Harmon Atticus Bunting,*—through which Xavier leafed with some distaste, yet, all fortuitously, as this proved the very volume he sought. For there had been slipped into the cumbersome volume a number of strips of foolscap, containing notes for sermons, drafts of sermons, et al., and, near the very back, drafts of those selfsame "anonymous" letters Xavier had been studying but a few hours earlier—!

So it was, Xavier blinked and stared, and could scarcely believe the evidence of his eyes: for though he had bemusedly entertained the notion that Reverend Harmon Bunting might have written the let-ters,—*might* have, like virtually any male citizen in Winterthurn—he must not have considered it seriously, to judge from the surprise he felt.

"The brute, the swine,—*he,* of all persons!—the sanctimonious hypocrite!" Thus Xavier's disgust broke from him, as, by the pale-glowering light of the window, he hurriedly perused the half-dozen drafts, taking note of how, even while sketching out his lewd remarks, Bunting had, all shrewdly, essayed to disguise his hand. "Yet it *is* his hand, as even the least professional eye might see," Xavier inwardly declared.

After some ten or fifteen minutes of scrupulous examination,

Xavier folded all the sheets of foolscap up,—including those pertaining to mere sermons—and slipped them, with care, into a secret inner pocket of his coat.

Yet he found himself unable to leave the rectory: for its dank and oppressive air was such, he pitied all who must remain in it: and it is no irresponsible flight of hyperbole to say that his heart fairly ached for the young widow who lay in her invalid's bed, but a floor above. How grievously abused Xavier's cousin had been, by the masculine sex!— whether her assailant Poindexter, or her husband Bunting, or, indeed, her wicked and unnatural father, many years before. (A veritable shudder of loathing ran through Xavier when, of a sudden, he thought of Erasmus Kilgarvan,—a figure out of the past, which is to say, out of Winterthurn, which he had not contemplated for more than twenty years. "*He*, the greatest of brutes,—the swine, the father of all," Xavier murmured. "If only he is truly dead—!")

Taking the stairs to the second floor in such determined haste, he bounded up two or three steps at a time, Xavier Kilgarvan went directly to the chamber in which Perdita lay, and saw, through the crack of the door, the girl Nell seated in a rocking chair; and, close by, in a bed of modest proportions, albeit charmingly canopied in white damask sprinkled with rosebuds, Perdita herself,—asleep, or unconscious, in so profound a stupor, her breath came gasping and arrhythmic, and her lips appeared parched, and even cracked with fever blisters; her skin had acquired the flawless dead-white tone of alabaster, as if she were, not a living woman, but a beauteous effigy of Death,—placed amidst a bower of spotless white linen, in a pose of mocking serenity!

She is dying,—she is near death—they have destroyed her, Xavier thought, stricken to the heart.

At this moment Nell glanced up from her knitting in alarm, and sprang to the door, to close it against him: her broad ruddy face expressing such fearful surprise, she might have been gazing at her mistress's assailant in the doorway, and not at Xavier Kilgarvan, whom she certainly knew. However, Xavier handily prevented the door being shut; and drew the trembling girl out into the corridor, to inform her that he had come to speak with Mrs. Bunting,—and that *she* was wanted straightaway downstairs, by the housekeeper. "Please, sir, Mr. Kilgarvan, sir," the girl said in a quavering voice, "you know I am forbidden to allow any visitors into this room; you know Mrs. Bunting is in a delirium,—she is very ill—Dr. Hatch has cautioned me, and Miss Thérèse—O please, sir—" Thus the blushing maidservant protested, very nearly weeping with distress, and embarrassment, and, it may have been, some degree of girlish excitement at Xavier's presence.

But Xavier sent her away, with dispatch; and entered the dim-lit bed-chamber, which, as a consequence of the drawn blinds, and a pale green-gold covering of tea-paper on the walls, possessed an eerie undersea quality. How quiet this perfumed chamber, save for its mistress's labored breathing! How gingerly, and with what reverence, Xavier approached the bed, to gaze upon the sleeping woman!—to see how Time had, subtly, yet incontestably, etched her forehead with fine, white, perplexed lines; and dulled the luster of her superb hair, now streaked with silver, in ore artless profusion than Xavier's own. Yet Perdita's beauty seemed the more haunting, for being so poignantly touched with mortality.

Scarcely daring to breathe, Xavier gazed hungrily upon her: and saw, with a stab of incalculable emotion, that she had removed her wedding band from her left hand, and now wore, on her smallest finger, an antique ruby ring of exquisite design: a child's ring, it seemed: and one which struck Xavier's eye as familiar,—ah, how wondrously familiar!

He bent over her, to stroke the disordered tresses on her pillow; and to murmur her magical name; and, with but a moment's hesitation, to kiss her cool cheek,—with the immediate consequence that her eyelids began to flutter, and blink; and, by degrees, consciousness, and recognition, flooded into her vision.

"My Perdita—!" Xavier whispered.

Xavier Kilgarvan's Investigation: The Embrace

While our daily lives commonly proceed with so little variation, one day is scarcely to be distinguished from the next, and an entire week,— nay, a month—may glide by with seamless ease, it is a predominant characteristic of a *criminal investigation* that each day is fraught with discovery, and oft-times with danger: and the passage of a mere twelve hours may so completely eclipse the day that preceded it, it constitutes a unit entire in itself. Now Fortune smiles; now frowns; now clues appear to "fall into place"; now the detective's theory is so cruelly injured, a giant's hand might well have swooped idly down, to brush all the chess pieces from the table—!

Thus, the painful contrast betwixt the events of September 15, which roused in Xavier Kilgarvan such rare emotion, he felt himself, for the first time in years, on the very brink of *contentment*,—and those of September 16, one of the most disagreeable days of his professional life.

Xavier was seated with Murre Pitt-Davies in the latter's handsome drawing room, sipping sherry, and talking of divers subjects,— listening, rather, as Murre inclined toward loquacity, and did not need to be drawn out by the detective,—when, shortly past five o'clock, word came that the fugitive Dovekie had been, at last, taken into custody by police; and brought to the Winterthurn County Jail, after a considerable struggle; and would be presently available for questioning by Xavier Kilgarvan.

So it was, Xavier sprang from his seat, in some excitement: for

424

he was convinced that Dovekie's testimony would clear him and, if all went well, provide evidence by which a case against Ellery Poindexter might be assembled.

(Since Xavier's nettlesome interview with Poindexter, he had questioned numerous persons about him, and, most specifically, about his relations with his late wife, Amanda: but the results were inconclusive indeed. On every side it was hinted that the Poindexters were mismatched, and, perhaps, Ellery Poindexter had not practiced the strictest fidelity in his marriage,—indeed, he was rumored to have a mistress in Rivière-du-Loup, and even to have sired bastard children, unknown to his family. It was hinted that Amanda Poindexter's anxiety over religious matters, and, indeed, her dependence upon Reverend Bunting and his counsel, might have sprung from marital discord. Yet, to Xavier Kilgarvan's frustration, no one wished to speak frankly. His promise that remarks would be held in strictest confidence proved of little help: one lady would frown, and stare pensively into her tea cup, and suggest to Xavier that he ask such questions of another lady: that lady would begin to speak, think better of it, fall frowningly silent, and then, with a sigh, aver that *she* was not the one to question: and so on, and so forth, until Xavier agonized that he had fallen into the midst of a veritable clan of sphinxes! Nor were the gentlemen of Winterthurn any less reticent: for, it seemed, they feared Ellery Poindexter for his wicked tongue, and his penchant for taking revenge in underhanded ways, against persons imagined to have offended him. Early on in the investigation, Xavier learned that the master of St. Bride's was known as an *indefatigable enemy* and naught but an *intermittent friend:* he gambled carelessly at his clubs, and at the horse track; "forgot" to pay his debts; and flew into a rage if it were suggested, however diplomatically, that he had done so. Seemingly for the sport of it, he set friends against one another; blackballed the very "up and coming" gentlemen of Winterthurn society, whom he appeared to be championing to their faces; and had been known to participate in business deals of a clouded nature, especially involving the Great Northern Pacific Railroad Development Company, in which he was the principal shareholder. Only Wilbur Elspeth spoke openly against him, telling Xavier, with a grim visage, that "the Devil himself might know where Poindexter had been, on the afternoon of the murders,"—but Xavier wondered how to credit this, since Elspeth and Poindexter had been feuding for years, on the Bishop's Standing Committee. No lady would say what she seemed to be thinking, albeit Murre's aunt, Miss Elvira Pitt-Davies, strongly hinted that Xavier should be discreet in his inquiries, as Poindexter was one to bear a grudge for years: he had once boastfully described himself, in her presence, as wishing neither to forget nor to forgive,—what sport did life hold otherwise? *Revenge is a dish best served cold*,—thus he had quoted a Spanish proverb, to the perplexity of his well-bred listeners. Of the servants in Poindexter's employ, no one would speak with Xavier save McPhearson Jones, whom Poindexter had discharged from his post for drunkenness, but two days after the murders: and Jones's allegations against his former employer,—that he chastised his wife in such uncouth language, the poor lady habitually burst into tears—struck Xavier as not altogether reliable. Whom could he believe? Whom could he approach? His cousin Thérèse, with whom he spoke but briefly, seemed to wish to shun him, saying that she knew very little of Ellery Poindexter,—knew little, and wanted to know less; and that the entire affair, involving the murders, and the tragedy that had befallen Perdita, left her so sickened, she cared not to speak of it at all. "No more would I," Xavier faintly protested, "save that it is my duty.")

Since the calamitous afternoon when, it seemed, Jabez Dovekie disappeared into thin air in the hilly scrubland beyond Jewett's Pond, a number of search parties had been organized throughout the valley, seeking the red-haired fugitive in such places as Mt. Moriah, and Mt. Provenance, and Nautauga Falls, to no avail: for, alas, one false lead followed another: with Dovekie, or his fearsome look-alike, being sighted virtually everywhere, oft-times in several towns at the same approximate hour,—*and with his bloody ax in hand.*

From the first, it had been Xavier Kilgarvan's casual suggestion that the police keep a close watch on the Dovekie family: for, knowing as little of Dovekie as he did, Xavier nonetheless speculated that the man, grown desperate, and doubtless limited in his resources, and in his imagination, would be drawn back toward home; and might very well seek a hiding place nearby. If this were the case, he would soon make contact with his family, Xavier reasoned, and it might be that someone,—doubtless a child—would be entrusted with bringing him food: whereupon the police had only to follow the child, and they would find their man.

So, happily, it turned out, on the fifth day following the murder: for Dovekie was at last discovered to be hiding, like an animal, in the cellar of an abandoned planing mill not a mile from his family: and, after a considerable struggle, was overcome by a dozen or more members of the posse, to be hauled in triumph to the county jail, bleeding from numberless wounds, and trussed and chained like a wild beast. (How recklessly,—nay, how valiantly—the red-haired giant fought his captors!—sensing, perhaps, how he was doomed, once the law took him into custody.)

By the time word came to Xavier Kilgarvan, at the Pitt-Davies house, that Dovekie was jailed, the man had evidently been in captivity for several hours; yet, even so, for clouded reasons, Xavier was required by the police chief to wait an additional forty minutes, before being allowed to visit with him. "I must plan my strategy to perfection," Xavier excitedly bethought himself, "not to confuse the wretch with 'leading' questions, but to allow him his freedom, to speak as artlessly and as directly as possible: for his every word,—nay, his every syllable—will be precious to me."

When, at last, Xavier was escorted to the dank windowless cell in which Dovekie was being held, the thought straightaway occurred to him that this man might be the murderer after all, and Perdita's assailant: so fierce, so brutish, so subhuman did Dovekie appear, hunched over on his cot, still in his handcuffs and leg-irons, and exuding an air of sickly animal panic, and, most intolerably, gazing at Xavier with the eerie flicker of a smile, or a twitch, about his blood-encrusted lips. ("Why, does he mock *me?*" Xavier thought in amazement. "Does he know who I am, and what power I have over him—?")

Nonetheless, addressing the brute in the most courteous and forthright of voices, Xavier essayed to put him at his ease, that he might tell all he knew of the murders,—*all* he knew; omitting no detail, however seemingly trivial; and assuring him that he, Xavier Kilgarvan, was prepared to honor his testimony, and had by no means judged him beforehand, as, it appeared, others had done. "Thus," the detective said, smiling as best he could under the strained circumstances, "I beg you to consider me an ally, and not an antagonist."

Despite these kindly words, Jabez Dovekie glared at Xavier in wrathful silence; and drew in long shuddering breaths, and released them, with such intensity, it seemed his lungs must burst, and his eyes, already bloodshot and somewhat protuberant, must bulge from their sockets. Xavier repeated his questions, phrasing them as simply and directly as possible, the while he took uneasy note of the defiant rigidity of Dovekie's facial muscles, about the jaws in particular.

"Nay, I am certain that this man was not her assailant," Xavier chided himself, "and, in any case, I must not judge him beforehand."

Though courteously questioned by Xavier, Dovekie did no more than grunt, and sigh, and make a writhing motion with his shoulders; and Xavier took uneasy note of an indefinable *queerness* about his face,—masklike, and imbecile, and darkly smoldering, as if the blood beat hard and hot beneath the coarse surface of the skin. Withal, the accused man *was* ugly, at least in his present condition: several of his teeth were missing, and his lips had been badly cut; his broad flat nose had been bloodied; his hair was that of a wild beast's, all matted, grizzled, and filthy; and his eyebrows, inordinately grizzled as well, lifted spikily from his forehead, like those of a hog. Yet more distressing, Dovekie's left eye began, of a sudden, to *wander*,—tracing a pattern in the air, it seemed, beyond Xavier's head, while the right eye continued to fix Xavier in its bulging glare.

"Is he mocking me?—is he mad?—what on earth is happening?" Xavier thought in alarm.

When the lurid motions of the eye stilled, and, it seemed, Dovekie was again attending Xavier's words,—or, at any rate, staring most intensely at him—Xavier repeated all he had said, even more clearly; and essayed to comfort Dovekie by telling him that, under Law, he had the right to retain legal counsel,—and should by no means proffer a "confession" at the urgings of the police.

"For it is invariably their wish to make things as tidy as possible,—to proclaim a *criminal* where, perhaps, there is naught but a *suspect*," Xavier said.

Even these sympathetic words failed to evoke any response from Dovekie, save a louder sigh, verging on a moan; and a series of convulsive motions, in which his entire body participated, the head and shoulders in particular. While the appalled detective stared, Dovekie's eyes rolled upward, showing the whites: and his lips hideously twitched, in a mockery of a smile: and a pink-flecked foam or froth appeared in his nostrils.

"Dear God, man, what is wrong!—tell me what is wrong!" Xavier cried, springing to his feet.

The doomed man likewise heaved himself up from his cot, swaying, and staggering, and making his way to Xavier: now drooling copiously from bloodied lips: his eyes careening out of focus, and every fiber of his being straining to speak. Yet, how queer it was, that naught but hissing sounds, and guttural moans, and nonsensical syllables escaped from him: "—iiiiiyyysssssss,—yyyyyyssssschch-chchxt,—ghpxytoloththth—" uttered in the most piteously intense of ways, as if, even in his extremity, Dovekie harbored some small margin of confidence that Xavier should understand.

All bravely, Xavier essayed to hold the staggering giant erect, and did not shrink from his grasp, when, in a wild and panicked motion, he raised his manacled arms above Xavier's head, to lower them into an embrace: albeit Dovekie must have weighed one hundred pounds more than Xavier, and stood a good six or eight inches taller. Thus, the dying man hissed, and babbled, and groaned, and grunted, and, in spasmodic stammers, mimicked, it seemed, the pattern and rhythm of an ordinary conversation, in which something urgent must be communicated: though, as it scarcely needs be said, poor Xavier could understand not a word,—nay, not a syllable!—and was unable to keep from crying aloud in pain, as Dovekie's embrace tightened, and tightened, and yet further tightened, squeezing the breath out of the detective, and threatening to crack his ribs.

Fortuitously, as it turned out, the wretched man was, in this struggle, *breathing his last:* and, with a final spasm of hisses, and a gargling noise that arose deep in his throat, he relaxed, of a sudden, his grip upon Xavier,—and crashed so heavily to the floor, he pulled the terrified Xavier with him.

So it transpired, that Jabez Dovekie, the sole suspect in the Grace Church murders, died within a few hours of his arrest, of causes subsequently deemed "natural" by Hans Deck, the Winterthurn county coroner (who felt obliged to perform the autopsy only at the repeated urgings of Xavier Kilgarvan): albeit it came to be whispered through Winterthurn, in the less affluent neighborhoods in particular, that, when taken into captivity by the police, Dovekie had been so struck, and pummeled, and kicked, about the head especially, it was a testament to his strength and vigor of being, that he had lived as long as he had—!

Nonetheless, as Dovekie was generally believed to be the ax murderer, and the loathsome assailant of Reverend Bunting's widow, it was pronounced a blessing of God that he had died when he had, whether of natural causes, or no: for would the murderer not have been hanged, in any case, within a few months? And, in thus dying so handily, he had,—poor wretch!—saved the taxpayers of Winterthurn County the needless expense of a trial, and a stay in jail, and a public execution.

"A disagreeable end to a disagreeable interlude," Police Chief Orrin Wick was reported to have said, when queried by the *Winterthurn Gazette*, "but, at least, it *is* an end: and we can now turn our thoughts to other things."

Postscript:
Xavier Kilgarvan's Vow

"It cannot be,—it cannot have happened,—the poor man,—the hapless brute,—my primary witness,—dying in my arms,—so irrevocably snatched from me, *the insult of it cannot be borne!*"

Thus Xavier Kilgarvan inwardly murmured, for days after the untimely death: glimpsed by observers in so dazed and disheveled a state, he might have himself been suffering from a cruel blow to the head.

For the import of Dovekie's death was unmistakable, in Xavier's eyes; and unmistakable, the cynical hand of Poindexter behind it,—bribing the police from Orrin Wick on down; and the coroner as well. "He imagines himself unassailable, in his bastion of wealth and prestige,—his *Winterthurn prestige*," Xavier thought, trembling, still, when he recalled the death shudder that had coursed through Dovekie's body, and his own, "but he is much mistaken, if he thinks he has thwarted me. Why, I shall never rest until Poindexter is run to earth: less for the cruelty to Dovekie and the others, and the insult to *my* poor honor, than for the outrage against Perdita. *That*, with God as my witness, I cannot,—I dare not—forget!"

The Talk of the Town (II)

After this tumultuous sequence of events, lasting less than a week, but fraught, it scarcely needs be said, with tragic consequences for all of Winterthurn, there ensued an interregnum of merciful calm; only Xavier Kilgarvan was given out to be dissatisfied.

(Both Murre Pitt-Davies and Miss Thérèse Kilgarvan were oft-times queried as to when Xavier Kilgarvan would be returning to Manhattan: for it struck Winterthurn as decidedly queer, and perhaps troublesome, that the detective had protracted his stay through the remainder of September, and well into October, *for no discernible reason*. The rumor had become solidly ensconced in society that Xavier felt no kinship, and very little warmth, for anyone in the city of his birth; and was so fired with contempt for the local police,—indeed, for all members of the local government—that he could not trust himself to comment upon them, when asked. He had severed ties with his agèd father, and with his brother Bradford; certainly, he was involved in no romantic attachment; and the murderer of the Buntings and Mrs. Poindexter had been found. Thus, why did he linger; why was he suddenly glimpsed about town, when his manner, though unfailingly courteous, communicated the repugnance,—nay, the hostility—he assuredly felt?

As to this, Murre Pitt-Davies simply replied that his friend was welcome to stay with him as long as he wished, and for whatever purpose he wished, while Miss Thérèse Kilgarvan more stiffly replied that she had spoken with her cousin but two or three times since his return, and could hardly count herself his confidante. "It may be that Mr. Kilgarvan's heart is more entangled in Winterthurn than he knows," the schoolmistress said, in a neutral tone, "and though he should like very much to leave, he cannot.")

During these chill autumn weeks, as, in stealth, Xavier Kilgarvan pressed on with his private investigation, several minor events occurred, of a problematic nature.

Mr. John Hathorne, the assistant pastor of Grace Church, found himself so bedeviled by an irksome spirit claiming to be the late Harmon Bunting, and warning him against "ascending to the pulpit" of Reverend Bunting's church, he suffered a nervous collapse at the very end of September, and had to be relieved of his pastoral duties; Henry Harder, the elderly sexton, complained of being similarly bedeviled by a spirit,—that of poor Letitia Bunting herself, who claimed only that she wanted to comfort her son, as he had been so grievously mistreated by one he had trusted; and the pretty Penistone twins received yet another "anonymous" letter!—this, a coarse missive in a hand very unlike that of the others. (Since his discovery of the drafts of the letters in Reverend Bunting's collection of sermons, Xavier Kilgarvan had pondered whether to divulge the secret identity of the original malefactor, or no: for, though he had not admired Bunting in life, he did not wish to blacken the man's reputation after his death; nor did he want to further distress Perdita by so scandalous a revelation. In the end, Xavier shared the secret only with his friend Murre, who, altogether astonished by the evidence, strongly advised Xavier to tell no one. "For it is repugnant enough that Harmon Bunting will be forever whispered of as a common adulterer," Murre said, "without adding to the ignominy, that he had written perverse letters to his own wife!")

Following an unidentified source, Winterthurn police raided a clandestine meeting of a fledgling chapter of the "Wobblies,"—the Industrial Workers of the World—in South Winterthurn, in early October, making the significant discovery that these persons had been connected with Jabez Dovekie: or so it was claimed. Whereupon a dozen arrests were made, on charges of sedition and mischief and conspiracy to commit further crimes against life and property. And when Reverend Bunting's widow, Perdita, continued in her malaise— oscillating, it was said, betwixt periods of fevered delirium and periods of listlessness and inertia—it was prescribed by her physician, Dr. Colney Hatch, that she be removed to more congenial surroundings, at the home of Contracoeur relatives: whereupon the invalid threw herself into a frenzy, claiming that she did not wish to leave Winterthurn, though it be the place of her damnation. (One can well imagine how indelicate it seemed to Thérèse that her sister, so lately bereft of her husband and her mother-in-law, should ply Thérèse with questions of their cousin Xavier!—at whose home he was dining, with whom he was seen, what was whispered of him, etc. Wishing only to shield the unhappy woman from needless excitement, Thérèse followed Dr. Hatch's counsel, in telling her that her husband's murderer had been apprehended, and Justice had been, by an act of God, meted out; that it was understood the case was closed, and the mystery resolved; and that Xavier Kilgarvan had subsequently returned to Manhattan, on very short notice. "He has not. He would not. Ah, you lie, Thérèse! You lie! He would not leave without telling me!" Thus the sickly woman exclaimed, fixing her sister with a look of childlike fury, and refusing to be placated.)

As to Ellery Poindexter,—where a lesser gentleman might have fled grief and scandal by going abroad, or, at the very least, withdrawing from the public eye, it was his strategy to "brazen it out," so to speak, by continuing in his usual routine, albeit dressed impeccably in mourning, and oft-times wearing a tall black silken hat. He soon became a conspicuous sight in the Poindexter pew in Grace Church, all prayerful, and reverent, and innocent of any flicker of boredom or irony, of the sort for which he had long been known; he conversed graciously, if rather soberly, with his acquaintances and business associates; he was adamant in establishing a memorial fund in Reverend Bunting's honor, for the admirable purpose of providing scholarships for deserving young seminarians. When he spoke of his late wife, Amanda, it was invariably in the most solemn and hushed of tones: it was said he arranged for flowers to be delivered to her gravesite each day, through the month of September; and that he had arranged for a well-known Winterthurn portraitist to paint her portrait,—this splendid work of art, measuring five feet by seven, based partly on daguerreotypes of Mrs. Poindexter and partly on the painter's memory. (Thus it was, Amanda Poindexter, in oils, possessed a far more radiant and youthful beauty than she had in life,—even in her youth; and, her ample womanly charms constrained by a crimson gown, she bespoke a remarkable synthesis of the imperial and the voluptuous, which had perhaps not been altogether her own while she lived. Yet, when viewers were shown the portrait, they did not dare evince any doubt to the widower regarding the authenticity of the likeness; but marveled with him, in hushed and reverent tones, that the artist had so brilliantly captured Mrs. Poindexter's personality. "Yes, indeed, it is very like Amanda,—it *is* Amanda," Ellery Poindexter said, stroking his mustache, and in a voice entirely devoid of irony, "as natural on canvas as she had ever been in life.")

True, if, as the weeks passed, Ellery Poindexter began to be seen again in his old haunts,—if he could not always resist a trip to the race-track, or a game of poker at his club; if, again, his lengthy absences from home were remarked upon,—it was supposed that these activities were intended to distract him from grief, and not to provide mere recreation.

The keener-eyed observers of Winterthurn society soon noted, however, that when Ellery Poindexter and Xavier Kilgarvan chanced to meet, a palpable tension in the air might be discerned: for it could never be foretold whether these gentlemen would stare intensely, and, as it were, avidly, at each other; or, more curious still, whether they would *look through each other*, in the most uncanny manner—! If Poindexter was a past master at snubbing those persons whom he considered his inferiors, or who had offended him in some wise, it soon became evident that the youngest Kilgarvan son was his match; or, it may have been, owing to the detective's chill gray gaze, he was even Poindexter's superior. One evening, when the two men were about to be introduced, in the drawing room of the Harrier Von Goelers, Ellery Poindexter gaily interrupted his charming hostess to say: "But Kilgarvan and I have already met, my dear,—several times, many times, a surfeit of times!"—whereupon the detective formally bowed and, with an admirable air of *sangfroid*, murmured: "No, we have not yet become acquainted,—the pleasure lies all before us."

Memento Mori

Winterthurn's splendid autumn darkened, by subtle yet inexorable gradations, to winter: the riotous late bloom of Indian summer was soon blasted away by November's winds: and the days,—ah, the pitiless progression of days!—grew ever more cruelly enshadowed, and chill: the while Xavier Kilgarvan immersed himself so fully in his solitary task, to prove Ellery Poindexter guilty, and to extract a confession from him, he could scarcely have said which season it was, if suddenly asked; or why, indeed, anyone of intelligence should be concerned with so trivial a fact.

Yet the detective had become, of late, queerly preoccupied,—nay, quite troubled—by the passage of Time, and Time's grave authority. For it seemed to him, he knew not why, that he *must* get his man before the turn of the year, or he would lose him forever: a notion, somewhat superstitious, that might have derived from the increasing darkness of winter; or from the fact that his fortieth birthday was approaching, several months hither. On some days he was provoked to near-frenzy, by a contemplation of Time, that he must work more quickly, to assemble a great mass of data, a veritable miniature galaxy, it seemed, proving Poindexter's guilt; on other days, alas, he felt near-paralyzed by the terrifying thought that, even as his pulses beat, *Time beat*, and though he labor at his task ten, or twelve, or fifteen, or eighteen,—or, indeed, twenty-four—hours a day, he could never hope to catch the phantom Poindexter; or even, for a scant minute, to still that dread passage of time.

So apprehensive was Xavier of repeating certain of the blunders that had led to the acquittal of Valentine Westergaard, he conspired to erect an "airtight" case against Poindexter, where, by degrees, he might wear his man down *from within*, as it were; for, painful as it is to admit, in this most definitive of histories, by this time in his turbulent career Xavier Kilgarvan had seriously lost faith in the judicial system of our great nation,—and had, in truth, lost faith in the integrity of the average law enforcement officer, long before Jabez Dovekie's "natural" death. (So preposterous a matter came to light, in the last week of October, it was some days before Xavier could bring himself to tell his friend Murre: evidently, the murder weapon itself, a fifty-four-inch ax with a powerful five-pound head, had been in some wise lost down at the police station!—and was never to be found again; nor to turn up anywhere, in any Crime Collection that I know of. "But how on earth can it be that an object of that size has been lost—?" Xavier asked the blushing Orrin Wick, with no attempt to conceal his outrage; whereupon the chief of police replied, in a sullen and defensive voice: "I did not say that the ax has been *lost*, Mr. Kilgarvan, but that it has been *misplaced*.")

So absorbed in his work was Xavier, he oft-times did not speak with his sole friend for days at a time; and was to be observed leaving the house, and returning, frequently disguised, at any hour of the day or night. His mealtimes were erratic; frequently he failed to dine at all, or, discovering himself ravenous, ate a hasty meal in a tavern close at hand; or bought food from a street vendor, to devour as he walked along. With the approach of the winter solstice, the daylight hours were lamentably truncated; with the inevitable result that, following his old custom, Xavier allowed himself to partake of alcoholic spirits earlier and earlier each day: there being some days when, it seemed, the sun neglected to appear at all, and "dusk" and "dawn" were most weirdly conjoined.

When his thrumming nerves were calmed by drink, and the piercing pain behind his eyes tempered, Xavier drew breath, as it were, and saw that his task was by no means an impossible one; for, over the past ten or twelve years, he had solved far more knotty cases, and aided in the restoration of Justice. Poindexter was clever,—devilishly clever,—and behaved much more circumspectly now than he had done in the past: but if Xavier applied himself unstintingly, he was confident that he would, one day soon, *get his man*,—and avenge Perdita's despoiled honor, and the pain and humiliation she had suffered, in the cuckold Poindexter's villainy. To that end, Xavier was amassing a prodigious quantity of evidence; and made it a point to trail the master of St. Bride's about, in disguise if he wished not to be detected, undisguised if he wished, for reasons of his own, to be recognized; and envisioned himself as a sort of *memento mori*, very like the human skull kept in a monk's cell, to remind him of his mortality. One evening when, by chance, both he and Poindexter appeared together on the doorstep of a Berwick Square townhouse, Xavier said, in a lowered voice: "I know you for what you are, and for what you have done; and am content to wait a very long time, until you make a mistake and reveal yourself to the world." With a show of bravado, Poindexter replied, "Why, then, you detective, you *shall* wait a very long time; and I hope you are not an impatient man."

Before the invalided Perdita was removed to Contracoeur, against her will, to what were deemed more hospitable surroundings, the lovers were able to meet several times, by stealth, in Perdita's very bedchamber; with the servant-girl Nell constrained to keep watch at the head of the stairs, to warn them against the approach of Mrs. Harwich, or Thérèse, or the busybody Hatch, who kept a jealous watch, as it were, over his patient. "I hope that Nell is as unfailingly loyal as you seem to believe her," Xavier said; whereupon Perdita said gaily: "Why, she knows her mistress's caprices so thoroughly, she should be frightened *not* to be loyal!"

During these idyllic, and oft-times somewhat giddy, interludes, such grave matters as *revenge*, and *justice*, and *Poindexter's villainy* were never directly addressed: for Perdita naturally shrank from speaking of them, or of her own condition: and Xavier, a gentleman to his fingertips, could not bring himself to broach the subject,—or to hint to Perdita the smoldering rage he felt that Poindexter, who had so brutally abused her, walked about Winterthurn a free man, his chin uplifted and his gaze, for the most part, unwavering. ("He is no less a monster than Valentine Westergaard," Xavier thought, with a shudder, *"but this time I shall not fail."*)

The reader will be gratified to learn that all was soon healed betwixt Xavier and Perdita: the one "forgiving" the other, for the hurt she had inflicted upon them both: and the other several times breaking into tempestuous tears of self-recrimination that she should have been so blind,—nay, so *demented*—as to have imagined that being the wife of a man of God might have had a whit to do with God!—or, indeed, as she so sadly phrased it, with earthly happiness.

"Albeit," she said in haste, while pressing herself agitatedly into Xavier's arms, "—albeit *I did love Mr. Bunting,* according to my bond; and have every reason to believe that he loved me. And my regard for poor Mrs. Bunting,—by which is meant, *Mother Bunting*—was no less high: for it is no exaggeration to say, as all of Winterthurn says, that that remarkable woman was a saint."

(Of Amanda Poindexter's death Perdita never spoke at all; so that Xavier came to wonder whether the full extent of the carnage below-stairs had been explained to her. It had been Thérèse's grim duty to break the news,—the which, following precisely Dr. Hatch's instructions,, she had broken by degrees: informing Perdita that her husband was "gravely afflicted," and then "critically ill," and then "not expected to live," etc. This most staggering of blows being dealt, and the widow forced to comprehend that she *was* a widow, Thérèse had then told her of Mrs. Bunting's death,—and then of Mrs. Poindexter's. But, as Xavier reasoned, it was altogether possible that Perdita had failed to absorb this additional news,—or that she had not "heard" it at all. For such vagaries of the human spirit had become commonplace to him, during the course of his career; he could recall a half-dozen cases, for instance, in which persons who knew very well that loved ones were dead, continued to speak of them as living, in the present tense,—there being an actual *deafness* operant. "Well, Perdita shall be steeped in these grisly details soon enough, when she rises from her sickbed," Xavier thought.)

Yet, ah!—how warmly suffused with love, and kittenish affection, Perdita now was!—so delighted to be reconciled with Xavier ("whom I feared I had irrevocably offended"), she brought a crimson flush to his face by kissing him full on the lips, as often, and as deeply, as impulse moved her; and of hugging him, and "clambering" (as she playfully called it) into his lap, from out her very sickbed—! Doubtless a certain measure of this exhilaration derived from a powerful reaction against the horrors that had transpired: yet it is certainly the case that Perdita was possessed of a wild and repentant sort of love for her cousin,—with whom she essayed to speak, very often, of the past: of what she called their "shared past," as if they had been children together, in any significant sense, in and about Glen Mawr Manor. ("Do you remember, Xavier," she would begin, thereby to chatter lightly of an event in which Xavier had not participated, so far as he could recall: "Ah, do you remember—! And Father was still living, then; and poor Georgina; and dear old Uncle Simon; and Jupiter,—do you remember Jupiter?")

Betwixt them, however, the opprobrious name *Poindexter* was never uttered; though Perdita must have understood Xavier's passion,—that he would be incapable of repose, or of ordinary contentment, until the "balance of Justice" was restored.

At their last stolen meeting, the tearful Perdita had seized his hands in hers, and again covered them in kisses, and rubbed them against her cheeks and bosom, that she might be warmed; and murmured the wish,—nay, it was very nearly a plea—that Xavier leave the business of Justice to others, or even to God. For, once the period of mourning was accomplished,—once she regained her health,—and the complications of the Bunting estate were settled (Perdita having inherited, it seemed, a tidy little fortune in properties and investments),—why, might they not be wed; was it not toward this long-awaited end that Fate at last directed them—?

"We will be wed, assuredly," Xavier declared, kissing his mistress's inflamed cheeks, and allowing his tears to mingle freely with hers, "but that cannot exclude the restoration of Justice, *as any Kilgarvan must know.*"

The Poisoned Benison

Though much of Xavier Kilgarvan's laboriously assembled evidence against Ellery Poindexter was to be destroyed by his own despairing hand, in late December, it is believed that the punctilious investigator had assembled an unprecedented quantity of "hard" data (but a single item, for instance, being a few grains of sandstone-and-oyster-shell gravel, identical to that used on the main drive at St. Bride's, which he had discovered betwixt the floorboards of Harmon Bunting's study); and that, in an exercise of great patience and ingenuity, rivaling that of any criminal investigator on this continent, or in Europe, he had essayed to construct a minute-by-minute time chart, recording the actual, hypothetical, probable, and "claimed" activities of some two dozen persons, through the daylight hours of September 11. (As unburnt sections of this chart were retrieved by Murre Pitt-Davies from the fireplace of Xavier's room, it is possible for us to reconstruct it in outline, if not in particulars, and to marvel at its ambition. It consisted of several sheets of stiff, plain shelving paper, taped together to form a whole, measuring some six feet by eight, onto which was transcribed, in the detective's clear angular hand, a staggering cornucopia of facts!—the Hours of the Day noted in a horizontal band, at the top of the sheet, and the Principal Actors noted vertically, in a band at the far left. [For, to his credit, it must be said that while Xavier knew that Poindexter was his man, he knew also that several other persons might have committed the crimes,—amongst them, for instance, McPhearson Jones, John Hathorne, and Henry Harder.] Doubtless Xavier had affixed this masterpiece of detective work to the wall of his bedroom that, even while lying abed, he might allow his restless eye to travel over it, seeking out here and there a clue, or a miscalculation, or a contradiction, or a remarkable new possibility, otherwise overlooked,—the euphoric nature of the enterprise being, *Xavier could not predict what might next spring to mind.* Needless to say, the elaborate chart concerned itself most obsessively with Ellery Poindexter,—in his *actual, hypothetical,* and *probable* emanations; but it contained fascinating, albeit mildly scandalous, details regarding numerous other principals as well; and odd, near-illegible scribbles here and there,—doubtless penned by the detective very late at night, or while sunk in an uncharacteristic mood, one of these being, in black ink, *Circumstance is all.*)

Like many another criminal investigator before him, Xavier Kilgarvan exulted in busyness, and movement,—indeed, a kind of *perpetual motion:* the which saw him in all parts of Winterthurn City, and even in the village of Rivière-du-Loup: at Poindexter's clubs, at Poindexter's favored racetrack, at St. Bride's itself (in disguise,—once as an itinerant peddler; another time as a cousin of Amanda Poindexter's from Missouri, who had not yet learned of her death; yet another time, by night and stealth, in a state of quasi-invisibility). Though oft-times revulsed by his fellow man, and harboring a very low opinion of Mankind's capacity for telling the truth, Xavier gloried in his interrogations, whether they yielded fruit, or no: for it gratified him to speak with persons otherwise unknown to him, of no connection with his solitary life. Thus a lengthy session with Mrs. Bessie Hyde, which threw light, as it were, on Harmon Bunting's inordinate dependence upon Letitia Bunting; thus a yet more lengthy session with Henry Harder, whose dislike of Reverend Bunting, and sympathy for his young wife, soon came to the fore; a conversation with the embittered McPhearson Jones, whose story shifted even while he repeated it,—the main constant being Mr. Poindexter's cruelty to Mrs. Poindexter, *whom he had several times threatened to divorce.* And, too, unsettling conversations with the rectory servants, who disagreed vehemently on the frequency with which Mrs. Poindexter had visited Harmon Bunting; and with the pale-faced John Hathorne, who betrayed a comical sort of apprehension that Xavier Kilgarvan, with his magical detective's prowess, should somehow prove *him* the murderer.

"A curious notion of the way in which a criminal investigation is directed—!" Xavier thought, in irritation.

He managed to obtain an interview, after some difficulty, with his elder brother Bradford: who insisted that, the case being closed, it only remained for Xavier to withdraw his services, and betake himself back to Manhattan,—"where, I have no doubt," Bradford said, "you are rather more at home than you are here." Showing a broad, sleek, ruddy face of perplexed innocence, Bradford Kilgarvan professed not to know anything pertaining to the mystery,—not to have been aware of anything, whether minor tensions betwixt Bunting and his parishioners, or rumors having to do with the adulterous affair, or Ellery Poindexter's clouded reputation. As the minutes passed, Bradford fell to interrupting his younger brother,—with such remarks as "Nonsense!" and "Not at all, my boy, *there* you are mistaken!"—and it soon became evident to the dismayed Xavier that Bradford *lied for the sheer pleasure of lying.* "This disagreeable person is my brother," Xavier bethought himself, sickened to the very marrow of his bones, "and yet I feel no more brotherly sentiment for him than I do for Poindexter himself."

Thus it was, the purposeless interview was concluded; and the two remaining Kilgarvan sons solemnly shook hands, with such finality, it seemed they had no wish ever to meet again.

It was Xavier's strategy, as I have noted, to follow Ellery Poindexter closely about Winterthurn: either in so overt a manner as to make it impossible for the vexed gentleman *not* to see him, or so cleverly disguised, even Poindexter's anxious eye could not detect him. *To wear his man down from within* seemed to Xavier the only hope, for no other strategy, under these peculiar circumstances, was likely to succeed.

To this end, Xavier often kept a vigil close by St. Bride's, that he might follow his prey downtown, where Poindexter made a pretense of keeping to professional hours. When Poindexter escorted a trio of elderly female relatives to Mrs. Poindexter's gravesite, Xavier observed him through a pair of binoculars, noting how the widower carelessly yawned behind his glove, and, when none of the ladies was turned toward him, essayed to dislodge mud from his shoes *by scraping them against his wife's very marker.* ("A monster!—pray God he is not conscienceless," Xavier thought, staring in revulsion.) Upon those occasions when Poindexter dined at the Rose Tree Club, or the Corinthian Club, or the Athletic Club, Xavier, alerted by his paid informers, hurried to keep the gentleman company, as it were: timing his cocktail hour, and his dinner hour, to coincide smoothly with Poindexter's. He observed him at billiards, and at cards, with a neutral expression; silent as a ghost, he stole up behind him in the cloakroom, to murmur a quiet greeting. When Poindexter journeyed to New York City at the end of November, allegedly for business purposes, Xavier slipped into the club car just behind him, and sat but two or three seats away, so that both gentlemen were facing a mirror, and the agitated

Poindexter had no choice but to stare in fascinated loathing at the detective's reflection. "You! Why do you persecute me! *Why cannot you let me go?*" the guilty man at last exclaimed.

But Xavier Kilgarvan, unyielding, implacable as Fate, did no more than keep his stony gray gaze affixed to Poindexter's, by way of the polished surface of the mirror. *You know why I cannot,* his heart intoned.

Not many days afterward an uncanny episode transpired, which Xavier found puzzling in the extreme.

In one of his favored disguises, he had been making his way, at dusk, through the lively pubs and taverns of lower Union Avenue when, quite by happenstance, he found himself standing at a crowded bar beside his very prey, Ellery Poindexter!—the flush-faced gentleman being already in a state of mild drunkenness, and altogether ignorant of Xavier's identity. (As much for the pleasure of the sport as for pragmatic reasons, Xavier had, that evening, cast himself into the mold of an itinerant salesman of "cultural" pretensions: with gray-powdered hair, and thick quizzical eyebrows, and muttonchop whiskers; and gold-rimmed glasses that fitted his face tightly; and upper eyelids so cunningly built up with flesh-colored putty, his eyes appeared smaller than they were, with a decided Slavic or Oriental cast. Studying himself in a mirror beforehand, Xavier had felt a grim thrill of euphoria, that he could not be recognized by anyone on earth,—that he had, indeed, slipped out of his nettlesome skin and was possessed of nearly as much power as if he were invisible. "Why, it is to be wondered whether Perdita herself would know me now," he thought, examining his countenance closely.)

So crowded was the tavern, The Sign of the Horn, and so motley and ill-assorted its patrons, the presence of a gentleman of Poindexter's stature went unnoticed, save by Xavier: albeit, in his somewhat disheveled state, with his Shetland wool coat badly rumpled and his mustache grown coarse and drooping, Ellery Poindexter struck a sorry note. With a brusque sort of camaraderie, suggesting that he knew not quite how to behave in such circumstances, Poindexter leaned in Xavier's direction, and, affixing his bloodshot eyes to Xavier's, asked him if he was a stranger to Winterthurn, and what was his trade; then plunging on, before receiving an answer, to say that *he* had lived in Winterthurn an entire lifetime, "though, in truth," Poindexter said, with a hoarse wheezing laugh, "it has seemed far longer."

Though greatly excited by this turn of events, Xavier naturally showed not a whit of the emotion he felt, but answered his man quietly and civilly; and took care, not to evince any inordinate curiosity. Whereupon Poindexter signaled to the barman, to bring them fresh drinks,—gin but faintly tinged with water—and launched into a rambling and abusive monologue, having to do with persons who had "betrayed" him, and "wished him Death," and "showed no mercy."

A tragedy had befallen him, Poindexter said, *but he was blameless.*

Scarcely daring to breathe, Xavier waited to hear what his man would confess: and felt keen disappointment when, swallowing one-third of his glass at once, Poindexter brooded over an incident that had occurred many years ago, when he was a boy. "Ah, on the very day of my confirmation into the Episcopal Church,—on the very day!" he exclaimed in a slurred voice. "Why, my friend, I did no more than pray to God, as I had been instructed, with the most astonishing results: *for God Himself appeared:* and gazed upon me with some droll bemusement, and no love that I could discern: and, finally,—ah, my friend, if you could have seen it!—finally waved me away in dismissal! 'Naught that Man *does* can overcome what Man *is*,' God allowed me to know, 'for Heaven will never be any closer than it is, at the present moment.' And, having said these damning words, do you know, my friend,—*God vanished.*"

Xavier observed, in a murmur, that it was unfortunate; but perhaps God would one day reappear.

"It is too late!—too late!" Poindexter said savagely. "You are much mistaken, my friend, if you believe I have been cooling my heels these many millennia, awaiting *His* return!"

Whereupon Xavier hurriedly murmured an apology, for he quite saw his companion's logic, if it be true that Man cannot overcome what he *is* by what he *does:* and yet more sobering was the revelation that Heaven culminates in the present moment,—*this* present moment, at any rate.

"You are right, sir!—you are right! But you are a stranger to Winterthurn, and can have no idea of what you say," Poindexter rejoined, with a blustering authority, the while, in an awkward pretense of familiarity, he continued to lean toward Xavier, and even to nudge Xavier's elbow with his own. He took a second immense swallow of his drink, and then a third, to drain the glass; and rubbed vigorously,—nay, cruelly—at his damp mustache, with the back of his gloved hand. His drunken monologue took up again its tone of reproach, and weary ire, turning upon "events ancient and modern," and "God's poisoned benison," and "Woman's poisoned love." While Xavier pricked up his ears, as it were, to hear every syllable that fell from the man's slack lips, Poindexter veered away from his subject, to dwell upon old disappointments and betrayals,—why, was he not speaking, at one point, of an insult borne by his paternal grandfather, who had been "royally snubbed" by his Federalist friends, and "ignobly snubbed" by the fool Jefferson? So rambling, so listless, so depressed was Poindexter, Xavier felt a stir of pity for him: then bethought himself that this was, after all, the manifestation of guilt: and he might be content that his man was *wearing down from within*.

Thus, an hour passed; and yet a second hour; Poindexter downing many more gins than Xavier, and alternating betwixt a piteous garrulousness and an abrupt sodden silence, the while, with as much caution as possible, Xavier essayed to query him on the source of his present unhappiness. But of that, it seemed, the wretched man could not bring himself to speak. Instead he informed Xavier, in a tone of commingled sorrow and bluster, that he, of all persons, was an object of envy in certain circles: for men who glimpsed only the outward man, and assessed a man's soul in naught but material terms, were fool enough to envy him: which irony struck him as so preposterous, Poindexter burst into a hacking and wheezing cough, of such protracted violence, Xavier feared he might collapse. Then, recovering feebly, he laid a heavy arm across Xavier's shoulders, and brought his head close to Xavier's, and said: "My secret is that I would gladly exchange positions in this world with anyone,—with anyone: with *you*, though you are but a stranger to me, for this poison of which I speak, why, it has so worn me down, and I am guilty of so foul a crime, *there is no one to whom I can confess*."

Xavier took care not to reply with overmuch alacrity; then averred, that it was likely his companion *exaggerated*: for gentlemen of refined conscience were wont to do so, while the common run of criminal suffered no pangs of regret at all.

These provocative words the drunken Poindexter seemed not to hear, for he continued in his lament, his saturnine complexion darkening, it seemed, by degrees, the while his close-set eyes filled with tears that threatened to spill on Xavier's very arm. With the dogged and repetitive vehemence of intoxication he declared that 'twas all God's blame, and none of his own: and the secret tragedy that had befallen him, some five years previous, had left him so worn and depleted, he was but the husk of a man,—the husk of a sinner: and, indeed—this declared in another outburst of wheezing laughter—he thought it a droll sort of comedy that there was a man in Winterthurn, a "detective," in fact, who so miscalculated him, he imagined him capable of a remarkable *crime of passion*, when, if the truth be known, he possessed as much "passion" as might be required to play a game of stud poker, or lift his glass to his mouth: and had been exiled from the bed of any woman for more years than he cared to admit. Moreover,—

Unfortunately, at this point Poindexter's unabashèd speech was cut short by a sudden fracas in the taproom, amongst a small gang of drunken dock workers: and it was not altogether clear whether the "traveling salesman" had even heard all that his drinking companion had been saying. Alas, so rudely jostled were these gentlemen, it looked for a precarious moment as if, all innocently, they might be caught up in the scuffle: for Poindexter caught a heavy blow to the chest, and Xavier was so violently shoved, his gold-rimmed eyeglasses flew from his face.

Being by far the more intoxicated of the two, Poindexter whirled about, and grabbed at shoulders and arms, cursing in a most imprudent way; and Xavier, fearing as much for his life as for his disguise, deemed it best to withdraw,—for he was a slender-bodied man, and could not have hoped to hold his own amidst a crowd of wildly fighting men. "Do not allow yourself to be drawn into it, sir!—do not, it is a mistake!" Xavier cried, with as much impulsive sympathy as if Ellery Poindexter were not, for that instant, his sworn enemy: but Poindexter paid him no attention, being, of a sudden, warmly absorbed in the excitement, and content to brush him aside as one might a gnat.

So it was, Xavier hastily retreated from The Sign of the Horn, knowing, with any professional detective, that valor and discretion cannot be evenly matched. His pulses all in a flurry, and his thoughts beating hot and riotous in his skull, he headed afoot for the bright-lit Berwick Avenue some blocks away, where he might have no difficulty in hailing a hackney cab to take him back to,—but where was he going?—where was it, he would be spending the night? An excess of gin-and-water, and, it may have been, an excess of mental stimulation, conspired together most potently to render the detective, for some perplexed minutes, in a state of suspension,—whereby he could not recall from whence he came, or whither he was headed. "Ah, what is it, —where am I,—where, and why?" Xavier numbly bethought himself, even as he raised his gloved hand to signal a cab.

And, waking some hours later, in a bed-chamber that seemed but dimly familiar to him, amidst fresh linens that should have consoled more than they did, he could not, for a space of five or ten minutes, recall where he was, or in whose home he stayed: and was tormented by the words, rising as it seemed out of nowhere, *Heaven will never be any closer than it is, at the present moment,—Heaven will never be any closer than it is, at the present moment—*

"Pray, God," Xavier whispered. "You are but jesting."

The Proposal

At this time, unbeknownst to Xavier, his cousin Thérèse and his friend Murre Pitt-Davies, companions and erstwhile "sweethearts" of old, found themselves growing yet more intimate, in their mutual concern for the detective's well-being. For, though his investigation into Ellery Poindexter's guilt was secret enough, and his renewed passion for Perdita unknown, it was clear to anyone who observed him that Xavier Kilgarvan had become so strangely obsessed with his work, his health had visibly deteriorated.

Moreover,—to his shame be it said—Xavier was more and more observed under the influence of alcoholic spirits: albeit, fortunately, he was a gentleman who, in the common parlance, knew how to hold his liquor.

Not a week passed, but that Miss Thérèse Kilgarvan, of the Parthian Academy for Girls, and Mr. Murre Pitt-Davies, headmaster of the Winterthurn Academy for Boys, had tea or dinner together in town, that they might compare notes, as it were; and speculate as to how best to approach the problem of Xavier. (Thérèse did not actually know, but strongly suspected, that Xavier and Perdita had renewed their love for each other, in the very shadow of Death: Harmon Bunting scarcely buried, and the "funeral meats" scarcely cold: and all of Winterthurn unwholesomely absorbed, in conjecture over the widow's fate,—whether she would ever marry again, and whom; whether, indeed, she would ever emerge from her state of collapse, to overcome the ignominy of what had befallen her. This suspicion troubled Thérèse, for she retained, still, her romantic feeling for Xavier; yet, as maturity had brought with it a healthsome equanimity regarding

447

what one *desires* and what one can *expect*, she oft-times wondered whether a love match betwixt Xavier and the troubled Perdita might not, in the end, prove lasting. ''For there is no gainsaying passion, after all,'' Thérèse sadly concluded.)

Of such delicate matters Thérèse and Murre shrank from speaking; but confined their discussion to the well-being of both Xavier and Perdita,—the latter having made some ''modest improvement'' in her health, since taking up residence in Contracoeur. Albeit the beauteous invalid quite distressed her relatives and her physician by refusing most foods, and by passing tormented sleepless nights, murmuring to herself in a delirium, and struggling, it seemed, with bodiless attackers,—whom she begged to ''spare my belovèd Harmon, if not myself.'' It was remarked upon too that she bribed servants to bring her forbidden newspapers, that she might greedily peruse them, searching, evidently, for news related to the murders, or news of Xavier Kilgarvan; and that she spent hours daily scribbling letters, which she hid in her bosom if anyone approached, and which she did not dare attempt to mail, as they would naturally have been intercepted. And, ah! did she not daily plead to be allowed to return to Winterthurn—though it be, as she wildly declared, the place of her ''damnation''?

One December afternoon, past dusk, Thérèse and Murre met for tea at the Winterthurn Arms: the one tall, and chastely attractive, in her black cashmere cape, and her kidskin gloves, and the hat she most favored,—stylish, yet not conspicuous, of smooth dark felt, with a wide brim, and numerous black swan's-down feathers; the other scarcely an inch or two above Thérèse's height, but stolidly built, with an agreeable countenance, and an air of gentlemanly solicitude. Both having spent full days at their respective schools, they spoke for a while of teaching, and of their students,—of whom, it seemed, they were, in the main, extremely fond; Miss Thérèse Kilgarvan returned to Murre Pitt-Davies his well-worn copy of Winwood Reade's *Martyrdom of Man*, which he had pressed upon her, for its high quality of discourse and its message of progress,—the which Murre took very much to heart, as it confirmed his own sentiment that, by way of evolving consciousness, and the development of science and rationality, Mankind could hope to obtain a Utopia of sorts, sometime in the near future. They spoke then of more personal matters: for Murre felt constrained to report that both he and his Aunt Elvira were quite distressed at so frequently hearing poor Xavier return to the house very late at night,—which is to say, very early in the morning: entering by way of his private entrance, and climbing the stairs unsteadily, oft-times muttering and quarreling with himself, in a state,—ah, how Murre winced to say it—of unmistakable inebriation.

At this, Thérèse did not trust herself to speak; but sat staring pensively at the delicate fluted rim of her tea cup. How wretched a turn of Fate that, since Xavier had failed to arrive in time to prevent the murders, he had arrived at all!—and now showed no sign of preparing to leave, as if caught fast in a web, the sinister dimensions of which he could not discern.

At last Thérèse bestirred herself to observe quietly that, at the very least, Xavier had in *him* the most loyal and selfless of friends: a better friend, perhaps, than he deserved, in his current state of preoccupation. "If only he would abandon the struggle, and return to Manhattan, and let Winterthurn be—!" Thérèse added, in a tone of uncharacteristic acerbity.

"Yet, it seems, some riddle, some vexation, some *unresolved mystery* holds him here," Murre frowningly said, "which, for my part, *I* cannot quite see: for assuredly poor Jabez Dovekie was the murderer!"

"Yes," said Thérèse at once, "yes,—you are correct—assuredly."

If, in the course of this narrative, I seem to have slighted so sweet-tempered and exemplary a gentleman as Murre Pitt-Davies, it is not, in truth, that other persons are more worthy of authorial attention; but rather that the much-loved headmaster of the Winterthurn Academy was, by all accounts, one of those individuals so devilishly difficult to capture in prose, I have long shrunk from the attempt. Which is to say, Thérèse's faithful suitor was so blessed with virtues (viz., intelligence, generosity, sincerity, warmth, Christian fortitude, and, withal, a total lack of pretension), and, it seemed, so innocent of any failings whatsoever (save the questionable failing of being, at times, excessively patient and overly "soft-hearted" toward problematic students), it is all but impossible to speak of him without risking the charge of implausibility—! He was forty-nine years old at this time, but wondrously vigorous and youthful; balding, and thick-set, and possessed of a somewhat overlarge nose, yet, withal, not unattractive; unfailingly good-hearted, yet by no means pious, or lacking in a robust sense of humor; taking pride in his work and in his accomplishments, yet by no means vain, or deluded as to his personal significance. It was whispered against him by a very few detractors that, in failing to insist upon corporeal discipline at the Academy, he was violating the school's tradition, and would "spoil" his young charges; but the great majority of the parents soundly supported him, and, needless to say, the Academy boys were near-unanimous in their fondness for him. Throughout Winterthurn, Murre Pitt-Davies was known as one of those persons to whom life appears a genuine blessing, and not a burden; his manner was forthright and exuberant, his

smile unpremeditated . . . And so forth, and so on!—for it is simply
the case that Xavier's friend was an entirely admirable man, and, while
villainous persons and "characters" invariably set well in prose, those
individuals whom we might call "the salt of the earth" fare less
easily: there being as much covert resistance to Goodness in art as
there is affection for it in life.

These things Thérèse knew, for she felt great esteem for Murre,
and affection, and, *almost*, love,—albeit, set beside Xavier Kilgarvan,
he seemed in some obscure wise less *manly*, as he was the more
human!

"Why then," Thérèse sternly bethought herself, "I must not indulge in idle romantic thoughts of,—my redoubtable cousin."

Upon this occasion in December, having spoken earnestly for
some time of various matters, Murre Pitt-Davies of a sudden renewed
his proposal of marriage: surprising both himself and his companion,
so that they blushed crimson, and Thérèse occupied herself in searching for her gloves, to disguise the agitation she felt. For, ah!—did
Murre's soft-voiced proposal not sound, this time, strangely reasonable?—inviting?—even, it might be said, seductive? Thérèse did not,
she could not—love him as she loved Xavier, and yet—

Seeing her upset, Murre warmly proffered his apologies, and
hoped he had not offended her,—as they had been speaking of grave
matters; and a personal importunity was perhaps out of place.

Thérèse, however, adjusting her veil, heard herself say in a
breathless voice that, perhaps, when the *mystery* was resolved,—if resolved it might be—when this atmosphere of dread, and malaise, and
Evil had passed,—why, then,—*then* she might rejoice in his proposal:
if, of course, he still wanted her as his wife.

—With which amazing words the handsome Miss Kilgarvan
rose to her feet, to conclude the conversation, before her incredulous
suitor could respond!

Xavier Kilgarvan's Investigation:
Hotel Paradise

———

The reader is now obliged to wrest his thoughts away from the genteel environs of the Winterthurn Arms, to a setting differing greatly from it, in both atmosphere and reputation,—this, the notorious village of Rivière-du-Loup, some ten miles north of Winterthurn City.

It had long been Xavier Kilgarvan's suspicion that the hypocrite Poindexter had secreted away a mistress, whom, since the day of the murders, he had not dared visit: and, surely, if Xavier waited patiently enough, and began to allow the beleaguered roué some measure of his old freedom, he would soon betray himself. Yet the weeks passed; and nothing, and no one, came to light; albeit twenty-odd informers had supplied the names and addresses of "Poindexter's whores" to Xavier, to send him on numberless futile chases through the back streets and alleys of the city,—these excursions oft-times proving dangerous, both to the detective's morals and to his sobriety.

(Alas, Xavier was beginning to despair of ever learning the truth about his adversary!—or even the name, the actual name, of Poindexter's mistress. For while some persons spoke vehemently of the man's "rapacity" amongst women,—McPhearson Jones being particularly strong on this point—others, doubtless fearing his wrath, declined to speak at all. Jones claimed that he had for years been employed in driving Poindexter to the gaming houses and bordellos of Rivière-du-Loup; another informer slyly suggested that Poindexter's true appetite was for young boys, of the poorer classes; yet other persons, who refused payment from Xavier, and struck him, consequently, as possessed of a higher degree of integrity, insisted they knew nothing of Ellery Poindexter's private life,—save that it had been cloaked in secrecy, and had best remain so. As to Xavier's shrewd question, whether this ''secrecy'' might have sprung from Poindexter's animosity toward his wife,—no one wished to venture an answer.)

Frustrated thus in his investigation, no matter with what diligence he labored, Xavier decided, of a sudden, to revisit Rivière-du-Loup: for it seemed the answer to his questions must reside there: and, no matter how long he waited, Ellery Poindexter would not lead him thither. ''For he has grown fearful, and cautious,'' Xavier thought, ''and as devious, perhaps, as I.''

All this while, it scarcely needs be recorded, the days grew ever darker, and bleaker, and windier: and snow began to fall near-daily, in great soft smothering clumps, or in stinging pellets, cruelly driven out of the northeast. This shifting of the Earth's poles,—this inexorable slide to the winter solstice—roused in the hapless detective, despite his rational judgment, a frequent sensation of panicked despair: for in him, still, was the child-soul, paralyzed by the specter of greedy and all-embracing Night.

As for the disreputable village of Rivière-du-Loup,—doubtless the reader is familiar in outline with its history, or, at the very least, its position vis-à-vis Winterthurn City: so I shall but briefly limn it here, before following Xavier Kilgarvan to the Hotel Paradise, and to his remarkable adventure there.

According to all reliable histories, this village of some fifteen hundred persons had had, from the days of its earliest settlement in the 1700s, a rough and scandalous reputation: being an Indian trading post for many years; and then one of the liveliest centers for lumbering; and, more recently, with the gradual decline of the lumbering business, a kind of ''free zone'' for men for all social ranks,—a lawless, and, indeed, unlicensed place where vices of every imaginable sort (whether drinking, or gambling, or consorting with females of the lewdest type, or betting on dog- and cock-fighting) were freely indulged. True, the county law enforcement officers essayed, now and then, to reform Rivière-du-Loup, or, perhaps, to regulate its excesses (for a goodly percentage of the county's crimes, including murder, were perpetrated there): but to no avail, as, it was whispered, the sheriff himself partook of the village's profits; and if raids ensued, very few arrests were actually made, and it was a rare conviction that resulted. Even as a schoolboy, Xavier had heard wild and alarming tales of the village; and his brother Wolf had made little secret of it, that *he*, from the precocious age of seventeen onward, made regular jaunts there, to such sporting houses as The Golden Vanity, The Peacock, The Black Elk Inn, and, not least, the despoiled ''gem'' of Rivière-du-Loup, the

Hôtel Paradis—or Hotel Paradise—which, in more prosperous lumbering days, had been a hotel of some legitimate prestige. (It had been Wolf's half-serious jest to "kidnap" his youngest brother, on the occasion of his eighteenth birthday, and take him to the Paradise to celebrate!—but so little did the chaste Xavier fall in with this foolery, Wolf did not pursue the subject.)

"Ah, if only I might be, still, that innocent prig, the boy Xavier!"—thus the detective laughingly murmured.

Needless to say, at this juncture of his life, Xavier Kilgarvan had few moral qualms about visiting the sporting houses of Rivière-du-Loup; and so practiced was he in suppressing his distaste for such excursions, he betook himself to the village with little delay, in a two-seater gig belonging to Murre. En route, he sternly warned himself against overindulging in drink; nor must he succumb to any feminine blandishments, and be drawn into a dangerous situation. For it might be the case, after all, that Poindexter had friends in this depraved place, or even business associates: and it would ill behoove Xavier to be discovered. Many were the tales he had heard, as a youth, of feckless gentlemen lured to their ruin at the gambling tables, or beaten and robbed, and left for dead in the hills: there being an especial danger for solitary men whose names and faces were unknown, and who did not live in the Winterthurn area.

Thus it was, Xavier arrived in Rivière-du-Loup shortly past dusk of a day in mid-December, skillfully, though not elaborately, costumed in a herringbone-tweed coat some years old, and a bowler hat of a subdued brown shade, and the red-dyed wig and goatee which he had worn on the day of his arrival back in September. (Since his gold-rimmed glasses had been broken, he had not troubled to replace them.) As one or another of his paid informers had named Ellery Poindexter a patron at all of the houses, Xavier felt obliged to visit each in turn, under the pretense of being an ordinary customer,—a businessman from Vanderpoel who had come to spend a few days in Winterthurn City, and had found his surroundings dull. He began, then, with the lowliest, and, in many ways, the least offensive of the houses, The Peacock: and worked his way up, so to speak, to the yet-resplendent Hotel Paradise,—a yellow clapboard structure of seven stories, with a grandiose portico, and ornately bracketed pillars in the style of the 1870s, and an air, surprisingly appealing on this grim December night, of tawdry prosperity. True, alarming tales had been told, over the years, of innocent young girls and women, many of immigrant stock, brought to the Paradise with the promise of honest employment, there to be drugged, and abused, and imprisoned, until such time as they would cooperate with their captors; and yet more alarming tales,—whispered, rather than spoken aloud—of hapless girls "bought" by well-to-do gentlemen, for a night's savage sport, which, upon some occasions, they did not survive.

So ablaze, however, was the Paradise, with lights, and music, and laughter, and so infectious its high masculine spirits, Xavier found himself thinking, as he entered, and was at once made welcome: "I suppose one cannot entirely blame a weak man like Poindexter, for seeking, in such a place, what low happiness might be his."

Though initially discountenanced by the rowdy gaiety of the high-ceilinged public rooms, Xavier partook but sparingly of alcoholic drink, and made his way about with shrewd discretion, as a "visitor to Winterthurn City who was not entirely a stranger,"—and who wished to make inquiries after an acquaintance of his, Mr. Ellery Poindexter, about whom he had become concerned of late. Unfortunately, no one Xavier encountered seemed to know the elusive Poindexter in person, though a fair number of the young women professed to have heard of him; and, it was hinted, he may well have been a regular patron of the Paradise, under one or another alias. (For, needless to say, the majority of the Winterthurn gentlemen who visited Rivière-du-Loup frequently,—those of high social rank, at any rate—were known by aliases and "nicknames" on this side of the river.) Might the person Xavier sought not be "Old Bull"?—or "Red"?—or "Buck"?—or "The Fox"? Might he not be "Trouble"?—or "Gnasher"?—or "Zach"?—or "Ironlocks"?—or "Bibs"?—or "Kooch"? Alas, even when Xavier generously proffered gold coins, to elicit more substantial information, his inquiries came to very little: for, as one young woman gaily averred, most of the well-heeled gentlemen of Winterthurn City visited Rivière-du-Loup from time to time, and it would be nigh impossible to remember them all—!

"Doubtless everyone in this place is in *his* pay," Xavier sullenly thought, "and it is a futile effort to make honest inquiries."

Thus it was, with the passage of hours, Xavier found himself drinking more heavily than he had planned, and somewhat promiscuously mixing drinks,—now a sherry, now a gin-and-water, now brandy, now Scotch—for he saw little purpose in returning to Jewett's Lane in the dark, alone and embittered, and, truth to tell, utterly baffled as to how next to proceed.

"Is't not the case that, at the age of thirty-nine, I am emulating, still, the 'Jashbers' of my boyhood," Xavier thought, in disgust, "while deluding myself, that I am an adult?—and have taken my rightful place amongst the adults of the world?" Seeing that, for the moment, he was unobserved, Xavier gave vent to his pique by roughly stripping the red goatee from his chin and shoving it into his pocket; for it had begun to irritate his sensitive skin, and served no purpose in any case. "Can it be, the majority of human beings live out their lives according to a child's scheme?—soon forgotten by the conscious mind, and 'buried over,' but operant nonetheless?" Xavier bethought himself, while, in the midst of a hurlyburly of drunken high spirits, to which he paid very little heed, he continued to sip at his drink: and felt so icily composed, he could not be vulnerable to anything so common as drunkenness.

"Nay," the detective murmured aloud, sighing, "I am one of those persons doomed, as it were, to *sobriety.*"

Nonetheless, it somehow came about,—whether at this time, or an hour or two later—that Xavier found himself in an upstairs room of the hotel, in the company of a full-bodied and heavily rouged woman of indeterminate age, with Indian-black hair, and a hawkish look about the eyes; whose simpering prattle quite belied the melancholy savagery of her countenance; and who roused him to both manly desire and annoyance, by her overfamilarity with his person. He was, it seemed, earnestly caught up in the attempt to explain to this woman that he had erred in accompanying her here, for he had given the pledge of his heart to another woman, and was not free: indeed, as Xavier excitedly insisted, in a slurred voice, *he had never been free.*

Even in his confusion, he was not so ungallant as to fail to press some bills into the woman's hand, and to close her moist, chill, trembling fingers about them: assuring her that he meant no insult to her, or harm: and apologizing for the violence of his response. (For, it seemed, Xavier had perpetrated some small damage in the room,— albeit he could not recall having done so: an overturned plush chair, a smashed vanity mirror, pillows and bedclothes tossed harmlessly about, in a sudden, and evidently short-lived, outburst of fury. Or had another gentleman caused this upset, and Xavier was not to be blamed—?)

Next, panting aloud, he found himself hurrying along the dim-lit corridor, that he might not be apprehended by any of the hotel's burly overseers: gloating in the cleverness of his escape, and making his way, with a shrewd simulation of knowledgeability, through the honeycomb-maze of corridors and back stairs. His excitation was such, he cared not precisely where his feet led him, so long as no one laid hands on him, and hauled him away downstairs. "Well,—for better or worse, I shall be faithful to Perdita," he thought, "though this wretched 'mystery' is never resolved, and we are never wed."

How long, in this state of mental confusion, Xavier wandered about in the overheated interior of the Paradise, is not known; nor could he have been able to recall, afterward, how many of the numerous floors he had traversed, and how often he had eluded discovery, by ducking around a corner, or hiding in an unoccupied room. (Yet, as it turned out, his wish to avoid detection was not steadfastly observed, for, upon one occasion, he found himself quietly inquiring, of a disheveled blond woman in a robe trimmed with black ostrich feathers, whether she knew firsthand of the shameless Poindexter; and of the Grace Church murders; and of the near-unbearable pressure being exerted upon *him* to proclaim the murderer's identity—!) One thing struck him above all, in this jumble of gas-jets, and banisters, and thick-piled carpets, and bursts of shrill bodiless laughter, and fleet mirrored images of a harried man who was, yet was not, Xavier Kilgarvan: the knowledge that the Hotel Paradise contained many more rooms, and, it certainly seemed, more floors, than one might have estimated, from the street; and that it must be altogether too easy to become lost in its labyrinthine passageways.

"A hellish sort of 'Paradise,' indeed," the detective thought, "wherein pleasure has no limit."

Had his senses been more acute, Xavier might, perhaps, have felt some premonitions of alarm, at the gradual increase in temperature, as he made his groping way down an ill-lit back stairs: there being, in addition, a steamy quality to the air, so that it became difficult to breathe; and an odor,—heady, rich, sweetly intoxicating, and somewhat sickening—of heated mammalian flesh. As he passed by degrees from the more lavishly decorated part of the hotel to a part distinctly older and shabbier, there came to him disjointed memories of the cruder sort of tales he had heard, from many years past: tales of "expendable" and "worthless" females, deemed insufficiently pretty, or healthy, or spirited, who were auctioned off to the highest bidders amongst the clientele, and taken off to the remoter corners of the hotel, to be dealt with as their buyers chose. There were, it was said, cork-lined subterranean chambers, wherein instruments of torture were available,—whips, and branding irons, and makeshift gallows, and "operating tables"—and the tiled floors were equipped with drains, that streams of blood might be carried away, with a minimum of perturbation. Why, had the amazed young Xavier not heard, by way of his older schoolmates, that there were even pens of a sort, in which luckless females were set upon, and torn to pieces by maddened pit bulls?—and cavernous ravines outside Rivière-du-Loup, where decaying bodies, sprinkled with quicklime, were unceremoniously dumped—?

Such horrors were, of course, highly doubtful: particularly as it was said they occurred so close to Winterthurn City. "Nay, they are naught but fancies,—the crudest sort of fancies," Xavier told himself, wiping his damp brow with a handkerchief, and fighting a growing sensation of nausea.

Now he searched assiduously for an exit: down a flight of stairs, and into another wing of the building: through a heavy oaken door, fortified with tin: and into a passageway so airless and low-ceilinged, it might have been a tunnel. Here, the commingled odors of food, and liquor, and perspiration, and soiled linen, and, it may have been, stale flesh, so throbbed with humid heat, Xavier found it ever more difficult to breathe, and worried that, of a sudden, he might faint, and lie undiscovered for many hours. He passed an open doorway, glimpsing, inside, amidst coils of steam, laundresses bent over their washboards, their soap-splashed arms bared to the shoulder, and their hair escaping in untidy strands from their white caps. How queer, that they took no note of him,—had not the strength, it seemed, to glance around in his direction.

Farther along, he believed he heard women shrieking in terror: but when he passed by a large, dim-lit, and, it seemed, sumptuously appointed chamber, he saw that they were carousing in a most drunken fashion, not unlike their sisters in the public rooms abovestairs: but here they were only part-clad, in soiled chemises and other scant undergarments, though a number of gentlemen moved freely amongst them. Ah, how careless these women were of their delicate flesh, as if it possessed no value whatsoever—!

In revulsion, Xavier turned away at once; and blundered through a door, to discover himself in a storage room of sorts, in which slop jars and ill-scoured chamber pots were piled. He gagged; retreated in haste; hurried up a short flight of steps; along yet another narrow passageway, which seemed,—he knew not why—to be leading in the desired direction. Hazy, fleet, broken, and dreamlike were the glimpses he had, into rooms past which his panicked feet led him: one in which, it seemed, his brother Bradford stood, wiping his bloodied hands on a towel; another in which shadowed figures coiled together, whimpering and moaning; yet another, in which a naked girl crouched before a black-garbed gentleman who held something poised above her,—a riding crop, by the look of it: the particular shock of the sight being, this chestnut-haired girl closely resembled Perdita as she had been twenty years before.

Nonetheless, Xavier pressed onward: for he did not dare pause.

At one spot, condensation had formed so thickly on the walls of the tunnel, it had gathered into rivulets, and, in the lowest section of the passageway, had drained into an actual puddle, or pool, some three inches deep, through which Xavier was obliged to splash. Water it was, surely; water, and nothing more; though he seemed to recall, from the dim past, that the entrapped females of the Paradise so copiously wept, their tears collected into a pool . . . "Nay, it is naught but fancy, and I shall give no more thought to it," Xavier sternly chided himself.

Alas, the detective's adventure was fast drawing to a close, and something very like a child's terror was beginning. For his affrighted heart now beat so violently, he could scarcely draw breath; and the pain behind his eyes was such, a frenzied bird might have been encased in his skull, beating its frenzied wings. "Where is the way out?—I must find the way out," Xavier exclaimed: by happenstance turning a corner, to come upon a candle-lit chamber, a private dining room, by the look of it: albeit malodorous, and low-ceilinged, with damp concrete walls, and a disagreeably wet concrete floor into which several drains had been set. A queer enough dining room, Xavier saw, as his eyes accustomed themselves to the gloom, in that a solitary gentleman in a bowler hat was being served, seated at a table rather too high for such purposes, over which an ill-laundered white sheet had been hastily arranged, as a tablecloth—!

Yet more remarkable was the identity of the diner,—the redoubtable Dr. Wilts, upon whom Xavier had not set eyes for many years! Genial and white-haired, with a high, tight, round little belly, and faded blue eyes crinkled in an expression of sly merriment, it *was* Dr. Holyrod Wilts, who had lately been barred from practicing medicine in the State: and here he sat, his brown bowler hat pushed back upon his head, and a somewhat stained white towel tucked into his shirt front as a napkin. Evidently he had been feasting upon a late-night supper of oysters on the half-shell; a near-depleted bottle of champagne was set before him; his starched white collar had been unfastened, for comfort's sake. Pink-skinned, he exuded an air of contentment and well-being, and showed very little surprise at Xavier's entrance,—or at Xavier's identity. (For, even in the tremulous candle-light, he had no difficulty recognizing Xavier Kilgarvan; albeit some remnants of the night's disguise yet clung to the detective.)

Thus, Dr. Wilts but squinted at Xavier, and greeted him with a smile, and reached out to shake hands,—apologizing for the greasiness of his own, and for the fact that, grown "stout" and "elderly," he found it too much effort to rise from his seat. While Xavier blushed in confusion and discomfort, the white-haired gentleman snapped his fingers at a servant, that a second chair be brought for his guest, and a fresh bottle of champagne: for, as he smilingly explained, it was at this hour he oft-times lapsed into melancholy and restlessness, a night's arduous labor being accomplished, and the dawn, when he might sleep the sleep of Death, yet far distant.

"For old Doc Wilts is kept wondrously busy, despite his age, and the weakened condition of his legs," he said, with a wink for Xavier, "there being no end to them, the requests from patients *to be granted Life yet longer.*"

So it was, a servant brought Xavier, not a chair, but a metal stool, upon which he seated himself with some reluctance: and a second bottle of champagne was uncorked, with little ceremony. It was Xavier's hope that he might at once inquire after Ellery Poindexter, and mince no words, but, alas, Dr. Wilts seemed so genuinely desirous of talking,—nay, of chattering—he found he could get very few words into the conversation, and these, as it were, *slantwise!*

It was the women who kept the elderly Wilts running, as he phrased it; nay, that was unfair,—it was the men too: women and men alike, embarked upon a single folly. For they were insatiable in their appetites; and not even the terrors of disease could dampen their ardor. Ah, the things *he* saw!—the things *he* was obliged to treat, or to make an outward show of treating! Pustules, and tubercles, and blobs, and lesions, and tumors, and scales, and crusts, and fissures, and scars, and papules; and blindness; and nocturnal convulsions; and, finally, idiocy and Death. Yet they were insatiable: they thought little of what lay ahead, or, at the very most, they put their faith in mercury treatments, and in Dr. Wilts himself. "Even your brother,—what is his name?— one of your older brothers—even he!" Dr. Wilts said with a sigh: yet smilingly, and, withal, with such an air of philosophic equanimity, one could not believe he was greatly concerned.

Before the startled Xavier could ask about his brother, however, Dr. Wilts, grown warmly garrulous with the late hour, and the pleasure of youthful company, and, not least, food and drink, shifted of a sudden to a topic that evidently stirred his especial ire: the distinguished reputation his colleague Colney Hatch had enjoyed through the Valley, for so many decades: while he, Holyrod Wilts, the scorned, the disparaged and disgraced, had in truth been a colleague of his,—having supplied his laboratory with many a scarcely cooled corpse, on a regular basis. Thus, the cruder sort of sensibility saw one gentleman as a loathsome *bodysnatcher,* and the other as a prominent *man of science*—*!* And, so far as ministering unto the female sex in their greatest hour of need,—in their anguish, and humiliation, and physical terror— Dr. Wilts believed it was he, and not his respected colleague, who had, over the years, performed the most absolute good: for an honest compendium of statistics would surely reveal to the world, that many more of Hatch's female patients had died, than had Wilts's.

Before Xavier could respond to these amazing disclosures, yet alone draw breath to make his inquiry, the elder gentleman, now grown somewhat impassioned, shifted to yet another subject, *Death:* about which, as he claimed with a lewd wink in Xavier's direction, he suspected he knew far more than a youth of Xavier's age,—whether he be a professional detective, or no. (It was soon revealed, to Xavier's surprise, that Holyrod Wilts had evidently followed his career with interest and sympathy; and had not been so wounded by Winterthurn City's disapproval of his own career as to fail to take civic pride in the sole Kilgarvan,—after "that old hellfire Erasmus"—who had achieved a modicum of public renown in the world beyond Winterthurn. "For, never doubt that we are all quite boastful of you, my boy," he said, carelessly splashing more champagne in Xavier's glass, "even those who count themselves your enemies, and wish you ill.")

Now fairly inebriated, Dr. Wilts laid a paternal hand on Xavier's arm, and brought his flushed face close to his, and began, in a lyrical tone, to rhapsodize on Death: which is to say, both the *Idea of Death* and *Death in Itself*,—two very different matters, as he scarcely needed to point out. ("Indeed," he said in an aside, "the physician chuckles at the philosopher's spurious authority, in speaking of such things: for, as I told your late uncle, Simon Esdras, upon several occasions, the *Idea of Death* has as much to do with *Death in Itself* as the word *oyster* has to do with eating the tasty little devils—!")

The experience of a long, turbulent, and, withal, courageous life, as a general practitioner, amongst all classes and species of Mankind, had taught Xavier's host that, though Death disguised itself in a protean manner, it was, in truth, naught but a single essence,—a single determined force: now seeking entry at one moment in Time, now, with equal ferocity, at another; now attempting to enter its victim by way of this orifice, and now that; by this means,—whether "natural," or "unnatural"—or by that. Xavier Kilgarvan, as a detective, was pledged to seek out the cause of death in terms of its *literal agent:* for common belief required that a murdered person necessitate a murder: that this murderer be wicked, and must be removed from the community: and that, once he was removed, the community would reside again in health, and justice, and good cheer, and whatever,—*the agent of Death being conquered.* But it was quite otherwise,—thus Dr. Wilts said, with a wink, and a squeeze of Xavier's arm—it was *quite* otherwise, so far as he was concerned.

"On the one hand," Wilts said, "we have this wondrous force, Death, whose strength is incalculable,—whose strength, it might be said, fills all of the universe, and all of Time: while on the other side, in feeble 'opposition' to it, we have a frail organism, indeed,—the *human body.* Protected by the skin, that thinnest and most easily violated of membranes; alerted against danger by the senses, known for their fallibility; and guided through life by the energies of the brain, ever susceptible to distraction, error, and breakdown: is't not a miracle, indeed, that our species has survived to this day, ill-equipped as it is, by and large, to do battle with so powerful an adversary? Ah, the numberless hopes and stratagems, throughout history,—the prayers, and pleas, and superstitions, and bargains; the rituals, and customs—the countermeasures, the philosophical devices whereby Death is forestalled but a little while, as if it were a game, indeed, with rules of fairness and justice, which, if obeyed, one might win—! My dear boy,—I hope I am not impertinent, in speaking thus, for I do feel affection for you—my dear Xavier, you, of all persons, as a 'professional detective,' employ your best energies in the struggle to understand how it was, that Death finally entered through one or another doorway; and it is your hope as well, I assume, that, by so understanding, you will prevent another assault,—another victory by the adversary. Yet, even as you barricade the door, another is being slyly tested; and perhaps even unlocked from within. For like cries out to like, for consummation,—and Death's ancient properties, in Life, insist upon their claim. The physician, like the detective, rushes hither and thither, to stop up this hole, and that; to deal with this emergency, and that; to see whether 'tis pneumonia this time, or heart failure, or cancer, or,—why, I know not—snakebite: the pretense being, there is not a single omnipotent adversary, but numberless adversaries, who might be conquered. Nonetheless, my detective friend," Wilts said, bringing his flushed face so close to Xavier's, he seemed about to embrace or kiss him, "nonetheless, I do admire you: and wish to congratulate you for your heroic optimism, and your abiding faith in Mankind."

This remarkable speech so discountenanced Xavier, he could not summon forth the strength to reply, for some pained moments: his poor skull ringing, and his eyes spilling tears: and the sensation of nausea rising so powerfully in him, he was in terror of making a sudden movement, and provoking a spasm of retching and vomiting. Unhappy Xavier! What remained there to say, or even to think after Holyrod Wilts's testimony!—which predicament the detective seems to have dealt with in the only way he knew: by turning his mind to a familiar issue.

Thus it was, he held himself very still; his dried and cracked lips moving, it seemed, in a semblance of childlike prayer; and, after a sufficient pause, finally made his long-planned inquiry regarding Mr. Ellery Poindexter,—whose guilt, he said, he did not doubt.

Amazing, then, was Dr. Wilts's reply, and altogether unexpected: for the white-haired old gentleman fell in with Xavier's mood at once, sneering, and nodding vehemently, and saying that he was correct,—he was quite correct: for *he* did not doubt Poindexter's guilt either, on any score; and wished the scoundrel all the bad luck due him, and more. For it was several years ago,—at least five, Wilts frowningly thought—that he had done Poindexter a prolonged service out here in Rivière-du-Loup: attending his mulatto mistress in her final illness, and even delivering her sickly bastard child: spending weeks,—nay, months—on this fool's errand, when it was no secret that the woman was doomed, as she suffered from a bone marrow disease for which there was no cure. That aspect of the piteous case Wilts minded less than the fact that, after the woman's death, Ellery Poindexter, out of sheer obstinacy, had refused to pay a penny of his fee—! "He blamed me for the whore's death,—as if anyone on earth could have saved her," Dr. Wilts said angrily. "And 'twas whispered, too, the madman blamed me for the condition of the bastard son: one of those diseased whelps, born prematurely, and so wizened and pinched, it should never have been allowed to draw breath: but might better have ended in the bottom of a bucket—!"

Thus Holyrod Wilts raved, the while Xavier stared, and blinked, and listened hard: unable to believe his great good fortune in that, at last, Ellery Poindexter's secret was being revealed.

For it turned out that Poindexter had set up his mistress ("a golden-skinned Barbados wench, and most attractive") in a stone cottage hardly a mile from the Hotel Paradise, where they had met: and that, after her death, he continued to finance a small household, consisting of a Negro nursemaid for the sickly child, and one or two other servants. Dr. Wilts, who had delivered the infant, recalled it as "dusky-skinned": though not black, or predominantly Negroid, it could certainly not pass in white circles; and would have to be hidden away forever. "As to how Poindexter has fared in the years since his sordid 'tragedy,' " Dr. Wilts said, with a discernible curl of his lip, "I neither know nor care, for I have broken off relations with the wretch entirely. It surprises me not a whit that his wife has been murdered,— his wife and her lover, as rumor would have it; and I cannot feel sorry for him, or for anyone connected with him. Indeed, yes, I wish Poindexter all the suffering due him," the white-haired gentleman said, gripping Xavier's arm hard, "and if it is suffering you promise to bring him, I can give you precise directions to his nigger household,—his 'honeymoon cottage' that was."

Which impassioned offer, Xavier Kilgarvan could hardly refuse.

The Honeymoon Cottage.
Poindexter's Defeat.
The End.

So it came about, that Xavier Kilgarvan's spirited pursuit of Ellery Poindexter ended, abruptly, and most unexpectedly, but a few hours following his conversation with the infamous Dr. Wilts: not entirely as Xavier would have wished it, but, alas, *with the villain's violent death.*

For, while peering into the interior of the "honeymoon cottage,"—an unprepossessing stone house, of weatherworn façade, on the bank of the Loup River—Xavier was taken by surprise, by a sudden commotion behind him: and turned to see, hurtling toward him, his sallow face contorted with rage, Ellery Poindexter himself!—crying, "You—it is *you! Here! Of all places, here! Ah, I cannot bear it! I will not bear it—*" Thus, choking on his words, scarcely able to draw breath, the enraged Poindexter threw himself upon his adversary, with the unmistakable intention of killing him.

Yet, within a few minutes, as it so confusedly transpired, not Xavier Kilgarvan lay dead in the sullied snow close by the house, but Ellery Poindexter himself,—his puffy face so mottled in shades of red, and crimson, and sickly white, and his expression so wildly deranged, it seemed he must have murdered himself: suffocating, as it were, upon his own fury: with a final snarled curse against Xavier on his lips,—albeit too faint to be clearly heard.

"Why, can it be?—can it be? He is dead? Poindexter,—dead?" Thus the dazed Xavier Kilgarvan queried himself, rising shakily to his feet, and crouching over his adversary's lifeless form. "And it is all over—?"

As the precise circumstances bearing upon this felicitous death have ever been confused, and the chronological sequence of events knotty in the extreme,—there having been no detached, disinterested, and unfailingly reliable witnesses—it were best for me to set forth, as simply and directly as possible, all that is known of that windy December morn.

When, at last, Xavier left the overheated confines of the Hotel Paradise, he betook himself on foot, with no delay, to the easternmost edge of the straggling village of Rivière-du-Loup, where, as Dr. Wilts had said, Ellery Poindexter had established his secret household: this, evidently, in a narrow two-story house, with badly rotted shutters, and a chimney in need of painting. Save for a light that burned within, in what appeared to be a kitchen, Xavier would have believed the house to be uninhabited: for it possessed a bleak air indeed, and scarcely one proportionate to Ellery Poindexter's wealth. ("This, then, is the abode of his shame," Xavier thought, with a pang of gratification.)

No sooner was Xavier within a hundred feet of the stone house, atop a snowy wooded slope, than he realized he was wanting his binoculars; and would be greatly disadvantaged without them. (Nor could he recall, for an anxious moment, whether he had even brought the binoculars along with him the previous night; whether he had forgotten them, or mislaid them; or had had them stolen from him, by one of the treacherous damsels of the Paradise—! For, it seems, the haphazard episodes of the night had had a deleterious effect upon his memory and his ratiocinative faculties; and his strength had been so steadily ebbing from him, for a period of many weeks, it might be said that the detective was not himself at this time,—albeit the effect of the wind-rocked December morn, with its savage blue sky and yet more savage sun, should have been tonic, and roused him from his somnolent state.)

Lacking his instrument for surveillance at a distance, Xavier was required to approach the house, as cautiously and as stealthily as possible: and taking pains that he should not be espied. In driving out from Winterthurn City the evening before, he had neglected to dress himself adequately, in the warmest of his several topcoats; and now he so felt the piercing cold, he could scarcely control his shivering. His hat had been misplaced, and, it seems, his gloves; even the red wig had vanished,—left behind, perhaps, when he had fled the bed-chamber of the black-haired woman. And it struck him as a painful,—nay, a very nearly preternatural—phenomenon, the violence with which diamond-hard grains of light were reflected from the snow, causing his weakened eyes to water.

"Yet, am I really here, at last? Shall I see, now, at last, one of

Poindexter's most shameful secrets?'' Thus Xavier inwardly marveled, the while his faint breath steamed about him, and he had all he could do, to keep from slipping and sliding on patches of ice.

Then, peering through a ground-floor window, he saw, of a sudden, a full-bodied female figure stooped over a baby, or a very small child, secured in a high-chair.

The woman was black,—wondrously black—large, and slackbodied, and altogether oblivious of his presence: in her mid-thirties, perhaps: possessed of ample swaying hips and an immense bosom, and fine-frizzed hair caught up in a red scarf. So deeply absorbed was she, in her task of feeding the child, not a thing else might have distracted her. Ah, how Xavier stared!—blinked and stared!—finding himself quite mesmerized, as if it were a distinct privilege for him to be standing here, shivering in the cold, and gazing into the kitchen of a weatherworn little house he knew naught of, for a purpose he could not readily recall.

In a brash movement Xavier drew as close to the window as he might, to note that the child, though hardly more than the size of an eighteen-month infant, was surely much older, to judge by its face,—four or five years, perhaps: but indisputably sickly, with underdeveloped, and even wizened, limbs: its fine features pinched: its expression listless and apathetic: and, most pitiable of all, its beautiful eyes set deep in their sockets, and not perfectly in focus.

''Poor thing,—that you are *his*,'' Xavier murmured aloud, with anxious-knit brows. (For Poindexter's bastard, though possessed of faint Negroid features,—about the lips predominantly—had otherwise the quality of an angel-child, a cherub, amazedly blighted by the hand of his Maker, as if in wrath, or in violent whimsy: possessed of a distinct beauty, delicate and unearthly, yet, as it was the product of disease and infamy, doomed.)

''*His*,'' Xavier numbly repeated, ''though you are no more stamped with your father's features than,—than,—''

Xavier's whispered words trailed off into silence; and, the while he stood gazing into the warm-lit kitchen, the teasing admonition came to him, he knew not whence, or why,—*Heaven will never be any closer than it is, at the present moment.*

It struck him then, though not with the force of a blow,—with the *frisson*, perhaps, of a feather, lightly drawn across the skin—that Ellery Poindexter might perhaps have been hidden away in this secret abode on the afternoon of the murders: and was too shamed,—too proud—to confess his whereabouts.

Which is to say,—

Then, of a sudden, the detective was sickened to the very marrow of his bones, to hear a shout behind him, and to know himself detected, in this graceless posture: the which infelicitous turnabout had rarely befallen him in his years of professional service—!

Turning, then, he was astounded to see his very adversary rushing toward him, shouting, and choking, and flailing his arms about!—Poindexter's sickly face so contorted with fury, one could scarcely have recognized him. For a scant moment Xavier stood affrighted and paralyzed as any boy, exposed in a guilty predicament: albeit his wily trained muscles alerted themselves to withstand physical assault; and his gaze leapt about to determine whether a weapon of any sort lay close at hand,—or whether he must defend his life against the madman bare-fisted.

Alas, there was nothing: not a tree limb,—not a club,—not a hammer or an ax: nothing whatsoever, for his panicked fingers to grasp.

"You!—it *is* you! And here! Of all places! Here! *I will not bear it. It is an insult God cannot ask me to bear!*" With which infuriated words Poindexter threw himself upon poor Xavier, his fingers essaying to close brutally about Xavier's throat.

Albeit the detective had been taken totally by surprise,—his flank undefended, as it were—he was agile enough to slip from the fiend's grasp, protecting himself with fists, and elbows, and feet: striking a blow all wildly here, and another there,—with the immediate result that Poindexter's nose spurted red, and he grew more maddened still, and began to scream, and seemed, of a sudden, suffused with a maniacal strength *to kill, to kill, to kill:* emitting now sounds partaking rather more of the bestial, than the human,—and gasping for breath,—and choking, while poor Xavier nearly collapsed beneath the sheer weight of his bulk; and again his fingers groped for Xavier's throat,—and squeezed, and squeezed—until, of a sudden, both men tumbling to the snow, and rolling and wrestling about, the pressure of Poindexter's fingers was relaxed: and Xavier knew himself spared, and his opponent lifeless. Apoplexy, perhaps; or heart failure; or a seizure of some kind,—thus, dazed and blinking, and himself wounded about the face, Xavier reasoned, while summoning forth the strength to crawl from beneath his opponent's bulk, and rise to his feet.

So this scene, ill-orchestrated as it has been, ends nonetheless in triumph, with Xavier Kilgarvan crouched trembling over his adversary's corpse, musing aloud: "Dead?—he is dead?—*he!*—at last?—Poindexter,—dead? *And it is all over—!*"

Epilogue

I

Certainly, in the narrative it should please me to write, and, doubtless, the reader to read, the mystery entitled *The Bloodstained Bridal Gown* would end at this dramatic juncture: the detective at last triumphant, after his long and torturous ordeal,—the villain dead by his own hand, in a manner of speaking,—and naught remaining but the judicious tying-up of a few loose threads, that the case be formally closed. Here, too, we have the additional benison, that some nine months later, not one but two devoted couples,—Xavier and Perdita, and Murre Pitt-Davies and Thérèse—are to be yoked in Holy Matrimony: the morbid infelicities of the past swept aside, and, with God's grace, a cloudless future in store for all principals.

This unlook'd-to double wedding does indeed take place, on a hazily warm morning in September: but, unfortunately, some exceedingly painful months lay between, during which time poor Xavier Kilgarvan suffered greatly,—the more so, in that the circumstances of his "nervous collapse" were never understood; and so many irresponsible rumors made their way through Winterthurn, it is all but impossible to sort out truth from fancy.

All that is known with certainty is that, scarcely a fortnight following the death of Ellery Poindexter, Xavier Kilgarvan was felled by some sort of debilitating illness, or condition, rising partly from physical exhaustion and partly from an overtaxed imagination: the which could not fail to have been exacerbated by alcoholic spirits. (For more than one scandalmonger had spread the news that Xavier Kilgarvan had taken to drink; and was no stranger to opium, besides—! Where-

467

upon cruel commentary was aired, yet again, on the *tainted blood* inherited from a distant ancestor, harking back at least to Colonial times, and to the fateful intermingling of pure English stock with Red Indians, native to the Winterthurn Valley.)

So far as Xavier's struggle with Ellery Poindexter was concerned, however, and the outcome of his investigation,—the reader may be somewhat surprised (as, indeed, I must confess I was) to learn that, as soon as Poindexter was buried, public sentiment swung strongly against him. Xavier Kilgarvan's highly detailed case against the suspect was doubtless convincing, but, it seemed, of a sudden, no one required convincing!—the consensus now being, on every level of society, that Poindexter, and not the luckless Jabez Dovekie, had committed the ax murders after all.

And why had he done it?—why had a gentleman of his wealth and rank stooped to so bestial an act?

Suddenly, through Winterthurn City, it was said to have been "generally known" that Amanda Poindexter and Harmon Bunting had been involved in an illicit liaison, which roused the cuckolded Ellery to the simple expedient of *revenge;* just as it was "known,"—nay, "it had been known all along"—that Poindexter, though making a pretense of Christian virtue, and invariably chairing the Bishop's Standing Committee with an iron hand, had been a shameless profligate and immoralist, since coming of age. The Peregrines, and the Goshawks, and the Von Goelers, and the De Forrests; the Elspeths, and the Westergaards, and the Penistones; why, even the Pitt-Davies,—even the Shaws (who had long been reticent about their son-in-law)—now spoke openly of the man's criminal excesses: his unpaid gambling debts, scattered about the state; his rudeness; his indifference as to grooming; his negligence as a husband, and father, and heir to the St. Bride's estate; and, not least, his predilection for such outposts of debauchery as Rivière-du-Loup. ("Why, sir, if Poindexter has whelped one nigger bastard, you may be sure he has whelped a dozen!" Thus the venerable Henry Peregrine himself said, one evening at cards: whereupon it quickly became common knowledge through town that Poindexter had fathered a dozen illegitimate children, or more,—and all with "nigger wenches" of the most depraved sort.)

To this consensus was added the whispered testimony of Amanda's elder sister, that she knew *for a fact* that Ellery Poindexter had penned the unspeakable letters received by several ladies,—as she had received one of these shocking missives herself, but had destroyed it at once, and told no one of it, out of a terror of her brother-in-law. Also, it was whispered, by certain lady friends of Amanda's, that though she was "altogether innocent" of any romantic attachment to Reverend

Bunting, had she not been, Ellery Poindexter's numberless infidelities would have driven her to it—!

Most damaging of all was the vehement testimony of Dr. Holyrod Wilts, who had been summoned to examine the fallen man, in Rivière-du-Loup, and had pronounced him dead of "those convulsive seizures of the central nervous system and paroxysms of the heart" common to syphilitic infection. Dr. Wilts, an old acquaintance of the deceased, boasted that he himself had had a hand in bringing the murderer to justice: for 'twas he who had provided Xavier Kilgarvan with invaluable information, leading him to Poindexter's secret household,—his *refuge of sin*—in Rivière-du-Loup. (For, it seems, Dr. Wilts had for weeks strongly suspected,—or, it might have been, had actually known—that Ellery Poindexter had butchered his wife and the Buntings, in order to be free to remarry: his present mistress being but a common whore, of sullied racial strain, employed at the Hotel Paradise. "Her identity is kept secret, and she herself is in terror of stepping forward," the white-haired physician said, "for fear of becoming implicated as an accessory to the crime: and as I am a gentleman, I have sworn not to expose her.")

Yet, though fulsomely praised on all sides as a detective of rare genius, and once again besieged by invitations to the most exclusive houses in Winterthurn, Xavier Kilgarvan took no evident joy in his triumph: and presented to the world so pale, flaccid, and remorseful a countenance, one might surmise he had not solved a devilishly knotty murder case, but, instead, lost his closest friend,—or his very brother!

One evening, partaking of an intimate dinner at the Pitt-Davies home,—there being only Thérèse, and Elvira Pitt-Davies, and, of course, Murre, as his companions—Xavier of a sudden laid down his fork and gripped his head in his hands, and murmured, through numbed lips, that he could not eat: nay, *he could not go on.*

A moment of stricken silence ensued; then Murre rose from his seat, to approach his friend, and inquire what was wrong; and poor Xavier, yet gripping his head in his hands, as if it pulsed with pain too violent to be borne, whispered that he did not know: he did not know what was wrong: he had no idea whatsoever, what was wrong, save that it *was* wrong,—and he could not continue.

Thereafter, all swiftly, he sank, it seems, into most surprising idleness, rarely left his suite of rooms, and rarely welcomed Murre in; ate very little; began drinking ever earlier in the day,—so unnaturally early, it might be said that he was never without a drink close at hand, save when lying senseless on his bed, or (thus the servants whispered) on the carpeted floor. "Xavier, what is wrong?—please answer—what is wrong?'' Murre worriedly inquired of him, several times a day; whereupon the detective, unshaven, and disheveled, and perplexed, it seemed, as Murre himself was perplexed, answered, *he did not know what was wrong.*

It was Xavier's stated intention to leave Winterthurn City and return to Manhattan, in order to take up, at once, his detective work,—there being, by this time, any number of fresh mysteries at hand, and clients begging in desperation for his services. Yet, it seemed, he lacked the requisite energy to make arrangements; and easily bent to Murre's suggestion that, as he was feeling still the debilitating effect of the ''Poindexter case,'' he might better stay where he was.

Ah, how peculiar a mystery it was!—that Xavier *did not know what was wrong, save that it* was *wrong—and he could not go on.*

His faithful friend Murre asked of him, whether he wished to see a physician: but Xavier's muttered reply was negative. Then, would he like to speak with any acquaintance?—or, if the lesions had healed betwixt them, his father?—or his brother Bradford?

''I have no father, in any accurate manner of speaking,'' Xavier sullenly said, ''nor, what is even more felicitous, any 'brother Bradford.' ''

When Murre brought news of Perdita, conveyed to him by Thérèse, it was observed that Xavier visibly brightened: for the widow's physician in Contracoeur now voiced a ''cautious hope'' regarding her full recovery, where, formerly, he had not wished to comment. ''Then she is well?—I mean, she is not ill?—I mean, not gravely ill?'' Xavier asked, his brow anxiously knit. ''But why does she not write?—or *does* she write, and her letters are lost? Yet, still, I shall write to her, this evening, perhaps, or tomorrow; I shall write to her; for there are many things to be said . . .'' Whereupon his voice trailed off into a listless silence; and, after a minute, he lapsed into his distracted state, scarcely knowing where he was.

In so spiritless a mood, Xavier shunned all festivities of the holiday season; and many were the days, I am sorry to say, in late December, when he did not trouble himself to dress completely, or to perform the most cursory rites of his toilet,—and this, at a time when he was fiercely pursued by Winterthurn hostesses; and served up, as it were, in altogether rhapsodic terms, in the newspapers of the Northeast. Letters and telegrams arrived daily at the Pitt-Davies home, and petitioners came in person, begging the detective's services, and proffering highly satisfactory fees: but, alas, Xavier would have none of them: and instructed the Pitt-Davies servants never to bother him with such trifles.

"Cannot you tell these persons that I am departed,—or dead?" Xavier irritably jested.

Thus it was, while all of Winterthurn celebrated Christmas, Xavier Kilgarvan kept to his retreat on the second floor of the Pitt-Davies house, and felt so little suffused with energy, he did not even stand at the window, to stare over at Grace Church, as he had been wont to do. Much of the time he lay part-dressed on his bed, sipping gin, and thinking, and thinking,—though what it was, of which he thought, he seemed not to know. If he tried to read, the print swirled and danced before his eyes; if he tried to sleep, his brain worked all the more frenetically, as it had been accustomed to working in the past several months: albeit now, it seemed, *he had nothing about which to think.*

"I am indeed a mirror suspended above an abyss," he thought, "possessed of no content, and reflecting nothing save motion. And now, alas, that motion appears to have stilled—!"

Though, with Ellery Poindexter's death, the mystery of the Grace Church murders would seem to have been resolved, Xavier could not forgo thinking of it; and soon lapsed into perusing his coded notes on the subject and staring, oft-times for long-benumbed periods at a stretch, at the several labyrinthine charts, graphs, and maps he had so meticulously devised,—in another phase of his life, it seemed. A sickly sort of fascination led him, yet again, to the "anonymous" letters he knew to have been penned by Harmon Bunting: the which he read, and reread; and shook his head over; and yet again, he knew not why, reread,—hearing a sinister voice in these rhythms:

> . . . 'Tis the Devil's very own delicacy you are, tho' chastely professing otherwise! . . . like many another wife of this quaint region in whose mouth (as the naughty expression would have it) *butter would not melt.* Nay, it is no secret to me, that Woman is but a gilded & primped sepulcher,—a chasm of sickly heat,—a bunghole, as St. Augustine would have it, into which Man falls to his damnation. Such frailties can be attributed to the Moon's tide, tho' I (who know the wicked heart of Woman well) should attribute them to a volition *diseased & spiteful & mischievous & wanton* . . .

"Whose voice?—*whose* voice do I hear?" the stricken man cried aloud.

It was this very letter (originally received, according to records, by the late Mrs. Poindexter herself) that was found gripped betwixt Xavier Kilgarvan's tight-closed fingers when a manservant discovered him the following morning: lying part-sensible, and raving, on the carpet beside his bed.

Hereafter, Xavier descended into a state of despondent torpor, beside which his previous mood appeared healthsome indeed. Now, he could be prevailed upon to eat virtually nothing; or, if he swallowed a few mouthfuls, he immediately sickened, and vomited it up again. Ofttimes, when Murre Pitt-Davies gingerly approached him, he burst into childish tears, saying that it had been *he*, and not Ellery Poindexter after all, who had committed the murders—!

"Why, Xavier, how is that possible?" Murre inquired, laying a cool hand against his friend's feverish brow.

"I—I know not— I cannot remember precisely— Albeit I do remember that I had cunningly arranged to *appear* to arrive in Winterthurn on the evening of—was it September eleventh?—yes, September eleventh—when in truth I had arrived the night before—in order to consummate a secret design— The dimensions of which," he said, faltering, "I cannot speak."

"And why cannot you speak of them, Xavier?" Murre gently inquired.

To which reasonable question, the distraught man could supply no answer,—no answer at all.

It was on a snow-swept New Year's Eve that the troubled detective consigned to the flames every shred of information he had so laboriously gathered regarding the infamous Poindexter case: his coded notes,—copies of numerous official documents from the coroner's office, the chief of police, etc.; dozens of "tips" from informants both identified and anonymous; the labyrinthine charts, graphs, and maps; and, not least, the collection of offensive letters received by the Winterthurn ladies. Alas, that such priceless papers were destroyed by Xavier's own hand, in a roaring conflagration in his suite—!

"Loathsome, loathsome,—loathsome," Xavier muttered, poking the evidence more forcibly into the flames. "Thus the 'Old Year' ends!"

And in the morning, when the New Year dawned frigid and silent, the detective was discovered in Grace Church Cemetery,— wandering shoeless and but part-clad, murmuring aloud, and laughing, and swiping at invisible adversaries amidst the snow-shrouded gravestones.

Ah, so dazed and contorted was the gentleman's face,—so bloodshot his eyes—and so silvery-white had his wavy hair become, in a matter of hours, he was scarcely to be recognized: and had to be carried bodily back to the Pitt-Davies home, that he might be positively identified by his shocked friend as,—*Xavier Kilgarvan*.

II

Thus, an interlude of some twenty weeks ensued, reaching well into spring: during which time the detective drank deep, as it were, of the waters of Pathos,—those of Tragedy being finally inappropriate, as, by pained and halting degrees, he did recover.

But, ah!—how pained and halting indeed, and how doubtful, was his convalescence!—and how frequently Murre Pitt-Davies and his dear friend Thérèse despaired that the patient would ever regain any measure of his former strength, and his former mental faculties, and, withal, his *former soul*,—though he had been placed under the rigorous care of a physician, and watched day and night, that he might adhere to a healthsome regimen of rest, and quiet, and prolonged sleep; and, it scarcely needs be said, naught but the most nourishing of foods and drink. (For all alcoholic beverages were now forbidden him: and though, in the first weeks, the piteous gentleman begged for strong drink,—essayed to seduce the servants into aiding him, and bullied, and threatened where he could—he soon came to see that his salvation lay in renouncing drink forever: and made the heroic resolve, in as firm a voice as he could summon forth, that *he would never allow a drop of alcohol to touch his lips again, so long as he lived.*)

By midwinter, I am sorry to say, newspapers throughout the Northeast had caught up, as it were, with their former hero: and, out of angry disappointment with his rumored "resignation" from the profession of detective, vied with one another to publish lurid, sensational, and altogether irresponsible accounts of his condition, for the titillation of their readers. In certain papers Xavier Kilgarvan was accused of "sordid and duplicitous dealings" with those very criminals he had sworn to combat; in others, of demanding such prohibitive fees for his services, he might stand accused as "a subtle species of blackmailer." His penchant for alcohol, womanizing, gambling, and divers lowlife preoccupations was emblazoned in print for all to ponder; no less than his "physical and mental collapse,"—suffered, it was said, as a consequence of injuries dealt to him by Mr. Ellery Poindexter in his death throes. The *Vanderpoel Sun* published a two-part "confidential interview" with an anonymous person, doubtless a servant at the Pitt-Davies home, who spoke at length, and cruelly, of the detective's ill-health, and his oft-reiterated despair in his profession: for, it was said, while caught up in alcoholic delirium, Xavier Kilgarvan was given to raving, and ranting, and vowing that, if he lived, he would repent of his ways,—"and never again lust after Evil."

Mr. Hearst's popular papers,—including, by this time, the *Winterthurn Gazette*, which he had bought from the Goshawks to save from bankruptcy—were particularly censorious: for it was charged against Xavier Kilgarvan that he had frequently indulged in a perverted practice of penning lewd "anonymous" letters to ladies of high social rank—! (Of these, the only one reproduced was a crude copy of the mysterious letter received by the Misses Penistone, in the late autumn: albeit the young ladies were scandalized at its appearance, and swore that they had not released it; but that it must have been stolen by a servant.)

Doubtless, in his demoralized state, Xavier Kilgarvan would have cared very little about such absurd public notices: but all effort was made to spare him shock and discomfort: and those few visitors allowed into his sickroom were cautioned, of course, against arousing his distress in any way, or asking him questions regarding crime, murder, mystery, and the like. (Amongst these visitors, the reader will be interested to learn, was the long-retired sheriff of Winterthurn County, Frank Shearwater, who, though well into his seventies by this time, was possessed of an enviable vigor and good humor: for, having withdrawn from that profession deemed "accursèd," and taking up, albeit belatedly, the profession of farming, he had acquired a somewhat different perspective on life, as he phrased it: and heartily recommended to Xavier that *he* consider a like pathway. Yet another visitor of Xavier's, no less unanticipated, was Mr. Lucas Kilgarvan himself, with whom, in early March, Xavier became reconciled after an estrangement of more than a dozen years. All credit for this reunion must go to Miss Thérèse Kilgarvan, who tirelessly sought out the reclusive old gentleman in his Wycombe Street quarters: refusing to be turned aside, or discouraged, by his rude claim that "he had no son in the world remaining to him, and no one to whom he might leave his savings,—nay, no family altogether'': and possessed of inordinate patience, in convincing him to glance in upon his youngest son, who had, it seemed, ventured perilously close to death.)

Thus, Xavier Kilgarvan's gradual recovery, under the watchful eye of his friend Murre: for he presented no difficulties of personality, but slipped with a surprising ease into the role of convalescent,— spending his time in reading matter of the lighter sort (albeit he soon came to rejoice in, and to laugh heartily at, the follies of the times,—primary amongst them the comical public squabble of President William Howard Taft and former President Teddy Roosevelt); and in games of a resolutely cheery and uncomplicated sort (which is to say, gin rummy rather than poker, and checkers rather than chess); and in moderate exercise, close about the grounds of the Pitt-Davies estate, and along Jewett's Lane, and, on good days, all the way around Jewett's Pond,—on whose grassy banks it was oft-times his practice to stand and meditate, for long minutes at a time.

Upon one curious occasion, accompanied by both Murre and Thérèse, Xavier drew from the pocket of his tweed jacket a pair of handsome cuff links,—of lapis lazuli, it appeared—and tossed them casually into the water, at a distance of about fifteen feet—! When queried by his surprised companions, as to why he had done so rash a thing, the pale-brow'd convalescent said simply: ''The pond appears so perfect, and so inviolable, a mirrored surface,—I wanted to see if metal would sink in it.''

With the advent of longer, sunnier, and, withal, more healthsome days, as the earth shifted in a felicitous wise upon its axis, Xavier Kilgarvan began to recover, by degrees, a modicum of his old resiliency; found food less nauseating than he had,—indeed, upon occasion, if he dined in the company of agreeable persons, did it not even afford a wondrous sort of pleasure? And, ah!—it was, at the very least, an *intriguing phenomenon* that he might stride to an opened window, and draw a luxuriant breath, with not the slightest temptation to throw himself thither, and to dash out his brains on the flagstone below—! (Nor did sashes, cords, neckties, belts, and ''innocent'' lengths of twine, which had slipped by the careful eye of Murre Pitt-Davies, put him invariably in mind of nooses; or butter knives and forks, in mind of a way in which, all surreptitiously, he might *open his jugular vein*.) By the time Jewett's Pond had begun at last to thaw, after the extremities of the long winter, and the winds out of the northeast did not inevitably set his teeth to chattering, he was capable of walking at a brisk pace for upward of two miles at a stretch; and of rejoicing inwardly that he possessed, still, the legs to carry him thus. In a book from out the Pitt-Davies library, by the problematic Henry David Thoreau, Xavier had discovered, and took passionately to heart, these words:

> Talk of mysteries!—Think of our life in nature,—daily to be shown matter, to come in contact with it,—rocks, trees, wind on our cheeks! the *solid* earth! the *actual* world! the *common sense! Contact! Contact! Who* are we? *where* are we?

—which may well strike the civilized ear, as, I must confess, they strike mine, as rather too vehement, and verging upon the illogical.

By degrees, too, Xavier Kilgarvan regained his old powers of concentration, and, with commingled skepticism and zest, delved into those philosophers of ancient, medieval, and modern times, whose weighty speculations were to be found entomed in the Pitt-Davies library,—not excluding the several abstruse *Treatises* of Simon Esdras Kilgarvan himself. These volumes, long out of print, and rare, indeed, had been acquired by Murre many years before; though, as that plain-speaking gentleman readily confessed, he had lacked the "steam" to make his way through the first section of the first volume; and had never quite grasped whether Xavier's uncle was a philosopher of rare genius, or a babbling madman. "Well,—is that not true for all the philosophers here at hand, ranged upon your library shelves?" Xavier artlessly rejoined. (In truth, Lucas Kilgarvan had happened to mention, with a dry chuckle, that his half-brother's controversial theories of knowledge and semantics appeared to be enjoying a sort of "posthumous vogue" in philosophical circles: and that a venerable publishing firm in London, England, had written him but the other day, requesting the rights to reprint all the *Treatises* in a single volume, with a lengthy introduction by an Englishman named Bertrand Russell,—the royalties to go to Mr. Kilgarvan and his heirs, of course. "Thus we are forced to conclude," Xavier's father said in mirth, "that madness can scarcely be counted madness, if it pays.")

Many a serene hour, sequestered in his bed-chamber, Xavier lay with one or another of the *Treatises* at hand: perusing it, or idly turning its pages, or, more frequently, gazing sightless at the sky beyond his window: certain questions rising to his consciousness,—

Who,—or what—am I?
Who,—or what—am "I"?
"Who,"—or what—am I?
Who, or "what"—am I?

—these queries defining themselves with no disagreeable urgency, but, rather, rising and falling and drifting about, weightless, lacking the power to terrify, like swan's-down borne upon a summery breeze, or the glossy fluff from a ripened milkweed pod. Oft-times, the convalescent's eyes moved to a mirror on the facing wall, and a mirrored image there which he knew to be his own: which is to say, *his*, yet not, it seemed, *him*.

A mild, unemphatic state of well-being, shading almost into contentment, suffused him at such times: for he knew himself suspended, as it were, betwixt the past (which, it seemed, he remembered but haphazardly) and the future (which was no one's responsibility, *as it did not yet exist*).

One hazily warm afternoon in April, seeing his friend resting in this wise, Xavier's gaze as grayly luminous, and as dreamy, as it had been in his youth, Murre Pitt-Davies ventured to ask him where his thoughts had drifted; and Xavier answered, with no hesitation, that they had drifted nowhere at all,—they dwelt within the length and breadth of his body, and were in perfect equilibrium. "As I have failed most conspicuously in my 'chosen' field, it seems that I will be spared the ignominy of failing in anything else," Xavier said, with not the slightest air of self-pity, or discontent. "Thus it is, I know myself saved."

Murre stared at the pale-brow'd Xavier; and saw how thoroughly, and how purely, his hair had shaded to a lustrous silver; and protested, in a faint stammering voice, that Xavier Kilgarvan, of all persons, should not take so despairing and pessimistic an attitude, as to imagine that he had *failed*: still less, that he had *failed completely*. "Why, Kilgarvan has probably succeeded with more distinction than any detective native to these shores," Murre said in an admonitory tone; whereupon Xavier smiled somewhat irritably, and murmured that such flattery,—whether based upon a modicum of truth, or no— was of no interest to him whatsoever.

"Indeed, Murre, if you are my friend," he said, "you must not humor me, for all the world knows, or should know by now, that I *have* failed: the proof of it being, I have lain helpless these many months beneath your roof, without a whit of shame. For no one can return to the art of crime detection who has once been broken, as I have been broken; and in this,—pray, Murre, *do not interrupt*—lies my salvation."

III

It was hardly more than a fortnight later, on a surpassingly fair spring afternoon, that Mrs. Perdita Bunting, the rector's young widow, reappeared of a sudden in Winterthurn,—and in a most unusual guise.

Indeed, the bereaved woman aroused amazement in all who chanced to see her, by bicycling unescorted in a public thoroughfare, in unabashèd daylight: pedaling from the rectory at Grace Church to the Pitt-Davies estate at the far end of Jewett's Lane, with no evident care in the world that she might be espied.

Ah, Perdita!—oblivious to censorious eyes; and, it seemed, very much absorbed in the tricky mechanics of keeping her balance while, with measured motions of her feet, she essayed to propel herself steadily forward. Her bicycle, whether her own, or merely rented, was set somewhat high from the ground, as was her seat; the wheels were many-spoked; and the handlebars wide-set. Her costume,—a most idiosyncratic *mourning costume*, indeed—was fashioned of blue-brown velveteen, so dark as to pass, very nearly, for black: consisting of a snug-fitting bolero jacket embroidered in gold thread, with full leg-o'-mutton sleeves; and bloomers fetchingly "bunched" at the knees, to give an impression of childlike piquancy. An ascot scarf of pastel blue she had knotted about her slender neck; and a pert tam-o'-shanter, in matching hues of blue and blue-brown, had been firmly affixed to her glossy braided hair. Black cotton gloves, and black silk stockings, and black patent leather shoes, fashioned in the new low-cut *déshabillé* style (over which some controversy yet raged) completed this lady cyclist's charming costume, which could not be faulted in

478

any detail: even by her late husband's parishioners, who thought it a scandalous fact that Perdita Bunting had recovered so quickly from her grief; and that she had recovered at all, from her shame.

So it was, Miss Thérèse Kilgarvan herself chanced to espy her pretty sister, pedaling her bicycle along Jewett's Lane, a grave little crease betwixt her brows, and her hands gripping the handlebars tight: for, emboldened as the minister's young widow assuredly was, she had no wish to topple over while on her wheeled contraption, for all to observe. "Why, it is Perdita,—and she is returned already, without having sent word to me," Thérèse inwardly exclaimed, not knowing if, in the exigency of the moment, she felt more wounded in her sisterly heart, or roused to simple anger at Perdita's forgetfulness. (For, of course, Perdita would have meant nothing by such an oversight: and her stammered explanation would be, proffered with an air of guilty surprise, that she had intended to dash off a note to Thérèse, but had somehow,—in some mysterious wise—been distracted.)

By happenstance, Thérèse was invited to the Pitt-Davies' for tea: and arrived but a few minutes after her sister: albeit, when Thérèse was escorted inside, to the glassed-in Garden Room at the rear of the house, she did not see her sister amongst the small circle of guests,—and began to wonder whether Perdita was there at all. (For Xavier Kilgarvan too was missing,—alas, an absence Thérèse noted at once, in looking anxiously about the room. She had brought her cousin a copy of the handsome red-bound English edition of *The Collected Poems of "Iphigenia,"* which had already gone into its third printing; and had hoped, it scarcely needs be said, to deliver it to him in person.)

Well,—it must be stoically borne that Xavier Kilgarvan had once again stayed away from a sociable tea, though he had known, surely, that she was to attend: and must have remembered that she was bringing him Georgina's poems. Thus, the wounded Thérèse took care to make no special inquiries after him, when Murre and his aunt Elvira came forward to greet her: but put on a brave front,—nay, a most smiling and composed front—as she was wont to do, in her role of schoolmistress most particularly. (Nor did Thérèse make any reference to Perdita,—who was, it seemed, all oddly, *not* a guest at the tea—and halfway wondered whether the spectacle of her sister bicycling along Jewett's Lane, in her tam-o'-shanter and bloomers, might not have been phantasmal—! "Perhaps she has died," Thérèse bethought herself, most queerly, and, I am bound to say, most uncharacteristically, "perhaps she has died in Contracoeur, of a sudden, and that was naught but a spirit.")

Not five minutes later, however, Thérèse was disabused of this eccentric notion.

All casually, she wandered off from the tea party, and outside, into the fragrant garden; and along a winding pink-graveled path; the volume of "Iphigenia's" verse clutched in her gloved hand, that she might, after all, press it into her cousin's hand, if she chanced to encounter him. For, ah!—she *did* feel some excitation, with the certainty that he was, very likely, somewhere near: somewhere very near: and that, if she hurried, she would find him,—*she would find him first.*

Unfortunately, this was not to be: and the reader can well imagine the high-strung Thérèse's commingled alarm and chagrin, and simple embarrassment, at witnessing, by accident, a shocking,—nay, a near-obscene—vision: the romantic reunion, as it were, of her cousin Xavier and her widowed sister, Perdita—! And this, in the bucolic depths of the Pitt-Davies' English garden.

Poor Thérèse happened upon the lovers in this way: having slipped from the quiet festivities in the house, she followed the curving path for some small distance, and turned a corner, to see, all unexpected, Xavier Kilgarvan himself seated on a stone bench, about fifteen feet away, an opened book on his knee: and, *at that selfsame moment*, Perdita, her cheeks flushed and her eyes unnaturally bright, stealing up noiselessly behind him.

Obeying impulse rather than premeditation, Thérèse drew back; and hid her trembling frame behind an evergreen shrub.

Ah, was there ever a more disconcerting sight, than this!—for the grave-browed Xavier was possessed of so melancholy and subdued an air, and appeared to be so intensely absorbed in his reading, Thérèse herself would have shrunk from disturbing him: yet the brazen Perdita stealthily approached him: and hesitated but for the space of a heartbeat, before,—alas, how shameless!—leaning rapturously forward to slide her arms about Xavier's neck and shoulders, from behind; and to grip him hard, though he flinched in her embrace; and to bury her heated face in his hair.

Thérèse felt a stab of rage in her heart: and the admonition rushed through her,—*She has come for him, as it has been ordained: and neither he nor you can forestall it.*

For a tense moment, however, it seemed that Xavier Kilgarvan would resist: for he froze stock-still in this amazing embrace: and paid not the slightest heed, that his book had dropped to the grass, and that a looped braid of Perdita's hair had fallen free, to brush, with sinuous grace, against his cheek.

How long this frieze of Eros endured,—whether for a full minute, or, what is more likely, naught but a few seconds—the sickened Thérèse could not have said: for, despite her upbringing, and the intrinsic maidenly restraint of her nature, she stared, and stared,—

and blinked, and stared—with as little compunction as if her mind had been blasted clean.

Then, as Perdita's clutching hands freed themselves, to greedily, and ah, how boldly!—caress her lover's body, Xavier wrenched from her, saying: "How dare you touch me,—*you!*"

Whereupon Perdita replied, in a low fierce voice, with scarcely a moment's hesitation: "Yet who has earned the right, dear Xavier, if not *I—?*"

Thus, for the space of a very long moment, the erstwhile lovers contemplated each other, trembling; until, of a sudden, to Thérèse's dismay, Xavier appeared to surrender, and, springing to Perdita, crushed her in his arms,—with very little ceremony.

At this, the hot-blushing Thérèse turned aside, for she *dared be a witness to animal passion no longer.*

Nor could the young woman bring herself, after so untrammeled a scene, to return to the amiable confines of the tea; but thought it more pragmatical to flee the park, and to make her solitary way afoot to Berwick Avenue. There, she caught a trolley home: and, while yet on the clattering vehicle, her cheeks heated; and the vision of the outlaw lovers still fresh in her thoughts, Thérèse drew from her handbag a notebook and pencil, and, breathless, dashed off a draft of the tender message she would send, by messenger, to Murre that very evening:

As to your question, my dear friend,—YES. If, pray God, you can forgive me my years of blindness; and if, at this juncture, you still want your Thérèse. . . .

IV

Mystery now being formally concluded, and naught but mere *Life*, and *Matrimony*, remaining, I am obliged to end my narrative forthwith: noting primarily that, the following September, both couples were at last wed, not in Winterthurn City, but, for decorum's sake, in Contra-coeur, where their histories were less known.

The double-ring ceremony, held at St. John's Episcopal Church, was modest in scale, and attended by very few persons: for Mrs. Perdita Bunting was judged nearly scandalous, in marrying Xavier Kilgarvan, of whom her late husband could not possibly have approved; and, in-deed, in marrying but a scant year and a fortnight after her husband's untimely death. As to Miss Thérèse Kilgarvan and Murre Pitt-Davies,—this union was naturally met with more favor; yet, the fact that Thérèse should so publicly align herself with her sister, in a ceremony of such solemnity, aroused waves of disapproval. ("One might have expected a higher degree of propriety ˙from the elder sister," the Winterthurn ladies complained, "—if not the younger.")

The Pitt-Davies lived, of course, in Winterthurn, each being greatly devoted to the education of the young; the Kilgarvans made it a point, it seemed, *not* to live in Winterthurn,—indeed, not even to return to their native city, for the briefest of visits. And though Xavier Kilgarvan was to try his hand at various enterprises in Manhattan and elsewhere,—some rather more suited to his talents than others—the chastened gentleman was never again, alas, despite the appeals of his admirers, to return to the accursèd art of crime detection. "Such ex-plorations are, perhaps, suited uniquely for *bachelors*," he was reported to have said, upon more than one occasion, "—and not at all fitting for a *husband*, and, of late, a *father*."

482

* Rivière-du-Loup

Wycombe Street

Winterthurn City

Parthian Square

Railroad Street

* Courth

* Devil's
Half-Acre

South W

Winterthurn City